Emma Orczy

THE LAUGHING CAVALIER
(& Its Sequel The First Sir Percy)

OK Publishing 2021

Emma Orczy
THE LAUGHING CAVALIER

(& Its Sequel The First Sir Percy)

Historical Adventure Novels, Prequels to Scarlet Pimpernel

Published by

MUSAICUM

Books

- Advanced Digital Solutions & High-Quality book Formatting -

musaicumbooks@okpublishing.info

2021 OK Publishing

ISBN 978-80-272-7867-1

Contents

The Laughing Cavalier

AN APOLOGY

Does it need one?

If so it must also come from those members of the Blakeney family in whose veins runs the blood of that Sir Percy Blakeney who is known to history as the Scarlet Pimpernel — for they in a manner are responsible for the telling of this veracious chronicle.

For the past eight years now — ever since the true story of The Scarlet Pimpernel was put on record by the present author — these gentle, kind, inquisitive friends have asked me to trace their descent back to an ancestor more remote than was Sir Percy, to one in fact who by his life and by his deeds stands forth from out the distant past as a conclusive proof that the laws which govern the principles of heredity are as unalterable as those that rule the destinies of the universe. They have pointed out to me that since Sir Percy Blakeney's was an exceptional personality, possessing exceptional characteristics which his friends pronounced sublime and his detractors arrogant — he must have had an ancestor in the dim long ago who was, like him, exceptional, like him possessed of qualities which call forth the devotion of friends and the rancour of enemies. Nay, more! there must have existed at one time or another a man who possessed that same sunny disposition, that same irresistible laughter, that same careless insouciance and adventurous spirit which were subsequently transmitted to his descendants, of whom the Scarlet Pimpernel himself was the most distinguished individual.

All these were unanswerable arguments, and with the request that accompanied them I had long intended to comply. Time has been my only enemy in thwarting my intentions until now — time and the multiplicity of material and documents to be gone through ere vague knowledge could be turned into certitude.

Now at last I am in a position to present not only to the Blakeneys themselves, but to all those who look on the Scarlet Pimpernel as their hero and their friend — the true history of one of his most noted forebears.

Strangely enough his history has never been written before. And yet countless millions must during the past three centuries have stood before his picture; we of the present generation, who are the proud possessors of that picture now, have looked on him many a time, always with sheer, pure joy in our hearts, our lips smiling, our eyes sparkling in response to his; almost forgetting the genius of the artist who portrayed him in the very realism of the personality which literally seems to breathe and palpitate and certainly to laugh to us out of the canvas.

Those twinkling eyes! how well we know them! that laugh! we can almost hear it; as for the swagger, the devil-may-care arrogance, do we not condone it, seeing that it has its mainspring behind a fine straight brow whose noble, sweeping lines betray an undercurrent of dignity and of thought.

And yet no biographer has — so far as is known to the author of this veracious chronicle — ever attempted to tell us anything of this man's life, no one has attempted hitherto to lift the veil of anonymity which only thinly hides the identity of the Laughing Cavalier.

But here in Haarlem — in the sleepy, yet thriving little town where he lived, the hard-frozen ground in winter seems at times to send forth a memory-echo of his firm footstep, of the jingling of his spurs, and the clang of his sword, and the old gate of the Spaarne through which he passed so often is still haunted with the sound of his merry laughter, and his pleasant voice seems still to rouse the ancient walls from their sleep.

Here too — hearing these memory-echoes whenever the shadows of evening draw in on the quaint old city — I had a dream. I saw him just as he lived, three hundred years ago. He had stepped out of the canvas in London, had crossed the sea and was walking the streets of Haarlem just as he had done then, filling them with his swagger, with his engaging personality, above all with his laughter. And sitting beside me in the old tavern of the "Lame Cow," in that self-same tap-room where he was wont to make merry, he told me the history of his life.

Since then kind friends at Haarlem have placed documents in my hands which confirmed the story told me by the Laughing Cavalier. To them do I tender my heartfelt and grateful thanks.

But it is to the man himself — to the memory of him which is so alive here in Haarlem — that I am indebted for the true history of his life, and therefore I feel that but little apology is needed for placing the true facts before all those who have known him hitherto only by his picture, who have loved him only for what they guessed.

The monograph which I now present with but few additions of minor details, goes to prove what I myself had known long ago, namely, that the Laughing Cavalier who sat to Frans Hals for his portrait in 1624 was the direct ancestor of Sir Percy Blakeney, known to history as the Scarlet Pimpernel.

EMMUSKA ORCZY.

Haarlem, 1913.

THE PROLOGUE

HAARLEM — MARCH 29TH, 1623

The day had been spring-like — even hot; a very unusual occurrence in Holland at this time of year.

Gilda Beresteyn had retired early to her room. She had dismissed Maria, whose chatterings grated upon her nerves, with the promise that she would call her later. Maria had arranged a tray of dainties on the table, a jug of milk, some fresh white bread and a little roast meat on a plate, for Gilda had eaten very little supper and it might happen that she would feel hungry later on.

It would have been useless to argue with the old woman about this matter. She considered Gilda's health to be under her own special charge, ever since good Mevrouw Beresteyn had placed her baby girl in Maria's strong, devoted arms ere she closed her eyes in the last long sleep.

Gilda Beresteyn, glad to be alone, threw open the casement of the window and peered out into the night.

The shadow of the terrible tragedy — the concluding acts of which were being enacted day by day in the Gevangen Poort of 'S Graven Hage — had even touched the distant city of Haarlem with its gloom. The eldest son of John of Barneveld was awaiting final trial and inevitable condemnation, his brother Stoutenburg was a fugitive, and their accomplices Korenwinder, van Dyk, the redoubtable Slatius and others, were giving away under torture the details of the aborted conspiracy against the life of Maurice of Nassau, Stadtholder of Holland, Gelderland, Utrecht and Overyssel, Captain and Admiral-General of the State, Prince of Orange, and virtual ruler of Protestant and republican Netherlands.

Traitors all of them — would-be assassins — the Stadtholder whom they had planned to murder was showing them no mercy. As he had sent John of Barneveld to the scaffold to assuage his own thirst for supreme power and satisfy his own ambitions, so he was ready to send John of Barneveld's sons to death and John of Barneveld's widow to sorrow and loneliness.

The sons of John of Barneveld had planned to avenge their father's death by the committal of a cruel and dastardly murder: fate and the treachery of mercenary accomplices had intervened, and now Grœneveld was on the eve of condemnation, and Stoutenburg was a wanderer on the face of the earth with a price put upon his head.

Gilda Beresteyn could not endure the thought of it all. All the memories of her childhood were linked with the Barnevelds. Stoutenburg had been her brother Nicolaes' most intimate friend, and had been the first man to whisper words of love in her ears, ere his boundless ambition and his unscrupulous egoism drove him into another more profitable marriage.

Gilda's face flamed up with shame even now at recollection of his treachery, and the deep humiliation which she had felt when she saw the first budding blossom of her girlish love so carelessly tossed aside by the man whom she had trusted.

A sense of oppression weighed her spirits down to-night. It almost seemed as if the tragedy which had encompassed the entire Barneveld family was even now hovering over the peaceful house of Mynheer Beresteyn, deputy burgomaster and chief civic magistrate of the town of Haarlem. The air itself felt heavy as if with the weight of impending doom.

The little city lay quiet and at peace; a soft breeze from the south lightly fanned the girl's cheeks. She leaned her elbows on the window-sill and rested her chin in her hands. The moon was not up and yet it was not dark; a mysterious light still lingered on the horizon far away where earth and sea met in a haze of purple and indigo.

From the little garden down below there rose the subtle fragrance of early spring — of wet earth and budding trees, and the dim veiled distance was full of strange sweet sounds, the call of night-birds, the shriek of sea-gulls astray from their usual haunts.

Gilda looked out and listened — unable to understand this vague sense of oppression and of foreboding: when she put her finger up to her eyes, she found them wet with tears.

Memories rose from out the past, sad phantoms that hovered in the scent of the spring. Gilda had never wholly forgotten the man who had once filled her heart with his personality, much less could she chase away his image from her mind now that a future of misery and disgrace was all that was left to him.

She did not know what had become of him, and dared not ask for news. Mynheer Beresteyn, loyal to the House of Nassau and to its prince, had cast out of his heart the sons of John of Barneveld whom he had once loved. Assassins and traitors, he would with his own lips have condemned them to the block, or denounced them to the vengeance of the Stadtholder for their treachery against him.

The feeling of uncertainty as to Stoutenburg's fate softened Gilda's heart toward him. She knew that he had become a wanderer on the face of the earth, Cain-like, homeless, friendless, practically kinless; she pitied him far more than she did Grœneveld or the others who were looking death quite closely in the face.

She was infinitely sorry for him, for him and for his wife, for whose sake he had been false to his first love. The gentle murmur of the breeze, the distant call of the water-fowl, seemed to bring back to Gilda's ears those whisperings of ardent passion which had come from Stoutenburg's lips years ago. She had listened to them with joy then, with glowing eyes cast down and cheeks that flamed up at his words.

And as she listened to these dream-sounds others more concrete mingled with the mystic ones far away: the sound of stealthy footsteps upon the flagged path of the garden, and of a human being breathing and panting somewhere close by, still hidden by the gathering shadows of the night.

She held her breath to listen — not at all frightened, for the sound of those footsteps, the presence of that human creature close by, were in tune with her mood of expectancy of something that was foredoomed to come.

Suddenly the breeze brought to her ear the murmur of her name, whispered as if in an agony of pleading:

"Gilda!"

She leaned right out of the window. Her eyes, better accustomed to the dim evening light, perceived a human figure that crouched against the yew hedge, in the fantastic shadow cast by the quaintly shaped peacock at the corner close to the house.

"Gilda!" came the murmur again, more insistent this time.

"Who goes there?" she called in response: and it was an undefinable instinct stronger than her will that caused her to drop her own voice also to a whisper.

"A fugitive hunted to his death," came the response scarce louder than the breeze. "Give me shelter, Gilda — human bloodhounds are on my track."

Gilda's heart seemed to stop its beating; the human figure out there in the shadows had crept stealthily nearer. The window out of which she leaned was only a few feet from the ground; she stretched out her hand into the night.

"There is a projection in the wall just there," she whispered hurriedly, "and the ivy stems will help you.... Come!"

The fugitive grasped the hand that was stretched out to him in pitying helpfulness. With the aid of the projection in the wall and of the stems of the century-old ivy, he soon cleared the distance which separated him from the window-sill. The next moment he had jumped into the room.

Gilda in this impulsive act of mercy had not paused to consider either the risks or the cost. She had recognised the voice of the man whom she had once loved, that voice called to her out of the depths of boundless misery; it was the call of a man at bay, a human quarry hunted and exhausted, with the hunters close upon his heels. She could not have resisted that call even if she had allowed her reason to fight her instinct then.

But now that he stood before her in rough fisherman's clothes, stained and torn, his face covered with blood and grime, his eyes red and swollen, the breath coming in quick, short gasps through his blue, cracked lips, the first sense of fear at what she had done seized hold of her heart.

At first he took no notice of her, but threw himself into the nearest chair and passed his hands across his face and brow.

"My God," he murmured, "I thought they would have me to-night."

She stood in the middle of the room, feeling helpless and bewildered; she was full of pity for the man, for there is nothing more unutterably pathetic than the hunted human creature in its final stage of apathetic exhaustion, but she was just beginning to co-ordinate her thoughts and they for the moment were being invaded by fear.

She felt more than she saw, that presently he turned his hollow, purple-rimmed eyes upon her, and that in them there was a glow half of passionate will-power and half of anxious, agonizing doubt.

"Of what are you afraid, Gilda?" he asked suddenly, "surely not of me?"

"Not of you, my lord," she replied quietly, "only for you."

"I am a miserable outlaw now, Gilda," he rejoined bitterly, "four thousand golden guilders await any lout who chooses to sell me for a competence."

"I know that, my lord ... and marvel why you are here? I heard that you were safe — in Belgium."

He laughed and shrugged his shoulders.

"I was safe there," he said, "but I could not rest. I came back a few days ago, thinking I could help my brother to escape. Bah!" he added roughly, "he is a snivelling coward...."

"Hush! for pity's sake," she exclaimed, "some one will hear you."

"Close that window and lock the door," he murmured hoarsely. "I am spent — and could not resist a child if it chose to drag me at this moment to the Stadtholder's spies."

Gilda obeyed him mechanically. First she closed the window; then she went to the door listening against the panel with all her senses on the alert. At the further end of the passage was the living-room where her father must still be sitting after his supper, poring over a book on horticulture, or mayhap attending to his tulip bulbs. If he knew that the would-be murderer of the Stadtholder, the prime mover and instigator of the dastardly plot was here in his house, in his daughter's chamber ... Gilda shuddered, half-fainting with terror, and her trembling fingers fumbled with the lock.

"Is Nicolaes home?" asked Stoutenburg, suddenly.

"Not just now," she replied, "but he, too, will be home anon.... My father is at home...."

"Ah!... Nicolaes is my friend ... I counted on seeing him here ... he would help me I know ... but your father, Gilda, would drag me to the gallows with his own hand if he knew that I am here."

"You must not count on Nicolaes either, my lord," she pleaded, "nor must you stay here a moment longer ... I heard my father's step in the passage already. He is sure to come and bid me good-night before he goes to bed...."

"I am spent, Gilda," he murmured, and indeed his breath came in such feeble gasps that he could scarce speak. "I have not touched food for two days. I landed at Scheveningen a week ago, and for five days have hung about the Gevangen Poort of 'S Graven Hage trying to get speech with my brother. I had gained the good will of an important official in the prison, but Grœneveld is too much of a coward to make a fight for freedom. Then I was recognized by a group of workmen outside my dead father's house. I read recognition in their eyes — knowledge of me and knowledge of the money which that recognition might mean to them. They feigned indifference at first, but I had read their thoughts. They drew together to concert over their future actions and I took to my heels. It was yesterday at noon, and I have been running ever since, running, running, with but brief intervals to regain my breath and beg for a drink of water — when thirst became more unendurable than the thought of capture. I did not even know which way I was running till I saw the spires of Haarlem rising from out the evening haze; then I thought of you, Gilda, and of this house. You would not sell me, Gilda, for you are rich, and you loved me once," he added hoarsely, while his thin, grimy hands clutched the arms of the chair and he half-raised himself from his seat, as if ready to spring up and to start running again; running, running until he dropped.

But obviously his strength was exhausted, for the next moment he fell back against the cushions, the swollen lids fell upon the hollow eyes, the sunken cheeks and parched lips became ashen white.

"Water!" he murmured.

She ministered to him kindly and gently, first holding the water to his lips, then when he had quenched that raging thirst, she pulled the table up close to his chair, and gave him milk to drink and bread and meat to eat.

He seemed quite dazed, conscious only of bodily needs, for he ate and drank ravenously without thought at first of thanking her. Only when he had finished did he lean back once again against the cushions which her kindly hand had placed behind him, and he murmured feebly like a tired but satisfied child:

"You are an angel of goodness, Gilda. Had you not helped me to-night, I should either have perished in a ditch, or fallen in the hands of the Stadholder's minions."

Quickly she put a restraining hand on his shoulder. A firm step had echoed in the flagged corridor beyond the oaken door.

"My father!" she whispered.

In a moment the instinct for life and liberty was fully aroused in the fugitive; his apathy and exhaustion were forgotten; terror, mad, unreasoning terror, had once more taken possession of his mind.

"Hide me, Gilda," he entreated hoarsely, and his hands clutched wildly at her gown, "don't let him see me … he would give me up … he would give me up…."

"Hush, in the name of God," she commanded, "he will hear you if you speak."

Swiftly she blew out the candles, then with dilated anxious eyes searched the recesses of the room for a hiding-place — the cupboard which was too small — the wide hearth which was too exposed — the bed in the wall….

His knees had given way under him, and, as he clutched at her gown, he fell forward at her feet, and remained there crouching, trembling, his circled eyes trying to pierce the surrounding gloom, to locate the position of the door behind which lurked the most immediate danger.

"Hide me, Gilda," he murmured almost audibly under his breath, "for the love you bore me once."

"Gilda!" came in a loud, kindly voice from the other side of the door.

"Yes, father!"

"You are not yet abed, are you, my girl?"

"I have just blown out the candles, dear," she contrived to reply with a fairly steady voice.

"Why is your door locked?"

"I was a little nervous to-night, father dear. I don't know why."

"Well! open then! and say good-night."

"One moment, dear."

She was white to the lips, white as the gown which fell in straight heavy folds from her hips, and which Stoutenburg was still clutching with convulsive fingers. Alone her white figure detached itself from the darkness around. The wretched man as he looked up could see her small pale head, the stiff collar that rose above her shoulders, her embroidered corslet, and the row of pearls round her neck.

"Save me, Gilda," he repeated with the agony of despair, "do not let your father hand me over to the Stadholder … there will be no mercy for me, Gilda … hide me … for the love of God."

Noiselessly she glided across the room, dragging him after her by the hand. She pulled aside the bed-curtains, without a word pointed to the recess. The bed, built into the wall, was narrow but sure; it smelt sweetly of lavender; the hunted man, his very senses blurred by that overwhelming desire to save his life at any cost, accepted the shelter so innocently offered him. Gathering his long limbs together, he was soon hidden underneath the coverlet.

"Gilda!" came more insistently from behind the heavy door.

"One moment, father. I was fastening my gown."

"Don't trouble to do that. I only wished to say good-night."

She pulled the curtains together very carefully in front of the bed: she even took the precaution of taking off her stiff collar and embroidered corslet. Then she lighted one of the candles, and with it in her hand she went to the door.

Then she drew back the bolt.

"May I not come in?" said Mynheer Beresteyn gaily, for she remained standing on the threshold.

"Well no, father!" she replied, "my room is very untidy … I was just getting into bed…."

"Just getting into bed," he retorted with a laugh, "why, child, you have not begun to undress."

"I wished to undress in the dark. My head aches terribly … it must be the spring air … Good-night, dear."

"Good-night, little one!" said Beresteyn, as he kissed his daughter tenderly. "Nicolaes has just come home," he added, "he wanted to see you too."

"Ask him to wait till to-morrow then. My head feels heavy. I can scarcely hold it up."

"You are not ill, little one?" asked the father anxiously.

"No, no … only oppressed with this first hot breath of spring."

"Why is not Maria here to undress you? I'll send her."

"Not just now, father. She will come presently. Her chattering wearied me and I sent her away."

"Well! good-night again, my girl. God bless you. You will not see Nicolaes?"

"Not to-night, father. Tell him I am not well. Good-night."

Mynheer Beresteyn went away at last, not before Gilda feared that she must drop or faint under the stress of this nerve-racking situation.

Even now when at last she was alone, when once again she was able to close and bolt the door, she could scarcely stand. She leaned against the wall with eyes closed, and heart that beat so furiously and so fast that she thought she must choke.

The sound of her father's footsteps died away along the corridor. She heard him opening and shutting a door at the further end of the passage, where there were two or three living rooms and his own sleeping chamber. For awhile now the house was still, so still that she could almost hear those furious heart-beats beneath her gown. Then only did she dare to move. With noiseless steps she crossed the room to that recess in the wall hidden by the gay-flowered cotton curtains.

She paused close beside these.

"My lord!" she called softly.

No answer.

"My lord! my father has gone! you are in no danger for the moment!"

Still no answer, and as she paused, straining her ears to listen, she caught the sound of slow and regular breathing. Going back to the table she took up the candle, then with it in her hand she returned to the recess and gently drew aside the curtain. The light from the candle fell full upon Stoutenburg's face. Inexpressibly weary, exhausted both bodily and mentally, not even the imminence of present danger had succeeded in keeping him awake. The moment that he felt the downy pillow under his head, he had dropped off to sleep as peacefully as he used to do years ago before the shadow of premeditated crime had left its impress on his wan face.

Gilda looking down on him sought in vain in the harsh and haggard features, the traces of those boyish good looks which had fascinated her years ago; she tried in vain to read on those thin, set lips those words of passionate affection which had so readily flown from them then.

She put down the candle again and drew a chair close to the bed, then she sat down and waited.

And he slept on calmly, watched over by the woman whom he had so heartlessly betrayed. All love for him had died out in her heart ere this, but pity was there now, and she was thankful that it had been in her power to aid him at the moment of his most dire peril.

But that danger still existed of course. The household was still astir and the servants not yet all abed. Gilda could hear Jakob, the old henchman, making his rounds, seeing that all the lights were safely out, the bolts pushed home and chains securely fastened, and Maria might come back at any moment, wondering why her mistress had not yet sent for her. Nicolaes too was at home, and had already said that he wished to see his sister.

She tried to rouse the sleeping man, but he lay there like a log. She dared not speak loudly to him or to call his name, and all her efforts at shaking him by the shoulder failed to waken him.

Lonely and seriously frightened now Gilda fell on her knees beside the bed. Clasping her hands she tried to pray. Surely God could not leave a young girl in such terrible perplexity, when her only sin had been an act of mercy. The candle on the bureau close by burnt low in its socket and its flickering light outlined her delicate profile and the soft tendrils of hair that escaped from beneath her coif. Her eyes were closed in the endeavour to concentrate her thoughts, and time flew by swiftly while she tried to pray. She did not perceive that after awhile the Lord of Stoutenburg woke and that he remained for a long time in mute contemplation of the exquisite picture which she presented, clad all in white, with the string of pearls still round her throat, her hands clasped, her lips parted breathing a silent prayer.

"How beautiful you are, Gilda!" he murmured quite involuntarily at last.

Then — as suddenly startled and terrified — she tried to jump up quickly, away from him, he put out his hand and succeeded in capturing her wrists and thus holding her pinioned and still kneeling close beside him.

"An angel of goodness," he said, "and exquisitely beautiful."

At his words, at the renewed pressure of his hand upon her wrists she made a violent effort to recover her composure.

"I pray you, my lord, let go my hands. They were clasped in prayer for your safety. You slept so soundly that I feared I could not wake you in order to tell you that you must leave this house instantly."

"I will go, Gilda," he said quietly, making no attempt to move or to relax his hold on her, "for this brief interval of sleep, your kind ministrations and the food you gave me have already put new strength into me. And the sight of you kneeling and praying near me has put life into me again."

"Then, since you are better," she rejoined coldly, "I pray you rise, my lord, and make ready to go. The garden is quite lonely, the Oude Gracht at its furthest boundary is more lonely still. The hour is late and the city is asleep … you would be quite safe now."

"Do not send me away yet, Gilda, just when a breath of happiness — the first I have tasted for four years — has been wafted from heaven upon me. May I not stay here awhile and live for a brief moment in a dream which is born of unforgettable memories?"

"It is not safe for you to stay here, my lord," she said coldly.

"My lord? You used to call me Willem once."

"That was long ago, my lord, ere you gave Walburg de Marnix the sole right to call you by tender names."

"She has deserted me, Gilda. Fled from me like a coward, leaving me to bear my misery alone."

"She shared your misery for four years, my lord; it was your disgrace that she could not endure."

"You knew then that she had left me?"

"My father had heard of it."

"Then you know that I am a free man again?"

"The law no doubt will soon make you so."

"The law has already freed me through Walburg's own act of desertion. You know our laws as well as I do, Gilda. If you have any doubt ask your own father whose business it is to administer them. Walburg de Marnix has set me free, free to begin a new life, free to follow at last the dictates of my heart."

"For the moment, my lord," she retorted coldly, "you are not free even to live your old life."

"I would not live it again, Gilda, now that I have seen you again. The past seems even now to be falling away from me. Dreams and memories are stronger than reality. And you, Gilda ... have you forgotten?"

"I have forgotten nothing, my lord."

"Our love — your vows — that day in June when you yielded your lips to my kiss?"

"Nor that dull autumnal day, my lord, when I heard from the lips of strangers that in order to further your own ambitious schemes you had cast me aside like a useless shoe, and had married another woman who was richer and of nobler birth than I."

She had at last succeeded in freeing herself from his grasp, and had risen to her feet, and retreated further and further away from him until she stood up now against the opposite wall, her slender, white form lost in the darkness, her whispered words only striking clearly on his ear.

He too rose from the bed and drew up his tall lean figure with a gesture still expressive of that ruthless ambition with which Gilda had taunted him.

"My marriage then was pure expediency, Gilda," he said with a shrug of the shoulders. "My father, whose differences with the Stadtholder were reaching their acutest stage, had need of the influence of Marnix de St. Aldegonde; my marriage with Walburg de Marnix was done in my father's interests and went sorely against my heart ... it is meet and natural that she herself should have severed a tie which was one only in name. A year hence from now, the law grants me freedom to contract a new marriage tie; my love for you, Gilda, is unchanged."

"And mine for you, my lord, is dead."

He gave a short, low laugh in which there rang a strange note of triumph.

"Dormant mayhap, Gilda," he said as he groped his way across the darkened room and tried to approach her. "Your ears have been poisoned by your father's hatred of me. Let me but hold you once more in my arms, let me but speak to you once again of the past, and you will forget all save your real love for me."

"All this is senseless talk, my lord," she said coldly, "your life at this moment hangs upon the finest thread that destiny can weave. Human bloodhounds you said were upon your track; they have not wholly lost the scent, remember."

Her self-possession acted like a fall of icy-cold water upon the ardour of his temper. Once more that hunted look came into his face; he cast furtive, frightened glances around him, peering into the gloom, as if enemies might be lurking in every dark recess.

"They shall not have me," he muttered through set teeth, "not to-night ... not now that life again holds out to me a cup brimful of happiness. I will go, Gilda, just as you command ... they shall not find me ... I have something to live for now ... you and revenge.... My father, my brother, my friends, I shall avenge them all — that treacherous Stadtholder shall not escape from my hatred the second time. Then will I have power, wealth, a great name to offer you. Gilda, you will remember me?"

"I will remember you, my lord, as one who has passed out of my life. My playmate of long ago, the man whom I once loved is dead to me. He who would stain his hands with blood is hateful in my sight. Go, go, my lord, I entreat you, ere you make my task of helping you to life and safety harder than I can bear."

She ran to the window and threw it open, then pointed out into the night.

"There lies your way, my lord. God only knows if I do right in not denouncing you even now to my father."

"You will not denounce me, Gilda," he said, drawing quite near to her, now that he could see her graceful figure silhouetted against the starlit sky, "you will not denounce me for unknown mayhap even to yourself, your love for me is far from dead. As for me I feel that I have never loved as I love you now. Your presence has intoxicated me, your nearness fills my brain as with a subtle, aromatic wine. All thought of my own danger fades before my longing to hold you just for one instant close to my heart, to press for one brief yet eternal second my lips against yours. Gilda, I love you!"

His arms quickly closed round her, she felt his hot breath against her cheek. For one moment did she close her eyes, for she felt sick and faint, but the staunch valour of that same Dutch blood which had striven and fought and endured and conquered throughout the ages past gave her just that courage, just that presence of mind which she needed.

"An you do not release me instantly," she said firmly, "I will rouse the house with one call."

Then, as his arms instinctively dropped away from her and he drew back with a muttered curse:

"Go!" she said, once more pointing toward the peaceful and distant horizon now wrapped in the veil of night. "Go! while I still have the strength to keep silent, save for a prayer for your safety."

Her attitude was so firm, her figure so rigid, that he knew that inevitably he must obey. His life was in danger, not hers; and she had of a truth but little to fear from him. He bowed his head in submission and humility, then he bent the knee and raising her gown to his lips he imprinted a kiss upon the hem. The next moment he had swung himself lightly upon the window sill, from whence he dropped softly upon the ground below.

For a few minutes longer she remained standing beside the open window, listening to his footfall on the flagged path. She could just distinguish his moving form from the surrounding gloom, as he crept along the shadows towards the boundary of the garden. Then as for one brief minute she saw his figure outlined above the garden wall, she closed the window very slowly and turned away from it.

The next moment she was lying in a swoon across the floor of her room.

CHAPTER I
NEW YEAR'S EVE

If the snow had come down again or the weather been colder, or wetter, or other than it was....

If one of the three men had been more thirsty, or the other more insistent....

If it had been any other day of the year, or any other hour of any other day....

If the three philosophers had taken their walk abroad in any other portion of the city of Haarlem....

If....

Nay! but there's no end to the Ifs which I might adduce in order to prove to you beyond a doubt that but for an extraordinary conglomeration of minor circumstances, the events which I am about to relate neither would nor could ever have taken place.

For indeed you must admit that had the snow come down again or the weather been colder, or wetter, the three philosophers would mayhap all have felt that priceless thirst and desire for comfort which the interior of a well-administered tavern doth so marvellously assuage. And had it been any other day of the year or any other hour of that same last day of the year 1623, those three philosophers would never have thought of wiling away the penultimate hour of the dying year by hanging round the Grootemarkt in order to see the respectable mynheer burghers and the mevrouws their wives, filing into the cathedral in a sober and orderly procession, with large silver-clasped Bibles under their arms, and that air of satisfied unctuousness upon their faces which is best suited to the solemn occasion of watch-night service, and the desire to put oneself right with Heaven before commencing a New Year of commercial and industrial activity.

And had those three philosophers not felt any desire to watch this same orderly procession they would probably have taken their walk abroad in another portion of the city from whence....

But now I am anticipating.

Events crowded in so thickly and so fast, during the last hour of the departing year, and the first of the newly-born one, that it were best mayhap to proceed with their relation in the order in which they occurred.

For look you, the links of a mighty chain had their origin on the steps of the Stadhuis, for it is at the foot of these that three men were standing precisely at the moment when the bell of the cathedral struck the penultimate hour of the last day of the year 1623.

Mynheer van der Meer, Burgomaster of Haarlem, was coming down those same steps in the company of Mynheer van Zilcken, Mynheer Beresteyn and other worthy gentlemen, all members of the town council and all noted for their fine collections of rare tulips, the finest in the whole of the province of Holland.

There was great rivalry between Mynheer van der Meer, Mynheer van Zilcken and Mynheer Beresteyn on the subject of their tulip bulbs, on which they expended thousands of florins every year. Some people held that the Burgomaster had exhibited finer specimens of "Semper Augustus" than any horticulturist in the land, while others thought that the "Schwarzer Kato" shown by Mynheer Beresteyn had been absolutely without a rival.

And as this group of noble councillors descended the steps of the Stadhuis, preparatory to joining their wives at home and thence escorting them to the watch-night service at the cathedral, their talk was of tulips and of tulip bulbs, of the specimens which they possessed and the prices which they had paid for these.

"Fourteen thousand florins did I pay for my 'Schwarzer Kato,'" said Mynheer Beresteyn complacently, "and now I would not sell it for twenty thousand."

"There's a man up at Overveen who has a new hybrid now, a sport of 'Schone Juffrouw' — the bulb has matured to perfection, he is putting it up for auction next week," said Mynheer van Zilcken.

"It will fetch in the open market sixteen thousand at least," commented Mynheer van der Meer sententiously.

"I would give that for it and more," rejoined the other, "if it is as perfect as the man declares it to be."

"Too late," now interposed Mynheer Beresteyn with a curt laugh, "I purchased the bulb from the man at Overveen this afternoon. He did not exaggerate its merits. I never saw a finer bulb."

"You bought it?" exclaimed the Burgomaster in tones that were anything but friendly toward his fellow councillor.

"This very afternoon," replied the other. "I have it in the inner pocket of my doublet at this moment."

And he pressed his hand to his side, making sure that the precious bulb still reposed next to his heart.

"I gave the lout fifteen thousand florins for it," he added airily, "he was glad not to take the risks of an auction, and I equally glad to steal a march on my friends."

The three men, who were leaning up against the wall of the Stadhuis, and who had overheard this conversation, declared subsequently that they learned then and there an entirely new and absolutely comprehensive string of oaths, the sound of which they had never even known of before, from the two solemn and sober town-councillors who found themselves baulked of a coveted prize. But this I do not altogether believe; for the three eavesdroppers had already forgotten more about swearing than all the burghers of Haarlem put together had ever known.

In the meantime the town councillors had reached the foot of the steps: here they parted company and there was a marked coldness in the manner of some of them toward Mynheer Beresteyn, who still pressed his hand against his doublet, in the inner pocket of which reposed a bit of dormant vegetation for which he had that same afternoon paid no less a sum than fifteen thousand florins.

"There goes a lucky devil," said a mocking voice in tones wherein ripples of laughter struggled for ever for mastery. It came from one of the three men who had listened to the conversation between the town-councillors on the subject of tulips and of tulip bulbs.

"To think," he continued, "that I have never even seen as much as fifteen thousand florins all at once. By St. Bavon himself do I swear that for the mere handling of so much money I would be capable of the most heroic deeds … such as killing my worst enemy … or … or … knocking that obese and self-complacent councillor in the stomach."

"Say but the word, good Diogenes," said a gruff voice in response, "the lucky devil ye speak of need not remain long in possession of that bulb. He hath name Beresteyn.…I think I know whereabouts he lives … the hour is late … the fog fairly dense in the narrow streets of the city … say but the word.…"

"There is an honest man I wot of in Amsterdam," broke in a third voice, one which was curiously high-pitched and dulcet in its tones, "an honest dealer of Judaic faith, who would gladly give a couple of thousand for the bulb and ask no impertinent questions."

"Say but the word, Diogenes …" reiterated the gruff voice solemnly.

"And the bulb is ours," concluded the third speaker in his quaint high-pitched voice.

"And three philosophers will begin the New Year with more money in their wallets than they would know what to do with," said he of the laughter-filled voice. "'Tis a sound scheme, O Pythagoras, and one that under certain circumstances would certainly commend itself to me. But just now.…"

"Well?" queried the two voices — the gruff and the high-pitched — simultaneously, like a bassoon and a flute in harmony, "just now what?"

"Just now, worthy Socrates and wise Pythagoras, I have three whole florins in my wallet, and my most pressing creditor died a month ago — shot by a Spanish arquebuse at the storming of Breda — he fell like a hero — God rest his soul! But as to me I can afford a little while — at any rate for to-night — to act like a gentleman rather than a common thief."

"Bah!" came in muffled and gruff tones of disgust, "you might lend me those three florins — 'twere the act of a gentleman.…"

"An act moreover which would effectually free me from further scruples, eh?" laughed the other gaily.

"The place is dull," interposed the flute-like tones, "'twill be duller still if unworthy scruples do cause us to act like gentlemen."

"Why! 'tis the very novelty of the game that will save our lives from dullness," said Diogenes lightly, "just let us pretend to be gentlemen for this one night. I assure you that good philosophers though ye both are, you will find zest in the entertainment."

It is doubtful whether this form of argument would have appealed to the two philosophers in question. The point was never settled, for at that precise moment Chance took it on herself to forge the second link in that remarkable chain of events which I have made it my duty to relate.

From across the Grootemarkt there, where stands the cathedral backed by a network of narrow streets, there came a series of ear-piercing shrieks, accompanied by threatening cries and occasional outbursts of rough, mocking laughter.

"A row," said Socrates laconically.

"A fight," suggested Pythagoras.

Diogenes said nothing. He was already half-way across the Markt. The others followed him as closely as they could. His figure which was unusually tall and broad loomed weirdly out of the darkness and out of the fog ahead of them, and his voice with that perpetual undertone of merriment rippling through it, called to them from time to time.

Now he stopped, waiting for his companions. The ear-piercing shrieks, the screams and mocking laughter came more distinctly to their ears, and from the several bye-streets that gave on the Market Place, people came hurrying along, attracted by the noise.

"Let us go round behind the Fleischmarkt," said Diogenes, as soon as his two friends had come within ear-shot of him, "and reach the rear of the cathedral that way. Unless I am greatly mistaken the seat of yonder quarrel is by a small postern gate which I spied awhile ago at the corner of Dam Straat and where methinks I saw a number of men and women furtively gaining admittance: they looked uncommonly like Papists and the postern gate not unlike a Romanist chapel door."

"Then there undoubtedly will be a row," said Socrates dryly.

"And we are no longer likely to find the place dull," concluded Pythagoras in a flute-like voice.

And the three men pulling their plumed hats well over their eyes, turned off without hesitation in the wake of their leader. They had by tacit understanding unsheathed their swords and were carrying them under the folds of their mantles. They walked in single file, for the street was very narrow, the gabled roofs almost meeting overhead at their apex, their firm footsteps made no sound on the thick carpet of snow. The street was quite deserted and the confused tumult in the Dam Straat only came now as a faint and distant echo.

Thus walking with rapid strides the three men soon found themselves once more close to the cathedral: it loomed out of the fog on their left and the cries and the laughter on ahead sounded once more clear and shrill.

The words "for the love of Christ!" could be easily distinguished; uttered pleadingly at intervals and by a woman's voice they sounded ominous, more especially as they were invariably followed by cries of "Spaniards! Spies! Papists!" and a renewal of loud and ribald laughter.

The leader of the little party had paused once more, his long legs evidently carried him away faster than he intended: now he turned to his friends and pointed with his hand and sword on ahead.

"Now, wise Pythagoras," he said, "wilt thou not have enjoyment and to spare this night? Thou didst shower curses on this fog-ridden country, and call it insufferably dull. Lo! what a pleasing picture doth present itself to our gaze."

Whether the picture was pleasing or not depended entirely from the point of view of spectator or participant. Certes it was animated and moving and picturesque; and as three pairs of eyes beneath three broad-brimmed hats took in its several details, three muffled figures uttered three simultaneous gurgles of anticipated pleasure.

In the fog that hung thickly in the narrow street it was at first difficult to distinguish exactly what was going on. Certain it is that a fairly dense crowd, which swelled visibly every moment as idlers joined in from many sides, had congregated at the corner of Dam Straat, there where a couple of resin torches fixed in iron brackets against a tall stuccoed wall, shed a flickering and elusive light on the forms and faces of a group of men in the forefront of the throng.

The faces thus exposed to view appeared flushed and heated — either with wine or ebullient temper — whilst the upraised arms, the clenched fists and brandished staves showed a rampant desire to do mischief.

There was a low postern gate in the wall just below the resin torches. The gate was open and in the darkness beyond vague, moving forms could be seen huddled together in what looked like a narrow, unlighted passage. It was from this huddled mass of humanity that the wails and calls for divine protection proceeded, whilst the laughter and the threats came from the crowd.

From beneath three broad-brimmed hats there once more came three distinct chuckles of delight and three muffled figures hugged naked swords more tightly under their cloaks.

CHAPTER II

THE FRACAS BY THE POSTERN GATE

Thus am I proved right in saying that but for the conglomeration of minor circumstances within the past half hour, the great events which subsequently linked the fate of a penniless foreign adventurer with that of a highly honourable and highly esteemed family of Haarlem never would or could have occurred.

For had the three philosophers adhered to their usual custom of retiring to the warmth and comfort of the "Lame Cow," situate in the Kleine Hout Straat, as soon as the streets no longer presented an agreeable lolling place, they would never have known of the tumult that went on at this hour under the very shadow of the cathedral.

But seeing it all going on before them, what could they do but join in the fun?

The details of the picture which had the low postern gate for its central interest were gradually becoming more defined. Now the figure of a woman showed clearly under the flickering light of the resin torches, a woman with rough, dark hair that hung loosely round her face, and bare arms and legs, of which the flesh, blue with cold, gleamed weirdly against the dark oak panelling of the gate.

She was stooping forward, with arms outstretched and feet that vainly tried to keep a foothold of the ground which snow and frost had rendered slippery. The hands themselves were not visible, for one of them was lost in the shadows behind her and the other disappeared in the grip of six or eight rough hands.

Through the mist and in the darkness it was impossible to see whether the woman was young or old, handsome or ill-favoured, but her attitude was unmistakable. The men in the forefront of the crowd were trying to drag her away from the shelter of the gate to which she clung with desperate obstinacy.

Her repeated cries of "For the love of Christ!" only provoked loud and bibulous laughter. Obviously she was losing her hold of the ground, and was gradually being dragged out into the open.

"For the love of Christ, let me go, kind sirs!"

"Come out quietly then," retorted one of the men in front, "let's have a look at you."

"We only want to see the colour of your eyes," said another with mock gallantry.

"Are you Spanish spies or are you not, that's all that we want to know," added a third. "How many black-eyed wenches are there among ye? Papists we know you are."

"Papists! Spanish spies!" roared the crowd in unison.

"Shall we bait the Papists too, O Diogenes?" came in dulcet tones from out the shadow of the stuccoed wall.

"Bah! women and old men, and only twenty of these," said his companion with a laugh and a shrug of his broad shoulders, "whilst there are at least an hundred of the others."

"More amusing certainly," growled Socrates under the brim of his hat.

"For the love of Christ," wailed the woman piteously, as her bare feet buried in the snow finally slid away from the protecting threshold, and she appeared in the full light of the resin torches, with black unkempt hair, ragged shift and kirtle and a wild terror-stricken look in her black eyes.

"Black eyes! I guessed as much!" shouted one of the men excitedly. "Spaniards I tell you, friends! Spanish spies all of them! Out you come, wench! out you come!"

"Out you come!" yelled the crowd. "Papists! Spanish spies!"

The woman gave a scream of wild terror as half a dozen stones hurled from the rear of the crowd over the heads of the ringleaders came crashing against the wall and the gate all around her.

One of these stones was caught in mid air.

"I thank thee, friend," cried a loud, mocking voice that rang clearly above the din, "my nose was itching and thou didst strive to tickle it most effectually. Tell me does thine itch too? Here's a good cloth wherewith to wipe it."

And the stone was hurled back into the thick of the crowd by a sure and vigorous hand even whilst a prolonged and merry laugh echoed above the groans and curses of the throng.

For an instant after that the shouts and curses were still, the crowd — as is usual in such cases — pausing to see whence this unexpected diversion had come. But all that could be seen for the moment was a dark compact mass of plumed hats and mantles standing against the wall, and a triple glint as of steel peeping from out the shadows.

"By St. Bavon, the patron saint of this goodly city, but here's a feast for philosophers," said that same laughter-loving voice, "four worthy burghers grappling with a maid. Let go her arm I say or four pairs of hands will presently litter the corner of this street, and forty fingers be scattered amongst the refuse. Pythagoras, wilt take me at two guilders to three that I can cut off two of these ugly, red hands with one stroke of Bucephalus whilst Socrates and thou thyself wilt only account for one apiece?"

Whilst the merry voice went rippling on in pleasant mocking tones, the crowd had had ample time to recover itself and to shake off its surprise. The four stalwarts on in front swore a very comprehensive if heterogeneous oath. One of them did certainly let go the wench's arm somewhat hastily, but seeing that his companions had recovered courage and the use of their tongue, he swore once again and more loudly this time.

"By that same St. Bavon," he shouted, "who is this smeerlap whose interference I for one deeply resent. Come out, girl, and show thyself at once, we'll deal with thy protector later."

After which there were some lusty shouts of applause at this determined attitude, shouts that were interrupted by a dulcet high-pitched voice saying quietly:

"I take thee, friend Diogenes. Two guilders to three: do thou strike at the pair of hands nearest to thee and while I count three...."

From the torches up above there came a sharp glint of light as it struck three steel blades, that swung out into the open.

"One — two — — "

Four pairs of hands, which had been dragging on the woman's arm with such determined force, disappeared precipitately into the darkness, and thus suddenly released, the woman nearly fell backwards against the gate.

"Pity!" said the dulcet voice gently, "that bet will never be decided now."

An angry murmur of protest rose from the crowd. The four men who had been the leaders of the gang were pushed forward from the rear amidst shouts of derision and brandishing fists.

"Cowards! cowards! cowards! Jan Tiele, art not ashamed? Piet, go for them! There are only three! Cowards to let yourselves be bullied!"

The crowd pushed from behind. The street being narrow, it could only express its desire for a fight by murmurs and by shouts, it had no elbow-room for it, and could only urge those in the forefront to pick a quarrel with the interfering strangers.

"The blessing of God upon thee, stranger, and of the Holy Virgin...." came in still quivering accents from out the darkness of the passage.

"Let the Holy Virgin help thee to hold thy tongue," retorted he who had name Diogenes, "and do thou let my friend Socrates close this confounded door."

"Jan Tiele!" shouted someone in the crowd, "dost see what they are doing? the gate is being closed...."

"And bolted," said a flute-like voice.

"Stand aside, strangers!" yelled the crowd.

"We are not in your way," came in calm response.

The three muffled figures side by side in close if somewhat unnumerical battle array had taken their stand in front of the postern gate, the heavy bolts of which were heard falling into their sockets behind them with a loud clang. A quivering voice came at the last from behind the iron judas in the door.

"God will reward ye, strangers! we go pray for you to the Holy Virgin...."

"Nay!" rejoined Diogenes lightly, "twere wiser to pray for Jan Tiele, or for Piet or their mates — some of them will have need of prayers in about five minutes from now."

"Shame! cowards! plepshurk! At them Jan! Piet! Willem!" shouted the crowd lustily.

Once more stones were freely hurled followed by a regular fusillade of snowballs. One of these struck the crown of a plumed hat and knocked it off the wearer's head. A face, merry, a trifle fleshy perhaps, but with fine, straight brow, eyes that twinkled and mocked and a pair of full, joyous lips adorned by a fair upturned moustache, met the gaze of an hundred glowering eyes and towered half a head above the tallest man there.

As his hat fell to the ground, the man made a formal bow to the yelling and hooting crowd:

"Since one of you has been so kind as to lift my hat for me, allow me formally to present myself and my friends here. I am known to my compeers and to mine enemies as Diogenes," he said gravely, "a philosopher of whom mayhap ye have never heard. On my left stands Pythagoras, on my right Socrates. We are all at your service, including even my best friend who is slender and is made of steel and hath name Bucephalus — he tells me that within the next few minutes he means to become intimately acquainted with Dutch guts, unless ye disperse and go peaceably back to church and pray God to forgive ye this act of cowardice on New Year's eve!"

The answer was another volley of stones, one of which hit Socrates on the side of the head:

"With the next stone that is hurled," continued Diogenes calmly, "I will smash Jan Tiele's nose: and if more than one come within reach of my hand, then Willem's nose shall go as well."

The warning was disregarded: a shower of stones came crashing against the wall just above the postern gate.

"How badly these Dutchmen throw," growled Socrates in his gruff voice.

"This present from thy friends in the rear, Jan Tiele," rejoined Diogenes, as he seized that worthy by the collar and brandished a stone which he had caught in its flight. "'Tis they obviously who do not like the shape of thy nose, else they had not sent me the wherewithal to flatten it for thee."

"I'll do that, good Diogenes," said Pythagoras gently, as he took both the stone and the struggling Jan Tiele from his friend's grasp, "and Socrates will see to Willem at the same time. No trouble, I give thee my word — I like to do these kind of jobs for my friends."

An awful and prolonged howl from Jan Tiele and from Willem testified that the jobs had been well done.

"Papists! Spaniards! Spies!" roared the crowd, now goaded to fury.

"Bucephalus, I do humbly beg thy pardon," said Diogenes as he rested the point of his sword for one moment on the frozen ground, then raised it and touched it with his forehead and with his lips, "I apologize to thee for using thee against such rabble."

"More stones please," came in a shrill falsetto from Pythagoras, "here's Piet whose nose is itching fit to make him swear."

He was a great adept at catching missiles in mid-air. These now flew thick and fast, stones, short staves, heavy leather pouches as well as hard missiles made of frozen snow. But the throwers were hampered by one another: they had no elbow-room in this narrow street.

The missiles for the most part fell wide of the mark. Still! the numbers might tell in the end. Socrates' face was streaming with blood: a clump of mud and snow had extinguished one of the torches, and a moment ago a stone had caught Diogenes on the left shoulder.

The three men stood close together, sword in hand. To the excited gaze of the crowd they scarcely seemed to be using their swords or to heed those of their aggressors who came threateningly nigh. They stood quite quietly up against the wall hardly making a movement, their sword hand and wrist never appeared to stir, but many who had been in the forefront had retired howling and the snow all around was deeply stained with red: Jan Tiele and Willem had broken noses and Piet had lost one ear.

The three men were hatless and the faces of two of them were smeared with blood. The third — taller and broader than the others — stood between them, and with those that pressed him closely he bandied mocking words.

"Spaniards! Papists!" yelled the crowd.

"If I hear those words again," he retorted pleasantly, "I'll run three of you through on Bucephalus as on a spit, and leave you thus ready for roasting in hell. We are no Spaniards. My father was English and my friend Pythagoras here was born in a donkey shed, whilst Socrates first saw the light of day in a travelling menagerie. So we are none of us Spaniards, and you can all disperse."

"Papists!"

"And if I hear that again I'll send the lot of you to hell."

"Art thou Samson then, to think thyself so strong?" shouted a shrill voice close to him.

"Give me thy jawbone and I'll prove thee that I am," he retorted gaily.

"Spies!" they cried.

"Dondersteen!" he shouted in his turn, swearing lustily, "I am tired of this rabble. Disperse! disperse, I tell ye! Bucephalus my friend wilt have a taste of Dutch guts? Another ear? a nose or two? What, ye will not go?"

"Spaniards! Spies! Papists!"

The crowd was gathering unto itself a kind of fury that greatly resembled courage. Those that were behind pushed and those that were in front could no longer retreat. Blood had begun to flow more freely and the groans of the wounded had roused the bellicose instincts of those whose skin was still whole. One or two of the more venturesome had made close and gruesome acquaintance with the silent but swift Bucephalus, whilst from the market place in the rear the numbers of the crowd thus packed in this narrow street corner swelled dangerously. The new comers did not know what had happened before their arrival. They could not see over the heads of the crowd what was going on at this moment. So they pushed from behind and the three combatants with their backs against the wall had much difficulty in keeping a sufficiently wide circle around them to allow their swords free play.

Already Socrates, dizzy from the blood that was streaming down his sharp, hooked nose, had failed to keep three of his foremost assailants at bay: he had been forced to yield one step and then another, and the elbow of his sword arm was now right up against the wall. Pythagoras, too, was equally closely pressed, and Diogenes had just sent an over bold lout sprawling on the ground. The noise was deafening. Every one was shouting, many were screaming or groaning. The town guard, realizing at last that a tumult of more than usual consequence was going on in some portion of the city, had decided to go and interfere; their slow and weighty steps and the clang of their halberds could be heard from over the Grootemarkt during the rare moments when shouts and clamour subsided for a few seconds only to be upraised again with redoubled power.

Then suddenly cries of "Help!" were raised from the further end of Dam Straat, there where it debouches on the bank of the Spaarne. It was a woman's voice that raised the cry, but men answered it with calls for the guard. The tumult in front of the postern gate now reached its climax, for the pressure from behind had become terrible, and men and women were being knocked down and trampled on. It seemed as if the narrow street could not hold another human soul, and yet apparently more and more were trying to squeeze into the restricted space. The trampled, frozen snow had become as slippery as a sheet of glass, and if the guard with their wonted ponderous clumsiness charged into the crowd with halberds now, then Heaven help the weak who could not elbow a way out for themselves; they would be sure to be trampled under foot.

Every one knew that on such occasions many a corpse littered the roads when finally the crowd disappeared. Those of sober sense realized all this, but they were but small units in this multitude heated with its own rage, and intoxicated with the first hope of victory. The three strangers who, bare-headed, still held their ground with their backs to the wall were obviously getting exhausted. But a little more determination — five minutes respite before the arrival of the guard, a few more stones skilfully hurled and the Papists, Spaniards or Spies — whatever they were — would have paid dearly for their impudent interference.

"Papists, have ye had enough?" yelled the crowd in chorus as a stone well thrown hit the sword arm of the tallest of the three men — he whose mocking voice had never ceased its incessant chatter.

"Not nearly enough," he replied loudly, as he quietly transferred faithful Bucephalus from his right hand to his left.

"We are just beginning to enjoy ourselves," came in dulcet tones from the small man beside him.

"At them! at them! Papists! Spies!"

Once more a volley of stones.

"Dondersteen! but methinks we might vary the entertainment," cried Diogenes lustily.

Quicker than a flash of lightning he turned, and once more grasping Bucephalus in the partially disabled hand he tore with the other the resin torch out of its iron socket, and shouting to his two companions to hold their ground he, with the guttering lighted torch charged straight into the crowd.

A wild cry of terror was raised, which echoed and re-echoed from one end of the street to the other, reverberated against the cathedral walls, and caused all peaceable citizens who had found refuge in their homes to thank the Lord that they were safely within.

Diogenes, with fair hair fluttering over his brow, his twinkling eyes aglow with excitement, held the torch well in front of him, the sparks flew in all directions, the lustiest aggressors fled to right and left, shrieking with horror. Fire — that most invincible weapon — had accomplished what the finest steel never could have done; it sobered and terrified the crowd, scattered it like a flock of sheep, sent it running hither and thither, rendering it helpless by fear.

In the space of three minutes the circle round the three combatants was several metres wide, five minutes later the corner of the street was clear, except for the wounded who lay groaning on the ground and one or two hideous rags of flesh that lay scattered among heaps of stones, torn wallets, staves and broken sticks.

From the precincts of the Grootemarkt the town guard were heard using rough language, violent oaths and pikes and halberds against the stragglers that were only too eager now to go peaceably back to their homes. The fear of burnt doublets or kirtles had effectually sobered these over-flowing tempers. There had been enough Papist baiting to please the most inveterate seeker after excitement this night.

A few youths, who mayhap earlier in the evening had indulged too freely in the taverns of the Grootemarkt, were for resuming the fun after the panic had subsided. A score of them or so talked it over under the shadow of the cathedral, but a detachment of town guard spied their manœuvres and turned them all back into the market-place.

The bell of the cathedral slowly struck the last hour of this memorable year; and through the open portals of the sacred edifice the cathedral choir was heard intoning the First Psalm.

Like frightened hens that have been scared, and now venture out again, the worthy burghers of Haarlem sallied out from the by-streets into the Grootemarkt, on their way to watch-night service: Mynheer the burgomaster, and mynheer the town advocate, and the mevrouws their wives, and the town councillors and the members of the shooting guilds, and the governors and governesses of the Alms-houses. With ponderous Bibles and prayer-books under their arms, and cloaks of fur closely wrapped round their shoulders, they once more filled the Grootemarkt with the atmosphere of their own solemnity. Their serving men carried the torches in front of them, waiting women helped the mevrouws in their unwieldy farthingales to walk on the slippery ground with becoming sobriety.

The cathedral bells sent forth a merry peal to greet the incoming year.

CHAPTER III
AN INTERLUDE

And at the corner of Dam Straat, where the low postern gate cuts into the tall stuccoed wall, there once more reigned silence as of the grave.

Those that were hurt and wounded had managed to crawl away, the town guard had made short work of it all; the laws against street brawling and noisy assemblies were over severe just now; it was best to hide a wound and go nurse it quietly at home. Fortunately the fog favoured the disturbers of the peace. Gradually they all contrived to sneak away, and later on in the night to sally forth again for watch-night revelries, looking for all the world as if nothing had happened.

"Tumult? Papist baiting? Was there really any Papist baiting this night? Ah! these foreign adventurers do fill our peaceful city with their noise."

In the Dam Straat the fog and the darkness reigned unchallenged. The second torch lay extinguished on the ground, trampled out under the heel of a heavy boot. And in the darkness three men were busy readjusting their mantles and trying to regain possession of their hats.

"A very unprofitable entertainment," growled Socrates.

"Total darkness, not a soul in sight, and cold! fit to chill the inner chambers of hell," assented Pythagoras.

"And no chance of adding anything to the stock of three guilders which must suffice us for to-night," concluded Diogenes airily.

He was carefully wiping the shining blade of Bucephalus with the corner of Pythagoras' mantle.

"Verrek jezelf! and what the d — — l?" queried the latter in a high falsetto.

"My mantle is almost new," said Diogenes reproachfully; "thou would'st not have me soil it so soon?"

"I have a hole in my head fit to bury those three guilders in," murmured Socrates, with a sigh.

"And I a blow in the stomach which has chilled me to the marrow," sighed Pythagoras.

"And I a bruised shoulder," laughed Diogenes, "which hath engendered an unquenchable thirst."

"I wouldn't sell my thirst for any money this night," assented Pythagoras.

"To the 'Lame Cow,' then, O Pythagoras, and I'll toss thee for the first drink of hot ale."

"Ugh! but my head feels mightily hot and thick," said Socrates, somewhat huskily.

"Surely thou canst walk as far as the 'Lame Cow'?" queried Pythagoras, anxiously.

"I doubt me," sighed the other.

"Ale!" whispered Diogenes, encouragingly; "warm, sparkling, spicy ale!"

"Hm! hm!" assented the wounded man feebly.

"Easy! easy, my friend," said Diogenes, for his brother philosopher had fallen heavily against him.

"What are we to do?" moaned Pythagoras, in his dulcet tones. "I have a thirst … and we cannot leave this irresponsible fool to faint here in the fog."

"Hoist him up by the seat of his breeches, then on to my back," retorted Diogenes lightly. "The 'Lame Cow' is not far, and I too have a thirst."

Socrates would have protested. He did not relish the idea of being tossed about like a bale of goods on his friend's back. But he could only protest by word of mouth, to which the others paid no heed; and when he tried to struggle he rolled, dizzy and faint, almost to the ground.

"There's nothing for it," piped Pythagoras with consummate philosophy. "I couldn't carry him if I tried."

Diogenes bent his broad back and rested his hands on his thighs, getting as firm hold of the slippery ground as he could. Socrates for the moment was like a helpless log. There was much groping about in the darkness, a good deal of groaning, and a vast amount of swearing. Socrates had, fortunately, not fainted, and after a little while was able to settle down astride on his friend's back, his arms around the latter's neck, Pythagoras giving vigorous pushes from the rear.

When Diogenes, firmly grasping the wounded man's legs, was at last able to straighten himself out again, and did so to the accompaniment of a mighty groan and still more mighty oath, he found himself confronted by two lanthorns which were held up within a few inches of his nose.

"Dondersteen!" he ejaculated loudly, and nearly dropped his half-conscious and swaying burden on the ground.

"What is it now, Jakob?" queried a woman's voice peremptorily.

"I cannot see clearly, lady," replied one of the lanthorn-bearers — "two men I think."

"Then do thy thoughts proclaim thee a liar, friend," said Diogenes lightly; "there are three men here at this lady's service, though one is sick, the other fat, and the third a mere beast of burden."

"Let me see them, Jakob," ordered the woman. "I believe they are the same three men who...."

The lanthorn-bearers made way for the lady, still holding the lanthorns up so that the light fell fully on the quaint spectacle presented by the three philosophers. There was Socrates perched up aloft, his bird-like face smeared with blood, his eyes rolling in their effort to keep open, his thin back bent nearly double so that indeed he looked like a huge plucked crow the worse for a fight, and perched on an eminence where he felt none too secure. And below him his friend with broad shoulders bending under the burden, his plumed hat shading his brow, his merry, twinkling eyes fixed a little suspiciously on the four figures that loomed out of the fog in front of him, his mocking lips ready framed for a smile or an oath, his hands which supported the legs of poor wounded Socrates struggling visibly toward the hilt of his sword. And peeping round from behind him the short, rotund form of Pythagoras, crowned with a tall sugar-loaf hat which obviously had never belonged to him until now, for it perched somewhat insecurely above his flat, round face, with the small, upturned nose slightly tinged with pink and the tiny eyes, round and bright as new crowns.

Undoubtedly the sight was ludicrous in the extreme, and the woman who looked on it now burst into a merry peal of laughter.

"O Maria! dost see them?" she said, turning to her companion, an elderly woman in sober black gown and coif of tinsel lace. "Hast ever seen anything so quaint?"

She herself was young, and in the soft light of the two lanthorns appeared to the three philosophers to be more than passing fair.

"Socrates, thou malapert," said Diogenes sternly, "take my hat off my head at once, and allow me to make obeisance to the lady, or I'll drop thee incontinently on thy back."

Then, as Socrates half mechanically lifted the plumed hat from his friend's head, the latter bowed as well as he could under the circumstances and said gallantly:

"Thy servants, lady, and eternally grateful are we for a sight of thee at this moment when the world appeared peculiarly fog-ridden and unpleasant. Having been the fortunate cause of thy merriment, might we now crave thy permission to continue our way. The weight of my friend up there is greater than his importance warrants, and I don't want to drop him ere we reach a haven of refuge, where our priceless thirst will soon, I hope, find solace."

The delicate face of the young girl had suddenly become more grave.

"Your pardon, gentle sirs," she said, with a pretty mixture of imperiousness and humility; "my levity was indeed misplaced. I know ye now for the same three brave fellows who were fighting a few moments ago against overwhelming odds, in order to protect a woman against a rowdy crowd. Oh, it was a valorous deed! My men and I were on our way to watch-night service, and saw it all from a distance. We dared not come nigh, the rabble looked so threatening. All I could do was to shout for help, and summon the town guard to your aid. It was you, was it not?" she added, regarding with great wondering blue eyes the three curious figures who stood somewhat sheepishly before her.

"Yes, fair lady," piped Pythagoras, in his neatest falsetto, "we were the three men who, in the face of well-nigh overwhelming odds, did save a defenceless woman from the insolent rabble. My friend who is perched up there was severely wounded in the fray, I myself received so violent a blow in the stomach that a raging thirst has since taken possession of my throat, and —— "

He stopped abruptly and murmured a comprehensive oath. He had just received a violent kick in the shins from Diogenes.

"What the h —— ?" he muttered.

But Diogenes paid no heed to him; looking on the dainty picture before him, with eyes that twinkled whilst they did not attempt to conceal the admiration which he felt, he said, with elaborate gallantry, which his position under the burden of Socrates' swaying figure rendered inexpressibly droll:

"For the help rendered to us all at the moment of distress, deign to accept, mejuffrouw, our humble thanks. For the rest, believe me, our deed was not one of valour, and such as it was it is wholly unworthy of the praise thou dost deign to bestow upon it. I would tell thee more," he added, whimsically, "only that my friend behind me is violently kicking the calves of my legs, which renders the elegant flow of language well nigh impossible. I stopped him talking just now — he retaliates ... it is but just."

"Gentle sir," said the girl, who obviously had much ado to preserve her gravity, "your modesty doth but equal your gallantry. This do I see quite plainly. But if at any time I can do aught to express in a more practical manner the real admiration which I feel for your worth I pray you command me. Alas! brave men are few these days! But my father's name is known throughout Holland; his wealth and influence are vast. I pray you tell me, can I do aught for you now?"

She spoke so artlessly and at the same time with such gentle dignity, it was small wonder that for the nonce even the most talkative of all philosophers was dumb, and that his habitual mocking banter failed to cross his lips. The girl was young and exquisitely pretty; the stiff, unwieldy costume of the time failed to conceal altogether the graceful slenderness of her figure, just as the prim coif of gold and silver tissue failed to hold the unruly golden curls in bondage. The light from the lanthorns fell full on her face, and round her throat, beneath her fur-lined cloak, there was a glimmer of starched linen and lace, whilst gems in her ears and on her breast lent her an air of elegance and even of splendour.

Pythagoras in the rear heaved a deep sigh; he drew in his breath preparatory to a long and comprehensive oration. "Can I do aught for ye?" the lady had said: a lady who was rich and influential and willing. Ye thunders and lightnings! when but three guilders stood between three philosophers and absolute penury! Ye hails and storms! what an opportunity! He would have approached the lady, only Diogenes' wide shoulders blocked him out from her view.

"Can I do aught for you now?" she reiterated gently.

"Raise thy hand to my lips," said Diogenes lightly; "momentarily I have not the use of mine own."

She hesitated, but only for a brief moment, then did just what he asked. She held her hand to his lips, mayhap one second longer than was absolutely necessary, and her eyes, large, deep and shy, looked for that one second into a pair of merry, mocking ones. Then she sighed, whether with satisfaction or embarrassment I would not undertake to say, and asked with a gracious smile:

"And what is your next wish, gentle sir?"

"Thy leave to continue our journey to the 'Lame Cow,'" he replied airily; "my friend up there is getting damnably heavy."

She drew back, visibly surprised and hurt.

"I do not detain ye," she said curtly, and without another word she turned to her lanthorn-bearers and ordered them to precede her; she also called to her duenna to follow; but she did not bestow another look on the three men, nor did she acknowledge the respectful farewell which came from the lips of the beast of burden.

The next moment she had already crossed the road toward the cathedral, and she and her escort were swallowed up by the fog.

"Well, of all the d — — d idiots that ever...." swore Pythagoras, in his shrillest tones.

Even Socrates pulled himself together in order to declare emphatically that Diogenes was a confounded fool.

"I pray thee raise thy hand to my lips," mimicked Pythagoras mockingly. "Verrek jezelf!" he muttered under his breath.

"If you do not hold your tongue, O wise Pythagoras," retorted Diogenes with all his wonted merriment, "I'll even have to drop Socrates on the top of you in order to break your head."

"But 'tis a fortune — the promise of a fortune which you let slip so stupidly."

"There is a certain wisdom even in stupidity sometimes, Pythagoras, as you will discover one day, when your nose is less red and your figure less fat. Remember that I have three guilders in my pocket, and that our thirst hath not grown less. Follow me now, we've talked enough for to-night."

And he started walking down the street with long and rapid strides. Socrates up aloft swaying about like a dummy figure in carnival time, and Pythagoras — still muttering a series of diversified oaths — bringing up the rear.

CHAPTER IV
WATCH-NIGHT

And am I not proved fully justified in my statement that but for many seemingly paltry circumstances, the further events which I am about to place on record, and which have been of paramount importance to the history of no less than two great and worthy families, never would have shaped themselves as they did.

For who could assert that but for the presence of three philosophers on the Grootemarkt on the eve of the New Year, and their subsequent interference in the fray outside the Papist convent door in the Dam Straat, who could assert, I say, that but for these minor circumstances Jongejuffrouw Beresteyn would ever have condescended to exchange half a dozen words with three out-at-elbows, homeless, shiftless, foreign adventurers who happened to have drifted into Haarlem — the Lord only knew for what purpose and with what hopes.

Jongejuffrouw Beresteyn had been well and rigidly brought up; she was well educated, and possessed more knowledge than most young girls of her social standing or of her age. Mynheer Beresteyn, her father, was a gentleman of vast consideration in Haarlem, and as his two children had been motherless as soon as the younger one saw the light of day, he had been doubly careful in his endeavours that his daughter should in no way feel the lack of that tender supervision of which it had pleased God to deprive her.

Thus she had been taught early in life to keep herself aloof from all persons save those approved of by her father or her brother — a young man of sound understanding, some half dozen years older than herself. As for the strangers who for purposes of commerce or other less avowable motives filled the town of Haarlem with their foreign ways — which oft were immoral and seldom sedate — she had been strictly taught to hold these in abhorrence and never to approach such men either with word or gesture.

Was it likely, then, that she ever would have spoken to three thriftless knaves? — and this at a late hour of the night — but for the fact that she had witnessed their valour from a distance, and with queenly condescension hoped to reward them with a gracious word.

The kiss imprinted upon her hand by respectful, if somewhat bantering, lips had greatly pleased her: such she imagined would be the homage of a vassal proud to have attracted the notice of his lady paramount. The curtly expressed desire to quit her presence, in order to repair to a tavern, had roused her indignation and her contempt.

She was angered beyond what the circumstance warranted, and while the minister preached an admirable and learned watch-night sermon she felt her attention drifting away from the discourse and the solemnity of the occasion, whilst her wrath against a most unworthy object was taking the place of more pious and charitable feelings.

The preacher had taken for his text the sublime words from the New Testament: "The greatest of these is charity." He thought that the first day of the New Year was a splendid opportunity for the good inhabitants of Haarlem to cast off all gossiping and back-biting ways and to live from this day forth in greater amity and benevolence with one another. "Love thy neighbour as thyself," he adjured passionately, and the burghers, with their vrouws in their Sunday best, were smitten with remorse of past scandal-mongering, and vowed that in the future they would live in perfect accord and good-will.

Jongejuffrouw Beresteyn, too, thought of all her friends and acquaintances with the kindliest of feelings, and she had not a harsh thought for anyone in her heart … not for anyone, at any rate, who was good and deserving.… As for that knavish malapert with the merry, twinkling eyes and the mocking smile, surely God would not desire her to be in charity with him; a more ungrateful, more impertinent wretch, she had never met, and it was quite consoling to think of all that Mynheer Beresteyn's influence could have done for those three ragamuffins, and how in the near future they must all suffer abominable discomfort, mayhap with shortage of food and drink, or absence of shelter, when no doubt one of them at least would remember with contrition the magnanimous offer of help made to him by gracious lips, and which he had so insolently refused.

So absorbed was Jongejuffrouw Beresteyn in these thoughts that she never even noticed that the watch-night service was over, and the minister already filing out with the clerk. The general exodus around her recalled her to herself and also to a sense of contrition for the absent way in which she had assisted at this solemn service.

She whispered to Maria to wait for her outside the church with the men.

"I must yet pray for a little while alone," she said. "I will join you at the north door in a quarter of an hour."

And she fell on her knees, and was soon absorbed in prayer.

Maria found the two serving men in the crowd, and transmitted to them her mistress's orders. The cathedral had been very full for the service, and the worshippers took a long time filing out; they lingered about in the aisles, exchanging bits of city gossip and wishing one another a happy New Year.

The verger had much ado to drive the goodly people out of the edifice, no sooner had he persuaded one group of chatterers to continue their conversation on the Grootemarkt outside, than another batch seemed to loom out of the shadows, equally determined to conclude its gossip here in the warmth, before sallying forth once more into the foggy midnight air.

"I must close the cathedral for the night," the worthy man repeated piteously, "do you think that I don't want to get home and eat my watch-night supper at a reasonable hour. Move on there, my masters, move out please! My orders are to have the church closed before one o'clock."

He came on a group of men who sat together in the shadow of a heavy pillar close behind the pulpit.

"Now then, mynheers," he said, "'tis closing time."

But those that were there made no sign to obey.

"All right, Perk," said one of them in a whisper, "we are not going just yet."

"Aye, but ye are," retorted the verger gruffly, for he was cross now and wanting his supper, "what should I allow ye to stay for?"

"For the memory of Jan!" was the whispered response.

The verger's manner changed in an instant, the few words evidently bore some portentous meaning of which he held the key — and I doubt not but that the key was made of silver.

"All right, mynheers," he said softly, "the church will be clear in a few minutes now."

"Go round, Perk," said he who had first spoken, "and let us know when all is safe."

The verger touched his forelock and silently departed. Those that were there in the shadow by the great pillar remained in silence awaiting his return. The congregation was really dispersing now, the patter of leather shoes on the flagstones of the floor became gradually more faint; then it died out altogether. That portion of the Groote Kerk where is situated the magnificent carved pulpit was already quite dark and wholly deserted save for that group of silent, waiting figures that looked like shadows within the shadows.

Anon the verger returned. He had only been absent a few minutes.

"Quite safe now, mynheers," he said, "the last of them has just gone through the main door. I have locked all the doors save the West. If you want anything you will find me there. I can leave this one light for you, the others I must put out."

"Put them out, Perk, by all means," was the ready response. "We can find our way about in the dark."

The verger left them undisturbed; his shuffling steps were heard gliding along the flagstones until their murmur died away in the vastness of the sacred edifice.

The group of men who sat behind the pulpit against the heavy pillar, now drew their rush chairs closer to one another.

There were six of them altogether, and the light from the lamp above illumined their faces, which were stern looking, dark and of set determination. All six of them were young; only one amongst them might have been more than thirty years of age; that a great purpose brought them here to-night was obvious from their attitude, the low murmur of their voices, that air of mystery which hung round them, fostered by the dark cloaks which they held closely wrapped round their shoulders and the shadows from the pillar which they sought.

One of them appeared to be the centre of their interest, a man, lean and pallid-looking, with hollow purple-rimmed eyes, that spoke of night vigils or mayhap of unavowed, consuming thoughts. The mouth was hard and thin, and a febrile excitement caused his lips to quiver and his hand to shake.

The others hung upon his words.

"Tell us some of your adventures, Stoutenburg!" said one of them eagerly.

Stoutenburg laughed harshly and mirthlessly.

"They would take years in telling," he said, "mayhap one day I'll write them down. They would fill many a volume."

"Enough that you did contrive to escape," said another man, "and that you are back here amongst us once more."

"Yes! in order to avenge wrongs that are as countless by now as the grains of sand on the sea-shore," rejoined Stoutenburg earnestly.

"You know that you are not safe inside Holland," suggested he who had first spoken.

"Aye, my good Beresteyn, I know that well enough," said Stoutenburg with a long and bitter sigh. "Your own father would send me to the gallows if he had the chance, and you with me mayhap, for consorting with me."

"My father owes his position, his wealth, the prosperity of his enterprise to the Stadtholder," said Beresteyn, speaking with as much bitterness as his friend. "He looked upon the last conspiracy against the life of the Prince of Orange as a crime blacker than the blackest sin that ever deserved hell....If he thought that I ...at the present moment...."

"Yes I know. But he has not the power to make you false to me, has he, Nicolaes?" asked Stoutenburg anxiously. "You are still at one with us?"

"With you to the death!" replied Beresteyn fervently, "so are we all."

"Aye! that we are," said the four others with one accord, whilst one of them added dryly:

"And determined not to fail like the last time by trusting those paid hirelings, who will take your money and betray you for more."

"Last February we were beset with bunglers and self-seekers," said Stoutenburg, "my own brother Grœneveld was half-hearted in everything save the desire to make money. Slatius was a vindictive boor, van Dyk was a busy-body and Korenwinder a bloated fool. Well! they have paid their penalty. Heaven have their souls! But for God's sake let us do the work ourselves this time."

"They say that the Stadtholder is sick unto death," said one of the men sombrely. "Disease strikes with a surer hand sometimes than doth the poniard of an enemy."

"Bah! I have no time to waste waiting for his death," retorted Stoutenburg roughly, "there is an opportunity closer at hand and more swift than the weary watching for the slow ravages of disease. The Stadtholder comes to Amsterdam next week; the burghers of his beloved city have begged of him to be present at the consecration of the Western Kerk, built by Mynheer van Keyser, as well as at the opening of the East India Company's new hall. He plays up for popularity just now. The festivals in connection with the double event at Amsterdam have tempted him to undertake the long journey from the frontier, despite his failing health. His visit to this part of the country is a golden opportunity which I do not intend to miss."

"You will find it very difficult to get near the Stadtholder on such an occasion," remarked Beresteyn. "He no longer drives about unattended as he used to do."

"All the escort in the world will not save him from my revenge," said Stoutenburg firmly. "Our position now is stronger than it has ever been. I have adherents in every city of Holland and of Zealand, aye, and in the south too as far as Breda and in the east as far as Arnhem. I tell you, friends, that I have spread a net over this country out of which Maurice of Orange cannot escape. My organisation too is better than it was. I have spies within the camp at

Sprang, a knot of determined men all along the line between Breda and Amsterdam, at Gouda, at Delft … especially at Delft."

"Why specially there?" asked Beresteyn.

"Because I have it in my mind that mayhap we need not take the risks of accomplishing our coup in Amsterdam itself. As you say it might be very difficult and very dangerous to get at the Stadtholder on a public occasion.… But Delft is on the way.… Maurice of Orange is certain to halt at Delft, if only in order to make a pilgrimage to the spot where his father was murdered. He will, I am sure, sleep more than one night at the Prinsenhof.… And from Delft the way leads northwards past Ryswyk — Ryswyk close to which I have had my headquarters three weeks past — Ryswyk, my friends!" he continued, speaking very rapidly almost incoherently in his excitement, "where I have arms and ammunition, Ryswyk, which is the rallying point for all my friends … the molens! you remember?… close to the wooden bridge which spans the Schie.… I have enough gunpowder stored at that molens to blow up twenty wooden bridges … and the Stadtholder with his escort must cross the wooden bridge which spans the Schie not far from the molens where I have my headquarters.… I have it all in my mind already.… I only wait to hear news of the actual day when the Stadtholder leaves his camp.… I can tell you more to-morrow, but in the meanwhile I want to know if there are a few men about here on whom I can rely at a moment's notice … whom I can use as spies or messengers … or even to lend me a hand at Ryswyk in case of need … thirty or forty would be sufficient … if they are good fighting men.… I said something about this in my message to you all."

"And I for one acted on your suggestion at once," said one of the others. "I have recruited ten stout fellows: Germans and Swiss, who know not a word of our language. I pay them well and they ask no questions. They will fight for you, spy for you, run for you, do anything you choose, and can betray nothing, since they know nothing. They are at your disposal at any moment."

"That is good, and I thank you, my dear Heemskerk."

"I have half a dozen peasants on my own estate on whom I can rely," said another of Stoutenburg's friends. "They are good fighters, hard-headed and ready to go through fire and water for me. They are as safe as foreign mercenaries, for they will do anything I tell them and will do it without asking the reason why."

"I have another eight or ten foreigners to offer you," said a third, "they come from a part of Britain called Scotland so I understand. I picked them up a week ago when they landed at Scheveningen and engaged them in my service then and there."

"And I can lay my hand at any moment on a dozen or so young apprentices in my father's factory," added a fourth, "they are always ready for a frolic or a fight and ready to follow me to hell if need be."

"You see that you can easily count on three dozen men," concluded Beresteyn.

"Three dozen men ready to hand," said Stoutenburg, "for our present needs they should indeed suffice. Knowing that I can reckon on them I can strike the decisive blow when and how I think it best. It is the blow that counts," he continued between set teeth, "after that everything is easy enough. The waverers hang back until success is assured. But our secret adherents in Holland can be counted by the score, in Zealand and Utrecht by the hundred. When Maurice of Orange has paid with his own blood the penalty which his crimes have incurred, when I can proclaim myself over his dead body Stadtholder of the Northern Provinces, Captain and Admiral General of the State, thousands will rally round us and flock to our banner. Thousands feel as we do, think as we do, and know what we know, that John of Barneveld will not rest in his grave till I, his last surviving son, have avenged him. Who made this Republic what she is? My father. Who gave the Stadtholder the might which he possesses? My father. My father whose name was revered and honoured throughout the length and breadth of Europe and whom an ingrate's hand hath branded with the mark of traitor. The Stadtholder brought my father to the scaffold, heaping upon him accusations of treachery which he himself must have known were groundless. When the Stadtholder sent John of Barneveld to the scaffold he committed a crime which can only be atoned for by his own blood. Last year we failed. The mercenaries whom we employed betrayed us. My brother, our friends went the way my father led, victims all of them of the rapacious ambition, the vengeful spite of the Stadtholder. But I escaped as by a miracle! — a miracle I say it was, my friends, a miracle wrought by the God of vengeance, who hath said: 'I will repay!' He hath also said that whosoever sheds the blood of man, by man shall his blood be shed! I am the instrument of his vengeance. Vengeance is mine! 'tis I who will repay!"

He had never raised his voice during this long peroration, but his diction had been none the less impressive because it was spoken under his breath. The others had listened in silence, awed, no doubt, by the bitter flood of hate which coursed through every vein of this man's body and poured in profusion from his lips. The death of father and brother and of many friends, countless wrongs, years of misery, loss of caste, of money and of home had numbed him against every feeling save that of revenge.

"This time I'll let no man do the work for me," he said after a moment's silence, "if you will all stand by me, I will smite the Stadtholder with mine own hand."

This time he had raised his voice, just enough to wake the echo that slept in the deserted edifice.

"Hush!" whispered one of his friends, "Hush! for God's sake!"

"Bah! the church is empty," retorted Stoutenburg, "and the verger too far away to hear. I'll say it again, and proclaim it loudly now in this very church before the altar of God: I will kill the Stadtholder with mine own hand!"

"Silence in the name of God!"

More than one muffled voice had uttered the warning and Beresteyn's hand fell heavily on Stoutenburg's arm.

"Hush, I say!" he whispered hoarsely, "there's something moving there in the darkness."

"A rat mayhap!" quoth Stoutenburg lightly.

"No, no … listen!… some one moves … some one has been there … all along.…"

"A spy!" murmured the others under their breath.

In a moment every man there had his hand on his sword: Stoutenburg and Beresteyn actually drew theirs. They did not speak to one another for they had caught one another's swift glance, and the glance had in it the forecast of a grim resolve.

Whoever it was who thus moved silently out of the shadows — spy or merely indiscreet listener — would pay with his life for the knowledge which he had obtained. These men here could no longer afford to take any risks. The words spoken by Stoutenburg and registered by them all could be made the stepping stones to the scaffold if strange ears had caught their purport.

They meant death to someone, either to the speakers or to the eavesdropper; and six men were determined that it should be the eavesdropper who must pay for his presence here.

They forced their eyes to penetrate the dense gloom which surrounded them, and one and all held their breath, like furtive animals that await their prey. They stood there silent and rigid, a tense look on every face; the one light fixed in the pillar above them played weirdly on their starched ruffs scarce whiter than the pallid hue of their cheeks.

Then suddenly a sound caught their ears, which caused each man to start and to look at his nearest companion with set inquiring eyes; it was the sound of a woman's skirt swishing against the stone-work of the floor. The seconds went by leaden-footed and full of portentous meaning. Each heart-beat beneath the vaulted roof of the cathedral to-night seemed like a knell from eternity.

How slow the darkness was in yielding up its secret!

At last as the conspirators gazed, they saw the form of a woman emerging out of the shadows. At first they could only see her starched kerchief and a glimmer of jewels beneath her cloak. Then gradually the figure — ghostlike in this dim light — came more fully into view; the face of a woman, her lace coif, the gold embroidery of her stomacher all became detached one by one, but only for a few seconds, for the woman was walking rapidly, nor did she look to right or left, but glided along the floor like a vision — white, silent, swift — which might have been conjured up by a fevered brain.

"A ghost!" whispered one of the young men hoarsely.

"No. A woman," said another, and the words came like a hissing sound through his teeth.

Beresteyn and Stoutenburg said nothing for a while. They looked silently on one another, the same burning anxiety glowing in their eyes, the same glance of mute despair passing from one to the other.

"Gilda!" murmured Stoutenburg at last.

The swish of the woman's skirt had died away in the distance; not one of the men had attempted to follow her or to intercept her passage.

Jongejuffrouw Beresteyn, no spy of course, just a chance eavesdropper! but possessed nevertheless now of a secret which meant death to them all!

"How much did she hear think you?" asked Stoutenburg at last.

He had replaced his sword in his scabbard with a gesture that expressed his own sense of fatality. He could not use his sword against a woman — even had that woman not been Gilda Beresteyn.

"She cannot have heard much," said one of the others, "we spoke in whispers."

"If she had heard anything she would have known that only the west door was to remain open. Yet she has made straight for the north portal," suggested another.

"If she did not hear the verger speaking she could not have heard what we said," argued a third somewhat lamely.

Every one of them had some suggestion to put forward, some surmise to express, some hope to urge. Only Beresteyn said nothing. He had stood by, fierce and silent ever since he had first recognized his sister; beneath his lowering brows the resolve had not died out of his eyes, and he still held his sword unsheathed in his hand.

Stoutenburg now appealed directly to him.

"What do you think of it, Beresteyn?" he asked.

"I think that my sister did hear something of our conversation," he answered quietly.

"Great God!" ejaculated the others.

"But," added Beresteyn slowly, "I pledge you mine oath that she will not betray us."

"How will you make sure of that?" retorted Stoutenburg, not without a sneer.

"That is mine affair."

"And ours too. We can do nothing, decide on nothing until we are sure."

"Then I pray you wait for me here," concluded Beresteyn. "I will bring you a surety before we part this night."

"Let me go and speak to her," urged Stoutenburg.

"No, no, 'tis best that I should go."

Stoutenburg made a movement as if he would detain him, then seemed to think better of it, and finally let him go.

Beresteyn did not wait for further comment from his friends but quickly turned on his heel. The next moment he was speeding away across the vast edifice and his tall figure was soon swallowed up by the gloom.

CHAPTER V
BROTHER AND SISTER

The verger on guard at the west door had quietly dropped to sleep. He did not wake apparently when Jongejuffrouw Beresteyn slipped past him and out through the door.

Beresteyn followed close on his sister's heels. He touched her shoulder just as she stood outside the portal, wrapping her fur cloak more snugly over her shoulders and looking round her, anxious where to find her servants.

"'Tis late for you to be out this night, Gilda," he said, "and alone."

"I am only alone for the moment," she replied quietly. "Maria and Jakob and Piet are waiting for me at the north door. I did not know it would be closed."

"But why are you so late?"

"I stayed in church after the service."

"But why?" he insisted more impatiently.

"I could not pray during service," she said. "My thoughts wandered. I wanted to be alone for a few moments with God."

"Did you not know then that you were not alone?"

"No. Not at first."

"But ... afterwards...?"

"Your voice, Nicolaes, struck on my ear. I did not want to hear. I wanted to pray."

"Yet you listened?"

"No. I did not wish to listen."

"But you heard?"

She gave no actual reply, but he could see her profile straight and white, the curved lips firmly pressed together, the brow slightly puckered, and from the expression of her face and of her whole attitude, he knew that she had heard.

He drew in his breath, like one who has received a blow and has not yet realized how deeply it would hurt. His right hand which was resting on his hip tore at the cloth of his doublet, else mayhap it would already have wandered to the hilt of his sword.

He had expected it of course. Already when he saw Gilda gliding out of the shadows with that awed, tense expression on her face, he knew that she must have heard ... something at least ... something that had horrified her to the soul.

But now of course there was no longer any room for doubt. She had heard everything and the question was what that knowledge, lodged in her brain, might mean to him and to his friends.

Just for a moment the frozen, misty atmosphere took on a reddish hue, his tongue clove to the roof of his mouth, a cold sweat broke out upon his forehead.

He looked around him furtively, fearfully, wondering whence came that hideous, insinuating whisper which was freezing the marrow in his bones. No doubt that had she spoken then, had she reproached or adjured, he would have found it impossible to regain mastery over himself. But she looked so unimpassioned, so still, so detached, that self-control came back to him, and for the moment she was safe.

"Will you tell me what you did hear?" he asked after awhile, with seeming calm, though he felt as if his words must choke him, and her answer strike him dead.

"I heard," she said, speaking very slowly and very quietly, "that the Lord of Stoutenburg has returned, and is trying to drag you and others into iniquity to further his own ambitious schemes."

"You wrong him there, Gilda. The Lord of Stoutenburg has certain wrongs to avenge which cry aloud to Heaven."

"We will not argue about that, Nicolaes," she said coldly. "Murder is hideous, call it what you will. The brand of Cain doth defame a man and carries its curse with it. No man can justify so dastardly a crime. 'Tis sophistry to suggest it."

"Then in sending Barneveld to the scaffold did the Prince of Orange call that curse upon himself, a curse which — please the God of vengeance! — will come home to him now at last."

"'Tis not for you, Nicolaes, to condemn him, who has heaped favours, kindness, bounties upon our father and upon us. 'Tis not for you, the Stadtholder's debtor for everything you are, for everything that you possess, 'tis not for you to avenge Barneveld's wrongs."

"'Tis not for you, my sister," he retorted hotly, "to preach to me your elder brother. I alone am responsible for mine actions, and have no account to give to any one."

"You owe an account of your actions to your father and to me, Nicolaes, since your dishonour will fall upon us too."

"Take care, Gilda, take care!" he exclaimed hoarsely, "you speak of things which are beyond your ken, but in speaking them you presume on my forebearance … and on your sex."

"There is no one in sight," she said calmly, "you may strike me without fear. One crime more or less on your conscience will soon cease to trouble you."

"Gilda!" he cried with sudden passionate reproach.

At this involuntary cry — in which the expression of latent affection for her struggled with that of his rage and of his burning anxiety — all her own tender feelings for him, her womanliness, her motherly instincts were re-awakened in an instant. They had only been dormant for awhile, because of her horror of what she had heard. And that horror of a monstrous deed, that sense of shame that he — her brother — should be so ready to acquiesce in a crime had momentarily silenced the call of sisterly love. But this love once re-awakened was strong enough to do battle in her heart on his behalf: the tense rigidity of her attitude relaxed, her mouth softened, her eyes filled with tears. The next moment she had turned fully to him and was looking pleadingly into his face.

"Little brother," she murmured gently, "tell me that it is not true. That it was all a hideous dream."

He looked down on her for a moment. It pleased him to think that her affection for him was still there, that at any rate his personal safety might prove a potent argument against the slightest thought of indiscretion on her part. She tried to read his thoughts, but everything was dark around them both, the outline of his brow and mouth alone stood clearly out from the gloom: the expression of his eyes she could not fathom. But womanlike she was ready to believe that he would relent. It is so difficult for a woman to imagine that one whom she loves is really prone to evil. She loved this brother dearly, and did not grasp the fact that he had reached a point in his life when a woman's pleading had not the power to turn him from his purpose. She did not know how deeply he had plunged into the slough of conspiracy, and that the excitement of it had fired his blood to the exclusion of righteousness and of loyalty. She hoped — in the simplicity of her heart — that he was only misled, that evil counsels had only temporarily prevailed. Like a true woman she still saw the child in this brother who had grown to manhood by her side.

Therefore she appealed and she pleaded, she murmured tender words and made fond suggestions, all the while that his heart was hard to everything except to the one purpose which she was trying to thwart.

Not unkindly but quite firmly he detached her clinging arms from round his neck.

"Let us call it a dream, little sister," he said firmly, "and do you try and forget it."

"That I cannot, Nicolaes," she replied, "unless you will promise me…."

"To betray my friends?" he sneered.

"I would not ask you to do that: but you can draw back … it is not too late….For our father's sake, and for mine, Nicolaes," she pleaded once more earnestly. "Oh think, little brother, think! It cannot be that you could countenance such a hideous crime, you who were always so loyal and so brave! I remember when you were quite a tiny boy what contempt you had for little Jakob Steyn because he told lies, and how you thrashed Frans van Overstein because he ill-treated a dog….Little brother, when our father was ruined, penniless, after that awful siege of Haarlem, which is still a hideous memory to him, the Prince of Orange helped him with friendship and money to re-establish his commerce, he stood by him loyally, constantly, until more prosperous days dawned upon our house. Little brother, you have oft heard our father tell the tale, think ... oh, think of the blow you would be dealing him if you lent a hand to conspiracy against the Prince. Little brother, for our father's sake, for mine, do not let yourself be dragged into the toils of that treacherous Stoutenburg."

"You call him treacherous now, but you loved him once."

"It is because I loved him once," she rejoined earnestly, "that I call him treacherous now."

He made no comment on this, for he knew in his heart of hearts that what she said was true. He knew nothing of course of the events of that night in the early spring of the year when Gilda had sheltered and comforted the man who had so basely betrayed her; but for her ministration to him then, when exhausted and half-starved he sought shelter under her roof, in her very room — he would not have lived for this further plotting and this further infamy, nor yet to drag her brother down with him into the abyss of his own disgrace.

Of this nocturnal visit Gilda had never spoken to anyone, not even to Nicolaes who she knew was Stoutenburg's friend, least of all to her father, whose wrath would have fallen heavily on her had he known that she had harboured a traitor in his house.

"Stoutenburg lied to me, Nicolaes," she now said, seeing that still her brother remained silent and morose, "he lied to me when he stole my love, only to cast it away from him as soon as ambition called him from my side. And as he lied then, so will he lie to you, little brother, he will steal your allegiance, use you for his own ends and cast you ruthlessly from him if he find you no longer useful. Yes, I did love him once," she continued earnestly, "when he thought of staining his hands with murder my love finally turned to contempt. This new infamy which he plots hath filled the measure of my hate. Turn from him, little brother, I do entreat you with my whole soul. He has been false to his God, false to his prince, false to me! he will be false to you!"

"It is too late, Gilda," he retorted sombrely, "even if I were so minded, which please God! I am not."

"It is never too late to draw back from such an abyss of shame."

"Be silent, girl," he said more roughly, angered that he was making no headway against her obstinacy. "God-verdomme! but I am a fool indeed to stand and parley here with you, when grave affairs wait upon my time. You talk at random and of things you do not understand: I had no mind to argue this matter out with you."

"I do not detain you, Nicolaes," she said simply, with a sigh of bitter disappointment. "If you will but call Maria and the men who wait at the north door, I can easily relieve you of my presence."

"Yes, and you can go home to your pots and pans, to your sewing and your linen-chest, and remember to hold your tongue, as a woman should do, for if you breathe of what you have heard, if you betray Stoutenburg who is my friend, it is me — your only brother — whom you will be sending to the scaffold."

"I would not betray you, Nicolaes," she said.

"Or any of my friends?"

"Or any of your friends."

"You swear it?" he urged.

"There is no need for an oath."

"Yes, there is a pressing need for an oath, Gilda," he retorted sternly. "My friends expect it of you, and you must pledge yourself to them, to forget all that you heard to-night and never to breathe of it to any living soul."

"I cannot swear," she replied, "to forget that which my memory will retain in spite of my will: nor would I wish to forget, because I mean to exert all the power I possess to dissuade you from this abominable crime, and because I mean to pray to God with all my might that He may prevent the crime from being committed."

"You may pray as much as you like," he said roughly, "but I'll not have you breathe a word of it to any living soul."

"My father has the right to know of the disgrace that threatens him."

"You would not tell him?" he exclaimed hoarsely.

"Not unless...."

"Unless what?"

"I cannot say. 'Tis all in God's hands and I do not know yet what my duty is. As you say I am only a woman, and my place is with my pots and pans, my sewing and my spindle. I have no right to have thoughts of mine own. Perhaps you are right, and in that case my father must indeed be the one to act. But this I do swear to you, Nicolaes, that before you stain your hand with the blood of one who, besides being your sovereign lord, is your father's benefactor and friend, I will implore God above, that my father and I may both die ere we see you and ourselves so disgraced."

Before he could detain her by word or gesture she had slipped past him and turned to walk quickly toward the façade of the cathedral. An outstanding piece of masonry soon hid her from his view. For the moment he had thoughts of following her. Nicolaes Beresteyn was not a man who liked being thwarted, least of all by a woman, and there was a sense of insecurity for him in what she had said at the last. His life and that of his friends lay in the hands of that young girl who had spoken some very hard words to him just now. He loved her as a brother should, and would not for his very life have seen her in any danger, but he had all a man's desire for mastery and hatred of dependence: she had angered and defied him, and yet remained in a sense his master.

He and his friends were dependent on her whim — he would not call it loyalty or sense of duty to be done — it was her whim that would hold the threads of a conspiracy which he firmly believed had the welfare of Holland and of religion for its object, and it was her whim that would hold the threat of the scaffold over himself and Stoutenburg and the others. The situation was intolerable.

He ground his heel upon the stone and muttered an oath under his breath. If only Gilda had been a man how simple would his course of action have been. A man can be coerced by physical means, but a woman ... and that woman his own sister!

It was hard for Nicolaes Beresteyn, to have to think the situation out calmly, dispassionately, to procrastinate, to let the matter rest at any rate until the next day. But this he knew that he must do. He felt that he had exhausted all the arguments, all the reasonings that were consistent with his own pride; and how could he hope to coerce her into oaths or promises of submission here in the open street and with Maria and Jakob and Piet close by — eavesdropping mayhap?

Gilda was obstinate and had always been allowed more latitude in the way of thinking things out for herself than was good for any woman; but Nicolaes knew that she would not take any momentous step in a hurry. She would turn the whole of the circumstances over in her mind and as she said do some praying too. What she would do afterwards he dared not even conjecture.

For the moment he was forced to leave her alone, and primarily he decided to let his friends know at once how the matter stood.

He found them waiting anxiously for his return. I doubt if they had spoken much during his absence. A chorus of laconic inquiry greeted him as soon as his firm step rang out upon the flagstones.

"Well?"

"She has heard everything," he said quietly, "but, she will not betray us. To this I pledge ye my word."

CHAPTER VI
THE COUNSELS OF PRUDENCE

Neither Stoutenburg nor any of the others had made reply to Beresteyn's firmly spoken oath. They were hard-headed Dutchmen, every one of them: men of action rather than men of words: for good or ill the rest of the world can judge them forever after by their deeds alone.

Therefore when the spectre of betrayal and of subsequent death appeared so suddenly before them they neither murmured nor protested. They could not in reason blame Beresteyn for his sister's presence in the cathedral this night, nor yet that her thoughts and feelings in the matter of the enmity between the Stadtholder and the Barneveld family did not coincide with their own.

Silently they walked across the vast and lonely cathedral and filed one by one out of the western door where Perk still held faithful watch. Stoutenburg, their leader, had his lodgings in a small house situate at the top of the Kleine Hout Straat, close to the well-known hostelry at the sign of the "Lame Cow." This latter was an hostelry of unimpeachable repute and thither did the six friends decide to go ere finally going home for the night.

It had been decided between them some time ago that those who were able to do so would show themselves in public as much as possible during the next few days, so as to ward off any suspicion of intrigue which their frequent consorting in secluded places might otherwise have aroused.

Out in the open they thought it best to disperse, electing to walk away two and two rather than in a compact group which might call forth the close attention of the night watchmen.

Stoutenburg linked his arm in that of Beresteyn.

"Let the others go on ahead," he said confidentially, "you and I, friend, must understand one another ere we part for this night."

Then as Beresteyn made no immediate reply, he continued calmly:

"This will mean hanging for the lot of us this time, Nicolaes!"

"I pray to God ..." exclaimed the other hoarsely.

"God will have nought to say in the matter, my friend," retorted Stoutenburg dryly, "'tis only the Stadtholder who will have his say, and do you think that he is like to pardon...."

"Gilda will never...."

"Oh, yes, she will," broke in Stoutenburg firmly; "be not deluded into thoughts of security. Gilda will think the whole of this matter over for four and twenty hours at the longest, after which, feeling herself in an impasse between her affection for you and her horror of me, she will think it her duty to tell your father all that she heard in the cathedral to-night."

"Even then," said Beresteyn, hotly, "my father would not send his only son to the gallows."

"Do you care to take that risk?" was the other man's calm retort.

"What can I do?"

"You must act decisively and at once, my friend," said Stoutenburg dryly, "an you do not desire to see your friends marched off to torture and the scaffold with yourself following in their wake."

"But how? how?" exclaimed Beresteyn.

His was by far the weaker nature of the two: easily led, easily swayed by a will stronger than his own. Stoutenburg wielded vast influence over him; he had drawn him into the net of his own ambitious schemes, and had by promises and cajolery won his entire allegiance. Now that destruction and death threatened Nicolaes through his own sister — whom he sincerely loved — he turned instinctively to Stoutenburg for help and for advice.

"It is quite simple," said the latter slowly. "Gilda must be temporarily made powerless to do us any harm."

"How?" reiterated Beresteyn helplessly.

"Surely you can think of some means yourself," retorted Stoutenburg somewhat impatiently. "Self-preservation is an efficient sharpener of wits as a rule, and your own life is in the hands of a woman now, my friend."

"You seem to forget that that woman is my sister. How can I conspire to do her bodily harm?"

"Who spake of bodily harm, you simpleton?" quoth Stoutenburg with a harsh laugh, "'tis you who seem to forget that if Gilda is your sister she is also the woman whom I love more than my life ...more than my ambition ...more even than my revenge...."

He paused a moment, for despite his usual self-control his passion at this moment threatened to master him. His voice rose harsh and quivering, and was like to attract the notice of passers-by. After a moment or two he conquered his emotion and said more calmly:

"Friend, we must think of our country and of our faith; we must think of the success of our schemes: and, though Gilda be dear to us both — infinitely dear to me — she must not be allowed to interfere with the great object which we hope to attain. Think out a way therefore of placing her in such a position that she cannot harm us: have her conveyed to some place where she can be kept a prisoner for a few days until I have accomplished what I have set out to do."

Then as Beresteyn said nothing, seeming to be absorbed in some new train of thought, Stoutenburg continued more persuasively:

"I would I could carry her away myself and hold her — a beloved prisoner — while others did my work for me. But that I cannot do: for 'twere playing the part of a coward and I have sworn before the altar of God that I would kill the Stadtholder with mine own hand. Nor would I have the courage so to offend her: for let me tell you this, Nicolaes, that soaring even above my most ambitious dreams, is the hope that when these have been realized, I may ask Gilda to share my triumph with me."

"Nor would I have the courage so to offend my sister ...my father," said Beresteyn. "You speak of carrying her off, and holding her a prisoner for eight days perhaps, or even a fortnight. How can I, her own brother, do that? 'Tis an outrage she would never forgive: my father would curse me ...disinherit me ...turn me out of house and home...."

"And will he not curse you now, when he knows — when to-morrow mayhap, Gilda will have told him that you, his son, have joined hands with the Lord of Stoutenburg in a conspiracy to murder the Prince of Orange — will he not disinherit you then? turn you out of house and home?"

"Hold on for mercy's sake," exclaimed Beresteyn, who bewildered by the terrible alternative thus put ruthlessly before him, felt that he must collect his thoughts, and must — for the moment at any rate — put away from him the tempter who insinuated thoughts of cowardice into his brain.

"I'll say no more, then," said Stoutenburg quietly, "think it all over, Nicolaes. My life, your own, those of all our friends are entirely in your hands: the welfare of the State, the triumph of our faith depend on the means which you will devise for silencing Gilda for a few brief days."

After which there was silence between the two men. Beresteyn walked more rapidly along, his fur-lined cloak wrapped closely round him, his arms folded tightly across his chest and his hands clenched underneath his cloak. Stoutenburg on the other hand was also willing to let the matter drop and to allow the subtle poison which he had instilled into his friend's mind to ferment and bring forth such thoughts as would suit his own plans.

He knew how to gauge exactly the somewhat vacillating character of Nicolaes Beresteyn, and had carefully touched every string of that highly nervous organization till he left it quivering with horror at the present and deathly fear for the future.

Gilda was a terrible danger, of that there could be no doubt. Nicolaes had realized this to the full: the instinct of self-preservation was strong in him; he would think over Stoutenburg's bold suggestion and would find a way how to act on it. And at the bottom of his tortuous heart Stoutenburg already cherished the hope that this new complication which had dragged Gilda into the net of his own intrigues would also ultimately throw her — a willing victim — into his loving arms.

CHAPTER VII
THREE PHILOSOPHERS AND THEIR FRIENDS

Whereupon Chance forged yet another link in the chain of a man's destiny.

I pray you follow me now to the tapperij of the "Lame Cow." I had not asked you to accompany me thither were it not for the fact that the "Lame Cow" situate in the Kleine Hout Straat not far from the Cathedral, was a well-ordered and highly respectable tavern, where indeed the sober merry-makers of Haarlem as well as the gay and gilded youth of the city were wont to seek both pleasure and solace.

You all know the house with its flat façade of red brick, its small windows and tall, very tall gabled roof that ends in a point high up above the front door. The tapperij is on your left as you enter. It is wainscotted with oak which was already black with age in the year 1623; above the wainscot the walls are white-washed, and Mynheer Beek, the host of the "Lame Cow," who is a pious man, has hung the walls round with scriptural texts, appropriate to his establishment, such as: "Eat, drink and be merry!" and "Drink thy wine with a merry heart!"

From which I hope that I have convinced you that the "Lame Cow" was an eminently orderly place of conviviality, where worthy burghers of Haarlem could drink ale and hot posset in the company of mevrouws, their wives.

And it was to this highly praised and greatly respected establishment that three tired-out and very thirsty philosophers repaired this New Year's night, instead of attending the watch-night service at one of the churches.

Diogenes, feeling that three guilders still reposed safely in his wallet, declared his intention of continuing his career as a gentleman, and a gentleman of course could not resort to one of those low-class taverns which were usually good enough for foreign adventurers.

And thus did Fate have her will with him and brought him here this night.

Moreover the tap-room of the "Lame Cow" wore a very gay appearance always on New Year's night. It was noted for its clientèle on that occasion, for the good Rhenish wine which it dispensed, and for the gay sight engendered by the Sunday gowns of the burghers and their ladies who came here after service for a glass of wine and multifarious relish.

As the night was fine, despite the hard frost, Mynheer Beek expected to be unusually busy. Already he had arranged on the polished tables the rows of pewter platters heaped up with delicacies which he knew would be in great request when the guests would begin to arrive: smoked sausage garnished with horseradish, roasted liver and slabs of cheese.

The serving wenches with the sleeves of their linen shifts tucked well up above their round red arms, their stolid faces streaming with perspiration, were busy polishing tables that already were over-polished and making pewter mugs to shine that already shone with a dazzling radiance.

For the nonce the place was still empty and the philosophers when they entered were able to select the table at which they wished to sit — one near the hearth in which blazed gigantic logs, and at which they could stretch out their limbs with comfort.

At Diogenes' suggestion they all made hasty repairs to their disordered toilet, and re-adjusted the set of their collars and cuffs with the help of the small mirror that hung close by against the wall.

Three strange forms of a truth that were thus mirrored in turns.

Socrates with a hole in his head, now freshly bandaged with a bit of clean linen by the sympathetic hand of a serving maid: his hooked nose neatly washed till it shone like the pewter handle of a knife, his pointed cranium but sparsely furnished with lanky black hair peeping out above the bandage like a yellow wurzel in wrappings of paper. His arms and legs were unusually long and unusually thin, and he had long lean hands and long narrow feet, but his body was short and slightly bent forward as if under the weight of his head, which also was narrow and long. His neck was like that of a stork that has been half-plucked, it rose from out the centre of his ruffled collar with a curious undulating movement, which suggested that he could turn it right round and look at the middle of his own back. He wore a brown doublet of duffle and brown trunks and hose, and boots that appeared to be too big even for his huge feet.

Beside him Pythagoras looked like the full stop in a semi-colon, for he was but little over five feet in height and very fat. His doublet of thick green cloth had long ago burst its buttons across his protuberent chest. His face, which was round as a full moon, was highly coloured even to the tip of his small upturned nose, and his forehead, crowned by a thick mass of red-brown hair which fell in heavy and lanky waves down to his eyebrows, was always wet and shiny. He had a habit of standing with legs wide apart, his abdomen thrust forward and his small podgy hands resting upon it. His eyes were very small and blinked incessantly. Below his double chin he wore a huge bow of starched white linen, which at this moment was sadly crumpled and stained, and his collar which also had seen more prosperous days was held together by a piece of string.

Like his friend Socrates, his trunk and hose were of worsted, and he wore high leather boots which reached well above the knee and looked to have been intended for a much taller person. The hat, with the tall sugar-loaf crown, which he had picked up after the fray in the Dam Straat, was much too small for his big round head. He tried, before the mirror, to adjust it at a becoming angle.

In strange contrast to these two worthies was their friend whom they called Diogenes. He himself, had you questioned him ever so closely, could not have told you from what ancestry or what unknown parent had come to him that air of swagger and of assurance which his avowed penury had never the power to subdue. Tall above the average, powerfully built and solidly planted on firm limbs he looked what he easily might have been, a gentleman to the last inch of him. The brow was fine and broad, the nose sensitive and well shaped, the mouth a perfect expression of gentle irony. The soft brown hair, abundant and unruly, lent perhaps a certain air of untamed wildness to the face, whilst the upturned moustache and the tiny tuft below the upper lip accentuated the look of devil-may-care independence which was the chief characteristic of the mouth.

But the eyes were the most remarkable feature of all. They shone with an unconquerable merriment, they twinkled and sparkled, and smiled and mocked, they winked and they beckoned. They were eyes to which you were obliged to smile in response, eyes that made you laugh if you felt ever so sad, eyes that jested even before the mouth had spoken, and the mouth itself was permanently curved into a smile.

Unlike his two companions, Diogenes was dressed not only with scrupulous care but with a show of elegance. His doublet though well-worn was fashioned of fine black cloth, the slashed sleeves still showed the remnants of gold embroidery, whilst the lace of his pleated collar was of beautiful design.

Having completed their toilet the three friends sat at their table and sipped their ale and wine in comparative silence for a time. Socrates, weary with his wound, soon fell asleep with his arms stretched out before him and his head resting in the bend of his elbow.

Pythagoras too nodded in his chair; but Diogenes remained wide awake, and no doubt Mynheer Beek's wine gave him pleasing thoughts, for the merry look never fled from his eyes.

Half an hour later you would scarce have recognised the tapperij from its previous orderly silence, for at about one o'clock it began to fill very fast. Mynheer Beek's guests were arriving.

It was still bitterly cold and they all came into the warm room clapping their hands together and stamping the frozen snow off their feet, loudly demanding hot ale or mulled wine, to be supplemented later on by more substantial fare.

The two serving wenches were more busy, hotter and more profusely streaming with moisture than they had ever been before. It was "Käthi here!" and "Luise, why don't you hurry?" all over the tapperij now; and every moment the noise became louder and more cheery.

Every corner of the low, raftered room was filled to over-flowing with chairs and tables. People sat everywhere where a perch was to be found — on the corners of the tables and on the window sill and many sat on the floor who could not find room elsewhere. The women sat on the men's knees, and many of them had children in their arms as well. For indeed, on watch-night, room had to be found for every one who wanted to come in; no one who wanted to drink and to make merry must be left to wander out in the cold.

A veritable babel of tongues made the white-washed walls echo from end to end, for Haarlem now was a mightily prosperous city, and there were a great many foreign traders inside her walls, and some of these had thought to make merry this night in the famed tap-room of the "Lame Cow." French merchants with their silks, English ones with fine cloths and paper, then there were the Jew dealers from Frankfurt and Amsterdam, and the Walloon cattle drovers from Flanders.

Here and there the splendid uniform of a member of one of the shooting guilds struck a note of splendour among the drabs and russets of worsted doublets and the brilliant crimson or purple sashes gleamed in the feeble light of the tallow candles which spluttered and flickered in their sconces.

Then amongst them all were the foreign mercenaries, from Italy or Brabant or Germany, or from God knows where, loud of speech, aggressive in appearance, carrying swords and wearing spurs, filling the place with their swagger and their ribaldry.

They had come to the Netherlands at the expiration of the truce with Spain, offering to sell their sword and their skin to the highest bidder. They seemed all to be friends and boon companions together, called each other queer, fantastic names and shouted their rough jests to one another across the width of the room. Homeless, shiftless, thriftless, they knew no other names save those which chance or the coarse buffoonery of their friends had endowed them with. There was a man here to-night who was called Wry-face and another who went by the name of Gutter-rat. Not one amongst them mayhap could have told you who his father was or who his mother, nor where he himself had first seen the light of day; but they all knew of one another's career, of one another's prowess in the field at Prague or Ghent or Magdeburg, and they formed a band of brothers — offensive and defensive — which was the despair of the town-guard whenever the law had to be enforced against anyone of them.

It was at the hour when Mynheer Beek was beginning to hope that his guests would soon bethink themselves of returning home and leaving him to his own supper and bed, that a party of these worthies made noisy interruption into the room. They brought with them an atmosphere of boisterous gaiety with their clanking spurs and swords, their loud verbiage and burly personality.

"Hech da!" yelled one of these in a stentorian voice, "whom have we there, snug and cosy in the warmest corner of this hole but our three well-beloved philosophers. Diogenes, old compeer," he shouted still louder than before, "is there room in your tub for your friends?"

"Plenty round this table, O noble Gutter-rat," shouted Diogenes in joyful response, "but let me give you warning that space as well as common funds are running short, and that every newcomer who wants to sit must stand the others a draught of ale apiece; that is the price of a corner of this bench on which ye may sit if ye have a mind."

"Done with you," agreed all the newcomers lustily, and with scant ceremony they pushed their way through the closely packed throng.

They took no notice of the mutterings of more sober customers, angered at seeing their mantles crushed or feeling their toes trodden on. It suddenly seemed as if the whole place belonged to these men and that the peaceful burghers of the city were only here on suffrance.

The three philosophers had already called for some old Rhenish wine on draught. Käthi and Luise brought pewter jugs and more goblets along. Soon Gutter-rat and his friends were installed at the table, squeezed against one another on the narrow wooden benches. Pythagoras had already rolled off his corner seat and was sitting on the floor; Diogenes was perched on the corner of the table.

Socrates roused by the noise, opened a pair of heavy eyes and blinked round him in astonishment. Gutter-rat deposited his bulky form close beside him and brought his large and grimy hand down on the shoulder of the sleepy philosopher.

"Hello, wise Socrates," he cried in his rough, husky voice, "I hope you have been having pleasant dreams."

"No, I have not," growled Socrates laconically.

"Take no heed of him," laughed Diogenes, "he has a hole in his head through which his good temper has been oozing out bit by bit. And yet if you'll all believe me he has been reposing there so peacefully and snoring so lustily that I thought he must be dreaming of Heaven and the last trumpet call."

"I was dreaming of all the chances which Pythagoras and I have missed to-night owing to your d —— d nonsense," said Socrates, who was more sulky now than he had been before he went to sleep.

Pythagoras uttered a prolonged sigh and gazed meditatively down into the depths of his mug of ale. Gutter-rat and the others looked inquiringly from one philosopher to the other.

"Diogenes been at his tricks again?" asked Gutter-rat.

Socrates and Pythagoras nodded in their gloomy response.

"Gallantry, eh? some beauteous damsel, to succour whom we throw our life, our best chances away?" continued the other with ironical sympathy, the while Diogenes' entire face was wreathed in one huge, all-embracing smile. Gutter-rat admonished him with solemn voice and uplifted finger.

"Conduct unworthy a philosopher," he said.

"If he had only injured himself," growled Socrates.

"And let us enjoy the gifts which a beneficent goddess was ready to pour into our lap," added Pythagoras dulcetly from the floor.

"Let's hear the story," concluded Gutter-rat.

The others clapped their mugs against the table-top and shouted: "The story! the story!" to the accompaniment of din that drowned all other noises in the room.

Pythagoras from his lowly position began his narrative in a faint, injured tone of voice. He related the incidents of this night from the moment when the chance of possessing oneself with but little trouble of a tulip bulb worth fifteen thousand florins was so airily flouted, down to the awful moment when a young and beauteous lady made offers of influence and of money which were equally airily refused.

Gutter-rat and the others listened attentively. They specially relished the exciting incidents connected with the affray in Dam Straat, the breaking of Jan Tiele's nose and the dispersal of the mob with the aid of a lighted torch.

"Bravo! splendid!" they shouted at intervals and loudly expressed their regret at having missed such furious fun.

Socrates threw in a word or two now and then, when Pythagoras did not fully explain his own valorous position in the fight, but Diogenes said nothing at all; he allowed his comrade to tell the tale his own way; the recollection of it seemed to afford him vast amusement for he hummed a lively tune to himself all the while.

Pythagoras now was mimicking his friend, throwing into this performance all the disgust which he felt.

"Raise thy hand to my lips, mejuffrouw," he said mincing his words, "momentarily I have not the use of mine own."

His round, beady eyes appealed to his listeners for sympathy, and there is no doubt that he got that in plenty. Gutter-rat more especially highly disapproved of the dénouement of what might have proved a lucrative adventure.

"The rich jongejuffrouw might even have fallen in love with you," he said sternly to Diogenes, "and endowed you with her father's wealth and influence."

"That's just my complaint," said Pythagoras, "but no! what else do you think he said earlier in the evening?"

"Well?"

"To-night we'll behave like gentlemen," quoted the other with ever-growing disgust, "and not like common thieves."

"Why to-night?" queried Gutter-rat in amazement. "Why more especially to-night?"

Pythagoras and Socrates both shrugged their shoulders and suggested no explanation. After which there was more vigorous clapping of mugs against the table-top and Diogenes was loudly summoned to explain.

"Why to-night? why to-night?" was shouted at him from every side.

Diogenes' face became for one brief moment quite grave — quite grave be it said, but for his eyes which believe me could not have looked grave had they tried.

"Because," he said at last when the shouts around him had somewhat subsided, "I had three guilders in my wallet, because my night's lodging is assured for the next three nights and because my chief creditor has died like a hero. Therefore, O comrades all! I could afford the luxury."

"What luxury?" sneered Gutter-rat in disgust, "to refuse the patronage of an influential burgher of this city, backed by the enthusiasm of the beauteous damsel, his daughter?"

"To refuse all patronage, good comrade," assented Diogenes with emphasis.

"Bah! for twenty-four hours!..."

"Yes! for twenty-four hours, friend Gutter-rat, while those three florins last and I have a roof over my head for which I have already paid ... I can for those four and twenty hours afford the luxury of doing exactly and only what it pleases me to do."

He threw up his head and stretched out his massive limbs with a gesture of infinite satisfaction, his merry mocking glance sweeping over the company of watch-night revellers, out-at-elbows ragamuffins, and sober burghers with their respectable vrouws, all of whom were gaping on him open-mouthed.

"For four and twenty hours, my dear Gutter-rat," he continued after a long sigh of contentment, "that is during this day which has just dawned and the night which must inevitably follow it, I am going to give myself the luxury of speaking only when I choose and of being dumb if the fancy so takes me ... while my three florins last and I know that I need not sleep under the stars, I shall owe my fealty only to my whim — I shall dream when and what I I like, sing what I like, walk in company or alone. For four and twenty hours I need not be the ivy that clings nor the hose that is ragged at the knee. I shall be at liberty to wear my sash awry, my shoes unbuckled, my hat tilted at an angle which pleases me best. Above all, O worthy rat of the gutter, I need not stoop for four and twenty hours one inch lower than I choose, or render aught to Cæsar for Cæsar will have rendered naught to me. On this the first day of the New Year there is no man or woman living who can dictate to me what I shall do, and to-night in the lodgings for which I have paid, when I am asleep I can dream that I am climbing up the heights toward a mountain top which mayhap doth not quite stretch as far as the clouds, but which I can reach alone. To-day and to-night I am a man and not a bit of ribbon that flutters at the breath of man or woman who has paid for the fluttering with patronage."

Gradually as he spoke and his fresh young voice, sonorous with enthusiasm rang clearly from end to end of the raftered room, conversation, laughter, bibulous songs were stilled and every one turned to look at the speaker, wondering who he could be. The good burghers of Haarlem had no liking for the foreign mercenaries for whom they professed vast contempt because of their calling, and because of the excesses which they committed at the storming of these very walls, which event was within the memory of most. Therefore, though they were attracted by the speaker, they were disgusted to find that he belonged to that rabble; but the women thought that he was goodly to look upon, with those merry, twinkling eyes of his, and that atmosphere of light-heartedness and a gaiety which he diffused around him. Some of the men who were there and who professed knowledge in such matters, declared that this man's speech betrayed him for an Englishman.

"I like not the race," said a pompous man who sat with wife and kindred round a table loaded with good things. "I remember the English Leicester and his crowd, men of loose morals and doubtful piety; braggarts and roisterers we all thought them. This man is very like some of them in appearance."

"Thou speakest truly, O wise citizen of this worthy republic," said Diogenes, boldly answering the man's low-spoken words, "my father was one of the roisterers who came in English Leicester's train. An Englishman he, of loose morals and doubtful piety no doubt, but your sound Dutch example and my mother's Dutch blood — Heaven rest her soul — have both sobered me since then."

He looked round at the crowd of faces, all of which were now turned toward him, kindly faces and angry ones, contemptuous eyes and good-natured ones, and some that expressed both compassion and reproof.

"By the Lord," he said, and as he spoke he threw back his head and burst into a loud and prolonged fit of laughter, "but I have never in my life seen so many ugly faces before."

There was a murmur and many angry words among the assembly. One or two of the men half rose from their seats, scowling viciously and clenching their fists. Master Beek perspiring with anxiety saw these signs of a possible fray. The thought drove him well-nigh frantic. An affray in his establishment on New Year's morning! it was unthinkable! He rushed round to his customers with a veritable dictionary of soothing words upon his tongue.

"Gentlemen! gentlemen," he entreated, "I beg of you to calm yourselves....I humbly beseech you to pay no heed to these men...."

"Plepshurk! Insolent rabble!" quoth a corpulent gentleman who was crimson with wrath.

"Yes, mynheer, yes, yes," stammered Beek meekly, "but they are foreigners ... they ... they do not understand our Dutch ways ... but they mean no harm ... they...."

Some of the younger men were not easily pacified.

"Throw them out, Beek," said one of them curtly.

"They make the place insufferable with their bragging and their insolence," muttered another.

Diogenes and his friends could not help but see these signs of latent storm, and Mynheer Beek's feeble efforts at pacifying his wrathful guests. Diogenes had laughed long and loudly, now he had to stop in order to wipe his eyes which were streaming; then quite casually he drew Bucephalus from its scabbard and thoughtfully examined its blade.

Almost simultaneously the fraternity of merry-makers at his table also showed a sudden desire to examine the blade of their swords and immediately half a dozen glints of steel caught the reflection of tallow candles.

I would not assert that order was restored because of these unconscious gestures on the part of the insolent rabble aforesaid, but certain it is that within the next few seconds decorum once more prevailed as if magic had called it forth.

Mynheer Beek heaved a sigh of relief.

"All that you said just now was well spoken, sir," broke in a firm voice which proceeded from a group of gentlemen who sat at a table next to the one occupied by the philosophers and their friends, "but 'twere interesting to hear what you propose doing on the second day of this New Year."

Diogenes was in no hurry to reply. The man who had just spoken sat directly behind him, and Bucephalus — so it seemed — still required his close attention. When he had once more replaced his faithful friend into its delicately wrought scabbard he turned leisurely round and from the elevated position which he still occupied on the corner of the table he faced his interlocutor.

"What I propose doing?" he quoth politely.

"Why yes. You said just now that for four and twenty hours you were free to dream and to act as you will, but how will it be to-morrow?"

"To-morrow, sir," rejoined Diogenes lightly, "I shall be as poor in pocket as the burghers of Haarlem are in wits, and then...."

"Yes? and then?"

"Why then, sir, I shall once more become an integral portion of that rabble to which you and your friends think no doubt that I rightly belong. I shall not have one silver coin in my wallet and in order to obtain a handful I shall be ready to sell my soul to the devil, my skin to the Stadtholder...."

"And your honour, sir?" queried the other with a sneer, "to whom will you sell that precious guerdon to-morrow?"

"To you, sir," retorted Diogenes promptly, "an you are short of the commodity."

An angry word rose to the other man's lips, but his eyes encountered those of his antagonist and something in the latter's look, something in the mocking eyes, the merry face, seemed to disarm him and to quench his wrath. He even laughed good-humouredly and said:

"Well spoken, sir. You had me fairly there with the point of your tongue. No doubt you are equally skilful with the point of your rapier...."

"It shall be at your service after to-morrow, sir," rejoined Diogenes lightly.

"You live by the profession of arms, sir? No offence, 'tis a noble calling, though none too lucrative I understand."

"My wits supply, sir, what my sword cannot always command."

"You are ambitious?"

"I told my friends just now wherein lay my ambition."

"Money — an independent competence ... so I understand. But surely at your age, and — if you will pardon mine outspokenness — with your looks, sir, women or mayhap one woman must play some part in your dreams of the future."

"Women, sir," retorted Diogenes dryly, "should never play a leading rôle in the comedy of a philosopher's life. As a means to an end — perhaps ... the final dénouement...."

"Always that one aim I see — a desire for complete independence which the possession of wealth alone can give."

"Always," replied the other curtly.

"And beyond that desire, what is your chief ambition, sir?"

"To be left alone when I have no mind to talk," said Diogenes with a smile which was so pleasant, so merry, so full of self-deprecating irony that it tempered the incivility of his reply.

Again the other bit his lip, checking an angry word; for some unexplained reason he appeared determined not to quarrel with this insolent young knave. The others stared at their friend in utter astonishment.

"What fly hath bitten Beresteyn's ear?" whispered one of them under his breath. "I have never known him so civil to a stranger or so unwilling to take offence."

Certainly the other man's good humour did not seem to have abated one jot; after an imperceptible moment's pause, he rejoined with perfect suavity:

"You do not belie your name, sir, I heard your friends calling you Diogenes, and I feel proud that you should look on me as Alexander and call on me to stand out of your sunshine."

"I crave your pardon, sir," said Diogenes somewhat more seriously, "my incivility is unwarrantable in the face of your courtesy. No doubt it had its origin in the fact that like my namesake I happened to want nothing at the moment. To-morrow, sir, an you are minded to pay for my services, to ask for my sword, my soul or my wits, and in exchange will offer me the chance of winning a fortune or of marrying a wife who is both rich and comely, why sir, I shall be your man, and will e'en endeavour to satisfy you with the politeness of my speech and the promptness and efficiency of my deeds. To-morrow, sir, you and the devil will have an equal chance of purchasing my soul for a few thousand guilders, my wits for a paltry hundred, my skin for a good supper and a downy bed — to-morrow the desire will seize me once again to possess wealth at any cost, and my friends here will have no cause to complain of my playing a part which becomes a penniless wastrel like myself so ill — the part of a gentleman. Until then, sir, I bid you good-night. The hour is late and Mynheer Beek is desirous of closing this abode of pleasure. As for me, my lodgings being paid for I do not care to leave them unoccupied."

Whereupon he rose and to Mynheer Beek — who came to him with that same ubiquitous smile which did duty for all the customers of the "Lame Cow" — he threw the three silver guilders which the latter demanded in payment for the wine and ale supplied to the honourable gentleman: then as he met the mocking glance of his former interlocutor he said with a recrudescence of gaiety:

"I still have my lodgings, gentle sir, and need not sell my soul or my skin until after I have felt a gnawing desire for breakfast."

With a graceful flourish of his plumed hat he bowed to the assembled company and walked out of the tap-room of the "Lame Cow" with swagger that would have befitted the audience chamber of a king.

In his wake followed the band of his boon companions, they too strode out of the place with much jingle of steel and loud clatter of heavy boots and accoutrements. They laughed and talked loudly as they left and gesticulated with an air of independence which once more drew upon them the wrathful looks and contemptuous shrugs of the sober townsfolk.

Diogenes alone as he finally turned once again in the doorway encountered many a timid glance levelled at him that were soft and kindly. These glances came from the women, from the young and from the old, for women are strange creatures of whims and of fancies, and there was something in the swaggering insolence of that young malapert that made them think of breezy days upon the sea-shore, of the song of the soaring lark, of hyacinths in bloom and the young larches on the edge of the wood.

And I imagine that their sluggish Dutch blood yielded to these influences and was greatly stirred by memories of youth.

CHAPTER VIII
THE LODGINGS WHICH WERE PAID FOR

And once again Chance set to with a will and forged yet another link in that mighty chain which she had in hand.

For was it not in the natural course of things that the three philosophers, weary and thirsty as they were, should go and seek solace and material comfort under the pleasing roof of the "Lame Cow" — which as I remarked before was reputed one of the best conducted hostelries in Haarlem, and possessing a cellar full of wines and ales which had not its equal even in Amsterdam.

And was it not equally natural since the Lord of Stoutenburg lodged not far from that self-same hostelry — again I repeat one of the soberest in Haarlem — that his friends should choose to join him in the tap-room there ere parting from one another on this eventful night.

Stoutenburg and his family were but little known in these parts and the hue and cry after the escaped traitor had somewhat abated these few months past: moreover he was well disguised with beard and cloak and he kept a broad-brimmed hat pulled well down over his brow. On watch-night too, the burghers and their vrouws as well as the civic and military dignitaries of the town had plenty to do to think on their own enjoyment and the entertainment of their friends: they certes were not on the look-out for conspiracies and dangerous enemies within their gates.

Stoutenburg had sat well screened from general observation within a dark recess of the monumental fireplace. Nicolaes Beresteyn, the most intimate of all his friends, sat close to him, but neither of them spoke much. Beresteyn was exceptionally moody; he appeared absorbed in thought and hardly gave answer to those who attempted to draw him into conversation. Stoutenburg, on the other hand affected a kind of grim humour, and made repeated allusions to scaffold or gallows as if he had already wholly resigned himself to an inevitable fate.

The others sipped their mulled wine and tried to cheat themselves out of the burning anxiety which Jongejuffrouw Beresteyn's presence in the cathedral had awakened in their hearts. They had made great efforts not to seem pre-occupied and to be outwardly at least as gay as any of the other watch-night revellers in the room.

But with their thoughts fixed upon that vision of awhile ago — a woman appearing before them within twenty paces of the spot where death to the Stadtholder had just been loudly proclaimed amongst them — with that vision fixed upon their minds, they found light conversation and ordinary manner very difficult to keep up.

The peroration of the young adventurer had proved a welcome diversion: it had immediately aroused Stoutenburg's interest. He it was who first drew Beresteyn's attention to it, and he again who checked the angry words which more than once rose to his friend's lips at the insolent attitude affected by the knave.

And now when the latter finally swaggered out of the room it was Stoutenburg who made a sign to Beresteyn and then immediately rose to go.

Beresteyn paid his account and went out too, in the wake of his friend.

With the advent of the small morning hours the snow once more began to fall in large sparse flakes that lay thick and glistening where they fell. At the end of the Kleine Hout Straat where the two men presently found themselves, the feeble light of a street lamp glimmered through this white fluttering veil: with its help the group of foreign mercenaries could be dimly seen in the distance as they took leave of one another.

The tall form of Diogenes, crowned with his plumed hat, was easily distinguishable amongst them. He with his two special friends, fat Pythagoras and lean Socrates, remained standing for a few moments at the corner of the street after the others had departed: then only did the three of them turn and walk off in the direction of the Oude Gracht.

For some reason, as unexplainable as that which had guided their conduct at the "Lame Cow," Beresteyn and Stoutenburg, quite unconscious of the cold, elected to follow.

Was it not Chance that willed it so? Chance who was busy forging a chain and who had need of these two men's extraordinary interest in a nameless adventurer in order to make the links of that chain fit as neatly as she desired.

At the bottom of the Kleine Hout Straat, where it abuts on the Oude Gracht, the three philosophers had again paused, obviously this time in order to take leave of one another. The houses here were of a peculiarly woe-begone appearance, with tiny windows which could not possibly have allowed either air or light to penetrate within, and doors that were left ajar and were creaking on their hinges, showing occasional glimpses of dark unventilated passages beyond and of drifts of snow heaped up against the skirting of the worm-eaten, broken-down wooden floors. They were miserable lodging-houses of flimsy construction and low rentals, which the close proximity of the sluggish canal rendered undesirable.

The ground floor was in most instances occupied by squalid-looking shops, from which fetid odours emanated through the chinks and cracks of the walls. The upper rooms were let out as night-lodgings to those who were too poor to afford better quarters.

Diogenes with all his swagger and his airs of an out-at-elbows gentleman evidently was one of those, for he was now seen standing on the threshold of one of these dilapidated houses and his two friends were finally bidding him good-night.

By tacit consent Beresteyn and Stoutenburg drew back further into the shadow of the houses opposite. There appeared to be some understanding between these two men, an understanding anent a matter of supremely grave import, which caused them to stand here on the watch with feet buried in the snow that lay thick in the doorways, silently taking note of every word spoken and of every act that occurred on the other side of this evil-smelling street.

There seemed to be no need for speech between them; for the nonce each knew that the other's thoughts were running in the same groove as his own; and momentarily these thoughts were centred into a desire to ascertain definitely if it was the tallest and youngest of those three knaves over there who lodged in that particular house.

It was only when the fat man and the lean one had finally turned away and left their comrade on the doorstep that the watchers appeared satisfied and nodding silently to one another made ready to go home. They had turned their steps once more toward the more salubrious and elegant quarter of the city, and had gone but a few steps in that direction when something occurred behind them which arrested their attention and caused them to look back once more.

The Something was a woman's cry, pitiful in the extreme: not an unusual sound in the streets of a prosperous city surely, and one which under ordinary circumstances would certainly not have aroused Stoutenburg's or Beresteyn's interest. But the circumstances were not ordinary; the cry came from the very spot where the two men had last seen the young stranger standing in the doorway of his lodgings and the appeal was obviously directed toward him.

"Kind sir," the woman was saying in a quavering voice, "half a guilder I entreat you for the love of Christ."

"Half a guilder, my good woman," Diogenes said in response, "'Tis a fortune to such as I. I have not a kreutzer left in my wallet, 'pon my honour!"

Whereupon the two men who watched this scene from the opposite side of the street saw that the woman fell on her knees, and that beside her there stood an old man who made ready to follow her example.

"It's no use wearing out your stockings on this snow-covered ground, my good girl," said Diogenes good-humouredly. "All the kneeling in the world will not put half a guilder into my pocket nor apparently into yours."

"And father and I must sleep under the canal bridge and it is so bitterly cold," the woman moaned more feebly.

"Distinctly an uncomfortable place whereat to spend a night," rejoined the philosopher, "I have slept there myself before now, so I know."

Seemingly he made an attempt to turn incontinently on his heel, for the woman put out her hands and held on to his cloak.

"Father is crippled with ague, kind sir, he will die if he sleeps out there to-night," she cried.

"I am afraid he will," said Diogenes blandly.

In the meanwhile, Pythagoras and Socrates, who evidently had not gone very far, returned in order to see what was going on, on their friend's doorstep. It was Pythagoras who first recognized the wench.

"Thunder and lightning," he exclaimed, "'tis the Papist!"

"Which Papist?" queried Diogenes.

"Yes, gentle sirs," said the woman piteously, "you rescued me nobly this evening from that awful, howling mob. My father and I were able to go to midnight mass in peace. May God reward you all. But," she added naïvely, "'twas no good preventing those horrid men from killing us, if we are to die from cold and hunger under the bridge of the canal."

All of which was not incomprehensible to the two men on the watch who had heard a graphic account of the affray in Dam Straat as it was told by Pythagoras in the tap-room of the "Lame Cow." And they both drew a little nearer so as not to lose a word of the scene which they were watching with ever growing interest. Neither of them attempted to interfere in it, however, though Beresteyn at any rate could have poured many a guilder in the hands of those two starving wretches, without being any the poorer himself and though he was in truth not a hard-hearted man.

"The wench is right," now said Diogenes firmly, "the life which we helped to save, we must not allow to be frittered away. I talked of stockings, girl," he added lightly, "but I see thy feet are bare.... Brrr! I freeze when I look at thee...."

"For a quarter guilder father and I could find a lodging...."

"But Dondersteen!" he exclaimed, "did I not tell thee that I have not one kreutzer in my wallet, and unless my friends can help thee...."

"Diogenes thou speakest trash," interposed Pythagoras softly.

"We must both starve of cold this night," moaned the woman in despair.

"Nay ye shall not!" said Diogenes with sudden decision. "There is a room in this very house which has been paid for three nights in advance. Go to it, wench, 'tis at the very top of the stairs, crawl thither as fast as thou canst, dragging thy ramshackle parent in thy wake. What ho there!" he shouted at the top of his ringing voice, "what ho my worthy landlord! What ho!"

And with his powerful fists he began pounding against the panels of the door which swung loosely under the heavy blows.

Stoutenburg and Beresteyn drew yet a little nearer: they were more deeply interested than ever in all that was going on outside this squalid lodging house.

The three philosophers were making a sufficiency of noise to wake half the street and within a very few minutes they succeeded in their purpose. Through one or two of the narrow frames overhead heads appeared enveloped in shawls or cloaks, and anon the landlord of the house came shuffling down the passage, carrying a lighted, guttering taper.

The two silent watchers could not see this man, but they could hear him grumbling and scolding audibly in short jerky sentences which he appeared to throw somewhat tentatively at his rowdy lodger.

"Late hour of the night," they heard him muttering. "New Year's morning.... Respectable house ... noise to attract the town guard...."

"Hadst thou turned out of thy bed sooner, O well-beloved lord of this abode of peace," said Diogenes cheerily, "there would have been less noise outside its portals. Had I not loved thee as I do, I would not have wakened thee from thy sleep, but would have acted in accordance with my rights and without bringing to thy ken a matter which would vastly have astonished thee in the morning."

The man continued to mutter, more impatiently this time:

"New Year's morning ... respectable citizen ... work to do in the morning ... undesirable lodgers...."

"All lodgers are desirable who pay for their lodging, O wise landlord," continued Diogenes imperturbably, "I have paid thee for mine, for three nights from this day and I herewith desire thee to place my palatial residence at the disposal of this jongejuffrouw and of mynheer her father."

The man's mutterings became still more distinct.

"Baggage ... how do I know?... not bound to receive them...."

"Nay! but thou art a liar, Master Landlord," quoth Diogenes still speaking quite pleasantly, "for the lodgings being mine, I have the right to receive in them anybody whom I choose. Therefore now do I give thee the option, either to show my guests straightway and with meticulous politeness into my room, or to taste the power and weight of my boot in the small of thy back and the hardness of my sword-hilt across thy shoulders."

This time the man's mutterings became inaudible. Nicolaes Beresteyn and Stoutenburg could only guess what was passing in the narrow corridor of the house opposite. The one moment there was a heart-rending howl, which suggested that the landlord's obduracy had lasted a few moments too long for the impatient temper of a philosopher; but the howl was not repeated and soon Diogenes' clear voice rang out lustily again:

"There! I knew that gentle persuasion would prevail. Dearly beloved landlord, now I pray thee guide the jongejuffrouw and mynheer her father to my sleeping chamber. It is at thy disposal, wench, for three nights," he added airily, "make the most of it; and if thou hast aught to complain of my friend the landlord, let me know. I am always to be found at certain hours of the day within the congenial four walls of the 'Lame Cow.' Good-night then and pleasant dreams."

What went on after that the watchers could, of course, not see. The wench and the old man had disappeared inside the house, where, if they had a spark of gratitude in them, they would undoubtedly be kneeling even now at the feet of their whimsical benefactor.

The next moment the interested spectators of this stirring little scene beheld the three philosophers once more standing together at the corner of the street under the feebly flickering lamp and the slowly falling snow; the door of the lodging-house had been slammed to behind them and the muffled heads had disappeared from out the framework of the windows above.

"And now, perhaps you will tell us what you are going to do," said Pythagoras in flute-like tones.

"There is not a bed vacant in the dormitory where I sleep," said Socrates.

"Nor would I desire to sleep in one of those kennels fit only for dogs which I cannot imagine how you both can stomach," quoth Diogenes lightly; "the close proximity of Pythagoras and yourself and of all those who are most like you in the world would chase pleasing sleep from mine eyelids. I prefer the Canal."

"You cannot sleep out of doors in this h — — l of a cold night," growled Socrates.

"And I cannot go back to the 'Lame Cow' for I have not a kreutzer left in my wallet wherewith to pay for a sip."

"Then what the d — — l are you going to do?" reiterated Pythagoras plaintively.

"I have a friend," said Diogenes after a slight pause.

"Hm?" was the somewhat dubious comment on this fairly simple statement.

"He will give me breakfast early in the morning."

"Hm!"

"'Tis but a few hours to spend in lonely communion with nature."

"Hm!"

"The cathedral clock has struck three, at seven my good Hals will ply me with hot ale and half his hunk of bread and cheese."

"Hals?" queried Socrates.

"Frans Hals," replied Diogenes; "he paints pictures and contrives to live on the proceeds. If his wife does not happen to throw me out, he will console me for the discomforts of this night."

"Bah!" ejaculated Pythagoras in disgust, "a painter of pictures!"

"And a brave man when he is sober."

"With a scold for a wife! Ugh! what about your playing the part of a gentleman now?"

"The play was short, O wise Pythagoras," retorted Diogenes with imperturbable good humour, "the curtain has already come down upon the last act. I am once more a knave, a merchant ready to flatter the customer who will buy his wares: Hech there, sir, my lord! what are your needs? My sword, my skin, they are yours to command! so many guilders, sir, and I will kill your enemy for you, fight your battles, abduct the wench that pleases you. So many guilders! and when they are safely in my pocket I can throw my glove in your face lest you think I have further need of your patronage."

"'Tis well to brag," muttered Pythagoras, "but you'll starve with cold this night."

"But at dawn I'll eat a hearty breakfast offered me by my friend Frans Hals for the privilege of painting my portrait."

"Doth he really paint thy portrait, O handsome Diogenes?" said Pythagoras unctuously.

"Aye! thou ugly old toad. He has begun a new one, for which I have promised to sit. I'll pay for the breakfast he gives me, by donning a gorgeous gold embroidered doubtlet which he once stole from somewhere, by putting my hand on my hip, tilting my hat at a becoming angle, and winking at him by the hour whilst he paints away."

"Hm! after a night of wandering by the canal in the fog and snow and sharing the meagre breakfast of a half-starved painter, methinks the portrait will be that of a knight of the rueful countenance."

"Indeed not, old compeer," said Diogenes with a hearty laugh, "it shall be the portrait of a Laughing Cavalier."

After this episode Chance had little to do with the further events of this veracious chronicle.

Men took their destiny in their own hands and laughed at Fate and at the links of the chain which she had been forging so carefully and so patiently ever since she began the business on the steps of the Stadhuis a few short hours ago.

Beresteyn and Stoutenburg walking home together in the small hours of New Year's morning spoke very little together at first. They strode along side by side, each buried in his own thoughts, and only a few curt remarks passed at intervals between them.

But something lay on the minds of both — something of which each desired to speak to the other, yet neither of them seemed willing to be the first to broach the absorbing topic.

It was Stoutenburg who at last broke the silence.

"A curious personality, that knave," he said carelessly after awhile, "an unscrupulous devil as daring as he is reckless of consequences I should say ... yet trustworthy withal ... what think you?"

"A curious personality as you say," replied Beresteyn vaguely.

"He might have been useful to us had we cared to pay for his services ... but now 'tis too late to think of further accomplices ... new men won or bought for our cause only mean more victims for the gallows."

"You take a gloomy view of the situation," said Beresteyn sombrely.

"No! only a fatalistic one. With our secret in a woman's keeping ... and that woman free and even anxious to impart it to one of my most bitter enemies ... I can see nought that can ward off the inevitable."

"Except...."

"Yes, of course," rejoined Stoutenburg earnestly, "if you, Nicolaes, are ready to make the sacrifice which alone could save us all."

"It is a sacrifice which will involve my honour, my sister's love for me, my father's trust...."

"If you act wisely and circumspectly, my friend," retorted Stoutenburg dryly, "neither your father nor Gilda herself need ever know that you had a share in ... in what you propose to do."

Beresteyn made no reply and he and his friend walked on in silence until they reached the small house close to the "Lame Cow" where Stoutenburg had his lodgings. Here they shook hands before parting and Stoutenburg held his friend's hand in his tightly grasped for a moment or two while he said earnestly:

"It is only for a few days, Nicolaes, a few days during which I swear to you that — though absent and engaged in the greatest task that any man can undertake on this earth — I swear to you that I will keep watch over Gilda and defend her honour with my life. If you will make the sacrifice for me and for our cause, Heaven and your country will reward you beyond your dreams. With the death of the Stadtholder my power in the Netherlands will be supreme, and herewith, with my hand in yours, I solemnly plight my troth to Gilda. She was the first woman I ever loved, and I have never ceased to love her. Now she fills my heart and soul even — at times — to the exclusion of my most ambitious hopes. Nicolaes — my friend — it is in your power to save my life as well as your own: an you will do it, there will be no bounds to my gratitude."

And Beresteyn replied calmly:

"The sacrifice which you ask of me I will make: I will take the risk for the sake of my country and of my faith. To-morrow at noon I will come to your lodgings and tell you in detail all the arrangements which I shall have made by then. I have no fear for Gilda. I believe that Heaven has guided my thoughts and footsteps to-night for the furtherance of our cause."

After which the two men took final leave of one another: Stoutenburg's tall lean form quickly disappeared under the doorway of the house, whilst Beresteyn walked rapidly away up the street.

Now it was close on ten o'clock of New Year's morning. Nicolaes Beresteyn had spent several hours in tossing restlessly under the warm eiderdown and between the fine linen sheets embroidered by his sister's deft hands. During these hours of sleeplessness a plan had matured in his mind which though it had finally issued from his own consciousness had really found its origin in the reckless brain of Willem van Stoutenburg.

Beresteyn now saw himself as the saviour of his friends and of their patriotic cause. He felt that in order to carry out the plan which he firmly believed that he himself had conceived, he was making a noble sacrifice for his country and for his faith, and he was proud to think that it lay in his power to offer the sacrifice. That this same sacrifice would have his own sister for victim, he cared seemingly very little. He was one of those men in whose hearts political aims outweigh every tender emotion, and he firmly believed that Gilda would be richly rewarded by the fulfilment of that solemn promise made by Stoutenburg.

Exquisite visions of satisfied ambition, of triumph and of glory chased away sleep: he saw his friend as supreme ruler of the State, with powers greater than the Princes of Orange had ever wielded: he saw Gilda — his sister — grateful to him for the part which he had played in re-uniting her to the man whom she had always loved, she too supreme in power as the proud wife of the new Stadtholder. And he saw himself as the Lord High Advocate of the Netherlands standing in the very shoes of that same John of Barneveld whose death he would have helped to avenge.

These and other thoughts had stirred Nicolaes Beresteyn's fancy while he lay awake during these the first hours of the New Year, and it was during those self-same hours that a nameless stranger whom his compeers called Diogenes had tramped up and down the snow-covered streets of Haarlem trying to keep himself warm.

I am very sorry to have to put it on record that during that time he swore more than once at his own softheartedness which had caused him to give up his hard but sheltered paillasse to a pair of Papists who were nothing to him and whom probably he would never see again.

"I begin to agree with that bloated puff-ball Pythagoras," he mused dejectedly once, when an icy wind, blowing straight from the North Sea, drove the falling snow into his boots, and under his collar, and up his sleeves, and nearly froze the marrow in his bones, "it is but sorry pleasure to play at being a gentleman. And I had not many hours of it either," he added ruefully.

Even the most leaden-footed hours do come to an end however. At one half after six Diogenes turned his steps toward the Peuselaarsteeg where dwelt his friend Frans Hals, the painter of pictures. Fortunately Mevrouw Hals was in a fairly good temper, the last portrait group of the officers of St. Joris' Shooting Guild had just been paid for, and there was practically a new commission to paint yet another group of these gentlemen.

And Mynheer van Zeller the deputy bailiff had brought the fancy picture too, for which that knave Diogenes had sat last year, so Mevrouw Hals was willing to provide the young man with a savoury and hot breakfast if he were willing once again to allow Frans to make a picture of his pleasant face.

Mevrouw Hals being in rare good humour, the breakfast was both substantial and savoury. Diogenes, who was starved with cold as well as with hunger, did great honour to all that was laid before him: he ate heartily while recounting his adventures of the past night to his friend.

"All that trouble for a Papist wench," said the painter as contemptuously as Pythagoras himself would have done, "and maybe a Spaniard too."

"Good-looking girl," quoth Diogenes dryly, "and would make you a good model, Frans. For a few kreutzers she'd be glad enough to do it."

"I'll have none of these vixens inside my house," interposed Mevrouw Hals decisively, "and don't you teach Frans any of your loose ways, my man."

Diogenes made no reply, he only winked at his friend. No doubt he thought that Hals no longer needed teaching.

The two men repaired to the studio, a huge bare room littered with canvases, but void of furniture, save for an earthenware stove in which fortunately a cheerful fire was blazing, a big easel roughly fashioned of deal, a platform for the model to stand on, and two or three rush-bottomed chairs: there was also a ramshackle dowry chest, black with age, which mayhap had once held the piles of homemade linen brought as a dowry by the first Mevrouw Hals: now it seemed to contain a heterogeneous collection of gaudy rags, together with a few fine articles of attire, richly embroidered relics of more prosperous days.

The artist went straight up to the chest and from out the litter he selected a bundle of clothes which he handed over to his friend.

"Slip into them as quickly as you can, old compeer," he said, "my fingers are itching to get to work."

And while he fixed the commenced picture on the easel and set out his palette, Diogenes threw off his shabby clothes and donned the gorgeous doubtlet and sash which the painter had given him.

CHAPTER X
THE LAUGHING CAVALIER

We all know every fold of that doubtlet now, with its magnificent sleeves, crimson-lined and richly embroidered, its slashings which afford peeps of snowy linen, and its accessories of exquisite lace; the immortal picture then painted by Frans Hals, and which he called the Laughing Cavalier, has put its every line on record for all times.

Diogenes wore it with delight. Its splendour suited his swaggering air to perfection: its fine black cloth, delicate lace and rich silk sash set off to perfection his well-proportioned massive figure.

A joy to the artist every bit of him, the tone, the pose, the line, the colour and that face full of life, of the joy of living, that merry twinkle in the eyes, that laugh that for ever hovers on the lips.

We all stand before it, marvelling at the artist's skill, for we know that the portrait is true to the life; we know that it is true, because we know the man; his whole character is there indelibly writ upon the canvas by the master-hand of a genius: — Diogenes the soldier of fortune is there, the man who bows to no will save to his own, too independent to bow to kindred or to power, the man who takes life as he finds it, but leavens it with his own gaiety and the priceless richness of his own humour: we know him for his light-hearted gaiety, we condone his swagger, we forgive his reckless disregard of all that makes for sobriety and respectability. The eyes twinkle at us, the mouth all but speaks, and we know and recognize every detail as true; only the fine, straight brow, the noble forehead, the delicate contour of the nose and jaw puzzle us at times, for those we cannot reconcile with the man's calling or with his namelessness, until we remember his boast in the tavern of the "Lame Cow" on New Year's morning: "My father was one of those who came in English Leicester's train."

So we see him now standing quite still, while the artist is absorbed in his work: his tall figure very erect, the head slightly thrown back, the well-shaped hand resting on the hip and veiled in folds of filmy lace. And so did Mynheer Nicolaes Beresteyn see him as he entered the artist's studio at ten o'clock of that same New Year's morning.

"A happy New Year to you, my good Hals," he said with easy condescension. "Vervloekte weather, eh — for the incoming year! there must be half a foot of snow in the by-streets by now."

With that same air of graciousness he acknowledged the artist's obsequious bow. His father Mynheer Councillor Beresteyn was an avowed patron of Frans Hals and the hour had not yet struck in civilized Europe when wealth would go hat in hand bowing to genius and soliciting its recognition. In this year of grace 1624 genius had still to hold the hat and to acknowledge if not to solicit the kindly favours of wealth.

Nicolaes Beresteyn did not know exactly how to greet the man with whom he had a few hours ago bandied arguments in the tap room of a tavern, and whom — to tell the truth — he had expressly come to find. The complaisant nod which he had bestowed on Frans Hals did not somehow seem appropriate for that swaggering young knight of industry, who looked down on him from the high eminence of the model's platform so that Nicolaes was obliged to look well up, if he wished to meet his glance at all.

It was the obscure soldier of fortune who relieved the pompous burgher of his embarrassment.

"Fate hath evidently not meant that we should remain strangers, sir," he said lightly, "this meeting after last night's pleasing amenities is indeed unexpected."

"And most welcome, sir, as far as I am concerned," rejoined Nicolaes pleasantly. "My name is Nicolaes Beresteyn and right glad am I to renew our acquaintance of last night. I had no idea that my friend Hals could command so perfect a model. No wonder that his pictures have become the talk of the town."

He turned back to Hals now with a resumption of his patronizing manner.

"I came to confirm my father's suggestion, my good Hals, that you should paint his portrait and at the price you named yourself. The officers of St. Joris' Guild are also desirous, as I understand, of possessing yet another group from your brush."

"I shall be honoured," said the artist simply.

"'Tis many an ugly face you'll have to paint within the next few months, my friend," added Diogenes lightly.

"My father is reckoned one of the handsomest men in Holland," retorted Beresteyn with becoming dignity.

"And the owner of the finest tulip bulbs in the land," said the other imperturbably. "I heard him tell last night that he had just given more florins for one bit of dried onion than I have ever fingered in the whole course of my life."

"Fortune, sir, has not dealt with you hitherto in accordance with your deserts."

"No! 'tis my sternest reproach against her."

"There is always a tide, sir, in a man's fortunes."

"Mine I feel, sir, is rising at your call."

There was a moment's pause now while the two men looked on one another eye to eye, appraising one another, each counting on his opponent's worth. Then Nicolaes suddenly turned back to Frans Hals.

"My good Hals," he said, "might I crave a favour from your friendship?"

"I am at your service, mynheer, now as always as you know," murmured the artist, who indeed was marvelling what favour so illustrious a gentleman could ask of a penniless painter of portraits.

"'Tis but a small matter to you," rejoined Nicolaes, "but it would be of great service to me. I desire to hold private conversation with this gentleman. Could I do so in your house without attracting anybody's attention?"

"Easily, sir. This room though none too comfortable is at your disposal. I have plenty of work to do in another part of my house. No one will come in here. You will be quite undisturbed."

"I am infinitely obliged to you. 'Tis but half-an-hour's privacy I desire … providing this gentleman will grant me the interview."

"Like my friend Hals," rejoined Diogenes suavely, "I am, sir, at your service. The tides are rising around me, I feel them swelling even as I speak. I have an overwhelming desire to ride on the crest of the waves, rather than to duck under them against my will."

"I hope this intrusion will not retard your work too much, my good Hals," said Beresteyn with somewhat perfunctory solicitude when he saw that the artist finally put his brushes and palette on one side, and in an abstracted manner began to dust a couple of rickety chairs and then place them close to the stove.

"Oh!" interposed Diogenes airily, "the joy of being of service to so bountiful a patron will more than compensate Frans Hals for this interruption to his work. Am I not right, old friend?" he added with just a soupçon of seriousness in the mocking tones of his voice.

Hals murmured a few words under his breath which certainly seemed to satisfy Beresteyn for the latter made no further attempt at apology, and only watched with obvious impatience the artist's slow progress out of the room.

As soon as the heavy oaken door had fallen-to behind the master of this house, Beresteyn turned with marked eagerness to Diogenes.

"Now, sir," he said, "will you accord me your close attention for a moment. On my honour it will be to your advantage so to do."

"And to your own, I take it, sir," rejoined Diogenes, as he stepped down from the elevated platform and sat himself astride one of the rickety chairs facing his interlocutor who had remained standing. "To your own too, sir, else you had not spent half an hour in that vervloekte weather last night pacing an insalubrious street in order to find out where I lodged."

Nicolaes bit his lip with vexation.

"You saw me?" he asked.

"I have eyes at the back of my head," replied the young man. "I knew that you followed me in company with a friend all the way from the door of the 'Lame Cow' and that you were not far off when I announced my intention of sleeping under the stars and asking my friend Frans Hals for some breakfast later on."

Beresteyn had quickly recovered his equanimity.

"I have no cause to deny it," he said.

"None," assented Diogenes.

"Something, sir, in your manner and your speech last night aroused my interest. Surely you would not take offence at that."

"Certainly not."

"And hearing you speak, a certain instinct prompted me to try and not lose sight of you if I could by some means ascertain where you lodged. My friend and I did follow you: I own it, and we witnessed a little scene which I confess did you infinite credit."

Diogenes merely bowed his head this time in acknowledgment.

"It showed, sir," resumed Nicolaes after a slight pause, "that you are chivalrous to a fault, brave and kindly: and these are just the three qualities which I — even like your illustrious namesake — have oft sought for in vain."

"Shall we add, also for the sake of truth, sir," said Diogenes pleasantly, "that I am obviously penniless, presumably unscrupulous and certainly daring, and that these are just the three qualities which you ... and your friend ... most require at the present moment in the man whom you wish to pay for certain services."

"You read my thoughts, sir."

"Have I not said that I have eyes at the back of my head?"

And Nicolaes Beresteyn wondered if that second pair of eyes were as merry and mocking and withal as inscrutable as those that met his now.

"Well," he said as if with suddenly conceived determination, "again I see no cause why I should deny it. Yes, sir, you have made a shrewd guess. I have need of your services, of your chivalry and of your valour and ... well, yes," he added after an instant's hesitation, "of your daring and your paucity of scruples too. As for your penury, why, sir, if you like, its pangs need worry you no longer."

"It all sounds very tempting, sir," said Diogenes with his most winning smile, "suppose now that we put preliminaries aside and proceed more directly with our business."

"As you will."

Nicolaes Beresteyn now took the other chair and brought it close to his interlocutor. Then he sat down and sinking his voice to a whisper he began:

"I will be as brief and to the point as I can, sir. There are secrets as you know the knowledge of which is oft-times dangerous. Such an one was spoken of in the cathedral last night after watch-night service by six men who hold their lives in their hands and are ready to sacrifice it for the good of their country and of their faith."

"In other words," interposed Diogenes with dry humour, "six men in the cathedral last night decided to murder some one for the good of this country and of their faith and for the complete satisfaction of the devil."

"'Tis false!" cried Beresteyn involuntarily.

"Be not angered, sir, I was merely guessing — and not guessing methinks very wide of the mark. I pray you proceed. You vastly interest me. We left then six men in the cathedral after watch-night service plotting for the welfare of Holland and the established Faith."

"Their lives, sir," resumed Beresteyn more calmly, "depend on the inviolability of their secret. You are good at guessing — will you guess what would happen to those six men if their conversation last night had been overheard and their secret betrayed."

"The scaffold," said Diogenes laconically.

"And torture."

"Of course. Holland always has taken the lead in civilization of late."

"Torture and death, sir," reiterated Beresteyn vehemently. "There are six men in this city to-day whose lives are at the mercy of one woman."

"Oho! 'twas a woman then who surprised those six men in their endeavour to do good to Holland and to uphold the Faith."

"Rightly spoken, sir! To do good to Holland and to uphold the Faith! those are the two motives which guide six ardent patriots in their present actions and cause them to risk their lives and more, that they may bring about the sublime end. A woman has surprised their secret, a woman pure and good as the stars but a woman for all that, weak in matters of sentiment and like to be swayed by a mistaken sense of what she would call her duty. A woman now, sir, holds the future happiness of Holland, the triumph of Faith and the lives of six stalwart patriots in the hollow of her hand."

"And 'tis with the lives of six stalwart patriots that we are most concerned at the moment, are we not?" asked Diogenes blandly.

"Put it as you will, sir. I cannot expect you — a stranger — to take the welfare of Holland and of her Faith so earnestly as we Dutchmen do. Our present concern is with the woman."

"Is she young?"

"Yes."

"Pretty?"

"What matter?"

"I don't know. The fact might influence mine actions. For of course you wish to put the woman out of the way."

"Only for a time and from my soul I wish her no harm. I only want to place her out of the reach of doing us all a grievous wrong. Already she has half threatened to speak of it all to my father. The idea of it is unthinkable. I want her out of the way for a few days, not more than ten days at most. I want her taken out of Haarlem, to a place of safety which I will point out to you anon, and under the care of faithful dependents who would see that not a hair on her head be injured. You see, sir, that what I would ask of you would call forth your chivalry and need not shame it; it would call forth your daring and your recklessness of consequences and if you will undertake to do me service in this, my gratitude and that of my friends as well as the sum of 2,000 guilders will be yours to command."

"About a tenth part of the money in fact which your father, sir, doth oft give for a bulb."

"Call it 3,000, sir," said Nicolaes Beresteyn, "we would still be your debtors."

"You are liberal, sir."

"It means my life and that of my friends, and most of us are rich."

"But the lady — I must know more about her. Ah sir! this is a hard matter for me — A lady — young — presumably fair — of a truth I care naught for women, but please God I have never hurt a woman yet."

"Who spoke of hurting her, man?" queried Nicolaes haughtily.

"This abduction — the State secret — the matter of life and death — the faithful dependent — how do I know, sir, that all this is true?"

"On the word of honour of a gentleman!" retorted Beresteyn hotly.

"A gentleman's honour is easily attenuated where a woman is concerned."

"The lady is my own sister, sir."

Diogenes gave a long, low whistle.

"Your sister!" he exclaimed.

"My only sister and one who is dearly loved. You see, sir, that her safety and her honour are dearer to me than mine own."

"Yet you propose entrusting both to me," said Diogenes with a mocking laugh, "to me, a nameless adventurer, a penniless wastrel whose trade lies in his sword and his wits."

"Which must prove to you, sir, firstly how true are my instincts, and secondly how hardly I am pressed. My instinct last night told me that in this transaction I could trust you. To-day I have realized more fully than I did last night that my sister is a deadly danger to many, to our country and to our Faith. She surprised a secret, the knowledge of which had she been a man would have meant death then and there in the chapel of the cathedral. Had it been a brother of mine instead of a sister who surprised our secret, my friends would have killed him without compunction and I would not have raised a finger to save him. Being a woman she cannot pay for her knowledge with her life; but her honour and her freedom are forfeit to me because I am a man and she a woman. I am strong and she is weak; she has threatened to betray me and my friends and I must protect them and our cause. I have decided to place her there where she cannot harm us, but some one must convey her thither, since I must not appear before her in this matter. Therefore hath my choice fallen on you, sir, for that mission, chiefly because of that instinct which last night told me that I could trust you. If my instinct should prove me wrong, I would kill you for having cheated me, but I would even then not regret what I had done."

He paused and for a moment looked straight into the laughter-loving face of the man in whose keeping he was ready to entrust with absolute callousness the safety and honour of one whom he should have protected with his life. The whole face, even now seemed still to laugh, the eyes twinkled, the mouth was curled in a smile.

The next moment the young adventurer had risen to his full height. He picked up his hat which lay on the platform close beside him and with it in his hand he made an elaborate and deep bow to Nicolaes Beresteyn.

"Sir?" queried the latter in astonishment.

"At your service, sir," said Diogenes gaily, "I am saluting a greater blackguard than I can ever hope to be myself."

"Insolent!" exclaimed Nicolaes hotly.

"Easy, easy, my good sir," interposed the other calmly, "it would not suit your purpose or mine that we should cut one another's throat. Let me tell you at once and for the appeasing of your anxiety and that of your friends that I will, for the sum of 4,000 guilders, take Jongejuffrouw Beresteyn from this city to any place you may choose to name. This should also ease your pride, for it will prove to you that I also am a consummate blackguard and that you therefore need not stand shamed before me. I have named a higher sum than the one which you have offered me, not with any desire to squeeze you, sir, but because obviously I cannot do this work single-handed. The high roads are not safe. I could not all alone protect the lady against the army of footpads that infest them, I shall have to engage and pay an escort for her all the way. But she shall reach the place to which you desire me to take her, to this I pledge you my word. Beyond that ...well! you have said it yourself, by her knowledge of your secret she has forfeited her own safety; you — her own brother — choose to entrust her to me. The rest lies between you and your honour."

An angry retort once more rose to Nicolaes Beresteyn's lips, but commonsense forced him to check it. The man was right in what he said. On the face of it his action in entrusting his own sister into the keeping of a knight of industry, a nameless wastrel whose very calling proclaimed him an unscrupulous adventurer, was the action of a coward and of a rogue. Any man with a spark of honour in him — would condemn Nicolaes Beresteyn as a blackguard for this deed. Nevertheless there was undoubtedly something in the whole personality of this same adventurer that in a sense exonerated Nicolaes from the utter dishonour of his act.

On the surface the action was hideous, monstrous, and cowardly, but beneath that surface there was the undercurrent of trust in this one man, the firm belief born of nothing more substantial than an intuition that this man would in this matter play the part of a gentleman.

But it is not my business to excuse Nicolaes Beresteyn in this. What guided him solely in his present action was that primary instinct of self-preservation, that sense which animals have without the slightest knowledge or experience on their part and which has made men play at times the part of a hero and at others that of a knave. Stoutenburg who was always daring and always unscrupulous where his own ambitious schemes were at stake had by a careful hint shown him a way of effectually silencing Gilda during the next few days. Beresteyn's mind filled to over-flowing with a glowing desire for success and for life had readily worked upon the hint.

And he did honestly believe — as hundreds of misguided patriots have believed before and since — that Heaven was on his side of the political business and had expressly led along his path this one man of all others who would do what was asked of him and whom he could trust.

CHAPTER XI
THE BARGAIN

There had been silence in the great, bare work-room for some time, silence only broken by Beresteyn's restless pacing up and down the wooden floor. Diogenes had resumed his seat, his shrewd glance following every movement of the other man, every varied expression of his face.

At last Nicolaes came to a halt opposite to him.

"Am I to understand then, sir," he asked, looking Diogenes straight between the eyes and affecting not to note the mocking twinkle within them, "that you accept my proposition and that you are prepared to do me service?"

"Absolutely, sir," replied the other.

"Then shall we proceed with the details?"

"An it please you."

"You will agree to do me service for the sum of 4,000 guilders?"

"In gold."

"Of course. For this sum you will convey Jongejuffrouw Beresteyn out of Haarlem, conduct her with a suitable escort and in perfect safety to Rotterdam and there deliver her into the hands of Mynheer Ben Isaje — the banker — who does a vast amount of business for me and is entirely and most discreetly devoted to my interests. His place of business is situated on the Schiedamsche Straat and is a house well known to every one in Rotterdam seeing that Mynheer Ben Isaje is the richest money-lending Jew in the city."

"That is all fairly simple, sir," assented Diogenes.

"You will of course tender me your oath of secrecy."

"My word of honour, sir. If I break that I would be as likely to break an oath."

"Very well," said Beresteyn after a moment's hesitation during which he tried vainly to scrutinize a face which he had already learned was quite inscrutable. "Shall we arrange the mode of payment then?"

"If you please."

"How to obtain possession of the person of the jongejuffrouw is not my business to tell you. Let me but inform you that to-day being New Year's day she will surely go to evensong at the cathedral and that her way from our home thither will lead her along the bank of the Oude Gracht between the Zijl Straat where our house is situate and the Hout Straat which debouches on the Groote Markt. You know the bank of the Oude Gracht better than I do, sir, so I need not tell you that it is lonely, especially at the hour when evensong at the cathedral is over. The jongejuffrouw is always escorted in her walks by an elderly duenna whom you will of course take to Rotterdam, so that she may attend on my sister on the way, and by two serving men whose combined courage is not, of course, equal to your own. This point, therefore, I must leave you to arrange in accordance with your desire."

"I thank you, sir."

"In the same way it rests with you what arrangements you make for the journey itself; the providing of a suitable carriage and of an adequate escort I leave entirely in your hands."

"Again I thank you."

"I am only concerned with the matter itself, and with the payment which I make to you for your services. As for your route, you will leave Haarlem by the Holy Cross gate and proceed straight to Bennebrock, a matter of a league or so. There I will meet you at the half-way house which stands at the cross-roads where a signpost points the way to Leyden. The innkeeper there is a friend of mine, whose natural discretion has been well nurtured by frequent gifts from me. He hath name Praff, and will see to the comfort of my sister and of her duenna, while you and I settle the first instalment of our business, quite unbeknown to her. There, sir, having assured myself that my sister is safe and in your hands, I will give over to you the sum of 1,000 guilders, together with a letter writ by me to the banker Ben Isaje of Rotterdam. He knows Jongejuffrouw Beresteyn well by sight, and in my letter I will ask him, firstly, to ascertain from herself if she is well and safe, and secondly to see that she is at once conveyed, still under your escort, to his private residence which is situate some little distance out of the city between Schiedam and Overschie on the way to Delft, and lastly, to hand over to you the balance of 3,000 guilders still due then by me to you."

He paused a moment to draw breath after the lengthy peroration, then, as Diogenes made no comment, he said somewhat impatiently:

"I hope, sir, that all these arrangements meet with your approval!"

"They fill me with profound respect for you, sir, and admiration for your administrative capacities," replied Diogenes, with studied politeness.

"Indeed I do flatter myself ..." quoth the other.

"Not without reason, sir. The marvellous way in which you have provided for the safety of three-fourths of your money, and hardly at all for that of your sister, fills me with envy which I cannot control."

"Insolent...."

"No, no, my good sir," interposed Diogenes blandly, "we have already agreed that we are not going to quarrel, you and I ... we have too great a need for one another; for that 3,000 guilders — which, after deductions, will be my profit in this matter — means a fortune to a penniless adventurer, and you are shrewd enough to have gauged that fact, else you had not come to me with such a proposal. I will do you service, sir, for the 3,000 guilders which will enable me to live a life of independence in the future, and also for another reason, which I would not care to put into words, and which you, sir, would fail to understand. So let us say no more about all these matters. I agree to your proposals and you accept my services. To-night at ten o'clock I will meet you at the half-way house which stands in the hamlet of Bennebrock at the cross-roads where a signpost points the way to Leyden."

"To-night! That's brave!" exclaimed Beresteyn. "You read my thoughts, sir, even before I could tell you that delay in this affair would render it useless."

"To-night then, sir," said Diogenes in conclusion, "I pray you have no fear of failure. The jongejuffrouw will sleep at Leyden, or somewhere near there, this night. The city is distant but half-a-dozen leagues, and we can reach it easily by midnight. From thence in the morning we can continue our journey, and should be in sight of Rotterdam twenty-four hours later. For the rest, as you say, the manner of our journey doth not concern you. If the frost continues and we can travel by sledge all the way we could reach Rotterdam in two days; in any event, even if a thaw were to set in we should not be more than three days on the way."

He rose from his chair and stood now facing Beresteyn. His tall figure, stretched to its full height, seemed to tower above the other man, though the latter was certainly not short; but Diogenes looked massive — a young lion sniffing the scent of the desert. The mocking glance, the curve of gentle irony were still there in eyes and mouth, but the nostrils quivered with excitement, with the spirit of adventure which never slept so soundly but that it awakened at a word.

"And now, sir," he said, "there are two matters both of equal importance, which we must settle ere I can get to work."

"What may these be, sir?"

"Firstly the question of money. I have not the wherewithal to make preparations. I shall have to engage a sleigh for to-night, horses, an escort as far as Leyden. I shall have to make payments for promises of secrecy...."

"That is just, sir. Would 200 guilders meet this difficulty?"

"Five hundred would be safer," said Diogenes airily, "and you may deduct that sum from your first payment at Bennebrock."

Beresteyn did not choose to notice the impertinent tone which rang through the other man's speech. Without wasting further words, he took a purse from his wallet, and sitting down on one corner of the model's platform, he emptied the contents of the purse upon it.

He counted out five hundred guilders, partly in silver and partly in gold. These he replaced in the purse and then handed it over to Diogenes. The latter had not moved from his position during this time, standing as he did at some little distance so that Beresteyn had to get up in order to hand him the money. Diogenes acknowledged its receipt with a courteous bow.

"And what is the other matter, sir?" asked Nicolaes, after he had placed the rest of his money back into his wallet, "what is the other matter which we have failed to settle?"

"The jongejuffrouw, sir....I am a comparative stranger in Haarlem....I do not know the illustrious lady by sight."

"True, I had not thought of that. But this omission can very easily be remedied ...if you, sir, will kindly call our friend Hals; he has, an I mistake not, more than one sketch of my sister in his studio and a half-finished portrait of her as well."

"Then I pray you, sir," rejoined Diogenes airily, "do you go and acquaint our mutual friend of your desire to show me the half-finished portrait of the jongejuffrouw, for I must now exchange this gorgeous doublet of a prosperous cavalier for one more suited to this day's purpose."

And he immediately proceeded to undress without paying the slightest heed to Beresteyn's look of offended dignity.

It was no use being angry with this independent knave; Nicolaes Beresteyn had found that out by now, therefore he thought it best to appear indifferent to this new display of impudence and himself to go and seek out Frans Hals as if this had been his own intention all along.

Inwardly fuming but without uttering another word he turned on his heel and went out of the room, slamming the door to behind him.

When Beresteyn returned to the studio in the company of Frans Hals they found Diogenes once more clad in his own well-fitting and serviceable doublet.

The artist looked bitterly disappointed at the sight, but naturally forbore to give vent to his feelings in the presence of his exalted patron.

Apparently he had been told what was required, for he went straight up to a large canvas which stood at the further end of the room with its face to the wall, and this he brought out now and placed upon the easel.

"It is an excellent likeness of my sister," said Nicolaes with his usual gracious condescension, to the artist, "and does your powers of faithful portraiture vast credit, my good Hals. I pray you, sir," he added calling to Diogenes, "come and look at it."

The latter came and stood in front of the easel and looked on the picture which was there exhibited for his gaze.

Among the hard lessons which varying Fortune teaches to those whom she most neglects, there is none so useful as self-control. Diogenes had learned that lesson early in his life, and his own good humour often had to act as a mask for deeper emotions. Now, when in the picture he recognized the woman who had spoken to him last night after the affray, in the Dam Straat, his face in no sense expressed surprise, it still smiled and mocked and twinkled, and neither of the two men who stood by guessed that he had seen the original of this dainty picture under peculiar circumstances not many hours before.

That portrait of Jongejuffrouw Beresteyn is one of the finest ever painted by Frans Hals, the intense naturalness of the pose is perfect, the sweet yet imperious expression of the face is most faithfully portrayed. Diogenes saw her now very much as he had seen her last night, for the artist had painted the young head against a dark background and it stood out delicate as a flower, right out of the canvas and in full light.

The mouth smiled as it had done last night when first she caught sight of the ludicrous apparition of one philosopher astride on the shoulders of the other, the eyes looked grave as they had done when she humbly, yet gracefully begged pardon for her levity. The chin was uplifted as it had been last night, when she made with haughty condescension her offers of patronage to the penniless adventurer, and there was the little hand soft and smooth as the petal of a rose which had rested for one moment against his lips.

And looking on the picture of this young girl, Diogenes remembered the words which her own brother had spoken to him only a few moments ago; "her honour and her safety are forfeit to me. I would kill you if you cheated me, but I would not even then regret what I had done."

The daughter of the rich city burgher was, of course, less than nothing to the nameless carver of his own fortunes; she was as far removed from his sphere of life as were the stars from the Zuyder Zee, nor did women as a sex play any serious part in his schemes for the future, but at the recollection of those callous and selfish words, Diogenes felt a wave of fury rushing through his blood; the same rage seized his temper now as when he saw a lout once plucking out the feathers of a song bird, and he fell on him with fists and stick and left him lying bruised and half-dead in a ditch.

But the hard lesson learned early in life stood him in good stead. He crossed his arms over his broad chest and anon his well-shaped hand went up to his moustache and it almost seemed as if the slender fingers smoothed away the traces of that wave of wrath which had swept over him so unaccountably just now, and only left upon his face those lines of mockery and of good-humour which a nature redolent of sunshine had rendered indelible.

"What think you of it, sir?" asked Beresteyn impatiently, seeing that Diogenes seemed inclined to linger over long in his contemplation of the picture.

"I think, sir," replied the other, "that the picture once seen would for ever be imprinted on the memory."

"Ah! it pleases me to hear you say that. I think too that it does our friend Hals here infinite credit. You must finish that picture soon, my good Frans. My father I know is prepared to pay you well for it."

Then he turned once more to Diogenes.

"I'll take my leave now, sir," he said, "and must thank you for so kindly listening to my proposals. Hals, I thank you for the hospitality of your house. We meet again soon I hope."

He took up his hat and almost in spite of himself he acknowledged Diogenes' parting bow with one equally courteous. Patron and employé stood henceforth on equal terms.

"And you desire to see me again to-day, sir," he said before finally taking his leave, "I shall be in the tapperij of the 'Lame Cow' between the hours of four and five and entirely at your service."

After that he walked out of the room escorted by Frans Hals, and Diogenes who had remained alone in the big, bare studio, stood in front of Jongejuffrouw Beresteyn's portrait and had another long look at it.

A whimsical smile sat round his lips even as they apostrophized the image that looked so gravely on him out of the canvas.

"You poor, young, delicate creature!" he murmured, "what of your imperious little ways now? your offers of condescension, your gracious wiping of your dainty shoes on the commoner herd of humanity? Your own brother has thrown you at the mercy of a rogue, eh? A rogue whose valour must needs be rewarded by money and patronage!... Will you recognise him to-night I wonder, as the rogue he really is? the rogue paid to do work that is too dirty for exalted gentlemen's hands to touch? How you will loathe him after to-night!"

He drew in his breath with a quaint little sigh that had a thought of sadness in it, and turned away from the picture just as Frans Hals re-entered the room.

"When this picture is finished," he said at once to his friend, "your name, my dear Hals, will ring throughout Europe."

"'Tis your picture I want to finish," said the other reproachfully, "I have such a fine chance of selling it the day after to-morrow."

"Why the day after to-morrow?"

"The Burgomaster, Mynheer van der Meer, comes to visit my studio. He liked the beginnings of the picture very much when he saw it, and told me then that he would come to look at it again and would probably buy it."

"I can be back here in less than a week. You can finish the picture then. The Burgomaster will wait."

The artist sighed a plaintive, uncomplaining little sigh and shrugged his shoulders with an air of hopelessness.

"You don't know what these people are," he said, "they will buy a picture when the fancy seizes them. A week later they will mayhap not even look at it. Besides which the Burgomaster goes to Amsterdam next week. He will visit Rembrandt's studio, and probably buy a picture there...."

His speech meandered on, dully and tonelessly, losing itself finally in incoherent mutterings. Diogenes looked on him with good-natured contempt.

"And you would lick the boots of such rabble," he said.

"I have a wife and a growing family," rejoined the artist, "we must all live."

"I don't see the necessity," quoth Diogenes lightly, "not at that price in any case. You must live of course, my dear Hals," he continued, "because you are a genius and help to fill this ugly grey world with your magnificent works, but why should your wife and family live at the expense of your manhood."

Then seeing the look of horror which his tirade had called forth in the face of his friend, he said with more seriousness:

"Would the price of that picture be of such vital importance then?"

"It is not the money so much," rejoined Frans Hals, "though God knows that that too would be acceptable, but 'tis the glory of it to which I had aspired. This picture to hang in the Stan-huis, mayhap in the reception hall, has been my dream these weeks past; not only would all the wealthy burghers of Haarlem see it there, but all the civic dignitaries of other cities when they come here on a visit, aye! and the foreign ambassadors too, who often come to Haarlem. My fame then would indeed ring throughout Europe....It is very hard that you should disappoint me so."

While he went on mumbling in his feeble querulous voice, Diogenes had been pacing up and down the floor apparently struggling with insistent thoughts. There was quite a suspicion of a frown upon his smooth brow, but he said nothing until his friend had finished speaking. Then he ceased his restless pacing and placed a hand upon Hals' shoulder.

"Look here, old friend," he said, "this will never do. It seems as if I, by leaving you in the lurch to-day, stood in the way of your advancement and of your fortune. That of course will never do," he reiterated earnestly. "You the friend, who, like last night, are always ready to give me food and shelter when I have been without a grote in my pocket. You who picked me up ten years ago a shoeless ragamuffin wandering homeless in the streets, and gave me a hot supper and a bed, knowing nothing about me save that I was starving ...for that was the beginning of our friendship was it not, old Frans?"

"Of course it was," assented the other, "but that was long ago. You have more than repaid me since then ...when you had the means ...and now there is the picture...."

"To repay a debt is not always to be rid of an obligation. How can I then leave you in the lurch now?"

"Why cannot you stay and sit for me to-day....The light is fairly good...."

"I cannot stay now, dear old friend," said the other earnestly, "on my honour I would do my duty by you now if I only could. I have business of the utmost importance to transact to-day and must see to it forthwith."

"Then why not to-morrow?...I could work on the doublet and the lace collar to-day, by putting them on a dummy model....All I want is a good long sitting from you for the head....I could almost finish the picture to-morrow," he pleaded in his peevish, melancholy voice, "and the Burgomaster comes on the next day."

Diogenes was silent for awhile. Again that puzzled frown appeared between his brows. To-morrow he should be leaving Leyden on his way to Rotterdam; 1,000 guilders would be in his pocket, and 3,000 more would be waiting for him at the end of his journey....To-morrow!...

Frans Hals' keen, restless eyes followed every varying expression in the face he knew so well.

"Why should you not give up your day to me to-morrow?" he murmured peevishly. "You have nothing to do."

"Why indeed not?" said the other with a sudden recrudescence of his usual gaiety. "I can do it, old compeer! Dondersteen, but I should be a smeerlap if I did not. Wait one moment.... Let me just think....Yes! I have the way clear in my mind now....I will be here as early as I was to-day."

"By half-past seven o'clock the light is tolerable," said the artist.

"By half-past seven then I shall have donned the doublet, and will not move off that platform unless you bid me, until the shadows have gathered in, in the wake of the setting sun. After that," he added with his accustomed merry laugh, "let Mynheer, the Burgomaster come, your picture shall not hang fire because of me."

"That's brave!" said Frans Hals more cheerily. "If you will come I can do it. You will see how advanced that sleeve and collar will be by half-past seven to-morrow."

His voice had quite a ring in it now; he fussed about in his studio, re-arranged the picture on the easel, and put aside the portrait of Jongejuffrouw Beresteyn; Diogenes watched him with amusement, but the frown had not quite disappeared from his brow. He had made two promises to-day, both of which he would have to fulfil at all costs. Just now, it was in a flash, that the thought came to him how he could help his friend and yet keep his word to Beresteyn. A quick plan had formed itself in his mind for accomplishing this — he saw in a mental vision the forced run on the ice back to Haarlem and back again in the wake of the sleigh. It could be done with much pluck and endurance and a small modicum of good luck, and already his mind was made up to it, whatever the cost in fatigue or privations might be.

But time was pressing now. After a renewed and most solemn promise he took leave of Frans Hals, who already was too deeply absorbed in work to take much notice of his friend. The glorious, self-centred selfishness of genius was in him. He cared absolutely nothing for any worry or trouble he might cause to the other man by his demand for that sitting on the morrow. The picture mattered — nothing else — and the artist never even asked his friend if he would suffer inconvenience or worse by sacrificing his day to it to-morrow.

An hour later in the tap-room of the "Lame Cow" Diogenes had finished explaining to his brother philosophers the work which he had in hand and for which he required their help. The explanation had begun with the words filled with portentous charm:

"There will be 500 guilders for each of you at the end of our journey."

And they knew from many and varied experiences of adventures undertaken in amicable trilogy that Diogenes would be as good as these words.

For the rest they did not greatly trouble themselves. There was a lady to be conveyed with respect and with safety, out of Haarlem and as far as Rotterdam, and it was in Rotterdam that the 500 guilders would reward each man for his obedience to orders, his circumspection at all times and his valour if necessity arose. From this hour onwards and throughout the journey friend Diogenes would provide for everything and see that his faithful compeers lacked in nothing. Temperance and sober conduct would be the order paramount, but with that exception the adventure promised to be as exciting as it was lucrative.

It was good to hear the guilders jingling in Diogenes' wallet, and though he was sparing of them in the matter of heady ale or strong wines, he scattered them liberally enough on smoked sausage, fried livers and the many other delicacies for which his brother philosophers had a fancy and for which the kitchen of the "Lame Cow" was famous.

When they had all eaten enough and made merry on a little good ale and the prospects of the adventure, they parted on the doorstep of the tavern, Diogenes to attend to business, the other two to see to the horses and the sleigh for this night. These were to be in readiness at the point where the street of the Holy Cross abuts on the left bank of the Oude Gracht. Three good saddle horses were wanted — thick-set Flanders mares, rough shod against the slippery roads; also a covered sledge, with two equally reliable horses harnessed there to and a coachman of sober appearance on the box. Socrates and Pythagoras were required to scour the city for these, and to bespeak them for seven o'clock this evening, Diogenes undertaking to make payment for them in advance. There were also some warm rugs and wraps to be bought, for the night would be bitterly cold and the lady not prepared mayhap with a cloak sufficiently heavy for a lengthy journey.

All these matters having been agreed upon, Socrates and Pythagoras started to walk toward the eastern portion of the city where several posting inns were situated and where they hoped to find the conveyance which they required as well as the necessary horses. Diogenes on the other hand turned his steps deliberately southwards.

After a few minutes brisk walking he found himself at the further end of the Kleine Hout Straat, there where stood the ricketty, half-mildewed and wholly insalubrious house which had previously sheltered him. The door as usual was loose upon its hinges and swinging backwards and forwards in the draught with a squeaking, melancholy sound. Diogenes pushed it further open and went in. The same fetid smells, peculiar to all the houses in this quarter of the city, greeted his nostrils, and from the depths of the dark and dank passage a dog gave a perfunctory bark.

Without hesitation Diogenes now began the ascent of the creaking stairs, his heavy footfall echoing through the silent house. On one or two of the landings as he mounted he was greeted by pale, inquiring faces and round inquisitive eyes, whilst ghostlike forms emerged out of hidden burrows for a moment to look on the noisy visitor and then equally furtively vanished again.

On the topmost landing he halted; here a small skylight in the roof afforded a modicum of light. Two doors confronted him, he went up to one of them and knocked on it loudly with his fist.

Then he waited — not with great patience but with his ear glued to the door listening to the sounds within. It almost seemed as if the room beyond was the abode of the dead, for not a sound reached the listener's ear. He knocked again, more loudly this time and more insistently. Still no response. At the other door on the opposite side of the landing a female figure appeared wrapped in a worsted rag, and a head half hidden by a linen coif was thrust forward out of the darkness behind it.

"They's won't answer you," said the apparition curtly. "They are strangers … only came last night, but all this morning when the landlord or his wife knocked at the door, they simply would not open it."

"But I am a friend," said Diogenes, "the best I fancy that these poor folk have."

"You used to lodge here until last night."

"Why yes. The lodgings are mine, I gave them up to these poor people who had nowhere else to go."

"They won't answer you," reiterated the female apparition dolefully and once more retired into its burrow.

The situation was becoming irritating. Diogenes put his mouth against the keyhole and shouted "What ho, there! Open!" as lustily as his powerful lungs would allow.

"Dondersteen!" he exclaimed, when even then he received no response.

But strange to relate no sooner was this expletive out of his mouth, than there came a cry like that of a frightened small animal, followed by a patter of naked feet upon a naked floor; the next moment the door was thrown invitingly open, and Diogenes was able to step across its thresh-hold.

"Dondersteen!" he ejaculated again, "hadst thou not opened, wench, I would within the next few seconds have battered in the door."

The woman stood looking at him with great, dark eyes in which joy, surprise and fear struggled for mastery. Her hair though still unruly was coiled around her head, her shift and kirtle were neatly fastened, but her legs and feet were bare and above the shift her neck and shoulders appeared colourless and attenuated. Eyes and hair were dark, and her skin had the olive tint of the south, but her lips at this moment looked bloodless, and there was the look of starvation in her wan face.

Diogenes walked past her into the inner room. The old man was lying on the bed, and on the coverlet close to him a much fingered prayer-book lay open. The woman slipped noiselessly past the visitor and quietly put the prayer-book away.

"You have come to tell us that we must go," she said in an undertone as she suddenly faced the newcomer.

"Indeed, that was not my purpose," he replied gaily, "I have come on the contrary to bring you good news, and it was foolish of you to keep me dangling on your doorstep for so long."

"The landlord hates us," she murmured, "because you forced him last night to take us in. He came thundering at the door early this morning, and threatened to eject us as vagabonds or to denounce us as Spanish spies. I would not open the door to him, and he shouted his threats at us through the keyhole. When you knocked just now I was frightened. I thought that he had come back."

Her voice was low and though she spoke Dutch fluently her throat had in it the guttural notes of her native land. A touch of the gipsy there must be in her, thought Diogenes as he looked with suddenly aroused interest on the woman before him, her dark skin, the long, supple limbs, the velvety eyes with their submissive, terrified look.

With embarrassed movements she offered the only chair in the room to her visitor, then cast shy, timorous glances on him as he refused to sit, preferring to lean his tall figure against the white-washed wall. She thought that never in her life had she seen any man so splendid and her look of bold admiration told him so without disguise.

"Well!" he said with his quaint smile, "I am not the landlord, nor yet an enemy. Art thou convinced of that?"

"Yes, I am!" she said with a little sigh, as she turned away from him in order to attend to the old man, who was moaning peevishly in bed.

"He has lost the use of speech," she said to Diogenes as soon as she had seen to the old man's wants, "and to-day he is so crippled that he can scarcely move. We ought never to have come to this horrible cold part of the country," she added with a sudden tone of fierce resentment. "I think that we shall both die of misery before we leave it again."

"Why did you come here then at all?" asked Diogenes.

"We wandered hither, because we heard that the people in this city were so rich. I was born not far from here, and so was my mother, but my father is a native of Spain. In France, in Brabant where we wandered before, we always earned a good living by begging at the church doors, but here the people are so hard...."

"You will have to wander back to Spain."

"Yes," she said sullenly, "as soon as I have earned a little money and father is able to move, neither of which seems very likely just now."

"Ah!" he said cheerily, "that is, wench, where I proclaim thee wrong! I do not know when thy father will be able to move, but I can tell thee at this very moment where and how thou canst earn fifty guilders which should take thee quite a long way toward Spain."

She looked up at him and once more that glance of joy and of surprise crept into her eyes which had seemed so full of vindictive anger just now. With the surprise and the joy there also mingled the admiration, the sense of well-being in his presence.

Already he had filled the bare, squalid room with his breezy personality, with his swagger and with his laughter; his ringing voice had roused the echoes that slept in the mouldy rafters and frightened the mice that dwelt in the wainscotting and now scampered hurriedly away.

"I," she said with obvious incredulity, "I to earn fifty guilders! I have not earned so much in any six months of my life."

"Perhaps not," he rejoined gaily. "But I can promise thee this; that the fifty guilders will be thine this evening, if thou wilt render me a simple service."

"Render thee a service," she said, and her low voice sounded quite cooing and gentle, "I would thank God on my knees if I could render thee a service. Didst thou not save my life...."

"By thy leave we'll not talk of that matter. 'Tis over and done with now. The service I would ask of thee, though 'tis simple enough to perform, I could not ask of anyone else but thee. An thou'lt do it, I shall be more than repaid."

"Name it, sir," she said simply.

"Dost know the bank of the Oude Gracht?" he asked.

"Well," she replied.

"Dost know the Oudenvrouwenhuis situated there?"

"Yes!"

"Next to its outer walls there is a narrow passage which leads to the Remonstrant Chapel of St. Pieter."

"There is, sir. I know it."

"This evening at seven o'clock then thou'lt take thy stand at the corner of this passage facing the Oude Gracht; and there thou wilt remain to ask alms from the passers-by. Thou'rt not afraid?"

"Afraid of what, sir?"

"The spot is lonely, the passage leads nowhere except to the chapel, which has been deserted these past five years."

"I am not afraid."

"That's brave! After evensong is over at the cathedral, one or two people will no doubt come thy way. Thou'lt beg them for alms in the usual way. But anon a lady will come accompanied by a duenna and preceded by two serving men carrying lanthorns. From her thou must ask insistently, and tell her as sad a tale of woe as thou canst think on, keeping well within the narrow passage and inducing her to follow thee."

"How shall I know the lady? There may be others who go past that way, and who might also be escorted by a woman and two serving men."

"The men wear green and purple livery, with peaked green caps trimmed with fur. Thou canst not mistake them even in the dark, for the light of the lanthorns which they carry will be upon them. But I will be in the passage close behind thee. When I see her coming I will warn thee."

"I understand," she said, nodding her head slowly once or twice as if she were brooding over what she thought. "But surely that is not all that I can do for thee."

"Indeed it is, and therefore none too difficult. Having drawn the lady into the shadow by thy talk, contrive to speak to her, telling her of thy troubles. If anything occurs after that to surprise or mayhap frighten thee, pay no heed to it, but take at once to thy heels and run straight home here, without looking to right or left. No one will molest thee, I give thee my word."

"I understand!" she reiterated once more.

"And wilt thou do as I ask?"

"Of course. My life is thine; thou didst save it twice. Thou hast but to command and I will obey."

"We'll call it that," he said lightly, "since it seems to please thee. To-night then at seven o'clock, I too, will be on the spot to place the fifty guilders in thy hand."

"Fifty guilders!" she exclaimed almost with ecstasy, and pressed her hands to her breast. "My father and I need not starve or be homeless the whole of this winter."

"Thou'lt make tracks for Spain very soon," he rejoined carelessly, for he had accomplished his business and was making ready to go.

She threw him a strange look, half defiant yet almost reproachful.

"Perhaps!" she said curtly.

He took leave of her in his usual pleasant, airy manner, smiling at her earnestness and at her looks that reminded him of a starving dog which he had once picked up in the streets of Prague and kept and fed for a time, until he found it a permanent home. When he gave the dog away to some kindly people who promised to be kind to it, it threw him, at parting, just such a look as dwelt in the dark depths of this girl's eyes now.

The old cripple on the bed had fallen into a torpor-like sleep. Diogenes cast a compassionate glance on him.

"Thou canst take him to better quarters in a day or two," he said, "and mayhap give him some good food....Dondersteen!" he exclaimed suddenly, "what art doing, girl?"

She had stooped and kissed his hand. He drew it away almost roughly, but at the timid look of humble apology which she raised to him, he said gently:

"By St. Bavon thou'rt a funny child! Well? what is it now?" he asked, for she stood hesitating before him, with a question obviously hovering on her lips.

"I dare not," she murmured.

"Art afraid of me then?"

"A little."

"Yet there is something thou desirest to ask?"

"Yes."

"What is it? Quickly now, for I must be going."

She waited for a moment or two trying to gain courage, whilst he watched her, greatly amused.

"What is it?" he reiterated more impatiently.

Then a whispered murmur escaped her lips.

"The lady?"

"Yes. What of her?"

"Thou dost love her?" she stammered, "and wilt abduct her to-night because of thy love for her?"

For a second or two he looked on her in blank amazement, marvelling if he had entrusted this vital business to a semi-imbecile. Then seeing that indeed she appeared in deadly earnest, and that her great, inquiring but perfectly lucid eyes were fixed upon him with mute insistence, he threw back his head and laughed till the very rafters of the low room shook with the echo of his merriment.

"Dondersteen!" he said as soon as he felt that he could speak again, "but thou truly art a strange wench. Whatever did put that idea into thy head?"

"Thou dost propose to abduct her, I know that," she said more firmly. "I am no fool, and I understand I am to be the decoy. The dark passage, the lonely spot, thy presence there ... and then the occurrence, as thou saidst, that might surprise or frighten me....I am no fool," she repeated sullenly, "I understand."

"Apparently," he retorted dryly.

"Thou dost love her?" she insisted.

"What is it to thee?"

"No matter; only tell me this, dost thou love her?"

"If I said 'yes,'" he asked with his whimsical smile, "wouldst refuse to help me?"

"Oh, no!"

"And if I said 'no'?"

"I should be glad," she said simply.

"Then we'll say 'no!'" he concluded lightly, "for I would like to see thee glad."

And he had his wish, for quite a joyous smile lit up her small, pinched face. She tripped quite briskly to the door and held it open for him.

"If thou desirest to speak with me again," she said, as he finally took his leave, "give four raps on the door at marked intervals. I would fly to open it then."

He thanked her and went down stairs, humming a lively tune and never once turning to look on her again. And yet she was leaning over the ricketty banisters watching his slowly descending figure, until it disappeared in the gloom.

CHAPTER XIV
AFTER EVENSONG

Jongejuffrouw Beresteyn had spent many hours in church this New Year's Day, 1624. In spite of the inclemency of the weather she had attended Morning Prayer and Holy Communion and now she was back again for Evensong.

The cathedral was not very full for it. Most people were making merry at home to celebrate the festival; so Gilda had a corner of the sacred building all to herself, where she could think matters over silently and with the help of prayer. The secret of which she had gained knowledge was weighing heavily on her soul; and heart-rending doubts had assailed her all night and throughout the day.

How could she know what was the right thing to do? — to allow a crime of which she had fore-knowledge, to be committed without raising a finger to prevent it? or to betray her own brother and his friends — a betrayal which would inevitably lead them to the scaffold?

Her father was of course her great refuge, and to-night through Evensong she prayed to God to guide her, as to whether she should tell everything to her father or not. She had warned Nicolaes that she might do so, and yet her very soul shrank from the act which to many would seem so like betrayal. Cornelius Beresteyn was a man of rigid principles and unyielding integrity. What he might do with the knowledge of the conspiracy in which his own son was taking a leading part, no one — not even his daughter — could foresee. In no case would she act hurriedly. She hoped against all hope that mayhap Nicolaes would see his own treachery in its true light and turn from it before it was too late, or that God would give her some unmistakable sign of what He willed her to do.

Perplexed and wretched she stayed long on her knees and left the church after every one else. The night was dark and though the snow had left off falling momentarily, the usual frosty mist hung over the city. Jongejuffrouw Beresteyn wrapped her fur-lined cloak closely round her shoulders and started on her homeward walk, with Maria by her side and Jakob and Piet on in front carrying their lanthorns.

Her way took her firstly across the Groote Markt then down the Hout Straat until she reached the Oude Gracht. Here her two serving men kept quite close in front of her for the embankment was lonely and a well-known resort for evil doers who found refuge in the several dark passages that run at right angles from the canal and have no outlet at their further end.

Jongejuffrouw Beresteyn followed rapidly in the wake of her lanthorn bearers and keeping Maria — who was always timorous on dark nights and in lonely places — quite close to her elbow. Every footstep of the way was familiar to her. Now the ground was frozen hard and the covering of snow crisp beneath her feet as she walked, but in the autumn and the spring the mud here was ankle-deep, save on one or two rare spots in front of the better houses or public buildings where a few stones formed a piece of dry pavement. Such a spot was the front of the Oudenvrouwenhuis with its wide oaken gateway and high brick walls. The unmade road here was always swept neatly and tidily; during the rainy seasons the mud was washed carefully away and in the winter it was kept free from snow.

Beyond it was a narrow passage which led to the Chapel of St. Pieter, now disused since the Remonstrants had fallen into such bad odour after the death of Olden Barneveld and the treachery of his sons. The corner of this passage was a favourite haunt for beggars, but only for the humbler ones — since there is a hierarchy even amongst beggars, and the more prosperous ones, those known to the town-guard and the night-watchmen, flocked around the church porches. In this spot where there were but a few passers-by, only those poor wretches came who mayhap had something to hide from the watchful eyes of the guardians of this city, those who had been in prison or had deserted from the army, or were known to be rogues and thieves.

Gilda Beresteyn, who had a soft heart, always kept a few kreutzers in the palm of her hand ready to give to any of these poor outcasts who happened to beg for alms along the embankment, but she never liked to stop here in order to give those other alms, which she knew were oft more acceptable than money — the alms of kindly words.

To-night, however, she herself felt miserable and lonely and the voice that came to her out of the darkness of the narrow passage which leads to the Chapel of St. Pieter was peculiarly plaintive and sweet.

"For the love of Christ, gentle lady," murmured the voice softly.

Gilda stopped, ready with the kreutzers in her hand. But it was very dark just here and the snow appeared too deep to traverse; she could not see the melancholy speaker, though she knew of course that it was a woman.

"Bring the lanthorn a little nearer, Jakob," she said.

"Do not stop, mejuffrouw, to parley with any of these scamps," said Maria as she clung fearsomely to her mistress's cloak.

"For the love of Christ, gentle lady!" sighed the pitiable voice out of the darkness again.

Jakob brought the lanthorn nearer.

Some half a dozen steps up the passage a pathetic little figure appeared to view, the figure of a woman — a mere girl — with ragged shift and bare legs half buried in the depths of the snow.

Gilda without hesitation went up to her, money in hand, her own feet sinking in ankle deep into the cold, white carpet below. The girl retreated as the kind lady advanced, apparently scared by the two men who had paused one at each corner of the passage holding their lanthorns well above their heads.

"Don't be frightened, girl," said Gilda Beresteyn gently, "here's a little money. You look so cold, poor child!"

The next moment a double cry behind her caused her to turn in a trice: she had only just time to take in the terrifying fact that Piet and Jakob had dropped their lanthorns to the ground even as thick dark cloths were thrown over their heads — before she found herself firmly seized round the waist by a powerful arm whilst some kind of scarf was wound quickly round her face.

She had not the time to scream, the enveloping scarf smothered her cry even as it formed in her throat. The last thing of which she was clearly conscious was of a voice — which strangely enough sounded familiar — saying hurriedly:

"Here, take thy money, girl, and run home now as fast as thy feet will take thee."

After that, though she was never totally unconscious, she was only dimly aware of what happened to her. She certainly felt herself lifted off the ground and carried for some considerable distance. What seemed to her a long, long time afterwards she became aware that she was lying on her back and that there was a smell of sweet hay and fresh straw around her. Close to her ear there was the sound of a woman moaning. The scarf still covered her face, but it had been loosened so that she could breathe, and presently when she opened her eyes, she found that the scarf only covered her mouth.

As she lay on her back she could see nothing above her. She was not cold for the straw around her formed a warm bed, and her cloak had been carefully arranged so as to cover her completely, whilst her feet were wrapped up snugly in a rug.

It was only when complete consciousness returned to her that she realized that she was lying in an object that moved: she became conscious of the jingling of harness and of occasional unpleasant jolting, whilst the darkness overhead was obviously caused by the roof of a vehicle.

She tried to raise herself on her elbow, but she discovered that loose, though quite efficient bonds held her pinioned down; her arms, however, were free and she put out her hand in the direction whence came the muffled sound of a woman moaning.

"Lord! God Almighty! Lord in Heaven!" and many more appeals of a like character escaped the lips of Gilda's companion in misfortune.

"Maria! Is it thou?" said Gilda in a whisper. Her hand went groping in the dark until it encountered firstly a cloak, then an arm and finally a head apparently also enveloped in a cloth.

"Lord God Almighty!" sighed the other woman feebly through the drapery. "Is it mejuf-frouw?"

"Yes, Maria, it is I!" whispered Gilda, "whither are they taking us, thinkest thou?"

"To some lonely spot where they can conveniently murder us!" murmured Maria with a moan of anguish.

"But what became of Piet and Jakob?"

"Murdered probably. The cowards could not defend us."

Gilda strained her ears to listen. She hoped by certain sounds to make out at least in which direction she was being carried away. Above the rattle and jingle of the harness she could hear at times the measured tramp of horses trotting in the rear, and she thought at one time that the sleigh went over the wooden bridge on the Spaarne and then under the echoing portals of one of the city gates.

Her head after awhile began to ache terribly and her eyes felt as if they were seared with coal. Of course she lost all count of time: it seemed an eternity since she had spoken to the girl in the dark passage which leads to the chapel of St. Pieter.

Maria who lay beside her moaned incessantly for awhile like a fretful child, but presently she became silent.

Perhaps she had gone to sleep. The night air which found its way through the chinks of the hood came more keen and biting against Gilda's face. It cooled her eyes and eased the throbbing of her head. She felt very tired and as if her body had been bruised all over.

The noises around her became more monotonous, the tramping of the horses in the rear of the sleigh sounded muffled and subdued. Drowsiness overcame Gilda Beresteyn and she fell into a troubled, half-waking sleep.

For a long time she had been half-awake, ever since the vehicle had stopped, which must have been ages and ages ago. She had lain in a kind of torpor, various sounds coming to her ear as through the veil of dreams: there was Maria snoring contentedly close by, and the horses champing their bits and pawing the hard-frozen ground, also there was the murmur of voices, subdued and muffled — but she could not distinguish words.

Not for a long time at any rate — an interminably long time!

Her body and limbs felt quite numb, pleasantly warm under the rugs and cloaks, only her face rejoiced in the cold blast that played around it and kept her forehead and eyes cool.

Once it seemed to her as if out of the darkness more than one pair of eyes were looking down on her, and she had the sense as of a warm rapid breath that mingled with the pure frosty air. After which some one murmured:

"She is still unconscious."

"I think not," was the whispered reply.

She lay quite still, in case those eyes came to look on her again. The murmuring voices sounded quite close to the sleigh now, and soon she found that by holding her breath, and straining her every listening faculty she could detach the words that struck her ear from all the other sounds around her.

Two men, she thought, were speaking, but their voices were never once raised above a whisper.

"You are satisfied?" she heard one of these saying quite distinctly.

"Entirely!" was the response.

"The letter to Ben Isaje?"

"I am not like to lose it."

"Hush! I heard a sound from under the hood."

"'Tis only the old woman snoring."

"I wish you could have found a more comfortable sledge."

"There was none to be had in Haarlem to-day. But we'll easily get one in Leyden."

In Leyden! Gilda's numbed body quivered with horror. She was being taken to Leyden and further on still by sleigh! Her thoughts at present were still chaotic but gradually she was sorting them out, one or two becoming more clear, more insistent than the rest.

"I would like the jongejuffrouw to have something to eat and drink," came once more in whispers from out the darkness. "I fear that she will be faint!"

"No! no!" came the prompt, peremptory reply, "it would be madness to let her realize so soon where she is. She knows this place well."

A halt on the way to Leyden! and thence a further journey by sledge! Gilda's thoughts were distinctly less chaotic already. She was beginning to marshal them up in her mind, together with her recollections of the events of the past twenty-four hours. The darkness around her, which was intense, and the numbness of her body all helped her to concentrate her faculties on these recollections first and on the obvious conclusions based upon her position at the present moment.

She was being silenced effectually because of the knowledge which she had gained in the cathedral last night. The Lord of Stoutenburg, frightened for his plans, was causing her to be put out of his way. Never for a moment did she suspect her own brother in this. It was that conscienceless, ambitious, treacherous Stoutenburg! at most her brother was blindly acquiescent in this infamy.

Gilda was not afraid. Not even when this conviction became fully matured in her mind. She was not afraid for herself, although for one brief moment the thought did cross her mind that mayhap she had only been taken out of Haarlem in order that her death might be more secretly encompassed.

But she was cast in a firmer mould than most women of her rank and wealth would be. She came of a race that had faced misery, death and torture for over a century for the sake of its own independence of life and of faith, and was ready to continue the struggle for another hundred years if need be for the same ideals, and making the same sacrifices in order to attain them. Gilda Beresteyn gave but little thought to her own safety. Life to her, if Stoutenburg's dastardly conspiracy against the Stadtholder was successful and involved her own brother, would be of little value to her. Nicolaes' act of treachery would break her father's heart; what matter if she herself lived to witness all that misery or not.

No! it was her helplessness at this moment that caused her the most excruciating soul-agony. She had been trapped and was being cast aside like a noxious beast, that is in the way of men. Like a child that is unruly and has listened at the keyhole of the door, she was being punished and rendered harmless.

Indeed she had no fear for her safety; the few words which she had heard, the presence of Maria, all tended to point out that there would be no direct attempt against her life. It was only of that awful crime that she thought, that crime which she had so fondly hoped that she might yet frustrate: it was of the Stadtholder's safety that she thought and of her brother's sin.

She also thought of her poor father who, ignorant of the events which had brought about this infamous abduction, would be near killing himself with sorrow at the mysterious disappearance of his only daughter. Piet and Jakob would tell how they had been set on in the dark — footpads would be suspected, the countryside where they usually have their haunts would be scoured for them, but the high road leading to Leyden would never mayhap be watched, and certainly a sleigh under escort would never draw the attention of the guardians of the peace.

While these thoughts whirled wildly in her brain it seemed that preparations had been and were being made for departure. She heard some whispered words again:

"Where will you put up at Leyden?"

"At the 'White Goat.' I know the landlord well."

"Will he be awake at so late an hour?"

"I will ride ahead and rouse his household. They shall be prepared for our coming."

"But...."

"You seem to forget, sir," came in somewhat louder tones, "that all the arrangements for this journey were to be left entirely to my discretion."

For the moment Gilda could catch no further words distinctly: whether a quarrel had ensued or not she could not conjecture, but obviously the two speakers had gone some little distance away from the sledge. All that she could hear was — after a brief while of silence — a quaint muffled laugh which though it scarce was distinguishable from the murmur of the wind, so soft was it, nevertheless betrayed to her keenly sensitive ear an undercurrent of good-humoured irony.

Again there seemed something familiar to her in the sound.

After this there was renewed tramping of heavy feet on the snow-covered ground, the clang of bits and chains, the creaking of trace, the subdued call of encouragement to horses:

"Forward!" came a cheery voice from the rear.

Once more they were on the move; on the way to Leyden — distant six leagues from her home. Gilda could have cried out now in her misery. She pictured her father — broken-hearted all through the night, sending messengers hither and thither to the various gates of the city, unable no doubt to get satisfactory information at this late hour: she pictured Nicolaes feigning ignorance of the whole thing, making pretence of anxiety and grief. Torturing thoughts kept her awake, though her body was racked with fatigue. The night was bitterly cold, and the wind, now that they had reached open country, cut at times across her face like a knife.

The sledge glided along with great swiftness now, over the smooth, thick carpet of snow that covered the long, straight road. Gilda knew that the sea was not far off: but she also knew that every moment now she was being dragged further and further away from the chance of averting from her father and from her house the black catastrophe of disgrace which threatened them.

CHAPTER XVI
LEYDEN

It seemed that from some church tower far away a clock struck the hour of midnight when the sledge at last came to a halt.

Worn out with nerve-racking thoughts, as well as with the cruel monotony of the past four hours, Gilda felt her soul and body numb and lifeless as a stone. There was much running and shouting round the vehicle, of horses' hoofs resounding against rough cobble-stones, of calls for ostler and landlord.

Then for awhile comparative quietude. Maria still snored unperturbed, and Gilda, wide-eyed and with beating heart, awaited further events. Firstly the hood of the sledge in which she lay was lifted off: she could hear the ropes and straps being undone, the tramp of feet all round her and an occasional volley of impatient oaths. Then out of the darkness a pleasant voice called her somewhat peremptorily by name.

"Mejuffrouw Beresteyn!"

She did not reply, but lay quite still, with wide-open eyes like a bird that has been tracked and knows that it is watched. Maria uttered a loud groan and tried to roll over on her side.

"Where have those murderers taken us to now?" she muttered through the veil that still enveloped her mouth.

The pleasant voice close to Gilda's ear, now called out more loudly:

"Here, Pythagoras, Socrates! lift the mevrouw out of the sleigh and carry her up to the room which the landlord hath prepared for the ladies."

Maria immediately gave vent to violent shrieks of protest.

"How dare ye touch me!" she screamed at the top of her voice, "ye murdering devils dare but lay a finger on a respectable woman and God will punish you with pestilence and dislocation and ..."

It must be presumed that neither Pythagoras nor Socrates were greatly upset by the mevrouw's curses, for Gilda, who was on the alert for every movement and for every sound, was well aware that Maria's highly respectable person was presently seized by firm hands, that the shawl round her face was pressed more tightly against her mouth — for her screams sounded more muffled — and that despite her struggles, her cries and her kicking she was lifted bodily out of the sledge.

When these disquieting sounds had died down the same pleasant voice broke in once again on Gilda's obstinate silence.

"Mejuffrouw Beresteyn!" it reiterated once again.

"Dondersteen! but 'tis no use lying mum there, and pretending to be asleep," it continued after awhile, since Gilda certainly had taken no notice of the call, "that old woman made enough noise to wake the dead."

Still not a sound from Gilda, who — more like a cowering bird than ever — was trying with widely-dilated eyes to pierce the darkness around her, in order to see something of the enemy. She saw the outline of a plumed hat like a patch of ink against the sky above, and also a pair of very broad shoulders that were stooping toward the floor of the sledge.

"Hey!" shouted the enemy with imperturbable cheerfulness, "leave that door wide open, I'll carry the jongejuffrouw in myself. She seems to be unconscious."

The words roused Gilda out of her attitude of rigid silence, — the words which she looked on as an awful threat, and also the sensation that the loose bonds which had pinioned her down to the vehicle were being undone.

"I am not unconscious," she said aloud and quite calmly, "and was quite aware just now that you laid rough hands on a helpless woman. Since I am equally helpless and in your power I pray you to command what I must do."

"Come! that's brave! I knew that you could not be asleep," rejoined the enemy with inveterate good-humour, "but for the moment, mejuffrouw, I must ask you to descend from this sleigh.

It has been a vastly uncomfortable vehicle for you to travel in, I fear me, but it was the best that we could get in Haarlem on New Year's day. An you will deign to enter this humble hostelry you will find the mevrouw there, a moderately good supper and something resembling a bed, all of which I am thinking will be highly acceptable to you."

While the enemy spoke, Gilda had a few seconds in which to reflect. Above all things she was a woman of sense and one who valued her own dignity; she knew quite well that the making of a scene outside an inn in a strange town and at this hour of the night could but result in a loss of that dignity which she so highly prized, seeing that she was entirely at the mercy of men who were not likely to yield either to her protests or to her appeals.

Therefore, when she felt that she was free to move, she made every effort to raise herself; uncomfortably these long hours of weary motionless lying on her back, had made her limbs so numb that they refused her service. She made one or two brave attempts to hide her helplessness, but when she wanted to draw up her knees, she nearly cried with the pain of trying to move them out of their cramped position.

"It were wiser methinks," quoth the enemy with a slight tone of mockery in his cheerful voice, "it were wiser to accept the help of my arms. They are strong, firm and not cramped. Try them, mejuffrouw, you will have no cause to regret it."

Quite involuntarily — for of a truth she shrank from the mere touch of this rascal who obviously was in the pay of Stoutenburg, and doing the latter's infamous work for him — quite involuntarily then, she placed her hand upon the arm which he had put out as a prop for her.

It was as firm as a rock. Leaning on it somewhat heavily she was able to struggle to her knees. This made her venturesome. She tried to stand up; but fatigue, the want of food, the excitement and anxiety which she had endured, combined with the fact that she had been in a recumbent position for many hours, caused her to turn desperately giddy. She swayed like a young sapling under the wind, and would have fallen but that the same strong arm firm as a rock was there to receive her ere she fell.

I suppose that dizziness deprived her of her full senses, else she would never have allowed that knave to lift her out of the sledge and then to carry her into a building, and up some narrow and very steep stairs. But this Diogenes did do, with but scant ceremony; he thought her protests foolish, and her attempts at lofty disdain pitiable. She was after all but a poor, helpless scrap of humanity, so slight and frail that as he carried her into the house, there was grave danger of his crushing her into nothingness as she lay in his arms.

Despite her pride and her aloofness he found it in his heart to pity her just now. Had she been fully conscious she would have hated to see herself pillowed thus against the doublet of so contemptible a knave; and here she was absolutely handed over body and soul to a nameless stranger, who in her sight, was probably no better than a menial — and this by the cynical act of one who next to her father was her most natural protector.

Yes, indeed he did pity her, for she seemed to him more than ever like that poor little songbird whom a lout had tortured for his own pleasure by plucking out its feathers one by one. It seemed monstrous that so delicate a creature should be the victim of men's intrigues and passions. Why! even! her breath had the subtle scent of tulips as it fanned his cheeks and nostrils when he stooped in order to look on her.

In the meanwhile he had been as good as his word. He had pushed on to Leyden in advance of the cortège, had roused the landlord of this hostelry and the serving wenches, and scattered money so freely that despite the lateness of the hour a large square room — the best in the house, and scrupulously clean as to the red-tiled floor and walnut furniture — was at once put at the disposal of the ladies of so noble a travelling company.

The maids were sent flying hither and thither, one into the kitchen to make ready some hot supper, the other to the linen press to find the finest set of bed linen all sweetly laid by in rosemary.

Diogenes, still carrying Gilda, pushed the heavy panelled door open with his foot, and without looking either to right or left of him made straight for the huge open hearth, wherein already logs of pinewood had been set ablaze, and beside which stood an armchair, covered with Utrecht velvet.

Into its inviting and capacious depths he deposited his inanimate burden, and only then did he become aware of two pairs of eyes, which were fixed upon him with very different expression. A buxom wench in ample wide kirtle of striped duffle, had been busy when he entered in spreading clean linen sheets upon the narrow little bed built in the panelling of the room. From under her quaint winged cap of starched lace a pair of very round eyes, blue as the Ryn, peeped in naïve undisguised admiration on the intruder, whilst from beneath her disordered coif Maria threw glances of deadly fury upon him.

Could looks but kill, Maria certes would have annihilated the low rascal who had dared to lay hands upon the noble jongejuffrouw. But our friend Diogenes was not a man to be perturbed either by admiring or condemning looks. He picked up a footstool from under the table and put it under the jongejuffrouw's feet; then he looked about him for a pillow, and with scant ceremony took one straight out of the hands of the serving wench who was just shaking it up ready for the bed. His obvious intention was to place it behind the jongejuffrouw's head, but at this act of unforgivable presumption Maria's wrath cast aside all restraint. Like a veritable fury she strode up to the insolent rascal, and snatched the pillow from him, throwing on him such a look of angry contempt as should have sent him grovelling on his knees.

"Keep thy blood cool, mevrouw," he said with the best of humour, "thy looks have already made a weak-kneed coward of me."

With the dignity of an offended turkey hen, Maria arranged the pillow herself under her mistress's head, having previously shaken it and carefully dusted off the blemish caused upon its surface by contact with an unclean hand. As for the footstool, she would not even allow it to remain there where that same unclean hand had placed it; she kicked it aside with her foot and drew up her small, round stature in a comprehensive gesture of outraged pride.

Diogenes made her a low bow, sweeping the floor with his plumed hat. The serving wench had much ado to keep a serious countenance, so comical did the mevrouw look in her wrath, and so mirth-provoking the gentleman with his graceful airs and unruffled temper. Anon laughter tickled her so that she had to run quickly out of the room, in order to indulge in a fit of uncontrolled mirth, away from the reproving glances of mevrouw.

It was the pleasant sound of that merry laughter outside the door that caused the jongejuffrouw to come to herself and to open wide, wondering eyes. She looked around her, vaguely puzzled, taking in the details of the cosy room, the crackling fire, the polished table, the inviting bed that exhaled an odour of dried rosemary.

Then her glance fell on Diogenes, who was standing hat in hand in the centre of the room, with the light from the blazing logs playing upon his smiling face, and the immaculate whiteness of his collar.

She frowned. And he who stood there — carelessly expectant — could not help wondering whether with that swift contemptuous glance which she threw on him, she had already recognized him.

"Mejuffrouw," he said, thus checking with a loud word the angry exclamation which hovered on her lips, "if everything here is not entirely in accordance with your desires, I pray you but to command and it shall be remedied if human agency can but contrive to do so. As for me, I am entirely at your service — your major domo, your servant, your outrider, anything you like to name me. Send but for your servant if you have need of aught; supper will be brought up to you immediately, and in the meanwhile I beg leave to free you from my unwelcome company."

Already there was a goodly clatter of platters, and of crockery outside, and as the wench re-entered anon bearing a huge tray on which were set out several toothsome things, Diogenes contrived to make his exit without encountering further fusillades of angry glances.

He joined his friends in the tap-room downstairs, and as he was young, vigorous and hungry he set to with them and ate a hearty supper. But he spoke very little and the rough jests of his brother philosophers met with but little response from him.

CHAPTER XVII
AN UNDERSTANDING

At one hour after midnight the summons came.

Maria, majestic and unbending, sailed into the tap-room where Pythagoras and Socrates were already stretched out full-length upon a couple of benches fast asleep and Diogenes still struggling to keep awake.

"The noble Jongejuffrouw Beresteyn desires your presence," she said addressing the latter with lofty dignity.

At once he rose to his feet, and followed Maria up the stairs and into the lady's room. From this room an inner door gave on another smaller alcove-like chamber, wherein a bed had been prepared for Maria.

Gilda somewhat curtly ordered her to retire.

"I will call you, Maria," she said, "when I have need of you."

Diogenes with elaborate courtesy threw the inner door open, and stood beside it plumed hat in hand while the mevrouw sailed past him, with arms folded across her ample bosom, and one of those dignified glances in her round eyes that should have annihilated this impious malapert, whose face — despite its airs of deference, was wreathed in an obviously ironical smile.

It was only when the heavy oaken door had fallen to behind her duenna that Gilda with an imperious little gesture called Diogenes before her.

He advanced hat in hand as was his wont, his magnificent figure very erect, his head with its wealth of untamed curls slightly bent. But he looked on her boldly with those laughter-filled, twinkling eyes of his and since he was young and neither ascetic nor yet a misanthrope, we may take it that he had some considerable pleasure in the contemplation of the dainty picture which she presented against the background of dull gold velvet: her small head propped against the cushions, and feathery curls escaping from under her coif and casting pearly, transparent shadows upon the ivory whiteness of her brow. Her two hands were resting each on an arm of the chair, and looked more delicate than ever now in the soft light of the tallow candles that burned feebly in the pewter candelabra upon the table.

Diogenes for the moment envied his friend Frans Hals for the power which the painter of pictures has of placing so dainty an image on record for all time. His look of bold admiration, however, caused Gilda's glance to harden, and she drew herself up in her chair in an attitude more indicative of her rank and station and of her consciousness of his inferiority.

But not with a single look or smile did she betray whether she had recognized him or not.

"Your name?" she asked curtly.

His smile broadened — self-deprecatingly this time.

"They call me Diogenes," he replied.

"A strange name," she commented, "but 'tis of no consequence."

"Of none whatever," he rejoined, "I had not ventured to pronounce it, only that you deigned to ask."

Again she frowned: the tone of gentle mockery had struck unpleasantly on her ear and she did not like that look of self-satisfied independence which sat on him as if to the manner born, when he was only an abject menial, paid to do dirty work for his betters.

"I have sent for you, sir," she resumed after a slight pause, "because I wished to demand of you an explanation of your infamous conduct. Roguery and vagabondage are severely punished by our laws, and you have brought your neck uncommonly near the gallows by your act of highway robbery. Do you hear me?" she asked more peremptorily, seeing that he made no attempt at a reply.

"I hear you, mejuffrouw."

"And what is your explanation?"

"That is my trouble, mejuffrouw. I have none to offer."

"Do you refuse then to tell me what your purpose is in thus defying the laws of the land and risking the gallows by laying hands upon me and upon my waiting woman in the open streets, and by taking me away by brute force from my home?"

"My purpose, mejuffrouw, is to convey you safely as far as Rotterdam, where I will hand you over into the worthy keeping of a gentleman who will relieve me of further responsibility with regard to your precious person."

"In Rotterdam?" she exclaimed, "what should I do in Rotterdam?"

"Nothing, I imagine," replied Diogenes dryly, "for you would not remain there longer than is necessary. I am the bearer of written orders to that same gentleman in Rotterdam that he shall himself conduct you under suitable escort — of which I no doubt will still form an integral part — to his private residence, which I am told is situate outside the city and on the road to Delft."

"A likely story indeed!" she rejoined vehemently, "I'll not believe it! Common theft and robbery are your purpose, nothing less, else you had not stolen my purse from me nor the jewels which I wore."

"I had to take your purse and your jewels from you, mejuffrouw," he said with perfect equanimity, "else you might have used them for the purpose of slipping through my fingers. Wenches at wayside inns are easily amenable to bribes, so are the male servants at city hostelries. But your purse and the trinkets which you wore are safely stowed away in my wallet. I shall have the honour of returning them to you when we arrive in Rotterdam."

"Of returning them to me," she said with a contemptuous laugh, "do knaves like you ever return stolen property?"

"Seldom, I admit," he replied still with unruffled good-humour. "Nevertheless an exception hath often proved a rule. Your purse and trinkets are here," he added.

And from his wallet he took out a small leather purse and some loose jewellery which he showed to her.

"And," he added ere he once more replaced them in his wallet, "I will guard them most carefully until I can return them to you in Rotterdam, after which time 'twill be some one else's business to see that you do not slip through his fingers."

"And you expect me to believe such a senseless tale," she rejoined contemptuously.

"There are many things in this world and the next, mejuffrouw," he said lightly, "that are true though some of us believe them not."

"Nay! but this I do believe on the evidence of mine own eyes — that you stole my money and my jewels and have no intention of returning them to me."

"Your opinion of me, mejuffrouw, is already so low that it matters little surely if you think me a common thief as well."

"My opinion of you, sir, is based upon your actions."

"And these I own stand in formidable array against me."

She bit her lip in vexation and her slender fingers began to beat a tattoo on the arm of her chair. This man's placidity and inveterate good-humour were getting on her nerves. It is hard when one means to wound, to find the surest arrows falling wide of the mark. But now she waited for a moment or two lest her irritation betrayed itself in the quiver of her voice; and it was only when she felt quite sure that it would sound as trenchant and hard as she intended that it should, that she said abruptly:

"Who is paying you, sir, for this infamy?"

"One apparently who can afford the luxury," he replied airily.

"You will not tell me?"

"Do you think, mejuffrouw, that I could?"

"I may guess."

"It should not be difficult," he assented.

"And you, sir," she continued more vehemently, "are one of the many tools which the Lord of Stoutenburg doth use to gain his own political ends."

"The Lord of Stoutenburg?"

It was impossible for Gilda Beresteyn to gauge exactly whether the astonishment expressed in that young villain's exclamation was real or feigned. Certainly his mobile face was a picture of puzzlement, but this may have been caused only by his wondering how she could so easily have guessed the name of his employer. For as to this she was never for a moment in doubt. It was easy enough for her to piece together the series of events which had followed her parting from her brother at the cathedral door. Stoutenburg, burning with anxiety and glowing with his ardent desire for vengeance against the Stadtholder, had feared that she — Gilda — would betray the secret which she held, and he had paid this knave to take her out of the way. Stoutenburg and his gang! it could be no one else! she dared not think that her own brother would have a share in so dastardly an outrage. It was Stoutenburg of course! and this smiling knave knew it well! aye! even though he murmured again and this time to the accompaniment of smothered oaths:

"Stoutenburg? Bedonderd!"

"Aye!" she said loftily, "you see that I am not deceived! 'tis the Lord of Stoutenburg who gave you money to play this trick on me. He paid you! paid you, I say, and you, a man who should be fighting for your country, were over ready to make war upon a woman. Shame on you! shame I say! 'tis a deed that should cause you to blush, if indeed you have a spark of honesty in you, which of a truth I do gravely doubt."

She had worked herself up into an outburst of indignation and flung insult upon insult on him in the vague hope indeed of waking some slumbering remnant of shame in his heart, and mayhap ruffling that imperturbable air of contentment of his, and that impudent look of swagger most unbecoming in a menial.

But by naming Stoutenburg, she had certainly brought to light many things which Diogenes had only vaguely suspected. His mind — keen and shrewd despite his follies — recalled his interview with Nicolaes Beresteyn in the studio of Frans Hals; all the details of that interview seemed suddenly to have gained significance as well as lucidity. The lofty talk anent the future of Holland and the welfare of the Faith was easily understandable in this new light which the name of Stoutenburg had cast upon it. Stoutenburg and the welfare of Holland! a secret the possession of which meant death to six selfless patriots or the forfeiture mayhap of her good name and her honour to this defenceless girl! Stoutenburg at the bottom of it all! Diogenes could have laughed aloud with triumph so clear now was the whole scheme to him! There was no one living who did not think that at some time or other Stoutenburg meant to come back and make yet one more attempt to wipe a blood-stain from the annals of his country by one equally foul.

One of Barneveld's sons had already paid for such an attempt with his life; the other had escaped only in order to intrigue again, to plot again, and again to fail. And this poor girl had by a fortuitous mishap overheard the discussion of the guilty secret. Stoutenburg had come back and meant to kill the Stadtholder: Nicolaes Beresteyn was his accomplice and had callously sacrificed his innocent sister to the success of his friend's schemes.

If out of this network of intrigues a sensible philosopher did not succeed in consolidating his independence with the aid of a substantial fortune, then he was neither so keen nor so daring as his friends and he himself supposed!

And Gilda wondered what went on in his mind for those twinkling eyes of his never betrayed any deeper thought: but she noticed with great mortification that the insults which she had heaped upon him so freely had not shamed him at all, for the good-humoured smile was not effaced from his lips, rather did the shapely hand wander up to the moustache in order to give it — she thought — a more provoking curl.

"I still await your answer," she said haughtily, seeing that his prolonged silence savoured of impertinence.

"I humbly crave your pardon, mejuffrouw," he said pleasantly, "I was absorbed in wonderment."

"You marvelled, sir, how easily I saw behind your schemes, and saw the hand which drove you in harness?"

"Your pardon, mejuffrouw. I was pondering on your own words. You deigned to say just now that I — a man should be fighting for my country."

"And you are worthy, sir, to be called a man."

"Quite so," he said whimsically. "But even if I did lay claim to the title, mejuffrouw, how could I fight for my country when my country doth not happen to be at war just now."

"Your country? What pray might your country be? Not that this concerns me in the least," she added hastily.

"Of course not," he rejoined blandly.

"What is your country, sir?"

"England."

"I do not like the English."

"Nor do I, mejuffrouw. But I was unfortunately not consulted as to my choice of a fatherland: nor doth it change the fact that King James of England is at peace just now with all the world."

"So you preferred to earn a dishonest living by abducting innocent women, to further the intrigues of your paymaster."

"It is a harsh exposition," he said blandly, "of an otherwise obvious fact."

"And you are not ashamed."

"Not more than is necessary for my comfort."

"And cannot I move you, sir," she said with sudden warmth, "cannot an appeal to you from my lips rouse a feeling of manhood within you. My father is a rich man," she continued eagerly, "he hath it in his power to reward those who do him service; he can do so far more effectually than the Lord of Stoutenburg. Sir! I would not think of making an appeal to your heart! no doubt long ago you have taught it to remain cold to the prayers of a woman in distress: but surely you will listen to the call of your own self-interest. My father must be nigh heart-broken by now. The hours have sped away and he knows not where to find me."

"No! I have taken very good care of that, mejuffrouw. We are at Leyden now, but we left Haarlem through the Groningen gate. We travelled North first, then East, then only South.... Mynheer Beresteyn would require a divining rod wherewith to find you now."

It seemed unnecessary cruelty to tell her that, when already despair had seized on her heart, but she would not let this abominable rogue see how deeply she was hurt. She feigned not to have noticed the purport of his words and continued with the same insistent eagerness:

"Torn with anxiety, sir, he will be ready with a rich reward for one who would bring his only daughter safely home to him. I know not what the Lord of Stoutenburg hath promised you for doing his abominable work for him, but this I do assure you that my father will double and treble whatever sum you choose to name. Take me back to him, sir, now, this night, and to-morrow morning you could count yourself one of the rich men of Haarlem."

But Diogenes with half-closed eyes and gentle smile slowly shook his head.

"Were I to present myself before Mynheer Beresteyn to-night, he would summon the town guard and I should count myself as good as hanged to-morrow."

"Do you measure other men's treachery then by your own?"

"I measure other men's wrath by mine, mejuffrouw — and if a rogue had stolen my daughter, I should not rest until I had seen him hanged."

"I pledge you my word —— " she began hotly.

"And I mine, mejuffrouw," he broke in a little more firmly than he had spoken hitherto, "that I will place you safely and I pray God in good health, into the care of a certain gentleman in Rotterdam. To this is my word of honour pledged and even such a mean vagabond as I is bound by a given word."

To this she made no reply. Perhaps she felt that in his last words there lurked a determination which it were useless to combat. Her pride too was up in arms. How could she plead further to this rascal who met the most earnest appeal with a pert jest? who mocked at her distress, and was impervious alike to prayers and to insults?

"I see," she said coldly, "that I do but waste my time in calling on your honour to forego this infamous trickery. Where there is no chivalry, there can be neither honour nor pity. I am in your hands, helpless because I am a woman. If it is the will of God that I should so remain, I cannot combat brute force with my feeble strength. No doubt He knows best! and also I believe doth oft give the devil power to triumph in the sight of men. After this night, sir, I will no longer defame my lips by speaking to you. If you have a spark of compassion left in your heart for one who hath never wronged you, I but ask you to relieve me of your presence as much as you can during the weary hours of this miserable journey."

"Have I your leave to go at once?" he said with unalterable cheerfulness and made haste to reach the door.

"Only one moment more must I detain you," she rejoined haughtily. "I wish you to understand that from this hour forth until such time as it pleaseth God to free me from this humiliating position, I will follow your commands to the best of my ability; not because I recognize your right to dictate them but because I am helpless to oppose you. If I and my waiting woman obey your orders meekly, if we rise when so ordered, are ready to start on the way whenever so compelled, get in or out of the vehicle at the first word from you, can we at least rest assured that we shall be spared further outrage?"

"Do you mean, mejuffrouw, that I must no longer attempt to lift you out of a coach or to carry you up to your chamber, even if as to-night you are faint and but half-conscious?" he asked with whimsical earnestness.

"I desire, sir, that you and those who help you in this shameful work, do in future spare me and my woman the insult of laying hands upon our persons."

He gave a long, low whistle.

"Dondersteen," he exclaimed flippantly, "I had no thought that so much hatred and malice could lurk in the frail body of a woman ...'tis true," he added with a shrug of the shoulders, "that a rogue such as I must of necessity know very little of the workings of a noble lady's mind."

"Had you known aught of mine, sir," she retorted coldly, "you would have understood that it is neither hatred nor malice which I feel for you and for those who are paying you to do this infamy ...what I feel is only contempt."

"Is that all?" he queried blandly. "Ah, well, mejuffrouw, then am I all the more indebted to you for the great honour which you have done me this hour past."

"Honour? I do not understand. It was not in my mind to do you honour."

"I am sure not. You did it quite unconsciously and the honour was enhanced thereby. You honoured me, mejuffrouw," he said while a tone of earnestness crept into his merry voice, "by trusting me — the common thief, the cut-throat, the hired brigand, alone in your presence for a whole hour, while the entire household here was abed and your duenna snoring contentedly in a room with locked door close by. During that hour your tongue did not spare my temper for one moment. For this recognition of manly forbearance and chivalry — even though you choose to deny their existence — do I humbly thank you. Despite — or perhaps because of your harsh estimate of me — you made me feel to-night almost a gentleman."

With his habitual elegance of gesture he swept her a deep bow, then without another word or look, and with firm, ringing steps he walked quickly out of the room.

Once the door safely closed behind him, he heaved a deep sigh as if of intense relief and he passed his hand quickly across his brow.

"By St. Bavon," he murmured, "my friend Diogenes, thou hast had to face unpleasantness before now — those arquebusiers at Magdeburg were difficult to withstand, those murderous blackguards in the forests of Prague nearly had thy skin, but verdommt be thou, if thou hast had to hold thy temper in bounds like this before. Dondersteen! how I could have crushed that sharp-tongued young vixen till she cried for mercy ...or silenced those venomous lips with a kiss!...I was sore tempted indeed to give her real cause for calling me a knave...."

In the tap-room downstairs he found Pythagoras and Socrates curled up on the floor in front of the hearth. They were fast asleep, and Diogenes did not attempt to wake them. He had given them their orders for the next day earlier in the evening and with the promise of 500 golden guilders to be won by implicit obedience the two worthies were not like to disobey.

He himself had his promise to his friend Hals to redeem ...the flight along the frozen waterways back to Haarlem, a few hours spent in the studio in the Peuselaarsteeg, then the return flight to rejoin his compeers and the jongejuffrouw at the little hamlet of Houdekerk off the main road; thither he had ordered them to proceed in the early morning there to lie perdu until his return. Houdekerk lay to the east of Leyden and so well off the beaten track that the little party would be safely hidden there during the day; — he intended to be with them again well before midnight of the next day. For the nonce he collected a few necessary provisions which he had ordered to be ready for him — a half bottle of wine, some meat and bread, then he made his way out of the little hostelry and across the courtyard to the stables where the horses had been put up. The night was singularly clear: the waning moon after she had emerged from a bank of low-lying clouds, lit up the surrounding landscape with a radiance that was intensely blue.

Groping his way about in the stables Diogenes found his saddle which he himself had lifted off his horse, and from out the holster he drew a pair of skates. With these hanging by their straps upon his arm, he left the building behind him and turned to walk in the direction of the river.

The little city lay quite peaceful and still under the weird brilliancy of the moon which threw many-hued reflections on the snow-covered surfaces of roofs and tall gables. It was piercingly cold, the silver ribbon of the Rhyn wound its graceful course westward to the North Sea and from beyond its opposite bank a biting wind swept across the dykes and over the flat country around, chasing myriads of crisp snowflakes from their rest and driving them in wanton frolic round and round into little whirlpools of mist that glistened like the facets of diamonds.

Diogenes had walked briskly along; the skates upon his arm clicked at every one of his movements with a pleasing metallic sound. He chose a convenient spot on the river bank whereon to squat on the ground, and fastened on his skates.

After which he rose and for a moment stood looking straight out northwards before him. But a few leagues — half a dozen at most — lay between him and Haarlem. The Rhyn as well as the innumerable small polders and lakes had left — after the autumn floods — their usual trail of narrow waterways behind them which, frozen over now, joining, intersecting and rejoining again formed a perfect, uninterrupted road from hence to the northern cities. It had been along these frozen ways that the daring and patriotic citizens of Leyden had half a century ago kept up communication with the outer world during the memorable siege which had lasted throughout the winter, and it was by their help that they were able to defy the mighty investing Spanish army by getting provisions into the beleaguered city.

A young adventurer stood here now calmly measuring in his mind the distance which he would have to traverse in the teeth of a piercing gale and at dead of night in order to satisfy the ambition of a friend. It was not the first time in his hazardous career that he had undertaken such a journey. He was accustomed to take all risks in life with indifference and good humour, the only thing that mattered was the ultimate end: an exciting experience to go through, a goodly competence to earn, a promise to fulfil.

Up above, the waning moon seemed to smile upon his enterprise; she lay radiant and serene on her star-studded canopy of mysterious ethereal indigo. Diogenes looked back on the little hostelry, which lay some little distance up the street at right angles to the river bank. Was it his fancy or one of those many mysterious reflections thrown by the moon? but it certainly seemed to him as if a light still burned in one of the upper windows.

The unpleasant interview with the jongejuffrouw had evidently not weighed his spirits down, for to that distant light he now sent a loud and merry farewell.

Then deliberately facing the bitter blast he struck out boldly along the ice and started on his way.

CHAPTER XIX
IN THE KINGDOM OF THE NIGHT

Heigh-ho! for that run along the ice — a matter of half a dozen leagues or so — at dead of night with a keen north-easterly wind whipping up the blood, and motion — smooth gliding motion — to cause it to glow in every vein.

Heigh-ho! for the joy of living, for the joy in the white, ice-covered world, the joy in the night, and in the moon, and in those distant lights of Leyden which gradually recede and diminish — tiny atoms now in the infinite and mysterious distance!

What ho! a dark and heavy bank of clouds! whence come ye, ye disturbers of the moon's serenity? Nay! but we are in a hurry, the wind drives us at breathless speed, we cannot stay to explain whence we have come.

Moon, kind moon, come out again! ah, there she is, pallid through the frosty mist, blinking at this white world scarce less brilliant than she.

On, on! silently and swiftly, in the stillness of the night, the cruel skates make deep gashes on the smooth skin of the ice, long even strokes now, for the Meer is smooth and straight, and the moon — kind moon! — marks an even silvery track, there where the capricious wind has swept it free of snow.

Hat in hand, for the wind is cool and good, and tames the hot young blood which a woman's biting tongue has whipped into passion.

"The young vixen," shouts a laughing voice through the night, "was she aware of her danger? how I could have tamed her, and cowed her and terrified her! Did she play a cat and mouse game with me I wonder....Dondersteen! if I thought that...."

But why think of a vixen now, of blue eyes and biting tongues, when the night with unerring hand clothes the landscape with glory. One word to the north-east wind and he sweeps the track quite clear and causes myriads of diamonds to fly aimlessly about, ere they settle like tiny butterflies on tortuous twigs, and rough blades of coarse grass. One call to the moon and she partially hides her face, painting the haze around her to a blood-red hue; now a touch of blue upon the ice, further a streak of emerald, and then the tender mauves of the regal mantle of frost.

Then the thousand sounds that rise all around: the thousand sounds which all united make one vast, comprehensive silence: the soughing of the wind in the bare poplar trees, the rattle of the tiny dead twigs and moaning of the branches; from far away the dull and ceaseless rumble which speaks of a restless sea, and now and again the loud and melancholy boom of the ice, yielding to the restless movements of the water beneath.

The sounds which make up silence — silence and loneliness, nature's perfect repose under its downy blanket of snow, the vast embrace of the night stretching out into infinity in monotonous flatnesses far away, to the mysterious mists which lie beyond the horizon.

Oh! for the joy of it all! the beauty of the night, the wind and the frost! and the many landmarks which loom out of the darkness one by one, to guide that flying figure on its way; the square tower of old Katwyk-binnen church, the group of pollard willows at the corner of Veenenburg Polder, the derelict boats on the bank of the Haarlemer Meer, and always from the left that pungent smell of the sea, the brine and the peculiar odour which emanates from the dykes close by, from the wet clay and rotting branches of willows that protect man against the encroachment of the ocean.

On, on, thou sole inhabitant of this kingdom of the night! fly on thy wings of metal — hour after hour — midnight — one — two — three — where are the hours now? There are no hours in the kingdom of the night! On, on, for the moon's course is swift and this will be a neck to neck race. Ah! the wicked one! down she goes, lower and lower in her career, and there is a thick veil of mist on the horizon in the west! Moon! art not afraid? the mists will smother thee! Tarry yet awhile! tarry ere thou layest down on the cold, soft bed! thy light! give it yet awhile! — two hours! one hour until thou hast outlined with silver the openwork tower of Haarlem's Groote Kirk.

On, on, for a brief hour longer how can one pause even to eat or drink? there is no hunger in the kingdom of night, no thirst, no fatigue! and this is a neck to neck race with the moon.

Ah Dondersteen! but thou art beaten, fair moon! Let the mists embrace thee now! sink! fall! die as thou list, there is the tower of St. Bavon! and we defy the darkness now!

Here it comes creeping like a furtive and stealthy creature wiping out with thick black cloth here a star and there the tip of a tall poplar tree, there a shrub, there a clump of grass! Take care, traveller, take care! that was not just the shadow from the bank, it was a bunch of reeds that entangle the feet and bring the skater down on to his face and will drag him, if he be not swift and alert, right under, into the water under the ice.

Take care! there is danger everywhere now in this inky blackness! danger on the ice, and upon the bank, danger in the shadows that are less dark than the night!

Darker and darker still, until it seemed as if the night's brush could not hold a more dense hue. The night — angered that she hath been so long defied — has overtaken the flying skater at last. She grips him, she holds him, he dare not advance, he will not retreat. Haarlem is there not one whole league away and he cannot move from where he is, in the midst of the Meer, on her icy bosom, with shadows as tangible as human bodies hemming him in on every side.

Haarlem is there! the last kiss of the moon before she fell into that bed of mist, was for St. Bavon's tower, which then seemed so near. Since then the night had wiped out the tower, and the pointed gables which cluster around, and the solitary skater is a prisoner in the fastnesses of the night.

CHAPTER XX
BACK AGAIN IN HAARLEM

They were terribly weary hours, these last two which the soldier of fortune, the hardened campaigner had to kill before the first streak of pallid, silvery dawn would break over the horizon beyond the Zuyder Zee.

Until then it meant the keeping on the move, ceaselessly, aimlessly, in order to prevent the frost from biting the face and limbs, it meant wearily waiting in incessant, nerve-racking movement for every quarter of an hour tolled by the unseen cathedral clock; it meant counting these and the intervening minutes which crawled along on the leaden stilts of time, until the head began to buzz and the brain to ache with the intensity of monotony and of fatigue. It meant the steeling of iron nerves, the bracing of hardy sinews, the keeping the mind clear and the body warm.

Two hours to kill under the perpetual lash of a tearing north wind, gliding up and down a half league of frozen way so as not to lose the track in the darkness and with a shroud of inky blackness to envelop everything around!

The hardened campaigner stood the test as only a man of abnormal physique and body trained to privations could have stood it. As soon as the thin grey light began to spread over the sky and picked out a few stunted snow-covered trees, one by one, he once more started on his way.

He had less than a league to cover now, and when at last the cathedral tower boomed out the hour of seven he was squatting on the back of the Oude Gracht in Haarlem, and with numbed fingers and many an oath was struggling with the straps of his skates.

A quarter of an hour later he was installed in his friend's studio in front of a comfortable fire and with a mug of hot ale in front of him.

"I didn't think that you really meant to come," Frans Hals had said when he admitted him into his house in response to his peremptory ring.

"I mean to have some breakfast now at any rate, my friend," was the tired wayfarer's only comment.

The artist was too excited and too eager to get to work to question his sitter further. I doubt if in Diogenes' face or in his whole person there were many visible traces of the fatigues of the night.

"What news in Haarlem?" he asked after the first draught of hot ale had put fresh life into his veins.

"Why? where have you been that you've not heard?" queried Hals indifferently.

"Away on urgent business affairs," replied the other lightly; "and what is the news?"

"That the daughter of Cornelius Beresteyn, the rich grain merchant and deputy burgomaster of this city, was abducted last night by brigands and hath not to my knowledge been found yet."

Diogenes gave a long, low whistle of well-feigned astonishment.

"The fact doth not speak much for the guardians of the city," he remarked dryly.

"The outrage was very cleverly carried out, so I've heard said; and it was not until close upon midnight that the scouts sent out by Mynheer Beresteyn in every direction came back with the report that the brigands left the city by the Groningen gate and were no doubt well on their way north by then."

"And what was done after that?"

"I have not heard yet," replied Hals. "It is still early. When the serving woman comes she will tell us the latest news. I am afraid I can't get to work until the light improves. Are you hungry? Shall I get you something more solid to eat?"

"Well, old friend," rejoined the other gaily, "since you are so hospitable...."

By eight o'clock he was once more ensconced on the sitter's platform, dressed in a gorgeous doublet and sash, hat on head and hand on hip, smiling at his friend's delight and eagerness in his work.

Hals in the meanwhile had heard further news of the great event which apparently was already the talk of Haarlem even at this early hour of the day.

"There seems no doubt," he said, "that the outrage is the work of those vervloekte sea-wolves. They have carried Gilda Beresteyn away in the hope of extorting a huge ransom out of her father."

"I hope," said Diogenes unctuously, "that he can afford to pay it."

"He is passing rich," replied the artist with a sigh. "A great patron of the arts ... it was his son you saw here yesterday, and the portrait which I then showed you was that of the unfortunate young lady who has been so cruelly abducted."

"Indeed," remarked Diogenes ostentatiously smothering a yawn as if the matter was not quite so interesting to him — a stranger to Haarlem — as it was to his friend.

"The whole city is in a tumult," continued Hals, who was busily working on his picture all the while that he talked, "and Mynheer Beresteyn and his son Nicolaes are raising a private company of Waardgelders to pursue the brigands. One guilder a day do they offer to these volunteers and Nicholaes Beresteyn will himself command the expedition."

"Against the sea-wolves?" queried the other blandly.

"In person. Think of it, man! The girl is his own sister."

"It is unthinkable," agreed Diogenes solemnly.

All of which was, of course, vastly interesting to him, since what he heard to-day would be a splendid guidance for him as to his future progress southwards to Rotterdam. Nicolaes Beresteyn leading an expedition of raw recruits in the pursuit of his sister was a subject humorous enough to delight the young adventurer's sense of fun; moreover it was passing lucky that suspicion had at once fallen on the sea-wolves — a notorious band of ocean pirates whose acts of pillage and abduction had long since roused the ire of all northern cities that suffered from their impudent depredations. Diogenes congratulated himself on the happy inspiration which had caused him to go out of Haarlem by its north gate and to have progressed toward Groningen for a quarter of an hour or so, leaving traces behind him which Nicolaes Beresteyn would no doubt know how to interpret in favour of the "sea-wolves" theory. He could also afford to think with equanimity now of Pythagoras and Socrates in charge of the jongejuffrouw lying comfortably perdu at a wayside inn, situated fully thirteen leagues to the south of the nearest inland lair, which was known to be the halting place of the notorious sea-robbers.

Indeed, his act of friendship in devoting his day to the interests of Frans Hals had already obtained its reward, for he had gathered valuable information, and his journey to Rotterdam would in consequence be vastly more easy to plan.

No wonder that Frans Hals as he worked on the picture felt he had never had such a sitter before; the thoughts within redolent of fun, of amusement at the situation, of eagerness for the continuation of the adventure seemed to bubble and to sparkle out of the eyes, the lines of quiet humour, of gentle irony appeared ever mobile, ever quivering around the mouth.

For many hours that day hardly a word passed between the two men while the masterpiece was in progress, which was destined to astonish and delight the whole world for centuries to come. They hardly paused a quarter of an hour during the day to snatch a morsel of food; Hals, imbued with the spirit of genius, begrudged every minute not spent in work and Diogenes, having given his time to his friend, was prepared that the gift should be a full measure.

Only at four o'clock when daylight faded, and the twilight began to merge the gorgeous figure of the sitter into one dull, grey harmony, did the artist at last throw down brushes and palette with a sigh of infinite satisfaction.

"It is good," he said, as with eyes half-closed he took a final survey of his sitter and compared the living model with his own immortal work.

"Have you had enough of me?" asked Diogenes.

"No. Not half enough. I would like to make a fresh start on a new portrait of you at once. I would try one of those effects of light of which Rembrandt thinks that he hath the monopoly, but which I would show him how to treat without so much artificiality."

He continued talking of technicalities, rambling on in his usual fretful, impatient way, while Diogenes stretched out his cramped limbs, and rubbed his tired eyes.

"Can I undress now?"

"Yes. The light has quite gone," said the artist with a sigh.

Diogenes stood for a long time in contemplation of the masterpiece, even as the shadows of evening crept slowly into every corner of the studio and cast their gloom over the gorgeous canvas in its magnificent scheme of colour.

"Am I really as good looking as that?" he asked with one of his most winning laughs.

"Good looking? I don't know," replied Hals, "you are the best sitter I have ever had. To-day has been one of perfect, unalloyed enjoyment to me."

All his vulgar, mean little ways had vanished, his obsequiousness, that shifty look of indecision in the eyes which proclaimed a growing vice. His entire face flowed with the enthusiasm of a creator who has had to strain every nerve to accomplish his work, but having accomplished it, is entirely satisfied with it. He could not tear himself away from the picture, but stood looking at it long after the gloom had obliterated all but its most striking lights.

Then only did he realise that he was both hungry and weary.

"Will you come with me to the 'Lame Cow,'" he said to his friend, "we can eat and drink there and hear all the latest news. I want to see Cornelius Beresteyn if I can; he must be deeply stricken with grief and will have need of the sympathy of all his well-wishers. What say you? Shall we get supper at the 'Lame Cow'?"

To which proposition Diogenes readily agreed. It pleased his spirit of adventure to risk a chance encounter in the popular tavern with Nicolaes Beresteyn or the Lord of Stoutenburg, both of whom must think him at this moment several leagues away in the direction of Rotterdam. Neither of these gentlemen would venture to question him in a public place; moreover it had been agreed from the first that he was to be given an absolutely free hand with regard to his plans for conducting the jongejuffrouw to her ultimate destination.

Altogether the afternoon and evening promised to be more amusing than Diogenes had anticipated.

CHAPTER XXI
A GRIEF-STRICKEN FATHER

Frans Hals had not been guilty of exaggeration when he said that the whole city was in a turmoil about the abduction of Gilda Beresteyn by that impudent gang of ocean-robbers who called themselves the sea-wolves.

On this subject there were no two opinions. The sea-wolves had done this deed as they had done others of a like nature before. The abduction of children of rich parents was one of their most frequent crimes: and many a wealthy burgher had had to pay half his fortune away in ransom for his child. The fact that a covered sledge escorted by three riders who were swathed in heavy mantles had been seen to go out of the city by the northern gate at seven o'clock last evening, was held to be sufficient proof that the unfortunate jongejuffrouw was being conveyed straightway to the coast where the pirates had their own lairs and defied every effort which had hitherto been made for their capture.

On this the 2nd day of January, 1624 — rather less than twenty-four hours after the abduction of Gilda Beresteyn, the tapperij of the "Lame Cow" presented an appearance which was almost as animated as that which had graced it on New Year's night. Everyone who took an interest in the terrible event went to the "Lame Cow" in the hope of finding another better informed than himself.

Men and women sat round the tables or leaned against the bars discussing the situation: every one, of course, had a theory to put forward, or a suggestion to offer.

"'Tis time the old law for the raising of a corps of Waardgelders by the city were put into force once more," said Mynheer van der Meer the burgomaster, whose words carried weight. "What can a city do for the preservation of law and order if it has not the power to levy its own military guard?"

"My opinion is," said Mynheer van Zeller, who was treasurer of the Oudemannenhuis and a personage of vast importance, "that we in this city ought to close out gates against all this foreign rabble who infest us with their noise and their loose ways. Had there not been such a crowd of them here for the New Year you may depend on it that Jongejuffrouw Beresteyn would not have had to suffer this dastardly abomination."

Others on the other hand thought that the foreign mercenaries now within the city could be utilised for the purpose of an expedition against the sea-wolves.

"They are very daring and capable fighters," suggested Mynheer van Beerenbrock — a meek, timid but vastly corpulent gentleman of great consideration on the town council, "and more able to grapple with desperate brigands than were a levy of raw recruits from among our young townsfolk."

"Set a rogue to fight a rogue, say I," assented another pompous burgher.

Cornelius Beresteyn sat at a table with his son and surrounded by his most influential friends. Those who knew him well declared that he had aged ten years in the past few hours. His devotion to his daughter was well known and it was pitiable to see the furrows in his cheeks wet with continuously falling tears. He sat huddled up within himself, his elbows resting on the table, his head often buried in his hands when emotion mastered him, and he felt unable to restrain his tears. He looked like a man absolutely dazed with the immensity of his grief, as if some one had dealt him a violent blow on the head which had half-addled his brain.

Throughout the day his house had been positively invaded by the frequent callers who, under a desire to express their sympathy, merely hid their eagerness to learn fresh details of the outrage. Cornelius Beresteyn, harassed by this well-meaning and very noisy crowd and feeling numb in mind and weary in body, had been too feeble to withstand the urgent entreaties of his friends who had insisted on dragging him to the "Lame Cow," where the whole situation — which had become of almost national importance — could be fully and comprehensively discussed.

"You want to get your daughter back, do you not, old friend?" urged Mynheer van der Meer the burgomaster.

"Of course," assented Beresteyn feebly.

"And you want to get her back as quickly as possible," added the pompous treasurer of the Oudemannenhuis.

"As quickly as possible," reiterated Beresteyn vaguely.

"Very well then," concluded the burgomaster, in tones of triumph which suggested that he had gained a great victory over the obstinate will of his friend, "what you must do, my good Beresteyn, is to attend an informal council which I have convened for this afternoon at the 'Lame Cow' and whereat we will listen to all the propositions put forward by our fellow-townsmen for the speedy capture of those vervloekte brigands and the liberation of your beloved daughter."

In the meanwhile an untoward accident had momentarily arrested the progress of the original band of volunteers who, under the leadership of Nicolaes Beresteyn, had started quite early in the morning on the Groningen route in pursuit of the sea-wolves. Nicolaes, namely, on remounting his horse after a brief halt at Bloemendal, had slipped on the snow covered ground; his horse jumped aside and reared and, in so doing, seriously wrenched Nicolaes' right arm, almost dislocating his shoulder and causing him thereby such excruciating pain that he nearly fainted on the spot.

Further progress on horseback became an impossibility for him, and two of the volunteers had much difficulty in conveying him back to Haarlem, where, however, he displayed the utmost fortitude by refusing to waste his time in being examined and tended by the bone-setter, and declaring that since he could not take an active part in the campaign against the vervloekte malefactors he would give every moment of his time and every faculty he possessed for the organisation of an effective corps of soldiery capable of undertaking a successful punitive expedition.

He joined his father in the tap-room of the "Lame Cow," and though he was obviously in great pain with his arm and shoulder which he had hastily and perfunctorily tied up with his sash, he was untiring in his suggestions, his advice, his offers of money and of well-considered plans.

Unbeknown to anyone save to him, the Lord of Stoutenburg sat in a dark recess of the tapperij deeply interested in all that was going on. He knew, of course, every detail of the plot which Nicolaes Beresteyn had hatched at his instigation and — hidden as he was in his obscure corner — it pleased his masterful mind to think that the tangled skein of this affair which these solemn and pompous burghers were trying to unravel had been originally embroiled by himself.

He listened contemptuously and in silence to the wild and oft senseless talk which went on around him; but when he caught sight of Diogenes swaggering into the room in the wake of the painter Frans Hals he very nearly betrayed himself.

Nicolaes Beresteyn too was dumbfounded. For the moment he literally gasped with astonishment, and was quite thankful that his supposedly dislocated shoulder furnished a good pretext for the string of oaths which he uttered. But Diogenes, sublimely indifferent to the astonishment of his patron, took a seat beside his friend at one of the vacant tables and ordered a substantial supper with a bottle of very choice wine wherewith to wash it down, all of which he evidently meant to pay for with Nicolaes' money. The latter could do nothing but sit by in grim silence while the man whom he had paid to do him service ate and drank heartily, cracked jokes and behaved for all the world as if he were a burgher of leisure plentifully supplied with money.

Time was going on: the subject of the expedition against the sea-wolves had been fully discussed and certain resolutions arrived at, which only lacked the assent of the burgomaster sitting in council and of Cornelius Beresteyn — the party chiefly interested in the affair — in order to take effect on the morrow.

Gradually the tap-room became less and less full: one by one the eager and inquisitive towns-folk departed in order to impart what news they had gleaned to their expectant families at home.

Nicolaes Beresteyn, inwardly fuming and fretting with rage, had been quite unable to stay on quietly while Diogenes sat not twenty paces away from him, wasting his patron's time and money and apparently in the best of humours, for his infectious laugh rang from end to end of the raftered room; he had soon assembled a small crowd of boon-companions round his table, whom he treated to merry jests as well as to Mynheer Beek's most excellent wine; but when he leaned forward bumper in hand and actually had the audacity loudly to pledge the noble Beresteyn family and to wish the heroic Nicolaes speedy mending of his broken bones, the latter rose with a muttered curse and, having taken a curt farewell from his friends, he strode glowering out of the room.

The Lord of Stoutenburg — as unobtrusive and silent as was his wont — rose quietly a few minutes later and followed in the wake of his friend.

Cornelius Beresteyn had now only a few of his most intimate friends beside him, and when Frans Hals had finished his supper he ventured to approach the rich patron of arts and to present his own most respectful expressions of sympathy.

Softened by grief the old man was more than usually gracious to the artist.

"'Tis a bitter blow, my good Hals," he said dully.

"Please God, those devils have only an eye on your money, mynheer," said the artist consolingly. "They will look on the jongejuffrouw as a valuable hostage and treat her with the utmost deference in the hopes of getting a heavy ransom from you."

"May you be speaking truly," sighed Cornelius with a disconsolate shake of the head, "but think what she must be suffering now, while she is uncertain of her own fate, poor child!"

"Alas!"

"This delay is killing me, Hals," continued the old man, who in the midst of his more pompous friends seemed instinctively drawn to the simple nature of this humble painter of pictures. "The burgomaster means well but his methods are slow and ponderous. All my servants and dependents have joined the first expedition toward Groningen, but God knows how they will get on, now that Nicolaes no longer leads them. They have had no training in such matters, and will hardly know how to proceed."

"You really want some one who is daring and capable, mynheer, some one who will be as wary as those vervloekte sea-wolves and beat them at their own game. 'Tis not so much the numbers that you want as the one brain to direct and to act."

"True! true, my good Hals! But our best men are all at the war fighting for our religious and political liberties, while we — the older citizens of our beloved country with our wives and our daughters — are left a prey to the tyranny of malefactors and of pirates. The burgomaster hopes to raise an efficient corps of volunteers by to-morrow ... but I doubt me if he will succeed.... I have sent for help, I have spared no money to obtain assistance ... but I am an old man myself, and my son alas! has been rendered helpless at the outset, through no fault of his own...."

"But surely there are young men left in Haarlem whom wanton mischief such as this would cause to boil with indignation."

"There are few young men left in Haarlem, my friend," rejoined Beresteyn sadly, "the Stadtholder hath claimed the best of them. Those who are left behind are too much engrossed in their own affairs to care greatly about the grief of an old man, or a wrong done to an innocent girl."

"I'll not believe it," said Hals hotly.

"Alas, 'tis only too true! Men nowadays — those at any rate who are left in our cities — no longer possess that spirit of chivalry or of adventure which caused our forebears to give their life's blood for justice and for liberty."

"You wrong them, mynheer," protested the artist.

"I think not. Think on it, Hals. You know Haarlem well; you know most people who live in the city. Can you name me one man who would stand up before me to-day and say boldly: 'Mynheer, you have lost your daughter: evil-doers have taken her from her home. Here am I ready to do you service, and by God do I swear that I will bring your daughter back to you!' So would our fathers have spoken, my good Hals, before commerce and prosperity had dulled the edge of reckless gallantry. By God! they were fine men in those days — we are mere pompous, obese, self-satisfied shopkeepers now."

There was a great deal of bitter truth in what Cornelius Beresteyn had said: Hals — the artist — who had listened to the complacent talk that had filled this room awhile ago — who knew of the commercial transactions that nowadays went by the name of art-patronage — he knew that the old man was not far wrong in his estimate of his fellow-countrymen in these recent prosperous times.

It was the impulsive, artistic nature in him which caused him to see what he merely imagined — chivalry, romance, primeval notions of bravery and of honour.

He looked round the room — now almost deserted — somewhat at a loss for words that would soothe Beresteyn's bitter spirit of resentment, and casually his glance fell on the broad figure of his friend Diogenes, who, leaning back in his chair, his plumed hat tilted rakishly across his brow, had listened to the conversation between the two men with an expression of infinite amusement literally dancing in his eyes. And it was that same artistic, impulsive nature which caused Frans Hals then to exclaim suddenly:

"Well, mynheer! since you call upon me and on my knowledge of this city, I can give you answer forthwith. Yes! I do know a man, now in Haarlem, who hath no thought of commerce or affairs, who possesses that spirit of chivalry which you say is dead among the men of Holland. He would stand up boldly before you, hat in hand and say to you: 'Mynheer, I am ready to do you service, and by God do I swear that I will bring your daughter back to you, safe and in good health!' I know such a man, mynheer!"

"Bah! you talk at random, my good Hals!" said Beresteyn with a shrug of the shoulders.

"May I not present him to you, mynheer?"

"Present him? Whom?...What nonsense is this?" asked the old man, more dazed and bewildered than before by the artist's voluble talk. "Whom do you wish to present to me?"

"The man who I firmly believe would out of pure chivalry and the sheer love of adventure do more toward bringing the jongejuffrouw speedily back to you than all the burgomaster's levies of guards and punitive expeditions."

"You don't mean that, Hals? — 'twere a cruel jest to raise without due cause the hopes of a grief-stricken old man."

"'Tis no jest, mynheer!" said the artist, "there sits the man!"

And with a theatrical gesture — for Mynheer Hals had drunk some very good wine after having worked at high pressure all day, and his excitement had gained the better of him — he pointed to Diogenes, who had heard every word spoken by his friend, and at this dénouement burst into a long, delighted, ringing laugh.

"Ye gods!" he exclaimed, "your Olympian sense of humour is even greater than your might."

At an urgent appeal from Hals he rose and, hat in hand, did indeed approach Mynheer Beresteyn, looking every inch of him a perfect embodiment of that spirit of adventure which was threatening to be wafted away from these too prosperous shores. His tall figure looked of heroic proportions in this low room and by contrast with the small, somewhat obese burghers who still sat close to Cornelius, having listened in silence to the latter's colloquy with the artist. His bright eyes twinkled, his moustache bristled, his lips quivered with the enjoyment of the situation. The grace and elegance of his movements, born of conscious strength, added dignity to his whole personality.

"My friend hath name Diogenes," said Frans Hals, whose romantic disposition revelled in this presentation, "but there's little of the philosopher about him. He is a man of action, an invincible swordsman, a — — "

"Dondersteen, my good Hals!" ejaculated Diogenes gaily, "you'll shame me before these gentlemen."

"There's naught to be ashamed of, sir, in the eulogy of a friend," said Cornelius Beresteyn with quiet dignity, "and 'tis a pleasure to an old man like me to look on one so well favoured as yourself. Ah, sir! 'tis but sorrow that I shall know in future....My daughter ...you have heard...?"

"I know the trouble that weighs on your soul, mynheer," replied Diogenes simply.

"You have heard then what your friend says of you?" continued the old man, whose tear-dimmed eyes gleamed with the new-born flicker of hope. "Our good Hals is enthusiastic, romantic ...mayhap he hath exaggerated ...hath in fact been mistaken...."

It was sadly pathetic to see the unfortunate father so obviously hovering 'twixt hope and fear, his hands trembled, there was an appeal in his broken voice, an appeal that he should not be deceived, that he should not be thrown back from the giddy heights of hope to the former deep abyss of despair.

"My daughter, sir ..." he murmured feebly, "she is all the world to me ... her mother died when she was a baby ... she is all the world to me ... they have taken her from me ... she is so young, sir ... so beautiful ... she is all the world to me ... I would give half my fortune to have her back safely in my arms...."

There was silence in the quaint old-world place after that — silence only broken by the suppressed sobs of the unfortunate man who had lost his only daughter. The others sat round the table, saying no word, for the pathos evoked by Beresteyn's grief was too great for words. Hals' eyes were fixed on his friend, and he tried in vain to read and understand the enigmatical smile which hovered in every line of that mobile face. The stillness only lasted a few seconds: the next moment Diogenes' ringing voice had once more set every lurking echo dancing from rafter to rafter.

"Mynheer!" he said loudly, "you have lost your daughter. Here am I to do you service, and by God I swear that I will bring your daughter safely back to you."

Frans Hals heaved a deep sigh of satisfaction. Cornelius Beresteyn, overcome by emotion, could not at first utter a word. He put out his hand, groping for that of the man who had fanned the flames of hope into living activity.

Diogenes, solemnly trying to look grave and earnest, took the hand thus loyally offered to him. He could have laughed aloud at the absurdity of the present situation. He — pledged by solemn word of honour to convey Jongejuffrouw Beresteyn to Rotterdam and there to place her into the custody of Ben Isaje, merchant of that city, he — carrying inside his doublet an order to Ben Isaje to pay him 3,000 guilders, he — known to the jongejuffrouw as the author of the outrage against her person, he was here solemnly pledging himself to restore her safely into her father's arms. How this was to be fulfilled, how he would contrive to earn that comfortable half of a rich Haarlem merchant's fortune, he had — we may take it — at the present moment, not the remotest idea: for indeed, the conveying of the jongejuffrouw back to Haarlem would be no difficult matter, once his promise to Nicolaes Beresteyn had been redeemed. The question merely was how to do this without being denounced by the lady herself as an impudent and double-dealing knave, which forsooth she already held him to be.

Cornelius and his friends, however, gave him no time now for further reflection. All the thinking out would have to be done presently — no doubt on the way between Haarlem and Houdekerk, and probably in a mist of driving snow — for the nonce he had to stand under the fire of unstinted eulogy hurled at him from every side.

"Well spoken, young man!"

"'Tis gallant bearing forsooth!"

"Chivalry, indeed, is not yet dead in Holland."

"Are you a Dutchman, sir?"

To this direct query he gave reply:

"My father was one of those who came in English Leicester's train, whose home was among the fogs of England and under the shadow of her white, mysterious cliffs. My mother was Dutch and he broke her heart...."

"Not an unusual story, alas, these times!" quoth a sober mynheer with a sigh. "I know of more than one case like your own, sir. Those English adventurers were well favoured and smooth tongued, and when they gaily returned to their sea-girt island they left a long trail behind them of broken hearts — of sorrowing women and forsaken children."

"My mother, sir, was a saint," rejoined Diogenes earnestly, "my father married her in Amsterdam when she was only eighteen. She was his wife, yet he left her homeless and his son fatherless."

"But if he saw you, sir, as you are," said Cornelius Beresteyn kindly, "he would surely make amends."

"But he shall not see me, sir," retorted Diogenes lightly, "for I hate him so, because of the wrong he did to my mother and to me. He shall never even hear of me unless I succeed in carving mine own independent fortune, or contrive to die like a gentleman."

"Both of which, sir, you will surely do," now interposed Beresteyn with solemn conviction. "Your acts and words do proclaim you a gentleman, and therefore you will die one day, just as you have lived. In the meanwhile, I am as good as my word. My daughter's safety, her life and her honour are worth a fortune to me. I am reputed a wealthy man. My business is vast, and I have one million guilders lying at interest in the hands of Mynheer Bergansius the world-famed jeweller of Amsterdam. One-half that money, sir, shall be yours together with my boundless gratitude, if you deliver my daughter out of the hands of the malefactors who have seized her person and bring her back safe and sound to me."

"If life is granted me, sir," rejoined Diogenes imperturbably, without a blush or a tremor, "I will find your daughter and bring her safely to you as speedily as God will allow me."

"But you cannot do this alone, sir ..." urged Cornelius, on whom doubt and fear had not yet lost their hold. "How will you set to work?"

"That, mynheer, is my secret," rejoined Diogenes placidly, "and the discussion of my plans might jeopardise their success."

"True, sir; but remember that the anxiety which I suffer now will be increased day by day, until it brings me on the threshold of the grave."

"I will remember that, mynheer, and will act as promptly as may be; but the malefactors have twenty-four hours start of me. I may have to journey far ere I come upon their track."

"But you will have companions with you, sir? Friends who will help and stand by you. Those sea-wolves are notorious for their daring and their cruelty ... they may be more numerous too than you think...."

"The harder the task, mynheer," said Diogenes with his enigmatical smile, "the greater will be my satisfaction if I succeed in fulfilling it."

"But though you will own to no kindred, surely you have friends?" insisted Beresteyn.

"Two faithful allies, and my sword, the most faithful of them all," replied the other.

"You will let me furnish you with money in advance, I hope."

"Not till I have earned it, mynheer."

"You are proud, sir, as well as chivalrous," retorted Cornelius.

"I pray you praise me not, mynheer. Greed after money is my sole motive in undertaking this affair."

"This I'll not believe," concluded Beresteyn as he now rose to go. "Let me tell you, sir, that by your words, your very presence, you have put new life, new hope into me. Something tells me that I can trust you ... something tells me that you will succeed.... Without kith or kindred, sir, a man may rise to fortune by his valour: 'tis writ in your face that you are such an one. With half a million guilders so earned a man can aspire to the fairest in the land," he added not without significance, "and there is no father who would not be proud to own such a son."

He then shook Diogenes warmly by the hand. He was a different man to the poor grief-stricken rag of humanity who had entered this tavern a few hours ago. His friends also shook the young man by the hand and said a great many more gracious and complimentary words to him which he accepted in grave silence, his merry eyes twinkling with the humour of it all.

The worthy burghers filed out of the tap-room one by one, in the wake of Cornelius. It was bitterly cold and the snow was again falling: they wrapped their fur-lined mantles closely round them ere going out of the warm room, but their hats they kept in their hands until the last, and were loth to turn their backs on Diogenes as they went. They felt as if they were leaving the presence of some great personage.

It was only when the heavy oaken door had fallen to for the last time behind the pompous soberly-clad figures of the mynheers and Diogenes found himself alone in the tapperij with his friend Frans Hals that he at last gave vent to that overpowering sense of merriment which had all along threatened to break its bonds. He sank into the nearest chair:

"Dondersteen! Dondersteen!" he exclaimed between the several outbursts of irrepressible laughter which shook his powerful frame and brought the tears to his eyes, "Gods in Olympia! have you ever seen the like? Verrek jezelf, my good Hals, you should go straight to Paradise when you die for having brought about this heaven-born situation. Dondersteen! Dondersteen! I had promised myself two or three hours' sleep, but we must have a bottle of Beek's famous wine on this first!"

And Frans Hals could not for the life of him understand what there was in this fine situation that should so arouse Diogenes' mirth.

But then Diogenes had always been an irresponsible creature, who was wont to laugh even at the most serious crisis of his life.

CHAPTER XXIII
A SPY FROM THE CAMP

"Come to my lodgings, Nicolaes. I have good news for you, and you do no good by cooling your temper here in the open."

Stoutenburg, coming out of his lodgings half an hour later to look for his friend, had found Beresteyn in the Hout Straat walking up and down like a caged beast in a fury.

"The vervloekte Keerl! the plepshurk! the smeerlap!" he ejaculated between his clenched teeth. "I'll not rest till I have struck him in the face first and killed him after!"

But he allowed Stoutenburg to lead him down the street to the narrow gabled house where he lodged. Neither of them spoke, however; fury apparently beset them both equally, the kind of fury which is dumb, and all the more fierce because it finds no outlet in words.

Stoutenburg led the way up the wooden stairs to a small room at the back of the house. There was no light visible anywhere inside the building, and Nicolaes, not knowing his way about, stumbled upwards in the dark keeping close to the heels of his friend. The latter had pushed open the door of his room. Here a tallow candle placed in a pewter sconce upon a table shed a feeble, flickering light around. The room by this scanty glimmer looked to be poorly but cleanly furnished; there was a curtained bed in the panelling of the wall, and a table in the middle of the room with a few chairs placed in a circle round it.

On one of these sat a man who appeared to be in the last stages of weariness. His elbows rested on the table and his head was buried in his folded arms. His clothes looked damp and travel-stained; an empty mug of ale and a couple of empty plates stood in front of him, beside a cap made of fur and a pair of skates.

At the sound made by the opening of the door and the entrance of the two men, he raised his head and seeing the Lord of Stoutenburg he quickly jumped to his feet.

"Sit down, Jan," said Stoutenburg curtly, "you must be dog-tired. Have you had enough to eat and drink?"

"I thank you, my lord, I have eaten my fill," replied Jan, "and I am not so tired now that I have had some rest."

"Sit down," reiterated Stoutenburg peremptorily, "and you too, my good Nicolaes," he added as he offered a chair to his friend. "Let me just tell you the news which Jan has brought, and which should make you forget even your present just wrath, so glorious, so important is it."

He went up to a cabinet which stood in one corner of the room, and from it took a bottle and three pewter mugs. These he placed on the table and filled the mugs with wine. Then he drew another chair close to the table and sat down.

"Jan," he resumed, turning to Beresteyn, "left the Stadtholder's camp at Sprang four days ago. He has travelled the whole way along the frozen rivers and waterways only halting for the nights. The news which he brings carries for the bearer of such splendid tidings its own glorious reward; Jan, I must tell you, is with us heart and soul and hates the Stadtholder as much as I do. Is that not so, Jan?"

"My father was hanged two years ago," replied Jan simply, "because he spoke disparaging words of the Stadtholder. Those words were called treason, and my father was condemned to the gallows merely for speaking them."

Stoutenburg laughed, his usual harsh, mirthless laugh.

"Yes! that is the way justice is now administered in the free and independent United Provinces," he said roughly; "down on your knees, ye lumbering Dutchmen! lick the dust off the boots of His Magnificence Maurice of Nassau Prince of Orange! kiss his hand, do his bidding! give forth fulsome praise of his deeds!... How long, O God? how long?" he concluded with a bitter sigh.

"Only for a few more days, my lord," said Jan firmly. "The Stadtholder left his camp the same day as I did. But he travels slowly, in his sledge, surrounded by a bodyguard of an hundred picked men. He is sick and must travel slowly. Yesterday he had only reached Dordrecht, to-day

— if my information is correct — he should sleep at Ijsselmunde. But to-morrow he will be at Delft where he will spend two days at the Prinsenhof."

"At Delft!" exclaimed Stoutenburg as he brought his clenched fist down upon the table. "Thank God! I have got him at last."

He leaned across nearer still to Nicolaes and in his excitement clutched his friend's wrists with nervy trembling fingers, digging his nails into the other man's flesh till Beresteyn could have screamed with pain.

"From Delft," he murmured hoarsely, "the only way northwards is along the left bank of the Schie, the river itself is choked with ice-floes which renders it impassable. Just before Ryswyk the road crosses to the right bank of the river over a wooden bridge which we all know well. Half a league to the south of the bridge is the molens which has been my headquarters ever since I landed at Scheveningen three weeks ago; there I have my stores and my ammunition. Do you see it all, friend?" he queried whilst a feverish light glowed in his eyes. "Is it not God who hath delivered the tyrant into my hands at last? I start for Ryswyk to-night with you to help me, Nicolaes, with van Does and all my friends who will rally round me, with the thirty or forty men whom they have recruited for placing at my disposal. The molens to the south of the wooden bridge which spans the Schie is our rallying point. In the night before the Stadtholder starts on his way from Delft we make our final preparations. I have enough gunpowder stowed away at the mill to blow up the bridge. We'll dispose it in its place during that night. Then you Nicolaes shall fire the powder at the moment when the Stadtholder's escort is half way across the bridge....In the confusion and panic caused by the explosion and the collapse of the bridge our men can easily overpower the Prince's bodyguard — whilst I, dagger in hand, do fulfil the oath which I swore before the altar of God, to kill the Stadtholder with mine own hand."

Gradually as he spoke his voice became more hoarse and more choked with passion; his excitement gained upon his hearers until both Nicolaes Beresteyn his friend and Jan the paid spy and messenger felt their blood tingling within their veins, their throats parched, their eyes burning as if they had been seared with living fire. The tallow-candle flickered in its socket, a thin draught from the flimsily constructed window blew its flame hither and thither, so that it lit up fitfully the faces of those three men drawn closely together now in a bond of ambition and of hate.

"'Tis splendidly thought out," said Beresteyn at last with a sigh of satisfaction. "I do not see how the plan can fail."

"Fail?" exclaimed Stoutenburg with a triumphant laugh, "of course it cannot fail! There are practically no risks even. The place is lonely, the molens a splendid rallying point. We can all reach it by different routes and assemble there to-morrow eve or early the next day. That would give us another day and night at least to complete our preparations. I have forty barrels of gunpowder stowed away at the mill, I have new pattern muskets, cullivers, swords and pistols ...gifts to me from the Archduchess Isabella ...enough for our coup....Fail? How can we fail when everything has been planned, everything thought out? and when God has so clearly shown that He is on our side?"

Jan said nothing for the moment; he lowered his eyes not caring just then to encounter those of his leader, for the remembrance had suddenly flashed through his mind of that other day — not so far distant yet — when everything too had been planned, everything thought out and failure had brought about untold misery and a rich harvest for the scaffold.

Beresteyn too was silent now. Something of his friend's enthusiasm was also coursing through his veins, but with him it was only the enthusiasm of ambition, of discontent, of a passion for intrigue, for plots and conspiracies, for tearing down one form of government in order to make room for another — but his enthusiasm was not kept at fever-heat by that all-powerful fire of hate which made Stoutenburg forget everything save his desire for revenge.

The latter had pushed his chair impatiently aside and now was pacing up and down the narrow room like some caged feline creature waiting for its meal. Beresteyn's silence seemed to irritate him for he threw from time to time quick, furtive glances on his friend.

"Nicolaes, why don't you speak?" he said with sudden impatience.

"I was thinking of Gilda," replied the other dully.

"Gilda? Why of her?"

"That knave has betrayed me I am sure. He has hidden her away somewhere, not meaning to stick to his bargain with me, and then has come back to Haarlem in order to see if he can extort a large ransom for her from my father."

"Bah! He wouldn't dare...!"

"Then why is he here?" exclaimed Beresteyn hotly. "Gilda should be in his charge! If he is here, where is Gilda?"

"Good God, man!" ejaculated Stoutenburg, pausing in his restless walk and looking somewhat dazed on his friend, as if he were just waking from some feverish sleep. "Good God! you do not think that...."

"That her life is in danger from that knave?" rejoined Beresteyn quietly. "Well, no! I do not think that.... I do not know what to think ... but there is a hint of danger in that rascal's presence here in Haarlem to-day."

He rose and mechanically re-adjusted his cloak and looked round for his hat.

"What are you going to do?" asked Stoutenburg.

"Find the knave," retorted the other, "and wring his neck if he does not give some satisfactory account of Gilda."

"No! no! you must not do that ... not in a public place at any rate ... the rascal would betray you if you quarrelled with him ... or worse still you would betray yourself. Think what it would mean to us now — at this moment — if it were known that you had a hand in the abduction of your sister ... if she were traced and found! think what that would mean — denunciation — failure — the scaffold for us all!"

"Must I leave her then at the mercy of a man who is proved to be both a liar and a cheat?"

"No! you shall not do that. Let me try and get speech with him. He does not know me; and I think that I could find out what double game he is playing and where our own danger lies. Let me try and find him."

"How can you do that?"

"You remember the incident on New Year's Eve, when you and I traced that cursed adventurer to his own doorstep?"

"Yes!"

"Then you remember the Spanish wench and the old cripple to whom our man relinquished his lodgings on that night."

"Certainly I do."

"Well! yesterday when the hour came for the rascal to seize Gilda, I could not rest in this room. I wanted to see, to know what was going on. Gilda means so much to me, that remorse I think played havoc with my prudence then and I went out into the Groote Markt to watch her come out of church. I followed her at a little distance and saw her walking rapidly along the bank of the Oude Gracht. She was accosted by a woman who spoke to her from out the depths of the narrow passage which leads to the disused chapel of St. Pieter. Gilda was quickly captured by the brute whom you had paid to do this monstrous deed, and I stood by like an abject coward, not raising a hand to save her from this cruel outrage."

He paused a moment and passed his hand across his brow as if to chase away the bitter and insistent recollection of that crime of which he had been the chief instigator.

"Why do you tell me all that?" queried Beresteyn sombrely. "What I did, I did for you and for the triumph of your cause."

"I know, I know," replied Stoutenburg with a sigh, "may Heaven reward you for the sacrifice. But I merely acted for mine own selfish ends, for my ambition and my revenge. I love Gilda beyond all else on earth, yet I saw her sacrificed for me and did not raise a finger to save her."

"It is too late for remorse," retorted Beresteyn roughly, "if Gilda had been free to speak of what she heard in the cathedral on New Year's Eve, you and I to-day would have had to flee the country as you fled from it once before, branded as traitors, re-captured mayhap, dragged before the tribunal of a man who has already shown that he knows no mercy. Gilda's freedom would have meant for you, for me, for Heemskerk, van Does and all the others, torture first and a traitor's death at the last."

"You need not remind me of that," rejoined Stoutenburg more calmly. "Gilda has been sacrificed for me and by God I will requite her for all that she has endured! My life, my love are hers and as soon as the law sets me free to marry she will have a proud position higher than that of any other woman in the land."

"For the moment she is at the mercy of that blackguard...."

"And I tell you that I can find out where she is."

"How?"

"The woman who accosted Gilda last night, who acted for the knave as a decoy, was the Spanish wench whom he had befriended the night before."

"You saw her?"

"Quite distinctly. She passed close to me when she ran off after having done her work. No doubt she is that rascal's sweetheart and will know of his movements and of his plans. Money or threats should help me to extract something from her."

"But where can you find her?"

"At the same lodgings where she has been these two nights, I feel sure."

"It is worth trying," mused Beresteyn.

"And in the meanwhile we must not lose sight of our knave. Jan, my good man, that shall be your work. Mynheer Beresteyn will be good enough to go with you as far as the tapperij of the 'Lame Cow,' and there point out to you a man whom it will be your duty to follow step by step this evening until you find out where he intends to pitch his tent for the night. You understand?"

"Yes, my lord," said Jan, smothering as best he could an involuntary sigh of weariness.

"It is all for the ultimate triumph of our revenge, good Jan," quoth Stoutenburg significantly, "the work of watching which you will do this night is at least as important as that which you have so bravely accomplished these past four days. The question is, have you strength left to do it?"

Indeed the question seemed unnecessary now. At the word "revenge" Jan had already straightened out his long, lean figure and though traces of fatigue might still linger in his drawn face, it was obvious that the spirit within was prepared to fight all bodily weaknesses.

"There is enough strength in me, my lord," he said simply, "to do your bidding now as always for the welfare of Holland and the triumph of our faith."

After which Stoutenburg put out the light, and with a final curt word to Jan and an appeal to Beresteyn he led the way out of the room, down the stairs and finally into the street.

CHAPTER XXIV
THE BIRTH OF HATE

Here the three men parted; Beresteyn and Jan to go to the "Lame Cow" where the latter was to begin his work of keeping track of Diogenes, and Stoutenburg to find his way to that squalid lodging house which was situate at the bottom of the Kleine Hout Straat where it abuts on the Oude Gracht.

It had been somewhat impulsively that he had suggested to Beresteyn that he would endeavour to obtain some information from the Spanish wench as to Diogenes' plans and movements and the whereabouts of Gilda, and now that he was alone with more sober thoughts he realised that the suggestion had not been over-backed by reason. Still as Beresteyn had said: there could be no harm in seeking out the girl. Stoutenburg was quite satisfied in his mind that she must be the rascal's sweetheart, else she had not lent him an helping hand in the abduction of Gilda, and since he himself was well supplied with money through the generosity of his rich friends in Haarlem, he had no doubt that if the wench knew anything at all about the rogue, she could easily be threatened first, then bribed and cajoled into telling all that she knew.

Luck in this chose to favour the Lord of Stoutenburg, for the girl was on the doorstep when he finally reached the house where two nights ago a young soldier of fortune had so generously given up his lodgings to a miserable pair of beggars. He had just been vaguely wondering how best he could — without endangering his own safety — obtain information as to which particular warren in the house she and her father inhabited, when he saw her standing under the lintel of the door, her meagre figure faintly lit up by the glimmer of a street-lamp fixed in the wall just above her head.

"I would have speech with thee," he said in his usual peremptory manner as soon as he had approached her, "show me the way to thy room."

Then as, like a frightened rabbit, she made ready to run away to her burrow as quickly as she could, he seized hold of her arm and reiterated roughly:

"I would have speech of thee, dost hear? Show me the way to thy room at once. Thy safety and that of thy father depend on thy obedience. There is close search in the city just now for Spanish spies."

The girl's pale cheeks took on a more ashen hue, her lips parted with a quickly smothered cry of terror. She knew — as did every stranger in these Dutch cities just now — that the words "Spanish spy" had a magical effect on the placid tempers of their inhabitants, and that many a harmless foreign wayfarer had suffered imprisonment, aye and torture too, on the mere suspicion of being a "Spanish spy."

"I have nothing to fear," she murmured under her breath.

"Perhaps not," he rejoined, "but the man who shelters and protects thee is under suspicion of abetting Spanish spies. For his sake 'twere wiser if thou didst obey me."

Stoutenburg had every reason to congratulate himself on his shrewd guess, for at his words all resistance on the girl's part vanished, and though she began to tremble in every limb and even for a moment seemed ready to swoon, she murmured words which if incoherent certainly sounded submissive, and then silently led the way upstairs. He followed her closely, stumbling behind her in the dark, and as he mounted the ricketty steps he was rapidly rehearsing in his mind what he would say to the wench.

That the girl was that abominable villain's sweetheart he was not for a moment in doubt, her submission just now, at the mere hint of the fellow's danger, showed the depth of her love for him. Stoutenburg felt therefore that his success in obtaining what information he wanted would depend only on how much she knew. In any case she must be amenable to a bribe for she seemed wretchedly poor; even in that brief glimpse which he had had of her by the dim light of the street-door lamp, he could not help but see how ragged was her kirtle and how pinched and wan her face.

On the landing she paused and taking a key from between the folds of her shift she opened the door of her lodging and humbly begged the gracious mynheer to enter. A tallow candle placed upon a chair threw its feeble light upon the squalid abode, the white-washed walls, the primitive bedstead in the corner made up of deal planks and covered with a paillasse and a thin blanket. From beneath that same blanket came the gentle and fretful moanings of the old cripple.

But Stoutenburg was far too deeply engrossed in his own affairs to take much note of his surroundings; as soon as the girl had closed the door behind her, he called her roughly to him and she — frightened and obedient — came forward without a word, standing now before him, with hanging arms and bowed head, whilst a slight shiver shook her girlish form from time to time.

He dragged a chair out to the middle of the room and sat himself astride upon it, his arms resting across the back, his booted and spurred feet thrust out in front of him, whilst his hollow, purple-rimmed eyes with their feverish glow of ever-present inward excitement were fixed upon the girl.

"I must tell thee, wench," he began abruptly, "that I mean to be thy friend. No harm shall come to thee if thou wilt answer truthfully certain questions which I would ask of thee."

Then as she appeared too frightened to reply and only cast a furtive, timorous glance on him, he continued after a slight pause:

"The man who protected thee against the rabble the other night, and who gave thee shelter afterwards, the man in whose bed thy crippled father lies at this moment — he is thy sweetheart, is he not?"

"What is that to you?" she retorted sullenly.

"Nothing in itself," he said quietly. "I merely spoke of it to show thee how much I know. Let me tell thee at once that I was in the tavern with him on New Year's Eve when his boon-companions told the tale of how he had protected thee against a crowd; and that I was in this very street not twenty paces away when in response to thy appeal he gave up his room and his bed to thee, and for thy sake paced the streets for several hours in the middle of the night and in weather that must have frozen the marrow in his bones."

"Well? What of that?" said the girl simply. "He is kind and good, and hath that pity for the poor and homeless which would grace many a noble gentleman."

"No doubt," he retorted dryly, "but a man will not do all that for a wench, save in expectation of adequate payment for his trouble and discomfort."

"What is that to you?" she reiterated, with the same sullen earnestness.

"Thou art in love with that fine gallant, eh, my girl?" he continued with a harsh, flippant laugh, "and art not prepared to own to it. Well! I'll not press thee for a confession. I am quite satisfied with thine evasive answers. Let me but tell thee this; that the man whom thou lovest is in deadly danger of his life."

"Great God, have pity on him!" she exclaimed involuntarily.

"In a spirit of wanton mischief — for he is not so faithful to thee as thou wouldst wish — he has abducted a lady from this city, as thou well knowest, since thou didst lend him thy help in the committal of this crime. Thou seest," he added roughly, "that denials on thy part were worse than useless, since I know everything. The lady's father is an important magistrate in this city, he has moved every process of the law so that he may mete out an exemplary punishment to the blackguard who has dared to filch his daughter. Hanging will be the most merciful ending to thy lover's life, but Mynheer Beresteyn talks of the rack, of quartering and of the stake, and he is a man of boundless influence in the administration of the law."

"Lord, have mercy upon us," once again murmured the wretched girl whose cheeks now looked grey and shrunken; her lips were white and quivering and her eyes with dilated pupils were fixed in horror on the harbinger of this terrible news.

"He will have none on thy sweetheart, I'll warrant thee unless...."

He paused significantly, measuring the effect of his words and of that dramatic pause upon the tense sensibilities of the girl.

"Unless ... what?" came almost as a dying murmur from her parched throat.

"Unless thou wilt lend a hand to save him."

"I?" she exclaimed pathetically, "I would give my hand ... my tongue ... my sight ... my life to save him."

"Come!" he said, "that's brave! but it will not be necessary to make quite so violent a sacrifice. I have great power too in this city and great influence over the bereaved father," he continued, lying unblushingly, "I know that if I can restore his daughter to him within the next four and twenty hours, I could prevail upon him to give up pursuit of the villain who abducted her, and to let him go free."

But these words were not yet fully out of his mouth, before she had fallen on her knees before him, clasping her thin hands together and raising up to his hard face large, dark eyes that were brimful of tears.

"Will you do that then, O my gracious lord," she pleaded. "Oh! God will reward you if you will do this."

"How can I, thou crazy wench," he retorted, "how can I restore the damsel to her sorrowing father when I do not know where she is?"

"But — — "

"It is from thee I want to hear where the lady is."

"From me?"

"Why yes! of course! Thou art in the confidence of thy lover, and knowest where he keeps the lady hidden. Tell me where she is, and I will pledge thee my word that thou and he will have nothing more to fear."

"He is not my lover," she murmured dully, "nor am I in his confidence."

She was still on her knees, but had fallen back on her heels, with arms hanging limp and helpless by her side. Hope so suddenly arisen had equally quickly died out of her heart, and her pinched face expressed in every line the despair and misery which had come in its wake.

"Come!" he cried harshly, "play no tricks with me, wench. Thou didst own to being the rascal's sweetheart."

"I owned to my love for him," she said simply, "not to his love for me."

"I told thee that he will hang or burn unless thou art willing to help him."

"And I told thee, gracious sir, that I would give my life for him."

"Which is quite unnecessary. All I want is the knowledge of where he keeps the lady whom he has outraged."

"I cannot help you, mynheer, in that."

"Thou wilt not!" he cried.

"I cannot," she reiterated gently. "I do not know where she is."

"Will fifty guilders help thy memory?" he sneered.

"Fifty guilders would mean ease and comfort to my father and to me for many months to come. I would do much for fifty guilders but I cannot tell that which I do not know."

"An hundred guilders, girl, and the safety of thy lover. Will that not tempt thee?"

"Indeed, indeed, gracious sir," she moaned piteously, "I swear to you that I do not know."

"Then dost perjure thyself and wilt rue it, wench," he exclaimed as he jumped to his feet, and with a loud curse kicked the chair away from him.

The Lord of Stoutenburg was not a man who had been taught to curb his temper; he had always given way to his passions, allowing them as the years went on to master every tender feeling within him; for years now he had sacrificed everything to them, to his ambition, to his revenge, to his loves and hates. Now that this fool of a girl tried to thwart him as he thought, he allowed his fury against her full rein, to the exclusion of reason, of prudence, or ordinary instincts of chivalry. He stooped over her like a great, gaunt bird of prey and his thin claw-like hand fastened itself on her thin shoulder.

"Thou liest, girl," he said hoarsely, "or art playing with me? Money thou shalt have. Name thy price. I'll pay thee all that thou wouldst ask. I'll not believe that thou dost not know!

Think of thy lover under torture, on the rack, burnt at the stake. Hast ever seen a man after he has been broken on the wheel? his limbs torn from their sockets, his chest sunken under the weights — and the stake? hast seen a heretic burnt alive...?"

She gave a loud scream of agony: her hands went up to her ears, her eyes stared out of her head like those of one in a frenzy of terror.

"Pity! pity! my lord, have pity! I swear that I do not know."

"Verdomme!" he cried out in the madness of his rage as with a cruel twist of his hand he threw the wretched girl off her balance and sent her half-fainting, cowering on the floor.

"Verdommt be thou, plepshurk," came in a ringing voice from behind him.

The next moment he felt as if two grapnels made of steel had fastened themselves on his shoulders and as if a weight of irresistible power was pressing him down, down on to his knees. His legs shook under him, his bones seemed literally to be cracking beneath that iron grip, and he had not the power to turn round in order to see who his assailant was. The attack had taken him wholly by surprise and it was only when his knees finally gave way under him, and he too was down on the ground, licking the dust of the floor — as he had forced the wretched girl to do — that he had a moment's respite from that cruel pressure and was able to turn in the direction whence it had come.

Diogenes with those wide shoulders of his squared out to their full breadth, legs apart and arms crossed over his mighty chest was standing over him, his eyes aflame and his moustache bristling till it stood out like the tusks of a boar.

"Dondersteen!" he exclaimed as he watched the other man's long, lean figure thus sprawling on the ground, "this is a pretty pass to which to bring this highly civilized and cultured country. Men are beginning to browbeat and strike the women now! Dondersteen!"

Stoutenburg, whose vocabulary of oaths was at least as comprehensive as that of any foreign adventurer, had — to its accompaniment — struggled at last to his feet.

"You ..." he began as soon as he had partially recovered his breath. But Diogenes putting up his hand hastily interrupted him:

"Do not speak just now, mynheer," he said with his wonted good-humour. "Were you to speak now, I feel that your words would not be characterized by that dignity and courtesy which one would expect from so noble a gentleman."

"Smeerlap! — " began Stoutenburg once more.

"There now," rejoined the other with imperturbable bonhomie, "what did I tell you? Believe me, sir, 'tis much the best to be silent if pleasant words fail to reach one's lips."

"A truce on this nonsense," quoth Stoutenburg hotly, "you took me unawares — like a coward...."

"Well said, mynheer! Like a coward — that is just how I took you — in the act of striking a miserable atom of humanity — who is as defenceless as a sparrow."

"'Tis ludicrous indeed to see a man of your calling posing as the protector of women," retorted Stoutenburg with a sneer. "But enough of this. You find me unarmed at this moment, else you had already paid for this impudent interference."

"I thank you, sir," said Diogenes as he swept the Lord of Stoutenburg a deep, ironical bow, "I thank you for thus momentarily withholding chastisement from my unworthiness. When may I have the honour of calling on your Magnificence in order that you might mete unto me the punishment which I have so amply deserved?"

"That chastisement will lose nothing by waiting, since indeed your insolence passes belief," quoth Stoutenburg hotly. "Now go!" he added, choosing not to notice the wilfully impertinent attitude of the other man, "leave me alone with this wench. My business is with her."

"So is mine, gracious lord," rejoined Diogenes with a bland smile, "else I were not here. This room is mine — perhaps your Magnificence did not know that — you would not like surely to remain my guest a moment longer than you need."

"Of a truth I knew that the baggage was your sweetheart — else I had not come at all."

"Leave off insulting the girl, man," said Diogenes whose moustache bristled again, a sure sign that his temper was on the boil, "she has told you the truth, she knows nothing of the whereabouts of the noble lady who has disappeared from Haarlem. An you desire information on that point you had best get it elsewhere."

But Stoutenburg had in the meanwhile succeeded in recovering — at any rate partially — his presence of mind. All his life he had been accustomed to treat these foreign adventurers with the contempt which they deserved. In the days of John of Barneveld's high position in the State, his sons would never have dreamed of parleying with the knaves, and if — which God forbid! — one of them had dared then to lay hands on any member of the High Advocate's family, hanging would certainly have been the inevitable punishment of such insolence.

Something of that old haughtiness and pride of caste crept into the attitude of the Lord of Stoutenburg now, and prudence also suggested that he should feign to ignore the rough usage which he had received at the hands of this contemptible rascal. Though he was by no means unarmed — for he never went abroad these days without a poniard in his belt — he had, of a truth, no mind to engage in a brawl with this young Hercules whose profession was that of arms and who might consequently get easily the better of him.

He made every effort therefore to remain calm and to look as dignified as his disordered toilet would allow.

"You heard what I said to this girl?" he queried, speaking carelessly.

"You screamed loudly enough," replied Diogenes lightly. "I heard you through the closed door. I confess that I listened for quite a long while: your conversation greatly interested me. I only interfered when I thought it necessary."

"So then I need not repeat what I said," quoth the other lightly. "Hanging for you, my man, unless you tell me where you have hidden Jongejuffrouw Beresteyn."

"I? What have I to do with that noble lady, pray?"

"It is futile to bandy words with me. I know every circumstance of the disappearance of the lady, and could denounce you to the authorities within half an hour, and see you hanged for the outrage before sunrise."

"Then I do wonder," said Diogenes suavely, "that your Magnificence doth not do this, for of a truth you must hate me fairly thoroughly by now."

"Hate you, man? I'd gladly see you hang, or better still broken on the wheel. But I must know from you first where you have hidden the jongejuffrouw."

"If I am to hang anyway, sir, why should I trouble to tell you?"

"The lady is my affianced wife," said Stoutenburg haughtily, "I have every right to demand an explanation from you, why you are here when by the terms of your contract with my friend Nicolaes Beresteyn you should at this moment be on your way to Rotterdam, escorting the jongejuffrouw to the house of Ben Isaje, the banker.... You see that I am well informed," he added impatiently, seeing that Diogenes had become suddenly silent, and that a curious shadow had spread over his persistently smiling face.

"So well informed, sir," rejoined the latter after a slight pause, and speaking more seriously than he had done hitherto, "so well informed that I marvel you do not know that by the terms of that same contract I pledged my word to convey the jongejuffrouw safely to a certain spot and with all possible speed, but that further actions on my part were to remain for mine own guidance. I also pledged my word of honour that I would remain silent about all these matters."

"Bah!" broke in Stoutenburg roughly, "knaves like you have no honour to pledge."

"No doubt, sir, you are the best judge of what a knave would do."

"Insolent ...do you dare...?"

"If you like it better, sir, I'll say that I have parleyed long enough with you to suit my temper. This room is mine," he added, speaking every whit as haughtily as did the other man. "I have business with this wench, and came here, desirous to speak with her alone, so I pray you go! this roof is too lowly to shelter the Lord of Stoutenburg."

At mention of his name Stoutenburg's sunken cheeks took on the colour of lead, and with a swift, instinctive gesture, his hand flew to the hilt of the dagger under his doublet. During this hot and brief quarrel with this man, the thought had never entered his mind that his identity might be known to his antagonist, that he — a fugitive from justice and with a heavy price still upon his head — was even now at the mercy of this contemptible adventurer whom he had learnt to hate as he had never hated a single human soul before now.

Prudence, however, was quick enough to warn him not to betray himself completely. The knave obviously suspected his identity — how he did that, Stoutenburg could not conjecture, but after all he might only have drawn a bow at a venture: it was important above all not to let him see that that bow had struck home. Therefore after the first instant of terror and surprise he resumed as best he could his former haughty attitude, and said with well-feigned carelessness:

"The Lord of Stoutenburg? Do you expect his visit then? What have you to do with him? 'Tis dangerous, you know, to court his friendship just now."

"I do not court his friendship, sir," replied Diogenes with his gently ironical smile; "the Lord of Stoutenburg hath many enemies these days; and, methinks, that if it came to a question of hanging he would stand at least as good a chance of the gallows as I."

"No doubt, an you knew how to lay hands on him; you would be over ready to denounce him to the Stadtholder for the sake of the blood-money which you would receive for this act."

"Well played, my lord," retorted Diogenes with a ringing laugh. "Dondersteen! but you apparently think me a fool as well as a knave. Lay my hands on the Lord of Stoutenburg did you say? By St. Bavon, have I not done so already? aye! and made him lick the dust, too, at my feet? I could sell him to the Stadtholder without further trouble — denounce him even now to the authorities only that I do not happen to be a vendor of swine-flesh — or else...."

A double cry interrupted the flow of Diogenes' wrathful eloquence: a cry of rage from Stoutenburg and one of terror from the girl, who all this while — not understanding the cause and purport of the quarrel between the two men — had been cowering in a remote corner of the room anxious only to avoid observation, fearful lest she should be seen.

But now she suddenly ran forward, swift as a deer, unerring as a cat, and the next moment she had thrown herself on the upraised arm of Stoutenburg in whose hand gleamed the sharp steel of his dagger.

"Murder!" she cried in a frenzy of borrow. "Save thyself! he will murder thee!"

Diogenes, as was his wont, threw back his head and sent his merry laugh echoing through the tumble-down house from floor to floor, until, in response to that light-heartedness which had burst forth in such a ringing laugh, pallid faces were lifted wearily from toil, and around thin, pinched lips the reflex of a smile came creeping over the furrows caused by starvation and misery.

"Let go his arm, wench," he cried gaily; "he'll not hurt me, never fear. Hatred has drawn a film over his eyes and caused his hand to tremble. Put back your poniard, my lord," he added lightly, "the penniless adventurer and paid hireling is unworthy of your steel. Keep it whetted for your own defence and for the protection of the gracious lady who has plighted her troth to you."

"Name her not, man!" cried Stoutenburg, whose arm had dropped by his side, but whose voice was still hoarse with the passion of hate which now consumed him.

"Is her name polluted through passing my lips? Yet is she under my protection, placed there by those who should have guarded her honour with their life."

"Touch my future wife but with the tips of thy fingers, plepshurk, and I'll hang thee on the nearest tree with mine own hands."

"Wait to threaten, my lord, until you have the power: until then go your way. I — the miserable rascal whom you abhor, the knave whom you despise — do give you your life and your freedom which, as you well know, I hold at this moment in the hollow of my hand. But remember that I give it you only because to my mind one innocent woman has already suffered quite enough because of you, without having to mourn the man whom she loves and being widowed ere she is a wife. Because of that you may go out of this room a free man — free to pursue your tortuous aims and your ambitious scheme. They are naught to me and I know nothing about them. But this I do know — that a woman has been placed in my charge by one who should deem her honour more sacred than his own; in this infamy I now see that you too, my lord, have had a hand. The lady, you say, is your future wife, yet you placed her under my care — a knave, a rascal — miserable plepshurk was the last epithet which you applied to me — you! who also should have guarded her good name with your very life. To suit your own ends, you entrusted her to me! Well! to suit mine own I'll not let you approach her, until — having accomplished the errand for which I am being paid — I will myself escort the lady back to her father. To this am I also pledged! and both these pledges do I mean to fulfil and you, my lord, do but waste your time in arguing with me."

The Lord of Stoutenburg had not attempted to interrupt Diogenes in his long peroration. All the thoughts of hatred and revenge that sprang in his mind with every word which this man uttered, he apparently thought wisest to conceal for the moment.

Now that Diogenes, after he had finished speaking, turned unceremoniously on his heel and left Stoutenburg standing in the middle of the room, the latter hesitated for a few minutes longer. Angry and contemptuous words were all ready to his lips, but Diogenes was paying no heed to him; he had drawn the girl with him to the bedside of the cripple, and there began talking quietly in whispers to her. Stoutenburg saw that he gave the wench some money.

Smothering a final, comprehensive oath the noble lord went quietly out of the room.

"How that man doth hate thee," whispered the girl in awe-struck tones, as soon as she saw that the door had closed behind him. "And I hate him, too," she added, as she clenched her thin hands, "he is cruel, coarse and evil."

"Cruel, coarse and evil?" said Diogenes with a shrug of his wide shoulders, "and yet there is a delicate, innocent girl who loves him well enough to forget all his crimes and to plight her troth to him. Women are strange creatures, wench — 'tis a wise philosopher who steers widely clear of their path."

CHAPTER XXV
AN ARRANT KNAVE

In the street below, not far from the house which he had just quitted, Stoutenburg came on Nicolaes and Jan ensconced in the dark against a wall. Beresteyn quickly explained to his friend the reason of his presence here.

"I came with Jan," he said, "because I wished to speak with you without delay."

"Come as far as the cathedral then," said Stoutenburg curtly. "I feel that in this vervloekte street the walls and windows are full of ears and prying eyes. Jan," he added, turning to the other man, "you must remain here and on no account lose sight of that rascal when he leaves this house. Follow him in and out of Haarlem, and if you do not see me again to-night, join me at Ryswyk as soon as you can, and come there prepared with full knowledge of his plans."

Leaving Jan in observation the two men made their way now in the direction of the Groote Markt. It was still very cold, even though there was a slight suspicion in the air of a coming change in the weather: a scent as of the south wind blowing from over the estuaries, while the snow beneath the feet had lost something of its crispness and purity. The thaw had not yet set in, but it was coquetting with the frost, challenging it to a passage of arms, wherein either combatant might completely succumb.

As Stoutenburg had surmised the porch of the cathedral was lonely and deserted, even the beggars had all gone home for the night. A tiny lamp fixed into the panelling of the wall flickered dimly in the draught. Stoutenburg sat down on the wooden bench — dark and polished with age, which ran alongside one of the walls, and with a brusque and febrile gesture drew his friend down beside him.

"Well?" he asked in that nervous, jerky way of his, "What is it?"

"Something that wilt horrify you, just as it did me," replied Beresteyn, who spoke breathlessly as if under stress of grave excitement. "When I parted from you awhile ago, I did what you asked me to do. I posted Jan outside the door of the tapperij after I had pointed out our rogue to him through the glass door. Imagine my astonishment when I saw that at that moment our rascal was in close conversation with my father."

"With your father?"

"With my father," reiterated Beresteyn. "That fool, Hals, was with him, and there were another half dozen busy-bodies sitting round the table. Our man was evidently the centre of interest; I could not then hear what was said, but at one moment I saw that my father shook him cordially by the hand."

"Vervloekte Keerl!" exclaimed Stoutenburg.

"I didn't know at first what to do. I didn't want to go into the tapperij and to show myself just then, but at all costs I wished to know what my father and that arrant rascal had to say to one another. So, bidding Jan on no account to lose sight of the man, I made my way round to the service door behind the bar, and there bribed one of the wenches to let me stand under the lintel and to remain on the watch. It was quite dark where I stood and I had a good view of the tapperij without fear of being seen, and as my father and that cursed adventurer were speaking loudly enough I could hear all that they said."

"Well?" queried Stoutenburg impatiently.

"Well, my friend," quoth Beresteyn with slow emphasis, "that vervloekte scoundrel was making a promise to my father to bring Gilda safely back to Haarlem, and my father was promising him a fortune as his reward."

"I am not surprised," remarked Stoutenburg calmly.

"But...."

"That man, my friend, is the most astute blackguard I have ever come across in the whole course of my life. His English blood I imagine hath made him into a thorough-going rogue. He has played you false — always did mean to play you false if it suited his purpose! By God, Nicolaes! what fools we were to trust one of these foreign adventurers. They'll do anything for money, and this man instead of being — as we thought — an exception to the rule, is a worse scoundrel than any of his compeers. He has simply taken Gilda a little way out of Haarlem, and then came back here to see what bargain he could strike with your father for her return."

"Gilda is some way out of Haarlem," rejoined Beresteyn thoughtfully. "Jan and I heard that knave talking to his friend Hals later on. Hals was asking him to sup and sleep at his house. But he declined the proffered bed, though he accepted the supper: 'I have a journey before me this night,' he said, 'and must leave the city at moonrise.' It seemed to me that he meant to travel far."

"She may be still at Bennebrock, or mayhap at Leyden — he could not have taken her further than that in the time. Anyhow it would be quite easy for him to go back to her during the night, and bring her into Haarlem to-morrow. Friend!" he added earnestly, "the situation is intolerable — unthinkable! After all that we have done, the risks which we have taken, Gilda's return now — a certain denunciation from her — and failure and death once more stare us in the face, and this time more insistently."

"It is unthinkable, as you say," cried Beresteyn vehemently, "but the situation is not so hopeless as you seem to think. I can go at once to my father and denounce the rogue to him. I can tell him that I have reason to believe that the man to whom he has just promised a fortune for the return of Gilda is the very man who hath abducted her."

"Impossible," said Stoutenburg calmly.

"Why?"

"Your father would have the man arrested, he would be searched, and papers and letters writ by you to Ben Isaje of Rotterdam will be found in his possession. These papers would proclaim you the prime mover in the outrage against your sister."

"True! I had not thought of that. But, instead of going to my father, I could denounce the rascal to the city magistrate on suspicion of having abducted my sister. Van der Meer would give me the command of the town guard sent out to arrest him, I could search him myself and take possession of all his papers ere I bring him before the magistrate."

"Bah! the magistracy of Haarlem moves with ponderous slowness. While that oaf, Van der Meer, makes preparations for sending out the town guard, our rogue will slip through our fingers, and mayhap be back in Haarlem with Gilda ere we find him again."

"Let me have Jan and one or two of Heemskerk's mercenaries," urged Beresteyn, "we could seize him and his papers to-night as soon as he leaves the city gates."

"Then, out of revenge," said Stoutenburg, "he will refuse to tell us what he hath done with Gilda."

"Bah!" retorted Beresteyn cynically, "here in Haarlem we can always apply torture."

"Then, if he speaks, Gilda can be back here in time to denounce us all. No, no, my friend," continued Stoutenburg firmly, "let us own at once that by trusting that scoundrel we have run our heads into a noose out of which only our wits can extricate us. We must meet cunning with cunning, treachery if need be with treachery. Gilda — of course — must not remain at the mercy of brigands, but she must not be given her freedom to do us the harm which she hath already threatened. Remember this, Nicolaes," he added, placing his hand upon his friend's shoulder and forcing him to look straight into his own feverishly glowing eyes, "remember that, when all these troubles are over, Gilda will become my wife. The devotion of my entire life shall then compensate her for the slight wrong which fate compels us to do her at this moment. Will you remember that, my friend?"

"I do remember it," replied the other, "but...."

"And will you try and trust me as you would yourself?"

"I do trust you, Willem, as I would trust myself; only tell me what you want to do."

"I want to bring that knave to the gallows without compromising you and the success of our cause," said Stoutenburg firmly.

"But how can you do it?"

"That I do not know yet; I have only vague thoughts in my mind. But hate, remember, is a hard and very efficient task-master, and I hate that man, Nicolaes, almost as much as I hate the Prince of Orange. But 'tis the Prince's death which I want first; because of this my hatred of the rascal must lie dormant just a few days. But it shall lose nothing by waiting, and already I see before me visions of an exemplary revenge which shall satisfy you and gratify my hate."

"Can I help you in any way?"

"Not at present; I have no definite plans just now. All I know is that we must possess ourselves of the rascal's person as well as of Gilda without the risk of compromising ourselves. In this, of course, we have now Jan's valuable help; he is a splendid leader and entirely trustworthy where the cause of his own hatred against the Prince is served."

"And, of course, you have the thirty or forty men — mercenaries and louts — whom Heemskerk, van Does and the others have been recruiting for you."

"Exactly. I can easily detail half a dozen of them to follow Jan. That is our first move, my good Beresteyn," he added emphatically, "to gain possession of Gilda, and to capture the rascal. Only tell me this, what are the papers now in that knave's possession which might compromise you if they were found?"

"I had to write a letter to Ben Isaje, telling him to convince himself that Gilda was safe and in good health, ere he paid the rascal a sum of 3,000 guilders. This letter is writ in mine own hand and signed with my name. Then there is a formal order to Ben Isaje to pay over the money, but that was writ in the usual way by the public scrivener and is signed with the cypher which I always use in all monetary transactions with the Jew. He keeps these formal documents in his archives and all his clients use a cypher in the same way."

"How is that formal order worded?"

"As far as I remember it runs thus: 'In consideration of valuable services rendered to me by the bearer of this note, I desire you to pay him the sum of 3,000 guilders out of my monies which lie with you at interest.' The cypher signature consists of the words 'Schwarzer Kato' surmounted by a triangle."

"And is that cypher known to anyone save to Ben Isaje?"

"Alas! it is known to my father. We both use it for private business transactions."

"But to Gilda?" insisted Stoutenburg. "Would Gilda know it if she saw it?"

"She could not be certain of it … though, of course, she might guess. 'Schwarzer Kato' is the name of a tulip raised by my father, and the triangle is a sign used sometimes by our house in business. But it would be mere conjecture on her part."

"Then everything will still be for the best, never fear, my good Beresteyn," exclaimed Stoutenburg, whose hard, cruel face was glowing with excitement. "Chance indeed has been on our side throughout this business. An you will trust me to finish it now; you'll have no cause for anxiety or regrets. Come! let us find Jan at once! I have a few orders to give him, and then mean to be on my way to Ryswyk to-night."

He rose to his feet and now the glitter in his hollow eyes appeared almost inhuman. He was a man whose whole soul fed upon hatred, upon vengeance planned and accomplished, upon desire for supreme power; and at this moment his scheme for murdering the Stadtholder was backed by one for obtaining possession of the woman he loved, and being revenged on the man who had insulted and jeered at him.

Beresteyn, always ready to accept the leadership of his friend, followed him in silence down the street. After awhile they once more came upon Jan, who apparently had never moved all this while from his post of observation.

"Well?" asked Stoutenburg in a scarce audible whisper, "has he not gone yet?"

"Not yet," replied Jan.

Stoutenburg cast a quick, almost furtive glance in the direction of the house where he had experienced such dire humiliation a brief half hour ago. A curious whistling sound escaped through his clenched teeth, a sound such as many a wild beast makes when expectant of prey.

Then he drew Jan further away from the house, fearful lest his words were wafted toward it on the wind.

"Keep him in sight, Jan," he commanded, "until he goes to the house of Mynheer Hals in the Peuselaarsteg, whither he means to go for supper. There you may safely leave him for an hour, and go directly to the house of my Lord of Heemskerk whom you know. Ask him for half a dozen of his foreign mercenaries; tell him they are for my immediate service. These men will then help you to keep our knave in sight. He will leave Haarlem at moonrise, and you must never lose his track for a moment. Presently he should be escorting a lady in the direction of Rotterdam. If he does this — if he travel south toward that city, do not molest him, only keep him in sight, and the moment he arrives at Rotterdam come and report to me at Ryswyk. But," he added more emphatically, "if at any time it appears to you that he is turning back with the lady toward Haarlem come upon him at once with your men and seize him together with any companions he may have with him. You understand?"

"Perfectly, my lord. While he travels southwards with the lady, we are only to keep him in sight; when he and the lady arrive at Rotterdam we must report to you at Ryswyk, but the moment he turns back toward Haarlem we are to fall on him and seize him and his companions."

"The lady you will treat with the utmost respect," resumed Stoutenburg with an approving nod, "the rascal and his companions you may mishandle as much as you like, without, however, doing them mortal injury. But, having taken the whole party prisoner, you will forthwith convey them to the molens at Ryswyk, where you will find me. Now is all that clear?"

"Nothing could be clearer, my lord," repeated Jan firmly. "We follow him while he travels south, but seize him with his company and the lady if he turn back toward Haarlem. Nothing could be easier."

"You will not let him slip through your fingers, Jan?" said Stoutenburg earnestly.

Jan laughed and shrugged his shoulders.

"You said that this work would help to forward our cause," he said simply. "I ask no questions. I believe you and obey."

"That's brave! And you will take great care of the lady, when she falls into your hands?"

"I understand that she is my lord's future lady," rejoined Jan, with the same calm simplicity which makes the perfect soldier and the perfect servant, and which promised obedience without murmur and without question.

"Yes, Jan. The lady is my future wife," said Stoutenburg. "Treat her as such. As for the man … I want him alive … do not kill him, Jan, even if he provoke you. And he will do that by his insolence, I know."

"My lord shall have his enemy alive," said Jan, "a helpless prisoner … but alive."

"Then good luck to you, Jan," concluded Stoutenburg with a sigh of satisfaction. "I am well pleased with you. In the near future I shall be happy to remember that the high offices of State and those around my person must be filled by those who have well deserved of them."

He put out his thin, nervy hand and Jan fell on one knee in order to kiss it with fervour and respect. The son of John of Barneveld could still count on the loyalty of a few who believed in him, and who looked on his crimes as a necessary means to a glorious end.

A few moments later Beresteyn and Stoutenburg had disappeared in the darkness of the narrow street, and Jan remained alone at his post of observation.

CHAPTER XXVI
BACK TO HOUDEKERK

And now back once more in the kingdom of the night and of the frost, of the darkness and of silence, back along the ice ways on a swift and uninterrupted flight.

The moon is less kind now, fitful and coy; she will not peep out from behind the banks of clouds save at rare intervals; and the clouds are heavy; great billows, clumsy in shape as if weighted with lead; the moon plays a restless game of hide and seek amongst them for the bewilderment of the skater, to whom last night she was so kind.

They come tumbling in more and more thickly from the south — those clouds — driven more furiously by the gusty wind. Brother north-easter has gone to rest, it is the turn of the south wind now — not the soft south wind of summer, but a turbulent and arrogant fellow who bellows as loudly as he can, and who means to have a frolic in this world of ice and snow from which his colder brethren have exiled him until now.

Straight at the head of the skater, it expended the brunt of its fury, sending his hat flying in one direction and in wanton delight leading him into a mad chase after it; then when once more he was on his way — hat in hand this time — it tore with impish glee at his hair, impeded his movements, blew doublet and sash awry.

What a chase! what a fight! what a run! But Dondersteen! we do defy thee, O frolicsome south wind! aye, and the darkness too! Back to Houdekerk, the first stage on the road to fortune.

It is not nearly so cold now that brother north-easter has yielded to his madcap brother from the south! gusty and rough and a hand-to-hand fight for progress all the time, with tears running down the cheeks, and breath coming in gasps from the chest! It is not so cold, and the ice is less crisp, its smooth skin is furrowed and wrinkled, soft and woolly beneath the touch of the steel blades; but the snow still lies thickly upon the low-lying ground, and holds in its luminous embrace all the reflections which the capricious moon will lend it.

For the first half hour, while the moon was still very brilliant and the night air very still, it seemed to Diogenes as if the loneliness around him was only fictitious, as if somewhere — far away mayhap — men moved in the same way as he did, swiftly and silently over the surface of the ice. It seemed to him in fact that he was being followed.

He tried to make sure of this, straining his ears to listen, and now and then he caught very distinctly the sound of the metallic click of several pairs of skates. His senses, trained to over-acuteness through years of hard fighting and of campaigning, could not easily be deceived; and presently there was no doubt in his mind that Nicolaes Beresteyn or the Lord of Stoutenburg had set spies upon his track.

This knowledge caused him only to set his teeth, and to strike out more vigorously and more rapidly than before; those who followed him were fairly numerous — over half a dozen he reckoned — the only chance of evading them was, therefore, in flight. He took to noting the rolling banks of cloud with a more satisfied eye, and when, after the first hour or so, the light of the waning moon became more dim and even at times disappeared completely, he took the first opportunity that presented itself of making a détour over a backwater of the Meer, which he knew must bewilder his pursuers.

Whether the pursuit was continued after that, he could not say. His eyes trying to pierce the gloom could tell him nothing; but there were many intricate little by-ways just south of the Meer over backwaters and natural canals, which he knew well, and over these he started on an eccentric and puzzling career which was bound to baffle the spies on his track.

Whenever he spoke subsequently of the many adventures which befell him during the first days of this memorable New Year, he never was very explicit on the subject of this night's run back to Houdekerk.

As soon as he had rid himself — as he thought — of his pursuers, he allowed his mind to become more and more absorbed in the great problem which confronted him since he had pledged his word to Mynheer Beresteyn to bring the jongejuffrouw safely back to him.

He now moved more mechanically over the iceways, taking no account of time or space or distance, only noting with the mere eye of instinct the various landmarks which loomed up from time to time out of the fast gathering darkness.

This coming darkness he welcomed, for he knew his way well, and it would prove his staunch ally against pursuit. For the rest he was conscious neither of cold, of hunger nor of fatigue. Pleasant thoughts helped to cheer his spirits and to give strength to his limbs. His brief visit to Haarlem had indeed been fruitful of experiences. A problem confronted him which he had made up his mind to solve during his progress across the ice in the night. How to keep his word to Nicolaes Beresteyn, and yet bring the jongejuffrouw safely back to her father.

She would not, of course, willingly follow him, and his would once again be the uncongenial task of carrying her off by force if he was to succeed in his new venture.

A fortune if he brought her back! That sounded simple enough, and the thought of it caused the philosopher's blood to tingle with delight.

A fortune if he brought her back! It would have to be done after he had handed her over into the care of Mynheer Ben Isaje at Rotterdam. He was pledged to do that, but once this was accomplished — his word to Nicolaes Beresteyn would be redeemed.

A fortune if he brought her back! And when he had brought her back she would tell of his share in her abduction, and instead of the fortune mayhap the gallows would be meted out to him.

'Twas a puzzle, a hard nut for a philosopher to crack. It would be the work of an adventurer, of a man accustomed to take every risk on the mere chance of success.

But Gilda's image never left him for one moment while his thoughts were busy with that difficult problem. For the first time now he realized the utter pathos of her helplessness. The proud little vixen, as he had dubbed her a while ago, was after all but a poor defenceless girl tossed hither and thither just to suit the ambitions of men. Did she really love that unscrupulous and cruel Stoutenburg, he wondered. Surely she must love him, for she did not look the kind of woman who would plight her troth against her will. She loved him and would marry him, her small white hand, which had the subtle fragrance of tulips, would be placed in one which was deeply stained with blood.

Poor young vixen, with the sharp tongue that knew how to hurt and the blue eyes that could probe a wound like steel! It was strange to think that their soft glances were reserved for a man whose heart was more filled with hate for men than with love for one woman.

"If I loved you, little vixen," he once murmured apostrophizing the elusive vision which lightened the darkness around him, "if I loved you, I would break my word to that dastard who is your brother … I would not take you to Rotterdam to further his ambition, but I would carry you off to please myself. I would take you to some distant land, mayhap to my unknown father's home in England, where the sounds of strife and hatred amongst men would only come as a faint and intangible echo. I would take you to where roses bloom in profusion, and where in the spring the petals of apple-blossoms would cover you like a mantle of fragrant snow. There I would teach that sharp tongue of yours to murmur words of tenderness and those perfect blue eyes to close in the ecstasy of a kiss. But," he added with his habitual light-hearted laugh, "I do not love you, little vixen, for heigh-ho! if I did 'twere hard for my peace of mind."

When Diogenes neared the town of Leyden he heard its church clocks ring out the hour of three. Close by the city walls he took off his skates, preferring to walk the short league which lay between him and Houdekerk.

He was more tired than he cared to own even to himself, and the last tramp along the road was inexpressibly wearisome. But he had seen or heard nothing more of his pursuers; he was quite convinced that they had lost track of him some hours ago. The south wind blew in heavy gusts from over the marshlands far away, and the half-melted snow clung sticky and dank against the soles and heels of his boots. A smell of dampness in the air proclaimed the coming triumph of the thaw. The roads, thought Diogenes, would be heavy on the morrow, impassable mayhap to a sledge, and the jongejuffrouw would have to travel in great discomfort in a jolting vehicle.

At last in the near distance a number of tiny lights proclaimed the presence of a group of windmills. It was in one of these that Pythagoras and Socrates had been ordered to ask for shelter — in the fifth one down the road, which stood somewhat isolated from the others; even now its long, weird arms showed like heavy lines of ink upon the black background of the sky.

Diogenes almost fell up against the door; he could hardly stand. But the miller was on the look-out for him, having slept only with half an eye, waiting for the stranger whose emissaries had already paid him well. He carried a lanthorn and a bunch of keys; his thin, sharp head was surmounted with a cotton nightcap and his feet were encased in thick woollen hose.

It took him some time to undo the many heavy bolts which protected the molens against the unwelcome visits of night marauders, and before he pushed back the final one, he peered through a tiny judas in the door and in a querulous voice asked the belated traveller's name.

"Never mind my name," quoth Diogenes impatiently, "and open thy door, miller, ere I break it in. I am as tired as a nag, as thirsty as a dog and as hungry as a cat. The jongejuffrouw is I trust safe: I am her major domo and faithful servant, so open quickly, or thy shoulder will have to smart for the delay."

I have Diogenes' own assurance that the miller was thereupon both obedient and prompt. He — like all his compeers in the neighborhood — found but scanty living in the grinding of corn for the neighbouring peasantry, there was too much competition nowadays and work had not multiplied in proportion. Optimists said that in a few years time the paralysing effects of the constant struggle against Spain would begin to wear off, that the tilling of the soil would once more become a profitable occupation and that the molens which now stood idle through many days in the year would once more become a vast storehouse of revenue for those who had continued to work them.

But in the meanwhile the millers and their families were oft on the verge of starvation, and some of them eked out a precarious livelihood by taking in wayfarers who were on their way to and from the cities and had sundry reasons — into which it was best not to inquire — for preferring to sleep and eat at one of these out-of-the-way places rather than in one of the city hostelries.

Diogenes had made previous acquaintance with his present landlord; he knew him to be a man of discretion and of boundless cupidity, two very useful qualities when there is a secret to be kept and plenty of money wherewith to guard it.

Therefore did Diogenes order his companions to convey the jongejuffrouw to the molens of Mynheer Patz, and there to keep guard over her until his own return.

Patz looked well after his belated guest's material comfort. There was some bread and cheese and a large mug of ale waiting for him in the wheel-house and a clean straw paillasse in a corner. The place smelt sweetly of freshly ground corn, of flour and of dry barley and maize, and a thin white coating of flour — soft to the touch as velvet — lay over everything.

Diogenes ate and drank and asked news of the jongejuffrouw. She was well but seemed over sad, the miller explained; but his wife had prepared a comfortable bed for her in the room next to the tiny kitchen. It was quite warm there and Mevrouw Patz had spread her one pair of linen sheets over the bed. The jongejuffrouw's serving woman was asleep on the kitchen floor; she declared herself greatly ill-used, and had gone to sleep vowing that she was so uncomfortable she would never be able to close an eye.

As for the two varlets who had accompanied the noble lady, they were stretched out on a freshly made bed of straw in the weighing-room.

Patz and his wife seemed to have felt great sympathy for the jongejuffrouw, and Diogenes had reason to congratulate himself that she was moneyless, else she would have found it easy enough to bribe the over-willing pair into helping her to regain her home.

He dreamt of her all night; her voice rang in his ear right through the soughing of the wind which beat against the ill-fitting windows of the wheel-house. Alternately in his dream she reviled him, pleaded with him, heaped insults upon him, but he was securely bound and gagged and could not reply to her insults or repulse her pleadings. He made frantic efforts to tear the gag from his mouth, for he wished to tell her that he had not lost his heart to her and cared nothing for the misery which she felt.

He only caught sight of the jongejuffrouw later on in the morning when she came out of the molens and stepped into the sledge which stood waiting for her at the door.

The thaw had not been sufficiently heavy, nor had it lasted a sufficient number of hours to make a deep impression on the thick covering of snow which still lay over the roads. The best and quickest mode of travelling — at any rate for the next few hours — would still be by sledge, the intervening half-dozen leagues that lay between Houdekerk and Rotterdam could be easily covered in the day provided an early start was made and no long halts allowed for meals.

Diogenes had made arrangements for the start to be made by seven o'clock. A dull light of pale rosy grey hung over the snow-covered landscape, and far away on the horizon line that same rose-grey light was just assuming a more brilliant hue. He sent Mevrouw Patz up to the jongejuffrouw to acquaint her with the plans for the day, and to beg her to give these her approval.

Mevrouw Patz returned with the message that the jongejuffrouw was ready to start at any hour which Mynheer would command and was otherwise prepared to obey him in all things.

So Diogenes, standing well out of sight, watched Gilda as she came out of the door of the molens and remained for one moment quite still, waiting for the sledge to draw up. She looked fragile this morning, he thought, and her face looked tiny and very pale within the soft frame of the fur hood which covered her head. For a second or two it seemed to him as if she was looking round somewhat anxiously, with a frown upon her smooth forehead — puzzled and almost frightened — as if she expected and at the same time feared to see some one or something.

The next second the cloud appeared to lift from her face and Diogenes even thought — but in this he may have been mistaken — that a sigh of relief escaped her lips.

After that she stepped into the sledge, closely followed by Maria.

Pythagoras and Socrates had been well drilled in their duties toward the jongejuffrouw and Diogenes noted with satisfaction that his brother philosophers did their best to make the lady as comfortable as possible with a pillow or two bought at Leyden the day previously and the warm rugs from Haarlem which they wrapped carefully round her feet. Maria, dignified and unbending, did her best to prevent those rascals from doing their duty in this manner, but soon her own wants got the better of her pride, and shivering with cold she was glad enough to allow Pythagoras to roll a thick horse-cloth about her knees.

A few moments later a start was made to the accompaniment of lusty cheering from the miller and his wife, both of whom were pleasant — even obsequious to the last.

The stolid peasant who held the reins urged his horses on to a brisk trot as soon as they had reached the flat open road. The three philosophers rode at some little distance behind the sledge, ready only to push forward if some marauder or footpad showed signs of molesting the sledge.

Diogenes caught only a few brief glimpses of the jongejuffrouw during the day; once at Zegwaard where there was a halt for dinner, then at Zevenhuisen and Hillegersberg where horses and men were ready for a rest. But she never seemed to see him, passing quickly in and out of the small huts or cottages to which Pythagoras or Socrates escorted her from a respectful distance. She never spoke to either of these worthies on those occasions, nor did she question any orders for halting or re-starting.

To those who attended on her, however, at the halting places, to the cottagers or millers who brought her milk and bread to eat she was graciousness itself, and whenever it was time to go, Diogenes before leaving had invariably to listen to the loud praises of the beautiful jongejuffrouw with the sweet, sad face.

As to his own existence, she seemed hardly aware of it; at Zevenhuisen, when she went back to the sledge, Diogenes was not very far from where she passed. Moreover he was quite sure that she had seen him, for her head was turned straight in the direction where he stood, hat in hand, waiting to see her comfortably settled in the sledge, before remounting. It was in the early part of the afternoon and once more bitterly cold — no doubt she felt the return of the frost, for she seemed to give a little shiver and pulled the hood more closely over her face.

The roads had been very heavy earlier in the day with their carpet of partially melted snow, but now this surface had frozen once more and the track was slippery like glass under the sledge, but terribly trying for the horses.

Progress was necessarily slow and wearisome both to man and beast, and the shades of evening were beginning to gather in very fast when at last the wooden spire of Rotterdam's Groote Kerk emerged out of the frozen mist.

Diogenes — as he had done before at Leyden and at Zegwaard — pushed on ahead now; he wanted to reach the house of Ben Isaje in advance of the jongejuffrouw and prepare the Hebraic gentleman against her coming. The little town with its intricate network of narrow streets intersected by canals did not seem imposing to the eye. Diogenes marvelled with what thoughts the jongejuffrouw would survey it — wondering no doubt if it would prove the end of her journey or merely a halt on the way to some other place more distant still from her home.

Ben Isaje appeared to be a person of some consequence in Rotterdam, for the moment he questioned a passer-by as to where the Jewish Mynheer resided, there were plenty of willing tongues ready to give him information.

Having followed accurately the instructions which were given to him, Diogenes found himself presently at the top of a street which was so narrow that he reckoned if he stretched out his legs, his feet would be knocking against opposite walls. Anyhow, it looked almost impassable for a rider. He peered down it somewhat dubiously. It was very badly lighted; two feeble lamps alone glimmered at either end of it, and not a soul was in sight.

Close to where his horse was standing at the corner of that same street the word "Tapperij" writ in bold letters and well lit by a lamp placed conveniently above it, invited the tired way-farer to enter. This philosopher was not the man to refuse so insinuating an invitation. He dismounted and leaving his horse in charge of an ostler, he entered the tap-room of the tiny hostel and, being both tired and thirsty, he refreshed himself with a draught of good Rhyn wine.

After which he collected more information about the house of Mynheer Ben Isaje. It was situate about midway down that narrow street round the corner, and was easily distinguishable through its crooked and woe-begone appearance, and the closely shuttered projecting window on the ground floor.

A very few minutes later Diogenes had identified the house from the several descriptions which had been given him. Ben Isaje's abode proved to be a tiny shop with a tall pointed gable sitting above it like a sugar-loaf hat. Its low casement window was securely barred with stout wooden shutters, held in place by thick iron bars. The upper part of the house looked to be at perpetual enmity with the lower, for it did not sit straight, or even securely above the humble ground floor below. The upper floor moreover projected a good three feet over the front door and the shop window, whilst the single gable sat askew over the lot.

From the house itself — as Diogenes stood somewhat doubtfully before it — there came the pungent odour of fried onions, and from the one next door an equally insistent one of damp leather. The philosopher thought that it was high time to swear, and this he did lustily, anathematizing in one comprehensive oath every dirty Hebrew and every insalubrious Dutch city that he had ever come across.

After which he examined the abode of Mynheer Ben Isaje more closely. In the pointed gable, just under the roof, a tiny window with a light behind it seemed to be blinking out of the darkness like the single eye of some inebriate loafer. Seeing that the small casement was partially open and concluding that some one at any rate must be making use of that light up there, Diogenes at last made up his mind to knock at the door; and as there was no knocker and he never carried a riding whip he gave the substantial oak panel a vigorous kick with his boot.

Whereupon the light up above immediately went out, just as if the one-eyed inebriate had dropped off to sleep.

This sudden extinguishing of the light, however, only served to prove to Diogenes that some one was up and astir inside the house, so without more ado he proceeded to pound more forcibly against the door with his foot, to shout at the top of his voice, and generally to make a rousing noise — an art of which he was past master.

Soon he heard a soft grating behind the judas, and he felt — more than he saw — that a pair of eyes were peering at him from within.

"Open, Mynheer Ben Isaje," he cried loudly and peremptorily, "ere I rouse this entire evil-smelling neighbourhood with my calls. Open I tell you ere I break in your door first and your nose — which I suspect to be over long and over ruddy — afterwards."

"'Tis too late to transact business now," came in a feeble high-pitched voice from behind the narrow judas, "too late and too dark. The shop is closed."

"'Tis not with your shop that I have to do, master," quoth Diogenes impatiently, "but with yourself, if indeed you are Mynheer Ben Isaje, as I gravely suspect that you are."

"What do you want with Ben Isaje?" queried the timorous voice, "he hath gone home for the night. His house is situate...."

"His house shall be verdommt if you parley any longer behind that grating, man; aye and this shop too, for if you do not open that door immediately I will break the windows, for my business brooks no delay, and I must needs get into this house as best I can."

But despite his threat, no attempt was made to draw the bolts from within, whereupon Diogenes, whose stock of patience was never inexhaustible, and who moreover wished to give value to his threats, took a step backwards and then with a sudden spring threw his whole weight against the oak door; a proceeding which caused the tumble-down house to shake upon its foundations.

The next moment the timorous voice was once more raised behind the judas:

"Kindly have patience, gentle sir. I was even now about to open."

Diogenes heard the drawing of more than one heavy bolt, then the grinding of a key in the lock; after which the door was partially opened, and a thin face with hooked nose and sunken cheeks appeared in the aperture.

To imagine that any man could hold a door against Diogenes when he desired to pass through it was to be totally unacquainted with that philosopher. He certainly would have smashed in the door of Ben Isaje's abode with his powerful shoulders had it been kept persistently closed against him; but as it was, he only gave it a push with his knee, flinging it wide open thereby, and then stepped coolly into the narrow ill-lighted passage.

There was a blank wall each side of him, and a door lower down on the left; straight ahead a narrow ladder-like staircase was half lost in the gloom.

The anxious janitor had hastily retreated down the dark passage at sight of the towering figure which now confronted him, and in his fright he must have dropped the lanthorn which apparently he had been carrying. There it lay on the floor, fortunately still alight, so Diogenes picked it up and holding it high above his head he took a closer survey of the man.

"You are Ben Isaje," he said calmly, as he held the light close to the man's face and then let it travel over his spare and shrinking form; "your dress and nose do proclaim your race. Then pray tell me what was the use of making such a to-do, seeing that I had business with you and therefore meant to come in.... Now take this lanthorn and lock your front door again, after which you had best conduct me to a room where I can talk privately with you."

No doubt there was something in the stranger's face and attitude which re-assured the Jew, for after a few more seconds of anxious hesitancy, he did take the lanthorn from Diogenes' hand and then shuffled back to the street door which he once more carefully barred and bolted.

After which with the aid of one of the many large keys which hung by a steel chain in a bunch from his waist, he unlocked the door in the passage and standing a little to one side he bade his belated guest walk in.

CHAPTER XXVIII
CHECK

The room into which Diogenes now stepped looked at first sight to be almost devoid of furniture: it was only when the Jew had entered and placed the lanthorn down upon a wooden table at one end of the room that the philosopher realized where he was.

The dark low walls showed themselves lined with solid oak chests and presses, each with massive hinges and locks, rusty and covered with dust, but firm enough to withstand for many an hour the depredations of thieves. Ben Isaje was obviously a jeweller by trade and this was the shop where he kept his precious goods: no wonder then that he looked with obvious fear on his belated visitor with the powerful shoulders and vigorous limbs, seeing that to all appearances he was at the moment alone in the house.

Like all jewellers settled in the Dutch cities at this time Ben Isaje carried on a number of other trades — some of which were perhaps not altogether avowable. He acted as banker and moneylender, and general go-between in financial transactions, some of which had political aims. Discretion was of necessity his chief stock-in-trade, and his small cargo of scruples he had thrown overboard long ago.

He was as ready now to finance a conspiracy against the Stadtholder as against the Archduchess or Don John, provided he saw huge monetary profits in the deal, and received bribes with a calm conscience both from Maurice of Nassau and the Lord of Stoutenburg. But once he was liberally paid he would hold to his bond: it was only by keeping the good graces of all political parties that he remained free from molestation.

Diogenes had known exactly what to expect when Nicolaes Beresteyn gave him the letter and bond to present to Ben Isaje; he was, therefore, not surprised in the least when he saw before him the true type of financial agent whom already he had met more than once in his life before.

Ben Isaje, who was the depositary of vast sums of money placed in his house by clients of substance and of note, wore a long, greasy kaftan of black cloth, which was worn thread-bare at the elbows and the knees, and the shop wherein he transacted business both for governments and private individuals which oft times involved several million guilders, had only a few very ricketty chairs, one or two tables blackened with dirt and age, and a piece of tattered carpet in one corner as sole expressions of comfort.

But all these facts were of course none of Diogenes' business. At his host's invitation he had sat down on one of the ricketty chairs and then proceeded to extract some papers from out the inner lining of his doublet.

"It would save time," he began dryly, and seeing that the man still eyed him with suspicion, "if you would cease to deny that you are Ben Isaje, jeweller of Rotterdam. I have here some papers which I must deliver into the said Ben Isaje's own hands: they are writ by Mynheer Nicolaes Beresteyn of Haarlem and do explain the purport of my visit here."

"From Nicolaes Beresteyn," quoth the other with an obvious sigh of relief. "Why did you not name him before, sir? I am always at Mynheer Nicolaes Beresteyn's commands. Indeed my name is Ben Isaje. An you have cause to doubt it, sir...."

"Dondersteen! but I never did doubt it, man, from the moment I saw the end of your hooked nose through the aperture of your door. So no more talk now, I pray you. Time is getting on. Here is the letter which Mynheer Beresteyn bade me present to you."

He handed over the letter to Ben Isaje which was writ in Beresteyn's own hand and duly signed with his own name. The Jew took it from him and drawing a chair close to the light on the table he unfolded the paper and began to read.

Diogenes the while examined him attentively. He was the man who after this night would have charge of Gilda, at the bidding of her own brother; he — Diogenes — would after this night become a free agent, his pledge to Beresteyn would be redeemed and he would be free — in an hour's time mayhap — to work for his own ends — to restore the jongejuffrouw to her sorrowing father, by taking her by force from this old Jew's keeping and returning with utmost speed and in utmost secrecy the very way he had just come. A fortune of 500,000 guilders awaited him in Haarlem, provided he could cajole or threaten Gilda in keeping his share of her original abduction a secret for all times.

How this could be done he had not yet thought on; but that it could be done he had no manner of doubt. An interview with the lady either this night or on the morrow, a promise to take her back to her father at once if she swore a solemn oath never to betray him, and he might be back in Leyden with her to-morrow eve and in possession of a fortune the following day.

No wonder then, that with these happy thoughts whirling in his head, he could scarcely restrain his temper while Ben Isaje read the long letter through, and then re-read it again a second time.

"Have you not finished, sir?" he exclaimed at last with marked impatience, "meseems the letter is explicit enough."

"Quite explicit, sir, I thank you," replied Ben Isaje, as he slowly folded up the letter and slipped it into the pocket of his kaftan. "I am to assure myself that the Jongejuffrouw Gilda Beresteyn, who is in your charge, is safe and well and hath no grave complaints to make against you, beyond that you did seize her by force in the streets of Haarlem. After which I am to see that she is conveyed with respect and safety to my own private house which is situate outside this city, or to any other place which I might think fitting, and there to keep her in comfort until such time as Mynheer Beresteyn desires. All that is quite clearly set forth in the letter, sir, and also that in payment for your services you are to receive the sum of 3,000 guilders which I am to give you in exchange for the formal bond which you will duly present."

The Jew spoke very deliberately — too deliberately, in fact, for Diogenes' endurance. Now he broke in impatiently.

"Is that all that is set forth in the letter?"

The Jew smiled somewhat sardonically.

"Not quite all," he said, "there is, of course, question in it of payment to myself."

"And certain conditions too, I imagine, attached to such payment. I know that Mynheer Nicolaes Beresteyn is prudent beyond his years."

"There is but one condition, sir, which enjoins me to keep a watchful eye on the jongejuffrouw once she is under my roof: to set a watch over her and her movements, and never, if possible, to let her out of my sight; he suggests that she might at any time make an attempt at escape, which he strictly commands me to frustrate, and in point of fact he desires me to look upon his sister as a prisoner of war not even to be let out on parole."

Diogenes' low, prolonged whistle was his only comment on what he had just heard.

"Mynheer Beresteyn also suggests to me, sir," continued the Jew with marked affability, "the advisability of keeping a watchful eye over you until such time as the jongejuffrouw is safely housed under my roof."

"You will find that injunction somewhat more difficult to follow, my friend, than you imagine," retorted Diogenes with a ringing laugh, "an you'll take my advice you will have extra watchmen posted outside your door."

"I have valuable things as well as monies stored in this house, sir," rejoined the Jew simply. "I have a picked guard of ten men sleeping here every night, and two watchmen outside my door until dawn."

Once more a long, low whistle escaped from the philosopher's lips.

"You are careful, my friend!" he said lightly.

"One has to be careful, sir, against thieves and house-breakers."

"And will your picked guard of ten men escort the jongejuffrouw to your private house this night?"

But the other slowly shook his head in response.

"The lady and her escort," he said "must, I fear me, accept the hospitality of this hovel for to-night."

"But...."

"My wife is away, sir, visiting her father in Dordrecht. She will only be home to-morrow. In the meanwhile my house is empty, and I am spending my nights here as well as my days."

"But...."

"It will not be a great hardship for the jongejuffrouw, sir," broke in the Jew again, "she will be made as comfortable for the night as maybe — she and her attendant too. I have a serving woman here who will see to the beds and the supper. Then to-morrow I can send a messenger to my private house to prepare my wife the moment she arrives, against the coming of the jongejuffrouw. 'Tis situate but half a league from here, and she would then be sure of a welcome equal to her worth."

Then as Diogenes was silent — since he felt perplexed and anxious at this unlooked-for turn of events and this first check to his plans — Ben Isaje continued with even greater affability than heretofore:

"Indeed, sir, and is it not better for the lady's own comfort? She will be over-fatigued when she arrives, and delighted — I know — at finding a nice bed and supper ready for her. Is it not all for the best?" he reiterated pleasantly.

But Diogenes was not satisfied. He did not like the idea of losing sight of Gilda altogether, quite so soon.

"I do not care to leave the jongejuffrouw," he said, "until I see her safely on her way to your house."

"Nor need you leave her, sir. There is a small room at the back of this shop, to which you are heartily welcome for the night. It is usually occupied by some of my guard, but they can dispose themselves in other rooms in the house. They are sturdy fellows, sir, and well-armed," continued the Jew, not without significance, "and I trust that they will not disturb you with their noise. Otherwise, sir, you are most welcome to sleep and sup under this roof."

Diogenes murmured vague thanks. Indeed, he was not a little troubled in his mind. The plans which he had formed for the second abduction of Gilda would prove more difficult of execution than he had supposed. The Jew had more than the customary prudence of his race, and Beresteyn had made that prudence and the measures which it suggested a condition of payment.

Between the prudence of Beresteyn and that of Ben Isaje, it was difficult to see how an adventurous plan could succeed. Three philosophers against a picked guard of ten men, with two more to keep watch outside the door, did not seem a promising venture. But Diogenes would not have been the happy-go-lucky soldier of fortune that he was, had he paused for long at this juncture in order to brood over likely failure, or had he not been willing to allow Chance a goodly share in the working out of his destiny.

It certainly was useless to argue any of these matters further with Ben Isaje; fate had willed it that the philosopher should spend this night under the same roof as the jongejuffrouw with a watch of twelve picked men — not counting the Jew himself — set over him, and to rebel against that fate now were puerile and useless.

So he murmured more audible thanks for the proffered hospitality, and put on as good-humoured an air over the matter as he could.

From the distance now there came the sound of jingling bells and the clatter of horses' hoofs upon the cobble-stones of the streets.

"'Tis the jongejuffrouw," exclaimed Diogenes, springing to his feet.

"The sledge cannot turn into this narrow way," rejoined Ben Isaje, "will you go meet the lady, sir, at the top of the street where she must needs dismount, and escort her hither, while I go to give orders to the serving woman. Your men," he added, as Diogenes at once rose and went to the door, "and the horses can put up at the hostelry close by where no doubt they have halted even now."

But already Diogenes was half way down the passage; soon he was at the front door fumbling in the dark for the heavy bolts. Ben Isaje followed him more deliberately, lanthorn in hand. He unlocked the door, and the next moment Diogenes was once more out in the street, walking rapidly in the direction whence came the occasional pleasing sound of the tinkling of sleigh-bells.

Though the jongejuffrouw seemed inexpressibly tired and weak, her attitude toward Diogenes lost nothing of its cold aloofness. She was peeping out under the hood of the sledge when he approached it, and at sight of him she immediately drew in her head.

"Will you deign to descend, mejuffrouw," he said with that slight tone of good-humoured mockery in his voice which had the power to irritate her. "Mynheer Ben Isaje, whose hospitality you will enjoy this night, lives some way up this narrow, insalubrious street, and he has bidden me to escort you to his house."

Silently, and with a great show of passive obedience, Gilda made ready to step out of the sledge.

"Come, Maria," she said curtly.

"The road is very slippery, mejuffrouw," he added warningly, "will you not permit me — for your own convenience' sake — to carry you as far as Ben Isaje's door?"

"It would not be for my convenience, sir," she retorted haughtily, "an you are so chivalrously inclined perhaps you would kindly convey my waiting woman thither in your arms."

"At your service, mejuffrouw," he said with imperturbable good temper.

And without more ado, despite her screams and her struggles, he seized Maria round her ample waist and round her struggling knees at the moment that she was stepping out of the sledge in the wake of her mistress.

The lamp outside the hostel at the corner illumined for a moment Gilda's pale, wearied face, and Diogenes saw that she was trying her best to suppress an insistent outburst of laughter.

"Hey there!" he shouted, "Pythagoras, Socrates, follow the jongejuffrouw at a respectful distance and see that no harm come to her while I lead the way with this featherweight in my arms."

Nor did he deposit Maria to the ground until he reached the door of Ben Isaje's house; here, when the mevrouw began to belabour him with her tongue and with her fists, he turned appealingly to Gilda:

"Mejuffrouw," he said merrily, "is this abuse not unmerited? I did but obey your behests and see how I must suffer for mine obedience."

But Gilda vouchsafed him no reply, and in the darkness he could not see if her face looked angered or smiling.

Ben Isaje, hearing the noise that went on outside his house, had already hastened to open the door. He welcomed the jongejuffrouw with obsequious bows. Behind him in the dark passage stood a lean and towzled-looking serving woman of uncertain years who was as obsequious as her master. When Gilda, confused and wearied, and mayhap not a little tired, advanced timorously into the narrow passage, the woman rushed up to her, and almost kneeling on the floor in the lowliness of her attitude, she kissed the jongejuffrouw's hand.

Diogenes saw nothing more of Gilda and Maria after that. They vanished into the gloom up the ladder-like staircase, preceded by the towzled but amiable woman, who by her talk and clumsy attempts at service had already earned Maria's fulsome contempt.

"You, too, must be hungry, sir," murmured a smooth affable voice close to Diogenes' elbow. "There is a bite and a drink ready for you; will you sup, sir, ere you go to bed?"

Before, however, following Ben Isaje into the shop Diogenes exchanged a few words with his brother philosophers, who, impassive and unquestioning, had escorted the jongejuffrouw to the door, and now stood there awaiting further orders. Diogenes suggested their getting supper and a bed in the hostelry at the top of the street in company with their driver; the horses too should all be stabled there.

"I am going to spend the night under this tumble-down roof," he said, "but remember to sleep with one eye open and be prepared for a summons from me at any hour of the night or morning. Until that comes, however, do not leave the hostel. Care well for the horses, we may have need of them to-morrow. Good-night! pleasant dreams! Do not forget that to-morrow five hundred guilders will fill each of your pockets. In the meanwhile here is the wherewithal to pay for bed and supper."

He gave them some money and then watched the two quaint figures, the long one and the round one, until they were merged in the blackness of the narrow street. Then he went within. Ben Isaje once more closed and bolted the front door and the two men then went together into the shop.

Here an appetizing supper had been laid ready upon the table and a couple of tallow candles burned in pewter sconces.

Ben Isaje at once invited his guest to eat and drink.

"Not before we have settled our business together, master," said the latter as he dragged a chair towards him, and sitting astride upon it, with his shapely legs thrust well out before him, he once more drew a paper from out the lining of his doublet.

"You are satisfied," he resumed after a slight pause, "that the lady whom I have had the honour of bringing into your house is indeed the Jongejuffrouw Gilda Beresteyn, sister of your client Mynheer Nicolaes Beresteyn of Haarlem?"

"I am quite satisfied on that point," replied the Jew, whose thin, bent form under the rigid folds of the black kaftan looked curiously weird in the feeble yellow light. His face was narrow and also waxlike in hue and the flickering candle-light threw quaint, distorted shadows around his long hooked nose.

"Then," said Diogenes blandly while he held out a folded paper to Ben Isaje, "here is the bond signed by Mynheer Beresteyn wherein he orders you to pay me the sum of 3,000 guilders in consideration of the services which I have rendered him."

But Ben Isaje did not take the paper thus held out to him.

"It is too late," he said quietly, "to transact business to-night."

"Too late!" exclaimed Diogenes with a blunt oath. "What in thunder do you mean?"

"I mean, sir, that you must try and curb your natural impatience until to-morrow."

"But I will not curb mine impatience another moment, plepshurk," cried the philosopher in a rage, "I have fulfilled my share of a bargain, 'tis only a verdommte Keerl who would shirk paying his own share on the nail."

"Nor would Mynheer Beresteyn desire me to shirk his responsibilities, I assure you," rejoined the Jew suavely, "and believe me, sir, that you will not lose one grote by waiting until the morrow. Let a good supper and a comfortable bed freely offered you atone for this unimportant delay. You still hold Mynheer Beresteyn's bond: to-morrow at the first business hour you shall be paid."

"But why any delay at all?" thundered Diogenes, who indeed misliked this way of doing business. "Why not pay me the money now? — at once, I will gladly forego the supper and sit all night upon your doorstep, but have my money in my pocket."

"Unfortunately, sir," said Ben Isaje with imperturbable amiability, "I am quite helpless in the matter. I am not the sole master of this business, my wife's brother shares my profits and my obligations. Neither of us is at liberty to pay out a large sum of money, save in the presence of the other."

"You and your partner know how to trust one another," said Diogenes with a laugh.

The Jew made no comment on this, only shrugged his shoulders in that calm manner peculiar to his race, which suggests the Oriental resignation to compelling fate.

Diogenes — inwardly fuming — thought over the matter very quietly for a few moments: it was obviously as useless to argue this matter out with Ben Isaje, as it had been to combat his dictum anent the jongejuffrouw spending the night under his roof, and as usual the wholesome lesson of life which the philosopher had learnt so thoroughly during his adventurous career stood him in good stead now: the lesson was the one which taught him never to waste time, temper or words over a purposeless argument.

That one shrug of Isaje's shoulders had told him with dumb eloquence that no amount of persuasion on his part would cause the banker to swerve from his determination. The money would be forthcoming on the morrow but not before, and there were ten picked men somewhere in the house at the present moment to prevent Diogenes from settling this matter in a primitive and efficient way by using his fists.

So in this instance too — disappointed though he was — he quickly regained his good humour. After all, the Jew was right: a night's delay would not spell a loss, and was well compensated for by a good supper and cosy bed.

With his habitual light-hearted laugh and careless shrug of the shoulders, he folded the paper up again and once more slipped it carefully into the inner lining of his doublet.

"You are right, sir," he said, "'twere foolish to allow choler to spoil the appetite. I am as hungry as the dog of a Spaniard. By your leave I'll test the strength of your ale and to-morrow ere I leave your house you shall pay me over the money in the presence of your trusting brother-in-law. Until then the bond remains with me, and I hold myself responsible for the safety of the jongejuffrouw. So I pray you be not surprised if I forbid her removal from this house until I have exchanged this bond for the sum of 3,000 guilders."

After which he drew his chair close to the table, and fell to all its good cheer with a hearty will. Ben Isaje, hospitable and affable to the last, waited on him with his own hands.

CHAPTER XXX
A NOCTURNE

It was only natural that, though tired as he was and enjoying an unusually contented mind, Diogenes was nevertheless unable to get to sleep.

He had had a very good supper and had parted at an early hour from his host. Ben Isaje had been amiable even deferential to the last, and indeed there had been nothing in the Jew's demeanour to arouse misgivings in the most suspicious mind.

The lean and towzled serving woman had prepared a clean and comfortable bed in the narrow alcove within the wall panelling of the small room which adjoined the shop, but though the weary philosopher wooed sleep with utmost persistence, it resolutely refused to be lured to his pillow. At first the arrival of the night watchmen had kept him awake: for they made their entrance with much jangling of swords and loud and lusty talk. There was apparently a good solid partition between his room and the shop because as soon as the watchmen were settled at their post their voices only reached Diogenes' ear like a muffled murmur.

A door gave from this room on the passage and this he had carefully locked; but it hung loosely on its hinges and the slightest noise in the house — a heavy footfall overhead or in the shop — would cause it to rattle with a weird, intermittent sound which sent sleep flying baffled away.

There were thoughts too which crowded in upon him — pleasant thoughts as well as others that were a trifle sad — the immediate future with its promise of a possible fortune loomed brightly enough, but the means to that happy end was vaguely disturbing the light-hearted equanimity of this soldier of fortune accustomed hitherto to grip Chance by the hair whenever she rushed past him in her mad, whirling career, and without heeding those who stood in his way.

But suddenly the whole thing seemed different, and Diogenes himself could not have told you why it was so. Thoughts of the future and of the promises which it held disturbed when they should have elated him: there was a feeling in him which he could not analyse, a feeling wherein a strange, sweet compassion seemed to form the main ingredient. The philosopher who had hitherto viewed life through the rosy glasses of unalterable good-humour, who had smiled at luck and ill-luck, laughed at misfortune and at hope, suddenly felt that there was something in life which could not be dismissed light-heartedly, something which really counted, though it was so intangible and so elusive that even now he could not give it a name.

The adventurer, who had slept soundly and dreamlessly in camp and on the field, in the streets of a sacked town or the still smouldering battlements of a fortress, could find no rest in the comfortable bed so carefully prepared for him in the house of Ben Isaje the Jew. The murmur of voices from the shop, low and monotonous, irritated his nerves, the rattling of the door upon its hinges drove him well-nigh distracted.

He heard every noise in the house as they died out one by one; the voice of the serving woman bidding the jongejuffrouw "good-night," the shuffling footsteps of the old Jew, the heavy tread of Maria overhead, and another, light and swift which — strangely enough — disturbed him more completely than the louder sounds had done.

At last he could stand his present state no longer, he felt an unpleasant tingling to the very tips of his fingers and the very roots of his hair; it seemed to him as if soft noiseless steps wandered aimlessly outside his door; furtive tiny animals with feet of velvet must have run down the stairs and then halted, breathless and terrified, on the other side of those rattling wooden panels.

He sat up in bed and groping for his tinder he struck a light; then he listened again. Not a sound now stirred inside the house, only the wind soughed through the loose tiles of the roof and found out the chinks and cracks of the ill-fitting window, through which it blew with a sharp, whistling sound. From the shop there came the faint murmur of some of the watchmen snoring at their post.

Beyond that, nothing. And yet Diogenes, whose keen ear was trained to catch the flutter of every twig, the movement of every beast, could have sworn that someone was awake at this moment, in this house besides himself — someone who breathed and trembled on the other side of the door.

Without a moment's hesitation he slipped on his clothes as quickly as he could, then he pulled the curtains across in front of the alcove and paused for one second longer in order to listen.

He had certainly not been mistaken. Through the stillness of the house he heard the soughing of the wind, the snoring of the watchmen, and that faint, palpitating sound outside in the passage — that sound which was as the breathing of some living, frightened thing.

Then he walked as noiselessly as he could up to the door, and with a sudden simultaneous turn of key and handle he opened it suddenly.

It opened outwards, and the passage beyond was pitch dark, but there in front of him now, white as a ghost, white as the garment which she wore, white as the marble statue of the Madonna which he had seen in the cathedral at Prague, stood the jongejuffrouw.

The candle which she carried flickered in the draught, and thus flickering it lit up her large blue eyes which she kept fixed upon him with an expression half defiant yet wholly terrified.

Frankly he thought at first that this was an apparition, a vivid embodiment of the fevered fancies which had been haunting him. No wonder therefore that he made no movement toward her, or expressed the slightest astonishment at seeing her there, all alone, in the middle of the night, not five paces away from him.

Thus they stood looking at one another for some time in absolute silence; she obviously very frightened, hesitating betwixt audacity and immediate flight, and he puzzled and with a vague sense of unreality upon him, a sense as of a dream which yet had in it the pulsating vividness of life.

She was the first to break this silence which was beginning to be oppressive. Gilda Beresteyn was not a timid woman nor was hers a character which ever vacillated once her mind was made up. The step which she had taken this night — daring and unconventional as it was — had been well thought out: deliberately and seriously she had weighed every danger, every risk which she ran, even those which in her pure-minded innocence she was not able fully to appreciate. Now though she was scared momentarily, she had no thought of turning back.

The old stiff-necked haughtiness of her race did not desert her for a moment, even though she was obviously at a disadvantage in this instance, and had come here as a suppliant.

"I wished to speak with you, sir," she said, and her voice had scarce a tremor in it, "my woman was too timorous to come down and summon you to my presence, as I had ordered her to do; so I was forced to come myself."

Though she looked very helpless, very childlike in her innocence, she had contrived to speak to him like a princess addressing a menial, holding her tiny head very high and making visible efforts to still the quivering of her lips.

There was something so quaint in this proud attitude of hers under the present circumstances, that despite its pathos Diogenes' keen sense of humour was not proof against it, and that accustomed merry smile of his crept slowly over every line of his face.

"I am ever at your service, mejuffrouw," he said as gravely as he could, "your major domo, your valet ... I always await your commands."

"Then I pray you take this candle," she said coldly, "and stand aside that I may enter. What I have to say cannot be told in this passage."

He took the candle from her, since she held it out to him, and then stepped aside just as she had commanded, keeping the door wide open for her to pass through into the room. She was holding herself very erect, and with perfect self-possession she now selected a chair whereon to sit. She wore the same white gown which she had on when first he laid hands on her in the streets of Haarlem, and the fur cloak wherein she had wrapped herself had partially slid from her shoulders.

Having sat down, close to the table, with one white arm resting upon it, she beckoned peremptorily to him to close the door and to put the candle down; all of which he did quite mechanically, for the feeling had come back to him that the white figure before him was only a vision — or mayhap a dream — from which, however, he hoped not to awaken too soon.

"At your command, mejuffrouw," was all that he said, and he remained standing quite close to the door, with half the width of the room between himself and her.

But to himself he murmured under his breath:

"St. Bavon and the Holy Virgin, do ye both stand by me now!"

"I do not know, sir," she began after awhile, "if my coming here at this hour doth greatly surprise you, but in truth the matter which brings me is so grave that I cannot give a thought to your feelings or to mine own."

"And mine, mejuffrouw, are of such little consequence," he said good-humouredly seeing that she appeared to wait for a reply, "that it were a pity you should waste precious time in considering them."

"Nor have I come to talk of feelings, sir. My purpose is of deadly earnestness. I have come to propose a bargain for your acceptance."

"A bargain?"

"Yes. A bargain," she reiterated. "One I hope and think that you will find it worth while to accept."

"Then may I crave the honour of hearing the nature of that bargain, mejuffrouw?" he asked pleasantly.

She did not give him an immediate reply but remained quite still and silent for a minute or even two, looking with wide-open inquiring eyes on the tall figure of the man who had — to her mind — done her such an infinite wrong. She noted and acknowledged quite dispassionately the air of splendour which became him so well — splendour of physique, of youth and of strength, and those laughing eyes that questioned and that mocked, the lips that always smiled and the straight brow with its noble sweep which hid the true secret of his personality. And once again — as on that evening at Leyden — she fell almost to hating him, angered that such a man should be nothing better than a knave, a mercenary rogue paid to lend a hand in unavowable deeds.

He stood her scrutiny as best he could, answering her look of haughty condescension with one of humble deference; but the smile of gentle irony never left his lips and tempered the humility of his attitude.

"You have owned to me, sir," resumed Gilda Beresteyn at last, "that you have been paid for the infamous work which you are doing now; for laying hands on me in the streets of Haarlem and for keeping me a prisoner at the good will of your employer. To own to such a trade, sir, is to admit oneself somewhat below the level of honest men. Is that not so?"

"Below the level of most men, mejuffrouw, I admit," he replied imperturbably.

"Had it not been for that admission on your part, I would never have thought of coming to you with a proposal which...."

"Which you never would have put before an honest man," he broke in with perfect equanimity, seeing that she hesitated.

"You anticipate my thought, sir: and I am glad to find that you will make my errand even easier than I had hoped. Briefly then let me tell you — as I told you at Leyden — that I know who your paymaster is. A man has thought fit to perpetrate a crime against me, for a reason which no doubt he deemed expedient and which probably he has not imparted to you. Reasons and causes I imagine, sir, are no concern of yours. You take payment for your deeds and do not inquire into motives. Is that not so?"

This time Diogenes only made a slight bow in acknowledgment of her question. He was smiling to himself more grimly than was his wont, for he had before him the recollection of the Lord of Stoutenburg — cruel, coarse, and evil, bullying and striking a woman — and of Nicolaes Beresteyn — callous and cynical, bartering his sister's honour and safety to ensure his own. To the one she had plighted her troth, the other was her natural protector, dear to her through those sweet bonds of childhood which bind brother and sister in such close affection. Yet both are selfish, unscrupulous rogues, thought the philosopher, though both very dear to her, and both honest men in her sight.

"That being so, sir," she resumed once more, "meseems that you should be equally ready to do me service and to ask me no questions, provided that I pay you well."

"That, mejuffrouw," he said quietly, "would depend on the nature of the service."

"It is quite simple, sir. Let me explain. While my woman and I were having supper upstairs, the wench who served us fell to gossiping, telling us the various news of the day which have filtered through into Rotterdam. Among other less important matters, sir, she told us that the Prince of Orange had left his camp at Sprang in order to journey northwards to Amsterdam. Yesterday he and his escort of one hundred men-at-arms passed close to this city; they were making for Delft where the Prince means to spend a day or two before proceeding further on his journey. He sleeps at the Prinzenhof in Delft this night."

"Yes, mejuffrouw?" he said, for suddenly her manner had changed; something of its coolness had gone from it, even if the pride was still there. While she spoke a warm tinge of pink flooded her cheeks; she was leaning forward, her eyes bright and glowing were fixed upon him with a look of eagerness and almost of appeal, and her lips were moist and trembling, whilst the words which she wished to speak seemed to be dying in her throat.

"What hath the progress of the Prince of Orange to do with your most humble and most obedient servant?" he asked again.

"I must speak with the Prince of Orange, sir," she said while her voice now soft and mellow fell almost like a prayer on his ear. "I must go to him to Delft not later than to-morrow. Oh! you will not refuse me this ... you cannot ... I...."

She had clasped her hands together, her eyes were wet with tears, and as she pleaded, she bent forward so low in her chair, that it seemed for a moment as if her knees would touch the ground. In the flickering candle-light she looked divinely pretty thus, with all the cold air of pride gone from her childlike face. A gentle draught stirred the fair curls round her head, the fur cloak had completely slipped down from her shoulders and her white dress gave her more than ever the air of that Madonna carved in marble which he had seen once in the cathedral at Prague.

The philosopher passed a decidedly shaking hand across his forehead: the room was beginning to whirl round him, the floor to give way under his feet. He fell to thinking that the mild ale offered to him by Ben Isaje had been more heady than he had thought.

"St. Bavon," he murmured to himself, "where in Heaven's name are ye now? I asked you to stand by me."

It was one of those moments — perfect in themselves — when a man can forget everything that pertains to the outer world, when neither self-interest nor ordinary prudence will count, when he is ready to jeopardize his life, his career, his future, his very soul for the ecstasy which lies in the one heaven-born minute. Thus it was with this philosopher, this man of the moment, the adventurer, the soldier of fortune; the world which he had meant to conquer, the fortune which he had vowed to win seemed to slip absolutely away from him. This dream — for it was after all only a dream, it was just too beautiful to be reality — the continuance of this dream seemed to him to be all that mattered, this girl — proud and pleading — a Madonna, a saint, a child of innocence, was the only perfect, desirable entity in this universe.

"St. Bavon, you rogue! you are playing me false!" he murmured, as the last vestige of self-control and of prudence threatened to fall away from him.

"Madonna," he said as with a quick movement he came forward and bent the knee before her, "I entreat you to believe that whatever lies in my power to do in your service, that will I gladly do. How can I refuse," he added whilst that immutable smile, gentle, humourous, faintly ironical, once more lit up his face as he looked straight into hers, "how can I refuse to obey since you deign to plead to me with those lips? how can I withstand your appeal when it speaks to me through your eyes?"

"You will let me do what I ask?" she exclaimed with a little cry of joy, for his attitude was very humble and his voice yielding and kind; he was kneeling at some little distance from her, which was quite becoming in a mercenary knave.

"If it be in my power, Madonna!" he said simply.

"Then will I pay you well," she continued eagerly. "I have thought it all out. I am rich you know, and my bond is as good as that of any man. Do you but bring me inkhorn and paper, I will give you a bond for 4,000 guilders on Mynheer Ben Isaje himself, he hath monies of mine own in trust and at interest. But if 4,000 guilders are not enough, I pray you name your price; it shall be what you ask."

"What do you desire me to do, Madonna?"

"I desire you to escort me to Delft so that I may speak with the Prince of Orange."

"The Prince of Orange is well guarded. No stranger is allowed to enter his presence."

"I am not a stranger to him. My father is his friend; a word from me to him, a ring of mine sent in with a request for an audience and he will not refuse."

"And having entered the presence of the Stadtholder, mejuffrouw, what do you propose to say to him?"

"That, sir, is naught to you," she retorted coldly.

"I pray you forgive me," he said, still humbly kneeling, "but you have deigned to ask my help, and I'll not give it unless you will tell me what your purpose is."

"You would not dare...."

"To make conditions for my services?" he said speaking always with utmost deference, "this do I dare, mejuffrouw, and my condition is for your acceptance or refusal — as you command."

"I did not ask for your help, sir," she said curtly. "I offered to pay you for certain services which I desire you to render me."

Already her look of pleading had gone. She had straightened herself up, prouder and more disdainful than before. He dared to make conditions! he! the mercenary creature whom anyone could buy body and soul for money, who took payment for doing such work as would soil an honest man's hands! It was monstrous! impossible, unthinkable. She thought that her ears had deceived her or that mayhap he had misunderstood.

In a moment at her words, at the scornful glance which accompanied them, he had risen to his feet. The subtle moment had gone by; the air was no longer oppressive, and the ground felt quite steady under him. Calm, smiling, good-tempered, he straightened out his massive figure as if to prepare himself for those shafts which her cruel little tongue knew so well how to deal.

And inwardly he offered up a thanksgiving to St. Bavon for this cold douche upon his flaming temper.

"I did not misunderstand you, mejuffrouw," he said lightly, "and I am ready to do you service — under a certain condition."

She bit her lip with vexation. The miserable wretch was obviously not satisfied with the amount which she had named as payment for his services, and he played some weak part of chivalry and of honour in order to make his work appear more difficult, and to extract a more substantial reward from her. She tried to put into the glance which she now threw on him all the contempt which she felt and which truly nauseated her at this moment. Unfortunately she had need of him, she could not start for Delft alone, marauders and footpads would stop her ever reaching that city. Could she have gone alone she were not here now craving the help of a man whom she despised.

"Meseems," she said coldly after a slight pause, "that you do wilfully misunderstand our mutual positions. I am not asking you to do anything which could offend your strangely susceptible honour, whose vagaries, I own, I am unable to follow. Will 10,000 guilders satisfy your erratic conscience? or did you receive more than that for laying hands on two helpless women and dragging one — who has never done you any wrong — to a depth of shame and sorrow which you cannot possibly fathom?"

"My conscience, mejuffrouw," he replied, seemingly quite unperturbed at her contemptuous glance and insulting speech, "is, as you say, somewhat erratic. For the moment it refuses to consider the possibility of escorting you to Delft unless I know what it is that you desire to say to the Prince of Orange."

"If it is a question of price...."

"It is not a question of price, mejuffrouw," he broke in firmly, "let us, an you will allow it, call it a question of mine erratic conscience."

"I am rich, sir ... my private fortune...."

"Do not name it, mejuffrouw," he said jovially, "the sound of it would stagger a poor man who has to scrape up a living as best he can."

"Forty thousand guilders, sir," she said pleading once more eagerly, "an you will take me to Delft to-morrow."

"Were it ten hundred thousand, mejuffrouw, I would not do it unless I knew what you wished to say to the Stadtholder."

"Sir, can I not move you," she implored, "this means more to me than I can hope to tell you." Once again her pride had given way before this new and awful fear that her errand would be in vain, that she had come here as a suppliant before this rogue, that she had humbled her dignity, entreated him, almost knelt to him, and that he, for some base reason which she could not understand, meant to give himself the satisfaction of refusing the fortune which she did promise him.

"Can I not move you," she reiterated, appealing yet more earnestly, for, womanlike, she could not forget that moment awhile ago, when he had knelt instinctively before her, when the irony had gone from his smile, and the laughter in his mocking eyes had yielded to an inward glow.

He shook his head, but remained unmoved.

"I cannot tell you, sir," she urged plaintively, "what I would say to the Prince."

"Is it so deadly a secret then?" he asked.

"Call it that, an you will."

"A secret that concerns his life?"

"That I did not say."

"No. It was a guess. A right one methinks."

"Then if you think so, sir, why not let me go to him?"

"So that you may warn him?"

"You were merely guessing, sir...."

"That you may tell him not to continue his journey," he insisted, speaking less restrainedly now, as he leaned forward closer to her, her fair curls almost brushing against his cheek as they fluttered in the draught.

"I did not say so," she murmured.

"Because there is a trap laid for him ... a trap of which you know...."

"No, no!" she cried involuntarily.

"A trap into which he may fall ... unknowingly ... on his way to the north."

"You say so, sir," she moaned, "not I...."

"Assassins are on his track ... an attempt will be made against his life ... the murderers lie in wait for him ... even now ... and you, mejuffrouw, who know who those murderers are...."

A cry of anguish rose to her lips.

"No, no, no," she cried, "it is false ... you are only guessing ... remember that I have told you nothing."

But already the tense expression on his face had gone. He drew himself up to his full height once more and heaved a deep breath which sounded like a sigh of satisfaction.

"Yet in your candour, mejuffrouw, you have told me much," he said quietly, "confirmed much that I only vaguely guessed. The Stadtholder's life is in peril and you hold in your feeble little hands the threads of the conspiracy which threatens him ... is that not why you are here, mejuffrouw ...a prisoner, as you say, at the good-will of my employer? I am only guessing, remember, but on your face, meseems that I can read that I do guess aright."

"Then you will do what I ask?" she exclaimed with a happy little gasp of renewed hope.

"That, mejuffrouw, is I fear me impossible," he said quietly.

"Impossible? But — just now...."

"Just now," he rejoined with affected carelessness, "I said, mejuffrouw, that I would on no account escort you to Delft without knowing what your purpose is with the Prince of Orange. Even now I do not know, I merely guessed."

"But," she entreated, "if I do own that you have guessed aright — partly at any rate — if I do tell you that the Stadtholder's life might be imperilled if I did not give him a timely word of warning, if...."

"Even if you told me all that, mejuffrouw," he broke in lightly, "if you did bring your pride down so far as to trust a miserable knave with a secret which he might sell for money on the morrow — even then, I fear me, I could not do what you ask."

"But why not?" she insisted, her voice choking in her throat in the agony of terrible doubt and fear.

"Because the man of whom you spoke just now, the man whom you love, mejuffrouw, has been more far-seeing, more prudent than you or I. He hath put it out of my power to render you this service."

"How?"

"By warning Mynheer Ben Isaje against any attempt at escape on your part, against any attempt at betrayal on mine. Mynheer Ben Isaje is prepared: he hath a guard of ten picked men on the watch, and two more men outside his door. If you tried to leave this house with me without his consent he would prevent you, and I am no match alas! for twelve men."

"Why should he guard me so?"

"Because he will not be paid if he keep not watch over you."

"But I'll swear to return straightway from Delft. I'll only speak with the Prince and return immediately.... Money! always money!" she cried with sudden vehemence, "a great man's life, the honour of a house, the salvation of the land, are these all to be sacrificed because of the greed and cupidity of men?"

"Shall I call Mynheer Ben Isaje?" asked Diogenes placidly, "mayhap, mejuffrouw, that you could persuade him more easily than me!"

But at this she rose to her feet as suddenly as if she had been stung: the colour in her cheeks deepened, the tears were dry in her eyes.

"You," she exclaimed, and there was a world of bitter contempt in the tone of her voice, "persuade you who have tricked and fooled me, even while I began to believe in you? You, who for the past half hour have tried to filch a secret from me bit by bit! with lying words you led me into telling you even more than I should! and I, poor fool I thought that I had touched your heart, or that at least there was some spark of loyalty in you which mayhap prompted you to guess that the Prince was in danger. Fool that I was! miserable, wretched fool! to think for a moment that you would lend a hand in aught that was noble and chivalrous! I would I had the power to raise the blush of shame in your cheeks, but alas! the shame is only for me, who trusting in your false promises and your lies have allowed my tongue to speak words which I would give my life now to unsay — for me who thought that there was in you one feeble spark of pity or of honour. Fool! fool that I was! when I forgot for one brief moment that it was your greed and cupidity that were the props without which this whole edifice of infamy had tottered long ago; persuade you to do a selfish deed! you the abductor of women, the paid varlet and mercenary rogue who will thieve and outrage and murder for money!"

She sank back in her chair and, resting her arms upon the table, she buried her face in them, for she had given way at last to a passionate fit of weeping. The disappointment was greater than she could bear after the load of sorrow which had been laid on her these past few days.

When she heard through the chatterings of a servant that the Stadtholder was at Delft this very night, the memory of every word which she had heard in the cathedral on New Year's Eve came back to her with renewed vividness. Delft! she remembered that name so well and Ryswyk close by, the only possible way for a northward journey! Then the molens which Stoutenburg had said were his headquarters, where he stored arms and ammunition and enough gunpowder to blow up the wooden bridge which spans the Schie and over which the Stadtholder and his bodyguard must pass.

Every word that Stoutenburg and her brother and the others had spoken that night, rang now in her ears like a knell: Delft, Ryswyk, the molens, the wooden bridge! Delft, Ryswyk, the molens, the wooden bridge! Delft....

Delft was quite near, less than four leagues away ... the Stadtholder was there now ... he could be warned before it was too late ... and she could warn him without compromising her brother and his friends.... Then it was that she remembered that in the room below there slept a knave who would do anything for gold.

Thus she had run down to him full of eagerness and full of hope. And now he had refused to help her, and worse still had guessed at a secret which, if he bartered or sold it, meant death to her brother and his friends.

Contempt and hate had broken down her spirit. Smothering both, she was even now ready to fall on her knees, to plead with him, to pray, to implore ... if only that could have moved him ... if only it meant safety for the Stadtholder, and not merely a useless loss of pride and of dignity.

Anger and misery and utter hopelessness! they were causing her tears, and she hated this man who had her in his power and mocked her in her misery: and there was the awful thought that the Stadtholder was so near — less than four leagues away! Why! had she been free she could have run all the way to him — that hideous crime, that appalling tragedy in which her brother would bear a hand, could be averted even now if she were free! Oh! the misery of it! the awful, wretched helplessness! in a few days — hours mayhap — the Stadtholder would be walking straight into the trap which his murderers had set for him ... the broken bridge! the explosion! the assassin at the carriage door! She saw it all as in a vision of the future, and her brother in the midst of it all with hands deeply stained in blood.

And she could avert it all — the crime, the sorrow, the awful, hideous shame if only she were free.

She looked up at last, ashamed of her tears, ashamed that a rogue should have seen how keenly she suffered.

She looked up and turned to him once more. The flickering light of the candles fell full upon his splendid figure and upon his face: it was the colour of ashes, and there was no trace of his wonted smile around his lips: the eyes too looked sunken and their light was hid beneath the drooping lids. Her shafts which she had aimed with such deadly precision had gone home at last: in the bitterness of her heart she apparently had found words which had cut him like a lash.

Satisfied at least in this she rose to go.

"There is nothing more to say," she said as calmly as she could, trying to still the quivering of her lips: "as you say, Mynheer Ben Isaje has carefully taken the measure of your valour and it cannot come up to a dozen picked men, even though life and honour, country and faith might demand at least an effort on their behalf. I pray you open the door. I would — for mine own sake as well as your own — that I had not thought of breaking in on your rest."

Without a word he went to the door, and had his hand on the latch ready to obey her, when something in his placid attitude irritated her beyond endurance. Woman-like she was not yet satisfied: perhaps a thought of remorse at her cruelty fretted her, perhaps she pitied him in that he was so base.

Be that as it may, she spoke to him again:

"Have you nothing then to say?" she asked.

"What can I say, mejuffrouw?" he queried in reply, as the ghost of his wonted smile crept swiftly back into his pale face.

"Methought no man would care to be called a coward by a woman, and remain silent under the taunt."

"You forget, mejuffrouw," he retorted, "that I am so much less than a man …a menial, a rogue, a vagabond — so base that not even the slightest fear of me did creep into your heart … you came to me, here, alone at dead of night with an appeal upon your lips, yet you were not afraid, then you struck me in the face like you would a dog with a whip, and you were no more afraid of me than of the dog whom you had thrashed. So base am I then that words of mine are not worthy of your ear. Whatever I said, I could not persuade you that for one man to measure his strength against twelve others were not an act of valour, but one of senseless foolishness. I might tell you that bravery lies oft in prudence but seldom in foolhardiness, but this I know you are not in a mood now to believe. I might even tell you," he continued with a slight return to his wonted light-hearted carelessness, "I might tell you that certain acts of bravery cannot be accomplished without the intervention of protecting saints, and that I have found St. Bavon an admirable saint to implore in such cases, but this I fear me you are not like to understand. So you see, mejuffrouw, that whatever I said I could not prove to you that I am less of a blackguard than I seem."

"You could at least prove it to this extent," she retorted, "by keeping silence over what you may have guessed."

"You mean that I must not sell the secret which you so nearly betrayed …have no fear, mejuffrouw, my knowledge of it is so scanty that the Stadtholder would not give me five guilders for it."

"Will you swear…."

"Such a miserable cur as I am, mejuffrouw," he said lightly, "is surely an oath-breaker as well as a liar and a thief — what were the good of swearing?…But I'll swear an you wish …" he added gaily.

"Surely you …" she began.

But with a quick gesture he interrupted her.

"Dondersteen, mejuffrouw," he said more firmly than he had yet spoken before, "if beauty in you is tempered with pity, I entreat you to spare me now: even knaves remember become men sometimes and my patron Saint Bavon threatens to leave me in the lurch."

He held open the door for her to pass through, and gravely held out one of the pewter candles to her. She could not help but take it, though indeed she felt that the last word between that rogue and herself had not by any means been spoken yet. But she hardly looked at him as she sailed past him out of the room, her heavy skirt trailing behind her with a soft hissing sound.

As soon as she heard the door shut to behind her, she ran up the stairs back to her own room with all speed, like a frightened hare.

Had she remained in the passage one instant longer she would have heard a sound which would have terrified her; it was the sound of a prolonged and ringing laugh which roused the echoes of this sleeping house, but which had neither mirth nor joy in its tone, and had she then peeped through a keyhole she would have seen a strange sight. A man who in the flickering candle-light looked tall and massive as a giant took up one of the wooden chairs in the room, and after holding it out at arm's length for a few seconds, he proceeded to smash it viciously bit by bit until it lay a mass of broken débris at his feet.

CHAPTER XXXI
THE MOLENS

Less than half a league to the southeast of Ryswyk — there where the Schie makes a sharp curve up toward the north — there is a solitary windmill — strange in this, that it has no companions near it, but stands quite alone with its adjoining miller's hut nestling close up against it like a tiny chick beside the mother hen, and dominates the mud flats and lean pastures which lie for many leagues around.

On this day which was the fourth of the New Year, these mud flats and the pasture land lay under a carpet of half-melted snow and ice which seemed to render the landscape more weird and desolate, and the molens itself more deserted and solitary. Yet less than half a league away the pointed gables and wooden spires of Ryswyk break the monotony of the horizon line and suggest the life and movement pertaining to a city, however small. But life and movement never seem to penetrate as far as this molens; they spread their way out toward 'S Graven Hage and the sea.

Nature herself hath decreed that the molens shall remain solitary and cut off from the busy world, for day after day and night after night throughout the year a mist rises from the mud flats around and envelops the molens as in a shroud. In winter the mist is frosty, in summer at times it is faintly tinged with gold, but it is always there and through it the rest of the living world — Ryswyk and 'S Graven Hage and Delft further away only appear as visions on the other side of a veil.

Just opposite the molens, some two hundred paces away to the east, the waters of the Schie rush with unwonted swiftness round the curve; so swiftly in fact that the ice hardly ever forms a thick crust over them, and this portion of an otherwise excellent waterway is — in the winter — impracticable for sleighs.

Beyond this bend in the river, however, less than half a league away, there is a wooden bridge, wide and strongly built, across which it is quite easy for men and beasts to pass who have come from the south and desire to rejoin the great highway which leads from Delft to Leyden.

In the morning of that same fourth day in the New Year, two men sat together in what was once the weighing-room of the molens; their fur coats were wrapped closely round their shoulders, for a keen north-westerly wind had found its way through the chinks and cracks of tumble-down doors and ill-fitting window frames.

Though a soft powdery veil — smooth as velvet to the touch and made up of flour and fine dust-lay over everything, and the dry, sweet smell of corn still hung in the close atmosphere, there was little else in this room now that suggested the peaceful use for which it had been originally intended.

The big weighing machines had been pushed into corners, and all round the sloping walls swords, cullivers and muskets were piled in orderly array, also a row of iron boxes standing a foot or so apart from one another and away from any other objects in the room.

The silence which reigned over the surrounding landscape did not find its kingdom inside this building, for a perpetual hum, a persistent buzzing noise as of bees in their hives, filtrated through the floor and the low ceiling of this room. Men moved and talked and laughed inside the molens, but the movement and the laughter were subdued as if muffled in that same mantle of mist which covered the outside world.

The two men in the weighing-room were sitting at a table on which were scattered papers, inkhorns and pens, a sword, a couple of pistols and two or three pairs of skates. One of them was leaning forward and talking eagerly:

"I think you can rest satisfied, my good Stoutenburg," he said, "our preparations leave nothing to be desired. I have just seen Jan, and together we have despatched the man Lucas van Sparendam to Delft. He is the finest spy in the country, and can ferret out a plan or sift a rumour quicker than any man I know. He will remain at Delft and keep the Prinzenhof under observation: and will only leave the city if anything untoward should happen, and then he will come straight here and report to us. He is a splendid runner, and can easily cover the distance between Delft and this molens in an hour. That is satisfactory is it not?"

"Quite," replied Stoutenburg curtly.

"Our arrangements here on the other hand are equally perfect," resumed Beresteyn eagerly, "we have kept the whole thing in our own hands ... Heemskerk and I will be at our posts ready to fire the gunpowder at the exact moment when the advance guard of the Prince's escort will have gone over the bridge ... you, dagger in hand, will be prepared to make a dash for the carriage itself ... our men will attack the scattered and confused guard at a word from van Does.... What could be more simple, more perfect than that? Yourself, Heemskerk, van Does and I ... all of one mind ... all equally true, silent and determined.... You seem so restless and anxious.... Frankly I do not understand you."

"It is not of our preparations or of our arrangements that I am thinking, Nicolaes," said Stoutenburg sombrely, "these have been thought out well enough. Nothing but superhuman intervention or treachery can save the Stadtholder — of that am I convinced. Neither God nor the devil care to interfere in men's affairs — we need not therefore fear superhuman intervention. But 'tis the thought of treachery that haunts me."

"Bah!" quoth Beresteyn with a shrug of the shoulders, "you have made a nightmare of that thought. Treachery? there is no fear of treachery. Yourself, van Does, Heemskerk and I are the only ones who know anything at this moment of our plans for to-morrow. Do you suspect van Does of treachery, or Heemskerk, or me?"

"I was not thinking of Heemskerk or of van Does," rejoined Stoutenburg, "and even our men will know nothing of the attack until the last moment. Danger, friend, doth not lie in or around the molens; it lurks at Rotterdam and hath name Gilda."

"Gilda! What can you fear from Gilda now?"

"Everything. Have you never thought on it, friend? Jan, remember, lost track of that knave soon after he left Haarlem. At first he struck across the waterways in a southerly direction and for awhile Jan and the others were able to keep him in sight. But soon darkness settled in and along many intricate backwaters our rogue was able to give them the slip."

"I know that," rejoined Beresteyn somewhat impatiently. "I was here in the early morning when Jan reported to you. He also told you that he and his men pushed on as far as Leyden that night and regained the road to Rotterdam the following day. At Zegwaard and again at Zevenhuizen they ascertained that a party consisting of two women in a sledge and an escort of three cavaliers had halted for refreshments at those places and then continued their journey southwards. Since then Jan has found out definitely that Gilda and her escort arrived early last night at the house of Ben Isaje of Rotterdam, and he came straight on here to report to you. Frankly I see nothing in all this to cause you so much anxiety."

"You think then that everything is for the best?" asked Stoutenburg grimly, "you did not begin to wonder how it was that — as Jan ascertained at Zegwaard and at Zevenhuizen — Gilda continued her journey without any protest. According to the people whom Jan questioned she looked sad certainly, but she was always willing to restart on her way. What do you make of that, my friend?"

Once more Beresteyn shrugged his shoulders.

"Gilda is proud," he said. "She hath resigned herself to her fate."

Stoutenburg laughed aloud.

"How little you — her own brother — know her," he retorted. "Gilda resigned? Gilda content to let events shape themselves — such events as those which she heard us planning in the Groote Kerk on New Year's Eve? Why, my friend, Gilda will never be resigned, she will never be content until she hath moved earth and heaven to save the Stadtholder from my avenging hand!"

"But what can she do now? Ben Isaje is honest in business matters. It would not pay him to play his customers false. And I have promised him two thousand guilders if he keeps her safely as a prisoner of war, not even to be let out on parole. Ben Isaje would not betray me. He is too shrewd for that."

"That may be true of Ben Isaje himself; but what of his wife? his sons or daughters if he have any? his serving wenches, his apprentices and his men? How do you know that they are not amenable to promises of heavy bribes?"

"But even then...."

"Do you not think that at Rotterdam every one by now knows the Prince's movements? He passed within half a league of the town yesterday; there is not a serving wench in that city at this moment who does not know that Maurice of Nassau slept at Delft last night and will start northwards to-morrow."

"And what of that?" queried Beresteyn, trying to keep up a semblance of that carelessness which he was far from feeling now.

"Do you believe then that Gilda will stay quietly in the house of Ben Isaje, knowing that the Prince is within four leagues of her door?... knowing that he will start northwards to-morrow ... knowing that my headquarters are here — close to Ryswyk ... knowing in fact all that she knows?"

"I had not thought on all that," murmured Beresteyn under his breath.

"And there is another danger too, friend, greater perhaps than any other," continued Stoutenburg vehemently.

"Good G — d, Stoutenburg, what do you mean?"

"That cursed foreign adventurer — — "

"What about him?"

"Have you then never thought of him as being amenable to a bribe from Gilda."

"In Heaven's name, man, do not think of such awful eventualities!"

"But we must think of them, my good Beresteyn. Events are shaping themselves differently to what we expected. We must make preparations for our safety accordingly, and above all realise the fact that Gilda will move heaven and earth to thwart us in our plans."

"But she can do nothing," persisted Beresteyn sullenly, "without betraying me. In Haarlem it was different. She might have spoken to my father of what she knew, but she would not do so to a stranger, knowing that with one word she can send me first and all of you afterwards to the scaffold."

Stoutenburg with an exclamation of angry impatience brought his clenched fist crashing down upon the table.

"Are you a child, Beresteyn," he cried hotly, "or are you wilfully blind to your danger and to mine? I tell you that Gilda will never allow me to kill the Prince of Orange without raising a finger to save him."

"But what can I do?"

"Send for Gilda at once, to-night," urged Stoutenburg, "convey her under escort hither ... in all deference ... in all honour ... she would be here under her brother's care."

"A woman in this place at such a moment," cried Beresteyn; "you are mad, Stoutenburg."

"I shall go mad if she is not here," rejoined the other more calmly, "the fear has entered into my soul, Nicolaes, that Gilda will yet betray us at the eleventh hour. That fear is an obsession ... call it premonition if you will, but it unmans me, friend."

Beresteyn was silent now. He drew his cloak closer round his shoulders, for suddenly he felt a chill which seemed to have crept into his bones.

"But it is unpractical, man," he persisted with a kind of sullen despair. "Gilda and another woman here ... to-morrow ... when not half a league away...."

"Justice will be meted out to a tyrant and an assassin," broke in Stoutenburg quietly. "Gilda is not a woman as other women are, though in her soul now she may be shrinking at the thought of this summary justice, she will be strong and brave when the hour comes. In any case," he added roughly, "we can keep her closely guarded, and in the miller's hut, with the miller and his wife to look after her, she will be as safe and as comfortable as circumstances will allow. We should have her then under our own eyes and know that she cannot betray us."

As usual Beresteyn was already yielding to the stronger will, the more powerful personality of his friend. His association with Stoutenburg had gradually blunted his finer feelings; like a fly that is entangled in the web of a spider, he tried to fight against the network of intrigue and of cowardice which hemmed him in more and more closely with every step that he took along the path of crime. He was filled with remorse at thought of the wrong which he had done to Gilda, but he was no longer his own master. He was being carried away by the tide of intrigue and by the fear of discovery, away from his better self.

"You should have thought on all that sooner, Stoutenburg," he said in final, feeble protest, "we need never have sent Gilda to Rotterdam in the company of a foreign adventurer of whom we knew nothing."

"At the time it seemed simple enough," quoth Stoutenburg impatiently, "you suggested the house of Ben Isaje the banker and it seemed an excellent plan. I did not think of distance then, and it is only since we arrived at Ryswyk that I realized how near all these places are to one another, and how easy it would be for Gilda to betray us even now."

Beresteyn was silent after that. It was easy to see that his friend's restless anxiety was eating into his own soul. Stoutenburg watched him with those hollow glowing eyes of his that seemed to send a magnetic current of strong will-power into the weaker vessel.

"Well! perhaps you are right," said Beresteyn at last, "perhaps you are right. After all," he added half to himself, "perhaps I shall feel easier in my conscience when I have Gilda near me and feel that I can at least watch over her."

Stoutenburg, having gained his point, jumped to his feet and drew a deep breath of satisfaction.

"That's bravely said," he exclaimed. "Will you go yourself at once to Rotterdam? with two or three of our most trusted men you could bring Gilda here with absolute safety; you only need to make a slight détour when you near Delft so as to avoid the city. You could be here by six o'clock this evening at the latest, and Jan in the meanwhile with a contingent of our stalwarts shall try and find that abominable plepshurk again and bring him here too without delay."

"No, no," said Beresteyn quickly, "I'll not go myself. I could not bear to meet Gilda just yet. I will not have her think that I had a hand in her abduction and my presence might arouse her suspicions."

Stoutenburg laughed unconcernedly.

"You would rather that she thought I had instigated the deed. Well!" he added with a careless shrug, "my shoulders are broad enough to bear the brunt of her wrath if she does. An you will not go yourself we will give full instructions to Jan. He shall bring Gilda and her woman hither with due respect and despatch, and lay the knave by the heels at the same time. Ten or a dozen of our men or even more can easily be spared to-day, there is really nothing for them to do, and they are best out of mischief by being kept busy. Now while I go to give Jan his instructions do you write a letter to Ben Isaje, telling him that it is your wish that Gilda should accompany the bearer of your sign-manual."

"But...."

"Tush, man!" exclaimed Stoutenburg impatiently, while a tone of contempt rang through his harsh voice, "you can so word the letter that even if it were found it need not compromise you in any way. You might just have discovered that your sister was in the hands of brigands, and be sending an escort to rescue her; Gilda will be grateful to you then and ready to believe in you. Write what you like, but for God's sake write quickly. Every moment's delay drives me well-nigh distraught."

With jerky, feverish movements he pushed paper and inkhorn nearer to Beresteyn, who hesitated no longer and at once began to write. Stoutenburg went to the door and loudly called for Jan.

Ten minutes later the letter was written, folded and delivered into Jan's keeping, who was standing at attention and recapitulating the orders which had been given him.

"I take a dozen men with me," he said slowly, "and we follow the course of the Schie as far as Rotterdam. Fortunately it is passable practically the whole of the way."

Stoutenburg nodded in approval.

"I present this letter to Mynheer Ben Isaje, the banker," continued Jan, "and ask him at once to apprise the jongejuffrouw that she deign to accompany us."

"Yes. That is right," quoth Stoutenburg, "but remember that I want you above all things to find that foreigner again. You said that he was sleeping last night in Mynheer Ben Isaje's house."

"So I understood, my lord."

"Well! you must move heaven and earth to find him, Jan. I want him here — a prisoner — remember! Do not let him slip through your fingers this time. It might mean life or death to us all. By fair means or foul you must lay him by the heels."

"It should not be difficult, my lord," assented Jan quietly. "I will pick my men, and I have no doubt that we shall come across the foreigner somewhere in the neighbourhood. He cannot have gone far, and even if he left the city we will easily come on his track."

"That's brave, Jan. Then come straight back here; two or three of your men can in the meanwhile escort the jongejuffrouw, who will travel by sledge. You must avoid Delft of course, and make a détour there."

"I had best get horses at Rotterdam, my lord; the sledge can follow the left bank of the Schie all the way, which will be the best means of avoiding Delft."

"And remember," concluded Stoutenburg in his most peremptory manner, "that you must all be back here before ten o'clock to-night. The jongejuffrouw first and you with the foreigner later. It is not much more than eight o'clock now; you have the whole day before you. Let the sledge pull up outside the miller's hut, everything will be ready there by then for the jongejuffrouw's reception; and let your watchwords be 'Silence, discretion, speed!' — you understand?"

"I understand, my lord," replied Jan simply as he gave a military salute, then quietly turned on his heel and went out of the room.

The two friends were once more alone, straining their ears to catch every sound which came to them now from below. Muffled and enveloped in the mist, the voice of Jan giving brief words of command could be distinctly heard, also the metallic click of skates and the tramping of heavily-booted feet upon the ground. But ten minutes later all these sounds had died away. Jan and his men had gone to fetch Gilda — the poor little pawn moved hither and thither by the ruthless and ambitious hands of men.

Beresteyn had buried his head in his hands, in a sudden fit of overpowering remorse. Stoutenburg looked on him silently for awhile, his haggard face appeared drawn and sunken in the pale grey light which found its way through the tiny window up above. Passion greater than that which broke down the spirit of his friend, was tearing at his heart-strings; ambition fought with love, and remorse with determination. But through it all the image of Gilda flitted before his burning eyes across this dimly-lighted room, reproachful and sweet and tantalizingly beautiful. The desire to have her near him in the greatest hour of his life on the morrow, had been the true mainspring which had prompted him to urge Beresteyn to send for her. It seemed to him that Gilda's presence would bring him luck in his dark undertaking so heavily fraught with crime, and with a careless shrug of the shoulders he was ready to dismiss all thoughts of the wrong which he had done her, in favour of his hopes, his desire, his certainty that a glorious future in his arms would compensate her for all that he had caused her to endure.

That same morning of this fourth day of the New Year found Gilda Beresteyn sitting silent and thoughtful in the tiny room which had been placed at her disposal in the house of Mynheer Ben Isaje, the banker.

A few hours ago she had come back to it, running like some frightened animal who had just escaped an awful — but unknown — danger, and had thrown herself down on the narrow bed in the alcove in an agony of soul far more difficult to bear than any sorrow which had assailed her during the last few days.

A great, a vivid ray of hope had pierced the darkness of her misery, it had flickered low at first, then had glowed with wonderful intensity, flickered again and finally died down as hope itself fell dying once more in the arms of despair.

The disappointment which she had endured then amounted almost to physical pain; her heart ached and beat intolerably and with that disappointment was coupled a sense of hatred and of humiliation, different to any suffering she had ever had to bear before.

A man could have helped her and had refused: he could have helped her to avert a crime more hideous than any that had ever blackened the pages of this country's history. With that one man's help she could have stopped that crime from being committed and he had refused ... nay more! he had first dragged her secret from her, word by word, luring her into thoughts of security with the hope that he dangled before her.

He knew everything now: she had practically admitted everything save the identity of those whose crime she wished to avert. But even that identity would be easy for the man to guess. Stoutenburg, of course, had paid him to lay hands on her ... but her brother Nicolaes was Stoutenburg's friend and ally, and his life and that of his friends were now in the hands of that rogue, who might betray them with the knowledge which he had filched from her.

No wonder that hour after hour she lay prostrate on the bed, while these dark thoughts hammered away in her brain. The Prince of Orange walking unknowingly straight to his death, or Nicolaes — her brother — and his friends betrayed to the vengeance of that Prince. Ghosts of those who had already died — victims to that same merciless vengeance — flitted in the darkness before her feverish fancy: John of Barneveld, the Lord of Grœneveld, the sorrowing widows and fatherless children ... and in their trail the ghost of the great Stadtholder, William the Silent murdered — as his son would be — at Delft, close to Ryswyk and the molens, where even now Nicolaes her brother was learning the final lesson of infamy.

When in the late morning Maria came into the room to bring her mistress some warm milk and bread, and to minister to her comforts, she found her dearly loved jongejuffrouw wide-eyed and feverish.

But not a word could she get out of Gilda while she dressed her hair, except an assurance that their troubles — as far as Maria could gauge them — would soon be over now, and that in twenty-four hours mayhap they would be escorted back to Haarlem.

"When, I trust, that I shall have the joy of seeing three impudent knaves swing on gibbets in the market place," quoth Maria decisively, "and one of them — the most impudent of the lot — drawn and quartered, or burnt at the stake!" she added with savage insistence.

When Gilda was ready dressed, she asked for leave to speak with Mynheer Ben Isaje. The Jew, obsequious and affable, received her with utmost deference, and in a few words put the situation before her. Mevrouw Isaje, he said, was from home: he had not been apprised of the jongejuffrouw's coming, or his wife would have been ready to receive her at his private house, which was situated but half a league out of Rotterdam. But Mevrouw Isaje would return from the visit which she had been paying to her father in the course of the afternoon, until that hour Mynheer Ben Isaje begged that the jongejuffrouw would look upon this miserable hovel as her property and would give what orders she desired for the furtherance of her comfort. In the afternoon, he concluded, an escort would once more be ready to convey the jongejuffrouw to that same private house of his, where there was a nice garden and a fine view over the Schie instead of the confined outlook on squalid houses opposite, which was quite unworthy of the jongejuffrouw's glance.

Gilda did not attempt to stay the flow of Ben Isaje's eloquence: she thanked him graciously for everything that he had already done for her comfort.

Maria — more loquacious, and bubbling over with indignation — asked him when this outrageous confinement of her person and that of her exalted mistress at the hands of brigands would cease, and if Mynheer Ben Isaje was aware that such confinement against the jongejuffrouw's will would inevitably entail the punishment of hanging.

But thereupon Mynheer Ben Isaje merely rubbed his thin hands together and became as evasive first and then as mute as only those of his race can contrive to be.

Then Gilda — making an effort to speak unconcernedly — asked him what had become of the men who had brought her hither from Haarlem.

"They spent half the night eating and drinking at the tavern, mejuffrouw," said the Jew blandly.

"Ah!" rejoined Gilda quietly, "methought one of them had found hospitality under your roof."

"So he had, mejuffrouw. But this morning when I called him — for I had some business to transact with him — I found his room already empty. No doubt he had gone to join his companions at the tavern. But the rascal's movements need not disturb the jongejuffrouw for one moment. After to-day she need never set eyes on him again."

"Save when he is hanging on a gibbet in the Groote Markt," broke in Maria viciously. "I for one never go to see such sights, but when that rascal hangs it shall be a holiday for me to go and get a last look at him."

Later on in the day, Ben Isaje, more affable and obsequious than he had ever been, came to announce to the jongejuffrouw that her sledge was awaiting her at the top of the street.

Silently and resignedly as had been her wont these past two days Gilda Beresteyn, wrapping her cloak and hood closely round her, followed Mynheer Ben Isaje out of the house. Maria walked immediately behind her, muttering imprecations against brigands, and threatening dire punishments against every Jew.

Though it was only three o'clock in the afternoon, it was already quite dark in this narrow street, where tall gables almost touched one another at the top: only from the tiny latticed windows feeble patches of yellow light glimmered weirdly through the fog.

The sledge was waiting at the top of the street, as Mynheer Ben Isaje had said. Gilda shuddered as soon as she caught sight of it again; it represented so much that was vivid and tangible of her present anxiety and sorrow. It stood upon an open market-place, with the driver sitting up at his post and three horses harnessed thereto. The small tavern was at the corner on the left, and as Gilda walked rapidly up to the sledge, she saw two of the men who had been escorting her hitherto, the thin man with the abnormally long legs, and the fat one with the red nose and round eyes: but of the third tall, splendid figure she did not catch one glimpse.

The two men nudged one another as she passed, and whispered excitedly to one another, but she could not hear what they said, and the next moment she found herself being handed into the vehicle by Ben Isaje, who thereupon took humble leave of her.

"You are not coming with us, mynheer?" she asked in astonishment.

"Not … not just yet, mejuffrouw," murmured the Jew somewhat incoherently, "it is too early yet in the afternoon … er … for me to … to leave my business…. I have the honour to bid the jongejuffrouw 'Godspeed.'"

"But," said Gilda, who suddenly misliked Ben Isaje's manner, yet could not have told you why, "the mevrouw — your wife — she is ready to receive me?"

"Of a truth — certainly," replied the man. Gilda would have given much to question him further. She was quite sure that there was something strange in his manner, something that she mistrusted; but just as she was about to speak again, there was a sudden command of "Forward!"

the driver cracked his whip, the harness jingled, the sledge gave a big lurch forward and the next moment Gilda found herself once more being rushed at great speed through the cold night air.

She could not see much round her, for the fog out in the open seemed even more dense than it was inside the city and the darkness of the night crept swiftly through the fog. All that she knew for certain was that the city was very soon left behind, that the driver was urging his horses on to unusual speed, and that she must be travelling along a river bank, because when the harness rattled and jingled less loudly than usual, she could hear distinctly the clink of metal skates upon the ice, as wayfarers no doubt were passing to and fro.

Solitary as she was — for Maria and her eternal grumblings were poor company — she fell to thinking again over the future, as she had done not only last night but through the past few interminable days; it almost seemed as if she had never, never thought of anything else, as if those same few days stretched out far away behind her into dim and nebulous infinity.

During those days she had alternately hoped and feared and been disappointed only to hope again: but the disappointment of last night was undoubtedly the most bitter that she had yet experienced. So bitter had it been that for a time — after its intense poignancy had gone — her faculties and power of thinking had become numbed, and now — very gradually, unknown at first even to herself, hope shook itself free from the grip of disappointment and peeped up at her out of the abyss of her despair.

Did that unscrupulous knave really have the last word in the matter? had his caprice the power to order the destiny of this land and the welfare of its faith?

Bah! the very thought was monstrous and impossible. Was the life of the Prince of Orange to be sacrificed because a rascal would not help her to give him that word of warning which might save him even now at the eleventh hour?

No! Gilda Beresteyn refused to believe that God — who had helped the armies of the Netherlands throughout their struggle against the might of Spain — would allow a rogue to have so much power. After all, she was not going to be shut up in prison! she was going to the house of ordinary, respectable burghers; true, they were of alien and of despised faith, but they were well-to-do, had a family, serving women and men.

Surely among these there would be one who — amenable to cajoleries or to promises — would prove to be the instrument sent by God to save the Stadtholder from an assassin's dagger!

Gilda Beresteyn, wrapped in this new train of thought, lost count of time, of distance and of cold: she lived during one whole hour in the happiness of this newly-risen hope, making plans, conjecturing, rehearsing over in her mind what she would say, how she would probe the loyalty, the kindness of those who would be around her to-night.

Delft was so near! and after all even Maria might be bribed to forget her fears and her grievances and to become that priceless instrument of salvation of which Gilda dreamed as the sledge flew swiftly along through the night.

It was Maria who roused her suddenly out of these happy fancies. Maria who said plaintively:

"Shall we never get to that verdommte house. The Jew said that it was only situate half a league from Rotterdam."

"We must be close to it," murmured Gilda.

"Close to it!" retorted Maria, "we seem to be burning the ground under the horses' hoofs — we have left Rotterdam behind us this hour past....It is the longest half league that I have ever known."

"Peep out under the hood, Maria. Cannot you see where we are?"

Maria peeped out as she was bid.

"I can see the lights of a city far away on our right," she said. "From the direction in which we have been going and the ground which we have covered I should guess that city to be Delft."

"Delft!" exclaimed Gilda, smothering a louder scream.

The driver had just pulled up his horses, allowing them to go at a walk so as to restore their wind and ease them for awhile. Gilda tried her best to peer through the darkness. All that she could see were those lights far away on the right which proclaimed the distant city.

A chill struck suddenly to her heart. Ben Isaje had lied! Why? She was not being taken to his house which was situate half a league outside Rotterdam ... then whither was she being taken? What new misery, what new outrage awaited her now?

The lights of the distant city receded further and further away from her view, the driver once more put his horses at a trot, the sledge moved along more smoothly now: it seemed as if it were going over the surface of the river. Delft was being left behind, and the sledge was following the course of the Schie ... on toward Ryswyk....

The minutes sped on, another quarter of an hour, another half hour, another hour in this dread suspense. The driver was urging his horses unmercifully: he gave them but little rest. It was only when for a few brief moments he put them at walking pace, that Gilda heard — all around her as it seemed — that metallic click of skates which told her that the sledge was surrounded by men who were there to watch over her and see that she did not escape.

CHAPTER XXXIII
THE CAPTIVE LION

Beresteyn was sitting at the table in the weighing-room of the molens: his elbows rested on the table, and his right hand supported his head; in the feeble light of the lanthorn placed quite close to him, his face looked sullen and dark, and his eyes, overshadowed by his frowning brows, were fixed with restless eagerness upon the narrow door.

Stoutenburg, with hands crossed over his chest, with head bare and collar impatiently torn away from round his neck, was pacing up and down the long, low room like a caged beast of prey.

"Enter!" he shouted impatiently in response to a loud knock on the door. Then as Jan entered, and having saluted, remained standing by the door, he paused in his feverish walk, and asked in a curiously hoarse voice, choked with anxiety:

"Is everything all right, Jan?"

"Everything, my lord."

"The jongejuffrouw?..."

"In the hut, my lord. There is a good fire there and the woman is preparing some hot supper for the lady."

"How does she seem?"

"She stepped very quietly out of the sledge, my lord, the moment I told her that we had arrived. She asked no questions, and walked straight into the hut. Meseemed that the jongejuffrouw knew exactly where she was."

"The woman will look after her comforts well?"

"Oh, yes, my lord, though she is only a rough peasant, she will try and do her best, and the jongejuffrouw has her own waiting woman with her as well."

"And the horses?"

"In the shed behind the hut."

"Look after them well, Jan: we may want to use them again to-morrow."

"They shall be well looked after, my lord."

"And you have placed the sentry outside the hut?"

"Two men in the front and two in the rear, as you have commanded, my lord."

Stoutenburg drew a deep breath of satisfaction: but anxiety seemed to have exhausted him, for now that his questions had been clearly answered, he sank into a chair.

"All well, Nicolaes," he said more calmly as he placed a re-assuring hand upon his friend's shoulder.

But Nicolaes groaned aloud.

"Would to God," he said, "that all were well!"

Smothering an impatient retort Stoutenburg once more turned to Jan.

"And what news of the foreigner?" he queried eagerly.

"We have got him, my lord," replied Jan.

"By G — d!" exclaimed Stoutenburg, "how did you do it?"

His excitement was at fever pitch now. He was leaning forward, and his attitude was one of burning expectancy. His hollow eyes were fixed upon Jan's lips as if they would extract from them the glad news which they held. Whatever weakness there was in Stoutenburg's nature, one thing in him was strong — and that was hatred. He could hate with an intensity of passion worthy of a fine cause. He hated the Stadtholder first, and secondly the nameless adventurer who had humiliated him and forced him to lick the dust: wounded in his vanity and in his arrogance he was consumed with an inordinate desire for revenge. The hope that this revenge was now at last in sight — that the man whom he hated so desperately was now in his power — almost caused the light of mania to dance in his glowing eyes.

"How did you do it, Jan?" he reiterated hoarsely.

"It was not far from the molens," said Jan simply, "until then he gave us the slip, though we spied him just outside Delft on our way to Rotterdam this morning. My impression is that he went back to Rotterdam then, and that he followed the jongejuffrouw's sledge practically all the way. Close to the molens he was forced to draw a little nearer as it was getting very dark and probably he did not know his way about. I am convinced that he wished to ascertain exactly whither we were taking the jongejuffrouw. At any rate, I and some of our fellows who had lagged in the rear caught sight of him then...."

"And you seized him?" cried Stoutenburg with exultant joy.

"He was alone, my lord," replied Jan with a placid smile, "and there were seven of us at the time. Two or three of the men, though, are even now nursing unpleasant wounds. I myself fared rather badly with a bruised head and half-broken collar-bone.... The man is a demon for fighting, but there were seven of us."

"Well done, Jan!" cried Beresteyn now, for Stoutenburg had become speechless with the delight of this glorious news; "and what did you do with the rogue?"

"We tied him securely with ropes and dragged him along with us. Oh! we made certain of him, my lord, you may be sure of that. And now I and another man have taken him down into the basement below and we have fastened him to one of the beams, where I imagine the north-west wind will soon cool his temper."

"Aye, that it will!" quoth Stoutenburg lustily. "Take the lanthorn, Jan, and let us to him at once. Beresteyn, friend, will you come too? Your hand like mine must be itching to get at the villain's face."

The two men took good care to wrap their cloaks well round their shoulders and to pull their fur caps closely round their ears. Thus muffled up against the bitterness of the night, they went out of the molens, followed by Jan, who carried the lanthorn.

Outside the door, steep, ladder-like steps led to the ground. The place referred to by Jan as "the basement" was in reality the skeleton foundations on which the molens rested. These were made up of huge beams — green and slimy with age, and driven deep down into the muddy flat below. Ten feet up above, the floor of the molens sat towering aloft. Darkness like pitch reigned on this spot, but as Jan swung his lanthorn along, the solid beams detached themselves one by one out of the gloom, their ice-covered surface reflected the yellow artificial light, and huge icicles of weird and fantastic shapes like giant arms and fingers stretched out hung down from the transverse bars and from the wooden framework of the molens above.

To one of the upright beams a man was securely fastened with ropes wound round about his body. His powerful muscles were straining against the cords which tied his arms behind his back. A compassionate hand had put his broad-brimmed hat upon his head, to protect his ears and nose against the frost, but his mighty chest was bare, for doublet and shirt had been torn in the reckless fight which preceded final capture.

Jan held up the lanthorn and pointed out to my lord the prisoner whom he was so proud to have captured. The light fell upon the pinioned figure, splendid in its air of rebellious helplessness. Here was a man, momentarily conquered it is true, but obviously not vanquished, and though the ropes now cut into his body, though the biting wind lashed his bare chest, and dark stains showed upon his shirt, the spirit within was as free and untrammelled as ever — the spirit of independence and of adventure which is willing to accept the knockdown blows of fate as readily and cheerfully as her favours.

Despite the torn shirt and the ragged doublet there was yet an air of swagger about the whole person of the man, swagger that became almost insolent as the Lord of Stoutenburg approached. He threw back his head and looked his sworn enemy straight in the face, his eyes were laughing still, and a smile of cool irony played round his lips.

"Well done, Jan!" quoth Stoutenburg with a deep sigh of satisfaction.

He was standing with arms akimbo and legs wide apart, enjoying to the full the intense delight of gazing for awhile in silence on his discomfited enemy.

"Ah! but it is good," he said at last, "to look upon a helpless rogue."

"'Tis a sight then," retorted the prisoner lightly, "which your Magnificence hath often provided for your friends and your adherents."

"Bah!" rejoined Stoutenburg, who was determined to curb his temper if he could, "your insolence now, my man, hath not the power to anger me. It strikes me as ludicrous — even pathetic in its senselessness. An I were in your unpleasant position, I would try by submission to earn a slight measure of leniency from my betters."

"No doubt you would, my lord," quoth Diogenes dryly, "but you see I have up to now not yet come across my betters. When I do, I may take your advice."

"Verdommte Keerl! What say you, Beresteyn," added Stoutenburg turning to his friend, "shall we leave him here to-night to cool his impudence, we can always hang him to-morrow."

Beresteyn made no immediate reply, his face was pale and haggard, and his glance — shifty and furtive — seemed to avoid that of the prisoner.

"You must see that the fellow is well guarded, Jan," resumed Stoutenburg curtly, "give him some food, but on no account allow him the slightest freedom."

"My letters to Ben Isaje," murmured Beresteyn, as Stoutenburg already turned to go. "Hath he perchance got them by him still?"

"The letters! yes! I have forgotten!" said the other. "Search him, Jan!" he commanded.

Jan put down the lanthorn and then proceeded to lay rough hands upon the captive philosopher; he had a heavy score to pay off against him — an aching collar-bone and a bruised head, and the weight of a powerful fist to avenge. He was not like to be gentle in his task. He tore at the prisoner's doublet and in his search for a hidden pocket he disclosed an ugly wound which had lacerated the shoulder.

"Some of us took off our skates," he remarked casually, "and brought him down with them. The blades were full sharp, and we swung them by their straps; they made excellent weapons thus; the fellow should have more than one wound about him."

"Three, my good Jan, to be quite accurate," said Diogenes calmly, "but all endurable. I had ten about me outside Prague once, but the fellows there were fighting better than you, and in a worthier cause."

Jan's rough hands continued their exhaustive search; a quickly smothered groan from the prisoner caused Stoutenburg to laugh.

"That sound," he said, "was music to mine ear."

Jan now drew a small leather wallet and a parchment roll both from the wide flap of the prisoner's boot. Stoutenburg pounced upon the wallet, and Beresteyn with eager anxiety tore the parchment out of Jan's hand.

"It is the formal order to Ben Isaje," he said, "to pay over the money to this knave. Is there anything else, Jan?" he continued excitedly, "a thinner paper? — shaped like a letter?"

"Nothing else, mynheer," replied Jan.

"Did you then deliver my letter to Ben Isaje, fellow?" queried Beresteyn of the prisoner.

"My friend Jan should be able to tell you that," he replied, "hath he not been searching the very folds of my skin."

In the meanwhile Stoutenburg had been examining the contents of the wallet.

"Jewellery belonging to the jongejuffrouw," he said dryly, "which this rogue hath stolen from her. Will you take charge of them, Nicolaes? And here," he added, counting out a few pieces of gold and silver, "is some of your own money."

He made as if he would return this to Beresteyn, then a new idea seemed to strike him, for he put all the money back into the wallet and said to Jan:

"Put this wallet back where you found it, Jan, and, Nicolaes," he added turning back to his friend, "will you allow me to look at that bond?"

While Jan obeyed and replaced the wallet in the flap of the prisoner's boot, Beresteyn handed the parchment to Stoutenburg. The latter then ordered Jan to hold up the lanthorn so that by its light he might read the writing.

This he did, twice over, with utmost attention; after which he tore off very carefully a narrow strip from the top of the document.

"Now," he said quietly, "this paper, wherever found, cannot compromise you in any way, Nicolaes. The name of Ben Isaje who alone could trace the cypher signature back to you, we will scatter to the winds."

And he tore the narrow strip which he had severed from the document into infinitesimal fragments, which he then allowed the wind to snatch out of his hand and to whirl about and away into space. But the document itself he folded up with ostentatious care.

"What do you want with that?" asked Beresteyn anxiously.

"I don't know yet, but it might be very useful," replied the other. "So many things may occur within the next few days that such an ambiguously worded document might prove of the utmost value."

"But …the signature …" urged Beresteyn, "my father…."

"The signature, you told me, friend, is one that you use in the ordinary way of business whilst the wording of the document in itself cannot compromise you in any way; it is merely a promise to pay for services rendered. Leave this document in my keeping; believe me, it is quite safe with me and might yet be of incalculable value to us. One never knows."

"No! one never does know," broke in the prisoner airily, "for of a truth when there's murder to be done, pillage or outrage, the Lord of Stoutenburg never knows what other infamy may come to his hand."

"Insolent knave!" exclaimed Stoutenburg hoarsely, as with a cry of unbridled fury he suddenly raised his arm and with the parchment roll which he held, he struck the prisoner savagely in the face.

"Take care, Stoutenburg," ejaculated Beresteyn almost involuntarily.

"Take care of what," retorted the other with a harsh laugh, "the fellow is helpless, thank God! and I would gladly break my riding whip across his impudent face."

He was livid and shaking with fury. Beresteyn — honestly fearing that in his blind rage he would compromise his dignity before his subordinates — dragged him by the arm away from the presence of this man whom he appeared to hate with such passionate intensity.

Stoutenburg, obdurate at first, almost drunk with his own fury, tried to free himself from his friend's grasp. He wanted to lash the man he hated once more in the face, to gloat for awhile longer on the sight of his enemy now completely in his power. But all around in the gloom he perceived figures that moved; the soldiers and mercenaries placed at his disposal by his friends were here in numbers: some of them had been put on guard over the prisoner by Jan, and others had joined them, attracted by loud voices.

Stoutenburg had just enough presence of mind left in him to realize that the brutal striking of a defenceless prisoner would probably horrify these men, who were fighters and not bullies, and might even cause them to turn from their allegiance to him.

So with desperate effort he pulled himself together and contrived to give with outward calm some final orders to Jan.

"See that the ropes are securely fastened, Jan," he said, "leave half a dozen men on guard, then follow me."

But to Beresteyn, who had at last succeeded in dragging him away from this spot, he said loudly:

"You do not know, Nicolaes, what a joy it is to me to be even with that fellow at last."

A prolonged laugh, that had a note of triumph in it, gave answer to this taunt, whilst a clear voice shouted lustily:

"Nay! we never can be quite even, my lord; since you were not trussed like a capon when I forced you to lick the dust."

Half-an-hour later, the Lord of Stoutenburg was in Gilda's presence. He was glad enough that Nicolaes Beresteyn — afraid to meet his sister — had refused to accompany him. He, too, felt nervous and anxious at thought of meeting her face to face at last. He had not spoken to her since that day in March when he was a miserable fugitive — in a far worse plight than was the wounded man tied with cords to a beam. He had been a hunted creature then, every man's hand raised against him, his life at the mercy of any passer-by, and she had given him shelter freely and fearlessly — shelter and kind words — and her ministrations had brought him luck, for he succeeded in reaching the coast after he parted from her, and finding shelter once more in a foreign land.

Since then her image had filled his dreams by night and his thoughts by day. His earlier love for her, smothered by ambition, rose up at once more strong, more insistent than before; it became during all these months of renewed intrigues and plots the one ennobling trait in his tortuous character. His love for Gilda was in itself not a selfish feeling; neither ambition nor the mere gratification of obstinate desire entered in its composition. He loved Gilda for herself alone, with all the adoration which a pious man would have given to his God, and while one moment of his life was occupied in planning a ruthless and dastardly murder, the other was filled with hopes of a happier future, with Gilda beside him as his idolized wife. But though his love was in itself pure and selfless, he remained true to his unscrupulous nature in the means which he adopted in order to win the object of his love.

Even now, when he entered her presence in the miserable peasant's hut where he chose to hold her a prisoner, he felt no remorse at the recollection of what she must have suffered in the past few days; his one thought was — now that he had her completely under his control — how he could best plead his cause first, or succeed in coercing her will if she proved unkind.

She received him quite calmly, and even with a gracious nod of the head, and he thought that he had never seen her look more beautiful than she did now, in her straight white gown, with that sweet, sad face of hers framed by a wealth of golden curls. In this squalid setting of white-washed walls and rafters blackened with age, she looked indeed — he thought — like one of those fairy princesses held prisoner by a wicked ogre — of whom he used to read long ago when he was a child, before sin and treachery and that insatiable longing for revenge had wholly darkened his soul.

With bare head and back bent nearly double in the depth of his homage he approached his divinity.

"It is gracious of you, mejuffrouw, to receive me," he said forcing his harsh voice to tones of gentleness.

"I had not the power to refuse, my lord," she replied quietly, "seeing that I am in your hands and entirely at your commands."

"I entreat you do not say that," he rejoined eagerly, "there is no one here who has the right to command save yourself. 'Tis I am in your hands and your most humble slave."

"A truce to this farce, my lord," she retorted impatiently. "I were not here if you happened to be my slave, and took commands from me."

"'Tis true mayhap that you would not be here, now, mejuffrouw," he said blandly, "but I could only act for the best, and as speedily as I could. The moment I heard that you were in the hands of brigands I moved heaven and earth to find out where you were. I only heard this morning that you were in Rotterdam...."

"You heard that I was in the hands of brigands," she murmured, almost gasping with astonishment, "you heard this morning that I was in Rotterdam...?"

"I sent spies and messengers in every direction the moment I heard of the abominable outrage against your person," he continued with well-feigned vehemence. "I cannot even begin to tell you what I endured these past three days, until at last, by dint of ruse and force, I was able to circumvent the villains who held you captive, and convey you hither in safety and profound respect until such time as I can find a suitable escort to take you back to your father."

"If what you say is true, my lord, you could lend me an escort at once, that I might return to my dear father forthwith. Truly he must have broken his heart by now, weeping for me."

"Have I not said that I am your slave?" he rejoined gently, "an you desire to return to Haarlem immediately, I will see about an escort for you as quickly as may be. The hour is late now," he added hypocritically, "but a man can do much when his heart's desire lies in doing the behests of a woman whom he worships."

Though she frowned at these last words of his, she leaned forward eagerly to him.

"You will let me go ... at once ... to-night?"

"At once if it lies in my power," he replied unblushingly, "but I fear me that you will have to wait a few hours; the night is as dark as pitch. It were impossible to make a start in it. To-morrow, however...."

"To-morrow?" she cried anxiously, "'Tis to-night that I wish to go."

"The way to Haarlem is long ..." he murmured.

"'Tis not to Haarlem, my lord, but to Delft that I long to go."

"To Delft?" he exclaimed with a perfect show of astonishment.

She bit her lip and for the moment remained silent. It had, indeed, been worse than folly to imagine that he — of all men in the world — would help her to go to Delft. But he had been so gentle, so kind, apparently so ready to do all that she asked, that for the moment she forgot that he and he alone was the mover of that hideous conspiracy to murder which she still prayed to God that she might avert.

"I had forgotten, my lord," she said, as tears threatened to choke her voice, "I had forgotten."

"Forgotten? What?" he asked blankly.

"That you are not like to escort me to Delft."

"Why not to Delft, an you wish to go there?"

"But ..." she murmured, "the Stadtholder...."

"Ah!" he exclaimed, "now I understand. You are thinking of what you overheard in the cathedral of Haarlem."

"Indeed, how could I forget it?"

"Easily now, Gilda," he replied with solemn earnestness. "The plans which my friends and I formed on that night have been abandoned."

"Abandoned?"

"Yes! Your brother was greatly impressed by all that you said to him. He persuaded us all to think more lengthily over the matter. Then came the news of the outrage upon your person, and all thoughts of my ambition and of my revenge faded before this calamity, and I have devoted every hour of mine existence since then to find you and to restore you to your home."

Bewildered, wide-eyed, Gilda listened to him. In all her life hitherto, she had never come into contact with lying and with deceit: she had never seen a man lying unblushingly, calmly, not showing signs of confusion or of fear. Therefore, the thought that this man could be talking so calmly, so simply, so logically, and yet be trying to deceive her, never for one moment entered her head. The events of the past few days crowded in upon her brain in such a maddening array, that, as she sat here now, face to face with the man whom she had been so ready to suspect, she could not disentangle from those events one single fact that could justify her suspicions.

Even looking back upon the conversation which she had had with that impudent rogue in Leyden and again last night, she distinctly remembered now that he had never really said a single thing that implicated the Lord of Stoutenburg or anyone else in this villainy.

She certainly was bewildered and very puzzled now: joy at the thought that after all the Stadtholder was safe, joy that her brother's hand would not be stained with murder, or his honour with treachery, mingled with a vague sense of mistrust which she was powerless to combat, yet felt ashamed to admit.

"Then, my lord," she murmured at last, "do you really tell me that the outrage of which I have been the victim was merely planned by villains, for mercenary motives?"

"What else could have prompted it?" he asked blandly.

"Neither you ... nor ... nor any of your friends had a hand in it?" she insisted.

"I?" he exclaimed with a look of profound horror. "I?... to do you such a wrong! For what purpose, ye gods?"

"To ... to keep me out of the way...."

"I understand," he said simply. "And you, Gilda, believed this of me?"

"I believed it," she replied calmly.

"You did not realize then that I would give every drop of my blood to save you one instant's pain?"

"I did not realize," she said more coldly, "that you would give up your ambition for any woman or for anything."

"You do not believe then, that I love you?"

"Speak not of love, my lord," she retorted, "it is a sacred thing. And you methinks do not know what love is."

"Indeed you are right, Gilda," he said, "I do not know what is the love of ordinary men. But if to love you, Gilda, means that every thought, every hope, every prayer is centred upon you, if it means that neither sleep nor work, nor danger can for one single instant chase your image from my soul, if to love you means that my very sinews ache with the longing to hold you in my arms, and that every moment which keeps me from your side is torture worse than hell; if love means all that, Gilda, then do I know to mine own hurt what love is."

"And in your ambition, my lord, you allowed that love to be smothered," she retorted calmly. "It is too late now to speak of it again, to any woman save to Walburg de Marnix."

"I'll speak of it to you, Gilda, while the breath in my body lasts. Walburg de Marnix is no longer my wife. The law of our country has already set me free."

"The law of God binds you to her. I pray you speak no more of such things to me."

"You are hard and cruel, Gilda."

"I no longer love you."

"You will love again," he retorted confidently, "in the meanwhile have I regained your trust?"

"Not even that, wholly," she replied.

"Let me at least do one thing in my own justification," he pleaded. "Allow me to prove to you now and at once that — great though my love is for you, and maddening my desire to have you near me — I could not be guilty of such an outrage, as I know that in your heart you do accuse me of."

"I did accuse you of it, my lord, I own. But how can you prove me wrong now and at once?"

"By bringing before you the only guilty person in this network of infamy," he replied hotly.

"You know him then?"

"For these three days now I and my faithful servants have tracked him. I have him here now a prisoner at last. His presence before you will prove to you that I at least bore no share in the hideous transaction."

"Of whom do you speak, my lord?" she asked.

"Of the man who dared to lay hands upon you in Haarlem...."

"He is here — now?" she exclaimed.

"A helpless prisoner in my hands," he replied, "to-morrow summary justice shall be meted out to him, and he will receive the punishment which his infamy deserves."

"But he did not act on his own initiative," she said eagerly, "another man more powerful, richer than he prompted him — paid him — tempted him...."

Stoutenburg made a gesture of infinite contempt.

"So, no doubt, he has told you, Gilda. Men of his stamp are always cowards at heart, even though they have a certain brutish instinct for fighting — mostly in self-defence. He tried to palliate his guilt before you by involving me in its responsibility."

"You," she whispered under her breath, "or one of your friends."

"You mean your brother Nicolaes," he rejoined quietly. "Ah! the man is even a more arrant knave than I thought. So! he has tried to fasten the responsibility for this outrage against your person, firstly on me who worship the very ground you walk on, secondly on the brother whom you love?"

"No, no," she protested eagerly, "I did not say that. It was I who...."

"Who thought so ill of me," broke in Stoutenburg with gentle reproach, "of me and of Nicolaes. You questioned the rogue, and he did not deny it, nay more he enlarged upon the idea, which would place all the profits of this abominable transaction in his hands and yet exonerate him from guilt. But you shall question him yourself, Gilda. By his looks, by his answers, by his attitude you will be able to judge if I or Nicolaes — or any of our friends, have paid him to lay hands upon you. Remember however," he added significantly, "that such a low-born knave will always lie to save his skin, so this do I entreat of you on my knees: judge by his looks more than by his words, and demand a proof of what he asserts."

"I will judge, my lord, as I think best," she retorted coldly. "And now, I pray you, send for the man. I would like to hear what he has to say."

Stoutenburg immediately turned to obey: there was a guard outside the door, and it was easy to send one of the men with orders to Jan to bring the prisoner hither.

Within himself he was frankly taken aback at Gilda's ready acquiescence — nay obvious desire to parley with the foreigner. A sharp pang of jealousy had shot through his heart when he saw her glowing eyes, her eagerness to defend the knave. The instinct that guided his fierce love for Gilda, had quickly warned him that here was a danger of which he had never even dreamed.

Women were easily swayed, he thought, by a smooth tongue and a grand manner, both of which — Stoutenburg was bound to admit — the rogue possessed in no scanty measure. Fortunately the mischief — if indeed mischief there was — had only just begun: and of a truth reason itself argued that Gilda must loathe and despise the villain who had wronged her so deeply: moreover Stoutenburg had every hope that the coming interview if carefully conducted would open Gilda's eyes more fully still to the true character of the foreign mercenary with the unctuous tongue and the chivalrous ways.

In any case the Lord of Stoutenburg himself had nothing to fear from that interview, and he felt that his own clever words had already shaken the foundations of Gilda's mistrust of him. Mayhap in desiring to parley with the knave, she only wished to set her mind at rest finally on these matters, and also with regard to her own brother's guilt. Stoutenburg with an inward grim smile of coming triumph passed his hand over his doublet where — in an inner pocket — reposed the parchment roll which was the last proof of Beresteyn's connivance.

Gilda did not know the cypher-signature, and the knave would have some difficulty in proving his assertion, if indeed, he dared to name Nicolaes at all: whilst if he chose to play the chivalrous part before Gilda, then the anonymous document would indeed prove of incalculable value. In any case the complete humiliation of the knave who had succeeded in gaining Gilda's interest, if nothing more, was Stoutenburg's chief aim when he suggested the interview, and the document with the enigmatical signature could easily become a powerful weapon wherewith to make that humiliation more complete.

And thus musing, speculating, scheming, the Lord of Stoutenburg sent Jan over to the molens with orders to bring the prisoner under a strong guard to the jongejuffrouw's presence, whilst Gilda, silent and absorbed, sat on in the tiny room of the miller's hut.

In spite of her loyalty, her love for her brother, in spite of Stoutenburg's smooth assertions, a burning anxiety gnawed at her heart — she felt wretchedly, miserably lonely, with a sense of treachery encompassing her all round.

But there was a strange glow upon her face, which of a truth anxiety could not have brought about; rather must it have been inward anger, which assailed her whenever thoughts of the rogue whom she so hated intruded themselves upon her brain.

No doubt too, the heat of the fire helped to enhance that delicate glow which lent so much additional beauty to her face and such additional brilliance to her eyes.

CHAPTER XXXV
THE WITNESS FOR THE DEFENCE

The Lord of Stoutenburg was the first to enter: behind him came Jan, and finally a group of soldiers above whose heads towered another broad white brow, surmounted by a wealth of unruly brown hair which now clung matted against the moist forehead.

At a word of command from Stoutenburg, Jan and the other soldiers departed, leaving him and the prisoner only before Gilda Beresteyn.

The man had told her on that first night at Leyden that his name was Diogenes — a name highly honoured in the history of philosophy. Well! — philosophy apparently was standing him in good stead, for truly it must be responsible for the happy way in which he seemed to be bearing his present unhappy condition.

They had tied his arms behind his back and put a pinion through them, his clothes were torn, his massive chest was bare, his shirt bore ugly, dark stains upon it, but his face was just the same, that merry laughing face with the twinkling eyes, and the gentle irony that lurked round the lines of the sensitive mouth: at any rate when Gilda — overcome with pity — looked up with sweet compassion on him, she saw that same curious, immutable smile that seemed even now to mock and to challenge.

"This is the man, mejuffrouw," began Stoutenburg after awhile, "who on New Year's day at Haarlem dared to lay hands upon your person. Do you recognize him?"

"I do recognize him," replied Gilda coldly.

"I imagine," continued Stoutenburg, "that he hath tried to palliate his own villainies by telling you that he was merely a paid agent in that abominable outrage."

"I do not think," she retorted still quite coldly, "that this … this … person told me that he was being paid for that ugly deed: though when I did accuse him of it he did not deny it."

"Do you hear, fellow?" asked Stoutenburg, turning sharply to Diogenes, "it is time that all this lying should cease. By your calumnies and evil insinuations you have added to the load of crimes which already have earned for you exemplary punishment; by those same lies you have caused the jongejuffrouw an infinity of pain, over and above the horror which she has endured through your cowardly attack upon her. Therefore I have thought it best to send for you now so that in her exalted presence at least you may desist from further lying and that you may be shamed into acknowledging the truth. Do you hear, fellow?" he reiterated more harshly as Diogenes stood there, seemingly not even hearing what the Lord of Stoutenburg said, for his eyes in which a quaint light of humour danced were fixed upon Gilda's hands that lay clasped upon her lap.

The look in the man's face, the soft pallor on the girl's cheek, exasperated Stoutenburg's jealous temper beyond his power of control.

"Do you hear?" he shouted once more, and with a sudden grip of the hand he pulled the prisoner roughly round by the shoulder. That shoulder had been torn open with a blow dealt by a massive steel blade which had lacerated it to the bone; even a philosopher's endurance was not proof against this sudden rending of an already painful wound. Diogenes' pale face became the colour of lead: the tiny room began dancing an irresponsive saraband before his eyes, he felt himself swaying, for the ground was giving way under him, when a cry, gentle and compassionate, reached his fading senses, and a perfume of exquisite sweetness came to his nostrils, even as his pinioned arms felt just enough support to enable him to steady himself.

"Gilda," broke in Stoutenburg's harsh voice upon this intangible dream, "I entreat you not to demean yourself by ministering to that rogue."

"My poor ministry was for a wounded man, my lord," she retorted curtly.

Then she turned once more to the prisoner.

"You are hurt, sir," she asked as she let her tender blue eyes rest with kind pity upon him.

"Hurt, mejuffrouw?" he replied with a laugh, which despite himself had but little merriment in it. "Ask his Magnificence there, he will tell you that such knaves as I have bones and sinews

as tough as their skins. Of a truth I am not hurt, mejuffrouw ...only overcome with the humour
of this situation. The Lord of Stoutenburg indignant and reproachful at thought that another
man is proficient in the art of lying."

"By heaven," cried Stoutenburg who was white with fury. "Insolent varlet, take...."

He had seized the first object that lay close to his hand, the heavy iron tool used for raking
the fire out of the huge earthenware stove; this he raised above his head; the lust to kill glowed
out of his eyes, which had become bloodshot, whilst a thin red foam gathered at the corners of
his mouth. The next moment the life of a philosopher and weaver of dreams would have been
very abruptly ended, had not a woman's feeble hand held up the crashing blow.

"Hatred, my lord, an you will," said Gilda with perfect sangfroid as she stood between the
man who had so deeply wronged her and the upraised arm of his deadly enemy, "hatred and
fair fight, but not outrage, I pray you."

Stoutenburg, smothering a curse, threw the weapon away from him: it fell with a terrific
crash upon the wooden floor. Gilda, white and trembling now after the agonizing excitement
of the past awful moment, had sunk half-swooning back against a chair. Stoutenburg fell on
one knee and humbly raised her gown to his lips.

"Your pardon, Madonna," he whispered, "the sight of your exquisite hands in contact with
that infamous blackguard made me mad. I was almost ready to cheat the gallows of their prey.
I gratefully thank you in that you saved me from the indignity of staining my hand with a vile
creature's blood."

Quietly and dispassionately Gilda drew her skirts away from him.

"An you have recovered your temper, my lord," she said coldly, "I pray you ask the prisoner
those questions which you desired to put to him. I am satisfied that he is your enemy, and
if he were not bound, pinioned and wounded he would probably not have need of a woman's
hand to protect him."

Stoutenburg rose to his feet. He was angered with himself for allowing his hatred and his
rage to get the better of his prudence, and tried to atone for his exhibition of incontinent rage
by a great show of dignity and of reserve.

"I must ask you again, fellow — and for the last time," he said slowly turning once more to
Diogenes, "if you have realized how infamous have been your insinuations against mine honour,
and that of others whom the jongejuffrouw holds in high regard? Your calumnies have caused
her infinite sorrow more bitter for her to bear than the dastardly crime which you did commit
against her person. Have you realized this, and are you prepared to make amends for your
crime and to mitigate somewhat the grave punishment which you have deserved by speaking
the plain truth before the jongejuffrouw now?"

"And what plain truth doth the jongejuffrouw desire to hear?" asked Diogenes with equal
calm.

Stoutenburg would have replied, but Gilda broke in quietly:

"Your crime against me, sir, I would readily forgive, had I but the assurance that no one in
whom I trusted, no one whom I loved had a hand in instigating it."

The ghost of his merry smile — never very distant — spread over the philosopher's pale face.

"Will you deign to allow me, mejuffrouw," he said, "at any rate to tell you one certain, un-
varnished truth, which mayhap you will not even care to believe, and that is that I would give
my life — the few chances, that is, that I still have of it — to obliterate from your mind the
memory of the past few days."

"That you cannot do, sir," she rejoined, "but you would greatly ease the load of sorrow which
you have helped to lay upon me, if you gave me the assurance which I ask."

The prisoner did not reply immediately, and for one brief moment there was absolute silence
in this tiny room, a silence so tense and so vivid that an eternity of joy and sorrow, of hope
and of fear seemed to pass over the life of these three human creatures here. All three had
eyes and ears only for one another: the world with its grave events, its intrigues and its wars

fell quite away from them: they were the only people existing — each for the other — for this one brief instant that passed by.

The fire crackled in the huge hearth, and slowly the burning wood ashes fell with a soft swishing sound one by one. But outside all was still: not a sound of the busy life around the molens, of conspiracies and call to arms, penetrated the dense veil of fog which lay upon the low-lying land.

At last the prisoner spoke.

"'Tis easily done, mejuffrouw," he said, and all at once his whole face lit up with that light-hearted gaiety, that keen sense of humour which would no doubt follow him to the grave, "that assurance I can easily give you. I was the sole criminal in the hideous outrage which brought so much sorrow upon you. Had I the least hope that God would hear the prayer of so despicable a villain as I am I would beg of Him to grant you oblivion of my deed. As for me," he added and now real laughter was dancing in his eyes: they mocked and challenged and called back the joy of life, "as for me, I am impenitent. I would not forget one minute of the last four days."

"To-morrow then you can take the remembrance with you to the gallows," said Stoutenburg sullenly.

Though a sense of intense relief pervaded him now, since by his assertions Diogenes had completely vindicated him as well as Nicolaes in Gilda's sight, his dark face showed no signs of brightening. That fierce jealousy of this nameless adventurer which had assailed him awhile ago was gnawing at his heart more insistently than before; he could not combat it, even though reason itself argued that jealousy of so mean a knave was unworthy, and that Gilda's compassion was only the same that she would have extended to any dog that had been hurt.

Even now — reason still argued — was it not natural that she should plead for the villain just as any tender-natured woman would plead even for a thief. Women hate the thought of violent death, only an amazon would desire to mete out death to any enemy: Gilda was warm-hearted, impulsive, the ugly word "gallows" grated no doubt unpleasantly on her ear. But even so, and despite the dictates of reason, Stoutenburg's jealousy and hatred were up in arms the moment she turned pleading eyes upon him.

"My lord," she said gently, "I pray you to remember that by this open confession this ... this gentleman has caused me infinite happiness. I cannot tell you what misery my own suspicions have caused me these past two days. They were harder to bear than any humiliation or sorrow which I had to endure."

"This varlet's lies confirmed you in your suspicions, Gilda," retorted Stoutenburg roughly, "and his confession — practically at the foot of the gallows — is but a tardy one."

"Do not speak so cruelly, my lord," she pleaded, "you say that ... that you have some regard for me ... let not therefore my prayer fall unheeded on your ear...."

"Your prayer, Gilda?"

"My prayer that you deal nobly with an enemy, whose wrongs to me I am ready to forgive...."

"By St. Bavon, mejuffrouw," here interposed the prisoner firmly, "an mine ears do not deceive me you are even now pleading for my life with the Lord of Stoutenburg."

"Indeed, sir, I do plead for it with my whole heart," she said earnestly.

"Ye gods!" he exclaimed, "and ye do not interfere!"

"My lord!" urged Gilda gently, "for my sake...."

Her words, her look, the tears that despite her will had struggled to her eyes, scattered to the winds Stoutenburg's reasoning powers. He felt now that nothing while this man lived would ever still that newly-risen passion of jealousy. He longed for and desired this man's death more even than that of the Prince of Orange. His honour had been luckily white-washed before Gilda by this very man whom he hated. He had a feeling that within the last half-hour he had made enormous strides in her regard. Already he persuaded himself that she was looking on him more kindly, as if remorse at her unjust suspicions of him had touched her soul on his behalf.

Everything now would depend on how best he could seem noble and generous in her sight; but he was more determined than ever that his enemy should stand disgraced before her first and die on the gallows on the morrow.

Then it was that putting up his hand to the region of his heart, which indeed was beating furiously, it encountered the roll of parchment which lay in the inner pocket of his doublet. Fate, chance, his own foresight, were indeed making the way easy for him, and quicker than lightning his tortuous brain had already formed a plan upon which he promptly acted now.

"Gilda," he said quietly, "though God knows how ready I am to do you service in all things, this is a case where weakness on my part would be almost criminal, for indeed it would be to a hardened and abandoned criminal that I should be extending that mercy for which you plead."

"Indeed, my lord," she retorted coldly, "though only a woman, I too can judge if a man is an abandoned criminal or merely a misguided human creature who doth deserve mercy since his confession was quite open and frank."

"Commonsense did prompt him no doubt to this half-confession," said Stoutenburg dryly, "or a wise instinct to win leniency by his conduct, seeing that he had no proofs wherewith to substantiate his former lies. Am I not right, fellow?" he added once more turning to the prisoner, "though you were forced to own that you alone are responsible for the outrage against the jongejuffrouw, you have not told her yet that you are also a forger and a thief."

Diogenes looked on him for a moment or two in silence, just long enough to force Stoutenburg's shifty eyes to drop with a sudden and involuntary sense of shame, then he rejoined with his usual good-humoured flippancy:

"It was a detail which had quite escaped my memory. No doubt your Magnificence is fully prepared to rectify the omission."

"Indeed I wish that I could have spared you this additional disgrace," retorted Stoutenburg, whose sense of shame had indeed been only momentary, "seeing that anyhow you must hang to-morrow. But," he added once more to the jongejuffrouw, "I could not bear you to think, Gilda, that I could refuse you anything which it is in my power to grant you. Before you plead for this scoundrel again, you ought to know that he has tried by every means in his power — by lying and by forgery — to fasten the origin of all this infamy upon your brother."

"Upon Nicolaes," she cried, "I'll not believe it. A moment ago he did vindicate him freely."

"Only because I had at last taken away from him the proofs which he had forged."

"The proofs? what do you mean, my lord?"

"When my men captured this fellow last night, they found upon him a paper — a bond which is an impudent forgery — purported to have been written by Nicolaes and which promised payment to this knave for laying hands upon you in Haarlem."

"A bond?" she murmured, "signed by Nicolaes?"

"I say it again, 'tis an impudent forgery," declared Stoutenburg hotly, "we — all of us who have seen it and who know Nicolaes' signature could see at a glance that this one was counterfeit. Yet the fellow used it, he obtained money on the strength of it, for beside the jewelry which he had filched from you, we found several hundred guilders upon his person. Liar, forger, thief!" he cried, "in Holland such men are broken on the wheel. Hanging is thought merciful for such damnable scum as they!"

And from out the pocket of his doublet he drew the paper which had been writ by the public scrivener and was signed with Nicolaes' cypher signature: he handed it to Gilda, even whilst the prisoner, throwing back his head, sent one of his heartiest laughs echoing through the raftered room.

"Well played, my lord!" he said gaily, "nay! but by the devils whom you serve so well, you do indeed deserve to win."

In the meanwhile Gilda, wide-eyed and horrified, not knowing what to think, nor yet what to believe, scarcely dared to touch the infamous document whose very presence in her lap seemed a pollution. She noticed that some portion of the paper had been torn off, but the wording of the main portion of the writing was quite clear as was the signature "Schwarzer Kato" with the triangle above it. On this she looked now with a curious mixture of loathing and of fear. Schwarzer Kato was the name of the tulip which her father had raised and named: the triangle was a mark which the house of Beresteyn oft used in business.

"O God, have mercy upon me!" she murmured inwardly, "what does all this treachery mean?"

She looked up from one man to the other. The Lord of Stoutenburg, dark and sullen, was watching her with restless eyes; the prisoner was smiling, gently, almost self-deprecatingly she thought, and as he met her frightened glance it seemed as if in his merry eyes there crept a look of sadness — even of pity.

"What does all this treachery mean?" she murmured again with pathetic helplessness, and this time just above her breath.

"It means," said Stoutenburg roughly, "that at last you must be convinced that this man on whom you have wasted your kindly pity is utterly unworthy of it. That bond was never written by your brother, it was never signed by him. But we found it on this villain's person; he has been trading on it, obtaining money on the strength of his forgery. He has confessed to you that he had no accomplice, no paymaster in his infamies, then ask him whence came this bond in his possession, whence the money which we found upon him. Ask him to deny the fact that less than twenty-four hours after he had laid hands on you, he was back again in Haarlem, bargaining with your poor, stricken father to bring you back to him."

He ceased speaking, almost choked now by his own eloquence, and the rapidity with which the lying words escaped his lips. And Gilda slowly turned her head toward the prisoner, and met that subtly-ironical, good-humoured glance again.

"Is this all true, sir?" she asked.

"What, mejuffrouw?" he retorted.

"That this bond promising you payment for the cruel outrage upon me is a forgery?"

"His Magnificence says so, mejuffrouw," he replied quietly, "surely you know best if you can believe him."

"But this is not my brother's signature?" she asked: and she herself was not aware what an infinity of pleading there was in her voice.

"No!" he replied emphatically, "it is not your brother's signature."

"Then it's a forgery?"

"We will leave it at that, mejuffrouw," he said, "that it is a forgery."

A sigh, hoarse and passionate in its expression of infinite relief, escaped the Lord of Stoutenburg's lips. Though he knew that the man in any case could have no proof if he accused Nicolaes, yet there was great satisfaction in this unqualified confession. Slowly the prisoner turned his head and looked upon his triumphant enemy, and it was the man with the pinioned arms, with the tattered clothes and the stained shirt who seemed to tower in pride, in swagger and in defiance while the other looked just what he was — a craven and miserable cur.

Once more there was silence in the low-raftered room. From Gilda's eyes the tears fell slowly one by one. She could not have told you herself why she was crying at this moment. Her brother's image stood out clearly before her wholly vindicated of treachery, and a scoundrel had been brought to his knees, self-confessed as a liar, a forger and a thief; the Lord of Stoutenburg was proved to have been faithful and true, and yet Gilda felt such a pain in her heart that she thought it must break.

The Lord of Stoutenburg at last broke the silence which had become oppressive.

"Are you satisfied, Gilda?" he asked tenderly.

"I feel happier," she replied softly, "than I have felt these four days past, at thought that my own brother at least — nor you, my lord — had a hand in all this treachery."

She would not look again on the prisoner, even though she felt more than she saw, that a distinctly humorous twinkle had once more crept into his eyes. It seemed however, as if she wished to say something else, something kind and compassionate, but Stoutenburg broke in impatiently:

"May I dismiss the fellow now?" he asked. "Jan is waiting for orders outside."

"Then I pray you call to Jan," she rejoined stiffly.

"The rogue is securely pinioned," he added even as he turned toward the door. "I pray you have no fear of him."

"I have no fear," she said simply.

Stoutenburg strode out of the room and anon his harsh voice was heard calling to Jan.

For a moment then Gilda was alone — for the third time now — with the man whom she had hated more than she had ever hated a human creature before. She remembered how last night and again at Leyden she had been conscious of an overpowering desire to wound him with hard and bitter words. But now she no longer felt that desire, since Fate had hurt him more cruelly than she had wished to do. He was standing there now before her, in all the glory of his magnificent physique, yet infinitely shamed and disgraced, self-confessed of every mean and horrible crime that has ever degraded manhood.

Yet in spite of this shame he still looked splendid and untamed: though his arms were bound to a pinion behind his back, his broad chest was not sunken, and he held himself very erect with that leonine head of his thrown well back and a smile of defiance, almost of triumph, sat upon every line of his face.

Anon she met his eyes; their glance compelled and held her own. There was nothing but kindly humour within their depths. Humour, ye gods! whence came the humour of the situation! Here was a man condemned to death by an implacable enemy who was not like to show any mercy, and Gilda herself — remembering all his crimes — could no longer bring herself to ask for mercy for him, and yet the man seemed only to mock, to smile at fate, to take his present desperate position as lightly and as airily as another would take a pleasing turn of fortune's wheel.

Conscious at last that his look of unconquerable good-humour was working upon her nerves, Gilda forced herself to break the spell of numbness which had so unaccountably fallen upon her.

"I should like to say to you, sir," she murmured, "how deeply I regret the many harsh words I spoke to you at Leyden and ...and also last night ...believe me there was no feeling in me of cruelty toward you when I spoke them."

"Indeed, mejuffrouw," he rejoined placidly, whilst the gentle mockery in his glance became more accentuated, "indeed I am sure that your harshness towards me was only dictated by your kindliness. Believe me," he added lightly, "your words that evening at Leyden, and again last night were most excellent discipline for my temper: for this do I thank you! they have helped me to bear subsequent events with greater equanimity."

She bit her lip, feeling vexed at his flippancy. A man on the point of death should take the last hours of his life more seriously.

"It grieved me to see," she resumed somewhat more stiffly, "that one who could on occasions be so brave, should on others stoop to such infamous tricks."

"Man is ever a creature of opportunity, mejuffrouw," he said imperturbably.

"But I remembered you — you see — on New Year's Eve in the Dam Straat when you held up a mob to protect an unfortunate girl; oh! it was bravely done!"

"Yet believe me, mejuffrouw," he said with a whimsical smile, "that though I own appearances somewhat belie me, I have done better since."

"I wish I could believe you, sir. But since then ...oh! think of my horror when I recognized you the next day — at Leyden — after your cowardly attack upon me."

"Indeed I have thought of it already, mejuffrouw. Dondersteen! I must have appeared a coward before you then!"

He gave a careless shrug of the shoulders, and very quaintly did that carelessness sit on him now that he was pinioned, wounded and in a relentless enemy's hands.

"Perhaps I am a coward," he added with a strange little sigh, "you think so; the Lord of Stoutenburg declares that I am a miserable cur. Does man ever know himself? I for one have never been worth the study."

"Nay, sir, there you do wrong yourself," she said gently, "I cannot rightly gauge what temptations did beset you when you lay hands upon a defenceless woman, or when you forged my brother's name ... for this you did do, did you not?" she asked insistently.

"Have I not confessed to it?" he retorted quietly.

"Alas! And for these crimes must I despise you," she added quaintly. "But since then my mind hath been greatly troubled. Something tells me — and would to God I saw it all more clearly — that much that you so bravely endure just now, is somehow because of me. Am I wrong?"

He laughed, a dry, gentle, self-mocking laugh.

"That I have endured much because of you, mejuffrouw," he said gaily, "I'll not deny; my worthy patron St. Bavon being singularly slack in his protection of me on two or three memorable occasions; but this does not refer to my present state, which has come about because half a dozen men fell upon me when I was unarmed and pounded at me with heavy steel skates, which they swung by their straps. The skates were good weapons, I must own, and have caused one or two light wounds which are but scraps of evil fortune that a nameless adventurer like myself must take along with kindlier favours. So I pray you, mejuffrouw, have no further thought of my unpleasant bodily condition. I have been through worse plights than this before, and if to-morrow I must hang...."

"No, no!" she interrupted with a cry of horror, "that cannot and must not be."

"Indeed it can and must, mejuffrouw. Ask the Lord of Stoutenburg what his intentions are."

"Oh! but I can plead with him," she declared. "He hath told me things to-day which have made me very happy. My heart is full of forgiveness for you, who have wronged me so, and I would feel happy in pleading for you."

Something that she said appeared to tickle his fancy, for at her words he threw his head right back and laughed immoderately, loudly and long.

"Ye gods!" he cried, while she — a little frightened and puzzled — looked wide-eyed upon him — "let me hear those words ringing in mine ears when the rope is round my neck. The Lord of Stoutenburg hath the power to make a woman happy! the words he speaks are joy unto her heart! Oh! ye gods, let me remember this and laugh at it until I die!"

His somewhat wild laugh had not ceased to echo in the low-raftered room nor had Gilda time to recover her composure, before the door was thrown violently open and the Lord of Stoutenburg re-entered, followed by Jan and a group of men.

He threw a quick, suspicious glance on Gilda and on Diogenes, the latter answered him with one of good-humoured irony, but Gilda — pale and silent — turned her head away.

Stoutenburg then pointed to Diogenes.

"Here is your prisoner," he said to Jan, "take him back to the place from whence you brought him. Guard him well, Jan, for to-morrow he must hang and remember that your life shall pay for his if he escapes."

Jan thereupon gave a brief word of command, the men ranged themselves around the prisoner, whose massive figure was thus completely hidden from Gilda's view; only — towering above the heads of the soldiers — the wide sweep of the brow caught a glimmer of light from the flickering lamp overhead.

Soon the order was given. The small knot of men turned and slowly filed out. The Lord of Stoutenburg was the last to leave. He bowed nearly to the ground when he finally left Gilda's presence.

And she remained alone, sitting by the fire, and staring into the smouldering ashes. She had heard news to-night that flooded her soul with happiness. Her brother whom she loved was innocent of crime, and God Himself had interfered. He had touched the heart of the Lord of Stoutenburg and stopped the infamous plot against the Stadtholder's life. Yet Gilda's heart was unaccountably heavy, and as she sat on, staring into the fire, heavy tears fell unheeded from her eyes.

CHAPTER XXXVI
BROTHER PHILOSOPHERS

And now for the clang of arms, the movement, the bustle, the excitement of combat! There are swords to polish, pistols to clean, cullivers to see to! Something is in the air! We have not been brought hither all the way to this God-forsaken and fog-ridden spot in order to stare on a tumble-down molens, or watch a solitary prisoner ere he hang.

Jan knows of course, and Jan is eager and alert, febrile in his movements, there is a glow in his hollow eyes. And Jan always looks like that when fighting is in the air, when he sniffs the scent of blood and hears the resonance of metal against metal. Jan knows of course. He has no thought of sleep, all night he wanders up and down the improvised camp. No fires allowed and it is pitch dark, but an occasional glimmer from a lanthorn lights up compact groups of men lying prone upon the frozen ground, wrapped in thick coats, or huddled up with knees to chin trying to keep warm.

A few lanthorns are allowed, far into the interior of that weird forest of beams under the molens where slender protection against a bitter north-westerly wind can alone be found.

Shoulder to shoulder, getting warmth one from the other, we are all too excited to sleep. Something is in the air, some fighting to be done, and yet there are only thirty or forty of us at most: but swords and cullivers have been given out, and half the night through my lord and his friends, served only by Jan, have been carrying heavy loads from the molens out toward the Schie and the wooden bridge that spans it.

Silently, always coming away with those heavy loads from the molens, and walking with them away into the gloom, always returning empty-handed, and served only by Jan. Bah, we are no cullions! 'tis not mighty difficult to guess. And by the saints! why all this mystery? Some of us are paid to fight, what care we how we do it? in the open with muskets or crossbows, or in the dark, with a sudden blow which no man knows from whence it comes.

All night we sit and wait, and all night we are under the eye of Jan. He serves his lord and helps him to carry those heavy boxes from the molens to some unknown place by the Schie, but he is always there when you least expect him, watching to see that all is well, that there is not too much noise, that no one has been tempted to light a fire, that we do not quarrel too hotly among ourselves.

He keeps a watchful eye too, upon the prisoner: poor beggar! with a broken shoulder and a torn hip, and some other wounds too, about his body. A good fighter no doubt! but there were seven against him, and that was a good idea to swing heavy skates by their straps and to bring him down with them. His head was too high, else a blow from those sharp blades might have ended his life more kindly than the Lord of Stoutenburg hath planned to do.

A merry devil too! full of quaint jokes and tales of gay adventure! By Gad! a real soldier of fortune! devil-may-care! eat and drink and make merry for to-morrow we may die. Jan has ordered him to be kept tied to a beam! God-verdomme! but 'tis hard on a wounded man, but he seems tougher than the beams, and laughter in his throat quickly smothers groans.

Tied to a beam, he is excellent company! Ye gods, how his hands itch to grip his sword. Piet the Red over there! let him feel the metal against his palms, 'twill ease his temper for sure! Jan is too severe: but 'tis my lord's rage that was unbridled. Ugh! to strike a prisoner in the face. 'Twas a dirty trick and many saw it.

Heigh-ho, but what matter! To-morrow we fight, to-morrow he hangs! What of that? To-morrow most of us mayhap will be lying stark and stiff upon the frozen ground, staring up at next night's moon, with eyes that no longer see! A rope round the neck, a hole in the side, a cracked skull! what matters which mode Dame Death will choose for our ultimate end. But 'tis a pity about the prisoner! A true fighter if there was one, a stoic and a philosopher. "The Cavalier" we pretty soon call him.

"What ho!" he shouts, "call me the Laughing Cavalier!"

Poor devil! he tries not to show his hurts. He suffers much what with that damnable wind and those ropes that cut into his tough sinews, but he smiles at every twinge of pain: smiles and laughs and cracks the broadest jokes that have e'er made these worm-eaten beams ring with their echo.

The Laughing Cavalier in sooth!

There! now we can ease him somewhat. Jan's back is turned: we dare not touch the ropes, but a cloak put between his back and the beam, and another just against his head.

Is that not better, old compeer?

Aye! but is it not good to be a villain and a rogue and herd with other villains and other rogues who are so infinitely more kind and gentle than all those noble lords?

Diogenes — his head propped against the rude cushion placed there by the hand of some rough Samaritan — has fallen into a fitful doze.

Whispers around him wake him with a start. Ye gods! was there ever so black a night? The whispers become more eager, more insistent.

"Let us but speak with him. We'll do no harm!"

St. Bavon tell us how those two scarecrows have got here! For they are here in the flesh, both of them, Diogenes would have spotted his brother philosophers through darkness darker than the blackest hell. Pythagoras rolling in fat and Socrates lean and hungry-looking, peering like a huge gaunt bird through the gloom. Someone is holding up a lanthorn and Pythagoras' tip-tilted nose shines with a ruddy glow.

"But how did you get here, you old mushroom-face?" asks one of the men.

"We had business with him at Rotterdam," quoth Socrates with one of his choicest oaths and nodding in the direction of the prisoner. "All day we have wondered what has become of him."

"Then in the afternoon," breaks in Pythagoras, to the accompaniment of a rival set of expletives, "we saw him trussed like a fowl and tied into a sledge drawn by a single horse, which started in the wake of a larger one wherein sat a lovely jongejuffrouw."

"Then what did you do?" queries some one.

"Do?" exclaimed the philosophers simultaneously and in a tone of deep disgust.

"Followed on his trail as best we could," rejoins Socrates simply, "borrowed some skates, ran down the Schie in the wake of the two sledges and their escort."

"And after that?"

"After that we traced him to this solitary God-forsaken hole, but presently we saw that this molens was not so deserted as it seemed, so we hung about until now … then we ventured nearer … and here we are."

Here they were of course, but how was it possible to contravene the orders of Jan? What could these scarecrows have to say to the Laughing Cavalier?

"Just to ask him if there's anything we can do," murmurs Socrates persuasively. "He's like to hang to-morrow, you said, well! grant something then to a dying man."

Grave heads shake in the gloom.

"Our orders are strict…."

"'Tis a matter of life and death it seems…."

"Bah!" quoth Pythagoras more insinuatingly still, "we are two to your thirty! What have ye all to fear?"

"Here! tie my hands behind my back," suggests Socrates. "I only want to speak with him. How could we help him to escape?"

"We would not think of such a thing," murmurs Pythagoras piously.

Anxious glances meet one another in consultation. More than one kindly heart beats beneath these ragged doublets. Bah! the man is to hang to-morrow, why not give pleasure to a dying man?

If indeed it be pleasure to look on such hideous scarecrows a few hours before death.

Jan is not here. He is with my lord, helping with those heavy boxes.

"Five minutes, you old mushroom-face," suggests he who has been left in charge.

And all the others nod approval.

But they will take no risks about the prisoner. Pleasure and five minutes' conversation with his friends, yes! but no attempt at escape. So the men make a wide circle sitting out of ear-shot, but shoulder to shoulder the thirty of them who happen to be awake. In the centre of the circle is the Laughing Cavalier tied to a beam, trussed like a fowl since he is to hang on the morrow.

Close beside his feet is the lanthorn so that he may have a last look at his friends, and some few paces away his naked sword which Jan took from him when the men brought him down.

He has listened to the whispered conversation — he knows that his brother philosophers are here. May the God of rogues and villains bless them for their loyalty.

"And now St. Bavon show me the best way to make use of them!"

There is still something to be done, which hath been left undone, a word hath been given and that pledge must be fulfilled, and the promised fortune still awaits him who will bring the jongejuffrouw safely to her father!

"My God, if it were not for that broken shoulder and that torn hip! ... there are many hours yet before the morrow."

"Old compeer!" came in a hoarse whisper close to his ear, "how did you come to such a pass?"

"They came and took the jongejuffrouw away from Rotterdam," he replied also speaking in a whisper. "I had just returned from Delft, where I had business to transact and I recognized Jan beside the sledge into which the jongejuffrouw was stepping even then. He had ten or a dozen men with him. I felt that they meant mischief — but I had to follow ... I had to find out whither they were taking her...."

"Verdommt!" growled Socrates under his breath. "Why did you not take us along?"

"I meant to come back for you, as soon as I knew ... but in the dark ... and from behind, seven of these fellows fell upon me ... they used their skates like javelins ... mine were still on my feet ... I had only Bucephalus.... A blow from one of the heaviest blades cracked my shoulder, another caught me on the hip. There were seven of them," he reiterated with a careless laugh, "it was only a question of time, they were bound to bring me down in the end."

"But who has done this?" queried Pythagoras with an oath.

"A lucky rogue on whom God hath chosen to smile. But," he added more seriously and sinking his voice to the lowest possible whisper, "never mind about the past. Let us think of the future, old compeers."

"We are ready," they replied simultaneously.

"A knife?" he murmured, "can you cut these confounded ropes?"

"They took everything from us," growled Socrates, "ere they let us approach you."

"Try with your hands to loosen the knots."

"What ho! you brigands, what are you doing there?"

In a moment the circle around broke up. A crowd of angry faces were gathered closely round the philosophers, and more than one pair of rough hands were laid upon their shoulders.

"Play fair, you two!" cried Piet the Red, who was in command, "or we'll tie you both to the nearest beams and await my lord's commands."

"Easy, easy, friend," quoth Diogenes with a pleasant laugh, "my nose was itching and my compeer held on to my arm while he tried to reach my nose in order to scratch it."

"Then if it itch again," retorted the man with an equally jovial laugh, "call for my services, friend. And now, you two scarecrows! the five minutes are over. Jan will be here in a moment."

But they formed up the circle once more, kind and compassionate. Jan was not yet here, and the rogues had had a warning: they were not like to be at their tricks again.

"Never mind about me," whispered Diogenes hurriedly as Pythagoras and Socrates, baffled and furious, were giving forth samples of their choicest vocabularies. "You see that Chance alone can favour me an she choose, if not ...'tis no matter. What you can do for me is far more important than cheating the gallows of my carcase."

"What is it?" they asked simply.

"The jongejuffrouw," he said, "you know where she is?"

"In the hut — close by," replied Socrates, "we saw the sledge draw up there...."

"But the house is well guarded," murmured Pythagoras.

"Nor would I ask you to run your heads in the same noose wherein mine will swing to-morrow. But keep the hut well in sight. At any hour — any moment now there may be a call of *sauve qui peut*. Every man for himself and the greatest luck to the swiftest runner."

"But why?"

"Never mind why. It is sure to happen. Any minute you may hear the cry ... confusion, terror ... a scramble and a rush for the open."

"And our opportunity," came in a hoarse whisper from Socrates. "I think that I begin to understand."

"We lie low for the present and when *sauve qui peut* is called we come straight back here and free you ... in the confusion they will have forgotten you."

"If the confusion occurs in time," quoth Diogenes with his habitual carelessness, "you may still find me here trussed like a fowl to this verdommte beam. But I have an idea that the Lord of Stoutenburg will presently be consumed with impatience to see me hang ... he has just finished some important work by the bridge on the Schie ... he won't be able to sleep and the devil will be suggesting some mischief for his idle hands to do. There will be many hours to kill before daylight, one of them might be well employed in hanging me."

"Then we'll not leave you an instant," asserted Pythagoras firmly.

"What can you do, you two old scarecrows, against the Lord of Stoutenburg who has thirty men here paid to do his bidding?"

"We are not going to lie low and play the part of cowards while you are being slaughtered."

"You will do just what I ask, faithful old compeers," rejoined Diogenes more earnestly than was his wont. "You will lie very low and take the greatest possible care not to run your heads into the same rope wherein mayhap mine will dangle presently. Nor will you be playing the part of cowards, for you have not yet learned the A B C of that part, and you will remember that on your safety and freedom of action lies my one chance, not so much of life as of saving my last shred of honour."

"What do you mean?"

"The jongejuffrouw — " he whispered, "I swore to bring her back to her father and I must cheat a rascal of his victory. In the confusion — at dawn to-morrow — think above all of the jongejuffrouw.... In the confusion you can overpower the guard — rush the miller's hut where she is ... carry her off ... the horses are in the shed behind the hut ... you may not have time to think of me."

"But...."

"Silence — they listen...."

"One of us with the jongejuffrouw — the other to help you — —"

"Silence ... I may be a dead man by then — the jongejuffrouw remember — make for Ryswyk with her first of all — thence straight to Haarlem — to her father — you can do it easily. A fortune awaits you if you bring her safely to him. Fulfil my pledge, old compeers, if I am not alive to do it myself. I don't ask you to swear — I know you'll do it — and if I must to the gallows first I'll do so with a cry of triumph."

"But you...."

"Silence!" he murmured again peremptorily, but more hoarsely this time for fatigue and loss of blood and tense excitement are telling upon his iron physique at last — he is well-nigh spent and scarce able to speak. "Silence — I can hear Jan's footsteps. Here! quick! inside my boot ... a wallet? Have you got it?" he added with a brief return to his habitual gaiety as he felt Socrates' long fingers groping against his shins, and presently beheld his wallet in his compeer's hand. "You will find money in there — enough for the journey. Now quick into the night, you two — disappear for the nonce, and anon when *sauve qui peut* rings in the air — to-night or at dawn or whenever this may be, remember the jongejuffrouw first of all and when you are ready give the cry we all know so well — the cry of the fox when it lures its prey. If I am not dangling on a gibbet by then, I shall understand. But quick now! — Jan comes! — Disappear I say!..."

Quietly and swiftly Socrates slipped the wallet with some of the money back into his friend's boot, the rest he hid inside his own doublet.

Strange that between these men there was no need of oaths. Pythagoras and Socrates had said nothing: silent and furtive they disappeared into the darkness. Diogenes' head sank down upon his breast with a last sigh of satisfaction. He knew that his compeers would do what he had asked. Jan's footsteps rang on the hard-frozen ground — silently the living circle had parted and the philosophers were swallowed up by the gloom.

Jan looks suspiciously at the groups of men who now stand desultorily around.

"Who was standing beside the prisoner just now?" he asks curtly.

"When, captain?" queries one of the men blandly.

"A moment ago. I was descending the steps. The lanthorn was close to the prisoner; I saw two forms — that looked unfamiliar to me — close to him."

"Oh!" rejoined Piet the Red unblushingly, "it must have been my back that you saw, captain. Willem and I were looking to see that the ropes had not given way. The prisoner is so restless...."

Jan — not altogether re-assured — goes up to the prisoner. He raises the lanthorn and has a good and comprehensive look at all the ropes. Then he examines the man's face.

"What ho!" he cries, "a bottle of spiced wine from my wallet. The prisoner has fainted."

CHAPTER XXXVII
DAWN

What a commotion when dawn breaks at last; it comes grey, dull, leaden, scarce lighter than the night, the haze more dense, the frost more biting. But it does break at last after that interminable night of excitement and sleeplessness and preparations for the morrow.

Jan has never closed an eye, he has scarcely rested even, pacing up and down, in and out of those gargantuan beams, with the molens and its secrets towering above his head. Nor I imagine did those noble lords and mynheers up there sleep much during this night; but they were tired and lay like logs upon straw paillasses, living over again the past few hours, the carrying of heavy iron boxes one by one from the molens to the wooden bridge, the unloading there, the unpacking in the darkness, and the disposal of the death-dealing powder, black and evil smelling, which will put an end with its one mighty crash — to tyranny and the Stadtholder's life.

Tired they are but too excited to sleep: the last few hours are like a vivid dream; the preparation of the tinder, the arrangements, the position to be taken up by Beresteyn and Heemskerk, the two chosen lieutenants who will send the wooden bridge over the Schie flying in splinters into the air.

Van Does too has his work cut out. General in command of the forces — foreign mercenaries and louts from the country — he has Jan for able captain. The mercenaries and the louts know nothing yet of what will happen to-morrow — when once the dawn has broken — but they are well prepared; like beasts of the desert they can scent blood in the air; look at them polishing up their swords and cleaning their cullivers! they know that to-morrow they will fight, even though to-night they have had no orders save to see that one prisoner tied with ropes to a beam and fainting with exposure and loss of blood does not contrive to escape.

But the Lord of Stoutenburg is more wakeful than all. Like a caged beast of prey he paces up and down the low, narrow weighing-room of the molens, his hands tightly clenched behind his back, his head bare, his cloak cast aside despite the bitter coldness of the night.

Restless and like a beast of prey; his nostrils quiver with the lust of hate and revenge that seethes within his soul. Two men doth he hate with a consuming passion of hatred, the Stadtholder Prince of Orange, sovereign ruler of half the Netherlands, and a penniless adventurer whose very name is unknown.

Both these men are now in the power of the Lord of Stoutenburg. The bridge is prepared, the powder laid, to-morrow justice will be meted out to the tyrant; God alone could save him now, and God, of a surety, must be on the side of a just revenge. The other man is helpless and a prisoner; despite his swagger and his insolence, justice shall be meted out to him too; God alone could save him, and God, of a surety, could not be on the side of an impudent rogue.

These thoughts, which were as satisfying to the Lord of Stoutenburg as food placed at an unattainable distance is to a starving beast, kept him awake and pacing up and down the room after he had finished his work under the bridge.

He could not sleep for thinking of the prisoner, of the man's insolence, of the humiliation and contempt wherewith every glance he had brought shame to his cheeks. The Lord of Stoutenburg could not sleep also for thinking of Gilda, and the tender, pitying eyes wherewith she regarded the prisoner, the gentle tone of her voice when she spoke to him, even after proof had been placed before her that the man was a forger and a thief.

The Lord of Stoutenburg could not sleep and all the demons of jealousy, of hatred and of revenge were chasing him up and down the room and whispering suggestions of mischief to be wrought, of a crime to be easily committed.

"While that man lives," whispered the demon of hate in his ear, "thou wilt not know a moment's rest. To-morrow when thy hand should be steady when it wields the dagger against the Stadtholder, it will tremble and falter, for thoughts of that man will unsettle thy nerves and cause the blood to tingle in thy veins."

"While that man lives," whispered the demon of revenge, "thou wilt not know a moment's rest. Thou wilt think of him and of his death, rather than of thy vengeance against the Stadtholder."

"While that man lives," whispered the demon of jealousy more insistently than did the other evil spirits, "Gilda will not cease to think of him, she will plead for him, she will try mayhap to save him and then — — "

And the Lord of Stoutenburg groaned aloud in the silence of the night, and paused in his restless walk. He drew a chair close to the table, and sat down; then resting his elbows upon the table, he buried his head in his hands, and remained thus motionless but breathing heavily like one whose soul is fighting a losing battle.

The minutes sped on. He had no means of gauging the time. It was just night, black impenetrable night. From down below came the murmur of all the bustle that was going on, the clang of arms, the measured footsteps which told of other alert human creatures who were waiting in excitement and tense expectancy for that dawn which still was far distant.

The minutes sped on, on the leaden feet of time. How long the Lord of Stoutenburg had sat thus, silent and absorbed, he could not afterwards have said. Perhaps after all he had fallen asleep, overcome with fatigue and with the constant sleeplessness of the past few days. But anon he was wide awake, slightly shivering with the cold. The tallow candle was spluttering, almost dying out. With a steady hand the Lord of Stoutenburg snuffed the smouldering wick, the candle flickered up again. Then he rose and quietly walked across the room. He pulled open the door and loudly called for Jan.

A few minutes later Jan was at the door, silent, sullen, obedient as usual.

"My lord called?" he asked.

"Yes," replied Stoutenburg, "what hour is it?"

"Somewhere near six I should say, my lord. I heard the tower-clock at Ryswyk strike five some time ago."

"How long is it before the dawn?"

"Two hours, my lord."

"Time to put up a gibbet, Jan? and to hang a man?"

"Plenty of time for that, my lord," replied Jan quietly.

"Then see to it, Jan, as speedily as you can. I feel that that man down below is our evil genius. While he lives Chance will be against us, of that I am as convinced as I am of the justice of our cause. If that man lives, Jan, the Stadtholder will escape us; I feel it in my bones: something must have told me this in the night — it is a premonition that comes from above."

"Then the man must not live, my lord," said Jan coldly.

"You recognize that too, Jan, do you not?" rejoined Stoutenburg eagerly. "I am compelled in this — I won't say against my will, but compelled by a higher, a supernatural power. You, too, believe in the supernatural, do you not, my faithful Jan?"

"I believe, my lord, first and foremost in the justice of our cause. I hate the Stadtholder and would see him dead. Nothing in the world must place that great aim of ours in jeopardy."

Stoutenburg drew a deep breath of satisfaction.

"Then see to the gibbet, my good Jan," he said in a firm almost lusty voice, "have it erected on the further side of the molens so that the jongejuffrouw's eyes are not scandalized by the sight. When everything is ready come and let me know, and guard him well until then, Jan, guard him with your very life; I want to see him hang, remember that! Come and tell me when the gallows are ready and I'll go to see him hang ...I want to see him hang...."

And Jan without another word salutes the Lord of Stoutenburg and then goes out.

And thus it is that a quarter of an hour later the silence of the night is broken by loud and vigorous hammering. Jan sees to it all and a gibbet is not difficult to erect.

Then men grumble of course; they are soldiers and not executioners, and their hearts for the most have gone out to that merry compeer — the Laughing Cavalier — with his quaint jokes and his cheerful laugh. He has been sleeping soundly too for several hours, but now he is awake. Jan has told him that his last hour has come: time to put up a gibbet with a few stiff planks taken from the store-room of the molens and a length of rope.

He looks round him quite carelessly. Bah! death has no terrors for such a splendid soldier as he is. How many times hath he faced death ere this? — why he was at Prague and at Madgeburg where few escaped with their lives. He bears many a fine scar on that broad chest of his and none upon his back. A splendid fighter, if ever there was one!

But hanging? Bah!

The men murmur audibly as plank upon plank is nailed. Jan directs operations whilst Piet the Red keeps guard over the prisoner. Two or three of the country louts know something of carpentering. They do the work under Jan's watchful eye. They grumble but they work, for no one has been paid yet, and if you rebel you are like to be shot, and in any case you lose your pay.

And Diogenes leaning up against the beam watches with lazy quaintly smiling eyes the preparations that are going on not a hundred paces away from him. After a while the darkness all around is beginning to yield to the slow insistence of dawn. It rises slowly behind the veils of mist which still envelop the distant East. Gradually an impalpable greyness creeps around the molens, objects begin to detach themselves one by one out of the gloom, the moving figures of the mercenaries, the piles of arms heaped up here and there out of the damp, the massive beams slimy and green which support the molens, and a little further on the tall erection with a projecting arm round which great activity reigns.

Diogenes watches it all with those same lazy eyes, and that same good-humoured smile lingering round his lips. That tall erection over there which still looks ghostlike through the mist is for him. The game of life is done and he has lost. Death is there at the end of the projecting arm on which even now Jan is fixing a rope.

"Death in itself matters but little," mused the philosopher with his gently ironical smile. "I would have chosen another mode than hanging ... but after all 'tis swift and sure; and of course now she will never know."

Know what, O philosopher? What is it that she — Gilda — with the fair curls and the blue eyes, the proud firm mouth and round chin — what is it that she will never know?

She will never know that a nameless, penniless soldier of fortune has loved her with every beat of his heart, every thought of his brain, with every sinew and every aspiration. She will never know that just in order to remain near her, when she was dragged away out of Rotterdam he affronted deliberately the trap into which he fell. She will never know that for her dear sake, he has borne humiliation against which every nerve of his splendid nature did inwardly rebel, owning to guilt and shame lest her blue eyes shed tears for a brother's sin. She will never know that the warning to the Stadtholder came from him, and that he was neither a forger nor a thief, only just a soldier of fortune with a contempt for death, and an unspoken adoration for the one woman who seemed to him as distant from him as the stars.

But there were no vain regrets in him now; no regret of life, for this he always held in his own hand ready to toss it away for a fancy of an ideal — no regret of the might-have-been because he was a philosopher, and the very moment that love for the unattainable was born in his heart he had already realized that love to him could only mean a memory.

Therefore when he watched the preparations out there in the mist, and heard the heavy blows upon the wooden planks and the murmurs of his sympathizers at their work, he only smiled gently, self-deprecatingly, but always good-humouredly.

If the Lord of Stoutenburg only knew how little he really cared.

CHAPTER XXXVIII

THE HOUR

A curiously timid voice roused the philosopher from his dreams.

"Is there aught I can do for you, sir? Alas! my friend the Lord Stoutenburg is deeply angered against you. I could do nothing with him on your behalf."

Diogenes turned his head in the direction whence had come the voice. He saw Nicolaes Beresteyn standing there in the cold grey mist, with his fur cloak wrapped closely up to his chin, and his face showing above the cloak, white and drawn.

The situation was not likely to escape Diogenes' irrepressible sense of humour.

"Mynheer Beresteyn," he exclaimed; "Dondersteen! what brings your Mightiness here at this hour? A man on the point of death, sir, has no call for so pitiable a sight as is your face just now."

"I heard from my Lord Stoutenburg what happened in the hut last night," said Beresteyn in a faltering voice, and determined not to heed the other's bantering tone. "You exonerated me before my sister ... sir, this was a noble act ... I would wish to thank you...."

"And do so with quaking voice and shaking knees," quoth Diogenes with unalterable good-humour, through which there pierced however an obvious undercurrent of contempt. "Ye gods!" he added with a quaint sigh, "these men have not even the courage of their infamy!"

The words, the tone, the shrug of the shoulders which accompanied these, stung Nicolaes Beresteyn's dormant dignity to the quick.

"I do not wonder," he said more firmly, "that you feel bitter contempt for me now. Your generosity for which I did not crave hath placed me momentarily at a disadvantage before you. Yet believe me I would not be outdone by you in generosity; were it not for my allegiance to the Lord Stoutenburg I would go straight to my sister now and confess my guilt to her.... You believe me I trust," he added, seeing that Diogenes' merry eyes were fixed mockingly upon him, "did fate allow it I would gladly change places with you even now."

"I am about to hang, sir," quoth Diogenes lightly.

"Alas!"

"And you are forced, you say, to play a craven's part; believe me, sir, I would not change places with you for a kingdom."

"I do believe you, sir," rejoined Beresteyn earnestly, "yet I would have you think of me as something less of a coward than I seem. Were I to make full confession to my sister now, I should break her heart — but it would not save your neck from the gallows."

"And a rogue's neck, sir, is of such infinitely less value than a good woman's heart. So I pray you say no more about it. Death and I are old acquaintances, oft hath he nodded to me en passant, we are about to become closer friends, that is all."

"Some day my sister shall know, sir, all that you have done for her and for me."

The ghost of a shadow passed over the Laughing Cavalier's face.

"That, sir, I think had best remain 'twixt you and me for all times. But this I would have you know, that when I accepted the ignoble bargain which you proposed to me in my friend Hals' studio, I did so because I thought that the jongejuffrouw would be safer in my charge then than in yours!"

Beresteyn was about to retort more hotly when Jan, closely followed by half a dozen men, came with swift, firm footsteps up to the prisoner. He saluted Beresteyn deferentially as was his wont.

"Your pardon, mynheer," he said, "my lord hath ordered that the prisoner be forthwith led to execution."

Nicolaes' pale face became the colour of lead.

"One moment, Jan," he said, "one moment. I must speak with my lord ... I...."

"My lord is with the jongejuffrouw," said Jan curtly, "shall I send to tell him that you desire to speak with him?"

"No — no — that is I ...I ..." stammered Nicolaes who, indeed, was fighting a cruel battle with his own weakness, his own cowardice now. It was that weakness which had brought him to the abject pass in which he now stood, face to face with the man he had affected to despise, and who was about to die, laden with the crimes which he Nicolaes had been the first to commit.

Stoutenburg's influence over him had been paramount, through it he had lost all sense of justice, of honour and of loyalty; banded with murderers he had ceased to recognize the very existence of honesty, and now he was in such a plight morally, that though he knew himself to be playing an ignoble rôle, he did not see the way to throw up the part and to take up that of an honest man. One word from him to Gilda, his frank confession of his own guilt, and she would so know how to plead for the condemned man that Stoutenburg would not dare to proceed with this monstrous act.

But that word he had not the courage to speak.

With dull eyes and in sullen silence he watched Piet the Red untying under Jan's orders the ropes which held the prisoner to the beam, and then securing others to keep his arms pinioned behind his back. The mist now was of a faint silvery grey, and the objects around had that mysterious hushed air which the dawn alone can lend. The men, attracted by the sight of a fellow creature in his last living moments, had gathered together in close knots of threes and fours. They stood by, glowering and sombre, and had not Jan turned a wilfully deaf ear to their murmurings he would have heard many an ugly word spoken under their breath.

These were of course troublous and fighting times, when every man's hand was against some other, when every able-bodied man was firstly a soldier and then only a peaceable citizen. Nor was the present situation an uncommon one: the men could not know what the prisoner had done to deserve this summary punishment. He might have been a spy — an informer — or merely a prisoner of war. It was no soldier's place to interfere, only to obey orders and to ask no questions.

But they gave to the splendid personality of the condemned man the tribute of respectful silence. Whilst Jan secured the slender white hands of the prisoner, and generally made those awful preparations which even so simple a death as hanging doth demand, jests and oaths were stilled one by one among these rough fighting men, not one head but was uncovered, not a back that was not straightened, not an attitude that was not one of deference and attention. Instinct — that unerring instinct of the soldier — had told them that here was no scamp getting his just reward, but a brave man going with a careless smile to his death.

"Has mynheer finished with the prisoner," asked Jan when he saw that Piet had finished his task and that the prisoner was ready to be led away. "Is there aught your greatness would still desire to say to him?"

"Only this," said Beresteyn firmly, "that were his hands free I would ask leave to grasp them."

A look of kindly amusement fell from the prisoner's eyes upon the pale face of the young man.

"I have never known you, sir, save by a quaint nick-name," continued Beresteyn earnestly, "but surely you have kith and kin somewhere. Have you no father or mother living whom you will leave to mourn?"

The prisoner made no immediate reply, the smile of kindly amusement still lingered round his lips, but presently with an instinctive gesture of pride, he threw back his head and looked around him, as one who has nothing to fear and but little to regret. He met the sympathetic glance cast on him by the man who had done him — was still doing him — an infinite wrong, and all round those of his mute and humble friends who seemed to be listening eagerly now for the answer which he would give to Mynheer. Then with a quick sweep his eyes suddenly rested on the wooden erection beyond the molens that loomed out so tragically through the mist, pointing with its one weird arm to some infinite distance far away.

Something in the gentle pathos of this humble deference that encompassed him, something mayhap in the solemnity of that ghostly arm suddenly seemed to melt the thin crust of his habitual flippancy. He looked back on Beresteyn and said softly:

"I have a friend, Frans Hals — the painter of pictures — tell him when next you see him that I am glad his portrait of me is finished, and that I asked God to bless him for all his goodness has meant to me in the past."

"But your father, sir," urged Beresteyn, "your kindred...."

"My father, sir," replied Diogenes curtly, "would not care to hear that his son had died upon the gallows."

Beresteyn would have spoken again but Jan interposes once more, humbly but firmly.

"My lord's orders," he now says briefly, "and time presses, mynheer."

Beresteyn stands back, smothering a sigh. Jan on ahead, then Piet the Red and the six soldiers with the prisoner between them. A few steps only divide them from the gruesome erection that looms more solidly now out of the mist. Beresteyn, wrapping his head up in his cloak to shut out sound and sight, walks rapidly away in the opposite direction.

CHAPTER XXXIX
"SAUVE QUI PEUT"

Then it is that, out of the thickness of the fog a figure suddenly emerges running and panting: a man has fallen up against the group of soldiers who have just halted beside the gibbet.

"It is Lucas of Sparendam come back from Delft," they cry as soon as they recognize the stained face, wet with the frost and the mist.

Already Jan — who with Piet's help was busy with the rope — has heard the name. His wan, thin face has become the colour of ashes.

"Lucas of Sparendam back from Delft," he murmurs, "the Lord save us all!"

Lucas of Sparendam was sent yesterday to Delft by the Lord of Stoutenburg to spy and to find out all that was going on inside the Prinzenhof where slept the Stadtholder and his bodyguard of one hundred men-at-arms: and now he has come back running and panting: his clothes torn, his face haggard and spent. He has run all the way from Delft — a matter of a league and a half! Why should a man half kill himself by endeavouring to cover a league and a half in one hour?

"A drop of hot wine for Lucas," cries one of the soldiers. "He is faint."

The other men — there are close on forty all told — crowd round the gibbet now, those in charge of the prisoner have much ado to keep the space clear. They don't say anything just yet, but there is a strange, restless look in their eyes and their lips tremble with all the unspoken questions. Only two men remain calm and silent, Jan has never ceased in his task of adjusting the ropes, and the prisoner stands quite still, bound with cords, and neither looking on Lucas nor yet on the gibbet above him. His eyes are half closed and there is a strained look on his merry face as if he were trying to listen to something that was too far off to hear.

But one man in the meanwhile is ready with the bottle of spiced wine, the best cordial there is for a fainting man. The others make way for him so that he can minister to Lucas. And Lucas drinks the wine eagerly, then he opens his eyes.

"We are betrayed," he murmurs.

"Great God!" exclaims Jan dully.

"Betrayed!"

"What does it mean?"

No one heeds the prisoner now. They all crowd around Lucas. Jan calls out his orders in vain: Piet the Red alone listens to what he says, the others all want to know what Lucas means. They had been in the thick of a plot of course, they all knew that: a guet-apens had been prepared by the Lord of Stoutenburg for the Stadtholder whom he hates. The heavy boxes of course — gunpowder ... to blow up the wooden bridge when the Stadtholder and his escort are half way across!

Of course they had all guessed it, thought on it all through the night while they polished the arms — the swords and the pistols and the cullivers — which had been served out to them. They had guessed of course — the foreign mercenaries who were always in the thick of every conspiracy and well paid for being so — they had been the first to guess and they had told the country louts who only grinned enjoying the prospect of the fun.

But now they were betrayed. Lucas of Sparendam had come back with the news, and even Jan stopped in his hideous task in order to listen to what he had to say.

"It all happened yesterday," quoth Lucas as soon as he had recovered his breath, "the rumour began in the lower quarters of the town. Nobody knows who began it. Some say that a foreigner came into the city in the early morning and sat down at one of the taverns to eat and drink with the Prince's soldiers."

"A foreigner?"

Jan turns to look on the prisoner and encounters his mocking glance. Smothering a curse he resumes his task of adjusting the rope upon the gibbet, but his fingers are unsteady and his work doth not progress.

"Yes, a foreigner," continued Lucas volubly, "though it all has remained very mysterious. The Prince's soldiers spoke of it amongst themselves ... the foreigner had said something about a guet-apens, a plot against the Stadtholder's life on his way to the North ... then one of the officers heard the rumour and carried it to one of his superiors.... By the evening it had reached the Stadtholder's ears."

"Then what happened?" they all asked eagerly.

"Nothing for some hours," replied Lucas, "but I know that spies were sent round in every direction, and that by midnight there was general talk in the city that the Stadtholder would not continue his journey to the North. When the captain of the guard came to him for orders the Prince said curtly: 'We do not start to-morrow!' As soon as I heard of this I made preparations. It was then an hour after midnight. I was still alert and listening: all around me — as I made ready to leave the city — I heard rumours among the soldiers and spies of the Stadtholder, of their knowledge of a lonely spot — a deserted molens — near Ryswyk where they declared many men did lately congregate. I heard too that soon after dawn the Prince's guard would make straight for the molens, so I put on my snow shoes and started to run, despite the darkness and the fog, for we are all betrayed and the Stadtholder's soldiers will be on us in a trice."

Hardly are the words out of Lucas Sparendam's mouth than the commotion begins, the disbanding; there is a roar and a bustle and a buzz: metal clashing, men rushing, cries of "we are betrayed! *sauve qui peut!*"

At first there is a general stampede for the places where the arms are kept — the muskets, the swords and cullivers — but these are thrown down almost as soon as they are picked up. They are no use now and worse than useless in a flight. But pistols are useful, in case of pursuit. "Quick, turn, fire!... so where are the pistols?... Jan, where are those pistols?"

There are not enough to go round: about a dozen were served out last night, and there are forty pairs of hands determined to possess one at least. So they begin to fight for them, tearing one another to pieces, shouting execrations, beating round with bare fists, since the other arms have already been laid down.

Now the confusion becomes worse than any that might reign among a herd of animals who are ready to rend one another: they tear the clothes off one another's back, the skin off one another's face: fear — hideous, overwhelming, abject fear, has made wild beasts of these men. The mist envelops them, it is barely light in this basement beneath the molens: lanthorns have long ago been kicked into extinction. The hot breath of forty panting throats mingles with the mist, and the heat of human bodies fever-heated with passion, fights against the strength of the frost. The frozen ground yields under the feet, clots of mud are thrown up by the stampede, from the beams up aloft the heavy icicles melt and drip monotonously, incessantly down upon those faces, red and perspiring in an agony of demented fear.

Jan and Piet the Red stand alone beside the prisoner: a sense of duty, of decency hath kept their blood cool. Until they are relieved from their post of guarding this man by orders from their lord, they will not move. Let the others rage and scream and tumble over one another, there must be at least a few soldiers among this rabble.

And the prisoner looks on all this confusion with eyes that dance and sparkle with the excitement of what is yet to come. Torn rags and broken accoutrements soon lie in a litter in the mud, trampled in by forty pairs of feet. There is not one face now that is not streaked with blood, not one throat that is not hoarse with terror — the terror of the unknown.

In vain Jan from his post beside the prisoner shouts, harangues, appeals, threatens! A fight? yes! defeat? why not? but betrayal!... no, no, let's away. The Stadtholder is fiercer than any Inquisitor of Spain ... his cruelty last February almost turned the nation against him. But now — this second conspiracy — Stoutenburg again! what hope for his followers?

The horrors of last February perpetrated in the Gevangen Poort of 'S Graven Hage still cause many a rough cheek to blanch at their recollection. Men had gone mad who had heard the cries which pierced those stone walls then. One executioner had thrown down his bloody tools and fled from the place like one possessed! Van Dyk and Korenwinder, Slatius and the rest had been in hell ere a merciful death at last released them from the barbaric cruelty of the Prince of Orange.

"No, no! such a fate cannot be risked. We are betrayed! let us fly!"

Suddenly one man starts to run.

"I am for the coast!" he shouts, and incontinently takes to his heels.

"Sauve qui peut!"

Like irresponsible creatures they throw down the very weapons for which they have been fighting. The one man has given the signal for the run. Everything now is thrown aside, there is no thought save for flight.

A splashing of the mud, a general shout, a scramble, a clatter — they run — they run — crying to those who are behind to follow and run too.

In five minutes the dark basement is clear of noise — a litter of broken arms lies in one heap close by, others are scattered all over the ground in the mud, together with torn clothing, rags of leather and of cloth and great red pools that mingle with the melted ice.

The mist surrounds it all, this abandoned battle field wherein fear was the victor over man. The swiftly flying figures are soon swallowed up by the grey wall which lies dense and heavy over the lowland around; for a time they appear like ghosts with blurred outlines of torn doublets and scraps of felt hats placed awry; then the outline gets more dim as they run, and the kindly mist hides them from view.

Under the molens all is silent now. Jan and Piet the Red guard the prisoner alone. The gallows are ready or nearly so, but there is no one to send to the Lord of Stoutenburg to tell him this — as he hath commanded — so that he may see this man hang whom he hates. And it would not be safe to leave the prisoner unguarded. Only from time to time Jan looks to see that the ropes still hold fast, but for the most part his eyes are fixed upon the mist on his left, for that way lies Delft, and from thence will loom out by and by the avenging hordes sent by the Prince of Orange.

Now that all those panting, perspiring human creatures have gone, the frost is more bitter, more biting than before; but neither Piet nor Jan seem to heed it, though their flesh is blue with the cold. Overhead there is a tramp of feet; the noble mynheers must have heard the confusion, they must have seen the flight; they are even now preparing to do in a slightly more dignified way what the foreign mercenaries and the louts from the country have done so incontinently.

The prisoner, hearing this tramp of feet over his head, looks more alertly around him. He sees that Jan and Piet have remained on guard even whilst the others have fled. He also sees the pile of heaped-up arms, the broken metal, the rags and the mud, and through the interstices of the wooden steps the booted feet of the mynheers running helter-skelter down; and a mad, merry laugh — that holds a world of joy in its rippling tones — breaks from his lips.

The next moment from far away comes a weird cry through the mist. A fox on the alert tries to lure his prey with that quaint cry of his, which appeals to the young birds and encourages them to come. What should a fox be doing on these ice-covered tracks? he must have strayed from very far, from over the moor mayhap beyond Gonda; hunger no doubt hath made a wanderer of him, an exile from his home.

Jan listens — greatly astonished — what should a fox be doing here? Piet is impassive, he knows nothing of the habits of foxes; sea-wolves are more familiar to him. With his eyes Jan instinctively questions the prisoner:

"What should a fox be doing here on these ice-bound flats?" he mutely asks.

But the prisoner apparently cares nothing about the marvels of nature, cares nothing about exiled foxes. His head is erect, his eyes dance with glee, a happy smile lights up his entire face.

Jan remembered that the others last night had called the wounded man the Laughing Cavalier. A Cavalier he looked, every inch of him; the ropes mattered nothing, nor the torn clothing; proud, triumphant, happy, he was laughing with all the light-hearted gaiety which pertains to youth.

The Laughing Cavalier forsooth. Lucky devil! if he can laugh! Jan sighed and marvelled when the Lord of Stoutenburg would relieve him from his post.

CHAPTER XL
THE LOSER PAYS

Nicolaes Beresteyn had not gone far when Lucas of Sparendam came running with the news. He heard it all, he saw the confusion, the first signs of *sauve qui peut.*

At first he was like one paralyzed with horror and with fear; he could not move, his limbs refused him service. Then he thought of his friends — some up in the molens, others at various posts on the road and by the bridge — they might not hear the confusion and the tumult, they might not see the coming *sauve qui peut*; they might not hear that the Stadtholder's spies are on the alert, and that his bodyguard might be here at any time.

Just then the disbanding began. Nicolaes Beresteyn pushed his way through the fighting, quarrelling crowd to where Lucas of Sparendam, still exhausted and weak, was leaning up against a beam.

"Their lordships up in the molens," he said in a voice still choked with fear, "and the Lord of Stoutenburg in the hut with the jongejuffrouw....Come and tell them at once all that you know."

And he dragged Lucas of Sparendam in his wake.

The Lord of Stoutenburg was at Gilda's feet when Beresteyn ran in with Lucas to tell him the news.

After he had given Jan the orders to prepare the gallows for the summary execution of the prisoner he had resumed his wild, restless pacing up and down the room. There was no remorse in him for his inhuman and cowardly act, but his nerves were all on the jar, and that perpetual hammering which went on in the distance drove him to frantic exasperation.

A picture of the happenings in the basement down below would obtrude itself upon his mental vision; he saw the prisoner — careless, contemptuous, ready for death; Jan sullen but obedient; the men murmuring and disaffected. He felt as if the hammering was now directed against his own head, he could have screamed aloud with the agony of this weary, expectant hour.

Then he thought of Gilda. Slowly the dawn was breaking, the hammering had ceased momentarily; silence reigned in the basement after the turbulence of the past hour. The Lord of Stoutenburg did not dare conjecture what this silence meant.

The thought of Gilda became more insistent. He snatched up a cloak and wrapping it closely round him, he ran out into the mist. Quickly descending the steps, he at once turned his back on the basement where the last act of the supreme tragedy would be enacted presently. He felt like a man pursued, with the angel of Nemesis close to his heels, hour-glass in hand to mark the hour of retribution.

He hoped to find rest and peace beside Gilda; he would not tell her that he had condemned the man to death. Let her forget him peaceably and naturally; the events of to-day would surely obliterate other matters from her mind. What was the life of a foreign vagabond beside the destinies of Holland which an avenging God would help to settle to-day?

The Lord of Stoutenburg had walked rapidly to the hut where he hoped to find Gilda ready to receive him. He knocked at the door and Maria opened it to him. To his infinite relief she told him that the jongejuffrouw had broken her fast and would gladly speak with him.

Gilda, he thought, looked very pale and fragile in the dim light of two or three tallow candles placed in sconces about the room. There were dark circles round her eyes, and a pathetic trembling of her lips proclaimed the near presence of tears.

But there was an atmosphere of peace in the tiny room, with its humble little bits of furniture and the huge earthenware stove from which the pleasing glow of a wood fire emanated and shed a cheerful radiance around.

The Lord of Stoutenburg felt that here in Gilda's presence he could forget his ambitions and his crimes, the man whom he was so foully putting to death, his jealousies and even his revenge.

He drew a low chair close to her and half-sitting, half-kneeling, began speaking to her as gently, as simply as his harsh voice and impatient temperament would allow. He spoke mostly about the future, only touching very casually on the pain which she had caused him by her unjust suspicions of him.

Gilda listened to him in silence for awhile. She was collecting all her will-power, all her strength of purpose for the task which lay before her — the task of softening a hardened and treacherous heart, of rousing in it a spark of chivalry and of honour so that it showed mercy there where it now threatened injustice, cruelty and almost inhuman cowardice.

A brave man's life was in the hands of this man, who professed love for her; and though Gilda rejected that love with contempt, she meant, womanlike, to use that love as a mainspring for the softened mood which she wished to call forth.

The first thought that had broken in upon her after a brief and troubled sleep was that a brave young life would be sacrificed to-day to gratify the petty spite of a fiend. She had been persuaded yesterday that the man who — though helpless and pinioned — stood before her in all the splendour of manhood and of a magnificent personality was nothing but a common criminal — a liar, a forger and a thief.

Though this thought should have made her contented, since by bringing guilt home to a man who was nothing to her, it exonerated her brother whom she loved, she had felt all night, right through the disturbing dreams which had floated through her consciousness, a leaden weight sitting upon her heart, like the sense of the committal of some great and irreparable wrong. Indeed, she felt that if here in this very place which he had filled last night with his exuberant vitality, she had to think of him as silent and cold for all eternity, such a thought would drive her mad.

The Lord of Stoutenburg's honeyed words fell unheeded on her ear; his presence near her filled her with horror; she only kept up a semblance of interest in him, because he held the fate of another man in the hollow of his hand.

She was preparing in her mind what she was going to say to him, she rehearsed the words which were most likely to appeal to his callous nature. Already she was nerving herself for the supreme effort of pleading for a brave man's life when suddenly the tramping of heavy feet outside the hut, confused shouts and clang of arms, caused Stoutenburg to jump to his feet.

The door was torn open, and Nicolaes Beresteyn stood for a moment on the threshold, pale, speechless, with body trembling and moisture thick upon his brow. Lucas of Sparendam was close behind him equally pale and still.

At first sight of her brother Gilda had uttered a little cry of joy; but that cry soon died upon her lips. Beresteyn had scarcely looked on her, his glance at once had found that of Stoutenburg, and the two men seemed to understand one another.

"We are betrayed?" cried Stoutenburg hoarsely.

Beresteyn nodded in reply.

"How?"

Lucas of Sparendam in short jerky sentences retold once more the tale of all that had happened at Delft: the Prince of Orange warned, the spies which he had sent broadcast, the bodyguard which even now was on its way.

"They know of this place," murmured Beresteyn between quivering lips, "they might be here at any moment."

Through the open door there came the noise of the men fighting, the cries of rage and of fear, the clatter of metal and the tramping of many feet.

"They are scared and half mad," said Lucas of Sparendam, "in five minutes the *sauve qui peut* will commence."

"We are quite near the coast," said Stoutenburg with outward calm, though his voice was choked and his tongue clove to the roof of his mouth, "go you and tell the others, Beresteyn," he added, turning to his friend, "then collect all our papers that are in the molens. Thank God there are only a few that might compromise us at all. Heemskerk and van Does will help you, they are not like to be seized with panic. We can then make quietly for Scheveningen, where the boats are ready. There is a sledge here and a pair of horses which I shall need; but it is less than a league to Scheveningen, and you can all walk it easily. Tell the others not to lose time and I will follow with the sledge as soon as may be. There is no cause for a panic and we can all save ourselves."

Beresteyn made ready to go. He took less pains than Stoutenburg to conceal his terror and his knees frankly shook under him. At the door he paused. He had suddenly remembered Gilda.

She had risen from her chair and stood now like a statue carved in stone, white to the lips, wide-eyed, her whole expression one of infinite horror.

It had all been lies then, all that Stoutenburg had told her yesterday! He had concealed the monstrous truth, lying to her with every word he uttered. Now he stood there pale and trembling, the traitor who in his turn has been betrayed. Fear and blind rage were fighting their last deathly battle in his soul. The edifice of his treachery was crumbling around him; God's hand — through an unknown channel — had set the limit to his crimes. Twice a traitor, he had twice failed. Already he could see the disbanding of his mercenary troops, the beginning of that mad, wild flight to the coast, and down the steps of the molens his friends too were running helter-skelter, without thought of anything save of their own safety.

It would be so immeasurably horrible to fall into the Stadtholder's hands.

And Gilda, pale and silent, stood between the two men who had lied to her, outraged her to the end. Nicolaes was a traitor after all; he had cast the eternal shroud of shame over the honour and peace of his house. An God did not help him now, his death would complete that shame.

She tried to hold his glance, but he would not look at her; she felt that his wrath of her almost bordered on hatred because he believed that she had betrayed them all. His eyes were fixed upon his leader and friend, and all the anxiety which he felt was for that one man.

"You must not delay, Nicolaes," said Stoutenburg curtly, "go, warn the others and tell them to make for Scheveningen. But do you wait for me — we'll follow anon in the sledge and, of course, Gilda comes with us."

And Beresteyn said firmly:

"Of course, Gilda comes with us."

She was not afraid, even when he said this, even when his fierce glance rested upon her, and she was too proud to make an appeal to him. It was her turn now to avert her glance from him; to the bottom of her soul she loathed his cowardice, and the contempt with which she regarded him now was almost cruel in its intensity.

He went out of the room followed by Lucas of Sparendam, and now she was once more alone with the Lord of Stoutenburg.

"Gilda," he cried with a fierce oath, "when did you do this?"

"It was not I, my lord," she replied calmly, "you and Nicolaes did all that lay in your power to render me helpless in this. God knows I would not have betrayed you ... it is His hand that hath pointed the way to one who was more brave than I."

"'Tis false," he exclaimed violently, "no one knew of our plans save those who now must flee because like us they have been betrayed. No sane man would wilfully put his head in the halter; and there are no informers amongst us."

"You need not believe me, my lord," she rejoined coldly, "an you do not wish. But remember that I have never learnt the art of lying, nor could I be the Judas to betray my own brother. Therefore do I pledge you my word that I had no share in this decree of God."

"If not yourself," he retorted, "you spoke of it to some one ... who went to the Stadtholder ... and warned him! to some one ... some one who.... Ah!" he cried suddenly with a loud and ghoulish scream wherein rage, horror and fear and a kind of savage triumph too rang out, "I see that I have guessed aright. You did speak of what you knew ... to the miserable knave whom Nicolaes paid to outrage you ... and you offered him money to betray your own brother."

"It is false!"

"It is true — I can read it in your face. That man went to Delft yesterday — he was captured by Jan on his way back to Rotterdam. He had fulfilled your errand and warned the Prince of Orange and delivered me and all my friends into hands that never have known mercy."

He was blind with passion now and looked on her with bloodshot eyes that threatened to kill. But Gilda was not cast in the same mould as was this traitor.

Baffled in his crime, fear had completely unmanned him, but with every cry of rage uttered by Stoutenburg she became more calm and less afraid.

"Once more, my lord," she said quietly in the brief interval of Stoutenburg's ravings and while he was forced to draw breath, "do I pledge my word to you that I had no hand in saving the Stadtholder's life. That God chose for this another instrument than I, I do thank Him on my knees."

While she spoke Stoutenburg had made a quick effort to regain some semblance of composure, and now he contrived to say quite calmly and with an evil sneer upon his face:

"That instrument of God is an I mistake not tied to a post with ropes like an ox ready for the butcher's hand. Though I have but sorry chances of escape myself and every minute hath become precious, I can at least spend five in making sure that his fate at any rate be sorrier than mine."

Her face became if possible even paler than before.

"What do you mean to do?" she murmured.

"The man who has betrayed me to the Prince of Orange is the same man who laid hands upon you in Haarlem — is that not so?"

"I cannot say," she said firmly.

"The same man who was here in this room yesterday, bound and pinioned before you?" he insisted.

"I do not know."

"Will you swear then that you never spoke to him of the Prince of Orange, and of our plans?"

"Not of your plans ..." she protested calmly.

"You see that you cannot deny it, Gilda," he continued with that same unnatural calm which seemed to her far more horrible than his rage had been before. "Willingly or unwittingly you let that man know what you overheard in the Groote Kerk on New Year's Eve. Then you bribed him into warning the Prince of Orange, since you could not do it yourself."

"It is false," she reiterated wildly.

Once more that evil sneer distorted his pale face.

"Well!" he said, "whether you bribed him or not matters to me but little. I do believe that willingly you would not have betrayed Nicolaes or me or any of our friends to the Stadtholder, knowing what he is. But you wanted to cross our plans, you wanted to warn the Stadtholder of his danger, and you — not God — chose that man for your instrument."

"It is not true — I deny it," she repeated fearlessly.

"You may deny it with words, Gilda, but your whole attitude proclaims the truth. Thank God!" he cried with a note of savage triumph in his voice, "that man is still a helpless prisoner in my hands."

"What do you mean?" she murmured.

"I mean that it is good to hold the life of one's deadliest enemy in the hollow of one's hand."

"But you would not slay a defenceless prisoner," she cried.

He laughed, a bitter, harsh, unnatural laugh.

"Slay him," he cried, "aye that I will, if it is not already done. Did you hear the hammering and the knocking awhile ago? It was Jan making ready the gibbet. And now — though the men have run away like so many verdommde cowards, I know that Jan at any rate has remained faithful to his post. The gibbet is still there, and Jan and I and Nicolaes, we have three pairs of hands between us, strong enough to make an enemy swing twixt earth and heaven, and three pairs of eyes wherewith to see an informer perish upon the gallows."

But already she had interrupted him with a loud cry of overwhelming horror.

"Are you a fiend to think of such a thing?"

"No," he replied, "only a man who has a wrong to avenge."

"The wrong was in your treachery," she retorted, even while indignation nearly choked the words in her throat, "no honest man could refuse to warn another that a murderous trap had been laid for him."

"Possibly. But through that warning given by a man whom I hate, my life is practically at an end."

"Life can only be ended by death," she pleaded, "and yours is in no danger yet. In a couple of hours as you say you will have reached the coast. No doubt you have taken full measures for your safety. The Stadtholder is sick. He hath scarce a few months to live; when he dies everything will be forgotten, you can return and begin your life anew. Oh! you will thank God then on your knees, that this last hideous crime doth not weigh upon your soul."

"A wrong unavenged would weigh my soul down with bitterness," he said sombrely. "My life is done, Gilda. Ambition, hope, success, everything that I care for has gone from me. Nicolaes may begin his life anew; he is young and his soul is not like mine consumed with ambition and with hatred. But for that one man, I were to-day Stadtholder of half our provinces and sole ruler of our United Netherlands, instead of which from this hour forth I shall be a fugitive, a pariah, an exile. All this do I owe to one man," he added fiercely, "and I take my revenge, that is all."

He made a feint as if ready to go. But Gilda with a moan of anguish had already held him back. Despite the loathing which the slightest contact with such a fiend caused her, she clung with both her hands to his arm.

"My lord!" she entreated, "in the name of your dear mother, in the name of all that is yet good and pure and noble in you, do not allow this monstrous crime to add to the heavy load of sin which rests upon your soul. God is just," she added earnestly, "God will punish us all if such an infamy is done now at this supreme hour when our destinies are being weighed in the balance."

But he looked down on her suddenly, with an evil leer which sent a chill right through her to her heart.

"Are you pleading for a man who mayhap hath sent your brother to the scaffold?" he asked.

His glance now was so dark and so cruel, the suspicion which lurked in it was so clear, that for the moment Gilda was overawed by this passion of hate and jealousy which she was unable to fathom. The quick hot blood of indignation rushed to her pale cheeks.

"It was of Nicolaes that I was thinking," she said proudly, "if that man dies now, I feel that such a dastardly crime would remain a lasting stain upon the honour of our house."

"The crime is on you, Gilda," he retorted, "in that you did betray us all. Willingly or un-wittingly, you did deliver me into the hands of my most bitter enemy. But I pray you, plead no more for a knave whom you surely must hate even more bitterly than I do hate him. The time goes by, and every wasted minute becomes dangerous now. I pray you make yourself ready to depart."

She had not given up all thoughts of pleading yet; though she knew that for the moment she had failed, there floated vaguely at the back of her mind a dim hope that God would not abandon her in this her bitterest need. He had helped her in her direst trouble; He had averted the hideous treachery which threatened to stain her father's honoured name and her own with a hideous mark of shame; surely He would not allow this last most terrible crime to be committed.

No doubt that vague frame of mind, born of intense bodily and mental fatigue, betrayed itself in the absent expression in her eyes, for Stoutenburg reiterated impatiently:

"I can give you a quarter of an hour wherein to make ready."

"A quarter of an hour," she murmured vaguely, "to make ready?...for what?"

"For immediate departure with me and your brother for Belgium."

Still she did not understand. A deep frown of puzzlement appeared between her brows.

"Departure? — with you? — what do you mean, my lord?" she asked.

"I mean," he replied roughly, "that out of the wreckage of all my ambitions, my desires and my hopes I will at least save something that will compensate me for all that I have lost. You said just now that life could only end in death. Well! next to mine ambition and my desire for vengeance, you, Gilda, as you know, do fill my entire soul. With you beside me I may try to begin life anew. I leave for the coast in less than half an hour; Nicolaes will be with us and he will care for you. But I will not go without you, so you must come with us."

"Never!" she said firmly.

But Stoutenburg only laughed with careless mockery.

"Who will protect you?" he said, "when I take you in my arms and carry you to the sledge, which in a quarter of an hour will be ready for you? Who will protect you when I carry you in my arms from the sledge to the boat which awaits us at Scheveningen?"

"Nicolaes," she rejoined calmly, "is my brother — he would not permit such an outrage."

An ironical smile curled the comers of his cruel lips. "Do you really think, Gilda," he said, "that Nicolaes will run counter to my will? I have but to persuade him that your presence in Holland will be a perpetual menace to our safety. Besides, you heard what he said just now; that you, of course, would come with us."

"My dead body you can take with you," she retorted, "but I — alive — will never follow you."

"Then 'tis your dead body I'll take, Gilda," he said with a sneer, "I will be here to fetch you in a quarter of an hour, so I pray you make ready while I go to deal with that meddlesome instrument of God."

She was spent now, and had no strength for more; a great numbness, an overpowering fatigue seemed to creep into her limbs. She even allowed him to take her hand and to raise it to his lips, for she was quite powerless to resist him; only when she felt those burning lips against her flesh a shudder of infinite loathing went right through her body.

Soon he turned on his heel and strode out of the room. She heard the thin wooden door fall to with a bang behind him; but she could no longer see, a kind of darkness had fallen over her eyes, a darkness, in which only one figure appeared clearly — the figure of a man upon a gibbet. All else was blackness around her, impenetrable blackness, almost tangible in its intensity, and out of the blackness which seemed like that of a dungeon there came cries as of human creatures in hell.

"Lord have mercy upon him!" her lips, cold and white, murmured vaguely and insistently, "Lord have mercy upon him! Lord have mercy upon us all!"

CHAPTER XLI
"VENGEANCE IS MINE"

It was like a man possessed of devils that the Lord of Stoutenburg ran out through the mist toward the molens.

The grey light of this winter's morning had only vaguely pierced the surrounding gloom, and the basement beneath the molens still looked impenetrably dark. Dark and silent! the soldier — foreign mercenaries and louts — had vanished in the fog, arms hastily thrown down littered the mud-covered ground, swords, pistols, muskets, torn clothing, here and there a neck-cloth, a steel bonnet, a bright coloured sash. Stoutenburg saw it all, right through the gloom, and he ground his teeth together to smother a cry of agonised impotence.

Only now and then a ghostly form flitted swift and silent among the intricate maze of beams, a laggard left behind in the general scramble for safety, or a human scavenger on the prowl for loot. Now and then a groan or a curse came from out the darkness, and a weird, shapeless, moving thing would crawl along in the mud like some creeping reptile seeking its lair. But Stoutenburg looked neither to right nor left. He paid no heed to these swiftly fleeting ghostlike forms. He knew well enough that he would find silence here, that three dozen men — cowards and mercenaries all — had been scattered like locusts before a gale. Overhead he heard the tramping of feet, his friends — Beresteyn, Heemskerk, van Does — were making ready for flight. His one scheme of vengeance — that for which he had thirsted and plotted and sinned — had come to nought, but he had yet another in his mind — one which, if successful, would give him no small measure of satisfaction for the failure of the other.

And ahead the outline of the hastily improvised gallows detached itself out of the misty shroud, and from the Lord of Stoutenburg's throat there came a fierce cry of joy which surely must have delighted all the demons in hell.

He hurried on, covering with swift eager steps the short distance that separated him from the gibbet.

He called loudly to Jan, for it seemed to him as if the place was unaccountably deserted. He could not see Jan nor yet the prisoner, and surely Piet the Red had not proved a coward.

The solid beams above and around him threw back his call in reverberating echoes. He called again, and from far away a mocking laugh seemed alone to answer him.

Like a frightened beast now he bounded forward. There were the gallows not five paces away from him; the planks hastily hammered together awhile ago were creaking weirdly, buffeted by the wind, and up aloft the rope was swinging, beating itself with a dull, eerie sound against the wood.

The Lord of Stoutenburg — dazed and stupefied — looked on this desolate picture like a man in a dream.

"My lord!"

The voice came feebly from somewhere close by.

"My lord! for pity's sake!"

It was Jan's voice of course. The Lord of Stoutenburg turned mechanically in the direction from whence it came. Not far from where he was standing he saw Jan lying on the ground against a beam, with a scarf wound loosely round his mouth and his arms held with a cord behind his back. Stoutenburg unwound the scarf and untied the cord, then he murmured dully:

"Jan? What does this mean?"

"The men all threw down their arms, my lord," said Jan as soon as he had struggled to his feet, "they ran like cowards when Lucas of Sparendam brought the news."

"I knew that," said Stoutenburg hoarsely, "curse them all for their miserable cowardice. But the prisoner, man, the prisoner? What have you done with him? Did I not order you to guard him with your life?"

"Then is mine own life forfeit, my lord," said Jan simply, "for I did fail in guarding the prisoner."

A violent oath broke from Stoutenburg's trembling lips. He raised his clenched fist, ready to strike in his blind, unreasoning fury the one man who had remained faithful to him to the last.

Jan slowly bent the knee.

"Kill me, my lord," he said calmly, "I could not guard the prisoner."

Stoutenburg was silent for a moment, then his upraised arm fell nervelessly by his side.

"How did it happen?" he asked.

"I scarce can tell you, my lord," replied Jan, "the attack on us was so quick and sudden. Piet and I did remain at our post, but in the rush and the panic we presently were left alone beside the prisoner. Two men — who were his friends — must have been on the watch for this opportunity, they fell on us from behind and caught us unawares. We called in vain for assistance; it was a case of sauve qui peut and every one for himself, in a trice the cords that bound the prisoner were cut, and three men had very quickly the best of us. Piet, though wounded in the leg, contrived to escape, but it almost seemed as if those three demons were determined to spare me. Though by God," added Jan fervently, "I would gladly have died rather than have seen all this shame! When they had brought me down they wound a scarf round my mouth and left me here tied to a beam, while they disappeared in the fog."

Stoutenburg made no comment on this brief narrative, even the power of cursing seemed to have deserted him. He left Jan kneeling there on the frozen ground, and without a word he turned on his heel and made his way once more between the beams under the molens back toward the hut.

Vengeance indeed had eluded his grasp. The two men whom on earth he hated most had remained triumphant while he himself had been brought down to the lowest depths of loneliness and misery. Friendless, kinless now, life indeed, as he had told Gilda, was at an end for him. Baffled vengeance would henceforth make him a perpetual exile and a fugitive with every man's hand raised against him, a price once more upon his head.

The world doth at times allow a man to fail in the task of his life, it will forgive that one failure and allow the man to try again. But a second failure is unforgivable, men turn away from the blunderer in contempt. Who would risk life, honour and liberty in a cause that has twice failed?

Stoutenburg knew this. He knew that within the next hour his friends would already have practically deserted him. Panic-stricken now they would accompany him as far as the coast, they would avail themselves of all the measures which he had devised for their mutual safety, but in their innermost hearts they would already have detached themselves from his future ill-fortunes; and anon, in a few months mayhap, when the Stadtholder had succumbed to the disease which was threatening his life, they would all return to their homes and to their kindred and forget this brief episode wherein their leader's future had been so completely and so irretrievably wrecked.

They would forget, only he — Stoutenburg — would remain the pariah, the exile, that carries the brand of traitor for ever upon the pages of his life.

And now the hut is once more in sight, and for one brief instant an inward light flickers up in Stoutenburg's dulled eyes. Gilda is there, Gilda whom he loves, and whose presence in the sorrow-laden years that are to come would be a perpetual compensation for all the humiliation and all the shame which he had endured.

To-day mayhap she would follow him unwillingly, but Stoutenburg's passion was proof against her coldness. He felt that he could conquer her, that he could win her love, when once he had her all to himself in a distant land, when she — kinless too and forlorn — would naturally turn to him for protection and for love. He had little doubt that he would succeed, and vaguely in his mind there rose the pale ray of hope that her love would then bring him luck, or at any rate put renewed energy in him to begin his life anew.

CHAPTER XLII
THE FIGHT IN THE DOORWAY

It seemed to Stoutenburg that from the back of the hut there came the sound of bustle and activity: he thought that mayhap Beresteyn had had the good idea of making the sledge ready for departure, and he called out loudly to his friend.

It was a mocking voice, however, that rose in response:

"Was your Magnificence perchance looking for me?"

Out of the mist which still hung round the small building Diogenes' tall figure suddenly loomed before the Lord of Stoutenburg. He was standing in the doorway of the hut, with his back to it; one hand — the right one — was thrust inside his doublet, the left was on the hilt of his sword; his battered hat was tilted rakishly above his brow and he was regarding his approaching enemy with a look of keen amusement and of scorn.

At first Stoutenburg thought that his fevered fancy was playing his eyes a weird and elusive trick, then as the reality of what he saw fully burst upon his senses he uttered a loud and hoarse cry like a savage beast that has been wounded.

"Plepshurk! smeerlap!" he cried fiercely.

"Rogue! Villain! Menial! Varlet! and all that you care to name me, my lord!" quoth the philosopher lightly, "and entirely at your service."

"Jan!" cried Stoutenburg, "Jan! In the name of hell where are you?"

"Not very far, my lord," rejoined the other. "Jan is a brave soldier but he was no match for three philosophers, even though one of them at first was trussed like a fowl. Jan stuck to his post, my lord, remember that," he added more seriously, "even when all your other followers and friends were scattered to the winds like a crowd of mice at the approach of a cat. We did not hurt Jan because he is a brave soldier, but we tied him down lest he ran to get assistance whilst assistance was still available."

"You insolent knave...."

"You speak rightly, my lord: I am an insolent knave, and do so rejoice in mine insolence that I stayed behind here — while my brother philosophers accomplish the task which I have put upon them — on purpose to exercise some of that insolence upon you, and to see what power a man hath to curb his temper and to look pleasant, whilst an insolent knave doth tell him to his face that he is an abject and degraded cur."

"Then by Heaven, you abominable plepshurk," cried Stoutenburg white with passion, "since you stayed here to parley with me, I can still give you so complete a retort that your final insolence will have to be spoken in hell. But let me pass now. I have business inside the hut."

"I know you have, my lord," rejoined Diogenes coolly, "but I am afraid that your business will have to wait until two philosophers named respectively Pythagoras and Socrates have had time to finish theirs."

"What do you mean? Let me pass, I tell you, or...."

"Or the wrath of your Magnificence will once more be upon mine unworthy head. Dondersteen! what have I not suffered already from that all-powerful wrath!"

"You should have been hanged ere this...."

"It is an omission, my lord, which I fear me we must now leave to the future to rectify."

"Stand aside, man," cried Stoutenburg, who was hoarse with passion.

"No! not just yet!" was the other's calm reply.

"Stand aside!" reiterated Stoutenburg wildly.

He drew his sword and made a quick thrust at his enemy; he remembered the man's wounded shoulder and saw that his right hand was temporarily disabled.

"Ah, my lord!" quoth Diogenes lightly, as with his left he drew Bucephalus out of its scabbard, "you had forgotten or perhaps you never knew that during your follower's scramble for safety my sword remained unheeded in an easily accessible spot, and also that it is as much at home in my left hand as in my right."

Like a bull goaded to fury Stoutenburg made a second and more vigorous thrust at his opponent. But Diogenes was already on guard: calm, very quiet in his movements in the manner of the perfect swordsman. Stoutenburg, hot with rage, impetuous and clumsy, was at once at a disadvantage whilst this foreign adventurer, entirely self-possessed and good-humoured, had the art of the sword at his finger-tips — the art of perfect self-control, the art of not rushing to the attack, the supreme art of waiting for an opportunity.

No feint or thrust at first, only on guard, quietly on guard, and Bucephalus seemed to be infinitely multiplied at times so quickly did the bright steel flash out in the grey light and then subside again.

Stoutenburg was at once conscious of his own disadvantage. He was no match for this brilliant sword play; his opponent did indeed appear to be only playing with him, but Stoutenburg felt all the time that the abominable knave might disarm him at any moment if he were so minded.

Nor could he see very clearly: the passionate blood in him had rushed to his head and was beating furiously in his temples, whilst the other man with the additional advantage of a good position against the wall, kept up a perfect fusillade of good-humoured comments.

"Well attacked, my lord!" he cried gaily, "Dondersteen! were I as fat as your Magnificence supposes, your sword would ere now have made a hole in my side. Pity I am not broader, is it not? or more in the way of your sword. There," he added as with a quick and sudden turn of the wrist he knocked his opponent's weapon out of his hand, "allow me to return you this most useful sword."

He had already stooped and picked up Stoutenburg's sword, and now was holding it with slender finger tips by the point of its blade, and smiling, urbane and mocking, he held it out at arm's length, bowing the while with courtly, ironical grace.

"Shall we call Jan, my lord," he said airily, "or one of your friends to aid you? Some of them I noticed just now seemed somewhat in a hurry to quit this hospitable molens, but mayhap one or two are still lingering behind."

Stoutenburg, blind with rage, had snatched his sword back out of the scoffer's hand. He knew that the man was only playing with him, only keeping him busy here to prevent his going to Gilda. This thought threw him into a frenzy of excitement and not heeding the other's jeers he cried out at the top of his voice:

"Jan! Jan! Nicolaes! What-ho!"

And the other man putting his hand up to his mouth also shouted lustily:

"Jan! Nicolaes! What ho!"

Had Stoutenburg been less blind and deaf to aught save to his own hatred and his own fury, he would have heard not many paces away, the sound of horses' hoofs upon the hard ground, the champing of bits, the jingle of harness. But of this he did not think, not just yet. His thoughts were only of Gilda, and that man was holding the door of the hut because he meant to dispute with him the possession of Gilda. He cast aside all sense of pride and shame. He was no match with a foreign mercenary, whose profession was that of arms; there was no disgrace in his want of skill. But he would not yield the ground to this adventurer who meant to snatch Gilda away from him. After all the man had a wounded shoulder and a lacerated hip; with the aid of Jan and of Nicolaes he could soon be rendered helpless.

New hope rose in the Lord of Stoutenburg's heart, giving vigour to his arm. Now he heard the sound of running footsteps behind him; Jan was coming to his aid and there were others; Nicolaes no doubt and Heemskerk.

"My lord! my lord!" cried Jan, horrified at what he saw. He had heard the clang of steel against steel and had caught up the first sword that came to his hand. His calls and those of Stoutenburg as well as the more lusty ones of Diogenes reached the ears of Beresteyn, who with his friend Heemskerk was making a final survey of the molens, to search for compromising papers that might have been left about. They too heard the cries and the clash of steel; they ran down the steps of the molens, only to meet Jan who was hurrying toward the hut with all his might.

"I think my lord is being attacked," shouted Jan as he flew past, "and the jongejuffrouw is still in the hut."

These last words dissipated Nicolaes Beresteyn's sudden thoughts of cowardice. He too snatched up a sword and followed by Heemskerk he ran in Jan's wake.

The stranger, so lately a prisoner condemned to hang, was in the doorway of the hut, with his back to it, his sword in his left hand keeping my Lord of Stoutenburg at arm's length. Jan, Nicolaes and Heemskerk were on him in a trice.

"Two, three, how many of you?" queried Diogenes with a laugh, as with smart riposte he met the three blades which suddenly flashed out against him. "Ah, Mynheer Beresteyn, my good Jan, I little thought that I would see you again."

"Let me pass, man," cried Beresteyn, "I must to my sister."

"Not yet, friend," he replied, "till I know what your intentions are."

For one instant Beresteyn appeared to hesitate. The kindly sentiment which had prompted him awhile ago to speak sympathetic words to a condemned man who had taken so much guilt upon his shoulders, still fought in his heart against his hatred for the man himself. Since that tragic moment at the foot of the gallows which had softened his mood, Beresteyn had learnt that it was this man who had betrayed him and his friends to the Stadtholder, and guessed that it was Gilda who had instigated or bribed him into that betrayal. And now the present position seemed to bring vividly before his mind the picture of that afternoon in the "Lame Cow" at Haarlem, when the knave whom he had paid to keep Gilda safely out of the way was bargaining with his father to bring her back to him.

All the hatred of the past few days — momentarily lulled in the face of a tragedy — rose up once more with renewed intensity in his heart. Here was the man who had betrayed him, and who, triumphant, was about to take Gilda back to Haarlem and receive a fortune for his reward.

While Heemskerk, doubtful and hesitating, marvelled if 'twere wise to take up Stoutenburg's private quarrels rather than follow his other friends to Scheveningen where safety lay, Jan and Beresteyn vigorously aided by Stoutenburg made a concerted attack upon the knave.

But it seemed as easy for Bucephalus to deal with three blades as with one: now it appeared to have three tongues of pale grey flame that flashed hither and thither; — backwards, forwards, left, right, above, below, parry, riposte, an occasional thrust, and always quietly on guard.

Diogenes was in his greatest humour laughing and shouting with glee. To anyone less blind with excitement than were these men it would soon have been clear that he was shouting for the sole purpose of making a noise, a noise louder than the hammerings, the jinglings, the knocking that was going on at the back of the hut.

To right and left of the front of the small building a high wooden paling ran for a distance of an hundred paces or so enclosing a rough yard with a shed in the rear. It was impossible to see over the palings what was going on behind them and so loudly did the philosopher shout and laugh, and so vigorously did steel strike against steel that it was equally impossible to perceive the sounds that came from there.

But suddenly Stoutenburg was on the alert: something had caught his ear, a sound that rose above the din that was going on in the doorway ... a woman's piercing shriek. Even the clang of steel could not drown it, nor the lusty shouts of the fighting philosopher.

For a second he strained his ear to listen. It seemed as if invisible hands were suddenly tearing down the wooden palisade that hid the rear of the small building from his view; before his mental vision a whole picture rose to sight. A window at the back of the hut broken in, Gilda carried away by the friends of this accursed adventurer — Jan had said that two came to his aid at the foot of the gallows — Maria screaming, the sledge in wait, the horses ready to start.

"My God, I had not thought of that," he cried, "Jan! Nicolaes! in Heaven's name! Gilda! After me! quick!"

And then he starts to run, skirting the palisade in the direction whence come now quite distinctly that ceaseless rattle, that jingle and stamping of the ground which proclaims the presence of horses on the point of departure.

"Jan, in Heaven's name, follow me!" cries Stoutenburg, pausing one instant ere he rounds the corner of the palisade. "Nicolaes, leave that abominable knave! Gilda, I tell you! Gilda! They are carrying her away!"

Jan already has obeyed, grasping his sword he does not pause to think. My lord has called and 'tis my lord whom he follows. He runs after Stoutenburg as fast as his tired limbs will allow. Heemskerk, forgetting his own fears in the excitement of this hand-to-hand combat, follows in their wake.

Nicolaes, too, at Stoutenburg's call, is ready to follow him.

He turns to run when a grasp of iron falls upon his arm, holding it like a vice. He could have screamed with the pain, and the sword which he held falls out of his nerveless fingers. The next moment he feels himself dragged by that same iron grasp through the open door into the hut, and hears the door slammed to and locked behind him.

"Your pardon if I have been rough, mynheer," said Diogenes' pleasant voice, "but there was no time to argue outside that door and you seemed in such a mighty hurry to run straight into that yawning abyss of disgrace."

The grasp upon his arm had not relaxed, but it no longer hurt. Yet it was so firm and so absolute that Nicolaes felt powerless to wrench himself away.

"Let me go!" he cried hoarsely.

"Not just yet, mynheer," rejoined Diogenes coolly, "not while this hot temper is upon you. Let the Lord of Stoutenburg and our friend Jan fight to their heart's content with a fat philosopher who is well able to hold his own against them, while the other who is lean and a moderately good coachman sees that a pair of horses do not rear and bolt during the fray."

"Let me go, man, I tell you," cried Beresteyn who was making frantic efforts to free himself from that slender white grapnel which held his arm as in a vice.

"One moment longer, mynheer, and you shall go. The horses of which I speak are harnessed to a sledge wherein is the jongejuffrouw your sister."

"Yes! verdommte Keerl! let me get to her or...."

"As soon as the fat philosopher has disposed of the Lord of Stoutenburg and of Jan he too will jump into the sledge and a minute later will be speeding on its way to Haarlem."

"And there will be three of us left here to hang you to that same gallows on which you should have dangled an hour ago," exclaimed Beresteyn savagely.

"Possibly," retorted Diogenes dryly, "but even so your sister will be on the way to Haarlem rather than to exile — whither the Lord of Stoutenburg and you — her brother — would drag her."

"And what is it to you, you abominable plepshurk, whither I go with my sister and my friend?"

"Only this, mynheer, that yesterday in this very room I proclaimed myself a forger, a liar and a thief before the jongejuffrouw in order that her love for her only brother should not receive a mortal wound. At that moment I did greatly care for that lie," he added with his wonted flippancy, "but time hath lent it enchantment: It is on the whole one of the finest lies I ever told in my life; moreover it carried conviction; the jongejuffrouw was deceived. Now I will not see that pet lie of mine made fruitless by the abominable action which you have in contemplation."

Beresteyn made no immediate reply. Easily swayed as he always was by a character stronger than his own, the words spoken by the man whom he had always affected to despise, could not fail to move him. He knew that that same abominable action of which he was being accused had indeed been contemplated not only by Stoutenburg but also by himself. It had only required one word from Stoutenburg — "Gilda of course comes with us" — one hint that her presence in Holland would be a perpetual menace to his personal safety, and he had been not only willing but fully prepared to put this final outrage upon the woman whom he should have protected with his life.

Therefore now he dared not meet the eager, questioning glance of this adventurer, in whose merry eyes the look of irrepressible laughter was momentary veiled by one of anxiety. He looked around him restlessly, shiftily; his wandering glance fell on the narrow inner door which stood open, and he caught a glimpse of a smaller room beyond, with a window at the further end of it. That window had been broken in from without, the narrow frame torn out of its socket and the mullion wrenched out of its groove.

Through the wide breach thus made in the lath and mud walls of the hut, Beresteyn suddenly saw the horses and the sledge out there in the open. The fight of awhile ago by the front door had now been transferred to this spot. A short fat man with his back to the rear of the sledge was holding the Lord Stoutenburg and Heemskerk at a couple of arm's lengths with the point of his sword. Jan was apparently not yet on the scene.

Another man, lean and tall, was on the box of the sledge, trying with all his might to hold a pair of horses in, who frightened by the clang of steel against steel, by the movement and the shouting, were threatening to plunge and rear at any moment.

Diogenes laughed aloud.

"My friend Pythagoras seems somewhat hard pressed," he said, "and those horses might complicate the situation at any moment. I must to them now, mynheer. Tell me then quickly which you mean to do; behave like an honest man or like a cur?"

"What right have you to dictate to me?" said Beresteyn sullenly. "I have no account to give to you of mine own actions."

"None I admit," rejoined the philosopher placidly, "but let me put the situation a little more clearly before you. On the one hand you must own that I could at this moment with very little trouble and hardly any scruples render you physically helpless first, then lock you up in this room, and go and join my friends outside. On the other hand you could leave this room sound in body and at heart an honest man, jump into the sledge beside your sister and convey her yourself safely back to the home from whence you — her own brother — should never have allowed her to be taken."

"I cannot do it," retorted Beresteyn moodily, "I could not meet my father face to face after what has happened."

"Think you Gilda would tell him that his only son has played the part of traitor?"

"She loathes and despises me."

"She has a horror of that treacherous plot. But the plot has come to naught; and she will consider that you are punished enough for it already, and feel happy that you are free from Stoutenburg's clutches."

"I cannot leave Stoutenburg now, and she must go with him. She hates me for the outrage which was committed against her."

"She does not know your share in it," said Diogenes quickly, "have I not told you that I lied admirably? She believes me to be the only culprit and to have forged your name to hide mine own infamy."

A hot flush rose to Beresteyn's pale cheeks.

"I cannot bear to profit by your generosity," he said dully.

"Pshaw man!" rejoined the other not without a tone of bitterness, "what matters what my reputation is in her sight? She despises me so utterly already that a few sins more or less cannot lower me further in her sight."

"No! no! I cannot do it," persisted Beresteyn. "Go to your friends, man," he added fiercely, "the fat one is getting sorely pressed, the other cannot cope with the horses much longer! go to their aid! and kill me if you are so minded. Indeed I no longer care, and in any case I could not survive all this shame."

"Die by all means when and where you list," said Diogenes placidly, "but 'tis your place first of all to take your sister now under your own protection, to keep her in the knowledge that whatever sins you may have committed you were at least true and loyal to herself. By Heaven man, hath she not suffered enough already in her person, in her pride, above all in her affections?

Your loyalty to her at this moment would be ample compensation for all that she hath suffered. Be an honest man and take her to her home."

"How can I? I have no home: and she is a menace to us all...."

"I am a menace to you, you weak-hearted craven," cried Diogenes whose moustache bristled with fury now, "for by Heaven I swear that you shall not leave this place with a whole skin save to do an honest man's act of reparation."

And as if to give greater emphasis to his words Diogenes gave the other man's arm a vigorous wrench which caused Beresteyn to groan and curse with pain.

"I may have to hurt you worse than this presently," said the philosopher imperturbably as he dragged Beresteyn — who by now felt dizzy and helpless — to the nearest chair and deposited him there. "Were you not her brother, I believe I should crack your obstinate skull; as it is ... I will leave you here to take counsel with reason and honesty until I have finally disposed of my Lord of Stoutenburg."

He ran quickly to the outer door, pushed the bolts home, gave the key an extra turn and then pulled it out of the lock and threw it out of the window. Beresteyn — somewhat stunned with emotion, a little faint with that vigorous wrench on his arm, and prostrate with the fatigue and excitement of the past two days — made no attempt to stop him. No doubt he realized that any such attempt would indeed be useless: there was so much vitality, so much strength in the man that his tall stature appeared to Nicolaes now of giant-like proportions, and his powers to savour of the supernatural.

He watched him with dull, tired eyes, as he finally went out of the room through the inner door; no doubt that this too he locked behind him. Beresteyn did not know; he half lay, half sat in the chair like a log, the sound of the fight outside, of the shouts that greeted Diogenes' arrival, of the latter's merry laughter that went echoing through the mist, only reached his dull perceptions like a far-off dream.

But in his mind he saw it all: the walls of the hut were transparent before his mental vision, he saw now the unequal fight; a perfect swordsman against Stoutenburg's unreasoning attacks and Heemskerk's want of skill. Jan too will have joined them by now, but he was loutish and clumsy. The issue would have been a foregone conclusion even without the aid of the fat knave who had held his own already for nearly ten minutes. Yet, though his thoughts were not by any means all clear upon the subject, Beresteyn made no attempt to go to his own friend's assistance. Vaguely some pleasing visions began to float through space around him. It seemed as if the magic personality of a nameless adventurer still filled this narrow room with its vitality, with its joy and with its laughter. The optimistic breeziness which emanated from the man himself had lingered here after he was gone. His cheerful words still hung and reverberated upon the cold, wintry air.

"After all, why not?" mused Beresteyn.

Gilda knew of his share in the conspiracy against the Stadtholder of course. But that conspiracy had now aborted; Gilda would never betray her brother's share in it either to the Stadtholder's vengeance or to her father's wrath.

And she had been made to believe that he was not the mover in the outrage against her person.

"Then — why not?"

She had been forcibly dragged out of this hut: she knew that Stoutenburg meant to take her away with him into exile; even if she had been only partially conscious since she was taken to the sledge, she would know that a desperate fight had been going on around her. Then if he, Nicolaes, now appeared upon the scene — if he took charge of her and of the sledge, and with the help of one or other of those knaves outside sped away with her north to Haarlem, would she not be confirmed in her belief in his loyalty, would he not play a heroic rôle, make her happy and himself free?

"Then — why not?"

All the papers relating to the aborted conspiracy which might have compromised him he had upon his person even now. He and Heemskerk had themselves collected them in the weighing-room of the molens after Lucas of Sparendam had brought his terrible news.

"Then — why not?"

He rose briskly from his chair. The outer door of the hut was locked — he crossed to the inner door. That was just on the latch and he threw it open. Before him now was the broken window frame through which peeped the dull grey light of this misty winter's morning. Out in the open through the filmy veil of the fog he could see the final phases of an unequal fight. Stoutenburg and Heemskerk were both disarmed and Jan had just appeared upon the scene. More far-seeing than were the Lord of Stoutenburg and Mynheer Heemskerk, he had very quickly realized that sword in hand no one was a match for this foreigner and his invincible blade. When the fighting was transferred from the doorway of the hut to the open road-way in the rear, he had at first followed in the wake of his chief, then he had doubled back, swiftly running to the molens, and in the basement from out the scattered litter of arms hastily thrown down, he had quickly picked up a couple of pistols, found some ammunition, quietly loaded the weapons and with them in his hand started to run back to the hut.

All this had taken some few minutes while Pythagoras had borne the brunt of a vigorous attack from the Lord of Stoutenburg and Mynheer Heemskerk, whilst Diogenes parleyed with Beresteyn inside the hut.

Beresteyn saw the whole picture before him. He had thrown open the door, and looked through the broken window at the precise moment when the Lord of Stoutenburg's sword flew out of his hand. Then it was that Jan came running along, shouting to my lord. Stoutenburg turned quickly, saw his faithful lieutenant and caught sight of the pistols which he held. The next second he had snatched one out of Jan's hand, and the pale ray of a wintry sun penetrating through the mist found its reflection in a couple of steel barrels pointed straight at a laughing philosopher.

Beresteyn from within felt indeed as if his heart stood still for that one brief, palpitating second. Was Fate after all taking the decision for the future — Gilda's and his — out of his hands into her own? Would a bullet end that vigorous life and still that merry laugh and that biting tongue for ever, and leave Nicolaes to be swayed once more by the dark schemes and arbitrary will of his friend Stoutenburg?

Fate was ready, calmly spinning the threads of human destinies. But there are some men in the world who have the power and the skill to take their destinies in their own hands. The philosopher and weaver of dreams, the merry Laughing Cavalier was one of these.

What the Lord of Stoutenburg had seen that he perceived equally quickly; he, too, had caught sight of Jan, and of the two steel barrels simultaneously levelled at him; he too, realized that the most skilled swordsman is but a sorry match against a pair of bullets.

But while Beresteyn held his breath and Stoutenburg tried to steady the trembling of his hand, he raised Bucephalus above his head and with a wild shout pointed toward the southern horizon far away.

"The Stadtholder's guard!" he cried lustily, "they are on us! *Sauve qui peut!*"

Three cries of mad terror rent the air, there was a double detonation, a great deal of smoke. The horses in the sledge reared and plunged wildly, forcing those who were nearest to the vehicle to beat a precipitate retreat.

"At the horses' heads, you wooden-headed bladder," shouted Diogenes lustily. Pythagoras did his best to obey, while Socrates was nearly dragged off the box by the frightened horses. Heemskerk had already incontinently taken to his heels. Jan had dropped his weapon which Diogenes at once picked up. The Lord of Stoutenburg was preparing to fire again.

"*Sauve qui peut*, my lord!" cried Diogenes, "before I change my mind and put a hole through your heel, which will prevent your running away fast enough to escape the Stadtholder's wrath."

There was another detonation. The horses reared and plunged again. When Beresteyn once more obtained a clear view of the picture, he saw the Lord of Stoutenburg stretched out on his back upon the ground in a position that was anything but dignified and certainly very perilous, for Diogenes towering above him was holding him by both feet. The tall soldierly figure of the foreigner stood out clearly silhouetted against the grey, misty light: his head with its wealth of unruly brown curls was thrown back with a gesture that almost suggested boyish delight in some impish mischief, whilst his infectious laugh echoed and re-echoed against the walls of the molens and of the hut.

Jan was on his hands and knees crawling toward those two men — the conqueror and the conquered — with no doubt a vague idea that he might even now render assistance to my lord.

"Here, Pythagoras, old fat head," cried Diogenes gaily, "see that our friend here does not interfere with me: and that he hath not a concealed poniard somewhere about his person, then collect all pistols and swords that are lying about, well out of harm's way. In the meanwhile what am I to do with his Magnificence? he is kicking like a vicious colt and that shoulder of mine is beginning to sting like fury."

"Kill me, man, kill me!" cried Stoutenburg savagely, "curse you, why don't you end this farce?"

"Because, my lord," said Diogenes more seriously than was his wont, "the purest and most exquisite woman on God's earth did once deign to bestow the priceless jewel of her love upon you. Did she know of your present plight, she would even now be pleading for you: therefore," he added more flippantly, "I am going to give myself the satisfaction of making you a present of the last miserable shred of existence which you will drag on from this hour forth in wretchedness and exile to the end of your days. Take your life and freedom, my lord," he continued in response to the invectives which Stoutenburg muttered savagely under his breath, "take it at the hands of the miserable plepshurk whom you so despise. It is better methinks to do this rather than fall into the hands of the Stadtholder, whose mercy for a fallen enemy would be equal to your own."

Then he shouted to Pythagoras.

"Here, old compeer! search his Magnificence for concealed weapons, and then make ready to go. We have wasted too much time already."

Despite Stoutenburg's struggles and curses Pythagoras obeyed his brother philosopher to the letter. His lordship and Jan were both effectually disarmed now. Then only did Diogenes allow Stoutenburg to struggle to his feet. He had his sword in his left hand and Pythagoras stood beside him. Jan found his master's hat and cloak and helped him on with them, and then he said quietly:

"The minutes are precious, my lord, 'tis a brief run to Ryswyk: my Lord of Heemskerk has gone and Mynheer Beresteyn has disappeared. Here we can do nothing more."

"Nothing, my good Jan," said Diogenes more seriously, "you are a brave soldier and a faithful servant. Take his Magnificence away to safety. You have well deserved your own."

Stoutenburg gave a last cry of rage and of despair. For a moment it seemed as if his blind fury would still conquer reason and prudence and that he meant once more to make an attack upon his victorious enemy, but something in the latter's look of almost insolent triumph recalled him to the peril of his own situation: he passed his hand once or twice over his brow, like a man who is dazed and only just returning to consciousness, then he called loudly to Jan to follow him, and walked rapidly away northwards through the fog.

Beresteyn went up to the broken window and watched him till he was out of sight, then he looked on Diogenes. That philosopher also watched the retreating figure of the Lord of Stoutenburg until the fog swallowed it up, then he turned to his friend.

"Pythagoras, old compeer," he said with a shrug of his broad shoulders, "what would you take to be walking at this moment in that man's shoes?"

"I wouldn't do it, friend," rejoined Pythagoras placidly, "for the possession of a running river of home-brewed ale. And I am mightily dry at the present moment."

"Jump up then on the box beside Socrates, you old wine-tub, and get to Leyden as quickly as these horses will take you. A halt at Voorburg will refresh you all."

"But you?" queried Socrates from his post of vantage.

"I shall make my way to Ryswyk first and get a horse there. I shall follow you at a distance, and probably overtake you before you get to Leyden. But you will not see me after this ... unless there is trouble, which is not likely."

"But the jongejuffrouw?" persisted Socrates.

"Hush! I shall never really lose sight of you and the sledge. But you must serve her as best you can. Someone will be with her who will know how to take care of her."

"Who?"

"Her own brother of course, Mynheer Beresteyn. Over the sill, mynheer!" he now shouted, calling to Nicolaes who still stood undecided, shamed, hesitating in the broken framework of the window, "over the sill, 'tis only three feet from the ground, and horses and men are quite ready for you."

He gave a lusty cheer of satisfaction as Beresteyn, throwing all final cowardly hesitations to the wind, suddenly made up his mind to take the one wise and prudent course. He swung himself through the window, and in a few moments was standing by Diogenes' side.

"Let me at least tell you, sir ..." he began earnestly.

"Hush! — tell me nothing now ..." broke in the other man quickly, "the jongejuffrouw might hear."

"But I must thank you — —"

"If you say another word," said Diogenes, sinking his voice to a whisper, "I'll order Socrates to drive on and leave you standing here."

"But...."

"Into the sledge, man, in Heaven's name. The jongejuffrouw is unconscious, her woman daft with fear. When the lady regains consciousness let her brother's face be the first sight to comfort her. Into the sledge, man," he added impatiently, "or by Heaven I'll give the order to start."

And without more ado, he hustled Nicolaes into the sledge. The latter bewildered, really not clear with himself as to what he ought to do, peeped tentatively beneath the cover of the vehicle. He saw his sister lying there prone upon the wooden floor of the sledge, her head rested against a bundle of rugs hastily put together for her comfort. Maria was squatting beside her, her head and ears muffled in a cloak, her hands up to her eyes; she was moaning incoherently to herself.

Gilda's eyes were closed, and her face looked very pale: Beresteyn's heart ached at the pitiful sight. She looked so wan and so forlorn that a sharp pang of remorse for all his cruelty to her shot right through his dormant sensibilities.

There was just room for him under the low cover of the sledge; he hesitated no longer now, he felt indeed as if nothing would tear him away from Gilda's side until she was safely home again in their father's arms.

A peremptory order: "En avant," struck upon his ear, a shout from the driver to his horses, the harness rattled, the sledge creaked upon its framework and then slowly began to move: Beresteyn lifted the flap of the hood at the rear of the vehicle and looked out for the last time upon the molens and the hut, where such a tragic act in his life's drama had just been enacted.

He saw Diogenes still standing there, waving his hat in farewell: for a few moments longer his splendid figure stood out clearly against the flat grey landscape beyond, then slowly the veil of mist began to envelop him, at first only blurring the outline of his mantle or his sash, then it grew more dense and the sledge moved away more rapidly.

The next moment the Laughing Cavalier had disappeared from view.

CHAPTER XLIII
LEYDEN ONCE MORE

After that Gilda had lived as in a dream: only vaguely conscious that good horses and a smoothly gliding vehicle were conveying her back to her home. Of this fact she was sure Nicolaes was sitting quite close under the hood of the sledge and when first she became fully aware of the reality of his presence, he had raised her hand to his lips and had said in response to a mute appeal from her eyes:

"We are going home."

After that a quiet sense of utter weariness pervaded her being, and she fell into a troubled sleep. She did not heed what went on around her, she only knew that once or twice during the day there was a halt for food and drink.

The nearness of her brother, his gentleness toward her, gave her a sense of well-being, even though her heart felt heavy with a great sorrow which made the whole future appear before her like an interminable vista of blank and grey dullness.

It was at her suggestion that arrangements were made for an all night halt at Leyden, which city they reached in the early part of the afternoon. She begged Nicolaes that they might put up at the hostelry of the "White Goat" on the further side of the town, and that from thence a messenger might be sent to her father, asking him to come and meet her there on the morrow.

Though Nicolaes was not a little astonished at this suggestion of Gilda's — seeing that surely she must be longing to be home again and that Haarlem could easily have been reached before night — he did not wish to run counter to her will. True enough, he dreaded the meeting with his father, but he knew that it had to come, and felt that, whatever might be the future consequences of it all — he could not possibly bear alone the burden of remorse and of shame which assailed him every time he encountered Gilda's tear-stained eyes, and saw how wearied and listless she looked.

So he called a halt at the "White Goat" and as soon as he saw his sister safely installed, with everything ordered for her comfort, and a tasteful supper prepared, he sent a messenger on horseback at once to Haarlem to his father.

Gilda had deliberately chosen to spend the night at the hostelry of the "White Goat" because she felt that in that quaint old building with its wide oak staircase — over which she had been carried five days ago, dizzy and half fainting — the blackened rafters would mayhap still echo with the sound of a merry laughter which she would never hear again.

But when the sledge finally turned in under the low gateway and drew up in the small court-yard of the inn — when with wearied feet and shaking knees she walked up those oaken stairs, it seemed to her that the vivid memories which the whole place recalled were far harder to bear than those more intangible ones which — waking and sleeping — had tortured her up to now.

The bedroom too, with the smaller one leading out of it, was the same in which she had slept. As the obsequious waiting-wench threw open the door for the noble jongejuffrouw to pass through she saw before her the wide open hearth with its crackling fire, the high-backed chair wherein she had sat, the very footstool which he had put to her feet.

It seemed to her at first as if she could not enter, as if his splendid figure would suddenly emerge out of the semi-darkness to confront her with his mocking eyes and his smiling face. She seemed to see him everywhere, and she had to close her eyes to chase away that all too insistent vision.

The waiting-wench did not help matters either, for she asked persistently and shyly about the handsome mynheer who had such an irresistible fund of laughter in him. Maria too, in her mutterings and grumblings, contrived — most unwittingly, since she adored Gilda — to inflict a series of tiny pin-pricks on an already suffering heart.

Tired in body and in mind, Gilda could not sleep that night. She was living over again every second of the past five days: the interview with that strangely winning person — a stranger still to her then — here in this room! how she had hated him at first! how she had tried to shame and wound him with her words, trying all the while to steel her heart against that irresistible gaiety and good humour which shone from him like a radiance: then that second interview in Rotterdam! did she still hate him then? and if not when was hatred first changed into the love which now so completely filled her soul?

Looking back on those days, she could not tell. All that she knew was that when he was brought before her helpless and pinioned she already loved him, and that since that moment love had grown and strengthened until her whole heart was given to that same nameless soldier of fortune whom she had first despised.

To live over again those few brief days which seemed now like an eternity was a sweet, sad pleasure which Gilda could endure, but what became intolerable in the darkness and in the silence of the night was the remembrance of the immediate past.

Clearly cut out before her mental vision were the pictures of her life this morning in the hut beside the molens: and indeed, it was a lifetime that had gone by in those few hours.

Firstly Stoutenburg's visit in the early morning, his smooth words and careless chatter! she, poor fool! under the belief all the time that the treacherous plot had been abandoned, and that she would forthwith be conveyed back to her father. Her thoughts of pleading for the condemned man's life: then the tramping of feet, the cries of terror, her brother's appearance bringing the awful news of betrayal. She lived over again those moments of supreme horror when she realized how Stoutenburg had deceived her, and that Nicolaes himself was but a traitor and a miserable liar.

She knew then that it was the adventurer, the penniless soldier of fortune whom she had tried to hate and to despise, who had quietly gone to warn the Stadtholder, and that his action had been the direct working of God's will in a brave and loyal soul: she knew also by a mysterious intuition which no good woman has ever been able to resist, that the man who had stood before her — self-convicted and self-confessed — had accepted that humiliation to save her the pain of fearing and despising her own brother.

The visions now became more dim and blurred. She remembered Stoutenburg's fury, his hideous threats of vengeance on the man who had thrown himself across his treacherous path. She remembered pleading to that monster, weeping, clinging to his arm in a passionate appeal. She remembered the soul agony which she felt when she realized that that appeal had been in vain.

Then she had stood for a moment silent and alone in the hut. Stoutenburg had left her in order to accomplish that hideous act of revenge.

After that she remembered nothing clearly. She could only have been half-conscious and all round her there was a confusion of sounds, of shouts and clash of arms: she thought that she was being lifted out of the chair into which she had fallen in a partial swoon, that she heard Maria's cries of terror, and that she felt the cold damp morning air striking upon her face.

Presently she knew that Nicolaes was beside her, and that she was being taken home. All else was a blank or a dream.

Now she was tossing restlessly upon the lavender-scented bed in this hostelry so full of memories. Her temples were throbbing, her eyes felt like pieces of glowing charcoal in her head. The blackness around her weighed upon her soul until she felt that she could not breathe.

Outside the silence of the night was being gravely disturbed: there was the sound of horses' hoofs upon the cobble-stones of the yard, the creaking of a vehicle brought to a standstill, the usual shouts for grooms and ostlers. A late arrival had filled the tranquil inn with its bustle and its noise.

Then once again all was still, and Gilda turned her aching head upon the pillow. Though the room was not hot, and the atmosphere outside heavy with frost, she felt positively stifled.

After a while this feeling of oppression became intolerable, she rose, and in the darkness she groped for her fur-lined cloak which she wrapped closely around her. Then she found her way across to the window and drew aside the curtain. No light penetrated through the latticed panes: the waning moon which four nights ago had been at times so marvellously brilliant, had not yet risen above the horizon line. As Gilda's fingers fumbled for the window-latch she heard a distant church clock strike the midnight hour.

She threw open the casement. The sill was low and she leaned out peering up and down the narrow street. It was entirely deserted and pitch dark save where on the wall opposite the light from a window immediately below her threw its feeble reflection. Vaguely she wondered who was astir in the small hostelry. No doubt it was the tap-room which was there below her, still lighted up, and apparently with its small casement also thrown open, like the one out of which she was leaning.

For now, when the reverberating echo of the chiming clock had entirely died away, she was conscious of a vague murmur of voices coming up from below, confused at first and undistinguishable, but presently she heard a click as if the casement had been pushed further open or mayhap a curtain pulled aside, for after that the sound of the voices became more distinct and clear.

With beating heart and straining ears Gilda leaned as far out of the window as she could, listening intently: she had recognized her father's voice, and he was speaking so strangely that even as she listened she felt all the blood tingling in her veins.

"My son, sir," he was saying, "had, I am glad to say, sufficient pride and manhood in him not to bear the full weight of your generosity any longer. He sent a special messenger on horseback out to me this afternoon. As soon as I knew that my daughter was here I came as fast as a sleigh and the three best horses in my stables could bring me. I had no thought, of course, of seeing you here."

"I had no thought that you should see me, sir," said a voice which by its vibrating tones had the power of sending the hot blood rushing to the listener's neck and cheeks. "Had I not entered the yard just as your sledge turned in under the gateway, you had not been offended by mine unworthy presence."

"I would in that case have searched the length and breadth of this land to find you, sir," rejoined Cornelius Beresteyn earnestly, "for half an hour later my son had told me the whole circumstances of his association with you."

"An association of which Mynheer Nicolaes will never be over-proud, I'll warrant," came in slightly less flippant accents than usual from the foreigner. "Do I not stand self-confessed as a liar, a forger and abductor of helpless women? A fine record forsooth: and ere he ordered me to be hanged my Lord of Stoutenburg did loudly proclaim me as such before his friends and before his followers."

"His friends, sir, are the sons of my friends. I will loudly proclaim you what you truly are: a brave man, a loyal soldier, a noble gentleman! Nicolaes has told me every phase of his association with you, from his shameful proposal to you in regard to his own sister, down to this moment when you still desired that Gilda and I should remain in ignorance of his guilt."

"What is the good, mynheer, of raking up all this past?" said the philosopher lightly, "I would that Mynheer Nicolaes had known how to hold his tongue."

"Thank God that he did not," retorted Cornelius Beresteyn hotly, "had he done so I stood in peril of failing — for the first time in my life — in an important business obligation."

"Not towards me, mynheer, at any rate."

"Yes, sir, towards you," affirmed Beresteyn decisively. "I promised you five hundred thousand guilders if you brought my daughter safely back to me. I know from mine own son, sir, that I owe her safety to no one but to you."

"Ours was an ignoble bargain, mynheer," said Diogenes with his wonted gaiety, and though she could not see him, Gilda could picture his face now alive with merriment and suppressed laughter. "The humour of the situation appealed to me — it proved irresistible — but the bargain in no way binds you seeing that it was I who had been impious enough to lay hands upon your daughter."

"At my son's suggestion I know," rejoined Beresteyn quietly, "and from your subsequent acts, sir, I must infer that you only did it because you felt that she was safer under your charge than at the mercy of her own brother and his friends....Nay! do not protest," he added earnestly, "Nicolaes, as you see, is of the same opinion."

"May Heaven reward you, sir, for that kindly thought of me," said Diogenes more seriously, "it will cheer me in the future, when I and all my doings will have faded from your ken."

"You are not leaving Holland, sir?"

"Not just now, mynheer, while there is so much fighting to be done. The Stadtholder hath need of soldiers...."

"And he will, sir, find none better than you throughout the world. And with a goodly fortune to help you...."

"Speak not of that, mynheer," he said firmly, "I could not take your money. If I did I should never know a happy hour again."

"Oh!"

"I am quite serious, sir, though indeed you might not think that I can ever be serious. For six days now I have had a paymaster: Mynheer Nicolaes' money has burned a hole in my good humour, it has scorched my hands, wounded my shoulder and lacerated my hip, it has brought on me all the unpleasant sensations which I have so carefully avoided hitherto, remorse, humiliation, and one or two other sensations which will never leave me until my death. It changed temporarily the shiftless, penniless soldier of fortune into a responsible human being, with obligations and duties. I had to order horses, bespeak lodgings, keep accounts. Ye gods, it made a slave of me! Keep your money, sir, it is more fit for you to handle than for me. Let me go back to my shiftlessness, my penury, my freedom, eat my fill to-day, starve to-morrow, and one day look up at the stars from the lowly earth, with a kindly bullet in my chest that does not mean to blunder. And if in the days to come your thoughts ever do revert to me, I pray you think of me as happy or nearly so, owning no master save my whim, bending my back to none, keeping my hat on my head when I choose, and ending my days in a ditch or in a palace, the carver of mine own destiny, the sole arbiter of my will. And now I pray you seek that rest of which you must be sorely in need. I start at daybreak to-morrow: mayhap we shall never meet again, save in Heaven, if indeed, there be room there for such a thriftless adventurer as I."

"But whither do you mean to go, sir?"

"To the mountains of the moon, sir," rejoined the philosopher lightly, "or along the milky way to the land of the Might-Have-Been."

"Before we part, sir, may I shake you by the hand?"

There was silence down below after that. Gilda listened in vain, no further words reached her ears just then. She tiptoed as quietly as she could across the room, finding her way with difficulty in the dark. At last her fumbling fingers encountered the latch of the door of the inner room where Maria lay snoring lustily.

It took Gilda some little time to wake the old woman, but at last she succeeded, and then ordered her, very peremptorily, to strike a light.

"Are you ill, mejuffrouw?" queried Maria anxiously even though she was but half awake.

"No," replied Gilda curtly, "but I want my dress — quick now," she added, for Maria showed signs of desiring to protest.

The jongejuffrouw was in one of those former imperious moods of hers when she exacted implicit obedience from her servants. Alas! the last few days had seen that mood submerged into an ocean of sorrow and humiliation, and Maria — though angered at having been wakened out of a first sleep — was very glad to see her darling looking so alert and so brisk.

Indeed — the light being very dim — Maria could not see the brilliant glow that lit up the jongejuffrouw's cheeks as with somewhat febrile gestures she put on her dress and smoothed her hair.

"Now put on your dress too, Maria," she said when she was ready, "and tell my father, who is either in the tap-room down below or hath already retired to his room, that I desire to speak with him."

And Maria, bewildered and flustered, had no option but to obey.

While Maria completed a hasty toilet, Gilda's instinct had drawn her back once more to the open window. The light from the room below was still reflected on the opposite wall, and from the tap-room the buzz of voices had not altogether ceased.

Cornelius Beresteyn was speaking now:

"Indeed," he said, "it will be the one consolation left to me, since you do reject my friendship, sir."

"Not your friendship, sir — only your money," interposed Diogenes.

"Well! you do speak of lifelong parting. But your two friends have indeed deserved well of me. Without their help no doubt you, sir, first and then my dearly loved daughter would have fallen victims to that infamous Stoutenburg. Will a present of twenty thousand guilders each gratify them, do you think?"

A ringing laugh roused the echoes of the sleeping hostelry.

"Twenty thousand guilders! ye gods!" exclaimed Diogenes merrily. "Pythagoras, dost hear, old bladder-face? Socrates, my robin, dost realize it? Twenty thousand guilders each in your pockets, old compeers. Lord! how drunk you will both be to-morrow."

Out of the confused hubbub that ensued Gilda could disentangle nothing definite; there was a good deal of shouting and clapping of pewter mugs against a table, and through it all that irresponsible, infectious laughter which — strangely enough — had to Gilda's ears at this moment a curious tone, almost of bitterness, as if its merriment was only forced.

Then when the outburst of gaiety had somewhat subsided she once more heard her father's voice. Maria was dressed by this time, and now at a word from Gilda was ready to go downstairs and to deliver the jongejuffrouw's message to her father.

"You spoke so lightly just now, sir, of dying in a ditch or palace," Cornelius Beresteyn was saying, "but you did tell me that day in Haarlem that you had kith and kindred in England. Where is that father of whom you spoke, and your mother who is a saint? Your irresponsible vagabondage will leave her in perpetual loneliness."

"My mother is dead, sir," said Diogenes quietly, "my father broke her heart."

"Even then he hath a right to know that his son is a brave and loyal gentleman."

"He will only know that when his son is dead."

"That was a cruel dictum, sir."

"Not so cruel as that which left my mother to starve in the streets of Haarlem."

"Aye! ten thousand times more cruel, since your dear mother, sir, had not to bear the awful burden of lifelong remorse."

"Bah!" rejoined the philosopher with a careless shrug of the shoulders, "a man seldom feels remorse for wrongs committed against a woman."

"But he doth for those committed against his flesh and blood — his son — — "

"I have no means of finding out, sir, if my father hath or hath not remorse for his wilful desertion of wife and child — England is a far-off country — I would not care to undertake so unprofitable a pilgrimage."

"Then why not let me do so, sir?" queried Cornelius Beresteyn calmly.

"You?"

"Yes. Why not?"

"Why should you trouble, mynheer, to seek out the father of such a vagabond as I?"

"Because I would like to give a man — an old man your father must be now — the happiness of calling you his son. You say he lives in England. I often go to England on business. Will you not at least tell me your father's name?"

"I have no cause to conceal it, mynheer," rejoined Diogenes carelessly. "In England they call him Blake of Blakeney; his home is in Sussex and I believe that it is a stately home."

"But I know the Squire of Blakeney well," said Cornelius Beresteyn eagerly, "my bankers at Amsterdam also do business for him. I know that just now he is in Antwerp on a mission from King James of England to the Archduchess. He hath oft told Mynheer Beuselaar, our mutual banker, that he was moving heaven and earth to find the son whom he had lost."

"Heaven and earth take a good deal of moving," quoth Diogenes lightly, "once a wife and son have been forsaken and left to starve in a foreign land. Mine English father wedded my mother in the church of St. Pieter at Haarlem. My friend Frans Hals — God bless him — knew my mother and cared for me after she died. He has all the papers in his charge relating to the marriage. It has long ago been arranged between us that if I die with ordinary worthiness, he will seek out my father in England and tell him that mayhap — after all — even though I have been a vagabond all my life — I have never done anything that should cause him to blush for his son."

Apparently at this juncture, Maria must have knocked at the door of the tapperij, for Gilda, whose heart was beating more furiously than ever, heard presently the well-known firm footsteps of her father as he rapidly ascended the stairs.

Two minutes later Gilda lay against her father's heart, and her hand resting in his she told him from beginning to end everything that she had suffered from the moment when after watch-night service in the Groote Kerk she first became aware of the murmur of voices, to that when she first realized that the man whom she should have hated, the knave whom she should have despised, filled her heart and soul to the exclusion of all other happiness in the world, and that he was about to pass out of her life for ever.

It took a long time to tell — for she had suffered more, felt more, lived more in the past five days than would fill an ordinary life — nor did she disguise anything from her father, not even the conversation which she had had at Rotterdam in the dead of night with the man who had remained nameless until now, and in consequence of which he had gone at once to warn the Stadtholder and had thus averted the hideous conspiracy which would have darkened for ever the destinies of many Dutch homes.

Of Nicolaes she did not speak; she knew that he had confessed his guilt to his father, who would know how to forgive in the fullness of time.

When she had finished speaking her father said somewhat roughly:

"But for that vervloekte adventurer down there, you would never have suffered, Gilda, as you did. Nicolaes...."

"Nicolaes, father dear," she broke in quietly, "is very dear to us both. I think that his momentary weakness will endear him to us even more. But he was a tool in the hands of that unscrupulous Stoutenburg — and but for that nameless and penniless soldier whose hand you were proud to grasp just now, I would not be here in your arms at this moment."

"Ah!" said Cornelius Beresteyn dryly, "is this the way that the wind blows, my girl? Did you not know then that the rascal — the day after he dared to lay hands upon you — was back again in Haarlem bargaining with me to restore you to my arms in exchange for a fortune?"

"And two days later, father dear," she retorted, "he endured insults, injuries, cruelties from Stoutenburg, rather than betray Nicolaes' guilt before me."

"Hm!" murmured Cornelius, and there was a humorous twinkle in his eyes as he looked down upon his daughter's bowed head.

"And but for that same rascal, father," she continued softly, "you would at this moment be mourning a dead daughter and Holland a hideous act of treachery."

"Hush, my dear!" cried the old man impulsively, as he put his kind protecting arms round the child whom he loved so dearly.

"I would never have followed the Lord of Stoutenburg while I lived," she said simply.

"Please God," he said earnestly, "I would sooner have seen you in the crypt beside your mother."

"Then, father, hath not the rascal you speak of deserved well of us? Can we not guess that even originally he took me away from Haarlem, only because he knew that if he refused the bargain, proposed to him by mine own brother, Stoutenburg would have found some other means of ensuring my silence."

"You are a good advocate, my girl," rejoined Cornelius with a sly wink which brought the colour rushing up to Gilda's cheeks. "I think, by your leave, I'll go and shake that vervloekte Keerl once more by the hand....And ...shall I tell him that you bear him no ill-will?" he added roguishly.

"Yes, father dear, tell him that," she said gently.

"Then will you go to bed, dear?" he asked, "you are overwrought and tired."

"I will sit by the window quietly for a quarter of an hour," she said, "after that I promise you that I will go peaceably to bed."

He kissed her tenderly, for she was very dear to him, but being a man of vast understanding and profound knowledge of men and things, the humorous twinkle did not altogether fade from his eyes as he finally bade his daughter "Good night," and then quietly went out of the room.

CHAPTER XLV
THE END

Diogenes sat beside the window in the tapperij listening with half an ear to the sounds in and about the hostelry which were dying out one by one. At first there had been a footfall in the room overhead which had seemed to him the sweetest music that man could hear. It had paced somewhat restlessly up and down and to the Laughing Cavalier, the gay and irresponsible soldier of fortune, it had seemed as if every creaking of a loose board beneath the featherweight of that footfall found its echo in his heart.

But anon Mynheer Cornelius Beresteyn was called away and then all was still in the room upstairs, and Diogenes burying his head in his hands evoked the picture of that room as he had seen it five days ago. The proud jongejuffrouw in her high-backed chair, looking on him with blue eyes which she vainly tried to render hard through their exquisite expression of appealing, childlike gentleness: and he groaned aloud with the misery of the inevitable which with stern finger bade him go and leave behind him all the illusions, all the dreams which he had dared to weave.

Had she not told him that she despised him, that his existence was as naught to her, that she looked on him as a menial and a knave, somewhat below the faithful henchmen who were in her father's service? Ye gods! he had endured much in his life of privations, of physical and mental pain, but was there aught on earth or in the outermost pits of hell to be compared with the agony of this ending to a dream.

The serving-wench came in just then. She scarcely dared approach the mynheer with the merry voice and the laughter-filled eyes who now looked so inexpressibly sad.

Yet she had a message for him. Mynheer Cornelius Beresteyn, she said, desired to speak with him once more. The wench had murmured the words shyly, for her heart was aching for the handsome soldier and the tears were very near her eyes. But hearing the message he had jumped up with alacrity and was immediately ready to follow her.

Mynheer Beresteyn had a room on the upper floor, she explained, as she led the way upstairs. The old man was standing on the narrow landing and as soon as Diogenes appeared upon the stairs, he said simply:

"There was something I did forget to say to you downstairs; may I trouble you, sir, to come into my room for a moment."

He threw open one of the doors that gave on the landing and politely stood aside that his visitor might pass through. Diogenes entered the room: he heard the door being closed behind him, and thought that Mynheer Beresteyn had followed him in.

The room was very dimly lighted by a couple of tallow candles that flickered in their sconces, and at first he could not see into the dark recesses of the room. But presently something moved, something ethereal and intangible, white and exquisite. It stirred from out the depths of the huge high-backed chair, and from out the gloom there came a little cry of surprise and of joy which was as the call of bird or angel.

He did not dare to move, he scarcely dared to breathe. He looked round for Mynheer Beresteyn who had disappeared.

Surely this could be only a dream. Nothing real on earth could be so exquisite as that subtle vision which he had of her now, sitting in the high-backed chair, leaning slightly forward toward him. Gradually his eyes became accustomed to the gloom: he could see her quite distinctly now, her fair curls round her perfect head, her red lips parted, her eyes fixed upon him with a look which he dared not interpret.

All around him was the silence and the darkness of the night, and he was alone with her just as he had been in this very room five days ago and then again at Rotterdam.

"St. Bavon, you rogue!" he murmured, "where are you? How dare you leave me in the lurch like this?"

Then — how it all happened he could not himself have told you — he suddenly found himself at her feet, kneeling beside the high-backed chair; his arms were round her shoulders and he could feel the exquisite perfume of her breath upon his cheek.

"St. Bavon," he cried exultingly to himself, "go away, you rogue! there's no need for your admonitions now."

Mynheer Beresteyn tiptoed quietly into the room. The roguish smile still played around his lips. He came up close to the high-backed chair and placed his hand upon his daughter's head.

Diogenes looked up, and met the kindly eyes of the old man fixed with calm earnestness upon him.

"Mynheer," he said, and laughter which contained a world of happiness as well as of joy danced and sparkled in every line of his face, "just now I refused one half of your fortune! But 'tis your greatest treasure I claim from you now."

"Nay! you rascal," rejoined Beresteyn, as he lifted his daughter's chin gently with one finger and looked into her deep blue eyes which were brimful of happiness, "methinks that that treasure is yours already!"

"Go back, good St. Bavon," cried the Laughing Cavalier in an ecstasy of joy, "your heaven — you rogue — is not more perfect than this."

The First Sir Percy

Chapter I – A Night on the Veluwe

1

A MOONLESS night upon the sandy waste – the sky a canopy of stars, twinkling with super-radiance through the frosty atmosphere; the gently undulating ground like a billowy sea of silence and desolation, with scarce a stain upon the smooth surface of the snow; the mantle of night enveloping every landmark upon the horizon beyond the hills in folds of deep, dark indigo, levelling every chance hillock and clump of rough shrub or grass, obliterating road and wayside ditch, which in the broad light of day would have marred the perfect evenness of the wintry pall.

It was a bitterly cold night of mid-March in that cruel winter of 1624, which lent so efficient a hand to the ghouls of war and of disease in taking toll of human lives.

Not a sound broke the hushed majesty of this forgotten corner of God's earth, save perhaps at intervals the distant, melancholy call of the curlew, or from time to time the sigh of a straying breeze, which came lingering and plaintive from across the Zuyder Zee. Then for awhile countless particles of snow, fanned by unseen breaths, would arise from their rest, whirl and dance a mad fandango in the air, gyrate and skip in a glistening whirlpool lit by mysterious rays of steel-blue light, and then sink back again, like tired butterflies, to sleep once more upon the illimitable bosom of the wild. After which Silence and Lifelessness would resume their ghostlike sway.

To right and left, and north and south, not half a dozen leagues away, humanity teemed and fought, toiled and suffered, unfurled the banner of Liberty, laid down life and wealth in the cause of Freedom, conquered and was down-trodden and conquered again; men died that their children might live, women wept and lovers sighed. But here, beneath that canopy dotted with myriads of glittering worlds, intransmutable and sempiternal, the cries of battle and quarrels of men, the wail of widows and the laughter of children appeared futile and remote.

2

But to an eye trained to the dreary monotony of winter upon the Veluwe, there were a few faint indications of the tracks, which here and there intersect the arid waste and link up the hamlets and cities which lie along its boundaries. There were lines – mere shadows upon the even sheet of snow – and tiny white hillocks that suggested a bordering of rough scrub along the edges of the roads.

That same trained eye could then proceed to trace those shadowy lines along their erratic way 'twixt Amersfoort and the Neder Rhyn, or else from Barneveld as far as Apeldoorn, or yet again 'twixt Utrecht and Ede, and thence as far as the Ijssel, from the further shores of which the armies of the Archduchess, under the command of Count Henri de Berg, were even then threatening Gelderland.

It was upon this last, scarcely visible track that a horse and rider came slowly ambling along in the small hours of the morning, on this bitterly cold night in March. The rider had much ado to keep a tight hold on the reins with one hand, whilst striving to keep his mantle closely fastened round his shoulders with the other.

The horse, only half-trusting his master, suspicious and with nerves a-quiver, ready to shy and swerve at every shadow that loomed out of the darkness, or at every unexpected sound that disturbed the silence of the night, would more than once have thrown his rider but for the latter's firm hand upon the curb.

The rider's keen eyes were searching the gloom around him. From time to time a forcible ejaculation, indicative of impatience or anxiety, escaped his lips, numb with cold, and with unconsidered vehemence he would dig his spurs into his horse's flanks, with the result that a fierce and prolonged struggle 'twixt man and beast would ensue, and, until the quivering animal was brought back to comparative quietude again, much time was spent in curses and recriminations.

Anon the rider pulled up sharply at the top of the rising ground, looked round and about him, muttered a few more emphatic 'Dondersteens' and 'verdommts.'

Then he veered his mount right round and started to go back down hill again – still at foot-pace – spied a side-track on his right, turned to follow it for a while, came to a halt again, and flung his head back in a futile endeavor to study the stars, about which he knew nothing.

Then he shook his head dolefully; the time had gone by for cursing – praying would have been more useful, had he known how to set about it – for in truth he had lost his way upon this arid waste, and the only prospect before him was that of spending the night in the saddle, vainly trying by persistent movement to keep the frost out of his limbs.

For the nonce, he had no idea in which direction lay Amersfoort, which happened to be his objective. Apparently he had taken the wrong road when first he came out of Ede, and might now be tending toward the Rhyn, or have left both Barneveld and even Assel considerably behind.

The unfortunate wayfarer did not of a surety know which to rail most bitterly against: his want of accurate knowledge as to the disposal of the stars upon a moonless firmament, so that he could not have told you, gaze on them how he might, which way lay the Zuyder Zee, the Ijssel, or the Rhyn; or that last mug of steaming ale of which he had partaken ere he finally turned his back on the hospitable doors of the "Crow's Nest" at Ede.

It was that very mug of the delicious spiced liquor – and even in this hour of acute misery, the poor man contrived to smack his half-frozen lips in retrospective enjoyment – which had somehow obscured his vision when first he found himself outside the city gates, confronted by the verfloekte waste, through which even a cat could not have picked its way on a night like this.

And now, here he was, hopelessly stranded, without drink or shelter, upon the most desolate portion of the Veluwe. In no direction could the lights of any habitation be seen.

"Dondersteen!" he muttered to himself finally, in despair. "But I must get somewhere in time, if I keep following my nose long enough!"

3

In truth, no more lonely spot could be imagined in a civilized land than that wherein the stranded traveler now found himself. Even by day the horizon seems limitless, with neither tower nor city nor homestead in sight. By night the silence is so absolute that imagination will conjure up strange and impossible sounds, such as that of the earth whistling through space, or of ceaseless rolls of drums and trampings of myriads of feet thousands of leagues away.

Strangely enough, however, once upon a time, in the far long ago and the early days of windmills, a hermit-miller – he must have been a hermit in very truth – did build one here upon the highest point of the Veluwe, close to the junction of the road which runs eastward from Amersfoort and Barneveld, with the one which tends southward from Assel, and distant from each a quarter of a league or so. Why that windmill was erected just there, far from the home of any peasant or farmer who might desire to have his corn ground, or who that hermit-miller was who dwelt in it before flocks of wild geese alone made it their trysting-place, it were impossible to say.

No trace of it remains these days, nor were there any traces of it left a year after the events which this veracious chronicle will presently unfold, for reasons which will soon appear obvious to anyone who reads. But there it stood in this year of grace 1624, on that cold night in March, when a solitary horseman lost his way upon the Veluwe, with serious consequences, not only to himself, but to no less a person than Maurice, Prince of Nassau, Stadtholder of the United Provinces of the Netherlands, and mayhap to the entire future history of that sorely tried country.

On a winter's night such as this, the mill looked peculiarly weird and ghost-like looming out of the darkness against the background of a star-studded firmament, and rising, sombre and dense, from out the carpet of glabrous snow, majestic in its isolation, towering above the immensity of the waste, its domed roof decked in virgin white like the mother-bosom of the wild. Built of weather-worn timber throughout, it had a fenced-in platform supported by heavy rafters all around it, like a girdle, at a height of twenty feet and more from the ground: and the gaunt, skeleton wings were stretched out to the skies, scarred, broken, and motionless, as if in piteous appeal for protection against the disfiguring ravages of time.

There were two small windows close under the roof on the south side of the building, and a large, narrow one midway up the same side. The disposal of these windows, taken in conjunction with the door down below, was so quaint that, viewed from a certain angle, they looked for all the world like the eyes, nose, and pursed-up mouth of a gargantuan, grinning face.

4

If a stranger travelling through Gelderland these days had thought it fit to inquire from a native whether that particular molen upon the Veluwe was doing work or was inhabited, he would of a certainty have been told that the only possible inhabitants of the molen were gnomes and sprites, and that if any corn was ground there it could only be in order to bake bread for the devil's dinner.

The mill was disused and uninhabited, had been for many years – a quarter of a century or more probably – so any and every native of Gelderland and Utrecht would have emphatically averred. Nevertheless, on this same memorable night in March, 1624, there were evident signs of life – human life – about that solitary and archaic molen on the Veluwe. Tiny slits of light showed clearly from certain angles through the chinks of the wooden structure; there were vague sounds of life and movement in and about the place; the weather-worn boards creaked and the timber groaned under more tangible pressure than that of the winds. Nay, what's more two horses were tethered down below, under the shelter afforded by the overhanging platform. These horses were saddled; they had nosebags attached to their bridles, and blankets thrown across their withers; all of which signs denoted clearly, methinks, that for once the mill was inhabited by something more material than ghosts.

More ponderous, too, than ghoulish footsteps were the sounds of slow pacing up and down the floor of the millhouse, and of two voices, now raised to loud argument, now sunk to a mere cautious whisper.

Two men were, in effect, inside the millhouse at this hour. One of them – tall, lean, dark in well-worn, almost ragged, black doublet and cloak, his feet and legs encased in huge boots of untanned leather which reached midway up his long thighs, his black bonnet pushed back from his tall, narrow forehead and grizzled hair – was sitting upon the steps of the steep, ladder-like stairs which led to the floor above; the other – shorter, substantially, even richly clad, and wearing a plumed hat and fur-lined cloak, was the one who paced up and down the dust-covered floor. He was younger than his friend, had fair, curly hair, and a silken, fair moustache, which hid the somewhat weak lines of his mouth.

An old, battered lanthorn, hanging to a nail in the wall, threw a weird, flickering light upon the scene, vaguely illumined the gaunt figure of the man upon the steps, his large hooked nose and ill-shaven chin, and long thin hands that looked like the talons of some bird of prey.

"You cannot stay on here forever, my good Stoutenburg, "the younger of the two men said, with some impatience. "Sooner or later you will be discovered, and —"

He paused, and the other gave a grim laugh.

"And there is a price of two thousand guilders upon my head, you mean, my dear Heemskerk?" he said dryly.

"Well, I did mean that," rejoined Heemskerk, with a shrug of the shoulders. "The people round about here are very poor. They might hold your father's memory in veneration, but there is not one who would not sell you to the Stadtholder if he found you out."

Again Stoutenburg laughed. He seemed addicted to the habit of this mirthless, almost impish laugh.

"I was not under the impression, believe me, my friend," he said, "that Christian charity or loyalty to my father's memory would actuate a worthy Dutch peasant into respecting my sanctuary. But I am not satisfied with what I have learned. I must know more. I have promised De Berg," he concluded firmly.

"And De Berg counts on you," Heemskerk rejoined. "But," he added, with a shrug of the shoulders, "you know what he is. One of those men who, so long as they gain their ambitious ends, count every life cheap but their own."

"Well," answered Stoutenburg, " 'tis not I, in truth, who would place a high price on mine."

"Easy, easy, my good man," quoth the other, with a smile. "Hath it, perchance, not occurred to you that your obstinacy in leading this owl-like life here is putting a severe strain on the devotion of your friends?"

I make no appeal to the devotion of my friends," answered Stoutenburg curtly. "They had best leave me alone."

"We cannot leave you to suffer cold and hunger, mayhap to perish of want in this God-forsaken eyrie."

"I'm not starving," was Stoutenburg's ungracious answer to the young man's kindly solicitude; "and have plenty of inner fire to keep me warm."

He paused, and a dark scowl contracted his gaunt features, gave him an expression that in the dim and flickering light appeared almost diabolical.

"I know," said Heemskerk, with a comprehending not. "Still those thoughts of revenge?"

"Always!" replied the other, with sombre calm.

"Twice you have failed."

"The third time I shall succeed," Stoutenburg affirmed with fierce emphasis. "Maurice of Nassau sent my father to the scaffold – my father, to whom he owed everything: money, power, success. The day that Olden Barneveldt died at the hands of that accursed ingrate I, his son, swore that the Stadtholder should perish by mine. As you say, I have twice failed in my attempt.

"My brother Groeneveld has gone the way of my father. I am an outlaw with a price upon my head, and my poor mother has three of us to weep for now, instead of one. But I have not forgotten mine oath, nor yet my revenge. I'll be even with Maurice of Nassau yet. All this fighting is but foolery. He is firmly established as Stadtholder of the United Provinces – the sort of man who sees others die for him. He may lose a town here, gain a city there, but he is the sovereign lord of an independent State, and his sacred person is better guarded than was that of his worthier father.

"But it is his life that I want," Stoutenburg went on fiercely, and his thin, claw-like hand clutched in imaginary dagger and struck out through the air as if against the breast of the hated foe. "For this I'll scheme and strive. Nay, I'll never rest until I have him at my mercy as Gerard in his day held William the Silent at his."

"Bah!" exclaimed Heemskerk hotly. "You would not emulate that abominable assassin!"

"Why not call me a justiciary?" Stoutenburg retorted dryly. "The Archduchess would load me with gifts. Spain would proclaim me a hero. Assassin or executioner – it only depends on the political point of view. But doubt me not for a single instant, Heemskerk. Maurice of Nassau will die by my hand."

"That is why you intend to remain here?"

"Yes. Until I have found out his every future plan."

"But how can you do it? You dare not show yourself abroad."

"That is my business," replied Stoutenburg quietly, "and my secret."

"I respect your secret," answered Heemskerk, with a shrug of the shoulders. "It was only my anxiety for your personal safety and for your comfort that brought me hither to-night."

"And De Berg's desire to learn what I have spied," Stoutenburg retorted, with a sneer.

"De Berg is ready to cross the Ijssel, and Isembourg to start from Kleve. De Berg proposes to attack Arnheim. He wishes to know what forces are inside the city and how they are disposed, and if the Stadtholder hath an army wherewith to come to their relief or to offer us battle, with any chance of success."

"You can tell De Berg to send you or another back to me here when the crescent moon is forty-eight hours older. I shall have all the information then that he wants."

"That will be good news for him and for Isembourg. There has been too much time wasted as it is."

"Time has not been wasted. The frosts have in the meanwhile made the Veluwe a perfect track for men and cannon."

"For Nassau's men and Nassau's cannon, as well as for our own," Heemskerk rejoined dryly.

"A week hence, if all's well, Maurice of Nassau will be too sick to lead his armies across the Veluwe or elsewhere," said Stoutenburg quietly, and looked up with such a strange, fanatical glitter in his deep-sunk eyes that the younger man gave an involuntary gasp of horror.

"You mean —" he ejaculated under his breath; and instinctively drawing back some paces away from his friend, stared at him with wide, uncomprehending eyes.

"I mean," Stoutenburg went on slowly and deliberately, "that De Berg had best wait patiently a little while longer. Maurice of Nassau will be a dying man ere long."

His harsh voice, sunk to a strange, impressive whisper, died away in a long-drawn-out sigh, half of impatience, wholly of satisfaction. Heemskerk remained for a moment or two absolutely motionless, still staring at the man before him as if the latter were some kind of malevolent and fiend-like wraith, conjured up by devilish magic to scare the souls of men. Nor did Stoutenburg add anything to his last cold-blooded pronouncement. He seemed to be deriving a grim satisfaction in watching the play of horror and of fear upon Heemskerk's usually placid features.

Thus for a space of a few moments the old molen appeared to sink back to its habitual ghost-haunted silence, whilst the hovering spirits of Revenge and Hate called up by the sorcery of a man's evil passions held undisputed sway.

"You mean —" reiterated Heemskerk after awhile, vaguely, stupidly, babbling like a child.

"I mean," Stoutenburg gave impatient answer, "that you should know me well enough by now, my good Heemskerk, to realize that I am no swearer of futile oaths. Last year, when I was over in Madrid, I cultivated the friendship of one Francis Borgia. You have heard of him, no doubt; they call him the Prince of Poets over there. He is a direct descendant of the illustrious Cesare, and I soon discovered that most of the secrets possessed by his far-famed ancestor were known to my friend the poet."

"Poisons!" Heemskerk murmured, under his breath.

"Poisons!" the other assented dryly. "And other things."

With finger and thumb of his right hand, he extracted a couple of tiny packets from a secret pocket of his doublet, toyed with them for awhile, undid the packets and gazed meditatively on their contents. Then he called to his friend. "They'll not hurt you," he said sardonically. "Look at this powder, now. Is it not innocent in appearance? Yet it is of incalculable value to the man who doth not happen to possess a straight eye or a steady hand with firearms. For add but a pinch of it to the charge in your pistol, them aim at your enemy's head, and if you miss killing him, or if he hold you at his mercy, you very soon have him at yours. The fumes from the detonation will cause instant and total blindness."

Despite his horror of the whole thing, Heemskerk had instinctively drawn nearer to his friend. Now, at these words, he stepped back again quickly, as if he had trodden upon an adder. Stoutenburg, with his wonted cynicism, only shrugged his shoulders.

"Have I not said that it would not hurt you?" he said, with a sneer. "In itself it is harmless enough, and only attains its useful properties when fired in connection with gunpowder. But when used as I have explained it to you, it is deadly and unerring. I saw it at work once or twice in Spain. The Prince of Poets prides himself on its invention. He gave me some of the precious powder, and I was glad of it. It may prove useful one day."

He carefully closed the first packet and slipped it back into the secret receptacle of his doublet; then he fell to contemplating the contents of the second packet – half a dozen tiny pillules, which he kept rolling about in the palm of his hand.

"These," he mused, "are of more proved value for my purpose. Have not De Berg," he added, with a sardonic grin, as he looked once more on his friend, "and the Archduchess, too, heard it noised abroad that Maurice of Nassau hath of late suffered from a mysterious complaint which already threatens to cut him off in his prime, and which up to now hath baffled those learned leeches who were brought over specially from England to look after the health of the exalted patient? Have not you and your friends, my good Heemskerk, heard the rumour too?"

The young man nodded in reply. His parched tongue seemed to cleave to the roof of his mouth; he could not utter a word. Stoutenburg laughed.

"Ah!" he said, with a nod of understanding. "I see that the tale did reach your ears. You understand, therefore, that I must remain here for awhile longer."

And with absolute calm and a perfectly steady hand, he folded up the pillules in the paper screw and put them back in his pocket.

"I could not leave my work unfinished," he said simply.

"But how —" Heemskerk contrived to stammer at last; and his voice to his own ears sounded hoarse and toneless, like a voice out of the grave.

"How do I contrive to convey these pillules into the Stadtholder's stomach?" retorted Stoutenburg, with a coarse chuckle. "Well, my friend, that is still my secret. But De Berg and the others must trust me a while longer – trust me and then thank me when the time comes. The Stadtholder once out of the way, the resistance of the United Provinces must of itself collapse like a house of cards. There need be no more bloodshed after that – no more sanguinary conflicts. Indeed, I shall be acclaimed as a public benefactor – when I succeed."

"Then – then you are determined to – to remain here?" Heemskerk murmured, feeling all the while that anything he said was futile and irrelevant.

But how can a man speak when he is confronted with a hideous spectre that mocks him, even whilst it terrifies?

"I shall remain here for the present," Stoutenburg replied, with perfect coolness.

"I – I'd best go, then," the other suggested vaguely.

"You had best wait until the daylight. 'Tis easy to lose one's way on the Veluwe."

The young man waited for a moment, irresolute. Clearly he was longing to get away, to put behind him this ghoul-infested molen, with its presiding genii of hatred and of crime. Nay, men like Heemskerk, cultivated and gently nurtured, understood the former easily enough. Men and women knew how to hate fiercely these days, and there were few sensations more thoroughly satisfying than that of holding an enemy at the sword's point.

But poison! The slow, insidious weapon that worked like a reptile, stealthily and in the dark! Bah! Heemskerk felt a dizziness overcome him; sheer physical nausea threatened to rob him of his faculties.

But there was undoubted danger in venturing out on the arid wild, in the darkness and with nought but instinct and a few half-obliterated footmarks to guide one along the track. The young man went to the door and pulled it open. A gust of ice-laden air blew into the great, empty place, and almost knocked the old lanthorn off its peg. Heemskerk stepped out into the night. He felt literally frightened, and, like a nervous child, had the sensation of someone or something standing close behind him and on the point of putting a spectral hand upon his shoulder.

But Stoutenburg had remained sitting on the steps, apparently quite unmoved. No doubt he was accustomed to look his abominable project straight in the face. He even shrugged his shoulders in derision when he caught sight of Heemskerk's white face and horror-filled eyes.

"You cannot start while this blind man's holiday lasts," he said lightly. "Can I induce you to partake of some of the refreshment you were good enough to bring for me?"

But Heemskerk gave him no answer. He was trying to make up his mind what to do; and Stoutenburg, with another careless laugh, rose from his seat and strode across the great barn-like space. There, in a remote corner, where sacks of uncrushed grain were wont to be stacked, stood a basket containing a few simple provisions; a hunk of stale bread, a piece of cheese and two or three bottles of wine. Stoutenburg stooped and picked one of these up. He was whistling a careless tune. Then suddenly he paused, his long back still bent, his arm with the hand that held the bottle resting across his knee, his face, alert and hawk-like, turned in an instant toward the door.

"What was that?" he queried hurriedly.

Heemskerk, just as swiftly, had already stepped back into the barn and closed the door again noiselessly.

"Useless!" commented Stoutenburg curtly. "The horses are outside."

"Where is Jan?" he added after an imperceptible pause, during which Heemskerk felt as if his very heart-beats had become audible.

"On the watch, outside," replied the young man.

Even whilst he spoke the door was cautiously opened from the outside, and a grizzled head wrapped in a fur bonnet was thrust in through the orifice.

"What is it, Jan?" the two men queried simultaneously.

"A man and horse," Jan replied in a rapid whisper.

"Coming from over Amersfoort way. He must have caught sight of the molen, for he has left the track and is heading straight for us."

"Some wretched traveler lost on this God-forsaken waste," Stoutenburg said, with a careless shrug of the shoulders. "I have seen them come this way before."

"But not at this hour of the night?" murmured Heemskerk.

"Mostly at night. It is easier to follow the track by day."

"What shall we do?"

"Nothing. Let the man come. We'll soon see if he is dangerous. Are we not three to one?"

The taunt struck home. Heemskerk looked abashed. Jan remained standing in the doorway, waiting for further orders. Stoutenburg went on quietly collecting the scanty provisions. He found a couple of mugs, and with a perfectly steady hand filled the first one and then the other with the wine.

"Drink this Heemskerk," he said lightly; and held out the two mugs at arm's length. "It will calm your nerves. You too, Jan."

Jan took the mug and drank with avidity, but Heemskerk appeared to hesitate.

"Afraid of the poison?" Stoutenburg queried with a sneer. Then, as the other, half-ashamed, took the mug and drank at a draught, he added coolly: "You need not be afraid. I could not afford to waste such precious stuff on you."

Then he turned to Jan.

"Remain outside," he commanded; "well wrapped in your blanket, and when the traveler hails you pretend to be wakened from pleasant dreams. Then leave the rest to chance."

Jan at once obeyed. He went out of the molen, closing the door carefully behind him.

Five minutes later, the hapless traveler had put his horse to a trot. He had perceived the molen looming at the top of the rising ground, dense and dark against the sky, and looking upon it as a veritable God-sent haven of refuge for wearied tramps, was making good haste to reach it, fearing lest he himself dropped from sheer exhaustion out of his saddle ere he came to his happy goal.

That terrible contingency, however, did not occur, and presently he was able to draw rein and to drop gently if somewhat painfully to the ground without further mishap. Then he looked about him. The mill in truth appeared to be uninhabited, which was a vast pity, seeing that a glass of spiced ale would – but no matter, 'twas best not to dwell on such blissful thoughts! A roof over one's head for the night was the most urgent need.

He led his horse by the bridle, and tethered him to a heavy, supporting rafter under the overhanging platform; was on the point of ministering to the poor, half-frozen beast, when his ear caught a sound which caused him instantly to pause first and then start on a tour around the molen. He had not far to go. The very next moment he came upon a couple of horses tethered like his own, and upon Jan, who was snoring lustily, curled up in a horse-blanket in the angle of the porch.

To hail the sleeper with lusty shouts at first, and then with a vigorous kick, was but the work of a few seconds; after which Jan's snores were merged in a series of comprehensive curses against the disturber of his happy dreams.

"Dondersteen!" he murmured, still apparently half asleep. "And who is this verfloekte plepshurk who ventures a weary traveler from his sleep?"

"Another weary traveler, verfloekte plepshurk yourself," the other cried aloud. Nor were it possible to render with any degree of accuracy the language which he subsequently used when Jan persistently refused to move.

"Then, dondersteen," retorted Jan thickly, "do as I do – wrap yourself up in a blanket and go to sleep."

"Not until I have discovered how it comes that one wearied traveler happens to be abroad with two equally wearied and saddled horses. And I am not mistaken, plepshurk, thou are but a varlet left on guard outside, whilst thy master feasts and sleeps within."

Whereupon, without further parley, he strode across Jan's outstretched body and, with a vigorous kick of his heavy boot, thrust open the door which gave on the interior of the mill.

Here he paused, just beneath the lintel, took off his hat, and stood at respectful attention; for he had realized at once that he was in the presence of his betters – of two gentlemen, in fact, one of whom had a mug of wine in his hand and the other a bottle. These were the two points which, as it were, jumped most directly to the eye of the weary, frozen, and thirsty traveler: two gentlemen who haply were now satiated, and would spare a drop even to a humble varlet if he stood before them in his full, pitiable plight.

"Who are you man? And what do you want?" one of these gentlemen queried peremptorily. It was the one who had a bottle of wine – a whole bottle – in his hand; but he looked peculiarly stern and forbidding, with his close-cropped, grizzled head and hard, bird-like features.

"Only a poor tramp, my lord," replied the unfortunate wayfarer, in high-pitched, flute-like tones, "who hath lost his way, and has been wandering on this verdommte plain since midnight."

"What do you want?" reiterated Stoutenburg sternly.

"Only shelter for the rest of the night, my lord, and – and – a little drink – a very little drink – for I am mightily weary, and my throat is dry as tinder."

"What is your name?"

At this very simple question the man's round, florid face with the tiny, upturned nose, slightly tinged with pink, and the small, round eyes, bright and shiny like new crowns, took on an expression of comical puzzlement. He scratched his head, pursed up his lips, emitted a prolonged and dubious whistle.

"I haven't a name, so please your lordship," he said, after a while. "That is, not a name such as other people have. I have a name, in truth, a name by which I am known to my friends; a name —"

"Thy name, plepshurk," command Stoutenburg roughly, "ere I throw thee out again into the night."

" 'So please your lordship." replied the man, "I am called Pythagoras – a name which I believe belongs by right to a philosopher of ancient times, but to which I will always answer, so please your High and Mightiness."

But this time his High and Mightiness did not break in upon the worthy philosopher's volubility. Indeed, at the sound of that highly ludicrous name – ludicrous, that is, when applied to its present bearer – he had deliberately put mug and bottle down, and then become strangely self-absorbed, even whilst his friend had given an involuntary start.

"H'm! Pythagoras!" his lordship resumed, after a while. "Have I ever seen thine ugly face before?"

"Not to my knowledge, my lord," replied the other, marvelling when it would please these noble gentlemen to give him something wherewith to moisten his gullet.

"Ah! Methought I had once met another who bore an equally strange name. Was it Demosthenes, or Euripides, or —"

"Diogenes, no doubt, my lord," replied the thirsty philosopher glibly. "The most gallant gentleman in the whole wide world, one who honours me with his friendship, was pleased at one time to answer to that name."

Now, when Pythagoras made his announcement he felt quite sure that lavish hospitality would promptly follow. These gentlemen had no doubt heard of Diogenes, his comrade in arms, the faithful and gallant friend for whom he – Pythagoras – would go through fire and water and the driest of deserts. They would immediately accord a welcome to one who had declared himself honoured by the friendship of so noble a cavalier. Great was the unfortunate man's disappointment, therefore, when his glib speech was received in absolute silence; and he himself was still left standing upon the lintel of the door, with an icy cold draught playing upon him from behind.

It was only after a considerable time that my lord deigned to resume his questionings again. "Where dost come from, fellow?" he asked.

"From Ede, so please your lordship," Pythagoras replied dolefully, "where I partook —"

"And whither art going?" Stoutenburg broke in curtly.

"I was going to Amersfoort, my lord, when I lost my way."

"To Amersfoort?"

" 'Yes, my lord."

"Mynheer Beresteyn hath a house at Amersfoort," Stoutenburg said, as if to himself.

"It was to Mynheer Beresteyn's house that I was bound, my lord, when I unfortunately lost my way."

"Ah!" commented my lord dryly. "Thou was on thy way to the house of Mynheer Beresteyn in Amersfoort?"

"Yes, my lord."

"With a message?"

"No, my lord. Not with a message; I was just going there for the wedding."

"The wedding?" ejaculated Stoutenburg, and it seemed to Pythagoras as if my lord's haggard face took on suddenly an almost cadaverous hue. "Whose wedding fellow?" he added more calmly.

"That of my friend Diogenes, so please your lordship, with the Jongejuffrouw Beresteyn, he —"

"Take care, man, take care!" came with an involuntary call of alarm from Heemskerk; for Stoutenburg, uttering a hoarse cry like that of a wounded beast, had raised his arm and now strode on the unfortunate philosopher with clenched fist and a look in his hollow eyes which boded no good to the harbinger of those simple tidings.

At sound of his friend's voice, Stoutenburg dropped his arm. He turned on his heel, ashamed no doubt that this stranger-varlet should see his face distorted as it was with passion.

This paroxysm of uncontrolled fury did not, however, last longer than a moment or two; the next instant the lord of Stoutenburg, outwardly calm and cynical as before had resumed his haughty questionings, looked the awe-struck philosopher up and down; and he, somewhat scared by the danger which he only appeared to have escaped through the timely intervention of the other gentleman, was marvelling indeed if he had better not take to his heels at once and run, and trust his safety and his life to the inhospitable wild, rather than in the company of this irascible noble lord.

I think, if fact, that he would have fled the very next moment, but that my lord with one word kept him rooted to the spot.

"So," resumed Stoutenburg coolly after awhile, "thou, fellow, art a bidden guest at the marriage feast, which it seems is to be solemnized 'twixt the Jongejuffrouw Beresteyn and another plepshurk as low as thyself. Truly doth democracy tread hard on the heels of such tyranny as the United Provinces have witnessed of late. Dost owe allegiance, sirrah, to the Stadtholder?"

"Where Diogenes leads, my lord," replied Pythagoras, with a degree of earnestness which sat whimsically upon his rotund person, "there do Socrates and I follow unquestioningly."

"Which means that ye are three rascals, ready to sell your skins to the highest bidder. Were ye not in the pay of the lord of Stoutenburg during the last conspiracy against the Stadtholder's life?"

"We may have been, your honour," the man replied naively; "although, to my knowledge, I have never set eyes on the lord of Stoutenburg."

" 'Twere lucky for thee knave, if thou didst," rejoined Stoutenburg with a harsh laugh, "for there's a price of two thousand guilders upon his head, and I doubt not but thy scurrilous friend Diogenes would add another two thousand to that guerdon."

Then, as Pythagoras, almost dropping with fatigue, was swaying upon his short, fat legs, he jerked his thumb in the direction where the tantalizing bottles and mugs were faintly discernible in the gloom. My lord continued curtly:

"There! Drink thy fill! Amersfoort is not far. My man will put thee on thy way when thou hast quenched thy thirst!"

Quench his thirst! Where was that cellar which could have worked this magic trick? In the corner to which my lord was pointing so casually there was but one bottle, which my lord had put down a while ago, and that, after all, was only half full.

Still, half a bottle of wine was better than no wine at all, and my lord, having granted his gracious leave, took no more notice of the philosopher and his unquenchable thirst, turned to his friend, and together the two gentlemen retired to a distant corner of the place and there whispered eagerly with one another.

Pythagoras tiptoed up to the spot where unexpected bliss awaited him. There was another bottle of wine there beside the half-empty one – a bottle that was full up to the neck, and the shape of which proclaimed that it came from Spain. Good, strong, heady Spanish wine!

And my lord had said "Drink thy fill!" Pythagoras did not hesitate, save for one brief second, while he marvelled whether he had accidentally wandered into Elysian fields, or whether he was only dreaming. Then he poured out for himself a mugful of wine.

Twenty minutes later, the last drop of the second bottle of strong, heady Spanish wine had trickled down the worthy Pythagoras' throat. He was in a state of perfect bliss, babbling words of supreme contentment, and seeing pleasing visions of gorgeous feasts in the murky angles of the old millhouse.

" 'Tis time the plepshurk got to horse," Stoutenburg said at last.

He strode across to where Pythagoras, leaning against the raftered wall, his round head on one side, his sugar-loaf hat set at the back of his head, was gazing dreamily into his empty mug.

"To horse, fellow!" he commanded curtly. " 'Tis but a league to Amersfoort, and thy friend will be waiting thee."

The old instinct of deference and good behaviour before a noble lord lent some semblance of steadiness to Pythagoras' legs. He struggled to his feet, vainly endeavored to keep an upright and dignified position – an attempt which, however, proved utterly futile.

Whereupon my lord called peremptorily to Jan, who appeared so suddenly in the doorway that, to Pythagoras' blurred vision, it seemed as if he had been put there by some kind of witchery. He approached his master, and there ensued a brief, whispered colloquy between those two – a colloquy in which Heemskerk took no part. After which, the lord of Stoutenburg said aloud:

"Set this worthy fellow on his horse, my good Jan, and put him on the track which leads to Amersfoort. He has had a rest and a good warm drink. He is not like to lose his way again."

Vaguely Pythagoras felt that he wished to protest. He did not want to be set on his horse, nor yet to go to Amersfoort just yet. The wedding was not until the morrow-- no, the day after the morrow – and for the nonce he wanted to sleep. Yes, sleep! Curled up in a blanket in any corner big enough and warm enough to shelter a dog.

Sleep! That was what he wanted; for he was so confoundedly sleepy, and this verfloekte darkness interfered with his eyes so that he could not see very clearly in front of him. All this he explained with grave deliberation to Jan, who had him tightly by the elbow and was leading him with absolutely irresistible firmness out through the door into the white, inhospitable open.

"I don't want to get to horse," the philosopher babbled thickly. "I want to curl up in a blanket and I want to go to sleep."

But, despite his protestations, he found himself presently in the saddle. How he got up there, he certainly could not have told you. Instinct, however, kept him there. Never could it be said that Pythagoras had tumbled off a horse. Anon he felt that the horse was moving, and that the air around him was bitterly cold.

The dull, even carpet of snow dazzled him, though it was pitch dark now both overhead and down below; of darkness that enveloped one like a mantle, and which felt as if it could have been cut through with a knife.

The horse went on at a steady trot, and another was trotting by its side, bearing a cavalier who wore a fur bonnet. Pythagoras vaguely imagined that this must be Jan. He owed Jan a grudge for taking him away from that hospitable molen, where half-bottles of wine were magically transformed into large ones, filled to overflowing with delicious liquor.

Presently Pythagoras began to feel cold again after the blissful warmth produced by that super-excellent Spanish wine.

"Is it far to Amersfoort?" he queried drowsily from time to time.

But he never seemed to get a reply. It appeared to him as if he had been hours in the saddle since last he felt comfortable and warm over in that hospitable molen. And he was very sleepy. His head felt heavy and his eyes would not keep open as hours and hours went by and the cold grew more and more intense.

"Is it far to Amersfoort?" he questioned whenever his head rolled forward with a jerk that roused him to momentary consciousness.

"Less than half a league now," Jan replied presently, and brought his own horse to a halt. "Follow the track before you and it will lead you straight to the city gates."

Pythagoras opened his eyes very wide. Straightway in front of him he perceived one or two tiny lights, which were too low down on the horizon for stars. The road, too, on which he found himself appeared straighter and more defined than those upon that verfloekte waste.

"Are those the lights of Amersfoort?" he murmured vaguely, and pointed in as straight a direction as his numbed arm would allow.

He expected an answer from Jan but there came none. The darkness appeared to have swallowed up horse and rider. Anyway, they had disappeared. Good old Jan! Pythagoras would have liked to thank him for his company, even though he did owe him a grudge for taking him away from the molen where there had been such wonderful —

The horse followed the track for a minute or two longer Pythagoras, left to his own devices, tried to keep awake. Suddenly the sharp report of a pistol rent the silence of the night. It was immediately followed by another.

Pythagoras felt a strange, sinking sensation in his stomach, a dizzy feeling in his head, a feeling which was no longer blissful like the one he had experienced after the third mugful of Spanish wine. A moment later, he fell forward on his horse's neck, then rolled out of the saddle down upon the bed of snow.

And at this spot, where the poor philosopher lay, the white pall which covered the Veluwe was dyed with a dark crimson stain.

5

A grey, dull light suffused the sky in the East when Jan once more knocked at the door of the old molen.

Stoutenburg's voice bade him enter.

"All well?" my lord queried, at sight of his faithful servant.

"All quiet, my lord," replied Jan. "That windbag, I'll warrant, will tell no tales."

"How far did you take him?"

"Nearly as far as Lang Soeren. I had to keep a track for fear of losing my way. But he lies eight leagues from Amersfoort now and six from Ede. His friends, I imagine, won't look for him thus far."

"And his horse?"

"It did not follow me. No doubt it will get picked up by some one in the morning."

Heemskerk shivered. It was certainly very cold inside this great, barn-like place at this hour just before sunrise; and the passing wayfarer had consumed the last measure of wine. The young man looked grimy, too, and untidy, covered with dust from the floor, where he had lain stretched out for the past three hours, trying to get a wink of sleep; whilst Stoutenburg, restless and alert, had kept his ears open and his nerves on the stretch for the first sound of Jan's return.

"You have been a long time getting to Lang Soeren and back," the latter remarked further to Jan.

I was guiding a drunken man on a wearied horse," the man replied curtly. "And I myself had been in the saddle all day."

"Then get another hour's rest now," Stoutenburg rejoined. "You will accompany my lord of Heemskerk back to Doesburg as soon as the sun is up."

Jan made no reply. He was accustomed to curt commands and to unquestioning obedience. Tired, saddle-sore and wearied, he would be ready to ride again, go anywhere until he dropped. So he turned on his heel and went out into the cold once more, in order to snatch that brief hour's rest which had been graciously accorded him.

Heemskerk gave an impatient sigh.

"I would the dawn were quicker in coming!" he murmured under his breath.

"The atmosphere of the Veluwe is getting oppressive for your fastidious taste," Stoutenburg retorted with a sneer. Then, as his friend made no other comment, he continued lightly: "Dead men tell no tales. I could not risk that blabbering fool going back to Amersfoort and speaking of what he saw. Even your unwonted squeamishness, my good Heemskerk, would grant me that."

"Or, rather," rejoined the other, almost involuntarily, "did not the unfortunate man suffer for being the messenger of evil tidings?"

Stoutenburg shrugged his shoulders with an assumption of indifference. "Perhaps," he said. "Though I doubt if the news was wholly unexpected. Yet I would have deemed Gilda Beresteyn too proud to wed that plepshurk."

"A man with a future," Heemskerk rejoined. "He is credited with having saved the Stadtholder's life, when the lord of Stoutenburg planned to blow up the bridge under his passage."

"And Beresteyn is grateful to him too," added Stoutenburg with a sarcastic curl of his thin lips, "for having rescued the fair Gilda from the lord of Stoutenburg's fierce clutches. But Nicolaes might have told me that his sister was getting married."

"Nicolaes?" ejaculated Heemskerk, with obvious surprise. "You have seen Nicolaes Beresteyn, then of late?"

For the space of a few seconds – less perhaps – Stoutenburg appeared confused, and the look which he cast on his friend was both furtive and searching. The next moment, however, he had recovered his usual cool placidity.

"You mistook, me, my friend," he said blandly. "I did not say that I had seen Nicolaes Beresteyn of late. I have not seen him, in fact, since the day of our unfortunate aborted conspiracy. Rumor reached me that he himself was about to wed the worthy daughter of some prosperous burgher. I merely wondered how the same rumor made no mention of the other prospective bride."

Once again the conversation flagged. Heemskerk regarded his friend with an anxious expression in his pale wearied face. He knew how passionately, if somewhat intermittently, Stoutenburg had loved Gilda Beresteyn. He knew of the original girl and boy affection between them, and of the man's base betrayal of the girl's trust. Stoutenburg had thrown over the humbler burgher's daughter in order to wed Walburg de Marnix, whom he promptly neglected, and who had since set him legally free. Heemskerk knew, too, how Stoutenburg's passion for the beautiful Gilda Beresteyn had since then burst into a consuming flame, and how the obscure soldier of fortune who went by the nick-name of Diogenes had indeed snatched the fair prize from his grasp.

Nigh on three months had gone by since then. Stoutenburg was still nurturing thoughts of vengeance and of crime, not only against the Stadtholder, but also against the girl who had scorned him. Well, this in truth was none of his friend's business. Hideous as was the premeditated coup against Maurice of Nassau, it would undoubtedly, if successful, help the cause of Spain in the Netherlands, and Heemskerk himself was that unnatural monster – a man who would rather see his country ruled by a stranger than by those of her sons whose political or religious views differed from his own.

Thus, when an hour later he took leave of Stoutenburg, he did so almost with cordiality, did not hesitate to grasp the had of a man whom he knew to be a scheming and relentless murderer.

"One of us will come out to wait on you in two days' time," he said at the last. "I go back to camp satisfied that you are not so lonely as you seem, and that there is some one who sees to it that you do not fare so ill even in this desolation. May I say this to De Berg?"

"If you like," Stoutenburg replied. "Anyway, you may assure him, and through him the Archduchess, that Maurice of Nassau will be in his grave before I, his judge and executioner, perish of hunger or of cold."

He accompanied his friend to the door, and stood there while the latter and Jan were getting to horse. Then, as they went out into the open, he waved them a last adieu. On the far distant east, the pale, wintry sun had tinged the mist with a delicate lemon gold. The vast immensity of the waste lay stretched out as if limitless before him. As far as the eye could see not a tower or column of smoke broke the even monotony of the undulating ground. The shadow of the great molen with its gaunt, mained wings lay, like patches of vivid blue upon the vast and glistening pall of snow.

The two riders put their horses to a trot. Soon they appeared like mere black specks upon a background of golden haze, whilst in their wake, upon the scarce visible track, the traces of their horses' hoofs, in stains of darker blue upon the virgin white, were infinitely multiplied.

Stoutenburg watched them until the mist-laden distance had completely hidden them from his view. Then, with a sigh of relief, he went within.

Chapter II – The Double Wedding

1

IT was one of those days when earth and heaven alike appear to smile. A day almost warm, certainly genial; for the wind had dropped, the sky was of a vivid blue, and the sun had a genuine feeling of warmth in its kiss. From the overhanging eaves the snow dropped down in soft, moist lumps, stained by the thaw, and the quay, where a goodly crowd had collected, was quickly transformed under foot into a sea of mud.

It almost seemed as if the little town was out on a holiday. People came and went, dressed in gay attire, stood about all along the bank of the river, staring up at the stately gabled house which looked so wonderfully gay with its decorations of flags and valuable tapestries and stuffs hanging from the numerous windows.

That house on the quay – and it was the finest house in the town – was indeed the centre of attraction. It was from there that the air of holiday-making emanated, and certainly from there that the gay sounds of music and revelry came wafted on the crisp, wintry air.

Mynheer Beresteyn had come to his house in Amersfoort, of which city he was chief civic magistrate, in order to celebrate the double wedding. No wonder such an event was made an excuse for a holiday. Burgomaster Beresteyn never did things by halves, and his hospitality was certain to be lavish. Already doles and largesse had been poured out at the porch of St. Maria Kerk; a crowd of beggars more or less indigent, crippled, sick, or merely greedy, had assembled there very early in the morning. Whoever was there was sure to get something. And there was plenty to see besides: the brides and bridegrooms and the wedding party; and of course His Highness the Stadtholder was a sight in himself. He did not often go abroad these days, for his health was no longer as good as it was. He had aged considerably, looked moody and ailing for the most part. There had been sinister rumours, too. The widowed Archduchess Isabella, Mistress of Flanders and Brabant, hated him because he held the United Provinces of the Netherlands free from the bondage of Spain. And in Spain the arts of poison and of secret assassination were carried on with as much perfection as they had ever been in Italy in the days of the Borgias.

However, all such dark thoughts must be put away for the day. This is a festive occasion for Amersfoort, when every anxiety for the fate of the poor fatherland – ever threatened and ever sore-pressed – must be laid to rest. Let the brides and bridegrooms see naught but merry faces – happy auguries of the auspicious days to come.

Here they come –the entire wedding party – walking down the narrow streets from the quay to the St. Maria Kerk. Every one is walking, even the Stadtholder. He is conspicuous by his great height, and the richness of his attire: embroidered doublet, slashed sleeves, priceless lace. His face looks thin and drawn, but he has lost nothing of his martial bearing, nor have his eyes lost their eagle glance. He had come over the previous afternoon from Utrecht, where he was in camp, and had deigned to grace Mynheer Beresteyn's house by sleeping under its roof. It was understood that he would return to Utrecht after the banquet which was to follow the religious ceremony, and he, too, for this one day was obviously making a valiant attempt to cast off the load of anxiety attendant upon ceaseless campaigning. In truth, the Archduchess Isabella, not content with the fairest provinces of Belgium, with Flanders, Brabant, and the Hainault, which her father, King Philip of Spain, had ceded to her absolutely, was even now striving to force some of the United Provinces back under the domination of Spain.

Small wonder then that the Stadtholder, wearied and sick, the shadow of his former self, was no longer sure of a whole-hearted welcome when he showed himself abroad. Nor had the people forgiven him the judicial murder of Olden Barneveldt – the trusted councillor in the past, afterwards the bitter opponent of his master's ambitions – of his severity towards Barneveldt's sons. His relentless severity toward those who offended him, his reckless ambition and stern disciplinarianism, had made him an object of terror rather than of affection. Nevertheless, he still stood for the upholder of the liberties of the United Provinces, the finest captain of his age, who by his endurance, his military skill, and his unswerving patriotism, kept his country's frontiers free from the incursions of the most powerful armies of the time. He still stood as the man who had swept the sacred soil of the Netherlands free from Spanish foes and Spanish tyranny, who had amplified and consolidated the work of his father and firmly established the independence of the Republic. Because of what he had done in the past, men like Mynheer Beresteyn and those of his kind still looked upon him with grave respect, as the chosen of God, the prophet sent to them from Heaven to keep the horrors of a new Spanish invasion away from their land.

And when Maurice of Nassau came to a small city like Amersfoort, as he had done today, he was received with veneration, if not with the old cheers and acclamations. His arbitrary temper was momentarily forgotten, his restless ambition condoned, in the joy of beholding the man who had fought for them, never spared himself until he had won for them all those civil and religious liberties which they prized above all the treasures of the earth.

All heads, then, were bowed in respectful silence as he walked by, with the brides one on each side of him. But the loving glances of the crowd, the jokes and whispered words of cheer and greeting, were reserved for Mynheer Beresteyn and for his family.

2

Two brides, and both comely! Jongejuffrouw Katharina van den Poele, the only child of the wealthy shipowner, member of the Dutch East India Company, a solid burgher both physically and financially, and one of the props of his country's overseas commerce. His daughter, in rich brocade, with stiff stomacher that vainly strove to compress her ample proportions, splashed through the mud on her high pattens beside the Stadtholder, her heavily be-ringed hands clinging to the folds of her gown, so as to save them from being soiled. Stolid and complacent, she heard with a satisfied smile the many compliments that rose from out the crowd on her dazzling complexion, her smoothly brushed hair and magnificent jewelry. The fair Katharina beamed with good-nature and looked the picture of happiness, despite the fact that her bridegroom, who walked immediately behind her, appeared somewhat moody, considering the occasion.

Nicolaes Beresteyn, the Burgomaster's only son, had in truth, no reason for surliness. His bride excited universal admiration, his own private fortune would be more than doubled by the dowry which the good Kaatje brought him along with her plump person, and all the disagreements between himself and his father, all the treachery and the deceit of the past three months, had been amply forgiven. It was all the more strange, therefore, that on this day his face alone should appear as a reflection of the Stadtholder's silent mood, and more than one comment was made thereon as he passed.

Of the other bride and bridegroom it is perhaps more difficult to speak. We all know the beautiful picture of Gilda Beresteyn which Frans Hals made of her some three months previously. That incomparable master of portraiture has rendered that indescribable air of force, coupled with extreme youthfulness, which was her greatest charm. Often she hath been called etherial, yet I do not see how that description could apply to one who was so essentially alive as Gilda Beresteyn. Her blue eyes always sparkled with vitality, and whenever she was moved – which was often enough – they became as dark as sloes. Probably the word came to be applied to her because there was always a little something mysterious about her – an enigmatic little smile, which suggested merriment that came from within rather than in response to an outside joke. Many have remarked that her smile was the gentle reflex of her lover's sparkling gaiety.

Him – that ardent lover, sobered bridegroom now – you cannot forget, not whilst Frans Hals' immortal work, whom he hath called "The Laughing Cavalier," depicts him in all is irrepressible joyousness, and gladdens the eye with its exhilaration and its magnificent gaite de coeur – a veritable nepenthe for jaded seek-sorrows.

For once in his life, as he walks gravely behind his bride, there is a look of seriousness not unmixed with impatience in his laughing eyes. A frown, too, between his brows. The crowd have at once taken him to its heart – especially the women. Those who have no sons wish for one at once, who would grow up just like him: tall and stately as a young sapling, with an air of breeding seldom seen in the sons of the Low Countries, and wearing his magnificent bridal attire as if he had never worn leather jerkin or worsted doublet in his life. The women admire the richly wrought doublet, the priceless lace at neck and wrists, the plumed hat that frames a face alike youthful and determined. But everyone marvels why a bridegroom should go to church in high riding-boots and spurred at this hour. Many whispered comments are exchanged as he goes by.

"A stranger, so they say."

"Though he has fought in the Netherlands."

"Ah, but he really comes from England."

"A romantic story. Never knew his father until recently."

Some said the bridegroom's name was really Blakeney, and that his father was a very rich and very great gentleman over in England. But there were others who remembered him well when he was just a penniless soldier of fortune who went by the name of Diogenes. No one knew him then by any other, and no one but Frans Hals, the painter over in Haarlem, knew whence he had come and what was his parentage. In those days his merry laughter would rouse the echoes of the old city where he and his two boon companions – such a quaint pair of loons! – were wont to dwell in the intervals of selling their swords to the highest bidders.

Ay, Jongejuffrouw Beresteyn's stranger bridegroom had fought in France and in Flanders, in Groningen and Brabant and 'twas said that recently he had saved the life of the Stadtholder at great risk of his own. Many more tales were whispered about him, which would take too long to relate, while the crowd stood agape all down the quay and up the Korte Gracht as far as the St. Maria Kerk.

3

Indeed, Mynheer Beresteyn had not done things by halves. He had chosen that the happy double event should take place at the old house at Amersfoort, where his children had been born, and where he had spent the few happy years of his married life, rather than at Haarlem, which was his business and official residence. He wished, for the occasion, to be just a happy father rather than the distinguished functionary, the head of the Guild of Armourers, one of the most important burghers of the Province, and second only in the council chamber to the Stadtholder.

The religious ceremony was over by noon. It was now mid-afternoon, and the wedding guests had assembled in the stately home on the quay for a gargantuan feast. The Stadtholder sat at a magnificently decked-out table at the far end of the panelled room, on a raised dais surmounted by a canopy of Flemish tapestry, all specially erected for the occasion. Around this privileged board sat the wedding party; Mynheer Beresteyn, grave and sedate, a man who had seen much of life, had suffered a great deal, and even now scarcely dared to give his sense of joy full play. He gazed from time to time on his daughter with something of anxiety as well as of pride. Then the worthy shipowner, member of the Dutch East India Company, and mejuroffluw, his wife – the father and mother of Nicolaes Beresteyn's bride, pompous and fleshy, and with an air of prosperous complacence about their persons which contrasted strangely with Mynheer Beresteyn's anxious earnestness. Finally, the two bridal couples, of whom more anon.

In the body of the nobly proportioned banqueting-hall, a vast concourse of guests had assembled around two huge tables, which were decked out with costly linen and plate, and literally groaned under the succulent dishes which serving-men repeatedly placed there for the delectation of the merry party. Roast capons and geese, fish from the Rhyn and from the sea, pasties made up of oysters and quails, and, above all, a constant supply of delicious Rhine or Spanish wines, according as the guests desired light or heady liquor.

A perpetual buzz of talk, intermingled with many an outburst of hilarity and an occasional song, filled the somewhat stuffy air of the room to the exclusion of any individual sound.

The ladies plied their fans vigorously, and some of the men, warmed by good cheer, had thrown their padded doublets open and loosened their leather belts. The brides-elect sat one on each side of the Stadtholder; a strange contrast, in truth. Kaatje van den Poele, just a young edition of her mother, her well-rounded figure already showing signs of the inevitable coming stoutness, comely to look at, with succulent cheeks shining like rosy apples, her face with the wide-open, prominent eyes, beaming with good-nature and the vigorous application of cold water. Well-mannered, too, for she never spoke unless spoken to, but sat munching her food with naive delight, and whenever her somewhat moody bridegroom hazarded a laboured compliment or joke, she broke into a pleasant giggle, jerked her elbow at him, and muttered a "Fie, Klaas!" which put and end to further conversation.

Gilda Beresteyn, who sat at the Stadtholder's right hand, was silent, too; demure, not a little prim, but with her, even the most casual observer became conscious that beneath the formal demeanor there ran an undercurrent of emotional and pulsating life. The terrible experience which she had gone through a few brief months ago had given to her deep blue eyes a glance that was vividly passionate, yet withal resposeful, and with a curiously childlike expression of trust within its depth.

The stiff bridal robes which convention decreed that she should wear gave her an air of dignity, even whilst it enhanced the youthfulness of her personality. There was all the roundness in her figure which is the attribute of her race; yet, despite her plump shoulders and full throat, her little round face and firm bosom, there remained something ethereal about her, a spirituality and a strength which inspired reverence, even whilst her beauty provoked admiring glances.

"Your Highness is not eating," she remarked timidly.

"My head aches," Maurice of Nassau replied moodily. "I cannot eat. I think I must be over-tired," he went on more pleasantly as he met the girl's kind blue eyes fixed searchingly upon him. "A little fresh air will do me good. Don't disturb any one," he continued hastily, as he rose to his feet and turned to go to the nearest open window.

Beresteyn quickly followed him. The prince looked faint and ill, and had to lean on his host's arm as he tottered towards the window. The little incident was noticed by a few. It caused consternation and the exchange of portentful glances.

A grave-looking man in sober black velvet doublet and sable hose quickly rose from the table and joined the Stadtholder and Mynheer Beresteyn at the window. He was the English physician especially brought across to watch over the health of the illustrious sufferer.

Gilda turned to her neighbour. Her eyes had suddenly filled with tears, but when she met his glance the ghost of a smile immediately crept around her mouth.

"It seems almost wicked," she said simply "to be so happy now."

Unseen by the rest of the company, the man next to her took her tiny hand and raised it to his lips.

"At times, even to-day," she went on softly, "it all seems like a dream. Your wooing, my dear lord, hath been so tempestuous. Less than three months ago I did not know of your existence —"

"My wooing hath been over-slow for my taste!" he broke in with a short, impatient sigh. "Three months, you say? And for me you are still a shadow, an exquisite sprite that eludes me behind an impenetrable, a damnable wall of conventions, even though my very sinews ache with longing to hold you in mine arms for ever and for aye!"

He looked her straight between the eyes, so straight and with such a tantalizing glance that a hot blush rose swiftly to her cheeks; whereupon he laughed again – a merry, a careless, infectious laugh it was – and squeezed her hand so tightly that he made her gasp.

"You are always ready to laugh, my lord," she murmured reproachfully.

"Always," he riposted. "And now, how can I help it? I must laugh, or else curse with impatience. It is scarce three o'clock now, and not before many hours can we be free of this chattering throng."

Then, as she remained silent, with eyes cast down now and the warm flush still lingering in her cheeks, he went on, with brusque impatience, his voice sunk to a quick, penetrating whisper:

"If anything should part me from you now, ma donna, I verily believe that I should kill someone or myself!"

He paused, almost disconcerted. It had never been his wont to talk of his feelings. The transient sentiments that in the past had grazed his senses, without touching his heart, had only led him to careless protestations, forgotten as soon as made. He himself marvelled at the depth of his love for this exquisite creature who had so suddenly come into his life, bringing with her a fragrance of youth and of purity, and withal of fervid passion, such as he had never dreamed of through the many vicissitudes of his adventurous life.

Still she did not speak, and he was content to look on her, satisfied that she was in truth too completely happy at this hour to give vent to her feelings in so many words. He loved to watch the play of emotions in her tell-tale face, the pursed-up little mouth, so ready to smile, and those violet-tinted eyes, now and then raised to him in perfect trust and abandonment of self, then veiled once more demurely under his provoking glance.

He loved to tease her, for then she blushed, and her long lashes drew a delicately pencilled shadow upon her cheeks. He loved to say things that frightened her, for then she would look up with a quick, inquiring glance, search his own with a palpitating expression that quickly melted again into one of bliss.

"You look so demure, ma donna," he exclaimed whimsically, "that I vow I'll create a scandal – leap across the table and kiss Kaatje, for instance – just to see if it would make you laugh!"

"Do not make fun of Kaatje, my lord," Gilda admonished. "She hath more depth of feeling than you give her credit for."

"I do not doubt her depth of feeling, dear heart," he retorted with mock earnestness. "But, oh, good St. Bavon help me! Have you ever seen so solid a yokemate, or," he added, and pointed to Nicolaes Beresteyn, who sat moody and sullen, toying with his food, beside his equally silent bride, "so ardent a bridegroom? Verily, the dear lady reminds me of those succulent fish pasties they make over in England, white and stodgy, and rather heavy on the stomach, but, oh, so splendidly nourishing!"

"Fie! Now you are mocking again."

"How can I help it, dear heart, when you persist in looking so solemn – so solemn, that, in the midst of all this hilarity, I am forcibly reminded of all the rude things you said to me that night at the inn in Leyden, and I am left to marvel how you ever came to change your opinion of me?"

"I changed my opinion of you," she rejoined earnestly, "when I learned how you were ready to give your life to save the Stadtholder from those abominable murderers; and almost lost it," she added under her breath, "to save my brother Nicolaes from the consequence of his own treachery."

"Hush! That is all over and done with now, ma donna," he retorted lightly. "Nicolaes has become a sober burgher, devoted to his solid Kaatje and to the cause of the Netherlands; and I have sold my liberty to the fairest tyrant that ever enslaved a man's soul."

"Do you regret it," she queried shyly, "already?"

"Already!" he assented gravely. "I am kicking against my bonds, longing for that freedom which in the past kept my stomach empty and my head erect."

"Will you never be serious?" she retorted.

"Never, while I live. My journey to England killed my only attempt at sobriety, for there I found that the stock to which I belonged was both irreproachable and grave, had been so all the while that I, the most recent scion of so noble a race, was roaming about the world, the most shiftless and thriftless vagabond it had ever seen. But in England" – he sighed and raised his eyes and hands in mock solemnity – "in England the climate is so atrocious that the people become grim-visaged and square-toed through constantly watching the rain coming down. Or else," he added, with another suppressed ripple of that infectious laugh of his, "the climate in England has become so atrocious because there are so many square-toed folk about. I was such a very little while in England," he concluded with utmost gravity, "I had not time to make up my mind which way it went."

"Methinks you told me," she rejoined, "that your home in England is beautiful and stately."

"It is both, dear heart," he replied more seriously; "and I shall learn to love it when you have dwelt therein. I should love it even now if it had ever been hallowed by the presence of my mother."

"She never went there?"

"No, never. My father came to Holland in Leicester's train. He married my mother in Haarlem, then deserted her and left her there to starve. My friend Frans Hals cared for me after she died. That is the whole of her history. It does not make for deep, filial affection, does it?"

"But you have seen your father now. Affection will come in time."

"Yes; I have seen him, thanks to your father, who brought us together. I have seen my home in Sussex, where one day, please God, you'll reign as its mistress."

"I, the wife of an English lord!" she sighed. "I can scarcely credit it."

"Nor can I, dear heart," he answered lightly; "for that you'll never be. Let me try and explain to you just how it all is, for, in truth, English honours are hard to understand. My father is an English gentleman with no handle to his name. Blake of Blakeney they call him over there; and I am his only son. It seems that he rendered signal services to his king of late, who thereupon desired to confer upon him one of those honours which we over here find it so difficult to apprise. My father, however, either because he is advanced in years or because he desired to show me some singular mark of favour, petitioned King James to bestow the proposed honour upon his only son. Thus am I Sir Percy Blakeney, it seems, without any merit on my part. Funny is it not? And I who, for years, was known by no name save Diogenes, one of three vagabonds, with perhaps more wits, but certainly no more worth, than my two compeers!"

"Then I should call you Sir Percy?" she concluded. "Yet I cannot get used to the name."

"You might even call me Percy," he suggested; "for thus was I baptized at my dear mother's wish. Though, in truth, I had forgotten it until my father insisted on it that I could not be called Diogenes by mine own servants, and that he himself could not present me to his Majesty the King of England under so fanciful a name."

"I like best to think of you as Diogenes," she murmured softly. "Thus I knew you first, and your brother philosophers, Socrates and Pythagoras – such a quaint trio, and all of you so unsuited to your names! I wish," she added with a sigh, "that they were here now."

"And they should be here," he assented. "I am deeply anxious. But Pythagoras —"

He broke off abruptly. Mynheer Beresteyn's voice called to him from the recess by the open window.

"A goblet of wine!" Mynheer commanded; "for his Highness."

Diogenes was about to comply with the order, but Nicolaes forestalled him. Already he had poured out the wine.

"Let me take it," he said curtly, took up the goblet and went with it to the window. He offered it to the Stadtholder, who drank greedily.

It was but a brief incident. Nicolaes had remained beside the prince while the latter drank; then he returned, with the empty goblet in his hand, to take his place once more beside his stolid and solid bride.

"You were speaking of Pythagoras, sir," Gilda rejoined, as soon as Diogenes was once more seated beside her. "I never know which is which of the two dear souls. Is Pythagoras the lean one with the deep, bass voice?"

"No. He is the fat one, with the round, red nose," Diogenes replied gravely. "He was at Ede the night before last, and was seen there, at the tavern of the Crow's Nest, somewhere after midnight, imbibing copious draughts of hot, spiced ale. After that all traces of him have vanished. But he must have started to join me here, as this had been pre-arranged, and I fear me that he lost his way on that verfloekte waste. I have sent Socrates, my lean comrade – to look for poor Pythagoras upon the Veluwe. They should be here, in truth, and —"

But the next word died in his throat. He jumped to his feet.

"The Stadtholder!" he exclaimed. "He hath fainted."

4

Indeed, there was quite a commotion now in the window recess, where Prince Maurice had remained all this while by the open casement, inhaling the fresh, keen air. The English physician stood beside him, and Mynheer Beresteyn was gazing with anxious eyes on the master to whom, in spite of all, he had remained so splendidly loyal. The dizziness had apparently come on quite suddenly, while the Stadtholder was acknowledging the acclamations of the crowd who had seen and cheered him. He tottered and would have fallen but for the physician's supporting arm.

Not many of the guests had noticed the incident. They were for the most part too much absorbed in their enjoyment of the feast to pay attention to what went on in other parts of the room. But Diogenes had seen it and was already over by the window; and Nicolaes Beresteyn, too, had jumped to his feet. He looked wide-eyed and scared, even whilst the stolid Kaatje, flushed with good cheer, remained perfectly unconcerned, munching some sweetmeats which seemed to delight her palate.

The Stadtholder, however, had quickly recovered. The faintness passed off as suddenly as it came, but it left the illustrious guest more silent and moody than before. His face had become of a yellowish pallor, and his eyes looked sunken as if consumed with fever. But he chose to return to his seat under the dais, and this time he called to Diogenes to give him the support of his arm.

"'Twas scarce worth while, eh, my friend," he said bitterly, "to risk your precious young life in order to save this precarious one. Had Stoutenburg's bomb done the assassin's work, it would only have anticipated events by less than three months."

"Your Highness is over-tired," Diogenes rejoined simply. "Complete rest in the midst of your friends would fight this insidious sickness far better than the wisest of physicians."

"What do you mean?" the Stadtholder immediately retorted, his keen, hawk-like glance searching the soldier's smiling face. "Why should you say 'in the midst of your friends?" he went on huskily. "You don't mean —?"

"What, your Highness?"

"I mean – you said it so strangely – as if —"

"I, your Highness?" Diogenes queried, not a little surprised at the Stadtholder's febrile agitation.

"I myself have oft wondered —"

Maurice of Nassau paused abruptly, rested his elbows on the table, and for a moment or two remained quite still, his forehead buried in his hands. Gilda gazed on him wide-eyed and tearful; even Kaatje ceased to munch. It seemed terrible to be so great a man, wielding such power, commanding such obedience, and to be reduced to a mere babbling sufferer, fearing phantoms and eagerly gleaning any words of comfort that might come from loyal lips.

Diogenes had remained silent, too; his eyes, usually so full of light-heartedness and merriment, had a strange, searching glitter in them now. A minute or two later the prince had pulled himself together, tried to look unconcerned, and assumed a geniality which obviously he was far from feeling. But it was to Diogenes that he spoke once more.

"Anyhow, I could not rest yet awhile, my friend," he said with a sigh; "whilst the Archduchess threatens Gelderland, the De Berg is making ready to cross the Ijssel."

"Your Highness's armies under your Highness's command," rejoined the soldier firmly, "can drive the Archduchess's hosts out of Gelderland, and send Henri de Berg back across the Ijssel. Maurice of Nassau is still the finest commander in Europe, even —"

He paused, and the Stadtholder broke in bitterly:

"Even though he is a dying man, you mean."

"No!" here broke in Gilda, with glowing fervour. "I swear that nothing was further from my lord's thoughts. Sir," she added, and turned boldly to her lover, "you spoke with such confidence just now. A toast, I pray you, so that we may all join in expressions of loyalty to our guest and sovereign lord, the Stadtholder!"

She poured a goblet full of wine. Diogenes gave her a quick glance of approval. Then he picked up the goblet, stood upon his seat, and placed one foot on the table.

"Long life to your Highness!" he cried aloud. "May it please God to punish your enemies and to give victory unto your cause!"

Then, holding the goblet aloft, he called at the top of his voice:

"Maurice of Nassau and the cause of Liberty!"

Every one rose, and a rousing cheer went echoing round the room. It was heard and taken up lustily by the crowd outside, until the very walls of the ancient city echoed the loyal toast, from the grim towers of Koppel Poort to the Vrouwetoren of St. Maria Kerk; from gateway to gateway, and rampart to rampart. And the bells of St. Joris and St. Maria took up the joyful call and sent peal after peal of bells resounding gleefully through the keen, wintry air.

"Maurice of Nassau!" rang the chimes. "Nassau and liberty!"

5

But after this manifestation of joy and enthusiasm, comparative silence fell upon the wedding assembly. None but those who had partaken over freely of Mynheer Beresteyn's good cheer could fail to see that the Stadtholder felt ill, and only kept up a semblance of gaiety by a mighty effort of his iron will. Thereafter, conversation became subdued. People talked in whispers, an atmosphere of constraint born of anxiety reigned there where light-hearted gaiety had a while ago held undisputed sway. The host himself did his best to revive the temper of his guests. Serving-men and maids were ordered to go around more briskly with the wine. One or two of the younger men hazarded the traditional jokes which usually obtained at wedding feasts; but those who laughed did so shamefacedly. It seemed as if a vague terror held erstwhile chattering tongues in check.

The Stadtholder, leaning back against the cushions of his chair, spoke very little. His long, nervy fingers played incessantly with crumbs and pellets of bread. He looked impatient and ill at ease, like a man who wants to get away yet fears to offend his host. He had kept Diogenes by his side this time, and Beresteyn was able to snatch a few last words with his daughter. Once she was married, her husband would take her to his home in England one day, and the thought of parting from the child he loved was weighing the father's spirit down.

" 'Tis the first time," he said sadly, "that you will pass out of my keeping. You were the precious heritage bequeathed to me your dead mother. Now 'tis to a stranger that I am entrusting my priceless treasure."

"A stranger, father," riposted Gilda quietly, "who hath proved himself worthy of the truth. And when we do go to England," she went on gaily, "there will only be a narrow strip of water between us, and that is easily crossed."

Beresteyn gave a quickly smothered sigh. He looked across at the stranger to whom, as he said, he was about to hand over the most precious gift he possessed. Handsome he was, that erstwhile penniless soldier of fortune; handsome and brave, frank and loyal, and with that saving grace of light-hearted gaiety in him which had helped him through the past terrible crisis in his life, and brought him to the safe haven of a stately home in England and wealthy father, eager to make amends for the wrongs committed long ago.

But still a stranger for all that, a man who had seen more of the seamy side of the world, who had struggled more, suffered more – ay, perhaps sinned more – than those of his rank in life usually did at his age. Something of that rough-and-tumble life of the soldier of fortune, without home or kindred, who sells his sword to the highest bidder, and knows no master save his own will, must have left its mark upon the temperament of the man. Despite the humorous twinkle in the eyes, the bantering curl on the lip, the man's face bore the impress of the devil-may-care existence that takes no heed of the morrow. And at times, when it was in repose, there was a strangely grim look in it of determination as well as of turbulent passions, not always held in check.

Beresteyn sighed with inward apprehension. His well-ordered mind, the mind of a Dutch middle-class burgher, precise and unemotional, could not quite fathom that of the Anglo-Saxon – the most romantic and the most calculating, and the most impulsive and the most studied, the most sensuous and most self-repressed temperament that ever set the rest of the world wondering. He could see the reckless scapegrace, the thoughtless adventurer, fuming and fretting under the restraint put upon him by the cut-and-dried conventions attendant upon these wedding ceremonies could watch him literally writhing under the knowing looks and time-honoured innuendos which custom deemed allowable on these occasions. His hands indeed must be itching to come in contact with the checks of mocking friends and smug relatives, all eager to give advice or to chaff the young bride, until the hot blood rushed to her cheeks and tears of annoyance gather in her eyes.

The whole atmosphere of noise and drinking – ay, of good-humour and complacency – did, in truth, grate upon Diogenes' nerves. He had not lied to Gilda nor yet exaggerated his sentiments when he said that his sinews ached with longing to seize her and carry her away into solitude and quiet, where nought would come to disturb their love-dream; away upon his horse, her soft arms encircling his neck her head resting on his shoulder, her dear face turned up to his gaze, with those heavenly eyes closed in rapture; the delicate mouth slightly parted, showing a vision of tiny teeth, a tear mayhap trembling on her lashes, a soft blush mantling on her cheek. Away! Across the ocean to that stately home in England, where the spring air was soft with the scent of violets and of fruit blossom, and where beside the river the reeds murmured a soft accompaniment to songs of passion and hymns of love. Away from all save the shrine which he had set up for her in his heart; from all save the haven of his arms.

To feel that, and then be forced to sit and discuss plans for the undoing of the Spanish commander or for the relief of Arnheim, was, in fact, more than Diogenes' restive temperament could stand. His attention began to wander, his answers became evasive; so much so that, after a while, the Stadtholder, eyeing him closely, remarked with the pale ghost of a smile:

" 'Tis no use fretting and fuming, my friend. Your English blood is too mutinous for this sober country and its multitude of stodgy conventions. One of these demands that your bride shall sit here till the last of the guests has departed, and only a few fussy and interfering old tantes are left to unrobe her and commiserate with her over her future lot – a slave to a bullying husband, a handmaid to her exacting lord. Every middle-aged frump in the Netherlands hath some story to tell that will bring tears to a young bride's eyes or a blush to her cheeks."

"Please God," Diogenes ejaculated fervently. "Gilda will be spared that."

"Impossible, you rogue!" the Stadtholder retorted, amused despite his moodiness by the soldier's fretful temper. "The conventions––"

"Verfloekt will be the conventions as far as we are concerned," Diogenes rejoined hotly. "And if your Highness would but help—" he added impulsively.

"I? What can I do?"

"Give the signal for dispersal," Diogenes entreated; "and graciously promise to forgive me if, for the first time in my life, I act with disrespect toward your Highness."

"But, man, how will that help you?" the Stadtholder demurred.

"I must get away from all this wearying bombast, this jabbering and scraping and all these puppy-tricks!" Diogenes exclaimed with comical fierceness. "I must get away ere my wife becomes a doll and a puppet, tossed into my arms by a lot of irresponsible monkeys! If I have to stay here much longer, your Highness," he added earnestly "I vow that I shall flee from it all, leave an angel to weep for my abominable desertion of what I hold more priceless than all the world, and an outraged father to curse the day when so reckless and adventurer crossed his daughter's path. But stand this any longer I cannot!" he concluded, and, with a quick sweep of the arm, he pointed to the chattering, buzzing crowd below. "And if your Highness will not help me —"

"Who said I would not help you, you hotheaded rashling?" the Stadtholder broke in composedly. "You know very well that I can refuse you nothing, not even the furtherance of one of your madcap schemes. And as for disrespect – why, as you say, in the midst of so much bowing and scraping some of us are eager for disrespect as an aging spinster for amorous overtures. By way of a change, you know."

He spoke quite simply and with an undercurrent of genuine sympathy in his tone, as a man towards his friend. Something of the old Maurice of Nassau seemed for the moment to have swept aside the arbitrary tyrant whom men had learned to hate as well as to obey. Diogenes' irascible mood melted suddenly in the sunshine of the Stadtholder's indulgent smile, the mocking glance faded out of his eyes, and he said with unwonted earnestness:

"No wonder that men have gone to death or to glory under your leadership."

"Would you follow me again if I called?" the prince retorted.

"Your Highness hath no need of me. The United Provinces are free, her burghers are free men. 'Tis time to sheathe the sword, and a man might be allowed, methinks, to dream of happiness."

"Is your happiness bound up with the mad scheme for which you want my help?"

"Ay, my dear lord!" Diogenes replied. "And, secure in your gracious promise, I swear that naught can keep me from the scheme now save mine own demise."

"There are more arbitrary things than death, my friend," the Stadtholder mused.

"Possibly, your Highness," the soldier answered lightly; "but not for me to-night."

6

More than one chronicler of the time hath averred that Maurice of Nassau had in truth a soft corner in his heart for the man who had saved him from the bomb prepared by the Lord of Stoutenburg, and would yield to the "Laughing Cavalier" when others, less privileged, were made to feel the weight of his arbitrary temper. Be that as it may, he certainly on this occasion was as good as his word. Wearied with all these endless ceremonials, he was no doubt glad enough to take his departure, and anon he gave the signal for a general breaking up of the party by rising, and, in a loud voice, thanking Mynheer Beresteyn for his lavish hospitality.

"An you will pardon this abrupt departure," he concluded with unwonted graciousness, "I would fain get to horse. By starting within the hour, I could reach Utrecht before dark."

All the guests had risen, too, and there was the usual hubbub and noise attendant on the dispersal of so large a party. That Stadtholder stepped down from the dais, Mynheer Beresteyn and the English physician remaining by his side, while the bridal party brought up the rear. Room was made for his Highness to walk down the room, the men standing bareheaded and the women curtseying as he passed. But he did not speak to any one, only nodded perfunctorily to those whom he knew personally. Obviously he felt ill and tired, and his moodiness was, for the most part, commented on with sympathy.

The brides and bridegrooms, on the other hand, had to withstand a veritable fusillade of banter, which Nicolaes Beresteyn received sulkily, and the solid Kaatje with much complacence. Indeed, this bride was willing enough to be chaffed, had even a saucy reply handy when she was teased, and ogled her friends slily as she went by. But Gilda remained silent and demure. I don't think that she heard a word that was said. She literally seemed to glide across the room like the veritable sprite her ardent lover had called her. Her tiny hand, white and slightly fluttering, rested on his arm, lost in the richly embroidered folds of his magnificent doublet. She was not fully conscious of her actions, moved along as in a dream, without the exertion of her will. She was wont to speak afterwards of this brief progress of hers through the crowded room with the chattering throng of friends all around, as a walk through air. Nothing seemed to her to exist. There was no room, , no crowd, no noise. She alone existed, and ethereally. Her lover was there, however, and she was fully conscious of his will. She knew that anon she would be a captive in his arms, to be dealt with my him as he liked; and this caused her to feel that fearful and yet wholly content.

He, Diogenes, on the other hand, was the picture of fretful impatience, squeezing his soft felt hat in his hand as if it were the throat of some deadly enemy. He never once looked at his bride; probably if he had he would have lost the last shred of self-control, would have seized her in his arms and carried her away then and there, regardless of the respect due to the Stadtholder and to his host.

But the trial, though severe to any ebullient temper, was not of long duration. Anon the Stadtholder was in the hall, booted once more and spurred, and surrounded by his equerries and by the bridal party.

His bodyguard encumbered the hall, their steel bonnets and short breastplates reflecting the wintry light which came, many-hued, through the tall, stained glass windows. In the rear the wedding guests were crowding forward to catch a last glimpse of the Stadtholder, and of the pageant of his departure. The great hall door had been thrown open, and through it, framed in the richness of the heavy oaken jambs, a picture appeared, gay, animated, brilliant, such as the small city had never before seen.

There was the holiday throng, moving ceaselessly in an ever flowing and glittering stream. The women in huge, winged hoods and short kirtles, the men in fur bonnets and sleeved coats, were strolling up and down the quay. There were the inevitable musicians with pipes, viols, and sackbuts, pushing their way through the dense mass of people, with a retinue behind them of young people and old, and of children, all stepping it to the measure of the tune. There was the swarthy foreigner with his monkey dressed out in gaily coloured rags, and the hawker with his tray full of bright handkerchiefs, of glass beads, chains, and amulets, crying out his wares. It was, in fact, a holiday crowd, drawn thither by Mynheer Beresteyn's largesse; the shopkeepers with their wives, who had been induced to shut down shop for the afternoon, as if some official function had been in progress; the apprentices getting in everybody's way, hilarious and full of mischief, trying to steal the hawkers' wares, or to play impish pranks on their employers; servant maids and sober apothecaries, out-at-elbow scriveners and stolid rustics, to-gether with the rag and tag of soldiery, the paid mercenaries of Maurice of Nassau's army, in their showy doublets and plumed bonnets, elbowing their way through with the air of masters.

And all this brilliant gathering was lit by a pale, wintry sun: and with the sleepy waters of the Eem, and the frowning towers of the Koppel-poort forming just the right natural-tinted background to the scene.

"Make way there!" the prince's herald shouted, whilst another rang a fanfare upon the trumpet. "Make way for his High and Mightiness, Maurice of Nassau, Prince of Orange, Stadtholder of the United Provinces of Holland, Friesland, Utrecht, Gelderland, Over Yssel, and Groningen! Make way!"

The equerries were bringing the prince's charger, the pikemen followed in gorgeous padded trunks and slashed hose. To the noise of the moving throng, the chatter and the laughter, the scraping of viols and piping of sackbuts, was now added the din of champing horses, rattle of bits and chains, the shouts of the men who were bringing the horses along. The crowd receded, leaving an open space in front of the house, where mounted men assembled so quickly that they seemed as if they had risen out of the ground.

The Stadtholder was taking final leave of his host listening with what patience he could master to lengthy, loyal speeches from the more important guests, and from the other bride and bridegroom. He had – deliberately methinks – turned his back on Diogenes, who, strangely enough, was booted and spurred too, had his sword buckled to his belt, and carried a dark cloak on his arm, presenting not at all the picture of a bridegroom in holiday attire.

And it all happened so quickly that neither the guests within, nor the soldiers, nor the crowd outside, had time to realize it or to take it in. No one understood, in fact, what was happening, save perhaps the Stadtholder, who guessed; and he engaged the sober fathers near him in earnest conversation.

A mounted equerry, dressed in rough leather jerkin and leading another horse by the bridle, had taken up his stand in the forefront of the crowd. Now at a signal unheard by all save him, he jumped out of the saddle and stood beside the stirrup leathers of the second charger. At that same instant Diogenes, with movements quick as lightning, had thrown the cloak, which he was carrying round Gilda's shoulders, and before she could utter a scream or even a gasp, he had stooped and picked her up in his arms as if she were a weightless doll.

Another second and he was outside the door, at the top of the steps which led down to the quay. For an instant he stood there, his keen eyes sweeping over the picture before him. Like a young lion that hath been caged and now scents liberty once more, he inhaled the biting air; a superb figure, with head tossed back, eyes and lips laughing with the joy of deliverance, the inert figure of the girl lying in his arms.

He felt her clinging more closely to him, and revelled in that intoxicating sense of power when the one woman yields who holds a world of happiness in her tiny hand. He felt the tightening of her hold, watched the look of contentment stealing over her face, saw her eyes close, her lips smile, and knew that they were ready for a kiss.

Then he caught sight of his horse, and of the man in the leather jerkin. He signalled to him to bring the horses near. The crowd understood his meaning and set up a ringing cheer. Many things had been seen in Dutch cities before, but never so romantic an abduction as this. The bridegroom carrying off his bride in the face of scandalized and protesting wedding guests! The Stadtholder even was seen to laugh. He could be seen in the background, reassuring the horrified guests, and trying by kind words and pressure of hand to appease Mynheer Beresteyn's agonized surprise.

"I knew of his mad project, and I must say I approved," the prince whispered to the agitated father. "He is taking her to Rotterdam to-night. Let the child be, Mynheer; she is safe enough in his arms."

Beresteyn was one of those men who throughout his life had always known how to accept the inevitable. Perhaps in his heart he knew that the Stadtholder was right.

"Give them your blessing, Mynheer," Maurice of Nassau urged. "English gentleman or soldier of fortune, the man is a man and deserves it. Your daughter loves him. Let them be."

Diogenes had encountered Beresteyn's reproachful glance. He did not move from where he stood, only his arms closed tighter still around Gilda's motionless form. It was an instinctive challenge to the father – almost a defiance. What he had would hold, in spite of all.

Beresteyn hesitated for the mere fraction of a second longer; then he, too, stepped out through the door and approached the man and his burden. He said nothing, but, in the face of the crowd, he stooped and pressed his lips against his daughter's forehead. Then Mynheer Beresteyn murmured something which sounded like a blessing, and added solemnly:

"May God's wrath descend upon you, my lord, if you ever cause her unhappiness."

"Amen to that!" responded Diogenes lightly. "She and I, Mynheer, will dream together for awhile in England, but I'll bring her back to you when our orchards are gay with apple-blossom and there is a taste of summer in the air."

He bowed his head to receive the father's blessing. The crowd cheered again; sackbuts and viols set up a lively tune. At every window of the house, along the quay eager faces were peering out, gazing on the moving spectacle. In the doorway of Mynheer Beresteyn's house the

Stadtholder remained to watch. For the moment he seemed better and brighter, more like his former self. The rest of the bridal party was still in the hall, but the wedding guests had gone back into the banqueting-room, whence they could see through the open windows what was going on.

7

Then it was that suddenly a curious spectacle presented itself to view. It was, in truth, so curious an one that those of the crowd who were in the rear withdrew their consideration from the romantic scene before them in order to concentrate it on those two strange-looking cavaliers who had just emerged from under the Koppel-port, and were slowly forging their way through the throng.

It was the ringing shout, reiterated twice in succession by one of these cavaliers, that had at first arrested the attention of the crowd, and had even caused Diogenes to pause in the very act of starting for his sentimental adventure. To him the voice that uttered such peremptory clamour was familiar enough, but what in St. Bavon's name did it all mean?

"Hola! you verdommte plepshurk!" came for the third time from the strange cavalier. "Make way there! We are for the house of Mynheer Beresteyn, where we are bidden as his guests."

A loud burst of hilarity greeted this announcement, and a mocking voice retorted lustily:

"Hey! Make way there for the honoured guests of Mynheer Beresteyn!"

In truth, it was small wonder that the aspect of these two cavaliers caused such wild jollity amongst the people, who at this precise moment were overready for laughter. One of them, as lean as a gatepost, sat high on his horse with long shanks covered in high leathern boots. A tall sugar-loaf hat sat precariously upon his head, and his hatchet face, with the hooked, prominent nose and sharp, unshaved chin, looked blue with the cold.

Behind him on a pillion rode – or rather clung – his companion, a short man as rotund as the other was lean, with round face which no doubt had once been of a healthy ruddy tint, but was now streaked and blotched with pallor. He, too, , wore a sugar-loaf hat, but it had slid down to the back of his head, and was held in place by a piece of black tape, which he had in his mouth like a horse has its bit. He was holding on very tightly with his short, fat arms to his companion's body, and his feet were tied together with thick cord beneath the horse's belly. His doublet and hose were smeared with mud and stained with blood, and altogether he presented a pitiable spectacle, more especially when he rolled his small, beady eyes and looked with a scared expression on the hilarious apprentices who were dancing and screaming around him.

But the other appeared quite indifferent to the jeers and mockeries of the crowd. He passed majestically through the gateway of the Koppel-poort that spans the river, not unlike the figure of that legendary knight of the rueful countenance of whom the SeÒor Cervantes had been writing of late.

Diogenes had remained on the top of the steps, perfectly still. His keen eyes, frowning now under the straight, square brow, watched the slow progress of those two quaint figures. Who will ever attempt to explain the subtle workings of that mysterious force which men term Intuition? Whence does it come? Where does it dwell? How doth it come knocking at a man's heart with cold, hard knuckles that bruise and freeze? Diogenes felt that sudden call. Gilda was still lying snugly in his arms; she had seen nothing. But he had become suspicious now, mistrustful of that Fate which had but a moment ago smiled so encourageingly upon him. All his exhilaration fell away from him like a discarded mantle, leaving him chilled to the soul and inert, and with the premonition of something evil looming from afar on the horizon of his Destiny.

The two quaint companions came nearer. Soon Diogenes could read every line upon the familiar countenances. He and those men had fought side by side, shoulder to shoulder, had bled together, suffered together, starved and triumphed together. There was but little the one thought that the others could not know. Even now, on Socrates; lean, lantern-jawed face Diogenes read plainly the message of some tragedy as yet uncomprehended by the other, but which Pythagoras' sorry plight had more that suggested. It was a deeper thing than Intuition; it was Knowledge. Knowledge that the hour of happiness had gone by, the hour of security and of repose, and that the relentless finger of Fate pointed once more to paths beset with sorrow and with thorns, to the path of an adventurer and of a soldier of fortune, rather than to the easy existence of a wealthy gentleman.

As Socrates swung himself wearily out of the saddle, Diogenes' piercing glance darted a mute, quick query toward his friend. The other replied by a mere nod of the head. They knew; they understood one another. Put into plain language, question and answer might have been put thus:

"Are we to go on the warpath again, old compeer?"

"So it seems. There's fighting to be done. Will you be in it, too?"

And Diogenes gave that quick impatient sigh which was so characteristic of him, and very slowly, very gently, as if she were a sheaf of flowers, he allowed his beloved to glide out of his arms.

Chapter III – The Great Interruption

1

THE next moment Diogenes was down on the quay, in time to help Socrates to lift his brother philosopher off the pillion.

Gilda, a little scared at first, not understanding, looked wonderingly around her, blinking in the glare, until she encountered her father's troubled glance.

"What is it?" she murmured, half-stupidly.

He tried to explain, pointed to the group down below, the funny, fat man in obvious pain and distress, being lifted off the horse and received in those same strong arms which had sheltered her – Gilda – but a moment ago.

The Stadtholder, too, was curious, asked many questions, and had to be waited on deferentially with replies and explanations, which were still of necessity very vague.

"Attend to his Highness, father," Gilda said more firmly. "I can look to myself now."

She felt a little strange, a little humiliated perhaps, standing here alone, as if abandoned by the very man who but a moment ago had seemed ready to defy every convention for her sake. Just now she had been the centre of attraction, the pivot round which revolved excitement, curiosity, interest. Even the Stadtholder had, for the space of those few minutes, forgotten his cares and his responsibilities in order to think of her and to plead with her father for her freedom and her happiness. Now she was all alone, seemed so for the moment, while her father and Mynheer van den Poele and the older men crowded around his Highness, and every one had their eyes fixed on the curious spectacle below.

But that sense of isolation and of disappointment was only transient. Gilda Beresteyn had recently gone through experiences far more bitter than this – experiences that had taught her to think and to act quickly and on her own initiative. She saw her lover remounting the steps now. He was carrying his friend in his arms as if the latter had been a child, his other compeer following ruefully. The rowdy 'prentices had been silenced; two or three kindly pairs of hands had proved ready to assist and to care for the horse, which looked spent. The holiday crowd was silent and sympathetic. Every one felt that in this sudden interruption of the gay and romantic adventure there lurked a something mysterious which might very well prove to be a tragedy.

It was Gilda who led the way into the house, calling Maria to open a guest-chamber forthwith, one where the bed was spread with freshly-aired linen. The English physician, at a word from the Stadtholder, was ready to minister to the sick man, and Mynheer Beresteyn himself showed the young soldier and his burden up the stairs, while the crowd of wedding guests and of the prince's bodyguard made way for them to pass through the hall.

What had been such a merry and excited throng earlier in the day was now more than ever subdued. The happenings in the house of Mynheer Beresteyn, which should have been at this hour solely centred around the Stadtholder and the wedding party, were strange enough indeed to call forth whispered comments and subdued murmurings in secluded corners. To begin with, the Stadtholder had put off his departure for an hour and more, and this apparently at the instance of Diogenes, who had begged for the assistance of the prince's English physician to minister to his friend.

People marvelled why the town leech should not have been called in. Why should a strange plepshurk's sickness interfere with his Highness's movements? Also the Stadtholder appeared agitated and fretful since Diogenes had had a word with him. Maurice of Nassau, acquiescing with unwonted readiness both in his physician remaining to look after the sick man and in the postponement of his own departure, had since then retired to a small private room on a floor above, in the company of Mynheer Beresteyn and several of the more important guests. The others were left to conjecture and to gossip, which they did freely, whilst Gilda was no longer to be seen, and the worthy Kaatje was left pouting and desolate beside her morose bridegroom.

Nicolaes Beresteyn, indeed, appeared more moody than any one, although the interruption could not in itself have interfered with his new domestic arrangements. At first he had thought of following his father and Stadtholder into the private chamber upstairs, but to this Mynheer Beresteyn had demurred.

"Your place, my son," he said, with a gently mocking smile, "is beside your Kaatje. His Highness will understand."

And when Nicolaes, trying to insist, followed his father up the stairs to the very threshold of the council room, Mynheer quite firmly and unceremoniously closed the door in his face.

2

Up in the guest-chamber, Diogenes was watching over his sick friend. The first moment that he was alone with his two old compeers, he had turned to Socrates and queried anxiously:

"What is it? What hath happened?"

"He'll tell you when he can speak," the other replied. "We found him lying in the snow outside Lang Soeren with two bullet-wounds in his back, after we had searched the whole verfloekte Veluwe for him all day. We took him into Lang Soeren, where there was a leech, who extracted the one bullet that had lodged under his shoulder blade; the other had only passed through the flesh along his ribs, where it made a clean hole but could not otherwise be found."

"Well, yes – and —" Diogenes went on impatiently, for the other was somewhat slow of speech.

"The leech," Socrates rejoined unperturbed, "said that the patient must lie still for a few days because of the fever; but what must this fool do but shout and rave the moment he is conscious that he must to Amersfoort to see you at once. And so loudly did he shout and so wildly did he rave, that the leech himself got scared and ran away. Whereupon I set the bladder-bellied loon upon the pillion behind me and brought him hither, thinking the ride would do him less harm than all that wild screeching and waving of arms. And here we are!" Socrates concluded blandly, and threw himself into the nearest chair; for he, too, apparently was exhausted with the fatigue of his perilous journey across the waste.

Just then the leech returned, and nothing more could be said. The sick man groaned a good deal under the physician's hands, and Socrates presently dropped off to sleep.

The noise in the street below had somewhat abated, but there was still the monotonous hubbub attendant on a huge crowd on the move. Diogenes went to the window and gazed out upon the throng. Even now the wintry sun was sinking slowly down in the west in a haze of purple and rose, licking the towers of St. Maria and Joris with glistening tongues of fire, and tinting the snow-covered roofs and gables with a rosy hue. The sluggish waters of the Eem appeared like liquid flame.

For a few minutes the Koppel-poort, the bridges, the bastions, the helmets and breastplates of the prince's guard threw back a thousand rays of multi-coloured lights. For a brief instant the earth glowed and blushed under this last kiss of her setting lord. Then all became sombre and dreary, as if a veil had been drawn over the light that illuminated the little city, leaving but the grey shadows visible, and the sadness of evening and the expectance of a long winter's night.

Diogenes gave a moody sigh. His fiery temper chafed under this delay. Not for a moment would he have thought of leaving his sick comrade until he had been reassured as to his fate; but if everything had happened as he had planned and wished, he would be half-way to Utrecht by now, galloping adown the lonely roads with a delicious burden upon his saddle-bow, and feeling the cold wintry wind whistling past his ears as he put the leagues behind him.

He turned away from the window, and tiptoed out of the room. The groans of the sick man, the measured movements of the leech, the snoring of Socrates, were grating on his nerves. Closing the door softly behind him, he strode down the gallery which ran in front of him along the entire width of the house. Up and down once or twice. The movement did him good, and he liked the solitude. The house was still full of a chattering throng; he could hear the murmur of conversation rising from below. Once he peeped over the carved balustrade of the gallery and down into the hall. The prince's bodyguard was still there, and two or three equerries. The clank of their spurs resounded up the stairs as they moved about on the flag-covered floor.

3

When Diogenes resumed his pacing up and down, he suddenly became aware of the soft and distant sound of a woman's voice, singing to the accompaniment of a quaint-toned virginal. He paused and listened. The voice was Gilda's, and the sentimental ditty which she sang had just that melancholy strain in it which is to be found in the songs of all nations that are foredoomed to suffer and to fight. Chiding himself for a fool, Diogenes, nevertheless, felt for a moment or two quite unable to move. It seemed as if Gilda's song – he could not catch the words – was tearing at his heart even whilst it reduced him to a state of silent ecstasy. Much against his will he felt the hot tears welling to his eyes. With his wonted impatience he swept them away with the back of his hand.

"Curse me for a snivelling blockhead!" he muttered; and strode resolutely in the direction whence had come the sweet sad sound.

Then it was that he noticed that one of the doors which gave on the gallery was ajar. It was through this that the intoxicating sound had come to his ears. After an instant's hesitation he pushed the door open. It gave on a small panelled room with deep-embrasured window, through which the grey evening light came in, shyly peeping. On the window-ledge a couple of pots of early tulips flaunted their crude colours against the neutral-tinted background, whilst on the shelves in a corner of the room gleamed the vivid blue of bright-patterned china plates. But the flowers and the china and the grey evening light were but momentary impressions, which did not fix themselves upon the man's consciousness. All that he retained clearly was the vision of Gilda sitting at the instrument, her delicate hands resting upon the keys. She had ceased to play, and was looking straight out before her, and Diogenes could see her piquant profile silhouetted against the pale, slivery light. She had changed her stiff bridal robes for a plain gown of dark-coloured worsted, relieved only by dainty cuffs and collar of filmy Flemish lace.

At the sound of her husband's footsteps she turned to look on him, and her whole face became wreathed in smiles. He was still booted and spurred, ready for the journey, with his long, heavy sword buckled to his belt; but he had put hat and mantle aside. The moment he came in Gilda put a finger to her lips.

"Sh-sh-sh!" she whispered. "If you make no noise they'll not know you are here."

She pointed across the room to where a heavy tapestry apparently masked another door.

"The Stadtholder is in there," she added naively, "with father and Mynheer van den Poele and a number of other grave seigneurs. Kaatje is weeping and complaining somewhere down in mejuffrouw van den Poele's arms. So I sat down to the virginal and left the door open, so that you might hear me sing; for if you heard I thought you would surely come. I was lonely," she added simply, "and waiting for you."

Quite enough in truth to make a man who is dizzy with love ten thousand times more dizzy still. And Diogenes was desperately in love, more so indeed than he had ever thought himself capable of being. He quietly unbuckled his sword, which clanged against the floor when he moved, and deposited in cautiously and noiselessly in an angle of the room. Then he tiptoed across to the virginal and knelt beside his beloved.

For a moment or two he rested his head against her cool white hands.

"To think," he murmured, with a sigh of infinite longing, "that we might be half-way to Rotterdam by now! But I could not leave my old Pythagoras till I knew that he was in no danger."

"What saith the physician, my lord?" she asked.

"I am waiting now for his final verdict. But he gives me every hope. In an hour I shall know."

He paused, trying to read the varying play of emotions upon her face. From the other side of the tapestry came the low sound of subdued murmurings.

"It would not be too late," he went on, slightly hesitating, taking her hands in his and forcing her glance to meet his. "You knew I meant to take you to England – to carry you away – to-night?"

She nodded.

"Yes, I knew," she replied. "And I was glad to go."

"Will you be afraid to come presently?" he urged, his voice quivering with excitement. "In the dark – I know the road well. We could make Rotterdam by midnight – and set sail for England To-morrow as I had prearranged —"

"Just as you wish, my dear lord," she assented simply.

"I could not wait, ma donna! I had planned it all – to ride with you Rotterdam to-night – and then to-morrow on the seas – with you – and England in sight, I could not wait!" he reiterated, almost pathetically, so great was his impatience.

"I am ready to start when you will, my lord," she said again, with a smile.

"And you'll not be afraid?" he insisted. "It will be dark – and cold. We could not reach Rotterdam before midnight."

"How should I be afraid of the darkness or of anything," she retorted, "when I am with you. And how should I be cold, when I am nestling in your arms?"

He had his arms round her in an instant. He would have kissed her if he dared. But with the kiss all restraint would of a surety have vanished, as doth the snow in the warm embrace of the sun. He would have seized her then and there once more and carried her away. And this time no consideration on earth would have stayed him. With a muttered exclamation, he jumped to his feet and passed his slender hand across his forehead.

"Good St. Bavon!" he murmured whimsically. "Why are you so unkind to me to-night?"

And she, a little disappointed because, in truth, she had been ready for the kiss, rejoined with a quaint little pout:

"You are always appealing to St. Bavon, my dear lord! Why is that?"

"Because," he replied very seriously, "St. Bavon is the patron saint of all men that are weak."

She fixed great, wondering eyes on him. The reply was ambiguous; she did not quite understand the drift of it.

"But you, my lord, are so strong," she objected.

It was perhaps too dark for her to see the expression in his face; but even so she felt herself unaccountably blushing under that gaze which she could not clearly see. Whereupon he uttered an ejaculation which sounded almost as if he were angered, and abruptly, without any warning, he turned on his heel and went out of the room, leaving Gilda alone once more beside the virginal.

But she no longer felt the desire to sing. The happiness which filled her entire soul was too complete even for song.

4

One of the equerries had awhile ago found his way to the guest-chamber where the sick man was lying, and had informed Diogenes that the Stadtholder was now ready to start on his way, but desired his presence that he might take his leave. Then it was that Diogenes sent an urgent message to his Highness, entreating him to remain but a little while longer. The sick man was better, would soon wake out of a refreshing sleep. Diogenes would then question him. Poor old Pythagoras had something to say, something that the Stadtholder himself must hear. Of this Diogenes was absolutely convinced.

"I know it," the young soldier asserted earnestly. "I seem to feel it in my bones."

Whereupon the Stadtholder had decided to wait, and Diogenes, after his brief glimpse of Gilda, felt easier in his mind, less impatient. Already he chided himself for his gloomy forebodings. Since his beloved was ready to entrust herself to him, the journey to England would only be put off by a few hours. What need to repine? Joy would be none the less sweet for this brief delay.

A quarter of an hour later Pythagoras was awake the physician out of the room, and Diogenes was sitting on the edge of the bed holding his faithful comrade's hand, and trying to disentangle some measure of coherence out of the other's tangled narrative, whilst Socrates stood by making an occasional comment or just giving an expressive grunt from time to time. It took both time and patience, neither of which commodities did Diogenes possess in super-abundance; but after the first few moments of listening to the rambling of the sick man, he became very still and attentive. The busy house, the noisy guests, the waiting Stadtholder down below, all slipped out from his ken. Holding his comrade's hand, he was with him on the snow-clad Veluwe, and had found his way with him into the lonely mill.

"It was the Lord of Stoutenburg," Pythagoras averred, with as much strength as he could command. "I'd stake my life on't! I knew him at once. How could I ever forget his ugly countenance, after all he made you suffer?"

"Well – and?" queried Diogenes eagerly.

"I knew the other man too, but could not be sure of his name. He was one of those who was with Stoutenburg that day at Ryswick, when you so cleverly put a spoke in their abominable wheel. I knew them both, I tell you!" the sick man insisted feverishly; "but I had the good sense not to betray what I knew."

"But Stoutenburg did not know you?" Diogenes insisted.

"Yes, he did," the other replied, sagely nodding his head. "That is why he ordered his menial to put a bullet into my back. The two noble gentlemen questioned me first," he went on more coherently; "then they plied me with wine. They wanted to make me drunk so as to murder me at their leisure."

"They little know they, eh, thou bottomless barrel?" Diogenes broke in with a laugh. "The cask hath not been fashioned yet that would contain enough liquor even to quench thy thirst, what?"

"They plied me with wine," Pythagoras reiterated gravely; "and then I pretended to get very drunk. For I soon remarked that the more drunk they thought I was, the more freely they talked."

"Well, and what did they say?"

"They talked of De Berg crossing the Ijssel with ten thousand men between Doesburg and Bronchorst; and of Isembourg coming up from Kleve at the same time. I make no doubt that the design is to seize Arnheim and Nijmegen. They talked a deal about Arnheim, which they thought was scantily garrisoned and could easily be taken by surprise and made to surrender. Having got these two cities, the plan is to march across the Veluwe and offer battle to the Stadtholder with a force vastly superior to his, if in the meanwhile —"

He paused. It seemed as if his voice, hoarse with fatigue, was refusing him service. Diogenes reached for the potion which stood on a small table beside the bed. The sick man made a wry face.

"Physic?" he ejaculated reproachfully. "From you, old compeer? Times were when––"

"There will be a time now," retorted the other gruffly, "when you'll sink back into a raging fever, and will be babbling bibulous nonsense if you don't do as you are told."

"I'll sink into a raging fever now," the sick man retorted fretfully, "if I have not something potable to drink ere long."

"You'll drink this physic now, old compeer," Diogenes insisted, and held the mug to his friend's parched lips, forcing him to drink. "Then I'll see what can be done for you later on."

He schooled himself to patience and gentleness. At all costs Pythagoras must complete his narrative. There was just something more that he wished to say, apparently – something fateful and of deadly import, but which for some obscure reason he found difficult to put into words.

"Now then, old friend, make an effort!" Diogenes urged insistently. "There is still something on your mind. What is it?"

Pythagoras' round, beady eyes were rolling in their sockets. He looked scared, like one who has gazed on what is preternatural and weird.

"Stoutenburg has a project," he resumed after a while, and sank his spent voice to the merest whisper. "Listen, my compeer; for the very walls have ears. Bend yours to me. There! That's better," he added, as Diogenes bent his long back until his ear was almost on a level with the sick man's lips. "Stoutenburg hath a project, I tell you. A damnable project, akin to the one which you caused to abort three months ago."

"Assassination?" Diogenes queried curtly.

The sick man nodded.

"Do you know the details?"

"Alas, no! But it is aimed at the Stadtholder. What form it is to take I know not, and they had evidently talked it all over before. It seemed almost as if the other man – Stoutenburg's friend – was horrified at the project. He tried to argue once or twice, and once I heard him say quite distinctly: 'Not that, Stoutenburg! Let us fight him like men; even kill him, like men kill one another. But not like that.' But my Lord Stoutenburg only laughed."

Diogenes was silent. He was deep in thought.

"You had no other indication?" he asked reflectively.

"No," Pythagoras replied. All I saw was that my lord kept the finger and thumb of his right hand in a hidden pocket of his doublet, and once he said: 'The Prince of Poets taught me to manufacture them; and I supply them to him you know of, wherever he can find an opportunity to come out here to me. He uses them at his discretion. But we can judge by results! And then he laughed because his friend appeared to shudder. I was puzzled," the sick man went on wearily, "because of it all; and I marvelled who the Prince of Poets might be, for I am no scholar and I thought that perhaps —"

"You are quite sure Stoutenburg said 'Prince of Poets'?" Diogenes insisted, frowning. "Your ears must have been buzzing by then."

"I am quite sure," Pythagoras asserted. "But I could not see what he had in his hand."

Diogenes said nothing more, and silence fell upon the stately chamber, the sombre panelling and heavy tapestries of which effectually deadened every sound that came from the outside. Only the monumental clock up against the wall ticked in a loud monotone. The sick man, wearied with so much talking, fell back against the pillows. The shades of evening were quickly gathering in now; the corners of the room were indistinguishable in the gloom. Only the bed-clothes still gleamed white in the uncertain light. From the distant tower of St. Maria Kerk a bell chimed the hour of seven. A few minutes went by. Anon there came a scratching at the door.

In response to Diogenes' loud "Enter!" the physician came in, preceded by a serving-man carrying two lighted candles in massive silver sconces.

"His Highness cannot wait any longer," the physician said, as soon as he had perceived Diogenes, still sitting pensive on the edge of the bed. "And as I have no anxiety about the patient now, I will, by your leave, place him in your hands."

Diogenes appeared to wake as if out of a dream. He rose and looked about him somewhat vaguely. The physician thought he must have been asleep.

"Will you pay your respects to his Highness?" the latter said. "I think he desires to see you."

Just for a moment Diogenes remained quite still. The physician had approached the sick man, and was surveying him with critical but obviously reassured attention. Socrates was again snoring somewhere in a far corner of the room, and the serving-man, having placed the candles on the table, stood waiting at the door.

"Yes. I'll to his Highness," Diogenes said abruptly; and , beckoning to the serving-man to precede him, he strode out of the room.

Outside on the landing he paused. Then, with a characteristic, impulsive gesture, he suddenly beat his forehead with the palm of his hand.

"The Prince of Poets, of course!" he murmured under his breath. "Francis Borgia, the true descendant of his infamous ancestors! Poison! And a slow one at that! Oh, the miserable assassins! Please God, this knowledge hath not come too late!" he added with earnest fervor.

5

A quarter of an hour later the Stadtholder was in possession of all the facts as they had been revealed to Diogenes by his comrade in arms.

"I seem fated," he said to Diogenes kindly, yet not without a measure of bitterness, "to owe my safety to you and your brother philosophers."

He was discussing De Berg's surprise plans on Arnheim and Nijmegen. Of that abominable crime, hatched with the chance aid of a poison-mongering Borgia, Diogenes had not as yet spoken one word. Accustomed to swift decisions and prompt action, he had already made up his mind that he would speak of it first to the English physician, whose business it would be to see to it that the insidious poison no longer reached the prince's lips, at the same time enjoining the strictest secrecy in the matter; for it would only be by rigid circumspection and ceaseless watching that the assisin's accomplice could be brought to justice.

Mynheer Beresteyn and some of his older friends were in the room with his Highness. They all put their grave heads together, for there was no doubt that the Archduchess's advisers had planned an invasion of the United Provinces on a grand scale.

"Arnheim is insufficiently defended, of that there's no doubt," the Stadtholder said. "It was my intention to reinforce all the frontier cities, and to keep their garrisons up to the requisite numbers. If I only had the strength--"

He paused. The feeling of physical weakness consequent on disease caused him endless and acute bitterness.

"It is not too late to send troops to Arnheim and to Nijmegen," Diogenes broke in, in his usual abrupt manner. "Three thousand in one city, four thousand in the other would be sufficient, if your Highness can act quickly."

"I cannot detach seven or eight thousand troops from my forces at the present moment," the prince rejoined. "If Spinola were to attack from the south I am only just strong enough to defend myself as it is."

"Marquet is in Overijssel, I believe," urged the soldier. "He hath three or four thousand troops. Let him push on to Arnheim to reinforce the garrison."

"And De Keysere is at Wageningen," the prince broke in, fired, despite himself, by the other's enthusiasm. "He hath three thousand mercenaries from Switzerland and Germany."

"Excellent fighters and well-seasoned," Diogenes asserted. "And trained under Maurice of Nassau, the first captain of this or any epoch!"

"Ay!" sighed Maurice wearily. "But time is against us. Marquet is at Vorden —"

"But Arnheim and Nijmegen can hold out for awhile," Diogenes argued forcefully.

"And would hold out to the last man," Mynheer Beresteyn added, "if they knew that succor would come in due course."

" 'Tis only uncertainty that paralyses the endurance of a garrison," Diogenes went on with firm emphasis. "Send to Arnheim and to Nijmegen, your Highness! Bid them hold out against any attack until you come with ten thousand troops to their aid. In the meanwhile, send orders to Marquet and to De Keysere to advance forthwith with reinforcements for these two garrisons. Then raise your standard once more in Friesland, Drenthe, and Groningen. I'll warrant you will have twenty thousand men there ready to fight once more for liberty and for you!"

His sonorous voice rang clear and metallic in the small, panelled room. His enthusiasm appeared almost like a living thing, a tangible force that touched the hearts and minds of all the solemn burghers here, causing their eyes to glow and their fists, not yet wholly unskilled in the use of the sword, to clench with inward excitement. The Stadtholder looked up at him with undisguised admiration.

"Is it the English blood in you, man," he said with a smile, "that makes you valorous in war and wise in counsel?"

Diogenes shrugged his broad shoulders.

"I fought for your Highness before now," he rejoined, with a quaint, self-deprecating laugh, "when I had nothing to lose save my skin, and still less to gain. The English blood in me dearly loves a fight, and all doth hate the Spaniard and all his tyrannies."

"Then I can reckon on you?" the prince riposted quickly.

"On me, your Highness?" the other exclaimed.

"On you, of course. With your mother's blood in your veins, the United Provinces have a double claim on you. You have fought for us before, as you say, unknown to us then, an obscure soldier of fortune with nothing to lose and but little to gain. Join us now, man, in the field and under the council tent. Get to horse to-night. You will find Marquet at Vorden, on his way south from Overijssel. Tell him to push on at once to Arnheim with all the troops he hath at his command. From thence I would bid you go straightway to De Keysere, who is at Wageningen, and order him to reinforce Nijmegen forthwith with three thousand men, if we have them. Tell both Marquet and De Keysere to fight and hold the towns. I'll to their aid as soon as may be. Then, man, join my brother Frederick, and help him to raise my standard in Gelderland and in Overijssel, and rally ten thousand men to our cause. I feel that success will attend our arms if we keep you by our side."

Maurice of Nassau had spoken with more vigor and verve than he had shown for the past three months. Indeed, his deeply anxious friends could not help but feel that the old fighting spirit of this peerless commander had not wholly been undermined by disease. Five pairs of eager eyes had scanned his features while he spoke; five hearts beat in response to his enthusiasm. Now, when he had finished speaking, Mynheer Beresteyn and the others turned their expectant gaze upon the stranger who had been so signally honoured; but he looked uncertain, gravely perturbed. In the flickering light of the wax candles his face appeared haggard and drawn, and a set line had crept around his ever-laughing lips.

"You seem to hesitate, my friend," the Stadtholder remarked, with that tone of bitterness which had become habitual to him. "Methought you said that the English blood in you dearly loved a fight. But in truth, I had forgotten! You have other claims upon you now – one, at least, which is paramount. An easy, untroubled life awaits you. No wonder you hesitate to embark on so perilous an adventure!" Then, as if loth to give up the thought that was foremost in his mind, he added, with persuasive insistence; "If you followed me, you'd have everything to gain – nothing to lose save a sentimental pastime."

Just then Diogenes caught Mynheer Beresteyn's eyes fixed steadily upon him. The old man who knew well enough what was going on in that wayward, turbulent mind – the doubts, the fears, the hideous, horrible disappointment.

Nothing to lose! Ye gods, at the hour when a whole life's happiness not only beckoned insistently, but was actually there to hand, like a bunch of ripe and luscious fruit, ready to drop into a yearning hand! Here was the end of a vagabond life, here was love and home and peace, and all to be given up as soon as found to the equally insistent call of honour and of duty!

The others did not speak; perhaps they, too, understood. Men in those days were used to stern sacrifices. They and there forebears had given up their all so that their children's children might live in freedom and security. They only marvelled if this stranger, with the combative English blood in him, would give up what was so infinitely dear to him – the exquisite wife to whom he had plighted his troth but a few hours ago – and if he would fight for them again as he had done in the past.

The Stadtholder remained moody and silent, and the close atmosphere of the heavily curtained room seemed to become suddenly still, hushed, as if expectant of the grave decision to come. The wax candles burned quite steadily, with just a tiny fillet of smoke rising up towards the low-raftered ceiling, almost like the incense of silent prayer rising unwaveringly to God.

To many the silence appeared absolute, but not to the man who stood in the midst of them all beside a table littered with papers and documents, his slender hand – the hand of an idealist, rendered firm and hard by action – resting lightly upon the board. A tense look in his eyes. Through the silence he could hear his beloved in the little room behind the heavy tapestry. He could hear the soft, insidious sound of the quaint-toned virginal, and her voice, tender and melancholy as the call of the bird to its mate, humming the sweet refrain gently under her breath. with every note she seemed to tear at his heart with an unendurable regret for what might have been.

Oh, it had been such a perfect dream! Gilda and that stately home over in England, and the ride through the night in pursuit of happiness which had proved as elusive as Fata Morgana, as unreal as the phantoms born in the mind of a rhapsodist.

Then the silence did, indeed, become absolute, even to him. Gilda had ceased her song. Only his straining ears caught the sound of her footsteps as she rose from the virginal, then moved swiftly about the room.

"Well," the Stadtholder reiterated, after awhile, "which is it to me, my friend? I start for Utrecht within the hour and if we are to save Arnheim and Nijmegen, you should be on your way to Vorden with the necessary moneys and my written orders to-night. Of course, I cannot compel you," he added simply "The decision rests with you, and if you —"

The words died on his lips, and in an instant all eyes were turned to that end of the room where a heavy portière divided it from the room beyond. A faint rustling sound had come from there, then the grating of metal rings upon the cornice-pole that held the tapestry. The next moment Gilda appeared in the doorway, shadowy, wraith-like in her sombre gown that melted into the gloom. Just her small, white face and delicate hands stood out against the murky background, and the gossamer lace at her throat and wrists.

For a moment she stood there, one hand still holding back the heavy portière, quite still, taking in the company at a glance. A sigh of longing and of renunciation came from an over-burdened heart, and was wafted up to the foot of Him who knows all and understands all. Then Gilda allowed the tapestry to fall together behind her, and she came quickly forward. In the other hand she was holding, firmly clasped, her husband's heavy sword.

She came close to him, and then said simply, with an ingenuous smile: "I thought you might wonder where you had left it. It was in the other room. You will be wanting it, my dear lord, if you start for Vorden within the hour."

With deft fingers she buckled the sword to his belt. This, in truth, was her decision, and she had acted with scarce a moment's hesitation, even whilst he marvelled how he could set to work to break her heart by leaving her this night.

Now, when their glances met, they understood one another. The power that lay within both their souls had met and, as it were, clasped hands. They accepted one another's sacrifice. Hers, mayhap, was the more complete of the two, because for her his absence would mean weary waiting, the dull heartache so terrible to bear.

For the man, the wrench would be eased by action, danger and hard fighting; for her there would be nothing to do but wait. But she acquiesced. No one had seen the struggle which it had cost her, over there in the little room, all alone with only the dumb virginal and the dying light to see the tears of rebellion and of agony which for one brief moment – for her an eternity – had seared her eyes. By the time the full meaning of what she had overheard from the other side of the portière had entered into her brain, she had recovered full outward calm, and had brought him his sword in token of her resolve.

Gilda Beresteyn came of a race that had learned to fight even from its infancy. She had handled her father's sword at an age when little maids are content with playthings. Now, when she made the buckles of her husband's sword secure, she met his glance with perfect serenity, and said simply and calmly:

"You will find me, as before, in the other room. I will be waiting there to bid you farewell."

Then she glided out of the room, wraith-like, ethereal, as she had come. And Diogenes woke as if out of a trance.

The Stadtholder jumped to his feet. "Then you're with us?" he exclaimed.

"If your Highness hath need of me," the soldier replied.

"Have I not said so?" the prince retorted. "Henceforth, Sir Percy Blakeney – for that is your name, is it not? – accompanies us as our Master of the Camp wherever we go!"

"Nay, " the other replied quite firmly and without even a sigh of regret this time, "my name is Diogenes, as it hath always been. It is the nameless and homeless adventurer, the son of the poor Dutch tramp, who once again places his sword at your Highness's disposal. Sir Percy Blakeney was only a myth, a shade that hath already been exorcized by the magic of your Highness's call, in the name of our faith and of liberty."

"Frankly, man," the Stadtholder retorted with a smile, "I could not picture you in the character of a placid and uxorious country gentleman, watching with unruffled complacence the life and death struggles of your friends."

"I should have waxed obese, your Highness," Diogenes assented whimsically; "and the horror of it would have sent me to my grave."

"Then, you inveterate mocker, are you ready to start?"

"Booted and spurred, your Highness, and a sword on my hip," replied the other lightly. "And my horse hath been waiting for me these two hours past."

Already Maurice of Nassau was on his feet. He took the sacrifice, the self-denial, as a matter of course; was unaware of it, probably. Every other thought was completely merged in that of the coming struggle – De Berg crossing the Ijssel, Spinola threatening from the south, and victory beckoning once more.

The burghers crowded round him, speaking words of loyalty and of encouragement. He responded with somewhat curt farewells. His thoughts were no longer here; they were across the Veluwe with Marquet and De Keysere; inside Arnheim and Nijmegen.

He kept Diogenes by his side, wrote out his orders in sign-manual, discussed plans, possibilities with the man in whose luck and resource he had unbounded belief.

It took time to get everything ready. There was the financial question, too, for some of the troops were mercenaries, who would be demanding their pay ere they engaged to start on a fresh expedition. For this the aid of the loyal burghers had again to be requisitioned. Arrangements had to be made for credits at Zutphen and Arnheim.

This part of the great adventure the Stadtholder was willing to leave in the hands of Mynheer Beresteyn and his friends. Money to him was dross, save as a means of gaining his great ends. For the nonce he was in a hurry to get away, to get back to his camp at Utrecht, and to make ready for the coming fight.

Then at last there came a moment when everything appeared settled. The messenger had his sealed orders, and the credit notes and the read money upon his person. The Stadtholder was back in the hall with his equerries around him, ready for departure, giving brief, decisive orders such as soldiers love to hear.

But Diogenes did not follow him immediately, and Mynheer Beresteyn remained behind with him. He was the only one who really understood what the once careless and thoughtless adventurer felt at this moment, in face of the inevitable farewell. It was an understanding born in a staunch heart that had known both love and sorrow.

Beresteyn had idolized his young wife, who had died leaving her baby-girl in his arms. That deep affection the lonely widower had thereupon transferred to his motherless daughter, had cherished and guarded her as his most precious treasure, and had only consented to relinquish her into the guardianship of another because he knew that the other was worthy of the trust.

He knew also what hungering passion means; he knew the bitterness of parting and of a burning disappointment with the prospect of loneliness through the vista of years. But, with that infinite tact which is the attribute of a self-less heart, he offered no words of consolation or even of comment.

"I will leave you to bid farewell to Gilda alone," was all that he said.

Diogenes nodded in assent. The most terrible moment of this terrible hour was yet to come, for Gilda, having precipitated his decision, was now waiting for the last kiss.

6

She was, in truth, waiting for him, submissive and composed. What she had done, when she with her own act had mutely bidden him to go, that she did not regret. She had done it not so much perhaps from a sense of duty or of patriotism, but rather because she knew that this course was the only one that he would never rue.

Hers was that perfect love that dwells on the other's happiness, and not on its own. She knew that, though for the time being he would find bliss and oblivion in her arms, he would soon repine in inactivity whilst others fought for that which he held sublime.

So now, when he pushed aside the tapestry and once more stood before her, with the lovelight in his eyes obscured by the shadow of this coming parting, she met him without a tear. The next moment he had her in his arms, and his hand rested lightly across her eyes, lest they should perceived that his were full of tears.

For a long while he could not speak; then he drew her closer to him and pressed his lips against hers, drinking in all the joy and rapture which he might never taste again.

"What is it that hath happened, my lord?" she murmured. " I could not hear everything, and did not wish to be caught prying. All that I heard was that the Stadtholder needed you, and that in your heart you knew that your place, whilst there was danger to our land, was by his side, and not by mine."

"Your father will explain more fully, my beloved," he replied. You are right. The Stadtholder hath need of every willing sword. This unfortunate land is gravely threatened. The Archduchess is throwing the full force of her armies against the Netherlands. His Highness thinks that I might help to save the United Provinces from becoming once more the vassals of Spain. As you say, my place is on this soil where I and my mother were born. I should be a coward indeed were I to turn my back now on this land when danger is so grave. So I am going, my beloved," he continued simply.

"To-night I go to Vorden on his Highness's business, thence on to Wageningen. I shall go, taking your dear image in my heart, and with your exquisite face before me always. For I love you with every fibre of my being, every bone in my body and with every beat of my heart. Try not to weep, my dear. I shall return one day soon to take you in my arms, as I shall clasp your spirit only until then. I shall return, doubt it not. Such love as ours was not created to remain unfulfilled. Whatever may happen, believe and trust in me, as I shall believe in you, and keep the remembrance of me in your heart without sadness and without regret."

He spoke chiefly because he dared not trust to the insidiousness of silence. He knew that she wept for the first time because of him. Yet how could it be otherwise? And sorrow made her sacred. When, overcome with grief, she lay half-swooning in his arms, he picked her up quite tenderly and laid her back against the cushions of the chair. Then, as she sat there, pale and wan-looking in the uncertain light of the wax candles, with those exquisite hands of hers lying motionless in her lap, he knelt down before her.

For a second or two he rested his head against those soft white palms, fragrant as the petals of a lily. Then he rose, and, without looking at her again, he walked firmly out of the room.

Chapter IV – Adder's Fork

NCOLAES Beresteyn accompanied his brother-in-law during the first part of the journey. He had insisted on this, despite Diogenes' preference for solitude. There was not much comradeship lost between the two men. Though the events of that memorable New Years Day, distant less than three months, were ostensibly consigned to oblivion, nevertheless, the bitter humiliation which Nicolaes had suffered at the hands of the then nameless soldier of fortune still rankled in his heart. Since then so many things had come to light which, to an impartial observer, more than explained Gilda Beresteyn's love for the stranger, and Mynheer her father's acquiescence in an union based on respect for so brave a man.

But Nicolaes had held aloof from the intimacy, and soon his own courtship of the wealthy Kaatje gave him every reason for withdrawing more and more from his own family circle. But to-night, after the tempestuous close of what should have been a merely conventional day, he sought Diogenes' company in a way he had never done before.

"Like you," he said, "I am wearied and sick with all this mummery. A couple of hours on the Veluwe will set me more in tune with life."

Diogenes chaffed him not a little.

"The lovely Kaatje will pout," he suggested, "and rightly, too. You have no excuse for absenting yourself from her side at this hour."

"I'll come with you as far as Barneveld," Nicolaes insisted. "A matter of less than a couple of hours' ride. It will do me good. And Kaatje is still closeted with her garrulous mother."

"You think it will do her good to be kept waiting," Diogenes retorted with good-natured sarcasm. "well, come, if you have a mind. But I'll not have your company further than Barneveld. I am used to the Veluwe, and intend taking a short cut over the upland, through which I would not care to take a companion less well acquainted with the waste than I."

Thus it was decided. Already the Stadtholder had gone with his numerous retinue, with his bodyguard and his pike-men and with his equerries, and those of the wedding-party who had come in his train from Utrecht, friends of Mynheer Beresteyn, who had ridden over for the most part with wife or daughter pillioned behind them, and all glad to avail themselves of the protection of his Highness's escort against highway marauders, none too scarce in these parts. Torch-bearers and linkmen completed the imposing cavalcade, for the night would be moonless, and the tracks across the moorland none too clearly defined.

Diogenes had waited with what patience he could muster until the last of the numerous train had defiled under the Koppel-poort. Then he, too, got to horse. Despite Socrates' many protestations, he was not allowed to accompany him.

"You must look after Pythagoras," was Diogenes' final word on the subject.

" 'Tis the first time," the other answered moodily, "that you go on such an adventure without us. Take care, comrade! The Veluwe is wide and lonely. That swag-bellied oaf up there hath cause to rue his solitary wanderings on that verfloekte waste."

"I'll be careful, old compeer," Diogenes retorted with a smile. "But mine errand is not one on which I desire to draw unnecessary attention, and I can remain best unperceived if I am alone. 'Tis no adventure I am embarking on this night. Only a simple errand as far as Vorden, a matter of ten leagues at most.

"And the whole of the verdommte Veluwe to traverse at dead of night!" the other muttered sullenly.

"I know every corner of it," Diogenes rejoined impatiently. "And it will not be the first time that I travel on it alone."

Thus Socrates was left grumbling, and anon Diogenes, accompanied by Nicolaes Beresteyn, started on his way.

At first the two men spoke little. The air was still cold and very humid, and the thaw was persisting. The horses stepped out briskly on the soft, sandy earth.

The distance between Amersfoort and Barneveld is but a couple of leagues. Within the hour the lights of the little city could be seen gleaming ahead. After a while Nicolaes Beresteyn became more loquacious, talked quite freely of the past.

"My father no longer trusts me," he said, with ill-concealed bitterness. "Did you see how he shut me out of the council-chamber?"

"Yet the Stadtholder himself told you everything that occurred subsequently," Diogenes retorted kindly, "including his own plans and mine errand at this hour. I think that your conscience troubles you unnecessarily, and you see a deliberate intention in every simple act."

"And if he did, you could scarce blame him. 'Tis only in the future you can prove your true worth. And methinks," he added, more seriously than he was usually wont to speak, "that you will have occasion to do this very soon."

"In the meanwhile, here's Barneveld ahead of us," Nicolaes rejoined, with a quick, indefinable sigh, and giving a sudden turn to the conversation. "I'll see you across the city, then return to the bosom of my family, there to live in uxorious idleness, whilst you, a stranger, are entrusted with the destinies of our land. A poor outlook for a man who is young and a patriot, you'll own."

To this Diogenes thought it best to make no reply. He knew well enough that the mistrust of which Nicolaes accused his father was a very real thing, and that it was indeed only time that would soften the proud burgher's heart toward his only son. It was not likely that one who but a brief while ago had conspired against the Stadtholder's life with that abominable Stoutenburg could be admitted readily into the councils of the very man whom he had plotted to assassinate. With every desire to forgive, it was but natural that Mynheer Beresteyn should fail entirely to forget.

No more, however, was said upon the subject now, and Nicolaes soon relapsed into that sullen mood which had of late become habitual to him. Thus Diogenes was glad enough to be rid of his company. At Barneveld he obtained a fresh horse, left his own in charge of a man known to him, with orders to ride it quietly on the morrow as far as Wageningen, where he himself would pick it up a couple of days later. His journey would now lie due east to Zutphen. There he meant to make a halt of a few hours, and thence proceed to Vorden, where Marquet was in camp, with four thousand seasoned troops, trained under Mansfeld, and rested now since the campaign in Groningen.

The Stadtholder's orders were that the general proceed, at once to Arnheim, ere the forces of the Archduchess had time to cross the Ijssel, and to cut off all access to so important a city.

From Vorden to Wageningen, which lies due south form Barneveld, the journey would be a long one, and, with De Berg's army so near, might even prove perilous. But De Keysere was at Wageningen, with three thousand troops and some artillery. His help would be of immense service to Nijmegen if the latter city, too, were to be attacked.

"How will you journey from Vorden to Wageningen?" Nicolaes asked Diogenes in the end. "You will have to avoid the Ijssel."

"I'll cut across to Lang Soeren," the other replied; "and thence go to Ede."

"There's scarce a track on the Veluwe just there," the other urged.

"Such as there is, I know," Diogenes retorted curtly. "And I must trust to luck."

They had brought their horses to a halt about a quarter of a league outside Barneveld, where the two men decided to part. The stretch of the great waste, with its undulating, barren hills, and narrow, scarce visible tracks, lay straight out before them. Diogenes was sniffing the frosty air out toward the east, where lay Vorden, and whence there came to his nostrils the sharp tang of the breeze, that cut like a knife. The thaw which had held sway in the cities and on the low-lying lands had been vanquished ere it reached the arid upland. The snow upon the Veluwe lay as even and as pure as before. Above, a canopy of stars seemed but a diamond-studded veil of mysterious indigo, stretched over a world of light, which it failed altogether to dim. The silence and desolation were absolute; but not so the darkness. To the keen eye of the adventurer, accustomed to loneliness, the vast stretches of open country and limitless horizons, there was no such thing as absolute darkness. He could perceive the slightest accidental upon the smooth carpet of snow, noted every tiny mound that marked a clump of rough shrub or grass, and every footmark of beast or bird, mere flecks of blue upon the virgin pall.

"Such track as there is, I know," he had carelessly asserted awhile ago, in response to a warning from Nicolaes. And now, without an instant's hesitation, and tossing to the other a last curt word of farewell, he gave his horse a slight taste of the spur, and soon became a mere speck upon the illimitable waste.

3

It was close on midnight when, weary, saddle-sore, his boots covered in half-melted snow, Mynheer Nicolaes Beresteyn demanded admittance into his native city.

At first the guard at the Koppel-poort, roused from his slumbers, refused to recognize in the belated traveler the bridegroom of a few hours ago. Had anyone ever heard, I ask you, of a bridegroom absenting himself on the very night of his nuptial until so late an hour? And then returning in a mood that was so irascible and inconsequent that the sergeant in command of the gate was on the point of ordering his detention in the guard-room, pending investigation and the orders of the burgomaster, whose decision on such points was final? But since the burgomaster, whose decision on such points was final? But since the burgomaster happened to be Mynheer Beresteyn, and as the weary and pugnacious traveler did, in truth, appear to be his only son – why, it was perhaps best on the whole to take the matter as a joke, and not to say too much about it. The sergeant did, indeed, as Nicolaes was finally allowed to ride over the bridge, essay one or two of the most time-honoured witticisms at the expense of the belated bridegroom; but Mynheer Nicolaes was clearly in no mood for chaff, and when he had passed by, the sergeant and one or two of the men, who had witnessed his strangely sullen mood, shook their heads in ominous prognostication of sundry matrimonial difficulties to come.

The house on the quay, plainly visible from the Koppel-poort, was dark enough to suggest that every one of its inmates was already abed. Nicolaes, however, did not ride up to the front door; but, after he had crossed the bridge, he went straight on through one or two narrow streets which lay at the back of his home until he reached the corner of the Korte Gracht, which, again, abuts on the quay. Thus he had gone round in a semicircle, in obvious avoidance of the paternal house, and now he brought his horse to a halt outside a tall and narrow door which was surmounted by a lanthorn let into the wall. A painted sign which hung from an iron bracket above the door indicated to the passing wayfarer that the place was one where rider and horse could find food and shelter.

Nicolaes dismounted, and going up to the door, he knocked against it with the point of his foot. This he had to do several times before the welcome sound of someone moving inside the house came to his ear. A moment or two later the door was opened cautiously. A man appeared on the threshold, wrapped in a night-robe and still wearing a night-bonnet on his head.

"Is that you, mynheer?" he queried drowsily.

"Who else should it be, you loon?" Nicolaes replied irritably. "here's your horse," he added, and without waiting for further commend or protest from the unfortunate landlord thus roused from his slumbers, he proceeded to tether the animal by the reins to one of the iron rings in the wall.

"It is so late, mynheer," the man protested dolefully; and so cold. Will you not take the horse round to the stable yourself? It is but a step to the right, and there's the gate —"

"It is late, as you say, and cold," Nicolaes retorted curtly. "And when I paid you so liberally for the horse, I did not bargain to take service with you as ostler in the middle of the night."

"But, mynheer —" urged the landlord, still protesting.

But Nicolaes did not listen. In faith, he had ceased to hear, for already he was striding rapidly down the Korte Gracht, and the next moment was back on the quay. A few steps brought him to the door of his father's house. Here he paused for a moment ere he mounted the stone steps that led up to the massive front door, stamped his feet so as to shake the melted snow from his boots, and with a few quick touches tried to re-establish some semblance of order in his clothes. Indeed, when presently he rapped vigorously with the iron knocker against the door, he looked no longer like a wearied and querulous traveler, but rather like a man just returned from a short and pleasant ride.

To his astonishment it was Maria, his sister Gilda's faithful tire-woman, who opened the door for him. She anticipated his very first query by a curt:

"Everyone is abed. The jongejuffrouw alone chose to wait for you, and I could not let her wait alone."

Nicolaes uttered an angry exclamation.

"Tell my sister to go to bed, too," he commanded briefly. "I'll go to my rooms at once, as it is so late."

Maria made no audible reply. She mumbled something about "Shameful conduct!" and "Wedding-night!" But Nicolaes paid no heed, strode quickly across the hall, and ran swiftly up the stairs.

But on the landing he came abruptly to a halt. He had almost fallen against his sister Gilda, who stood there waiting for him.

Behind her, a little way down the passage, a door stood ajar, and through it there came a narrow fillet of light. At sight of him, and before he could utter a sound, she put a finger to her lip, then let the way along the passage. The door which stood ajar was the one which gave on her own room. She went in, and he followed her, his heart beating with something like shame or fear.

"Hush!" she whispered, and gently closed the door behind him. "Make no noise!" Kaatje has at last sobbed herself to sleep. She hath been put to bed in her mother's room. 'Twere a shame to disturb her." Then, as Nicolaes muttered something that sounded very like a curse, the girl added reproachfully: "Poor Kaatje! You have shown very little ardour toward her, Klaas."

"I lost my way in the dark," he answered. "I had no thought it could be so late."

Just then the tower clock of St. Maria Kerk chimed the midnight hour.

Gilda hazarded timidly: "You should not have thought of accompanying my lord. He was ready to start out alone; and your place, Klaas, was beside your wife!"

"Are you going to lecture me about my duty, Gilda?" he said irritably. "You must not think that because —"

"I think nothing," she broke in simply, "save that Kaatje wept when the evening wore on and you did not return; and that the more she wept the greater was our father's anger against you."

"He knew that I meant to accompany your husband a part of the way," Nicolaes retorted. "In truth, had he done me the justice to read my thoughts, he himself would have bade me go."

"It was kind of you," she rejoined somewhat coolly, to be concerned as to my lord's safety. But I can assure you —"

" 'Twas not concern for his safety," he broke in gruffly, "that caused me to accompany him to-night."

"What then?"

But he gave no reply, but his lip and turned away from her, with the air of one who fears that he hath said too much and cares not to be questioned again.

"I'd best go now," he said abruptly.

He looked around for his gloves, which he had thrown down upon the table. His manner seemed so strange that Gilda was suddenly conscious of a nameless kind of fear; the sort of premonition that comes to highly sensitive natures, at times when hitherto unsuspected danger suddenly looms upon the cloudless sky of life. She forced him to return her searching glance.

"You are hiding something from me, Klaas," she said determinedly. "What is it?"

"I?" he riposted, feigning surprise. "Hiding something? Why should I have something to hide?"

"That I know not," she replied. "But there was some hidden meaning in your words just now when you said that 'twas not concern for my lord's safety that caused you to accompany him this night. What, then, was it?" she insisted, seeing that he remained silent, even though he met her gaze with a look that appeared both fearful and pitying.

She had her back to the door now, looked like some timid creature brought to bay by a cruel and hitherto unsuspected enemy.

"You must not ask me for my meaning, Gilda," Nicolaes said at last. "There are things which concern men only, and with which women should have no part."

His tone of ill-concealed compassion stung her like a cut from a whip across the face.

"There is nothing that concerns my lord," she retorted proudly, "in which he would not desire me to bear my part."

"Then let him tell you himself."

"What?"

She threw the question at him like a challenge, stepped up to him and seized him by the wrist – no longer a timid creature at bay. But a strong, determined woman, who feels in some mysterious way that the man whom she loves is being attacked, and who is prepared, with every known and unknown weapon almighty love can suggest, to defend him, his life or his honour, or both.

"You are not going out of this room, Klaas, until you have explained!" she said with unquestionable determination. "What is it that my lord should tell me himself?"

"Why he, newly wed and a stranger, was so determined on this, his wedding night, to carry the Stadtholder's message across the Veluwe."

Nicolaes spoke abruptly, almost fiercely now, as if wearied of this wrangling, and burdened with a secret he could no longer hold. But she did not at first understand his meaning.

"I do not understand what you mean," she murmured vaguely, a perplexed frown between her eyes.

"There were plenty there eager and willing to go," Nicolaes went on roughly. "Nay, the errand was not in itself perilous. Speed was required, yes; and a sound knowledge of the country. But a dozen men at least who were in this house to-day know the Veluwe as well as this stranger, and any good horse would cover the ground fast enough. But he wanted to go – he, this man whom none of us know, who was married this day, and whose bride had the first call on his attention. He insisted with the Stadtholder, and he went — And I went with him; would have gone all the way if he had not forced me to go back. Why did he wish to go, Gilda? Why did he leave you deliberately this night? Think! Think! And why did he insist on going alone, with not even one of those besotted boon companions of his to share in his adventure? A message to Marquet – my God!" he added with a sneer. "A message to the Archduchess, more like, to cross the Ijssel ere it be too late!"

"You devil!"

She hissed out the words through set lips and teeth clenched in an access of fierce and overwhelming passion. And before he could recover himself, before he could guess her purpose, she had seized his heavy, leathern gloves, which were lying on the table, and struck him with them full in the face. He staggered, and put his hand up to his eyes.

"Go!" she commanded briefly.

He tried to laugh the situation off, said almost flippantly:

"I'll punish you for this, you young vixen!"

But she did not move, and her glance seemed to freeze the words upon his lips.

"Go!" she commanded once more.

He shrugged his shoulders.

"I understand your indignation, Gilda. Nay, I honour it. But remember my warning! Your stranger lord," he went on with slow and deliberate emphasis, "will be returning anon to the

Stadtholder's camp, a courted and honoured man; but 'tis the armies of the Archduchess who will have crossed the Ijssel by then, whilst the orders to Marquet will have reached that commander too late."

Then he turned on his heel and went out of the room, and anon Gilda heard his footstep resounding along the passage. She listened until she heard the opening and closing of a distant door, after which she sighed and murmured, "Poor Kaatje!" That was all; but there was a world of meaning in the sorrowful compassion wherewith she said those words.

Then she raised her left hand, round the third finger of which glittered a plain gold ring. The ring she pressed long and lingeringly against her lips, and in her heart she prayed, "God guard you, my dear lord!"

1

AS for Diogenes, he reached Zutphen in the small hours of the morning, and after a few hours' rest pushed on to Vorden at dawn. He himself would have deprecated any suggestion of making of this journey across the Veluwe a romantic adventure. The upland, under its covering of snow, held neither terrors nor secrets for him. The wind, the stars, an unerring instinct and sound knowledge of the scarce visible tracks, guided him across the arid waste. A real child of the open, he had less difficulty in finding his way across such a God-forsaken wild than he would through the intricate streets of a city.

Messire Marquet, encamped outside Vorden, welcomed the Stadtholder's messenger effusively. His troops, for the most part composed of mercenaries from Germany, were getting restive in idleness; once or twice they had used threats when demanding their pay. Diogenes, bringing both money and the prospect of a fight, was doubly welcome. His stay at the camp was brief. By late morning he was once more on his way, with the intention of re-crossing the Ijssel at Dieren and of reaching Wageningen before dark. He had but half a dozen leagues to cover, and eight hours of daylight wherein to do it. Weather, too, and circumstances favored him. The thaw, which had been so completely vanquished upon the upland, had remained sole monarch in the plain. The air was mild and intensely humid. A dense sea-fog lay over the river and the surrounding marshes. The numerous little tributaries of the Ijssel and the intervening canals and ditches were already free from ice, and as Diogenes put his horse to an easy gallop in the direction of the river, the animal sank fetlock deep in mud.

The road was solitary, and, as far as the eye could reach through the mist, seemed entirely deserted. The countryside here had the desolate appearance peculiar to districts that have been fought over. The few thatched cottages, which from time to time loomed out of the mist, still bore the marks of passing fire and sword; the trees were truncated and sparse, the marshland was riddled with the scars of ceaseless tramping of men, of wagons, and of beasts. The inevitable windmills, gaunt-looking and ghost-like through the humid atmosphere, appeared neglected and forlorn.

But the solitary rider had no eyes for landscape just now. He could have wished for a clearer day, for it was impossible even for his keen eyes to see what was going on behind that impenetrable wall of fog. If Pythagoras' ears had not played him false, De Berg was there, not very far away, waiting to cross the Ijssel when opportunity arose.

Thanks to that faithful hypertrophied loon, the ambitious designs of the Archduchess could still be frustrated. De Berg's armies were still on the right bank of the Ijssel, and if Marquet got his men on the move by midday, as he had promised he would do, the crossing of the enemy troops would become difficult, mayhap impossible.

These were pleasing thoughts for the man on whose speed and resource these important plans depended. All that he chafed against was the imperative slowness of his progress, as the mist enveloped him more closely the nearer he got to the river. But withal it protected him, too, hid him mayhap from the prying eyes of vedettes on the watch. Already, judging by certain landmarks that met him on the way, Brummen was half a league behind him on his right, Hengles far away on the left, and Dieren not more than another league on ahead. For the last quarter of an hour he had heard from time to time the heavy booming sound, akin to the reverberation of distant cannonade, which came from the breaking and cracking of the ice as it drifted downstream. He put his horse to slow trot, as he pried through the mist for the first indication of a short cut he knew of, which would take him to the river bank in less than half an hour.

2

The next moment he had spied the narrow track and set his horse to follow it; when suddenly, out of the mist, there came a loud report, and Diogenes heard the whistle of a bullet close to his ear. It almost grazed his shoulder. Without an instant's pause, without turning to look whence had come this unexpected greeting, he set spurs to his horse and galloped at breakneck speed toward the river. Over fields and ditches; no thought of prudence now, only of speed! Mud and water flew out in all directions under the horse's frantic gallopade, the plucky beast sinking at times almost to his knees in the marshy ground. A few minutes later – five, perhaps – Diogenes heard the sound of many hoofs behind him, obviously in pursuit. He turned to look this time, and through the mist vaguely discerned some three or four cavaliers, who were distant from him then less than two hundred yards. So far, so good! The Ijssel was close by now, and if, when he reached the banks, he turned off in the direction of the stream, he could easily reach the ford on this side of Brummen and get across – on foot, if need be, if his horse proved an obstacle to rapid progress.

A few more minutes now and the river was in sight, with, far away on the opposite bank, Brummen, nestling at the foot of the rising ground, the gate of the Veluwe. With renewed vigor the rider sped along, his blood whipped up by the chase, his whole body exhilarated by this sensation of danger and of one of those sportive races for life for which three months of idleness and luxury had given him a hitherto unsuspected longing.

Ah, there was the shore at last, the group of three windmills close to the bank, an unmistakable landmark. Here, too, within two hundred paces on ahead, was the ford, which no amount of drifting ice would cause the daring adventurer to miss. Already he was within a few yards of the low-lying bank, searching the approach to the ford with eyes now doubly keen, when, with staggering suddenness, another cavalier appeared, straight in front of him this time, and barring the way to the river-brink.

No time to note his face; just a second wherein to decide what had best be done, not only to save his own life, but also the message which he must carry to Wageningen, at whatever cost. Then the cavalier turned for one brief second in his saddle, to call to some companions as yet unseen. A brief second, did I say? 'Twas but a fraction. The next moment Diogenes had whipped out a pistol from his saddlebow, and with a steady hand fired at his foe. The cavalier reeled in his saddle and fell, just as half a dozen others issued with a shout from out the mist, and those in pursuit put fresh spurs to their mounts.

It had been madness to attempt the ford now. The young soldier, sore-pressed, might in truth have sold his life dearly, but with it, too, he would have sold Nijmegen and the possible success of the Stadtholder's plans. Ofttimes before, in the course of his adventurous life, he had been in as tight a place, where life and death hung quite evenly in the scales of Fate; but never before had he been quite so anxious to flee. He could not trust the valor of his sword, his own well-nigh unexampled skill in a fight against odds that would have made the bravest pause. No! It meant running away, away as fast as his horse would take him, and faster if the poor brute gave out. A short gallop along the bank, the cavalier behind him warming to the pursuit; keeping closer and closer to the low-lying bank, till the horse began to flounder in what was sheer morass.

The ford now lay well behind him. The waters of the Ijssel, tossed for awhile upon the shallows, flowed with increased swiftness here. Huge ice-blocks floated seaward upon the heaving bosom of the stream. The foremost of the pursuing cavaliers was then less than fifty yards behind, and more than one bullet had whizzed past the fleeing rider, one of them piercing his hat, the other grazing his thigh, but none doing him serious injury. Already the rallying cry of the pursuers had turned to one of triumph as the distance lessened between them and their quarry, when, with a sudden jerk of the reins, Diogenes plunged headlong into the river.

The Ijssel at this point is close on a quarter of a mile wide, her current is no longer sluggish, whilst the drifting ice-blocks constitute a peril which had to be boldly faced. But the mist, which hung thickly over the river, was the daring adventurer's most faithful ally.

Strangely enough, Diogenes' first thought, when his horse, finally losing its foothold upon the rapidly shelving bank, started to swim, was of Gilda, and of that ride which he had promised himself, with her dear arms clinging around him, her fair hair, tossed by the wind, brushing against his face. It was one of those sweet, sad visions which some mocking sprite seems to conjure up at moments such as this when life – ay, and honour too! – are trembling in the balance. Sad and swift! It vanished almost as quickly as it came, giving place to thoughts of De Keysere, still unsuspecting at Wageningen, and of Marquet, who haply had already started. Was there a trap waiting for him, too? Was this just an outpost of De Berg's armies; and had they indeed been mysteriously warned by traitor or spy, as Diogenes more than half suspected?

But what was the use of speculating? Indeed, every conjecture was futile, for this now was a supreme struggle – a tussle with Death, who was watching, uncertain whence and how he would strike. For the moment the adventurer was at grips with the flood and with the ice, guiding his horse as best he could toward mid-stream, where the current kept the threatening floes at bay. His pursuers had come to a halt upon the bank. Indeed, not one of them had the mind to follow his quarry on this perilous adventure. They stood there, some half-dozen of them, holding council, their eyes peering through the mist in search of the one black speck – horse and rider – now appearing clearly silhouetted against the silvery water, now vanishing again under cover of the floes. Then one of them raised his musket and took steady aim at the valiant swimmer, who had succeeded at last in reaching mid-stream.

The bullet whizzed through the mist. Diogenes' horse, hit through the neck, plunged and reared, pawed the waters wildly for a moment, then gave that heart-rending scream which is so harrowing to the ears of all animal-lovers. But already the rider had his feet clear of the stirrups, and as the waters finally swept over the head of the stricken beast, he slid out of the saddle and struck out for the opposite shore.

Chapter VI – A Nest of Scorpions

1

OF the extraordinary events which threatened to make March 21, 1624, one of the most momentous dates in the history of the Netherlands we have not much in the way of detail. The broad facts we know chiefly through Van Aitzema's ponderous and minute "Saken v. Staet," whilst De Voocht was, of course, a friend of the Beresteyn family, and, as I understand it, was present in the house at Amersfoort when the terrible catastrophe was so auspiciously and mysteriously averted.

The one thing, however, which neither he nor Van Aitzema have made quite clear is the motive which prompted the Stadtholder to go to Amersfoort in person. He had quite a number of knights and gentlemen around him whom he could have fully trusted to take even so portentous a message and such explicit orders as he desired to send. De Voocht, indeed, suggests that it was Nicolaes Beresteyn who persuaded him, urging the obstinacy of his father, the burgomaster, and of the burghers of the city, who had steadily opposed the Stadtholder's wishes when he – Nicolaes – had been sent to convey them.

Nicolaes Beresteyn had joined his sovereign lord at the camp at Utrecht a couple of days after his wedding. Wearied of sentimental dalliance with the stolid Kaatje, he was glad enough that his duty demanded his presence in camp rather than in the vicinity of his young wife's apron-strings.

It was but natural that, when the Stadtholder desired to send orders to Amersfoort, he should do so through the intermediary of Nicolaes. But on that day, which was March 20, the young man returned, vowing that these were not being obeyed; not a matter of disloyalty, of course, just of tenacity. Civic dignitaries, conscious of their worth and of the sacrifices they had made in the common cause, were wont to wax obstinate where the affairs of their own cities were concerned. But, on the other hand, resistance to his will had invariably the effect of rousing the Stadtholder's arbitrary temper to a point of unreasoning anger. Olden Barneveldt had expiated his contumacy on the scaffold, and I doubt not that, when Nicolaes returned from Amersfoort that evening and delivered his report, the fate of even so trusted a councillor as Mynheer Beresteyn hung for awhile in the balance.

That the matter was one of supreme importance it were impossible to doubt. Maurice of Nassau would not lightly have left his camp at Utrecht that day. The forces of the Archduchess Isabella, who, under the leadership of De Berg and of Isembourg, were threatening Gelderland from two sides, had succeeded on the one part in crossing the Ijssel. His own army was threatened by that of Spinola from the south. On the other hand, the messenger whom he had sent across the Veluwe to urge Marquet and De Keysere to concentrate inside Arnheim and Nijmegen had not yet returned. Nevertheless, he chose, by this suddenly planned excursion to Amersfoort, to expose his valuable person to serious danger; a fact which subsequent events proved only too conclusively.

Nicolaes Beresteyn was sent back at dawn the following morning to warn the burgomaster of the Stadtholder's coming, and enjoining the strictest secrecy. The young man was under orders to say nothing beyond that fact. When closely questioned, however, by his father and also by others, he did admit that fugitives from Ede had succeeded in reaching the camp.

Fugitives from Ede? What did that mean? Why should there be fugitives from Ede, when the armies of the Archduchess were so many leagues away?

Nicolaes Beresteyn shrugged his shoulders. "The Stadtholder will explain," was all that he said.

He appeared impatient and consequential, made them all feel that he could say more if he cared. He had been kept out of the prince's councils while he was under the paternal room, but now he had gained a place in the camp which had always been his by right. These solemn burghers – important enough within the purlieus of their own city – had become insignificant, mere civilians, now that the fate of the country rested upon those who were young enough to bear arms.

Nicolaes tried to meet his sister's glance.

Her indifference toward him galled his sense of importance, and he wished her to know that he neither repented nor was ashamed of what he had said the other night. Anon, when he had succeeded in forcing her eyes to meet his, he gave her a look charged with a mocking challenge. Up to this hour, she had said nothing to her father; now Nicolaes appeared to dare her to speak. But his sneers had not the power to disturb her sublime trust in the man she loved. That some mystery did cling to his journey across the Veluwe she could no longer doubt; but her fears upon the subject dwelt solely on any personal danger that might have overtaken him.

As for her father and his friends, they had apparently decided to possess their souls in patience. There was, indeed, nothing to do but to wait the Stadtholder's arrival, and in the meanwhile to try and hold those fears in check which had been aroused by the ominous words, "Fugitives from Ede."

2

The Stadtholder arrived in the course of the morning. Mynheer Beresteyn did not receive him on the doorstep, as he would have done had the visit been an open one. As it was, the passers-by on the busy quay did not bestow more than a passing glance on the plainly clad cavalier who swung himself out of the saddle outside the burgomaster's house. A message from the camp, probably, they thought. Mynheer Nicolaes had been backward and forward from Utrecht several times these past two or three days. The burgomaster awaited his exalted guest in the hall. His attitude and the expression of his face were alike pregnant with eager questionings. The Stadtholder gave curt acknowledgement to the greetings of Mynheer Beresteyn, of his family, and of his friends, and then strode deliberately into the banqueting-hall.

It looked vast and deserted at this early hour of a winter's morning. Nothing of the animation, the riotous gaiety of that day, less that a week ago, seemed to linger in its sombre, panelled walls. The dais upon which the brides and bridegrooms and the wedding party had sat, and which had crowned so brilliant a spectacle, had been removed, and the magnificent gold and silver plate, the fine linens and priceless crystals been carefully stowed away. Serving-men and sweepers were busy airing and dusting the room when the door was thrown open, and His Highness came in, ushered in by his host. They fled at sight of these great gentlemen, like so many rabbits into carefully hidden burrows.

The Stadtholder went up to the long centre table and faced Mynheer Beresteyn and those who had come in with him – the members of his family and half a dozen burghers, men of importance in the little city. Every one could see that His Highness's anger was bitter against them all. "And so, mynheer," he began curtly, and in tones of marked irritation, and addressing himself more particularly to the burgomaster, "you have thought fit to defy my orders."

"Your Highness!" protested Mynheer Beresteyn.

"Yet they were clear enough," the Stadtholder went on, not heeding the interruption. "Or did your son Nicolaes fail to explain?"

"He told us, your Highness, that it was feared the armies of the Archduchess had crossed the Ijssel —"

"The armies of the Archduchess crossed the Ijssel three days ago," Maurice of Nassau broke in impatiently. "Since then they have overrun Gelderland and occupied Ede, putting that city to fire and sword."

There came a sound like the catching of breath, the rise of a gasp of horror and anguish in every one's throat. But it was quickly suppressed, and His Highness was listened to in silence until the end. Even now, when he paused, no one spoke. All eyes were cast to the ground in self-centered meditation. The whole thing had come as a thunderbolt out of a cloudless sky. Ede had always seemed so safe, so remote. A little city which led nowhere save to the Zuyder Zee, and in the very heart of the United Provinces. What could be the motive of the Archduchess's commanders to adventure thus far into a country which was so universally hostile to them, even to the most miserable peasant, who would pollute every well and stream rather than see the enemy overrun the land?

But all these men – ay, and the women, too – had seen so much, suffered so much; fire and sword were such familiar dangers before their eyes, that for them the time had gone when sighs and lamentations would ease their overburdened hearts. They had learned to receive every fresh blow from God's hands in silence, but with determination to fight on, to fight again and to the death once more, if need be, for their liberties, their rights, and the welfare of their children. It was indeed Mynheer Beresteyn who took the next words out of the Stadtholder's mouth.

"Then Amersfoort, too, is threatened?" he said simply.

The prince nodded.

"Think you," he retorted, "that I would have ordered the evacuation of the town had there not been imperative necessity for such a course? Now, you may pray God that your wilful disobedience hath not placed your city in jeopardy."

" 'Twas but yesterday we had the order," one of the burghers urged. "And —"

" 'Twas yesterday it should have been obeyed," the Stadtholder broke in roughly. "You would then have saved me a perilous journey, for the country already is infested with spies and vedettes, outposts of the Spanish armies."

"We are all ready to guard your Highness with our lives," the burgomaster said quietly.

" 'Tis your wits I want, mynheer," the prince riposted dryly, "not your blood. Indeed, I do fear that Amersfoort is threatened, though I know not if De Berg will spend his forces on you, or, rather, concentrate them on Arnheim. But you must be prepared," he added with stern emphasis.

"You are not in a position to defend yourselves, and I cannot detach any of my troops to come to your assistance if you are attacked. Therefore, my orders were: 'Evacuate the town.' You, mynheer burgomaster, must issue your proclamation at once. Let every one go who can, taking women and children with them. Those who remain do so at their risk. Some of you can go north to Amsterdam, others west to Utrecht. Let De Berg find an empty shell when he comes."

3

Only those who had ever had the sorry task of abandoning a home in the face of an advancing enemy can have any conception of what this peremptory order meant to these burghers – fathers of families for the most part, who after the terrible privations which they had suffered for over half a century, had begun but a few years ago to reconstitute their country and their homes, to resume their interrupted industries, their commerce, their splendid art, to re-establish the wealth and power which had been their birthright, and which the tyranny of a bigoted and jealous overlord had wilfully wrested from them.

Now it meant laying aside spindles and looms once again, lathes, chisels, or books, in order to buckle on swords which threatened to rust in their scabbards, and to don steel helmets. It meant leaving the women to weep, the children fatherless.

Anxious eyes searched the Stadtholder's drawn, moody face; more than one mind reverted to memories of this peerless and fearless commander, the hero of Turnhout and Ostend. Would he have spoken in those days of "evacuation" and of "helplessness"? Would he have dreaded Spinola or the hosts of the Archduchess?

Ah, that subtle, insidious disease had indeed done its work! What mysterious poison was it that had shaken this great man's nerve, made him gloomy and fretful, weakened that in-domitable will which had once made the tyrant of Madrid quake for the future of his kingdom?

"De Berg would not dare —" one of the burghers hazarded timidly.

"He may not," His Highness answered. "In which case it might be safe for you all to return to your homes a few days hence. But some of those who fled from Ede believe that De Berg intends to detach some of his troops and with them push on as far as the Zuyder Zee, leaving it to others to join Isembourg, who is coming up from Kleve, and with his help capture Nijmegen first and then Arnheim."

"Marquet by now," observed Beresteyn, "must be well on the way to Arnheim, and De Keysere close to Nijmegen. They can intercept Isembourg and cut him off from Ede and De Berg. Your Highness's messenger —"

"Our messenger," the prince broke in curtly, "failed to deliver our messages. Marquet is not on his way to Arnheim, and De Keysere was still at Wageningen when the first fugitives from Ede ran terror-stricken into our camp."

The words were scarce out of his mouth when the sound of a low, quickly suppressed cry came from the rear of the little group that had gathered around His Highness. Few heard it, or guessed whence it had come. Only Mynheer Beresteyn, turning swiftly, caught his daughter's eyes fixed with a set expression upon him. With an almost imperceptible glance he beckoned to her, and she pushed her way through to his side, and slid her cold little hand into his firm grasp. Encouraged by her father's nearness, it was Gilda who uttered the word of protest which had risen to more than one pair of lips.

"Impossible, your Highness!" she said resolutely.

"Impossible!" Maurice of Nassau retorted curtly. "Why impossible, mejuffrouw?"

"Because my lord is a brave man, as full of resource as he is of courage. He undertook to deliver your Highness's commands to Messire Marquet and Mynheer de Keysere. He is not a man to fail."

She looked brave and determined, without a trace of self-consciousness, even though the rigid education meted out to girls in these times forbade their raising a voice in the councils of their lords. But in this case she had been voicing what was in more than one mind, and when she looked around her with a kind of timid defiance, she only encountered kindly glances.

Her father pressed her hand in tender encouragement. The Stadtholder himself appeared gracious and indulgent. It was only her brother's gaze that was unendurable, for it was charged with sarcasm, not unmixed with malevolence. Did Nicolaes hate her, then? A sickening sense of horror filled the poor girl's soul at the thought. Klaas, her little brother, whom she had loved and mothered, though he was her elder.

Ofttimes had she stood between his childish peccadillos and his father's wrath. And now — she could not even bear to meet his glance. She knew that he triumphed, and that he rejoiced in his triumph, even though he must know that she was wounded to the quick. His warning was ringing in her ear, his warning which had, in truth, proved prophetic: "The orders to Marquet will reach that commander too late!"

As in a dream, she listened to the Stadtholder's words. The whole situation appeared unreal — impossible.

"Your defense of your husband," the prince was saying, "does you honour, mejuffrouw. But this is not a time for sentiment, but for facts. And these it is our duty to face. We placed our every hope on Marquet's co-operation, but Arnheim and Nijmegen are in peril at this hour because certain messages which I sent failed to reach their destination. We have not the leisure to discuss the causes of this failure; rather must we take immediate measures for the safety of our subjects here."

Gilda perforce had to remain silent. To the others, in fact, the matter was only important, in so far that the messenger's failure to arrive had placed Arnheim and Nijmegen in jeopardy. What cared they for her heart-breaking anxiety on account of her beloved?

She looked up at her father, because from him she could always expect sympathy. But he, too, was over-preoccupied just now; patted her hand gently, then let it go, absorbed as he was in listening to the Stadtholder's orders for the speedy evacuation of Amersfoort.

She turned away with a bitter sigh, all the more resolutely suppressed as her brother's mocking glance followed her every movement. The men now were in close conference, the Stadtholder sitting at the table, the burgomaster beside him, with pen and ink, drafting the necessary proclamation, the others grouped around, discussing and tendering advice. Every one was busy, every one had something to think about.

Gilda, heavy-hearted, took the opportunity of slipping unseen out of the room.

4

What prompted her to run up to the very top of the house, like some stricken bird seeking an eyrie, she could not herself have told you. There is such a thing as instinct, and instinct takes innumerable forms according to the most pressing needs of the heart. For the moment, Gilda's most pressing need was a sight of her beloved. Quite apart from the importance of his presence now with news from the threatened cities, she longed to see him, to feel his arms round her, to warm her starved soul in the sunshine of his love and his never absent smile. This longing it was that drove her up to the attic chambers, under the apex of the roof; for these chambers had tiny dormer windows which commanded extensive views of the countryside far beyond the ramparts and beyond the Eem.

Gilda wandered into one of the attic chambers and threw open the narrow casements that gave on the back of the house. Leaning against the window frame, she looked out over the river and beyond it into the mist-laden distance. The sharp, humid air did her good, with its savour of the sea and the tang of spring already lurking in the atmosphere. The sea-fog which had hung over the country for some days still made a dense white veil that enveloped all the life that lay beyond the ramparts, and gave to the little city a strange air of isolation, as if the very world ended on the other side of its walls. From where Gilda stood, high above a forest of roofs and gables, she could see the picturesque fortifications, the monumental gates and turrets, and the Joris Poort and Nieuwpoort, which spanned the Eem on this side. Far away on her right was Utrecht; on her left Barneveld, beyond which stretched the arid upland which held in its cruel breast the secret of her husband's fate.

The girl felt inexpressibly alone, weighted with that sense of forlornness from which only the young are wont to suffer. With the years there comes a more complete self-sufficiency, a greater desire for solitude. Gregariousness is essentially the attribute of youth. And Gilda had no one in whom she could confide. Her father, in truth, had been all to her that a mother might have been; but just now the girl was pining for one of her own sex, for some one who would not be busy with many things, with politics and wars and dissensions, but whose breast would be warm and soft to pillow a head that was weary.

The tears gathered in Gilda's eyes and fell unheeded down her cheeks. It seemed to her as if every moment now she must see a rider galloping swiftly toward her as if she must hear that merry laugh ringing right across the marshland. But all that she saw was the sleepy little city, stretching out before her until it seemed to melt and merge in the arms of the mist; the network of narrow streets, the crow's foot gables, the dormer windows and ornamental corbellings; and, above everything, the tower of St. Maria and St. Joris, with quaint market-place alive with people that looked like ants, fussy and minute.

Even as she gazed, wide-eyed and tearful, the bell of St. Maria began to toll. The slow monotonous reverberation seemed in itself a presage of evil. From the height, Gilda could see the human ants pause awhile in their activities. Their very attitude, the grouping of individual figures, a kind of arrested action in the entire life of the town, proclaiming brooding terror. A moment or two later the sharp clang of the town-crier's bell mingled with the majestic booming, and people started to run toward the market-place from every direction.

Gilda watched this gathering, could see the narrow streets waxing dark with moving forms. She saw the casements thrown open one by one, heads and shoulders filling the dark squares of the window frames. And down below, the arrival of the town-crier, with his halberd and his bell, a crowd of diminutive ant-like forms pressed round his heels. A grey picture, yet all alive with movement, like unto one over which an impatient artist has hastily passed an obliterating brush; the outlines blurred, the colours dull and hazy in the humid atmosphere. It all seemed so dreamlike, so remote. Only a week ago life had appeared so exquisitely gay and so easy! An ardent lover, a happy future, home, adventure! Everything was tumbling out fulsomely from the Cornucopia of Fate. And now all the tragedy represented by those running people below; the enemy at the gates; the abandoned homes; the devastated city; crying children and starving women – a whole herd of fugitives wandering over the desolate marshland, seeking shelters in cities already over-filled, asking for food where so little was to be had.

It was cruel! Oh, horribly cruel! And aweful to see the children dancing around the town-crier, teasing by pulling at his doublet or trying to steal his bell. The crowd in the market-place had become very dense, and still people came running out of the side streets. The steps of St. Maria Kerk were black with the moving throng, and Gilda thought with added heartache of that same crowd, five short days ago, rallying for a holiday, cheering her and her handsome lover, wishing her joy and prosperity in the endless days to come.

Soon the city appeared weltering in confusion. The town-crier continued to ply his bell, and to call the proclamation ordered by the burgomaster. He went on so that every citizen in turn might hear, and now the crowd no longer tended all one way. Some had heard and were hurrying home to consult with their families, to make arrangements either for speedy departure or for weathering the terrible alternative of an invading army. Others lingered in groups on the market-place or at street corners, discussing or lamenting, according to their temperament, pausing to ask friends what they would do or what they thought of the terrible situation.

Gilda, up at the attic casement, could almost guess by the attitude, the gestures of the scared human ants, just how unsteady had become their mental balance. It was all so unexpected, and there was nothing that anyone could do to help in this terrible emergency. The Stadtholder was going back to camp. He had declared that he could not help. Threatened from every side, he could not spare his forces to come to the aid of so small a place as Amersfoort. And he – the stranger with the happy smile and the gay, inconsequent temper – who had been sent across the Veluwe to obtain succour – had failed to return. There was no garrison at Amersfoort, so there was nothing for it but to flee.

5

At what precise moment Gilda became aware of the solitary rider galloping tete baissee toward the city, it were impossible to say. He came out of the mist from the direction of Utrecht, and Gilda saw him long before the sentry at the Joris Poort challenged him. Apparently he had papers and all necessaries in order, for he was admitted without demur; and at the sight Gilda turned away from her point of vantage, ran across the attic chamber and down the stairs. It was such a very short distance between the Joris Poort and the front door of the burgomaster's house, and she wanted so much to be the first to welcome him.

It was then half an hour before noon. The city by this time was in the throes of a complete upheaval. The noise in the streets had become incessant and deafening. Church bells tolling, town-criers bawling, the clang of the halberds of the city guards mingling with the rattle of cart-wheels upon the cobble-stones, with the tramping of hundreds of feet and stamping of innumerable horses' hoofs. The air was resonant with shrieks and cries, with the grating and jarring of metal, with peal of bells and the hubbub of a throng on the move. Gilda, when she reached the foot of the stairs, found herself facing the wide-open doorway, and through it saw the quay alive with people running, with horses and driven cattle, with crowds scrambling into the boats down below, with carts and dogs and children and barrows piled up with furniture and luggage hastily tied together.

The confusion bewildered her. Determined not to allow futile terror to overmaster her, she, nevertheless, felt within her whole being the sense of an impending catastrophe. She could not approach the door, because the crowd was swarming up the stone steps, and her father's serving-men, armed with stout sticks and cudgels, had much ado to keep some of the more venturesome or more terrified among that throng from invading the house.

How that solitary rider whom she had spied in the distance would succeed in forging his way through the dense mass of surging humanity, she could not imagine; and yet through all the turmoil, the din, the terror she was more conscious of his nearness than of any other sensation. The longing to see him was, in a certain sort of way, appeased. She knew that he lived and that time alone stood between her present and past longing and the bliss of nestling once more in his arms.

Oh, the crowd! It was rapidly becoming unmanageable. The serving-men plied their cudgels in vain. There were men and women there stronger and bolder than others who were determined to have a word with the burgomaster.

"I am Mynheer Beresteyn's friend!" was shouted authoritatively to the helpless guardians of their master's privacy. Or, "You know me, Anton? Make way for me there. I must speak with the burgomaster!"

"The burgomaster is busy!" the serving-men bawled out until they were hoarse. "No one can be admitted!"

But it was difficult for any man to raise a stick against well-known burghers of the city, friends and acquaintances who had supped here in the house at Mynheer's own table; and the pressure became more and more difficult to withstand every moment. Some of the people had actually pushed their way into the hall, making it impossible for Gilda to get near the door; and the longing was irresistible to be close at hand when he dismounted, so that her smile might be the first to greet him as he ran up the steps. She pictured it all – his coming, his appearance, the way he would look about him, knowing that she must be near.

Then all at once something awful happened. Gilda, from where she stood, could neither see nor hear what it was; and yet she knew, just from looking at the crowd, that something more immediately terrifying had turned this seething mass of humanity into a horde of scared beasts. Their movements suddenly became more swift; it seemed as if some fearsome goad had been applied to the entire population of the city, and the desire, to get away, to run, to flee had become more insistent.

Those who had swarmed up the steps of the burgomaster's house ran down again. They had no longer the desire to speak with anyone, or to appeal to the servants to let them pass. They only wanted to run like the others, the few more grave ones gathering their scattered families around them like a mother hen does her chicks.

And, oh, the awful din! It had intensified a thousand-fold, and seemed all of a sudden like hell let loose. So many people shrieked, the women and the children for the most part. And the boatmen down on the water, plying for hire their small craft, already dangerously overloaded with fugitives and their goods. But now everyone on the quay appeared obsessed with the desire to get into the boats. There was scrambling and fighting upon the quay, shrieks of terror followed by ominous splashes in the murky waters. Gilda closed her eyes, not daring to look.

And still the clang of the church bells tolling and the hideous cacophony of a whole population stampeding in a mad panic.

The hall, the doorway, the outside steps were now deserted. Life and movement and din were all out on the quay and in the streets around. The serving-men even had thrown down their sticks and cudgels. Some of them had disappeared altogether, others stood in groups, skulking and wide-eyed. Gilda tried to frame a query. Her pale, anxious face no doubt expressed the words which her lips could not utter, for one of the men in the hall replied in a husky whisper:

"The Spaniards! They are on us!"

She wanted to ask more, for at first it did not seem as if this were fresh news. The Spaniards were at Ede, the town was being evacuated because of them. What had occurred to turn an ordered evacuation into so redoubtable a stampede?

And still no sign of my lord.

Then suddenly the doors of the banqueting-hall were thrown open, and the burgomaster appeared. Had Gilda doubted for a moment that something catastrophic had actually happened, she would have felt her doubts swept aside by the mere aspect of her father. He, usually so grave, so dignified, was trembling like a reed, his hair was dishevelled, his cheeks of a grey, ashen colour. The word "Gilda" was actually on his lips when he stepped across the threshold, and quite a change came over him the moment he caught sight of his daughter. Before he could call to her she was already by his side, and in an instant he had her by the hand and dragged her with him back into the banqueting-hall.

"What has happened?" she asked, in truth more bewildered than frightened.

"The Spaniards!" her father replied briefly. "They are on us."

"Yes," she ventured, frowning; "but —"

"Not three leagues away," he broke in curtly. "Their vanguard will be here by nightfall."

She looked round her, puzzled to see them all so calm in contrast to the uproar and the confusion without. The Stadtholder was sitting beside the table, his head resting on his hand. He looked woefully ill. Nicolaes Beresteyn was beside him, whispering earnestly.

"What are you going to do, father dear?" Gilda asked in a hurried whisper.

"My fellow-burghers and I are remaining at our posts," Beresteyn replied quietly. "We must do what we can to save our city, and our presence may do some good."

"And Nicolaes?" she asked again.

"Nicolaes has his horse ready. He will take you to Utrecht in His Highness's train." Then, as Gilda made no comment on this, only gave his hand a closer pressure, he added tentatively: "Unless you would prefer to go with Mynheer van den Poele and his family. He is taking Kaatje and her mother to Amsterdam."

"I would prefer to remain with you," she said simply.

"Impossible, my dear child!" he retorted.

"My place is here," she continued firmly, "and I'll not go. Oh, can't you understand?" she pleaded, with a break in her voice. "If you sent me away, I should go mad or die!"

"But, Gilda —" the poor man protested.

"My lord is here," Gilda suddenly broke in more calmly.

"My lord? What do you mean?"

"I saw him awhile ago. I was up in the attic-chamber, he came through the Joris Poort."

"Your eyes deceived you. He would be here by now."

"He should be here," she asserted. "I cannot understand what has happened. Perhaps the crowd —"

"Your eyes deceived you," he reiterated, but more doubtfully this time. Then, as just at that moment the Stadtholder and caught his eye, Beresteyn called to him, "My daughter says that my lord has returned."

"Impossible!" burst forth impulsively from Nicolaes.

"Why should it be impossible?" Gilda retorted quickly, and fixed coldly challenging eyes upon her brother. "Why should you say that it is impossible?" she insisted, seeing that Nicolaes now looked shamefaced and confused. "What do you know about my lord?"

"Nothing, nothing!" Nicolaes stammered. "I did not mean that, of course; it only seems so strange —" And he added roughly, "Then why is he not here?"

"The crowd is very dense about the streets," one of the burghers suggested. "My lord, mayhap hath found it difficult to push his way through."

"Why should he be coming to Amersfoort?" mused Mynheer Beresteyn.

"He came from the direction of Utrecht," Gilda replied. "Some one at the camp must have told him that His Highness was here."

"No one knew I was coming hither," the Stadtholder broke in impatiently.

"My sister more like hath been troubled with visions," Nicolaes rejoined with a sneer. "Nor have we the time," he added, "to wait on my lord's pleasure. If your Highness is ready, we should be getting to horse."

"But surely," Gilda protested with pitiful earnestness, "your Highness will wait to see your messenger. He must be bringing news from Messire Marquet. He —"

"Yes," the Stadtholder broke in decisively, "I'll see him. Let some one go out into the streets at once and find the man. Tell him that we are waiting —"

"He knows his way about the town," Nicolaes interposed, with an ill-concealed note of spite in his voice. "Why should he need a pilot.?"

There was a moment's silence. Every one looked nervy and worried. Then the Stadtholder turned once more to the burgomaster, and queried abruptly:

"Are those two companions of my lord's still in your house, mynheer? Can you not send one of them?"

The suggestion met with universal approval. And Mynheer Beresteyn himself urged the advisability of finding my lord's friends immediately. He took his daughter's hand. It was cold as ice, and quivered like a wounded bird in his warm grasp. He patted it gently, reassuringly. Her wild eyes frightened him. He knew what she suffered, and in his heart condemned his son for those insinuations against the absent. But this was not a moment for delicacy or for scruples. The hour was a portentous one, and fraught with peril for a nation and its chief. The individual matters so little at such times. The feelings, the sufferings, the broken heart of one women or one man – how futile do they seem when a whole country is writhing in the throes of her death agony?

"Go, my dear child," Beresteyn admonished firmly. "Obey His Highness's commands. Find my lord's friends and tell them to go at once, and return hither with my lord. Go," he added; and whispered gently in Gilda's ear, as he led her, reluctant yet obedient, to the door, "Leave your husband's honour in my hands."

She gave him a grateful look, and he gave her hand a last reassuring pressure. Then he let her go from him, only urging her to hurry back.

It must not be supposed for a moment that he did not feel for her in her anxiety and her misery. But the man in question was a stranger – an Englishman, what? – and Mynheer Beresteyn was above all a patriot, a man who had suffered acutely for his country, had sacrificed his all for her, and was ready to do it again whenever she called to him. The Stadtholder stood for the safety and the integrity of the United Provinces; he was the champion and upholder of her civil and religious liberties. His personal safety stood, in the minds of Beresteyn and his fellow burghers, above every consideration on earth.

Gilda knew this, and though she trusted her father implicitly, she knew that her beloved would be ruthlessly sacrificed, even by him, if, through misadventure or any other simple circumstance entirely beyond his control, he happened to have failed in the enterprise which had been entrusted to him. Nicolaes, of course, was an avowed enemy. Why? Gilda could not conjecture. Was it jealousy, or petty spite only? If so, what advantage could he reap from the humiliation of one who already was a member of his own family? But she felt herself encompassed with enemies. No one had attempted to defend my lord's honour when it was so ruthlessly impugned save her father, and he was too absorbed, too much centered in thoughts of his country's peril, to do real battle for the absent.

It was with a heavy heart that she turned to go up the stairs in search of the two men who alone were ready to go through fire in the defense of their friend. A melancholy smile hovered round Gilda's lips. She felt that with those two quaint creatures she had more in common at this hour than with her father, whom she idolized. In those too poor caitiffs she had all that her heart had been hungering for: simple hearts that understood her sorrow, loyal souls that never wavered. For evil or for good, through death-peril or through seeming dishonour, their friend whom they reverenced could count upon their devotion. And as Gilda went wearily up the stairs, her mind conjured up the picture of those two ludicrous vagabonds, with their whimsical saws and rough codes of honour, and she suddenly felt less lonely and less sad.

7

Great was her disappointment, therefore, when she reached the guest-chamber, which they still occupied, to find that it was empty. The whole house was by this time in a hopeless state of turmoil and confusion. Serving-men and maids rushed aimlessly hither and thither, up and down the stairs, along the passages, in and out of the rooms; or stood about in groups, whispering or cowering in corners. Some of them had already fled; the few who remained looked like so many scared chickens, fussy and inconsequent, – the maids, with kirtles awry and hair unkempt, the men striving to look brave and determined, putting on the air of masters, and adding to the maids' distress by their aimless, hectoring ways.

There was nothing in the house now left of that orderly management which is the pride of every self-respecting housewife. Doors stood open, displaying the untidiness of the rooms; there was noise and bustle everywhere, calls of distress and loud admonitions. From no one could Gilda learn what she desired to know. She was forced to seek out Maria, her special tiring-woman, who, it was to be hoped, had some semblance of reason left in her. Maria, however, had no love for the two rapscallions, who were treated in the house as if they were princes, and knew nothing of the respect due to their betters. She replied to her young mistress's inquiries by shrugging her shoulders and calling heaven to witness her ignorance of the whereabouts of those abominable louts.

"Spoilt, they have been," the old woman asserted sententiously. "Shamefully spoilt. They have neither order nor decency, nor the slightest regard for the wishes of their betters —"

"But, Maria, whither have the two good fellows gone?" Gilda broke in impatiently.

"Gone? Whither have they gone? Maria ejaculated, in pious ignorance of such probable wickedness. "Nay, that ye cannot expect any self-respecting woman to know. They have gone, the miserable roysterers! Went but an hour ago, without saying by your leave. This much I do know. And my firm belief is that they were naught but a pair of Spanish spies, come to hand us all, body and soul, to —"

"Maria, I forbid thee to talk such rubbish!" Gilda exclaimed wrathfully.

And, indeed, her anger and her white and worried look did effectually silence the garrulous woman's tongue.

Even the waiting-maids! Even these ignorant fools! Gilda could have screamed with the horror of it all, as if she had suddenly landed in a nest of scorpions and their poison encompassed her everywhere. This story of spies! God in Heaven, how had it come about? Whose was the insidious tongue that had perverted her brother Nicolaes first, and then every trimmer and rogue in the house? Gilda felt as if it might ease her heart to run around with a whip, and lash all these base detractors into acknowledgment of their infamy. But she forced herself to patience.

A vague instinct had already whispered to her that she must not go back to the banqueting-hall with the news that my lord's friends had gone, and that no one had any knowledge of their whereabouts. She felt that if she did that, her brother's sneers would become unendurable, and that she might then be led to retort with accusations against her only brother which she would afterwards forever regret.

So she waited for awhile, curtly bade Maria to be gone, and to leave her in peace. She wanted to think, to put a curb on her fears and her just wrath against this unseen army of calumniators; for wrath and fear are both evil counsellors. And above all, she wanted to see her beloved.

He was in the town. She knew it as absolutely as that she was alive. Were her eyes likely to be deceived? Even now, when she closed her eyes, she could see him, as she had done but a few minutes ago, walking his horse through the Joris Poort, his plumed hat shading the upper part of his face. She could see him, with just that slight stoop of his broad shoulders which denoted almost unendurable fatigue. She had noted this at the moment, with a pang of anxiety, and then forgotten it all in the joy of seeing him again. She remembered it all now. Oh, how could they think that she could be deceived?

Just for a second or two she had the mind to run back to the casement in the attic-chamber and see if she could not from thence spy him again. But surely this would be futile. He must have reached the quay by now, would be at the front door, with no one to welcome him. In truth, the longing to see him had become sheer physical pain.

So Gilda once more made her way down into the hall.

1

DOWN below, in the banqueting-hall, Gilda's departure had at first been followed by a general feeling of obsession, which caused the grave men here assembled to remain silent for awhile and pondering. There was no lack of sympathy, I repeat; not even on the part of the Stadtholder, whose heart and feelings were never wholly atrophied. But there had sprung up in the minds of these grave burghers an unreasoning feeling of suspicion toward the man whom they had trusted implicitly such a brief while ago.

Terror at the imminence of their danger, the appearance of the dreaded foe almost at their very gates, had in a measure – as terror always will – blurred the clearness of their vision, and to a certain extent warped their judgements. The man now appeared before them as a stranger, therefore a person to be feared, even despised to the extent of attributing the blackest possible treachery to him. They forgot that the closest possible ties of blood and of tradition bound the English gentleman to the service of the Prince of Orange. Sir Percy Blakeney now, and Diogenes the soldier of fortune of awhile ago, were one and the same. But no longer so to them. The adder's fork had bitten into their soul and left its insidious poison of suspicion and of misbelief.

So none of them spoke, hardly dared to look on Mynheer Beresteyn, who, they felt, was not altogether with them in their distrust. The Stadtholder had lapsed into one of his surly moods. His lean, brown hands were drumming a devil's tattoo upon the table.

Then suddenly Nicolaes broke into a harsh and mirthless laugh.

"It would all be a farce," he exclaimed with bitter malice, "if it did not threaten to become so tragic." Then he turned to the Stadtholder, and his manner became once more grave and earnest. "Your Highness, I entreat," he said soberly, "deign to come away with me at once, ere you fall into some trap set by those abominable spies —"

"Nicolaes," his father broke in sternly, "I forbid you to make these base insinuations against your sister's husband."

"I'll be silent if you command me," Nicolaes rejoined quietly. "But methinks that his Highness's life is too precious for sentimental quibbles. Nay," he went on vehemently, and like one who is forced into speech against his will, "I have warned Gilda of this before. While were all waiting here calmly, trusting to that stranger who came, God knows whence, he was warning De Berg to effect a quick crossing"

"It is false!" protested the burgomaster hotly.

"Then, I pray you," Nicolaes insisted hotly, "tell me how it is that De Berg did forestall his Highness's plans? Who was in the council-chamber when the plans were formulated save yourselves? Who knew of the orders to Marquet? Marquet hath not gone to relieve Arnheim, and the armies of the Archduchess are at our gates!"

He paused, and a murmur of assent went round the room, and when Mynheer Beresteyn once more raised his voice in protest, saying firmly: "I'll not believe it! Let us wait at least until we've heard what news my lord hath brought!" No one spoke in response, and even the Stadtholder shrugged his shoulders, as if the matter of a man's honour or dishonour had no interest for him.

"Your Highness," Nicolaes went on with passionate earnestness, "let me beg of you on my knees to think of your noble father, of the trap into which he fell, and of his assassin, Gerard – a stranger, too —"

"But this man saved my life once!" the Stadtholder said, with an outburst of generous feeling in favour of the man to whom, in truth, he owed so much.

"He hated Stoutenburg then, your Highness," Nicolaes retorted, and boldly looked his father in the face – his father who knew his own share in that hideous conspiracy three months ago. "He loved my sister Gilda. It suited his purpose then to use his sword in your Highness's service.

But remember, he is only a soldier of fortune after all. Have we not all of us heard him say a hundred times that he had lived hitherto by selling his sword to the highest bidder?"

This time his tirade was greeted by a distinct murmur of approval. Only the burgomaster raised his voice admonishingly once more.

"Take care, Nicolaes!" he exclaimed. "Take care!"

"Take care of what?" the young man retorted with all his wonted arrogance, and challenged his father with a look.

"Would you give your only son away," that look appeared to say, "in order to justify a stranger?"

Then, as indeed Mynheer Beresteyn remained silent, not exactly giving up the contention, but forced into passive acquiescence by the weight of public opinion and that inalienable feeling of family and kindred which makes most men or women defend their own against any stranger, Nicolaes continued, with magnificent assumption of patriotic fervor:

"Have we the right hazard so precious a thing as his Highness's life for the sake of sparing my sister's feelings?"

In this sentiment every one was ready to concur. They did not actually condemn the stranger; they were not prepared to call him a traitor and a potential assassin, or to believe one half of Nicolaes Beresteyn's insinuations. They merely put him aside, out of their minds, as not entering into their present schemes. And even the burgomaster could not gainsay the fact that his son was right.

The most urgent thing at the present juncture was to get the Stadtholder safely back to his camp at Utrecht. Every minute spent in this garrisonless city was fraught with danger for the most precious life in the United Provinces.

"Where is his Highness's horse?" he asked.

"Just outside," Nicolaes replied glibly; "in charge of a man I know. Mine is ready too. Indeed, we should get to horse at once."

The Stadtholder did not demur.

"Have the horses brought to," he said quickly. "I'll be with you in a trice."

2

Nicolaes hurried out of the room, his Highness remaining behind for a moment or two, in order to give his final instructions, a last admonition or two to the burghers.

"Do not resist," he said earnestly. "You have not the means to do aught but to resign yourselves to the inevitable. As soon as I can, I will come to your relief. In the meanwhile, conciliate De Berg by every means in your power. He is not a harsh man, and the Archduchess has learnt a salutary lesson from the discomfiture of Alva. She knows by now that we are a stiff-necked race, whom it is easier to cajole than to coerce. If only you will be patient! Can you reckon on your citizens not to do anything rash or foolish that might bring reprisals upon your heads?"

"Yes," the burgomaster replied. "I think we can rely on them for that. When your Highness has gone we'll assemble on the market place, and I will speak to them. We'll do our best to stay the present panic and bring some semblance of order into the town."

Their hearts were heavy. 'Twas no use trying to minimize the deadly peril which confronted them. There was a century of oppression, of ravage, and pillage, and bloodshed to the credit of the Spanish armies. It was difficult to imagine that the spirit of an entire nation should have changed suddenly into something more tolerant and less cruel.

However, for the moment, there was nothing more to be said, and alas! it was not as if the whole terrible situation was a novel one. They had all been through it before, at Leyden and Bergen-op-Zoom, at Haarlem and Delft, when they were weeping their land free from the foreign tyrant; and it was useless at this hour to add to the Stadtholder's difficulties by futile lamentations. All the more as Nicolaes had now returned with the welcome news that the horses were there, and everything ready for his Highness's departure. He appeared more excited than before, anxious to get away as quickly as may be.

"There is a rumour in the town," he said, "that Spanish vedettes have been spied less than a league away."

"And have you heard any rumour as to the arrival of our Diogenes?" the Stadtholder asked casually.

Nicolaes hesitated a moment ere he replied: "I have heard nothing definite."

3

A minute later the Stadtholder was in the hall. The doors were open and the horses down below in the charge of an equerry.

Nicolaes, half way down the outside stone steps, looked the picture of fretful impatience. With a dark frown upon his brow, he was scanning the crowd, and now and again a curse broke through his set lips when he saw the Stadtholder still delayed by futile leave-takings.

"In the name of heaven, let us to horse!" he exclaimed almost savagely.

Just at that moment his Highness was taking a kindly farewell of Gilda.

"I wish, mejuffrouw," he was saying, "that you had thought of taking shelter in our camp."

Gilda forced herself to listen to him, her lips tried to frame the respectful words which convention demanded. But her eyes she could not control, nor yet her thoughts, and they were fixed upon the crowd down below, just as were those of her brother Nicolaes. She thought that every moment she must catch sight of that plumed hat, towering above the throng, of those sturdy shoulders, forging their way to her. But all that she saw was the surging mass of people. A medley of colour. Horses, carts, the masts of ships. People running. And children. Numberless children, in arms or on their tiny feet; the sweet, heavy burdens that made the present disaster more utterly catastrophic.

Then suddenly she gave a loud cry.

"My lord!" she called, at the top of her voice. Then something appeared to break in her throat, and it was with a heart-rending sob that she murmured almost inaudibly: "Thank God! It is my lord!"

The Stadtholder turned, was across the hall and out in the open in a trice.

"Where?" he demanded.

She ran after him, seized his surcoat with a trembling hand, and with the other pointed in the direction of the Koppel-poort.

"A plumed hat!" she murmured vaguely, for her teeth were chattering so that she could scarcely speak. "All broken and battered with wind and weather – a torn jerkin – a mud-stained cloak. He is leading his horse. He has a three days' growth of beard on his chin, and looks spent with fatigue. There! Do you not see him?"

But Nicolaes already had interposed.

"To horse, your Highness!" he cried.

He would have given worlds for the privilege to seize the Stadtholder then and there by the arm, and to drag him down the steps and set him on his horse before the meeting which he dreaded could take place. But Maurice of Nassau, torn between his desire to get out of the threatened city as quickly as possible and his wish to speak with the messenger whom an inalienable instinct assured him that he could trust, was lingering on the steps trying in his turn to catch sight of Diogenes.

"Beware of the assassin's dagger, your Highness!" Nicolaes whispered hoarsely in his ear. "In this crowd who can tell? Who knows what deathly trap is being laid for you?"

"Not by that man, I'll swear!" the Stadtholder affirmed.

"Nay, if he is loyal he can follow you to the camp and report to you there. But for God's sake remember your father and the miscreant Gerard. There too, a crowd; the hustling, the hurry! In the name of your country, come away!"

There was no denying the prudence of this advice. Another instant's hesitation, the obstinacy of an arbitrary temperament that abhors being dictated to, the Stadtholder was ready to go. Gilda, on the top of the steps, was more like a stone statue of expectancy than like a living woman. Nay, all that she had alive in her were just her eyes, and they had spied her beloved. He was then by the Koppel-poort, some hundred yards or more on the other side of the quay, with a seething mass of panic-stricken humanity between him and the steps of Mynheer Beresteyn's house.

He had dismounted and was leading his horse. The poor beast, spent with fatigue, looked ready to drop, and, indeed, appeared too dazed to pick his own way through the crowd. As it was, he was more than a handful for his equally wearied master, whose difficulties were increased a hundredfold by the number of small children who were for ever getting in the way of the horse's legs, and were in constant danger of being kicked or trampled on.

But Gilda never lost sight of him now that she had seen him. With every beat of her heart she was measuring the footsteps that separated him from the Stadtholder. And the more Nicolaes fretted to hurry his Highness away, the more she longed and yearned for the quick approach of her beloved.

4

Amongst all those here present, Gilda was the only one who scented some unseen danger for them all in Nicolaes' strangely feverish haste. What the others took for zeal, she knew by instinct was naught but treachery. What form this would take she could not guess; but this she knew, that for some motive as sinister as it was unexplainable, Nicolaes did not wish the Stadtholder and his messenger to meet. That same motive had caused him to utter all those venomous accusations against her husband, and was even now wearing him into a state of fretfulness which bordered on dementia.

"My lord!" she cried out to her beloved at one time; and felt that even through all the din and clatter her voice had reached his ear, for he raised his head, and it even seemed to her as if his eyes met hers above the intervening crowd and as if the supernal longing for him which was in her heart had drawn him with its mystic power over every obtruding obstacle.

For, indeed, the next moment he was right at the foot of the steps, not five paces from the Stadtholder.

Nicolaes spied him in a moment, and a loud curse broke from his lips.

"That skulking assassin!" he cried; and with a magnificent gesture covered the Stadtholder with his body. "To horse, your Highness, and leave me to deal with him!"

Maurice of Nassau, indeed was one of the bravest men of his time, but the word "assassin" was bound to ring unpleasantly in the ears of a man whose father had met his death at a murderer's hand. Half-ashamed of his fears, he nevertheless did take advantage of Nicolaes' theatrical attitude to slip behind him and mount his horse as quickly as he could. But with his foot already in the stirrup compunction appeared to seize him. Wishing to palliate the gross insult which was being hurled at the man who had once saved his life at imminent peril of his own, he now turned and called to him in gracious, matter-of-fact tones:

"Why, man, what made you tarry so long? Come with us to Utrecht now. We can no longer wait."

With this he swung himself in the saddle.

"Not another step man, at your peril!"

This came from Nicolaes Beresteyn, who was still standing in a dramatic pose between Diogenes and the Stadtholder, with his cloak wrapped around his arm.

"Stand back, you fool!!" retorted the other loudly, and would have pushed past him, when suddenly Nicolaes disengaged his arm from his cloak wrapped around his arm.

For one fraction of a second the gleam of steel flashed in the humid air; then, without a word of warning, swift as a hawk descending on his prey, he struck at Diogenes with all his might.

It had all happened in a very few brief seconds. Diogenes, spent with fatigue, or actually struck, staggered and half fell against the bottom step. But Gilda, with a loud cry, was already by his side, and as Nicolaes raised his arm to strike once again, she was on him like some lithe pantheress.

She seized his wrist, and gave it such a violent twist that he uttered a cry of pain, and the dagger fell with a clatter to the ground. After which everything became a blur. She heard her brother's loudly triumphant shout:

"His Highness's life was threatened. Mine was but an act of justice!" even as he in his turn swung himself into the saddle.

5

The Stadtholder looked dazed. It had all happened so quickly that he had not the time to visualize it all. De Voocht, who was in the hall of the burgomaster's house from the moment when the Stadtholder bade farewell to Gilda until that when he dug his spurs into his horse and scattered the crowd in every direction, tells us in his "Brieven" – the one which is dated March 21, 1626 – that the incidents followed on one another with such astounding rapidity that it was impossible for any one to interfere.

All that he remembers very clearly is seeing his Highness getting to horse, then the flash of steel in the air and Nicolaes Beresteyn's arm upraised ready to strike. He could not see if any one had fallen. The next moment he heard Gilda's heart-piercing shriek, and saw her running down the stone steps – almost flying, like a bird.

Mynheer Beresteyn followed his daughter as rapidly as he could. He reached the foot of the steps just as his son put his horse to a walk in the wake of his Highness. He was wont to say afterwards that at the moment his mind was an absolute blank. He had heard his daughter's cry and seen Nicolaes strike; but he had not actually seen Diogenes. Now he was just in time to see his son's final dramatic gesture and to hear his parting words:

"There, father," Nicolaes shouted to him, and pointed to the ground, "is the pistol which the miscreant pointed at the Stadtholder when I struck him down like a dog!"

The people down on the quay had hardly perceived anything. They were too deeply engrossed in their own troubles and deadly peril.

When the horses reared under the spur they scattered like so many hens out of the way of immediate danger; but a second or two later they were once more surging everywhere, intent only on the business of getting away.

Gilda, at the foot of the steps, saw and heard nothing more. The sudden access of almost manlike strength wherewith she had fallen on her brother and wrenched the murderous dagger from his grasp had as suddenly fallen from her again. Her knees were shaking; she was almost ready to swoon.

She put out her arms and encountered those of her father, which gave her support. Her brother's voice, exultant and cruel, reached her ears as through a veil.

"My lord!" she murmured, in a pitiful appeal.

She did not know how severely he had been struck; indeed, she had not seen him fall. Her instinct had been to rush on Nicolaes first and to disarm him. In this she succeeded. Then only did she turn to her beloved.

But the crowd, cruelly indifferent, was all around like a surging sea. They pushed and they jostled; they shouted and filled the air with a medley of sounds. Some actually laughed. She saw some comely faces and ugly ones; some that wept and others that grinned. It seemed to her even for a moment that she caught sight of a round red face and of lean and lanky Socrates. She tried to call to him, to beg him to explain. She turned to her father, asking him if in truth she was going mad.

For she called in vain to her beloved. He was no longer here.

Chapter VIII – Devil's-Writ

1

WHEN Diogenes, taken wholly unawares by Nicolaes' treacherous blow, had momentarily lost his balance, he would have been in a precarious position indeed had not his faithful friends been close at hand at the moment.

It is difficult to surmise how terribly anxious the two philosophers had been these past few days. Indeed, their anxiety had proved more than a counterpart to that felt by Gilda, and had, with its simple-hearted sympathy, expressed in language more whimsical than choice, been intensely comforting to her.

Both these worthies had been inured to blows and hurts from the time when as mere lads, they first learned to handle a sword, and Pythagoras' wound, which would have laid an ordinary man low for a fortnight, was, after four days, already on the mend. To keep a man of that type in bed, or even within four walls, when he began to feel better was more than any one could do. And when he understood that Diogenes had been absent four days on an errand for the Stadtholder, that the jongejuffrouw was devoured with anxiety on his behalf, and that that spindle-legged gossoon Socrates was spending most of the day and one half of the night on horseback, patrolling the ramparts watching for the comrade's return; when he understood all that, I say, it was not likely that he – Pythagoras – an able-bodied man and a doughty horseman at that, would be content to lie abed and be physicked by any grovelling leech.

Thus the pair of them were providentially on the watch on that memorable March 21, and they both saw their comrade-in-arms enter the city by the Joris Poort. They followed him as best they could through the crowd, cursing and pushing their way, knowing well that Diogenes' objective could be none other than a certain house they wot of on the quay, where a lovely jongejuffrouw was waiting in tears for her beloved.

Remember that to these two caitiffs the fact that the Spaniards were said to be at the very gates of Amersfoort was but a mere incident. With their comrade within the city, they feared nothing, were prepared for anything. They had been in far worse plights than this many a time in their career, the three of them, and had been none the worse for it in the end.

Of course, now matters had become more complicated through the jongejuffrouw. She had become the first consideration, and though it was impossible not to swear at Diogenes for thus having laid this burden on them all, it was equally impossible to shirk its responsibilities.

The jongejuffrouw above all. That had become the moral code of these two philosophers, and with those confounded Spaniards likely to descend on this town – why, the jongejuffrouw must be got out of it as soon as may be! No wonder that Diogenes had turned up just in the nick of time! Something evidently was in the wind, and it behooved for comrades-in-arms to be there, ready to help as occasion arose.

A simple code enough, you'll admit; worthy of simple, unsophisticated hearts. Socrates, being the more able-bodied of the two, then took command, dismounted, and left his lubberly compeer in charge of the horses at a comparatively secluded corner of the market-place.

"If you can get hold of one more horse," he said airily, "one that is well-saddled and looks sprightly and fresh, do not let your super-sensitive honesty stand in your way. Diogenes' mount looked absolutely spent, and I'm sure he'll need another.

With which parting admonition he turned on his heel and made his way toward the quay.

2

Thus it was that Socrates happened to be on the spot, or very near it, when Diogenes was struck by the hand of a traitor, and, wearied, sick, and faint, lost his footing and fell for a moment helpless against the steps, whilst Nicolaes Beresteyn dug his spurs into his horse's sides and urged the Stadtholder to immediate haste.

A second or two later these two were lost to sight in the crowd. It was Socrates who received his half-swooning friend in his arms, and who dragged him incontinently into the recess formed by the side of the stone steps and the wall of the burgomaster's house.

By great good fortune, the dagger-thrust aimed by the abominable miscreant had lost most of its virulence in the thick folds of Diogenes' cloak. The result was just a flesh wound in the neck, nothing that would cause so hardened a soldier more than slight discomfort. His scarf, tied tightly around his shoulders by Socrates' rough, but experienced hands, was all that was needed for the moment. It had only been fatigue, and perhaps the unexpectedness of the onslaught, that had brought him to his knees for that brief second, and rendered him momentarily helpless. Time enough, by mischance for Nicolaes to drag the Stadtholder finally out of sight.

But by the time Diogenes' faithful comrade had found shelter for him in the angle of the wall the feeling of sickness had passed away.

"The Stadtholder," he queried abruptly, "where is he?"

"Gone!" Socrates grunted through clenched teeth. "Gone, together with that spawn of the devil who —"

"After him!" Diogenes commanded, speaking once more with that perfect quietude which is the attribute of men of action at moments of acute peril. "Get me a horse, man! Mine is spent."

"In the market-place," Socrates responded laconically. "Pythagoras is in charge. You can have the beast, and we'll follow." Then he added, under his breath: "And the jongejuffrouw? She was so anxious--"

Diogenes made no reply, gave one look up at the house which contained all that for him was dearest on God's earth. But he did not sigh. I think the longing and the disappointment were too keen even for that. The next moment he had already started to push his way through the throng along the quay, and thence into Vriese Straat in the direction of the market-place, closely followed by his long-legged familiar.

As soon as the Groote Market lay open before him, his sharp eyes searched the crowd for a sight of the Stadtholder's plumed bonnet. Soon he spied his Highness right across the place, with Nicolaes riding close to his stirrup.

The two horsemen were then tending toward Joris Laan, which leads straight to the poort.

At that end of the markt the crowd was much less dense, and Joris Laan beyond appeared practically deserted. It was, you must remember, from that side that the enemy would descend upon the city when he came, and the moving throng, if viewed from a height, would now have looked like a column of smoke when it is all blown one way by the wind. Already the Stadtholder and Nicolaes had been free to put their horses to a trot. Another moment and they would be galloping down Joris Laan, which is but three hundred yards from the poort.

"Oh, God, grant me wings!" Diogenes muttered, between his teeth.

"What are you going to do?" Socrates asked.

"Prevent the Stadtholder from falling into an abominable trap, if I can," the other replied briefly.

Socrates pointed to the distant corner of the markt, where Pythagoras could be dimly perceived waiting patiently beside three horses.

"I see the ruffian has stolen a horse," he said. "So long as it is a fresh one —"

"I shall need it." Diogenes remarked simply.

"I told him only to get the best, but you can't trust that loon since good fortune hath made him honest."

The next few seconds brought them to the spot. Pythagoras hailed them with delight. He was getting tired of waiting. Three horses, obviously fresh and furnished with excellent saddlery, were here ready. Even Socrates had a word of praise for his fat compeer's choice.

"Where did you get him from?" he queried, indicating the mount which Diogenes had without demur selected for himself.

Pythagoras shrugged his shoulder. What did it matter who had been made the poorer by a good horse? Enough that it was here now, ready to do service to the finest horseman in the Netherlands. Already Diogenes had swung himself into the saddle, and now he turned his horse toward Nieuwpoort.

"Where do we go?" the others cried.

"After me!" he shouted in reply.

3

Nose to heels, the three riders thundered through the city. It was deserted at this end of it, remember. Thank God for that! And now for a host of guardian angels to the rescue! Down the Oude Straat they galloped, their horses' hoofs raising myriads of sparks from the uneven cobblestones. "God grant me wings!" the leader had cried ere he set spurs to his horse, and the others followed without an instant's thought as to the whither or the wherefore. "After me!" he had called; and they who had fought beside him so often, who had bled with him, suffered with him, triumphed at times, been merry always, were well content to follow him now and forget everything in the exhilaration of this chase.

A chase it was! They could not doubt it, even though they seemed at this moment to be speeding in the opposite direction to that pursued by the Stadtholder and Nicolaes Beresteyn. But they well knew their friend's way, when he let his mount have free rein and threw up his head with that air of intense vitality which in him was at its height when life and death were having a tussle somewhere at the end of a ride.

Down the Oude Straat, which presently abuts on the ramparts. Then another two hundred yards to Nieuwpoort. No one in sight now. This part of the city looks like one of the dead. Doors open wide, litter of every sort encumbering the road. The din from afar, even the ceaseless tolling of St. Maria bell, seem like dream-sounds, ghost-like and unreal. Now the poort. Still no one insight. No guard. No sentry. The gate left open. Here two or three halberds hastily thrown down in some hurried flight. There a culverin, forlorn looking, gaping wide-mouthed, like some huge toad yawning, as if astonished or wearied to find itself deserted. Then again, a pile of muskets. It must have been a sudden panic that drove the guard from their post. But, thank God, the gate!

Diogenes is already through; after him his two compeers. A quarter of a league further on they suddenly draw rein. The horses rear, snorting and tossing, panting with the excitement and fretted with the curb. The riders blink for a second or two in the glare. The white mist is positively blinding here, where its sovereignty is unfettered. Just a clump of trees, way out on the right, here and there a hut with thatched roof and a piece of low fencing, or the gaunt arms of a windmill stretched with eerie stillness to the silvery sky. And above it all the mist — a pale shroud that envelopes everything.

To the east and the south the arid upland plunges head-long through it into infinity, cloaks within its stern bosom the secrets of the lurking enemy – the armies of De Berg, the Spanish outposts, the ambuscades. To the west Utrecht, unseen – and just now two tiny specks speeding along its road – the Stadtholder and Nicolaes Beresteyn. They came out into the open through Joris Poort, and are now some four hundred yards or less from the spot where three panting but exhilarated philosophers were now filling their lungs with the crisp, humid air.

They looked neither to right nor left. The Stadtholder, easily recognizable by his plumed bonnet, rides a length or less in advance of his companion. The fog has not yet swallowed them up. Diogenes takes all this in. A simple enough picture – the sea-fog and two riders speeding towards Utrecht. But a swift intaking of his breath, a tight closing of his firm lips, indicate to the others that all is not as simple as it seems.

4

Then a very curious thing happened. At first it seemed nothing. But to the watchers outside Nieuwpoort it had the same effect as a flash of lightning would have in an apparently cloudless sky. It began with Nicolaes Beresteyn drawing his horse close up to the Stadtholder, on his Highness's right. Then for another few seconds the two riders went along side by side, like one black speck now, still quite distinguishable through the fog. Socrates and Pythagoras had their eyes on Diogenes. But Diogenes did not move. He was frowning, and his face had a set and tense expression. He had his horse tightly on the curb, and appeared almost wilfully to fret the animal, who was pawing the wet, sandy ground and covering itself with lather – a picture of tearing impatience.

"What do we do now?" Pythagoras exclaimed at last, unable, just like the horse, to contain his excitement.

"Wait," Diogenes replied curtly. "All may be well after all."

"In which case?" queried Socrates.

"Nothing!"

A groan of disappointment rose to a couple of parched throats; but it was never uttered. What went on in the mist on the road to Utrecht, four hundred yards away, had stifled it at birth.

The Stadtholder's horse had become restive. A simple matter enough; but in this case unexplainable, because Maurice of Nassau was a splendid horseman. He could easily have quietened the animal if there had not been something abnormal in its sudden antics. It reared and tossed for no apparent reason, would have thrown a less experienced rider.

"The brute is being teased with a goad," Pythagoras remarked sententiously.

That was clear enough. Even in the distance, and experienced eye could have perceived that the horse became more and more unmanageable every moment, and the Stadtholder's seat more and more precarious. Then suddenly there came the sharp report of a pistol. The horse, goaded to madness, took the bit between its teeth, and with a final plunge bolted across country, away from that strident noise, which, twice repeated at intervals, had turned its fretfulness into blind panic.

It was at the first report that Socrates and Pythagoras again glanced at their leader. A gurgle of delight escaped them when they caught his eye. They had received their orders. The next moment all three had dug their spurs in their horses' flanks and were galloping over sand and ditch.

Diogenes' horse, given free rein at last, after the maddening curb of awhile ago, was soon half a dozen lengths ahead of the others, tearing along with all its might at right angles to the direction in which the Stadtholder's panic-stricken animal was rushing like one possessed. That direction was Ede.

5

In truth, the low-lying land veiled in sea-fog must at that moment have presented a very curious spectacle. Maurice of Nassau, Prince of Orange, the hope and pride of the Netherlands, helpless upon a horse that was running away with him straight in the direction of the nearest Spanish outposts.

Three soldiers of fortune, strangers, in the land hastening to intercept him, and a couple of hundred yards or so behind the Stadtholder, Nicolaes Beresteyn, puzzled and terror-filled at this unexpected check to his manoeuvre, pushing along for dear life.

It had been such a splendid scheme, evolved over there in the lonely mill on the Veluwe, between a reprobate and a traitor. The Spaniards on the watch. The Stadtholder helpless, whilst his mount carried him headlong into their hands. What a triumph for Stoutenburg, who had planned it all, and for Nicolaes Beresteyn, the worker of the infamous plot! The

Stadtholder prisoner in the hands of the Archduchess! His life the price of the subjection of the Netherlands!

And all to be frustrated by a foolish mischance! Three riders intent upon intercepting that runaway horse! Who in thunder were they? The mist, remember, would have blurred Nicolaes' vision. His thoughts were not just then on the man whom he hated. They were fixed upon the possibility – remote, alas! – of convincing the Stadtholder after this that the goaded horse had been the victim of a series of accidents.

Even at this moment the foremost of the three riders had overtaken the runaway. He galloped for a length or two beside it, then, with a dexterous and unerring grip, he seized the panic-stricken animal by the bridle. A few seconds of desperate struggle 'twixt man and beast. Then man remained the conqueror. The horse, panting, quivering in every limb, covered in sweat and foam, was finally brought to a standstill, and the Stadtholder in an instant had his feet clear of the stirrups and swung himself out of the saddle.

6

Then, and then only, did Nicolaes Beresteyn recognize the man who for the second time had frustrated his nefarious plans – the man whom, because of his easy triumphs, the humiliation which he had inflicted upon him, because of his careless gaiety and his very joy of life, he hated with a curious, sinister intensity.

A ferocious imprecation rose to his lips. For awhile everything became a blank. The present, the future, even the past. Everything became chaos in his mind, he could no longer think. All that he had planned became a blur, as if the sea-fog had enveloped his senses as well as the entire landscape.

But this confused mental state only lasted a very little while – a few seconds perhaps. Slowly, while he gazed on that distant group of men and horses, his perceptions became clearer once more. And even before the imprecation had died on his lips it gave place to a smile of triumph. Nicolaes Beresteyn had remembered that his Majesty the devil might well be trusted to care for his own. Had he not served the hell-born liege lord well?

For the nonce he brought his horse to a halt. It would be worse than folly to go on. With recognition of those three horsemen over there had also come the certainty that he was now irretrievably unmasked. The Stadtholder, his father, his sister, even his young wife, would turn from him in horror, as from a traitor and an outcast – a pariah, marked with the brand of Cain.

No! Henceforth, for good or for evil, his fortunes must be linked openly with Stoutenburg – with the man who wielded such a strange cabalistic power over him that he (Nicolaes) – rich, newly wed, in a highly enviable worldly position – had been ready to sacrifice his all in his cause, and to throw in the last shred of his honour into the bargain. In Stoutenburg's cause – ay, and in order to be revenged on the man who had never wronged him save in his conceit – that most vulnerable spot in the moral armour of such contemptible rogues as was Nicolaes Beresteyn.

The spot where he had brought his horse to a halt was immediately behind a low, deserted hut, which concealed him from view. Here he dismounted and, throwing the reins over his arm, advanced cautiously to a point of vantage at the angle of the little building, whence he could see what those four men were doing over there but himself remain unseen.

They, too, had dismounted, and were obviously intent on examining the Stadtholder's horse. A sinister scowl spread over Nicolaes Beresteyn's face. There was still a chance, then, of putting a bullet in one or other of those two men – the hated enemy or the Stadtholder. Nicolaes pondered; the scowl on his face became almost satanic in its expression of cruelty. Awhile ago, he had replaced his pistol in the holster, after it had served its nefarious purpose. Now he took it out again and examined it thoroughly.

It had one more charge in it, the devilish charge invented by the Borgias, the secret of which one of that infamous race had confided to Stoutenburg. The fumes from the powder when it struck the eyes must cause irretrievable blindness. Indeed, it had proved its worth already.

Nicolaes, from his hiding-place, could see those four men quite clearly. The Stadtholder, Diogenes, the two caitiffs, all standing round the one horse. Then Diogenes took something out of his belt. He raised his arm, and the next moment a sharp report rang through the mistladen air. The poor animal rolled over instantly into the mud.

The scowl on Nicolaes' face now gave place once more to a smile of triumph – more sinister than the frown. With the gesture of a conqueror, he clutched the pistol more firmly. The potent fumes had, in truth, wrought their fiendish work on the innocent beast. Diogenes had just put it out of its misery, and his two familiars were preparing to mount one of the horses, whilst he and the Stadtholder had the other two by the reins.

Why not?

The miscreant was sure enough of his aim, and the others would be unprepared. He was sure, too, of the swiftness of his horse, and the Spanish outposts were less than a quarter of a league away, whilst within half that distance Stoutenburg was on the watch with a vedette, waiting to capture the Stadtholder on his runaway horse as it had been prearranged.

Once there he – Nicolaes – would be amongst friends.

Then, why not?

Already the riders had put their horses to a trot. Diogenes and the Stadtholder on ahead, the two loons some few lengths in their rear. In less than three minutes they would be within range of Nicolaes' pistol and its blinding fumes. And Diogenes was riding on the side nearest to his enemy.

Nicolaes Beresteyn grasped his weapon more firmly. He realized with infinite satisfaction that his arm was perfectly steady. Indeed, he had never felt so absolutely calm. The measured tramp of the horses keyed him up to a point of unswerving determination. He raised his arm. The horses were galloping now. They would pass like a flash within twenty paces of him.

The next moment the sharp report of the pistol rang stridently through the mist. There was a burst, a flash, a column of smoke. Nicolaes jumped into the saddle and set spurs to his horse. The other riders went galloping on for a few seconds – not more. Then one of them swayed in his saddle. Nicolaes then was a couple of hundred yards away.

"You are hit, man!" the Stadtholder exclaimed. "That abominable assassin —"

But the words died in his throat. The reins had slipped out of Diogenes' grasp, and he rolled down into the mud.

7

A sudden jerk brought the Stadtholder's horse to a halt. He swung himself out of the saddle, ran quickly to his companion.

"You are hit, man!" he reiterated; this time with an unexplainable feeling of dread.

The other seemed so still, and yet his clothes and the soft earth around him showed no stains of blood.

Pythagoras now was also on the spot. He had slid off the horse as soon as the infamous assassin had started to ride away. Socrates was trying to give chase. Even now two pistol-shots rang out in quick succession right across the moorland. But the hell-hound was well mounted, and the avenging bullets failed to reach their mark. All this the Stadtholder took in with a rapid glance, even whilst Pythagoras, round-eyed and scared, was striving with gentle means to raise the strangely inert figure.

"He hath swooned," the Stadtholder suggested.

The stricken man had one arm across his face. His had had fallen from his head, leaving the fine, square brow free and the crisp hair weighted by the sweat of some secret agony. The mouth, too, was visible, and the chin, with its four days' growth of beard, the mouth that was always ready with a smile. It was set now in an awesome contraction of pain, and, withal, that terrible immobility.

Now Socrates was arriving. A moment or two later he, too, had dismounted, cursing lustily that he had failed to hit the hell-hound. A mute query, an equally mute reply, was all that passed between him and Pythagoras.

Then the stricken man stirred as if suddenly roused to consciousness.

"Are you hit, man?" the Stadtholder queried again.

"No – no!" he replied quickly. "Only a little dazed. That is all."

He raised himself to a sitting posture, helping himself up with his hands, which sank squelching into the mud; whereat he gave a short laugh, which somehow went a cold shiver down the listener's spines.

"Where is my hat?" he asked. "Pythagoras, you lazy loon, get me my hat."

He must indeed have been still dazed, for when his friend picked up the hat and gave it to him, his hand shot out for it quite wide of the mark. He gave another laugh, short and toneless as before, and set the hat on his head, pulling down well over his eyes.

"I had a mugful of hot ale at Amersfoort before starting," he said. "It must have got into my head."

He made no attempt to get to his feet, but just sat there, with his two slender hands all covered with mud, tightly clasped between his knees.

"Can you get to horse?" his Highness queried at last.

"No," Diogenes replied, "not just yet, an' it please you, I verily think that I would roll out of my saddle again, which would, in truth, be a disgusting spectacle."

"But we cannot leave you here, man," the Stadtholder rejoined, with a slight tone of impatience.

"And why not, I pray you?" he retorted. "Your Highness must get to Utrecht as quickly as may be. A half-drunken lout like me would only be a hindrance."

His voice was thick now and halting, in very truth like that of a man who had been drinking heavily. He rested his elbows on his knees and held his chin between his mud-stained hands.

"Socrates, you lumpish vagabond," he exclaimed all of a sudden, "don't stand gaping at me like that! Bring forth his Highness's horse at once, and see that you accompany him to Utrecht without further mishap, or 'tis with us you'll have to deal on your return!"

"But you, man!" the Stadtholder exclaimed once more.

He felt helpless and strangely disturbed in his mind, not understanding what all this meant; why this man, usually so alert, so keen, so full of vigour, appeared for the moment akin to a babbling imbecile.

"I'll have a good sleep inside that hut, so please you," the other replied more glibly. "These two ruffians will find me here after they have seen your gracious Highness safely inside your camp."

Then, as the Stadtholder still appeared to hesitate, and neither of the others seemed to move, Diogenes added, with an almost desperate note of entreaty:

"To horse, your Highness, I beg! Every second is precious. Heaven knows what further devilry lies in wait for you, if you linger here."

"Or for you, man," the Stadtholder murmured involuntarily.

"Nay, not for me!" the other retorted quickly. "The Archduchess and her gang of vultures fly after higher game than a drunken wayfarer lost on the flats. To horse, I entreat!"

And once more he pressed his hands together, and so tightly that the knuckles shone like polished ivory, even through their covering of mud.

The Stadtholder then gave a sign to the two men. It was obviously futile to continue arguing here with a man who refused to move. He himself had very rightly said that every second was precious. And every second, too, was fraught with danger. Already his Highness had well-nigh been the victim of a diabolical ambuscade, might even at this hour have been a prisoner in the hands of the enemy, a hostage of incalculable value, even if his life had been spared, but for the audacious and timely interference of this man, who now appeared almost like one partially bereft of reason.

"We'll see you safely inside the hut, at any rate," was his Highness's last word.

"And I'll not move," Diogenes retorted with a kind of savage obstinacy, "until the mist has swallowed up your gracious Highness on the road to Utrecht."

After that there was nothing more to be said. And we may take it that the Stadtholder got to horse with unaccountable reluctance. Something in that solitary figure sitting there, with the plumed hat tilted over his eyes and the slender, mud-stained hands tightly locked together, gave him a strange feeling of nameless dismay, like a premonition of some obscure catastrophic tragedy.

But his time and his safety did not belong to himself alone. They were the inalienable property of a threatened country, that would be grasping in her death-throes if she were deprived of him at this hour of renewed and deadly danger. So he gathered the reins in his hands and set spurs to his horse, and once he had started he did not look behind him, lest his emotion got the better of his judgement.

The two gossoons immediately followed in his wake. This they did because the friend they had always been wont to obey had thus commanded, and his seeming helplessness rendered his orders doubly imperative at this hour. They rode a length or two behind the Stadtholder, who presently put his horse to a gallop. Utrecht now was only a couple of leagues away.

The three horsemen galloped on for a quarter of a league or less at the same even, rapid pace. Then Pythagoras slackened speed. The others did not even turn to look at him, he seemed to have done it by tacit unspoken consent. The Stadtholder and Socrates sped on in the direction of Utrecht and Pythagoras turned his horse's head round toward the direction whence he had come.

8

The afternoon lay heavy and silent upon the plain. There was as yet no sign of the approach of the enemy from the south, and the low-lying land appeared momentarily hushed under its veil of mist, as if conscious of the guilty secret enshrined within its bosom. The fog, indeed, had thickened perceptibly. It lay like a wall around that lonely figure, still sitting there on the soft earth, with its head buried in its hands.

Far away, the gaunt-looking carcase of the dead horse appeared as the only witness of a hideous deed as yet un-recorded. Each a blurred and uncertain mass – the dead horse and the lonely figure, equally motionless, equally pathetic – were now the sole occupants of the vast and silent immensity.

Not far away, in the little town of Amersfoort, humanity, panic-stricken and terrorized, filled the air with clamour and with wails. Here, beneath the ghostly shroud of humid atmosphere, everything was stilled as if in ghoulish expectancy of something mysterious, indiscernible which was still to come. It was like the arrested breath before the tearing cry, the hush which precedes a storm.

Overhead, a flight of rooks sent their melancholy cawing through the air.

When Pythagoras was within fifty yards of his friend he dismounted, and, leading his horse by the bridle, he walked toward him. When he was quite near Diogenes put out a hand to him.

"I knew you would come back, you fat-witted nonny," he said simply.

"Socrates had to go on with the Stadtholder," the other remarked, "or he'd be here, too." Then he added tentatively: "Will you lean on my arm?"

"Yes, I'll have to do that now, old crony, shall I not?" Diogenes replied. "That devil," he murmured under his breath, "has blinded me!"

Chapter IX – Mala Fides

1

NICOLAES Beresteyn, riding like one possessed had reached Stoutenburg's encampment one hour before nightfall. He brought the news of the failure of his plan for the capture of the Stadtholder, spoke with many a muttered oath of the Englishman and his two familiars, and of how they had interposed just in the nick of time to stop the runaway horse.

"But for that cursed rogue!" he exclaimed savagely, "Maurice of Nassau would now be a prisoner in our hands. We would be holding him to ransom, earning gratitude, honours, wealth at the hands of the Archduchess. Whereas – now —"

But there was solace to the bitterness of this disappointment. The blinding powder, invented by the infamous Borgia, had done its work. The abominable rogue, the nameless adventurer, who had twice succeeded in thwarting the best-laid schemes of his lordship of Stoutenburg, had paid the full penalty for his audacity and his arrogant interference.

Blind, helpless, broken, an object now of contemptuous pity rather than of hate, he was henceforth powerless to wreak further mischief.

"Just before I put my horse to a swift gallop," Nicolaes Beresteyn had concluded, "I saw him sway in the saddle and roll down into the mud. One of the vagabonds tried to chase me; but my horse bore me well and I was soon out of his reach."

That news did, indeed compensate Stoutenburg for all the humiliation which he had endured at the hands of his successful rival in the past. A rival no longer; for the Laughing Cavalier, blind and helpless, was not like ever to return to claim his young wealthy wife and to burden her with his misery. This last tribute to the man's pluck and virility Stoutenburg paid him unconsciously. He could not visualize that splendid creature, so full of life and gaiety, and conscious of might strength, groping his way back to the side of the woman whom he had dazzled by his power.

"He would sooner die in a ditch," he muttered to himself, under his breath, "than excite her pity!"

"Then the field is clear for me!" he added exultantly; and fell to discussing with Nicolaes his chances of regaining Gilda's affections. "Do you think she ever cared for the rogue?" he queried, with a strange quiver of emotion in his harsh voice.

Nicolaes was doubtful. He himself had never been in love. He liked his young wife well enough; she was comely and rich. But love? No, he could not say.

"She'll not know what has become of him," Stoutenburg said, striving to allay his own doubts. "And women very quickly forget."

He sighed, proud of his own manly passion that had survived so many vicissitudes, and was linked to such a tenacious memory.

"We must not let her know," Nicolaes insisted.

Stoutenburg gave a short, sardonic laugh. "Are you afraid she might kill you if she did?" he queried.

Then, as the other made no reply, but stood there brooding, his soul a prey to a sudden horror, which was not unlike a vague pang of remorse, Stoutenburg concluded cynically:

"I'll give the order that every blind beggar found wandering around the city be forthwith hanged on the nearest tree. Will that allay your fears?"

Thereafter he paid no further heed to Nicolaes, whom, in his heart, he despised for a waverer and a weakling; but he gave orders to his master of the camp to make an immediate start for Amersfoort.

Amersfoort had, in the meanwhile, so De Voocht avers, become wonderfully calm. Those whose nerves would not stand the strain of seeing the hated tyrants once more within the gates of their peace-loving little city, those who had no responsibilities, and those who had families, fled at the first rumour of the enemy's approach. Indeed, for many hours the streets and open places, the quays and the sleepy, sluggish river, had on the first day been nothing short of a pandemonium. Then everything gradually became hushed and tranquil. Those who were panic-stricken had all gone by nightfall; those who remained knew the risk they were taking, and sat in their homes, waiting and pondering. Amersfoort that evening might have been a city of the dead.

Darkness set in early, and the sea-fog thickened at sundown. Some wiseacres said that the Spaniards would not come until the next day. They proved to be right. The dawn had hardly spread o'er the whole of the eastern sky on the morning of the twenty-second, when the master of the enemy's camp was heard outside the ramparts, demanding the surrender of the city.

The summons was received in absolute silence. The gates were open, and the mercenaries marched in. In battle array, with banners flying, with pikemen, halberdiers and arquebusiers; with fifes and drums and a trainload of wagons and horses, and the usual rabble of beggarly camp followers, they descended on the city like locusts; and soon every tavern was filled to overflowing with loud-voiced, swarthy, ill-mannered soldiery, and all the streets and places encumbered with their carts and their horses and their trappings.

They built a bonfire in the middle of the market-place, and all around it a crowd of out-at-elbows ruffians, men, women, and children, filled the air with their shrieks and their bibulous songs. Some four thousand troops altogether, so De Voocht states, spread themselves out over the orderly, prosperous town, invaded the houses, broke open the cellars and storehouses, made the day hideous with their noise and their roistering.

As many as could found shelter in the deserted homes of the burghers; others used the stately kerks as stabling for their horses and camping ground for themselves. The inhabitants offered no resistance. A century of unspeakable tyranny ere they had gained their freedom had taught them the stern lesson of submitting to the inevitable. The Stadtholder had ordered them to submit. Until he could come to their rescue they must swallow the bitter cup of resignation to the dregs. It could not be for long. He who before now had swept the Spanish hordes off the sacred soil of the United Provinces could do so again. It was only a case for a little patience. And patience was a virtue which these grave sons of a fighting race knew how to practise to its utmost limit.

And so the burghers of Amersfoort who had remained in the city in order to watch over its fate and over their property submitted without murmur to the arrogant demands of the invaders. Their wives ministered in proud silence to the wants of the insolent rabble. The saw their dower-chests ransacked, their effects destroyed or stolen, their provisions wasted and consumed. They waited hand and foot, like serving wenches, upon their tyrants; for, indeed, it had been the proletariat who had been the first to flee.

They even succeeded in keeping back their tears when they saw their husbands – the more noted burghers of the town – dragged as hostages before the commander of the invading troops, who had taken up his quarters in the burgomaster's house.

That commander was the Lord of Stoutenburg. In high favour with the Archduchess now, he had desired leave to carry through this expedition to Amersfoort. Private grudge against the man who had robbed him of Gilda, or lust for revenge against the Stadtholder for the execution of Olden Barneveldt, who can tell? Who can read the inner workings of a tortuous brain, or appraise the passions of an embittered heart?

Attended by all the sinister paraphernalia which he now affected, the Lord of Stoutenburg entered Amersfoort in the late afternoon as a conqueror, his eyes glowing with the sense of triumph over a successful rival and of power over a disdainful woman. The worthy citizens of the little town gazed with astonishment and dread upon his sable banner, broidered in silver with a skull and crossbones – the emblem of his relentlessness, now that the day of reckoning had come.

He rode through the city, hardly noticing its silent death-like appearance. Not one glance did he bestow on the closed shutters to the right or left of him. His eyes were fixed upon the tall pinnacled roof of the burgomaster's house, silhouetted against the western sky, the stately abode on the quay where, in the days long since gone by, he had been received as an honoured guest. Since then what a world of sorrow, of passion, of endless misery had been his lot! It seemed as if, on the day when he became false to Gilda Beresteyn in order to wed the rich and influential daughter of Marnix de St. Aldegonde, fickle fortune had finally turned her back on him. His father and brother ended their days of the scaffold; his wife, abandoned by him and broken-hearted; he himself a fugitive with a price upon his head, a potential assassin, and that vilest thing on earth, a man who sells his country to her enemies.

No wonder that, at a comparatively early age, the Lord of Stoutenburg looked a careworn and wearied man. The lines on his face were deep and harsh, his hair was turning grey at the temples. Only the fire in his deepset eyes was fierce and strong, for it was fed with the fire of an ever-enduring passion – hatred. Hatred of the Stadtholder; hatred of the nameless adventurer who had thwarted him at every turn; hatred of the woman who had shut him out wholly from her heart.

But now the hour of triumph had come. For it had schemed and lied and striven and never once given way to despair. It had come, crowned with immeasurable success. The Stadtholder – thanks to the subtle poison of an infamous Borgia, administered by a black-hearted assassin – was nothing but a physical wreck; whilst those who had brought him – Stoutenburg – to his knees three short months ago were at his mercy at last. A longing as cruel as it was vengeful had possession of his soul whenever he thought of these two facts.

His schemes were not yet mature, and he had not yet arrived at any definite conclusion as to how he would reach the ultimate goal of his desires; but this he did know – that the Stadtholder was too sick to put up a fight for Amersfoort, and that Gilda and her stranger lover were definitely parted, and both of them entirely in his power. Their fate was as absolutely in his hands as his had once been in theirs. And the Lord of Stoutenburg, with his eyes raised to the pinnacled roof of the house that sheltered the woman whom he still loved with such passionate ardour, felt that for the first time for this man a year he might count himself as almost happy.

3

Nicolaes Beresteyn was among the last to enter his native city. He did so as a shameless traitor, a dishonoured gambler who had staked his all upon a hellish die. Indeed now he seemed like a man possessed, careless of his crime, exulting in it even. The vague fear of meeting his father and Gilda eye to eye seemed somehow to add zest to his adventure. He did not know how much they knew, or what they guessed, but felt a strange thrill within his tortuous soul at the thought of standing up before them as their master, of defying them and deriding their reproaches.

His young wife he knew to be away. Her father had started off for Amsterdam with his family and his servants at the first rumour of the enemy's approach. In any case she was his. She and her wealth and Mynheer van den Poele's influence and business connexions. He – Nicolaes – who had always been second in his father's affections always subservient to Gilda and to Gilda's interests, and who since that affair in January had been treated like a skulking schoolboy in the paternal home, would now rule there as a conqueror, a protector on whose magnanimity the comfort of the entire household would depend.

These and other thoughts – memories, self-pity, rage, too, and hatred, and imputations against fate – coursed through his mind as he rode into his native city at the head of the rearguard of Stoutenburg's troops. He drew rein outside his father's house. Not the slightest stirring of his dormant conscience troubled him as he ran swiftly up the familiar stone steps.

With the heavy basket-hilt of his rapier he rapped vigorously against the stout oak panels of the door, demanding admittance in the name of the Archduchess Isabella, Sovereign Liege Lady of the Netherlands. At once the doors flew open, as if moved by a spring. Two elderly serving-men stood alone in the hall, silent and respectful.

At the sight of their young master they both made a movement as if to run to him, deluded for the moment into hopes of salvation, relief from this awful horror of imminent invasion. But he paid no heed to them. His very look chilled them and froze the words of welcome upon their lips, as he strode quickly past them into the hall.

The shades of evening were now rapidly drawing in. Except for the two serving-men, the house appeared deserted. In perfect order, but strangely still and absolutely dark. As he looked about him, Nicolaes felt as if he were in a vault. A cold shiver ran down his spine. Curtly he bade the men bring lighted candles into the banqueting-hall.

Here, too, silence and darkness reigned. In the huge monumental hearth a few dying embers were still smouldering, casting a warm glow upon the red tiles, and flicking the knobs and excrescences of the brass tools with minute crimson sparks.

Nicolaes felt his nerves tingling. He groped his way to one of the windows, and with an impatient hand tore at the casement. Stoutenburg's troops were now swarming everywhere. The quay was alive with movement. Some of the soldiers were bivouacking against the house, had build up a fire, the ruddy glow of which, together with the flicker of resin torches, thew a weird and uncertain light into the room. Nicolaes felt his teeth chattering with cold. His hands were like fire. Could it be that he was afraid – afraid that in a moment or two he would hear familiar footsteps coming down the stairs, that in a moment or two he would have to face the outraged father, come to curse his traitor son?

Bah! This was sheer cowardice! But a brief while ago he had exulted in his treachery, gloried in his callous disregard of his monstrous crime. How it seemed to him that a pair of sightless yet still mocking eyes glared at him from out the gloom. With a shudder and a quickly smothered cry of horror, Nicolaes buried his face in his hands.

The next moment the two serving-men came in, carrying lighted candles in heavy silver candelabra. These they set upon the table; and one of them, kneeling beside the hearth, plied the huge bellows, coaxing the dying embers into flame. After which they stood respectfully by, awaiting further commands. Obviously they had had their orders – absolute obedience and all those outward forms of respect which they were able to accord. Nicolaes looked at them with a fierce, defying glance. He knew them both well. Greybeards in the service of his father, they had seen the young master grow up from cradle to this hour when he stood, a rebel and a skunk, on the paternal hearth.

But they did not flinch under his glance. They knew that they had been specially chosen for the unpleasant task of waiting upon the enemy commanders because their tempers had no longer the ebullience of youth, and they might be trusted to remain calm in the face of arrogance or even of savagery – even in the face of Mynheer Nicolaes, the child they had loved, the youth they had admired, now a branded traitor, who had come like a thief in the night to barter his honour for a crown of shame.

4

A certain commotion outside on the quay proclaimed the fact that the commander of the troops, the Lord of Stoutenburg, had entered the town at the head of his bodyguard, and followed by his master of the camp and his equerries.

He, too, made straight for the burgomaster's house, brought his horse to a halt at the foot of the stone steps. With a curt nod, Nicolaes bade the old crones to run to the front door and receive his Magnificence. In this, as in everything else, the men obeyed at once and in silence.

But already Stoutenburg, preceded by his equerries and his torchbearers, had stepped across the threshold. He knew his way well about the house. As boys, he and his brother Groeneveld had played their games in and around the intricate passages and stairs. As a young man he had sat in the deep window embrasures, holding Gilda's hand, taking delight in terrifying her with his impetuous love, and forcing her consent to his suit by his masterful wooing. A world of memories, grave and gay, swept over him as he entered the banqueting-hall, where, but for his many misfortunes – as he callously called h is crimes – he would one day have sat at the bridegroom's table beside Gilda, his plighted wife.

Both he and Nicolaes felt unaccountably relieved at meeting one another here. For both of them, no doubt, the silence and gloom of this memory-haunted house would in the long run have proved unendurable.

"I did not know that I should meet you here," Stoutenburg exclaimed, as he grasped his friend by the hand.

"I thought it would be best," Nicolaes replied curtly.

But this warm greeting from the infamous arch-traitor, in the presence of the two loyal old servants, brought a hot flush to the young man's brow. The last faint warning from his drugged conscience, mayhap. But the feeling of shame faded away as swiftly as it had come, and the next moment he was standing by, impassive and seemingly unconcerned, while the Lord of Stoutenburg gave his orders to the men.

These orders were to prepare the necessary beds for my lord and for Mynheer Nicolaes Beresteyn, also for the equerries, and proper accommodation for my lord's bodyguard, which consisted of twenty musketeers with their captain. Moreover, to provide supper for his Magnificence and mynheer in the banqueting-hall, and for the rest of the company in some other suitable room, without delay.

The two old crones took the orders in silence, bowed, and prepared to leave the room.

"Stay," my lord commanded. "Where is the burgomaster?"

"In his private apartments, so please you," one of the men replied.

"And his daughter?"

"The jongejuffrouw is with Mynheer the Burgomaster."

"Tell them both I want them to sup here with me and Mynheer Nicolaes."

Again the men bowed with the same silent dignity. It was impossible to gather from their stolid, mask-like faces what their thoughts might be at this hour. When they had gone, Stoutenburg peremptorily dismissed his equerries.

"If you have anything to complain of in this house," he said curtly, "come and report to me at once. To-morrow we leave at dawn."

Both the equerries gave a gasp of astonishment.

"To-morrow?" one of them murmured, apparently quite taken aback by this order.

"At dawn," Stoutenburg reiterated briefly.

This was enough. Neither did the equerries venture on further remarks. They had served for some time now under his Magnificence, knew his obstinacy and the irrevocableness of his decisions when once he had spoken.

"No further commands until then, my lord?" was all that the spokesman said.

"None for you," Stoutenburg replied curtly. "But tell Jan that the moment – the moment, you understand – that the burgomaster enters this room, he is to be prevented from doing any mischief. If he carries a weapon, he must at once be disarmed; if he resists, there should be a length of rope handy wherewith to tie his hands behind his back. But otherwise I'll not have him hurt. Understand?"

"Perfectly, my lord," the equerry gave answer. " 'Tis simple enough."

5

Now the two friends – brothers in crime – were alone in the vast, panelled hall.

Nicolaes had said nothing, made no movement of indignation or protest, when the other delivered his monstrous and treacherous commands against the personal liberty of the burgomaster. He had sat sullen and glowering, his head resting against his hand.

Stoutenburg looked down on him for a moment or two, his deep-set eyes full of that contempt which he felt for this weak-kneed and conscience-plagued waverer. Then he curtly advised him to leave the room.

"You might not think it seemly," he remarked with a sneer, "to be present when I take certain preventive measures against your father. These measures are necessary, else I would not take them. You would not have him spitting some of our men, or mayhap do himself or Gilda some injury, would you?"

"I was not complaining," Nicolaes retorted dryly.

Indeed, he obeyed readily enough. Now that the time had come to meet his father, he shrank from the ordeal with horror. It would have come, of course; but, like all weak natures, Nicolaes was always on the side of procrastination. He rose without another word, and, avoiding the main door of the banqueting-hall, he went out by the back one, which gave on a narrow antechamber and thence on the service staircase.

"I'll remain in the ante-chamber," he said. "Call me when you wish."

Stoutenburg shrugged his shoulders. He was glad to remain alone for awhile – alone with that wealth of memories which would not be chased away. Memories of childhood, of adolescence, of youth untainted with crime; of love, before greed and ambition had caused him to betray so basely the girl who had believed in him.

"If Gilda had remained true to me," he sighed, with almost cynical inconsequence, exacting fidelity where he had given none. "If she had stuck to me that night in Haarlem everything would have been different."

He went up to the open window, and, leaning his arm against the mullion, he gazed upon the busy scene below. The current of cold, humid air appeared to do him good. His arquebusiers and pikemen, bivouacking round the spluttering fires, striving to keep the damp air out of their stiffening limbs; the shouts, the songs, the peremptory calls; the shrieks of frightened women and children; the loud Spanish oaths; the medley of curses in every tongue – all this confused din pertaining to strife seemed to work like a tonic upon his brooding spirit. A blind beggar soliciting alms among the soldiery chased all softer thoughts away.

"Hey, there!" he shouted fiercely, to one of the soldiers who happened just then to have caught his eye, "Have I not given orders that every blind beggar lurking around the city be hung to the nearest tree?"

The men laughed. A monstrously tyrannical order such as that suited their present mood.

"But this one was inside the city, so please your Magnificence," one of them protested with a cynical laugh, "when we arrived."

"All the more reason why he should be hung forthwith!" Stoutenburg riposted savagely in reply.

A loud guffaw greeted this inhuman order. His Magnificence was loudly cheered, his health drunk in deep goblets of stolen wine. Then a search was made for the blind beggar. But he, luckily for himself, had in the meanwhile taken to his heels.

6

The next moment a slight noise behind him caused the Lord of Stoutenburg to turn on his heel. The door had been thrown open, and the burgomaster, having his daughter on his arm, stood upon the threshold. He was dressed in his robes of office, with black cloak and velvet bonnet; but he wore a steel gorget round his neck and rapier by his side.

At the sight of his arch enemy, he had paused under the lintel, and the ashen pallor of his cheeks became more marked. But he had no time to move, for in an instant Jan and three or four men were all around him.

At this treacherous onslaught a fierce oath escaped Beresteyn's lips. In an instant his sword was out of its scabbard, he himself at bay, covering Gilda with his body, and facing the men who had thus scurrilously rushed on him out of the gloom.

But obviously resistance was futile. Already he was surrounded and disarmed, Gilda torn forcibly away from him, thrust into a corner, whilst he himself was rendered helpless, even though he fought and struggled magnificently. The whole unequal combat had only lasted a few seconds; and now the grand old man stood like a fettered lion, glowering and defiant, his hands tied behind his back with a length of rope, against which he was straining with all his might.

One of the most disloyal pitfalls ever devised against an unsuspecting civilian – and he the chief dignitary of a peace-loving city. Stoutenburg watched the scene with an evil glitter in his restless eyes. Shame and compunction did, in truth, bear no part in his emotions at this moment. He was exulting in the thought of his vile stratagem, pleased that he had thought of enticing Gilda hither by summoning her father at the same time. It was amusing to watch them both – the burgomaster still dignified, despite his helplessness, and Gilda beautiful in her indignation. By St. Bavon, the girl was lovely, and still desirable. And thank Beelzebub and all the powers of darkness who lent their aid in placing so exquisite a prize in the hands of the conqueror.

Stoutenburg could have laughed aloud with glee. As it was, he made an effort to appear both masterful and indifferent. He knew that he could take his time, that any scheme which he might formulate for his own advancement and the satisfaction of his every ambition was now certain of success. The future was entirely his, to plan and mould at will.

So now he deliberately turned back to the window, closed it with a hand that had not the slightest tremor in it. Then he returned to the centre of the room, sat down beside the table, and took on a cool and judicial air. All his movements were consciously slow. He looked at the burgomaster and at Gilda with ostentatious irony, remained silent for awhile as if in pleasant contemplation of their helplessness. "You are in suspense," his silence seemed to express. "You know that your fate is in my hands. But I can afford to wait, to take mine ease. I am lord of the future, and you are little better than my slaves."

"Was it not foolishness to resist, mynheer?" he said at last, in a tone of gentle mockery. "Bloodshed, eh? In truth, the role of fire-eater ill becomes your dignity and your years."

"Spare me your insults, my lord," Beresteyn retorted, with calm dignity. "What is your pleasure with my daughter and with me?"

"I will tell you anon," Stoutenburg replied coolly, "when you are more composed."

"I am ready now to hear your commands."

"Quite submissive, eh?" the other retorted with a sneer.

"No; only helpless, and justly indignant at this abominable outrage."

"Also surprised – what? – at seeing me here to-night?"

"In truth, my lord, I had not expected to see the son of Olden Barneveldt at the head of enemy troops."

"Or your son in his train, eh?"

The burgomaster winced at the taunt. But he rejoined quite simply:

"If what rumour says is true, my lord, then I have no son."

"If," Stoutenburg retorted dryly, "rumour told you that Nicolaes Beresteyn hath returned to his allegiance, then the jade did not lie. Your son, mynheer, hath shown you which way loyalty lies. Not in the service of a rebel prince, but in that of Archduchess Isabella, our Sovereign Liege."

He paused, as if expecting some word of reply from the burgomaster; but as the latter remained silent, he went on more lightly:

"But enough of this. Whether you, Mynheer Beresteyn, and your son do make up your differences presently is no concern of mine. You will see him anon, no doubt, and can then discuss your family affairs at your leisure. For the nonce, I do desire to know whether your city intends to be submissive. I have exercised great leniency up to this hour; but you must remember that I am equally ready to punish at the slightest sign of contumely or of resistance to my commands."

"For the leniency to which the Lord of Stoutenburg lays claim," Beresteyn rejoined with perfect dignity, "in that, up to this hour he has not murdered our peaceful citizens, burned down our houses, or violated our homes, we tender him our thanks. As for the future, the treacherous pitfall into which I have fallen, and the unwarrantable treatment that is meted out to me, will mayhap prove to my unfortunate fellow-citizens that resistance to overwhelming force is worse than useless."

"Excellent sentiments, mynheer!" Stoutenburg retorted. "Dictated, I make no doubt, by one who knows the usages of war."

"We do all of us," the burgomaster gave quiet answer, "obey the behests of our Stadtholder, our Sovereign Liege."

"The rebel prince, mynheer, who, by commanding you to submit, hath for once gauged rightly the temper of the Sovereign whom he hath outraged. Will you tell me, I pray you," Stoutenburg added, with a sardonic grin, "whether the jongejuffrouw your daughter is equally prepared to obey Maurice of Nassau's behests and submit to my commands?"

At this cruel thrust an almost imperceptible change came over the burgomaster's calm, dignified countenance; and even this change was scarce noticeable in the uncertain, flickering light of the wax candles. Perhaps he had realized, for the first time, the full horror of his position, the full treachery of the snare which had been laid for him, and which left him, pinioned and helpless, at the mercy of an unscrupulous and cowardly enemy. Not only him, but also his daughter.

A groan like that of a wounded beast escaped his lips, and his powerful arms and shoulders strained at the cords that fettered him. Nevertheless, after a very brief moment of silence he rejoined with perfect outward calm:

"My daughter, my lord, was under my protection until vile treachery rendered me helpless. Now that her father can no longer watch over her, she is under the protection of every man of honour."

"That is excellently said, mynheer," Stoutenburg replied. "And in a few words you have put the whole situation tersely and clearly. You have orders from the Stadtholder to obey my commands; therefore I do but make matters easier for you by having you removed to your apartments, instead of merely commanding you to return thither – an order which, if you were free, you might have been inclined to disobey."

"A truce on your taunts, my lord!" broke in the burgomaster firmly. "What is your pleasure with us?"

"Just what I have had the honour to tell you," Stoutenburg replied coolly. "That you return forthwith to your apartments."

"But my daughter, my lord?"

"She sups here, with her brother Nicolaes and with me."

" 'Tis only my dead body you'll drag away from here," the burgomaster rejoined quietly.

Once more Stoutenburg broke into that harsh, mirthless laugh which had become habitual to him and which seemed to find its well-spring in the bitterness of his soul.

"Fine heroics, mynheer!" he said derisively. "But useless, I fear me, and quite unnecessary. Were I to assure you that your daughter hath ceased to rouse the slightest passion in my heart or to stir my senses in any way, you would mayhap not credit me. Yet such is the case. The jongejuffrouw, I'll have you believe, will be as safe with me as would the ugliest old hag out of the street."

"Nevertheless, my lord," Beresteyn rejoined with calm dignity, "whilst I live I remain by my daughter's side."

Stoutenburg shrugged his shoulders.

"Jan," he called, "take mynheer the burgomaster back to his apartments. I have no further use for him."

7

Mynheer Beresteyn was still a comparatively young and vigorous man. In his day, he had been counted one of the finest soldiers in the armies of the Prince of Orange, and had accomplished prodigies of skill and valour at Turnhout and Ostend. The feeling that at this moment, when he would have given his life to protect his daughter, he was absolutely helpless, was undoubtedly the most cruel blow he had ever had to endure at the hands of Fate. His eyes, pathetic in their mute appeal for forgiveness, sought those of Gilda. She had remained perfectly still all this while, silent in the dark corner whither Jan and the soldiers had thrust her at their first onslaught on the burgomaster. But she had watched the whole scene with ever-increasing horror, not at thought of herself, of her own danger, only of her father and all that he must be suffering. Now her one idea was to reassure him, to ease the burden of sorrow and of wrath which his own impotence must have laid upon his brave soul.

Before any of the men could stop her, she had evaded them. Swift and furtive as a tiny lizard, she had wormed her way between them to her father's side. Now she had her arms round his neck, her head against his breast.

"Do not be anxious because of me, father dear," she whispered under her breath. "God hath us all in His keeping. Have no fear for me."

A deep groan escaped the old man's breast. His eyes, fierce and indignant, rested with an expression of withering contempt upon his enemy.

"Jan," Stoutenburg broke in harshly, "didst not hear my commands?"

Four pairs of hands immediately closed upon the burgomaster. He, like a creature at bay, started to struggle.

"Some one knock that old fool on the head!" his lordship shouted with a fierce oath.

And Jan raised his fist, overwilling to obey. But, with a loud cry of indignation, Gilda had already interposed. She seized the man's wrist with her own small hands and turned flaming eyes upon Stoutenburg.

"Violence is unnecessary, my lord," she said, vainly striving to speak coolly and firmly. "My father will go quietly, and I will remain here to listen to what you have to say."

"Bravely spoken!" Stoutenburg rejoined with a sneer. "And you, Mynheer Beresteyn, would do well to learn wisdom at so fair a source. You and your precious daughter will come to no harm if you behave like reasonable beings. There is such a thing," he added cynically, "as submitting to the inevitable."

"Do not trust him, Gilda," the old man cried. "False to his country, false to his wife and kindred, every word which he utters is a lie or a blasphemy."

"Enough of this wrangle," Stoutenburg exclaimed, wrathful and hoarse. "Jan, take that ranting dotard away!"

Then it was that, just before the men had time to close in all round the burgomaster, Gilda, placing one small, white hand upon her father's arm, pointed with the other to the door at the far end of the room. Instinctively the old man's glance turned in that direction. The door was open, and Nicolaes stood upon the threshold. He had heard his father's voice, Stoutenburg's brutal commands, his sister's cry of indignation.

"Nicolaes is here, father dear," Gilda said simply. "God knows that he is naught but an abominable traitor, yet methinks that even he hath not fallen so low as to see his own sister harmed before his eyes."

At sight of his son an indefinable look had spread over the burgomaster's face. It seemed as if an invisible and ghostly hand had drawn a filmy grey veil all over it. And a strange hissing sound – the intaking of a laboured sigh – burst through his tightly set lips.

"Go!" he cried to his son, in a dull, toneless voice, which nevertheless could be heard, clear and distinct as a bell, from end to end of the vast hall. "A father's curse is potent yet, remember!"

Nicolaes broke into a forced and defiant laugh, tried to assume a jaunty, careless air, which ill agreed with his pallid face and wild, scared eyes. But, before he could speak, Jan and the soldiers had finally seized the burgomaster and forcefully dragged him out of the room.

Chapter X – A Prince of Darkness

1

GILDA had seen her father dragged away from her side without a tear. Whatever tremor of apprehension made her heart quiver after she had seen the last of him, she would not allow these two men to see.

She was not afraid. When a woman has suffered as Gilda had suffered during these past two days, there is no longer in her any room for fear. Not for physical fear, at any rate. All her thoughts, her hopes, her anxieties were concentrated on the probable fate of her beloved. That unerring instinct which comes to human beings when they are within measurable distance of some acute, unknown danger amounts at times to second sight. This was the case with Gilda. With the eyes of her soul she could see and read something of what went on in her enemy's tortuous brain. She could see that he knew something about her beloved, and that he meant to use that knowledge for his own abominable ends. What these were she could not divine. Prescience did not go quite so far. But it had served her in this, that when her father was taken away she had just sufficient time and strength of will to brace herself up for the ordeal which was to come.

It is always remarkable when a woman, young and brought up in comparative seclusion and ignorance, is able to face moral danger with perfect calm and cool understanding. It was doubly remarkable in the case of a young girl like Gilda. She was only just twenty, had been the idol of her father; motherless, she had no counsels from those of her own sex, and there are always certain receptacles in a woman's soul which she will never reveal to the most loving, most indulgent father.

Three months ago, this same absolutely innocent, unsophisticated girl had suddenly been confronted with the vehement, turbulent passions of men. She had seen them in turmoil all round her – love, hatred, vengeance, treachery – she herself practically the pivot around which they raged. Out of the deadly strife she had emerged pure, happy in the arms of the man whom her wondrous adventures as much as his brilliant personality had taught her to love.

Since then her life had been peaceful and happy. She had allowed herself to be worshipped by that strangely captivating lover of hers, whose passionately wilful temperament, tempered by that persistent, sunny gaiety she had up to now only half understood. He made her laugh always made her taste a strange and exquisite bliss when he held her in his arms. But withal she had up till now kept an indulgent smile in reserve for his outbursts of vehemence, for his wayward, ofttimes irascible moods, his tearing impatience when she was away from him. Her love for him in the past had been almost motherly in its tenderness.

Somehow, with his absence, with the danger which threatened him, all that had become changed, intensified. The tenderness was still in her heart for him, an exquisite tenderness which caused her sheer physical ache now, when her mind conjured up that brief vision which she had had of him yesterday morning, wearied, with shoulders bent, his face haggard above a three-day's growth of beard, his eyes red-rimmed and sunken. But with that tenderness there was mingled at this hour a feeling which was akin to fierceness – the primeval desire of the woman to defend and protect her beloved – that same tearing impatience with Fate, of which he had been wont to suffer, for keeping him away from her sheltering arms.

Oh, she understood his vehemence now! No longer could she smile at his fretfulness. She, too, was a prey at this hour to a wildly emotional mood, tempest-tossed and spirit-stirring; her very soul crying out for him. And she hated – ay, hated with an intensity which she herself scarcely could apprise – this man whom she knew to be his deadly enemy.

"Sit down, sister; you are overwrought."

Nicolaes' cool, casual words brought her straightway back to reality. Quietly, mechanically she took the seat which he was offering – a high-backed, velvet-covered chair – the one in which the Stadtholder had sat at her wedding feast. She closed her eyes, and sat for a moment or two quite still. Visions of joy and of happiness must not obtrude their softly insidious presence beside the stern demands of the moment. Stoutenburg brought a footstool, and placed it to her feet. She felt him near her, but would not look on him, and he remained for awhile on his knees close beside her, she unable to move away from him.

"How beautiful you are!" he murmured, under his breath.

Her hand was resting on the arm of her chair. She felt his lips upon it, and quickly drew it back, wiping it against her gown as if a slimy worm had left its trail upon her fingers Seeing which, he broke into a savage curse and jumped to his feet.

"I thank you for the reminder, mejuffrouw," he said coldly.

After which he sat down once more beside the long centre table, at some little distance from her, but so that the light from the candles fell upon her dainty figure, graceful and dignified against the background of the velvet-covered chair, the while his own face remained in shadow. Nicolaes, nervous and restless, was pacing up and down the room.

3

"Allow me, mejuffrouw," Stoutenburg began coolly after awhile, "to tender you my sincere regrets for the violence to which necessity alone compelled me to subject the burgomaster; a worthy man, for whom, believe me, I entertain naught but sincere regard."

"I pray you, my lord," she retorted with complete self-possession, "to spare me this mockery. Had you not determined to put an insult on me, an insult which, apparently, you dared not formulate in the presence of my father. You had not, of a certainty subjected him to such an outrage."

"You misunderstand my motives, mejuffrouw. There was, and is, no intention on my part to insult you. Surely, as you yourself very rightly said just now, your brother's presence is sufficient guarantee for that."

"I said that, in order to quieten my father's fears. The treacherous snare which you laid for him, my lord, is proof enough of your cowardly intentions."

"You do yourself no good, mejuffrouw," rejoined the lord of Stoutenburg harshly, "by acrimony or defiance. I had to lure your father hither, else he would not have allowed you to come. Violence to you – though you may not believe it – would be repellent to me. But, having got you both here, I had to rid myself of him, using what violence was necessary."

"And why, I pray you, had you, as you say, to rid yourself of my father? Were you afraid of him?"

"No," he replied; "but I am compelled to put certain matters before you for your consideration, and did not desire that you should be influenced by him."

A quick sigh of satisfaction – or was it excitement? – escaped her breast. Fretful of all these preliminaries, which she felt were but the opening gambits of his dangerous game, she was thankful that, at last, he was coming to the point.

"Let us begin, mejuffrouw," Stoutenburg resumed, after a moment's deliberation, "by assuring you that the whereabouts of that gallant stranger who goes by the name of Diogenes are known to me and to your brother Nicolaes. To no one else."

He watched her keenly while he spoke. Shading his eyes with his hand, he took in every transient line of her face, noted the pallor of her cheeks, the pathetic droop of the mouth. But he was forced to own that at that curt announcement, wherewith he had intended to startle and to hurt, not the slightest change came over her. She still sat there, cool and impassive, her head resting against the velvet cushion of the chair, the flickering light of the candle playing with the loose tendrils of her golden hair. Her eyes he could not see, for they were downcast, veiled by the delicate, blue-veined lids; but of a surety, not the slightest quiver marred the perfect stillness of her lips.

In truth, she had expected some such statement from that execrable traitor. Her intuition had not erred when it told her that, in some subtle, devilish way, he would use the absence of her beloved as a tool wherewith to gain what he had in view. Now what she realized most vividly was that she must not let him see that she was afraid. Not even let him guess if she were hurt. She must keep up a semblance of callousness before her enemy for as long as she could. With her self-control, she would lose her most efficacious weapon. Therefore, for the next minute or two, she dared not trust herself to speak, lest her voice, that one uncontrollable thing, betrayed her.

"I await your answer, mejuffrouw," Stoutenburg resumed impatiently, after awhile.

"You have asked me no question, my lord," she rejoined simply. "Only stated a fact. I but wait to hear your further pleasure."

"My pleasure, fair one," he went on lightly, "is only to prove to you that I, as ever before, am not only your humble slave but also your sincere friend."

"A difficult task, my lord. But let me see, without further preamble, I pray you, how you intend to set about it."

"By trying to temper your sorrow with my heartfelt sympathy," he murmured softly.

"My sorrow?"

"I am forced to impart sad news to you, alas!"

"My husband is dead?" The cry broke from her heart, and this time she was unable to check it. Will and pride had been easy enough at first. Oh, how easy! But not now. Not in the face of this! She would have given worlds to appear calm, incredulous. But how could she? How could she, when such a torturing vision had been conjured up before her eyes?

For a moment it seemed as if reason itself began to totter. She looked on the man before her, and he appeared like a ghoulish fiend, with grinning jaws and sinister eyes, the play of light behind him making his face appear black and hideous. She put her hands up to her face, closed her eyes, and, oh, Heaven, how she prayed for strength!

None indeed but an implacable enemy, a jealous suitor, could have seen such soul-agony without relenting. But Stoutenburg was one of those hard natures which found grim pleasure in wounding and torturing. His love for Gilda, intensely passionate but never tender, was nothing now but fierce desire for mastership of her and vengeance upon his successful rival. The girl's involuntary cry of misery had been as balm to his evil soul. Now her hands dropped once more on her lap. She looked at him straight between the eyes, her own still a little wild, lit by a feverish brightness.

"You have killed him," she said huskily. "Is that it? Answer me! You have killed him?"

He put up his hand, smiling, as if to soothe a crying child.

"Nay! On my honour!" he replied quietly. "I have not seen that gallant adventurer these three months past."

"Well, then?"

"Ask your brother Nicolaes, fair one. He saw him but a few hours ago."

"Ay, yesterday," she retorted. "When he tried to assassinate him. I saw the murderous hand uplifted; I saw it all I tell you! And in my heart I cursed my only brother for the vile traitor that he is. But, thank Heaven, my lord was only hurt. I believe —"

She paused, put her hand up to her throat. The glance in Stoutenburg's eyes gave her a feeling as if she were about to choke.

"You are quite right, mejuffrouw," he broke in drily, "in believing that the intrepid Englishman who, for reasons best known to himself, hath chosen to meddle in the affairs of this country – that he, I say, was only hurt when your brother interposed yesterday betwixt him and the Stadtholder. The two ragamuffins who usually hang around him did probably save him from further punishment at the moment. But not altogether. Nicolaes will tell you that, half an hour later, that same intrepid and meddlesome English gentleman did once more try to interfere in the affairs of our Sovereign Liege the Archduchess Isabella. This time with serious consequences to himself."

"My brother Nicolaes," she murmured, more quietly this time, "hath killed my husband?"

"No, no!" here broke in Nicolaes at last. "The whole thing, I vow, was the result of an accident."

"What whole thing?" she reiterated slowly. "I pray you to be more explicit. What hath happened to my husband?"

"The explosion of a pistol," Nicolaes stammered, shamed out of his defiance at seeing his sister's misery, yet angered with himself for this weakness. "He is not dead, I swear!"

"Maimed?" she asked.

"Blind," Nicolaes replied, "but otherwise well. I swear it!" he protested, shutting his ears to Stoutenburg's scornful laugh, his eyes to the other's sardonic grin, his miserably weak nature swaying like a pendulum 'twixt his ambition, his hatred of the once brilliant soldier of fortune, and his dormant tenderness for the sweet and innocent sister to whom his treacherous hand had dealt such a devilish blow.

There was silence in the room now. Gilda had uttered no cry when that same blow fell on her like a crash. It had seemed to snap the very threads that held her to life. One sigh, and one only, came through her lips, like the dying call of a wounded bird. All feeling, all emotion, seemed suddenly to have died out of her, leaving her absolutely numb, scarcely conscious, with wide, unseeing eyes staring straight out before her, striving to visualize that splendid creature, that embodiment of gaiety, of laughter, of careless insouciance, stricken with impotence; those merry, twinkling eyes sightless. The horror of it was so appalling that it placed her for the moment beyond the power of suffering. She was not a human being now at all; she had no soul, no body, no life. Her senses had ceased to be. She neither saw nor heard nor felt. She was just a thing, a block of insentient stone into which life would presently begin to trickle slowly, bringing with it a misery such as could not be endured even by lost souls in hell.

How the time went by she did not know.

Just before this awful thing had happened she had chanced to look at the clock. It was then five minutes to eight. But all this was in the past. She no longer heard the ticking of the clock, nor her enemy's laboured breathing, nor Nicolaes' shuffling footsteps at the far end of the room. Fortunately, she could not see the triumph, the ominous sparkle, which glittered in Stoutenburg's eyes. He knew well enough what she suffered, or would be suffering anon when consciousness would return. Knew and revelled in it. He was like those inquisitors, the unclean spirits that waited on Spanish tyranny, who found their delight in watching the agony of their victims on the rack; who treasured every groan, exulted over every cry, wrung by unendurable bodily pain. Only with him it was the moral agony of those whom he desired to master that caused him infinite bliss. His stygian nature attained a demoniacal satisfaction out of the mental torture which he was able to inflict.

It is an undoubted fact that even the closest scrutiny of contemporary chronicles has failed to bring to light a single redeeming feature in this man's character, and all that the most staunch supporters of the Barneveldt family can bring forward in mitigation of Stoutenburg's crimes is the fact that his whole soul had been warped by the judicial murder of his father and of his elder brother, by his own consequent sufferings and those of his unfortunate mother.

4

"You will, I hope, mejuffrouw, give me the credit of having tried to break this sad news to you as gently as I could."

The words, spoken in smooth, silky tones were the first sounds that reached Gilda's returning perceptions. What had occurred in between she had not the vaguest idea. She certainly was still sitting in the same chair, with that sinister creature facing her, and her brother Nicolaes skulking somewhere in the gloom. The fire was still cracking in the hearth, the clock still ticking with insentient monotony. A tiny fillet of air caused the candle-light to flicker, and sent a thin streak of smoke upwards in an ever-widening spiral.

That streak of smoke was the first thing that Gilda saw. It arrested her eyes, brought her back slowly to consciousness. Then came Stoutenburg's hypocritical tirade. Her senses were returning one by one. She even glanced up at the clock. It marked three minutes before eight. Only two minutes had gone by. One hundred and twenty seconds. And they appeared longer than the most phantasmagoric conception of eternity. Two minutes! And she realized that she was alive, that she could feel, and that her beloved was sightless. Was it at all strange that, with return to pulsating life, there should arise within her that indestructible attribute of every human heart – a faint germ of hope?

When first the awful truth was put before her by her bitterest foe, she had not been conscious of the slightest feeling of doubt. Nicolaes' stammering protests, his obvious desire to minimise his own share of responsibility, had all helped to confirm the revelation of a hideous crime.

"He is not dead, I swear!" and "He is not otherwise hurt!" which broke from the dastard's quaking lips at the moment, had left no room for doubt or hope. At least, so she thought. And even now that faint ray of light in the utter blackness of her misery was too elusive to be of any comfort. But it helped her to collect herself, to look those two craven miscreants in the face. Nicolaes obviously dared not meet her glance, but Stoutenburg kept his eyes fixed upon her, and the look of triumph in them whipped up her dormant pride.

And now, when his double-tongued Pharisaism reached her ear, she swallowed her dread, bade horror be stilled. She knew that he was about to place an "either--or" before her which would demand her full understanding, and all the strength of mind and body that she could command. The fate of her beloved was about to be dangled before her, and she would be made to choose – what?

"You began, my lord," she said, with something of her former assurance – and God alone knew what it cost her to speak – "by saying that you desired to place certain matters before me for my consideration. I have not yet heard, remember, what those matters are."

"True – true!" he rejoined, with hypocritical unction. "But I felt it my duty – my sad duty, I may say —"

"A truce on this hollow mockery!" she riposted. "I pray you, come to the point."

"The point is, fair one, that both Nicolaes and I desire to compass your welfare," he retorted blandly.

"This you can do best at this hour, my lord, by allowing me to return to the privacy of mine apartments."

"So you shall, myn engel – so you shall," he rejoined suavely. "You will need time to prepare for departure."

She frowned, puzzled this time.

"For departure?" she asked, a little bewildered.

"I leave this town to-morrow at the head of my troops."

"Thank God for that!" she rejoined earnestly.

"And you, mejuffrouw," he added curtly, "will accompany us."

"I?" she asked, not altogether understanding, the frown more deeply marked between her brows.

"Methought I spoke clearly," he went on, in his habitual harsh, peremptory tone. "I only came to this town in order to fetch you, myn engel. To-morrow we go away together."

"The folly of human grandeur hath clouded your brain, my lord!" she said coldly.

"In what way?" he queried, still perfectly bland and mild.

"You know well that I would sooner die than follow you."

"I know well that most women are over-ready with heroics. But," he added, with a shrug of the shoulders, "these tantrums usually leave me cold. You are an intelligent woman, mejuffrouw, and you have seen your valiant father resign himself to the inevitable."

"I pray you waste no words, my lord," she rejoined coolly. "Three months ago, when at Ryswick, your crimes found you out, and you strove to involve me in your own disgrace and ruin, I gave you mine answer – the same that I do now. My dead body you can take with you, but I, alive, will never follow you!"

" 'Twas different then," he retorted, with a cynical smile. "You had a fortune-hunting adventurer to hand who was determined to see that your father's shekels did not lightly escape his grasp. To-day––"

"To-day," she retorted, and rose to her feet, fronted him now, superb with indignation, "he is sightless, absent, impotent, you would say, to protect me against your villainy! You miserable, slinking cur!"

Stoutenburg's harsh, forced laugh broke in upon her wrath.

"Ah!" he exclaimed lightly. "You little spit-fire! In very truth, I like you better in that mood. Heroics do not become you, myn schat, and they are so unnecessary. Did you perchance imagine that it was love for you that hath influenced my decision to take you away from here?"

"I pray God, my lord, that I be not polluted by as much as a thought from you!"

"Your prayers have been granted, fair one," he retorted with a sneer. " 'Tis but seldom I think of you now, save as an exquisite little termagant whom it will amuse me to tame. But this is by the way. That pleasure will lose nothing by procrastination. You know me well enough by now to realise that I am not likely to be lenient with you after your vixenish treatment of me. For the nonce, I pray you to keep a civil tongue in your head," he added roughly. "On your conduct at this hour will depend your future comfort. Nicolaes will not always be skulking in dark corners, ready to interfere if my manner become too rough."

"He is here now," she said boldly, "and if there is a spark of honour left in him he will conduct me to my rooms!"

With this she turned and walked steadily across the room. Even so his harsh laugh accompanied her as far as the door. When her hand was upon the knob, he called lightly after her:

"The moment you step cross the threshold, myn schat, Jan will bring you back here – in his arms!"

5

Instinctively she paused, realizing that the warning had come just in time – that the next moment, in very truth, she would be in the hands of those vile traitors who were there ready to obey their master's every command. She paused, too, in order to murmur a quick prayer for Divine guidance, seeing that human protection was denied her at this hour. What could she do? She was like a bird caught in a snare from which there seemed to be no issue. Stoutenburg's sneering laugh rang in her ear. He was beside her now, took her hand from the knob and held it for a moment forcibly in his. His glance, charged with cruel mockery, took in every line of her pallid face.

"Heroics again, fair one!" he said, with an impish grin. "Must I assure you once more that you are perfectly safe with me? See, if you were in danger from me, would not your brother interfere? Bah! Nicolaes knows well enough that passion doth not enter into my schemes at this hour. My plans are too vast to be swayed by your frowns or your smiles. I have entered this city as a conqueror. As a conqueror I shall go out of it to-morrow, and you will come with me. I shall go hence because I choose, and for reasons which I will presently make clear to you.

"But you shall come with me. When you are with me in my camp, I may honour you as my future wife, or cast you from me as I would a beggar. That will depend on my mood, and upon your temper. Nicolaes will not be there to run counter to my will. Therefore, understand me, my pretty fire-eater, that from this hour forth you are as absolutely my property as my dogs are, my horse, or the boots which I wear. I am the master here," he concluded with strangely sinister calm, "And my will alone is law."

"A law unto yourself," she retorted, faced him with absolute composure, neither defiant nor afraid, her nerves quiescent, her voice perfectly steady, "and mayhap unto your cringing sycophants. But above your will, my lord, is that of God; and neither death nor life are your slaves."

"Ay! But methinks they are, myn engel," he answered drily. "Yours in any case."

"No human being, my lord, can lose the freedom to die."

"You think not?" he sneered. "Well, we shall see."

He let go her hand, then quietly turned and walked to the window, threw open the casement once more, then beckoned to her. Strangely stirred, she followed, moved almost mechanically by something she could not resist.

At a sign from him she looked out upon the busy scene on the quay below – the enemy soldiers in possession, their bivouac fires, their comings and goings, the unfortunate citizens running hither and thither at their bidding, fetching and carrying, hustled, pushed, beaten, ordered about with rough words or the persuasive prod of pike or musket. A scene, alas, which already as a child had been familiar to her. A peaceable town in the hands of ruthless soldiery; the women fleeing from threatened insults, children clinging to their mother's skirts, men standing by, grim and silent, not daring to protest lest mere resentment brought horrible reprisals upon the city.

Gilda looked out for awhile in silence, her heart aching with the misery which she beheld, yet could not palliate. Then she turned coldly inquiring eyes on the prime mover of it all.

"I have seen a reign of terror such as this before, my lord," she said. "I was at Leyden, as you well know, and I have not forgotten."

"A reign of terror, you call it, mejuffrouw?" he retorted coolly. "Nay, you exaggerate. What is this brief occupation? To-morrow we go, remember. Is there a single house demolished at this hour, a single citizen murdered? You are too young to recollect Malines of Ghent, the reign of Alva over these recalcitrant countries. I have been lenient so far. I have spared fire and sword. Amersfoort still stands. It will stand to-morrow, even after my soldiers have gone," he went on speaking very slowly, "if —"

"If what, my Lord?" she asked, for he had paused.

The moment had come, then, the supreme hour when that dreaded "either--or" would be put before her. Even now he went on with that same sinister quietude which seemed like the voice of some relentless judge, sent by the King of Darkness to sway her destiny.

"If," Stoutenburg concluded drily, "you mejuffrouw, will accompany me. Oh," he added quickly, seeing that at once she had resumed that air of defiance which irritated even whilst it amused him. "I do not mean as an unwilling slave, pinioned to my chariot-wheel or strapped into a saddle, nor yet as a picturesque corpse, with flowing hair and lilies 'twixt your lifeless hands. No, no, fair one! I offer you the safety of your native city, the immunity of your fellow-citizens, in exchange for a perfectly willing surrender of your live person into my charge."

She looked on him for awhile, mute with horror, then murmured slowly:

"Are you a devil, that you should propose such an execrable bargain?"

He laughed and shrugged his shoulders.

"I am what you and my native land have made me," he replied. "As to that, the Stadtholder never offered to bargain with me for my father's life."

"Who but a prince of darkness would dream of doing so?" she retorted.

"Call me that, an you wish, fair one," he put in lightly; "and come back to the point."

"And the point is, my Lord?"

"That I will respect this city if you come to-morrow, willing and submissive, with me,"

"That, never!" she affirmed hotly.

"In that case," he riposted coldly, "my soldiers will have a free hand ere they quit the town, to sack it at their pleasure. Pillage, arson, will be rewarded; looting will be deemed a virtue, as will murder and outrage. Even your father —"

"Enough, my lord!" she exclaimed, with passionate indignation. "Tell me, I pray, which of the unclean spirits of Avernus did suggest this infamy to you?" Then, as he met her burning glance with another careless shrug and a mocking laugh, she turned to Nicolaes, and cried out to him, almost with entreaty: "Klaas! You at least are not a party to such hideous villainy!"

But he, sullen and shamefaced, only threw her an angry look.

"You make it very difficult for us, Gilda," he said moodily, "by your stupid obstinacy."

"Obstinacy?" she retorted, puzzled at the word. Then reiterated it once or twice. "Obstinacy – obstinacy? My God, hath the boy gone mad?"

"What else is it but obstinacy?" he rejoined vehemently. "You know that, despite all he says, Stoutenburg hath never ceased to love you. And now that he is master here you are lucky indeed to have him as a suitor. He means well by you, by us all, else I were not here. Think what it would mean to me, to father, to everyone of us, if you were Stoutenburg's wife. But you jeopardize my future and the welfare of us all by those foolish tantrums."

She gazed on him in utter horror – on this brother whom she loved; could scarcely believe her ears that it was he – really he – who was uttering such odious words. She felt her gorge rising at this callous avowal of a wanton and insulting treachery. And he, feeling the contempt which flashed on him from her glowing eyes, avoided her glance, tried to shift his ground, to argue his point with the sophistry peculiar to a traitor, and sank more deeply every moment into the mire of dishonour.

"It is time you realized, Gilda," he said, "that our unfortunate country must sooner or later return to her true allegiance. The Stadtholder is sick. His arbitrary temper hath alienated some of his staunchest friends. The Netherlands are the unalienable property of Spain; though two rebel princes have striven to wrest them from their rightful master, the might of Spain was sure to be felt in the end. 'Twas folly ever to imagine that this so-called Dutch Republic would ever abide; and the hour, though tardy, has struck at last when such senseless dreams must come to an end."

"Well spoken, friend Nicolaes!" Stoutenburg put in lustily. "In verity, our Liege Lady the Archduchess Isabella, whom may God protect, could with difficulty find a more eloquent champion."

"Or our noble land so vile a traitor!" Gilda murmured, burning now with shame. "Thank Heaven, Nicolaes, that our poor father is not here, for the disgrace of it all would have struck him dead at your feet. Would to God," she murmured under her breath, "that it killed me now!"

"An undutiful prayer, myn engel," Stoutenburg rejoined, "seeing that its fulfilment would mean that Amersfoort and her citizens would be wiped off the face of the earth."

This time he spoke quite quietly, without any apparent threat, only with determination, like one who knows that he is master and hath full powers to see his will obeyed. She looked at him keenly for a moment or two, wondering if she could make him flinch, if she could by word or prayer shake him in that devilish purpose which in truth must have found birth through the whisperings of uncanny fiends.

Gilda gazed critically at his lean, hard face with the sunken, restless eyes that spoke so eloquently of disappointed hopes and frustrated ambitions; the mouth, thin-lipped and set; the unshaven chin; the hollow temples and grizzled hair. She took in every line of his tall, gaunt figure; the shoulders already bent, the hands fidgety and claw-like; the torn doublet and shabby boots, all proclaiming the down-at-heel adventurer who has staked his all – honour, happiness, eternity – for ambition; has staked all he possessed and played a losing game.

But for pity or compunction Gilda sought in vain. The glance which after awhile was raised to hers revealed nothing but unholy triumph and a cruel, callous mockery. In truth, that glance had told her that she could expect neither justice nor mercy from him, and had spared her the humiliation of a desperate and futile appeal.

A low moan escaped her lips. She tottered slightly, and felt her knees giving way under her.

Vaguely she put out her hand, fearing that she might fall. Even so, she swayed backwards, feeling giddy and sick. But the dread of losing consciousness before this man whom she loathed and despised kept up both her courage and her endurance. She felt the panelling of the window-embrasure behind her, and leaned against it for support.

6

Stoutenburg had made no effort to come to her assistance, neither had Nicolaes. Probably both of them knew that she would never allow either of them to touch her. But Stoutenburg's mocking glance had pursued her all through her valiant fight against threatening unconsciousness. Now that she leaned against the framework of the window, pale and wraith-like, only her delicate profile vaguely distinguishable in the semi-gloom, her lips parted as if to drink in the cold evening air, she looked so exquisite, so desirable, that he allowed his admiration of her to override every other thought.

"You are lovely, myn schat," he said quietly. "Exquisite and worthy to be a queen. And, by Heaven," he exclaimed with sudden passion, "you'll yet live to bless this hour when I broke your obstinacy. Hand in hand, myn engel, you and I, we'll be masters of this beautiful land. I feel that I could do great things if I had you by my side. Listen, Gilda," he went on eagerly, thinking that because she remained silent and motionless she had given up the fight, and was at last resigned to the inevitable – "listen, my beautiful little vixen! The Archduchess will wish to reward me for this; the capture of Amersfoort is no small matter, and I have further projects in mind. In the meanwhile, De Berg hath already hinted that she might re-establish the republic under the suzerainty of Spain, and appoint me as her Stadtholder. Think, myn Geliefde: think what a vista of glorious, satisfied ambition lies before us both! Nay, before us all. Your father, chief pensionary; Nicolaes, general of our armies; your family raised above every one in the land. You'll thank me, I say; thank me on your knees for my constancy and for my unwavering loyalty to you. And even to-night, presently, when you are quite calm and at rest, you'll pray to your God, I vow, for His blessing upon your humble and devoted slave."

He bent the knee when he said this, still scornful even in this affectation of humility, and raised the hem of her gown to his lips. She did not look down on him, nor did she snatch her skirts out of his hand. She just stared straight out before her, and said slowly, with great deliberation:

"To-night – presently – when I am at rest – I will pray God to kill you ere you put your monstrous threat into execution."

With a light laugh he jumped to his feet.

"Still the shrewish little vixen, what?" he said carelessly. "Yet, see what a good dog I am. I'll not bear resentment, and you shall have the comfort of your father's company at the little supper party which I have prepared. Only the four of us, you and the burgomaster, and Nicolaes and I; and we can discuss the arrangements for our forthcoming wedding, which shall be magnificent, I promise you. But be sure of this, fair one," he went on harshly, drew up his gaunt figure to its full height, "that what I've said I've said. To-morrow at sunrise I go hence, and you come with me, able-bodied and willing, to a place which I have in mind. But this city will be the hostage for your good behaviour. My soldiers remain here under the command of one Jan, who obeys all my behests implicitly and without question, because he hates the Stadtholder as much as I do, and hath a father's murder to avenge against that tyrant, just as I have. Jan will stay in Amersfoort until I bid him go. But at one word from me, this city will be reduced to ashes, and not one man, woman or child shall live to tell the tale of how the jongejuffrouw Gilda Beresteyn set her senseless obstinacy above the lives of thousands.

"Think not that I'll relent," he concluded, and once more turned to the open window, gazed down upon the unfortunate city which he had marked as the means to his fiendish ends. His restless eyes roamed over the busy scene; his soldiers, his – the executioners who would carry out his will! Never had he been so powerful; never had his ambition been so near its goal! It had all come together – the humiliation of the Stadtholder, his own success in this daring enterprise, Gilda entirely at his mercy! Success had crowned all his nefarious schemes at last.

"Nothing will change me from my purpose," he said, with all the harsh determination which characterized his every action – "nothing! Neither your tears nor your frowns nor your prayers. There is no one, understand me, no one who can stand between me and my resolve."

"No one but God," she murmured under her breath. "Oh, God, protect me now! My God, save me from this!"

Dizzy, moving like a sleep-walker, she tried to hold herself erect, tried to move from the window, and from the propinquity of that execrable miscreant.

"Have I your permission to go now?" she murmured faintly.

"Yes," he replied; "to your father. I'll order Jan to release our worthy burgomaster, and you and he can pray for my demise at your leisure. Whether you confide in him or not is no concern of mine. I would have you remember that my promise to respect this city and her inhabitants only holds good if you, of your own free will, come with me to-morrow. Amersfoort shall live if you come willingly. You are the best judge whether your father would be the happier for this knowledge. Methinks it would be kinder to let him think that you come to-morrow as my willing bride. But that is for you to decide. I want him here anon to give his blessing upon our future union in the presence of your brother Nicolaes. I wish the bond to be made irrevocable as soon as may be. If you or your father break it afterwards, it will be the worse for Amersfoort. Try and believe that the alternative is one of complete indifference to me. I have everything in the world now that I could possibly wish for. My ambition is completely satisfied. To have you as my wife would only be the pandering to a caprice. And now you may go, myn schat," he concluded. "The destinies of your native city are in your dainty hands."

He watched her progress across the room with a sarcastic grin. But in his heart he was conscious of a bitter disappointment. Unheard by her, he muttered under his breath:

"If only she would care, how different everything might be!"

Aloud he called to Nicolaes: "Escort your sister, man, into the presence of the burgomaster! And see that Jan and a chosen few form a guard of honour on the passage of the future Lady of Stoutenburg."

Nicolaes hastened to obey. Gilda tried to check him with a brief. "I thank you; I would prefer to go alone!"

But already he had thrown open the door, and anon his husky voice could be heard giving orders to Jan.

Gilda, at the last, turned once more to look on her enemy. He caught her eye, bowed very low, his hand almost touching the ground ere he brought it with a sweeping flourish back to his breast, in the most approved fashion lately brought in from France.

"In half an hour supper will be served," he said. "I await the honour of the burgomaster's company and of your own!"

And he remained in an attitude of perfect deference whilst she passed silently out of the room.

Chapter XI – The Danger-Spoke

1

GILDA had refused her brother's escort, preferring to follow Jan; and Nicolaes, half indifferent, half ashamed, watched her progress up the stairs, and when she had disappeared in the gloom of the corridor above, he went back to his friend.

The two old serving-men were now busy in the banqueting-hall, bringing in the supper. They set the table with silver and crystal goblets, with jugs of Spanish and Rhenish wines, and dishes of cooked meats. They came and went about their business expeditiously and silently, brought in two more heavy candelabra with a dozen or more lighted candles in their sconces, so that the vast room was brilliantly lit. They threw fresh logs upon the fire, so that the whole place looked cosy and inviting.

Stoutenburg had once more taken up his stand beside the open window. Leaning his arm against the mullion, he rested his head upon it. Bitterness and rage had brought hot tears to his eyes. Somehow it seemed to him as if in the overflowing cup of his triumph something had turned to gall. Gilda eluded him. He could not understand her. The experience which he had of women had taught him that these beautiful and shallow creatures, soulless for the most part and heartless, were easily to be cajoled with soft words and bribed with wealth and promises. Yet he had dangled before Gilda's eyes such a vision of glory and exalted position as should have captured, quite unconditionally, the citadel of her affections, and she had remained indifferent to it all.

He had owned himself still in love with her, and she had remained quite callous to his ardour. He had tried indifference, and had only been paid back in his own coin. To a man of Stoutenburg's intensely egotistical temperament, there could only be one explanation to this seeming coldness. The wench's senses – it could be nothing more – were still under the thrall of that miserable adventurer who, thank Beelzebub and his horde, had at last been rendered powerless to wreak further mischief. There could be, he argued to himself, no aversion in her heart for one who was so ready to share prosperity, power, and honour with her, to forgive and forget all that was past, to raise her from comparative obscurity to the most exalted state that had ever dazzled a woman's fancy and stormed the inmost recesses of her soul.

She was still infatuated with the varlet, and that was all. A wholly ununderstandable fact. Stoutenburg never could imagine how she had ever looked with favour on such an adventurer, whose English parentage and reputed wealth were, to say the least, problematical. Beresteyn had been a fool to allow his only daughter to bestow her beauty and her riches on a stranger, about whom in truth he knew less than nothing. The girl, bewitched by the rascallion, had cajoled her father and obtained his consent. Now she was still under the spell of a handsome presence, a resonant voice, a provoking eye. It was, it could be, nothing more than that. When once she understood what she had gained, how utterly inglorious that once brilliant soldier of fortune had become, she would descend from her high attitude of disdain and kiss the hand which she now spurned.

But, in anticipation of that happy hour, the Lord of Stoutenburg felt moody and discontented.

2

Nicolaes' voice, close to his elbow, roused him from his gloomy meditations.

"You must be indulgent, my friend," he was saying in a smooth conciliatory voice. "Gilda had always a wilful temper."

"And a tenacious one," Stoutenburg retorted. "She is still in love with that rogue."

"Bah!" the other rejoined, with a note of spite in his tone. "It is mere infatuation! A woman's whimsey for a good-looking face and a pair of broad shoulders! She should have seen the scrubby rascal as I last caught sight of him – grimy, unshaven, broken. No woman's fancy would survive such a spectacle!"

Then, as Stoutenburg, still unconsoled, continued to stare through the open window, muttering disjointed phrases through obstinately set lips, he went on quite gaily:

"You are not the first by any means, my friend, whose tempestuous wooing hath brought a woman, loving and repentant, to heel. When I was over in England with my father, half a dozen years ago, we saw there a play upon the stage. It had been writ by some low-born mountebank, one William Shakespeare. The name of the play was 'The Taming of the Shrew.' Therein, too, a woman of choleric temper did during several scenes defy the man who wooed her. In the end he conquered; she became his wife, and as tender and submissive an one as e'er you'd wish to see. But, by St. Bavon, how she stormed at first! How she professed to hate him! I was forcibly reminded of that play when I saw Gilda defying you awhile ago; and I could have wished that you had displayed the same good-humour over the wrangle as did the gallant Petruchio – the hero of the piece."

Stoutenburg was interested.

"How did he succeed in the end?" he queried. "Your Petruchio, I mean."

"He starved the ranting virago into submission," Nicolaes replied, with an easy laugh. "Gave her nothing to eat for a day and a night; swore at her lackeys; beat her waiting-maids. She was disdainful at first, then terrified. Finally, she admired him, because he had mastered her."

"A good moral, friend Nicolaes!"

"Ay! One you would do well to follow. Women reserve their disdain for weaklings, and their love for their masters."

"And think you that Gilda —"

"Gilda, my friend, is but a woman after all. Have no fear, she'll be your willing slave in a week."

Stoutenburg's eyes glittered at the thought.

"A week is a long time to wait," he murmured. "I wish that now--"

He paused. Something that was happening down below on the quay had attracted his attention – unusual merriment, loud laughter, the strains of a bibulous song. For a minute or two his keen eyes searched the gloom for the cause of all this hilarity. He leaned far out the window, called peremptorily to a group of soldiers who were squatting around their bivouac fire.

"Hey!" he shouted. "Peter! Willem! – whatever your confounded names may be! What is that rascallion doing over there?"

"Making us all laugh, so please your lordship," one of the soldiers gave reply; "by the drollest stories and quips any of us have ever heard."

"Where does he come from?"

"From nowhere, apparently," the man averred. "He just fell among us. The man is blind, so please you," he added after a moment's hesitation.

Stoutenburg swore.

"How many times must I give orders," he demanded roughly, "that every blind beggar who comes prowling round the camps be hanged to the nearest post?"

"We did intend to hang him," the soldier replied coolly; "but when first he came along he was so nimble that, ere we could capture him, he gave us the slip."

"Well," Stoutenburg rejoined harshly, "it is not too late. You have him now."

"So we have, Magnificence," the man replied, hesitated for a second or two, then added: "But he is so amusing, and he seems a gentleman of quality, too proud for the hangman's rope."

"Too proud is he?" his lordship retorted with a sneer. "A gentleman of quality, and amusing to boot? Well, let us see how his humour will accommodate itself to the gallows. Here, let me have a look at the loon.

There was much hustling down below after this; shouting and prolonged laughter; a confused din, through which it was impossible to distinguish individual sounds. Stoutenburg's nerves were tingling. He was quite sure by now that he had recognised that irrepressible merry voice. A gentleman of quality! Blind! Amusing! But, if Nicolaes' report of yesterday's events were true, the man was hopelessly stricken. And what could induce him to put his head in the jackal's mouth, to affront his triumphing enemy, when he himself was so utterly helpless and abject?

Not long was the Lord of Stoutenburg left in suspense. Even whilst he gazed down upon the merry, excited throng, he was able to distinguish in the midst of them all a pair of broad shoulders that could only belong to one man. The soldiers, laughing, thoroughly enjoying the frolic, were jostling him not a little for the sheer pleasure of measuring their valour against so hefty a fellow. And he, despite his blindness, gave as good as he got; fought valiantly with fist and boot and gave his tormentors many a hard knock, until, with a loud shout of glee, some of the men succeeded in seizing hold of him, and hoisted him up on their shoulders and brought him into the circle of light formed by the resin torches.

A double cry came in response – one of amazement from Stoutenburg and one of horror from Nicolaes. But neither of them spoke. Stoutenburg's lips were tightly set; a puzzled frown appeared between his brows. In truth, for once in the course of his devilish career, he was completely taken aback and uncertain what to do. The man whom he saw there before him, in ragged clothes, unshaved and grimy, blinking with sightless eyes, was the man whom he detested above every other thing or creature on earth – the reckless soldier of fortune of the past, for awhile the proud and successful rival; now just a wreck of humanity, broken, ay, and degraded, and henceforth an object of pity rather than a menace to his rival's plans. His doublet was in rags, his plumed hat battered, his toes shone through the holes in his boots. The upper part of his face was swathed in a soiled linen bandage. This had, no doubt, been originally intended to shield the stricken eyes; but it had slipped, and those same eyes, with their horrible fixed look, glittered with unearthly weirdness in the flickering light.

"Salute his Magnificence, the lord and master of Amersfoort and of all that in it lies!" one of the soldiers shouted gaily.

And the blind man forthwith made a gesture of obeisance swept with a wide flourish his battered plumed hat from off his head.

"To his Magnificence!" he called out in response. "Though mine eyes cannot see him, my voice is raised in praise of his nobility and his valour. May the recording angels give him his full deserts."

3

The feeling of sheer horror which had caused Nicolaes to utter a sudden cry was, in truth, fully justified.

"It can't be!" he murmured, appalled at what he saw.

Stoutenburg answered with a hoarse laugh. "Nay, by Satan and all his myrmidons it is!"

Already he was leaning out of the window, giving quick orders to the men down below to bring that drunken vagabond forthwith into his presence. After which he turned once more to his friend.

"We'll soon see," he said, "if it is true, or if our eyes have played us both an elusive trick. Yet, methinks," he added thoughtfully, "that the pigwidgeon who of late hath taken my destiny in hand is apparently intent on doing me a good turn."

"In what way?" the other asked.

"By throwing my enemy across my path," Stoutenburg replied drily.

"You'll hang him of course?" Nicolaes rejoined.

"Yes; I'll hang him!" Stoutenburg retorted, with a snarl. "But I must make use of him first."

"Make use of him? How?"

"That I do not know as yet. But inspiration will come, never you fear, my friend. All that I want is a leverage for bringing the Stadtholder to his knees and for winning Gilda's love."

"Then, in Heaven's name, man," Nicolaes rejoined earnestly, "begin by ridding yourself of the only danger-spoke in your wheel!"

"Danger-spoke?" Stoutenburg exclaimed, threw back his head and laughed. "Would you really call that miserable oaf a serious bar to mine ambition or a possible rival in your sister's regard?"

And, with outstretched hand he pointed to the door.

There, under the lintel – pushed on by Jan and two or three men who, powerfully built though they were, looked like pigmies beside the stricken giant, drunk as an owl, his hat awry above that hideous bandage, dirty, unkempt, and ragged – appeared the man who had once been the brilliant inspiration of Franz Hals' immortal "Laughing Cavalier."

At sight of him Nicolaes Beresteyn gave a loud groan and collapsed into a chair; burying his face in his hand. He was ever a coward, even in villainy; and when the man whom he had once hated so bitterly, and whom his craven hand had struck in such a dastardly manner, lurched into the room, and as he fell against the table uttered an inane and bibulous laugh, his nerve completely forsook him.

At a peremptory sign from Stoutenburg, Jan closed the doors which gave on the hall; but he and two of the men remained at attention inside the room.

The blind man groped with his hands till they found a chair, into which he sank, with powerful limbs outstretched, snorting like a dog just come out of the water. With an awkward gesture he pushed his hat from off his head, and in so doing he dislodged the grimy bandage so that it sat like a scullion's cap across his white forehead.

Stoutenburg watched him with an expression of cruel satisfaction. It is not often given to a man to have an enemy and a rival so completely in his power, and the exultation in Stoutenburg's heart was so great that he was content to savour it in silence for awhile. Nicolaes was beyond the power of speech, and so the silence for a moment or two remained absolute.

Then the blind man suddenly sat up, craning his neck and rolling his sightless eyes.

"I wonder where the devil I am!" he murmured through set lips. He appeared to listen intently; no doubt caught the sound of life around him, for he added quickly: "Is anybody here?"

"I am here," Stoutenburg replied curtly. "Do you know whom I am, sirrah?"

"In truth, I do not," Diogenes replied. "But by your accent I would judge you to be a man who at this moment is mightily afraid."

"Afraid?" Stoutenburg retorted, with a loud laugh. I, afraid of a helpless vagabond who has been fool enough to run his head into a noose which I had not even thought of preparing for him?"

"Yet you are afraid my lord," the other rejoined quietly, "else you would not have ordered your bodyguard to watch over your precious person whilst you parleyed with a blind man."

"My bodyguard is only waiting for final orders to take you to the gallows," Stoutenburg rejoined roughly. "You may as well know now as later that it is my intention to hang you."

"As well now as later," the blind man assented, with easy philosophy. "I understand that for the nonce, whoever you Magnificence may be, you are master in Amersfoort. As such, you have a right to hang anyone you choose. Me or another. What matters? I was very nearly hung once, you must know, by the Lord of Stoutenburg. I did not mind much then; I'd mind it still less now. People talk of a hereafter. Well, whatever it is, it must be a better world that this, so I would just as soon as not, go and find out for myself."

He struggled to his feet, still groping with his hands for support, found the edge of the table and leaned up against it.

"Let's to the hangman, my lord," he said thickly. "If I'm to hang, I prefer it to be done at once. And if we tarry too long I might get sober ere I embark on the last adventure. But," he added, and once more appeared to search the room with eyes that could not see, "there's someone else here besides your lordship. Who is it?"

"My friend and yours," Stoutenburg replied. "Mynheer Nicolaes Beresteyn."

There was a second or two of silence. Nicolaes made as if he would speak, but Stoutenburg quickly put a finger up to his lips, enjoining him to remain still. The blind man passed his trembling hand once or twice in front of his eyes as if to draw aside an unseen veil that hid the outer world from his gaze.

"Ah!" he murmured contentedly. "My friend Klaas! He is here too, is he? That is indeed good news. For Nicolaes was ever my friend. That time three months ago – or was it three years, or three centuries? I really have lost count – that time that the Lord of Stoutenburg was on the point of hanging me, Klaas would have interposed on my behalf, only something went wrong with his heart at the moment, or his nerves, I forget which."

" 'Twere no use to rely on mynheer's interference this time," Stoutenburg put in drily. "There is but one person in the world now who can save you from the gallows."

"You mean the Lord of Stoutenburg himself?" the blind man queried blandly.

"Nay! He is determined to hang you. But there is another."

"Then I pray your lordship to tell me who that other is," Diogenes replied.

"You might find one, sirrah, in the jongejuffrouw Gilda Beresteyn, the Lord of Stoutenburg's promised wife."

Diogenes made no reply to this. He was facing the table now, still clinging to it with one hand, whilst the other wandered over the objects on the table. Suddenly they encountered a crystal jug which was full of wine. An expression of serene beatitude overspread his face. He raised the goblet to his lips, but ere he drank he said carelessly:

"Ah, the jongejuffrouw Beresteyn is the promised wife of the Lord of Stoutenburg?"

"My promised wife!" Stoutenburg put in roughly. "Methought you would ere this have recognized the man whom you tried to rob of all that he held most precious."

"Your lordship must forgive me," the blind man rejoined drily. "But some unknown miscreant – whom may the gods punish – interfered with me yesterday forenoon, when I was trying to render assistance to my friend Klaas. In the scuffle that ensued, I received a cloud of stinking fumes in the face, which has totally robbed me of sight."

As he spoke he raised his eyes, blinking in that pathetic and inconsequent manner peculiar to the blind. Nicolaes gave an audible groan. He could not bear to look on those sightless orbs, which in the flickering light of the wax candles appeared weird and unearthly.

"Oh," Stoutenburg put in carelessly, "is that how the – er – accident occurred?"

"So, please your lordship, yes," Diogenes replied. "And I was left stranded on the moor, since those two unreclaimed varlets, Pythagoras and Socrates by name, did effectually ride off in the wake of the Stadtholder, leaving me in the lurch. A pitiable plight, your lordship will admit."

"So pitiable," the other retorted with a sneer, "that you thought to improve your condition by bearding the Lord of Stoutenburg in his lair."

"I did not know your lordship was in Amersfoort," Diogenes replied imperturbably. "I thought – I hoped —"

He paused, and Stoutenburg tried in vain to read what went on behind that seemingly unclouded brow. The blind man appeared serene, detached, perfectly good-humoured. His slender hand, which looked hard beneath its coating of grime, was closed lovingly around the crystal jug. Stoutenburg vaguely wondered how far the man was really drunk, or whether his misfortune had slightly addled his brain. So much unconcern in the face of an imminent and shameful death gave an uncanny air to the whole appearance of the man. Even now, with a gently apologetic smile, he raised the jug once more to his lips. Stoutenburg placed a peremptory hand upon his arm.

"Put that down, man," he said harshly. "You are drunk enough as it is, and you'll have need of all your wits to-night."

"There you are wrong my lord," Diogenes retorted, and quietly transferred the jug to his other hand. "A man, meseems, needs no wits to hang gracefully. And I feel that I could do that best if I might quench my thirst ere I met my friend the hangman."

"You may not meet him at all."

"But just now you said —"

"That it was my intention to hang you," Stoutenburg assented. "So it is. But I am in rare good humour to-night, and —"

"So it seems, my lord," the blind man put in carelessly. "So it seems."

He appeared to be swaying on his feet, and to have some difficulty in retaining his balance. He still clung to the edge of the table with one hand. In the other he had the jug fill of wine.

"The jongejuffrouw Gilda Beresteyn," Stoutenburg went on, "will sup with me this night to celebrate our betrothal. The fulfillment of this, my great desire, hath caused me to feel lenient toward mine enemies."

"Have I not always asserted," Diogenes broke in with comical solemnity – "always ass-asserted that your lordship was a noble and true gentleman?"

"Women, we know," his lordship continued, ignoring the interruption, "are wont to be ten-derhearted where their – their former swains are concerned. And I feel that if the jongejuffrouw herself did make appeal to me on your behalf, I would relent towards you."

"B-b-but would that not be an awkward – a very awkward decision for your lordship?" Dio-genes riposted, turning round vacant eyes on Stoutenburg.

"Awkward? How so?

"If I do not hang, the jongejuffrouw, 'stead of being my widow, would still be my wife. And the laws of this country —"

"I have no concern with the laws of this country" Stoutenburg rejoined drily, "in which, anyhow, you are an alien. As soon as the Archduchess our Liege Lady is once more mistress here, we shall again be at war with England."

"Poor England!"

Diogenes sighed, and solemnly wiped a tear from his blinking eyes.

"And every English plepshurk will be kicked out of the country. But that is neither here nor there."

"Neither here nor there," the other assented, with owlish gravity. "But before England is s-sh-s-swept off the map, my lordship, what will happen?"

"My marriage to the jongejuffrouw," Stoutenburg replied curtly. "She hath consented to be my wife, and my wife she will be as soon as I have mind to take her. So you may drink to our union, sirrah. I'll e'en pledge you in a cup."

He poured himself out a goblet of wine, laughing to himself at his own ingenuity. That was the way to treat the smeerlap. Make him feel what a pitiable, abject knave he was! Then show him up before Gilda, just as he was – drunk, ragged, unkempt, an object of derision in his misfortune rather than of pity.

"Nay," the rascal objected, his speech waxing thicker and his hand more unsteady, "I cannot pledge you, my lord, in drinking to your union with my own wife, unless – unless my friend Klaas will drink to that union, too. Mine own brother by the law, you see, my lord, and —"

"Mynheer Nicolaes will indeed drink to his sister's happy union with me," Stoutenburg re-torted, with a sneer. "His presence here is a witness to my good intentions toward the wench. So you may drink, sirrah. The jongejuffrouw herself is overwilling to submit to my pleasure —"

But the imperious words were smothered in his throat, giving place to a fierce exclamation of choler. The blind man had at his invitation raised the jug of wine to his lips, but in the act his feet apparently slipped away from under him. The jug flew out of his hand, would have caught the Lord of Stoutenburg on the head had he not ducked just in time. But even so his Magnificence was hit on the shoulder by the heavy crystal vessel, and splashed from head to foot with the wine, whilst Diogenes collapsed on the floor with a shamed and bibulous laugh.

A string of savage oaths and tempestuous abuse poured from Stoutenburg's lips, which were in truth livid with rage. Already Jan had rushed to his assistance, snatched up a serviette from the table, and soon contrived to wipe his lordship's doublet clean.

The blind man in the meanwhile did his best to hoist himself up on his feet once more, clung to the edge of the table; but the sight of him released the last floodgate of Stoutenburg's tempestuous wrath. He turned with a vicious snarl upon the unfortunate man, and it would indeed have fared ill with the defenceless creature, for the Lord of Stoutenburg was not wont to measure his blows by the helplessness of his victims, had not a sudden exclamation from Nicolaes stayed the hand that was raised to strike.

"Gilda!" the young man cried impulsively.

Stoutenburg's arm dropped to his side. He turned toward the door. Gilda had just entered with her father, and was coming slowly down the room.

Chapter XII – Tears, Sighs, Hearts

1

GILDA caught sight of her beloved the moment she entered. To say that their eyes met would indeed be folly. Certain it is, however, that the blind man turned his sightless gaze in her direction. She only gave a gasp, pressed her hands to her heart as if the pain there was unendurable, and at the moment even the beauty of her face was marred by the look of soul-racking misery in her eyes and the quivering lines around her mouth.

The next moment, even while Jan and the soldiers retired, closing the doors behind them, she was in her husband's arms. Ay, even though Stoutenburg tried to intercept her. She did not hear his mocking laugh, or her brother's vigorous protest, nor yet her father's cry of horror. She just clung to him who, blind, fallen, degraded an you will, was still the beloved of her heart, the man to whom she had dedicated her soul.

She swallowed her tears, too proud to allow those who had wrought his ruin to see how mortally she was hurt.

She passed her delicate hands, fragrant as the petals of flowers, over his grimy face, those poor, stricken eyes, the noble brow so deeply furrowed with pain. She murmured words of endearment and of tenderness such as a mother might find to soothe the trouble of a suffering child. All in a moment. Stoutenburg had not even the time to interfere, to utter the savage oaths which rose from his vengeful heart at sight of the loving pity which this beautiful woman lavished on so contemptible an object.

Nor had the blind man time to encircle that exquisite form in his trembling arms. He had put them out at first, with a pathetic gesture of infinite longing. It was just a flash, a vision of his past self, an oblivion of the hideous, appalling present. Her arms at that moment were round his neck, her head against his breast, her soft, fair hair against his lips.

2

Then something happened. A magnetic current seemed to pass through the air. Diogenes freed himself with a sudden jerk from Gilda's clinging arms, staggered back against the table, swaying on his feet and uttering an inane laugh; whilst she, left standing alone, turned wide, bewildered eyes on her brother Nicolaes, who happened to be close to her at the moment. I think that she was near to unconsciousness then, and that she would have fallen, but that the burgomaster stepped quickly to her side and put his arms round her.

"May God punish you," he muttered between his teeth, and turned to Stoutenburg, who had watched the whole scene with a sinister scowl, "for this wanton and unnecessary cruelty!"

"You wrong me, mynheer," Stoutenburg retorted, with a shrug "I but tried to make your daughter's decision easier for her."

Then, as the burgomaster made no reply, but, with grim, set look on his face, drew his daughter gently down to the nearest chair, Stoutenburg went on lightly, speaking directly to Gilda:

"In the course of my travels, mejuffrouw, I came across a wise philosopher in Italy. He was a man whom an adverse fate had robbed of most things that he held precious; but he told me that he had quite succeeded in conquering adversity by the following means. He would gaze dispassionately on the objects of his past desires, see their defects, appraise them at their just value, and in every case he found that their loss was not so irreparable as he had originally believed."

"A fine moral lesson, my lord," the burgomaster interposed, seeing that Gilda either would not or could not speak as yet. "But I do not see its point."

" 'Tis a simple one, mynheer," Stoutenburg retorted coldly. "I pray you, look on the man to whom, an you had your way, you would even now link your daughter."

Instinctively Beresteyn turned his lowering gaze in the direction to which his lordship now pointed with a persuasive gesture. Diogenes was standing beside the table, his powerful frame drawn up to its full height, his sightless eyes blinking and gleaming with weird inconsequence in the flickering light of the candles. His hands were clasped behind his back, and on his face there was a curious expression which the burgomaster was not shrewd enough to define – one of self-deprecation, yet withal of introspection and of detachment, as if the helpless body alone were present and the mind had gone a-roaming in the land of dreams. The burgomaster tried manfully to conceal the look of half-contemptuous pity which, much against his will, had crept into his eyes.

"The man," he rejoined calmly, "is what Fate and a dastard's hand have made him, my lord. Many a fine work of God hath been marred by an evildoer's action."

"That is as may be mynheer," Stoutenburg riposted coolly. "But 'tis of the present and of the future you have to think now – not of the past."

"Even so, my lord, I would sooner see my daughter in the arms of the stricken lion than in those of a wily jackal."

"Am I the wily jackal?" Stoutenburg put in, with a sneer. Then, as the burgomaster made no reply, he added tersely: "I see that the jongejuffrouw hath told you —"

"Everything," Beresteyn assented calmly.

"And that I await your blessing on our union?"

"My blessing you cannot have, my lord, as you well know," the burgomaster retorted firmly. " 'Twas blasphemy to invoke the name of God on such an unholy alliance. My daughter is the lawfully wedded wife of an English gentleman, Sir Percy Blakeney by name, and until the law of this country doth sever those bonds she cannot wed another."

Stoutenburg gave a strident laugh.

"That is, indeed, unfortunate for the English gentleman with the high-sounding name," he said, with a sneer, "whom I gravely suspect of being naught but the common varlet whom we all know so well in Haarlem. But, gentleman or churl," he added, with a cynical shrug, " ' tis all one to me. He hangs to-morrow, unless —"

A loud cry of burning indignation escaped the burgomaster's lips.

"You would not further provoke the wrath of God," he exclaimed, "by this foul and cowardly crime!"

"And why not, I pray you?" the other coolly retorted. "Nor do I think that the Almighty would greatly care what happened to this drunken knave. The refuse of human kind, the halt, the lame, and the blind, are best out of the way."

"A man, my lord," the burgomaster protested, "Who when he had you in his power, generously spared your life!"

"The more fool he!" Stoutenburg riposted drily. " 'Tis my turn now. He hangs to-morrow, unless, indeed —"

"Unless, what, my lord?"

"Unless," Stoutenburg went on, with an evil leer, "my future wife will deign to plead with me for him – with a kiss."

A groan like that of a wounded beast broke from the burgomaster's heavy heart. For a moment a light that was almost murderous gleamed in his eyes. His fists were clenched; he murmured a dark threat against the man who goaded him wellnigh to madness. Then, suddenly, he met Stoutenburg's mocking glance fixed upon him, and a huge sob rose in his throat, almost choking him. Gilda, with a pitiful moan, had hidden her face against her father's sleeve.

" 'Tis but anticipating the happy time by a few hours," Stoutenburg went on, with calm cynicism. "But I have a fancy to hold my future wife in my arms now – at this moment – and to grant her in exchange for her first willing kiss the life of a miserable wretch whose life or death are, in truth, of no account to me."

He took a step or two forward in the direction where Gilda sat, clinging with desperate misery to her father. Then, as the burgomaster, superb with indignation, grand in his dignity,

Instinctively interposed his burly figure between his daughter and the man whom she loathed, Stoutenburg added, with well-assumed carelessness:

"If the jongejuffrouw prefers to put off the happy moment until we are alone in my camp to-morrow, we'll say no more about it. Let the rogue hang; I care not!"

"My lord," – the burgomaster spoke once more in a vigorous protest, which, alas, he knew to be futile – "what you suggest is monstrous, inhuman! God will never permit —"

"I pray you, mynheer," Stoutenburg broke in fiercely, "let us leave the Almighty out of our affairs. I have read my Bible as assiduously as you when I was younger, and in it I learned that God hath enjoined all wives to submit themselves to their husbands. A kiss from my betrothed, a word or gentle pleading, are little enough to ask in exchange for an act of clemency. And you, Heer Burgomaster, do but stiffen my will by your interference. Will you, at least, let the jongejuffrouw decide on the matter for herself, and, in her interests and your own, give to all that she does your unqualified consent!"

"My consent you'll never wring from me, as you well know, my lord. I and my daughter are powerless to withstand your might, but if we bend to the yoke it is because it hath pleased God that we should wear it, not because we submit with a free will. By exulting in such a monstrous crime you do but add to the loathing which we both feel for you —"

"Silence!" Stoutenburg broke in fiercely. "Silence, you dolt! What good, think you, you do yourself or your daughter by provoking me beyond endurance? She knows my decision, and so, methinks, do you. If the jongejuffrouw feels such unqualified hatred for me, let her return to your protecting arms and leave Amersfoort to its fate. As for that sightless varlet, let him hang, I say! I am a fool, indeed to listen to your gibberish! Jan!" he called, and strode to the door with a great show of determination, staking his all now on this card which he had decided to play.

But the card was a winning one, as well he knew. Already Gilda, as if moved by an unseen voice, had jumped to her feet and intercepted him ere he reached the door. Her whole appearance had changed – the expression of her eyes, her tone, her gestures.

"My father is overwrought, my lord," she said firmly. "He hath already promised me that he would offer no opposition to my wishes."

She looked him straight in the eyes, and he returned her gaze, his restless eyes seeming to search her very soul. she had, in truth, changed most markedly. She was, of course, afraid – afraid for that miserable plepshurk's life. But the change was something more than that – at least, Stoutenburg chose to think so. There was something in her glance at this moment that he did not quite understand, that he did not dare understand. A wavering – almost he would have called it a softness, had he dared. He came nearer to her, and, though at first she drew back from him, she presently held her ground, still gazing on him like a bird when it is fascinated and cannot move.

Now he was quite sure that her blue eyes looked less hard, and certainly her mouth was less tightly set. Her lips were slightly parted, and her breath came quick and panting. Ah, women were queer creatures! Had Nicolaes been right when he quoted the English play? Gilda had certainly begun by falling against that contemptible rascal's breast, but since then? Had her wayward fancy been repelled by that whole air of physical degradation which emanated from the once brilliant cavalier, or had it been merely dazzled by visions of power and of wealth, which had their embodiment in him who was her future lord?

He himself could not say. All that he knew, all that he felt of a certainty now, was that he held more than one winning card in this gamble for possession of an exquisite and desirable woman. Still holding her gaze, he took her hands. She did not resist, did not attempt to draw away from him, and he murmured softly:

"What are your wishes, myn engel?"

"To submit to your will, my lord," she replied firmly.

"At last!" he exclaimed, on a note of triumph, drew her still closer to him. "A kiss, fair one, to clinch this bargain, which hath made me the happiest of men!"

He had lost his head for the moment. Satisfaction, and an almost feverish sense of exultation, had turned his blood to liquid fire. All that he saw was this lovely woman, whom he had nearly conquered. Nearly, but not quite. At his desire for a kiss he felt that she stiffened. She closed her eyes, and even her lips became bloodless. She appeared on the verge of a swoon. Bah! Even this phase would pass away. Nicolaes was right. Women reserved their contempt for weaklings. In the end 'twas the master whom they adored.

"A kiss, fair one!" he called again. "And the rogue shall live or hang according as your lips are sweet or bitter!"

He was on the point of snatching that kiss at last, when suddenly there came so violent a crash that the whole room shook with the concussion, and even the windows rattled in their frames. The blind man, more unsteady than ever on his feet, had tried to get hold of a chair, lost his balance in the act, and, in the endeavour to save himself from falling, had lurched so clumsily against the table that it overturned, and all the objects upon it – silver, crystal, china dishes, and candelabra – fell with a deafening clatter on the floor.

Stoutenburg, uttering one of his favourite oaths, had instinctively turned to see whence had come this terrific noise. In turning, his hold on Gilda's wrists had slightly relaxed; sufficiently, at any rate, to enable her to free herself from his grasp and to seek shelter once more beside her father. Diogenes alone had remained unruffled through the commotion. Indeed, he appeared wholly unconscious that he had brought it about. He had collapsed amidst the litter, and now sprawled on the floor, surrounded by a medley of broken glass, guttering candles, hot food and liquor, convulsed with laughter, whist his huge, dark eyes, with the dilated pupils and pale, narrow circles of blue light, looked strangely ghostlike in the gloom.

"Who in thunder," he muttered inarticulately, "is making this confounded din?"

3

At the noise, too, the men had come running in from the hall. The sound had been akin to the detonation of a dozen pistols, and they had rushed along, prepared for a fight. With the fall of the candelabra, the vast banqueting hall had suddenly been plunged into semi-darkness. Only a couple of wax candles in tall sconces, which had originally set on the sideboard, vaguely illumined the disorderly scene.

Diogenes, with his infectious laugh, did in truth succeed in warding off the punishment which his Magnificence already held in preparation for him. As it was, Stoutenburg caught sight of Gilda's look of anxiety, and this at once put him into a rare good humour. He had had his wish. Gilda had been almost kind, had practically yielded to him in the presence of the man whom he desired to humiliate and to wound, as he himself had been humiliated and wounded in the past.

Whether the blind man's keen sense of hearing had taken in every detail of the scene, it was of course impossible to say. But one thing he must have heard – the brief soliloquy at the door, when Gilda, in response to his ardent query. "What are your wishes, myn engel?" had replied quite firmly: "To submit to your will, my lord!" That moment must, in truth, have been more galling and more bitter to the once gallant Laughing Cavalier than the rattle of the rope upon the gallows, or the first consciousness that he was irremediably blind.

Indeed, Stoutenburg had had something more than his wish. To make a martyr of the rogue, he would have told you, was not part of his desire. All that he wanted was to obliterated the man's former brilliant personality from Gilda's mind; that he should henceforth dwell in her memory as she last saw him, abject in his obvious impotence, owing his life to the woman whom he had wooed and conquered in the past with the high hand of a reckless adventurer. After that, the rogue might hang or perish in a ditch: his lordship did not care. What happened to blind men in these days of fighting when none but the best men had a chance to live at all, he had never troubled his head to inquire. At any rate, he knew that a sightless lion was less harmful than a keen-eyed mouse. Ah, in truth he had had more than his wish and satisfied now as to the present and the future, the thought that the moment had come to let well alone, and to remove from Gilda's sight the spectacle which, by some subtle reaction, might turn her heart back to pity for the knave. He gave Jan a significant nod.

But Gilda, whose glowing eyes had watched his every movement, was quick to interpose.

"My lord," she cried in protest, "I hold you to your bargain!"

"Have no fear, myn chat," he answered suavely. I will not repudiate it. The fellow's life is safe enough whilst you and the Heer Burgomaster honour me by supping with me. After that, the decision rests with you. As I said just now, he shall live or hang according as your lips are sweet or bitter. For the nonce, I am wearied and hungry. We'll sup first, so please you."

And Gilda had to stand by whilst she saw her husband dragged away from her presence. He offered no resistance; indeed, accepted the situation with that good-humoured philosophy which was so characteristic of him. But, oh, if she could have conveyed to him by a look all the tenderness, the sorrow, the despair, that was torturing her heart! If she could have run to him just once more, to whisper into his ear those burning words of love which would have eased his pain and hers!

If she could have defied that abominable tyrant who gloated over her misery, and, hand in hand with her beloved, have met death by his side, with his arms around her, her spirit wedded to his, ere they appeared together before the judgement seat of God!

But, as that arrogant despot had reminded her, she had even lost the freedom to die. The destinies of her native city were in her hands. Unless she bowed her willing neck to his will, Amersfoort and all its citizens would be wiped off the face of the earth. And as she watched the chosen of her heart led like a captive lion to humiliation if not to death those monstrous words rang in her ears, that surely must provoke the wrath of God.

Therefore, she watched his departure dry-eyed and motionless. Ay! envying him in her heart, that he, at least, was not called upon to make such an appalling sacrifice as lay now before her. She had indeed come to that sublimity of human suffering that she almost wished to see those dear, sightless eyes closed in their last long sleep, rather than that he should be forced to endure what to him would be ten thousand times worse than death – her submission to that miscreant – her willing union; and he, ignorant of how the tyrant had wrung this submission from her.

Chapter XIII – The Stygian Creek

1

THE Lord or Stoutenburg was conscious of a great feeling of relief when the blind man was finally removed from his presence. While the latter stood there, even in the abjectness of his plight, Stoutenburg felt that he was a living menace to the success of all his well-thought-out schemes. He kept his eyes fixed on Gilda with a warning look, that should be a reminder to her of the immutability of his resolve. He tried, in a manner, to surround her with a compelling fluid that would engulf her resistance and leave her weak and passive to his will.

There was of necessity a vast amount of confusion and din ere order was restored among the debris; and conversation was impossible in the midst of the clatter that was going on – men coming and going, the rattle of silver and glass. Gilda, the while, sat quite still, her blue eyes fixed with strange intensity on the door through which her beloved had disappeared. Her father stood beside her, holding her hand, and she rested her cheek against his.

The burgomaster, throughout the last scene, had not once looked at Diogenes. A dark, puzzled frown lingered between his brows whilst he stared moodily into the fire. He absolutely ignored the presence of his son, putting into practice his stern dictum that henceforth he had no son, whilst Nicolaes, who was becoming inured to his shameful position, put on a careless and jaunty air, spoke with easy familiarity to Stoutenburg, and peremptorily to the men.

Then at last the table was once more set, the candles relit, and the board again spread for supper. Stoutenburg, with an elegant flourish, invited his guests to sit, offered his arm to Gilda to lead her to the table. She, moved by a pathetic desire to conciliate him, a forlorn hope that a great show of submission on her part would soften his cruel heart and lighten the fate of her beloved, placed her hand upon his sleeve, and when she met his admiring glance a slight flush drove the pallor from her cheeks.

"You are adorable, myn geloof!" he murmured.

He appeared highly elated, sat at the head of the table, with Gilda on his right and the burgomaster on his left, whilst Nicolaes sat beside his sister.

The two old crones served the supper, coming and going with a noiselessness and precision acquired in long service in the well-conducted house of the burgomaster. They knew the use of the two pronged silver utensils which Mynheer Beresteyn had acquired of late direct from France, where they were used at the table of gentlemen of quality for conveying food to the mouth. They knew how to remove each service from the centre of the table without unduly disturbing the guests, and how to replace one cloth with another the moment it became soiled with sauce or wine.

Jan stood at the Lord of Stoutenburg's elbow and served him personally and with his own hands. Every dish, before it was handed to his lordship, was placed in front of the burgomaster, who was curtly bidden to taste of it. His Magnificence, adept in the poisoner's art, was taking no risks himself.

The cook had done his best, and the supper was, I believe, excellent. The Oille, the most succulent of dishes, made up of quails, capons, and ducks and other tasty meats, was a marvel of gastronomic art, and so were the tureens of beef with cucumber and the breast of veal larded and garnished with hard-boiled eggs. In truth it was all a terrible waste, and sad to see such excellent fare laid before guests who hardly would touch a morsel. Gilda could not eat, her throat seemed to close up every time she tried to swallow. Indeed, she had to appeal to the very last shred of her pride to keep up a semblance of dignity before her enemy. The burgomaster, too, flushed with shame at the indignity put upon him, did no more than taste of the dishes as they were put before him by the surly Jan.

The Lord of Stoutenburg, on the other hand, put up a great show of hilarity, talked much and drank deeply, discussed in a loud, arrogant voice with Nicolaes the Archduchess's plans for the subduing of the Netherlands. And Nicolaes, after he had imbibed two or three bumpers of heady Spanish wine, felt more assured, returned Gilda's reproachful glances with indifference, and his father's contempt with defiance.

2

What Gilda suffered it were a vain attempt to describe. How she contrived to remain at the table; to appear indifferent almost gay; to glance up now and again at a persuasive challenge from Stoutenburg, will for ever remain her secret. She never spoke of that hour, of that hateful, harrowing supper, like an odious nightmare, which was wont in after years to sent a shudder of horror right through her whenever she recalled it.

The burgomaster remained at first obstinately silent, whilst the Lord of Stoutenburg talked with studied insolence of the future of the Netherlands. The happy times would now come back, the traitor vowed, when the United Provinces, dissolved into feeble and separate entities, without form or governance, would once more return to their allegiance and bow the knee before the might of Spain; when the wholesome rule of another Alva would teach these stiffnecked and presumptuous burghers that comfort and a measure of welfare could only be obtained by unconditional surrender and submission to a high, unconquerable Power.

"Freedom!" Liberty!" he sneered. "Ancient Charters! Bah! Empty, swaggering words, I say, which their masters will soon force them to swallow. Then will follow an era more suited to all this beggarly Dutch rabble, one that will teach them a lesson which will at last stick in their memories. The hangman, that's what they want! The stake! The rack! Our glorious Inquisition, and the relentlessness which, alas, for the nonce hath lain buried with our immortal Alva!"

He drank a loyal toast to the coming new era, to the Archduchess, to King Philip IV, who in his glorious reign would see Spain once more unconquered, the Netherlands subdued, England punished at last. Nicolaes joined him with many a lustful shout, whilst the burgomaster sat with set lips, his eyes glowing with suppressed indignation. Once or twice it seemed as if his stern self-control would give way, as if his burning wrath would betray him into words and deeds that might cause abysmal misery to hundreds of innocent people whilst not serving in any way the cause which he would have given his life to uphold.

Indeed, in the book of heroic deeds of which God's angel hath a record, none stand out more brilliantly than the endurance of the Burgomaster of Amersfoort and of his daughter on this memorable occasion. Nor is there in the whole valorous history of the Netherlands a more glorious page than that which tells of the sacrifice made by father and daughter in order to save the city which they loved from threatened annihilation.

3

But like all things, good and evil, the trial came to an end at last. The Lord of Stoutenburg gave the signal, and the burgomaster and Gilda rose from the table both, in truth, with a deep sigh of thankfulness.

Stoutenburg remained deferential until the end – deferential, that is, with an undercurrent of mockery, which he took no pains to conceal, His bow, as he finally took leave of his guests, bidding the burgomaster a simple farewell and Gilda au revoir until the dawn on the morrow, was so obviously ironical that Beresteyn was goaded into an indignant tirade, which he regretted almost as soon as he had uttered it.

"Let him who stands," he said firmly, and with all of his wonted dignity, "take heed lest he fall. The Netherlands are not conquered yet, my lord, because your mercenary troops have succeeded, for the time being, in overrunning one of her provinces. Ede may have fallen. Amersfoort may for the moment, be under your heel –"

"Arnheim and Nijmegen may have capitulated by now," Stoutenburg broke in derisively. "Sold to De Berg, like Amersfoort and Ede, by the craven smeerlap to whom you have given your daughter."

"Even that may have happened," the burgomaster riposted hotly, "if so be the will of God. But we are a race of fighters. We have beaten and humiliated the Spaniard and driven him from off our land before now. And Maurice of Nassau, the finest captain of the age, is unconquered still!"

"Mightily sick, so I'm told," the other put in carelessly. "He was over-ready, methinks, to abandon Amersfoort to its fate."

"Only to punish you more effectually in the end. Take heed, my lord, take heed! The multiplicity of your crimes will find you out soon enough."

" 'Sblood!" retorted Stoutenburg, unperturbed; "but you forget, mynheer burgomaster, that, whate'er betide me, your daughter's fate is henceforth linked to mine own."

Then it was that Beresteyn repented of his outburst, for indeed he had gained nothing by it, and Stoutenburg had used the one argument which was bound to silence him. What, in truth, was the use of wrangling? Dignity was sure to suffer, and that mocking recreant would only feel that his triumph was more complete.

Even now he only laughed, pointed with an ironical flourish of his arm to the widely open doors, through which in the dimly lighted hall, a group of men could be perceived, sitting or standing around the centre table, with Diogenes standing in their midst, his fair head crowned by the hideous bandage, and his broad shoulders towering above the puny, swarthy Spanish soldiery. He had a mug of ale in his hand, and holding it aloft he was singing a ribald song, the refrain of which was taken up by the men. In the vague and flickering light of resin torches, his sightless orbs looked spectral, like those of a wraith.

"You should be grateful to me, mynheer," Stoutenburg added with a sneer, "for freeing your daughter from such a yoke."

He returned to Gilda, took her unresisting hand and raised it to his lips. Above it, he was watching her face. She was looking beyond him, straight at the blind man; and though Stoutenburg at that moment would have bartered much for the knowledge of what was in her thoughts, he could not define the expression of her eyes. At one time he thought that they had softened, that the fulfilment of all his hopes was hanging once more in the balance. It seemed for the moment as if she would snatch away her hand and seek shelter, as she had done before, against the heart of her beloved; that right through that outer husk of misery and degradation she saw something that puzzled her rather than repelled. A question seemed to be hovering on her lips. A question of a protest. Or was it a mute appeal for forgiveness?

Stoutenburg could not tell. But he felt that for a space of a few seconds the whole edifice of his desires was tottering, that Fate might, after all, still be holding a thunderbolt in store for him, which would hurl him down from the pinnacle of this momentary triumph. Gilda – as a woman – was still unconquered. Neither her heart nor her soul would ever be his. Somehow it was the glance wherewith she regarded the blind man that told the Lord of Stoutenburg this one unalterable fact.

The sortilege which he had tried to evoke, by letting her look on the pitiful wreck who had once been her lover, had fallen short in its potent charm. His own brilliant prospects, his masterful personality, ay, his well-assumed indifference, had all failed to cast their spells over her. Unlike the valiant Petruchio of the English play, he had not yet succeeded in taming this beautiful shrew. In the past she had resisted his blandishments; if she succumbed at all, it would be beneath the weight of his tyranny.

Well, so be it! Nicolaes, no doubt, had been right when he said that women reserved their disdain for weaklings. It was the man of iron who won a woman's love. The thought sent a fierce glow of hatred coursing through his blood. Mythical and fatalistic as he was, he believed that his lucky star would only begin to rise when he had succeeded in winning Gilda for his own. He had deemed women an easy conquest in the past. This one could not resist him for long. Even men were wont to come readily under his way – witness Nicolaes Beresteyn, who was as wax in his hands. In the past, he had delighted in wielding a kind of cabalistic power, which he undoubtedly possessed, over many a weak or shifty character. His mother even was wont to call him a magician, and stood not a little in awe of the dark-visaged, headstrong child, and later on of the despotic, lawless youth, who had set the crown on her manifold sorrows by his callousness and his crimes.

That power had been on the wane of late. But it was not – could not – be gone from him forever. Nicolaes was still his sycophant. Jan and his kind were willing to go to death for him. His own brain had devised a means for bringing that obstinate burgomaster and the beautiful Gilda to their knees. Then, of a surety, in the Cornucopia of Fate there was something more comforting, more desirable, than a thunderbolt!

Was he not a man the master of his destiny?

Bah! What was a woman's love, after all? Why not let her go – be content with worldly triumphs? The sacking of Amersfoort, which would yield him wealth and treasure; the gratitude of the Archduchess: a high – if not the highest – position in the reconquered provinces! Why not be content with those? And Stoutenburg groaned like a baffled tiger, because in his heart of hearts he knew these things would not content him in the end. He wanted Gilda! Gilda, of the blue eyes and the golden hair, the demure glance and fragrant hands. His desire for her was in his bones, and he felt that he would indeed go raving mad if he lost her after this – if that beggarly drunkard, unwashed, dishonoured, and stricken with blindness, triumphed through his very abasement and the magnitude of his misfortune.

"This, at any rate, I can avert!" he murmured under his breath. And somehow the thought eased the racking jealousy that was torturing him – jealousy of such an abject thing. He waited until Gilda had passed out of the room, and when she was standing in the hall, so obviously bidding a last farewell in her heart to the man she loved so well, he called peremptorily to Jan:

"Take the varlet," he commanded roughly, "and hang him on the Koppel-poort!"

At the word Gilda turned on him like an infuriated tigress. Pushing past her father, past the men, who recoiled from her as if from a madwoman, she was back beside the execrable despot who thus put the crown on his hideous cruelties.

"Your bargain, my lord!" she cried hoarsely. "You dare not – you dare not —"

"My bargain, fair one?" Stoutenburg retorted coolly. "Nay, you were so averse to fulfilling your share of it, that I have repented me of proposing it. The varlet hangs. That is my last word."

His last word! And Jan so ready to obey! The men were already closing in around her beloved; less than a minute later they had his hands securely pinioned behind his back. Can you wonder that she lost her head, that she fought to free herself from her father's arms, and, throwing reserve, dignity to the winds, threw herself at the feet of that inhuman monster and pleaded with him as no woman on earth had, mayhap, ever pleaded before?

We do not like to think of that exquisite, refined woman kneeling before such an abominable dastard. Yet she did it! Words of appeal, of entreaty, poured from her quivering lips. She raised her tear-stained face to his, embraced his knees with her arms. She forgot the men that stood by, puzzled and vaguely awed – Jan resolute, her father torn to the heart. She forgot everything save that there was a chance – a remote chance – of softening a cruel heart, and she could not – no, could not! – see the man she loved dragged to shameful death before her eyes.

She promised – oh, she promised all that she had to give!

"I'll be your willing slave, my lord, in all things," she pleaded, her voice broken and hoarse. "Your loving wife, as you desire. A kiss from me? Take it, an you will. I'll not resist! Nay, I'll return it from my heart, in exchange for your clemency."

Then it was that the burgomaster succeeded at last in tearing her away from her humiliating position. He dragged her to her feet, drew her to his breast, tried by words and admonition to revive in her her sense of dignity and her self-control. Only with one word did he, in his turn, condescend to plead.

"An you have a spark of humanity left in you, my lord," he said loudly, "order your executioners to be quick about their business."

For the Lord of Stoutenburg had, with a refinement of cruelty almost unbelievable, were it not a matter of history, stayed Jan from executing his inhuman order.

"Wait!" his glittering eyes appeared to say to the sycophant henchman who hung upon his looks. "Let me enjoy this feast until I am satiated."

Then, when Gilda lay at last, half-swooning in the shelter of her father's arms, he said coolly:

"Have I not said, fair one, that if you deigned to plead the rascal should not hang? See! The potency of your charm upon my sensitive heart! The man who hath always been my most bitter enemy, and whom at last I have within my power, shall live because your fair arms did encircle my knees, and because of your free will you offered me a kiss. Mynheer Burgomaster," he added, with easy condescension, "I pray you lead your daughter to her room. She is over-wrought and hath need of rest. Go in peace, I pray you. That drunken varlet is safe now in my hands."

The burgomaster could not trust himself to reply. Only his loving hands wandered with a gentle, soothing gesture over his beloved daughter's hair, whilst he murmured soft, endearing words in her ear. Gradually she became more calm, was able to gather her wits together, to realize what she had done and all that she had sacrificed, probably in vain. Stoutenburg had spoken soft words, but how could she trust him, who had ever proved himself a liar and a cheat? She was indeed like a miserable, captive bird, held, maimed and bruised, in a cruel trap set by vengeful and cunning hands. It seemed almost incredible why she should be made to suffer so.

What had she done? In what horrible way had she sinned before God, that His hand should lie so heavily upon her? Even her sacrifice – sublime and selfless – failed to give her the consolation of duty nobly accomplished. Everything before her was dreary and dark. Life itself was nought but torture. The few days – hours – that must intervene until she knew that Amersfoort was safe confronted her like the dark passage into Gehenna. Beyond them lay death at last, and she, a young girl scarce out of adolescence, hitherto rich, beautiful, adulated, was left to long for that happy release from misery with an intensity of longing akin to the sighing of souls in torment.

Chapter XIV – Treachery

1

Throughout this harrowing scene the blind man had stood by, pinioned, helpless, almost lifeless in his immobility. The only sign of life in him seemed to be in those weird, sightless orbs, in which the flickering light of the resin torches appeared to draw shafts of an unearthly glow. He was pinioned and could not move. Half a dozen soldiers had closed in around him. Whether he heard all that went on, many who were there at the time declared it to be doubtful. But, even if he heard, what could he have done? He could not even put his hands up to his ears to shut out that awful sound of his beloved wife's hoarse, spent voice pleading desperately for him.

One of the men who was on guard over him told De Voocht afterwards that he could hear the tough sinews cracking against the bonds that held the giant captive, and that great drops of sweat appeared upon the fine, wide brow. When Gilda, leaning heavily upon her father's arm, finally mounted the stairs which led up to her room, the blind man turned his head in that direction. But the jongejuffrouw went on with head bent and did not glance down in response.

All this we know from De Voocht, who speaks of it in his "Brieven." But he was not himself present on the scene and hath it only from hearsay. He questioned several of the men subsequently as he came in contact with them, and, of course, the burgomaster's testimony was the most clear and the most detailed. Mynheer Beresteyn admitted that, throughout that awful, ne'er-to-be-forgotten evening, he could not understand the blind man's attitude, was literally tortured with doubts of him. Was he, in truth, the craven wretch which he appeared to be – the miserable traitor who had sold the Stadtholder's original plans to De Berg, betrayed Marquet and De Keysere, and hopelessly jeopardized the whole of Gelderland, if not the entire future of the Netherlands? If so, he was well-deserving of the gallows, which would not fail to be his lot.

But was he? Was he?

The face, of course, out of which the light of the eyes had vanished, was inscrutable. The mouth, remember, was partially hidden by the three days' growth of beard, and grime and fatigue had further obliterated all other marks of expression. Of course, the man must have suffered tortures of humiliation and rage, which would effectually deaden all physical pain. But at the time he seemed not to suffer. Indeed, at one moment it almost seemed if he were asleep, with sightless eyes wide open, and standing on his feet.

2

After Gilda and her father had disappeared on the floor above, the Lord of Stoutenburg, like a wild and caged beast awaiting satisfaction, began pacing up and down the long banqueting-hall. The doors leading into it from the hall had been left wide open, and the men could see his lordship in his restless wanderings, his heavy boots ringing against the reed-covered floor. He held his arms folded across his chest, and was gnawing – yes, gnawing – his knuckles in the excess of his excitement and his choler.

Then he called Jan, and parleyed with him for awhile, consulted Mynheer Nicolaes, who was more taciturn and gloomy than ever before.

The soldiers knew what was coming. They had witnessed the scene between the jongejuffrouw and his Magnificence and some of them who had wives and sweethearts of their own, had felt uncomfortable lumps, at the time, in their throats. Others, who had sons, fell to wishing that their offsprings might be as finely built, as powerful as that poor, blind, intoxicated wretch who, in truth, now had no use for his magnificent muscles.

But what would you? These were troublous times. Life was cheap – counted for nothing in sight of such great gentlemen as was the Lord of Stoutenburg. The varlet, it seems, had offended his lordship awhile ago. Jan knew the story, and was very bitter about it, too. Well, no man could expected to be treated with gentleness by a great lord whom he had been fool enough to offend. The blind rascallion would hang, of that there could be no doubt. The jongejuffrouw had been pacified with soft words and vague promises, but the rascal would hang. Any man there would have bet his shirt on the issue. You had only to look at his lordship. A more determined, more terrifying look it were impossible to meet. Even Jan looked a little scared. When his Magnificence looked like that it boded no good to any one. All the rancour, the gall, that had accumulated in his heart against everything that pertained to the United Provinces and to their Stadtholder would effectively smother the slightest stirring of conscience or pity. Perhaps, when the jongejuffrouw knelt at his feet, he had thought of his mother, who, equally distraught and equally humiliated, had knelt in vain at the Stadtholder's feet, pleading for the life of her sons. Oh, yes, all that had made the Lord of Stoutenburg terribly hard and callous.

But the men were sorry for the blind vagabond, for all that. He had had nothing to do with the feuds between the Stadtholder and the sons of Olden Barneveldt. He had done nothing, seemingly, save to win the love of the beautiful lady whom his Magnificence had marked for his own. He was brave, too. You could not help admiring him as he stood between you and your comrades, his head thrown back, a splendid type of virility and manhood. Half-seas over he may have been. His misfortunes were, in truth, enough to make any man take a drink; but you could not help but see that there was an air of spirituality about the forehead and the sensitive nostrils which redeemed the face from any suggestion of sensuality. And now and again a quaint smile would play round the corners of his mouth, and the whole wan face would light up as if with a sudden whimsical thought.

Then all at once he threw back his head and yawned.

Such a droll fellow! Yawning on the brink of eternity! It was, in truth, a pity he should hang!

3

Yes, the blind man yawned, loudly and long, like one who is ready for bed. And the harmless sound completed Stoutenburg's exasperation. He once more gave the harsh word of command:

"Take the varlet out and hang him!"

Obviously this time it would be irrevocable. There was no one here to plead, and there was Jan, stolid and grim as was his wont, already at attention under the lintel – a veritable tower of strength in support of his chief's decisions.

Jan was not in the habit of arguing with his lordship. This, or any other order, was as one to him. As for the blind vagabond – well, Jan was as eager as his Magnificence to get the noose around the rascal's throat. There were plenty of old scores to settle between them – the humiliation of three months ago, which had sent Stoutenburg, disgraced and a fugitive, out of the land, had hit Jan severely, too.

And that never-to-be-forgotten discomfiture was entirely due to this miserable caitiff, who, indeed would get naught but his deserts.

The task, in truth, was a congenial one to Jan. A blind man was easy enough to deal with, and this one offered but little resistance. He had been half-asleep, it seems, and only woke to find himself on the brink of eternity. Even so, his good-humour did not forsake him.

"Odd's fish!" he exclaimed when, roughly shaken from his somnolence, he found himself in the hands of the soldiery. "I had forgotten this hanging business. You might have left a man to finish his dreams in peace."

He appeared dazed, and his speech was thick. He had been drinking heavily all the evening, and, save for an odd moment or so of lucid interval, he had been hopelessly fuddled all along. And he was merry in his cups; laughter came readily to his lips; he was full of quips and sallies, too, which kept the men in rare good-humour. In truth, the fellow would joke and sing apparently until the hangman's rope smothered all laughter in his throat.

But he had an unquenchable thirst; entreated the men to bring him a jug of wine.

"Spanish wine," he pleaded. "I dote on Spanish wine, but had so little of it to drink in my day. That villainous rascal Pythagoras – some of you must have known the pot-bellied loon – would always seize all there was to get. He and Socrates. Two scurvy runagates who should hang 'stead o' me. Give me a mug of wine, for mercy's sake!"

The men had none to give, and the matter was referred to Jan.

"Not another drop!" Jan declared with unanswerable finality. "The knave is quite drunk enough as it is."

"Ah!" the blind man protested with ludicrous vehemence. "But there thou'rt wrong, worthy Jan. No man is ever – is ever drunk enough. He may be top-heavy, he may be as drunk as a lord, or as fuddled as David's sow. He may be fuzzy, fou, or merely sottish; but sufficiently drunk? No!"

A shout of laughter from the men greeted this solemn pronouncement. Jan shrugged his shoulders impatiently.

"Well, that is as may be!" he rejoined gruffly. "But not another drop to drink wilt thou get from me."

"Oh, Jan," the poor man protested, with a pitiable note of appeal, "my good Jan, think on it! I am about to hang! Wouldst refuse the last request of a dying man?"

"Thou'rt about to hang," Jan assented, unmoved. "Therefore, 'twere a pity to waste good liquor on thee."

"I'll pay the well, my good Jan," Diogenes put in, with a knowing wink of his sightless eyes.

"Pay me?" Jan retorted, with a grim laugh. " 'Tis not much there's left in thy pockets, I'm thinking."

"No," the blind man agreed, nodding gravely. "These good men here did, in truth – empty my pockets effectually awhile ago. 'Twas not with coin I meant to repay thee, good Jan —"

"With what, then?"

"Information, Jan!" the blind man replied, sinking his voice to a hoarse whisper. "Information for the like of which his Lordship of Stoutenburg would give his ears."

Jan laughed derisively. The men laughed openly. They thought this but another excellent joke on the part of the droll fellow.

"Bah! Jan said, with a shrug of the shoulder. "How should a varlet like thee know aught of which his lordship hath not full cognisance already?"

"His lordship," the other riposted quickly, even whilst a look of impish cunning overspread his face – "his lordship never was in the confidence of the Stadtholder. I was!"

"What hath the Stadtholder to do with the matter?"

"Oh, nothing, nothing!" the blind man replied airily. "Thou art obstinate, my good Jan, and 'tis not I who would force thee to share a secret for the possession of which, let me assure thee, his lordship would repay me not only with a tankard of his best wine, but with my life! Ay, and with a yearly pension of one thousand guilders to boot."

These last few words he had spoken quite slowly and with grave deliberation, his head nodding sagely while he spoke. The look of cunning in those spectral orbs had lent to his pale, wan face an air of elfin ghoulishness. He was swaying on his feet, and now and again the men had to hold him up, for he was on the very point of measuring his length on the hall floor.

Jan did not know what to make of it all. Obviously the man was drunk. But not so drunk that he did not know what he was talking about. And the air of cunning suggested that there was something alive in the fuddled brain. Jan looked across the hall in the direction of the banqueting-room.

The doors were wide open, and he could see that his lordship, who at first had paced up and down the long room like a caged beast, had paused quite close to the door, then advanced on tip-toe out into the hall, where he had remained for the last minute or two, intent and still, with eager, probing glance fixed upon the blind man. Now, when Jan questioned him with a look, he gave his faithful henchman a scarce perceptible sign, which the latter was quick enough to interpret correctly.

"Thou dost set my mouth to water," he said to the blind man, with well-assumed carelessness, "By all this talk of yearly pensions and of guilders. I am a poor man, and not so young as I was. A thousand guilders a year would keep me in comfort for the rest of my life."

"Yet art so obstinate," Diogenes riposted with a quaint, inane laugh, "as to deny me a tankard of Spanish wine, which might put thee in possession of my secret – a secret, good Jan, worth yearly pensions and more to his lordship."

"How do I know thou'rt not a consummate liar?" Jan protested gruffly.

"I am!" the other riposted, wholly unruffled. "I am! Lying hath been my chief trade ever since I was breeched. Had I not lied to the Stadtholder he would not have entrusted his secrets to me, and I could not have bartered those secrets for a tankard of good Spanish wine."

"Thy vaunted secrets may not be worth a tankard of wine."

"They are, friend Jan, they are! Try them and see."

"Well, let's hear them and, if they are worth it, I'll pay thee with a tankard of his lordship's best Oporto."

But the blind man shook his head with owlish solemnity.

"And then sell them to his lordship," he retorted, "for pensions and what not, whilst thine own hand, mayhap, puts the rope around my neck. No, no, my good Jan, say no more about it. I'd as lief see his lordship and thee falling into the Stadtholder's carefully laid trap, and getting murdered in your beds, even while I am on my journey to kingdom come."

"Who is going to murder us?" Jan queried, frowning and puzzled, trying to get his cue once more from his master. "And how?"

"I'll not tell thee," the blind man replied, with a quick turn to that obstinacy which so oft pertains to the drunkard, "not if thou wert to plunge me in a bath of best Oporto."

Some of the men began to murmur.

"We might all share?" one or two of them suggested.

"Let's hear what it is," others declared.

"I'll tell thee, knave, what I'll do," Jan rejoined decisively. "I'll bring thee a tankard of Oporto to loosen thy tongue. Then, if thy secret is indeed as important as thou dost pretend, I'll see that the hangman is cheated of thy carcass."

For awhile the blind man pondered.

"Loosen my hands then, friend Jan," he said, "for, in truth, I am trussed like a fowl; then let's feel the handle of that tankard. After that we'll talk."

4

The soldiers sat around the table, watching the blind man with grave attention. At a sign from Jan they soon loosened his bonds. There was something magnetic in the air just then, something that sent sensitive nerves aquiver, and of which these rough fellow were only vaguely conscious. They could not look on that drunken loon without laughing. He was more comical than ever now, with that air of bland beatitude upon his face as his slender fingers closed around the handle of the tankard which Jan had just placed in his hand.

"I would sell my soul for a butt of this nectar," he said; and drank in the odour of the wine with every sign of delight, even before he raised the tankard to his lips.

The Lord of Stoutenburg watched the blind man, too. A deep furrow between his brows testified to the earnest concentration of his thoughts. The man knew something, or thought he knew, of that his lordship could not be in doubt. The question was, was that knowledge of such importance as the miserable wretch averred, or was he merely, like any rogue who sees the rope dangling before his eyes, trying to gain a respite, by proposing vain bargains or selling secrets that had only found birth in his own fuddled brain. Stoutenburg, remember, was no psychologist. Indeed, psychology did not exist as a science in these days when men were over-busy with fighting, and had no time or desire to probe into the inner workings of one another's soul.

On the other hand, here was a man, thus his lordship argued to himself, who might know something of the Stadtholder's plans. He was wont, before he rolled so rapidly down the hill of manhood and repute, to be an inimate of Maurice of Nassau. He might, as lately as yesterday, have been initiated into the great soldier's plans for repelling this sudden invasion of the land which he had thought secure. The Stadtholder, in truth, was not the man to abandon all efforts at resistance just because his original plans had failed.

True, the attempt to rescue Arnheim and Nijmegen had ended in smoke. Marquet and De Keysere were, thanks to timely warning, being held up somewhere by the armies of Isembourg and De Berg. But Maurice of Nassau would not of a certainty, thus lightly abandon all hopes of saving Gelderland. He must have formulated a project, and Stoutenburg, who was no fool, was far from underestimating the infinite brain power and resourcefulness of that peerless commander. Whether he had communicated that project to this besotted oaf was another matter.

Stoutenburg searched the blind man's face with an intent glance that seemed to probe the innermost thoughts behind that fine, wide brow. For the moment, the face told him nothing. It was just vacant, the sightless eyes shone with delight, and the tankard raised to the lips effectually hid all expression around the mouth.

Well, there was not much harm done, the waste of a few moments, if the information proved futile. Jan was ready with the rope, if the whole thing proved to be a mere trick for putting off the fateful hour. As the Lord of Stoutenburg gazed on the blind man, trying vainly to curb his burning impatience, he instinctively thought of Gilda. Gilda, and his hopeless wooing of her, her coldness toward him and her passionate adherence to this miserable caitiff, who, in truth, had thrown dust in her eyes by an outward show of physical courage and a mock display of spurious chivalry.

What if the varlet had been initiated in the Stadtholder's projects? What if he betrayed them now – sold them in exchange for his own worthless life, and stood revealed, before all the world, as an abject coward, as base as any Judas who would sell his master for thirty pieces of silver? The thought turned the miscreant giddy, so dazzling did this issue appear before his mental vision. What a revelation for a fond and loyal woman, who had placed so worthless an object on a pinnacle of valour! What a disillusionment! She had staunchly believed in his integrity up to now. But after this?

In truth, what more can a man desire than to see the honour of a rival smirched in the eyes of a woman who spurns him? That was the main thought that coursed through Stoutenburg's brain, driving before it all obstinacy and choler, ay, even soothing his exacerbated nerves.

He gave a sign to Jan.

"Bring that varlet here to me," he commanded. "I'll speak to him myself."

The sound of his voice chased the look of beatitude from the blind man's face, which took on an expression of bewildered surprise.

"I had no thought his lordship was here," he said, with a self-conscious, inane laugh.

The men were murmuring audibly. Some of them had seen visions of good reward, shared amongst them all, after the blind man had been made to speak. But Jan paid no heed to their discontent. In a trice he had seen the blind man secure once more, with arms tied as before behind his back. Diogenes had uttered a loud cry of protest when the empty tankard was torn out of his hand.

"Jan," he shouted, in a thick, hoarse voice, "if thou'rt a knave and dost not keep faith with me, the devil himself will run away with thee."

"His Magnificence will hear what thou hast to say," Jan retorted gruffly. "After that, we'll see."

He led the prisoner through into the banqueting-hall, and despite the men's murmurings, he closed the door upon them. He sat the blind man down in a chair, opposite his lordship. The poor loon had begun to whimper softly, just like a child, and continued to appeal pitiably to Jan.

"If his lordship is satisfied," he murmured confidingly, "you'll see to it, Jan, that I do not hang."

"Jan has his orders!" his lordship put in roughly. "But take heed, sirrah! If your information is worth having, you may go to hell your own way; I care nought! But remember," he added, with slow and stern emphasis, "if you trick me in this, 'twil not be the rope for you at dawn – but the stake!

Diogenes gave a quick shudder.

"By the lord," he said blandly, "how very unpleasant! But I am a man of my word. Jan put good wine into me. He shall be paid for it. And I'll tell you what the Stadtholder hath planned for the defeat of the Lord of Stoutenburg."

"Well," his lordship retorted curtly. "I wait!"

There was silence for a moment whilst the blind man apparently collected his thoughts. He sat, trussed and helpless in the chair, with his head thrown back, and the full light of the candles playing upon his pale face – the latter still vacant and with a childish expression of excitement about those weird, dark orbs. The Lord of Stoutenburg, master of the situation, sat in a high-backed chair opposite him, his chin resting in his hand, his eyes, glowering and fierce, searching that strange, mysterious face before him. Strange and mysterious, in truth, with those sightless eyes, that glittered uncannily whenever the flickering candle-light caught the abnormally dilated pupils, and those quavering lips which every moment broke into a whimsical and inane smile.

"Jan, my friend," the blind man asked after a while, "art here?"

"Ay!" Jan replied gruffly. "I'm here right enough to see that thou'rt up to no mischief."

"How can I be that, worthy Jan?" the other retorted blandly, "since thou hast again trussed me like a capon?"

"Well, the sooner thou hast satisfied his lordship," Jan rejoined with stolid indifference, "the sooner thou wilt be free —"

"To go to hell mine own way!" Diogenes put in with a hiccough. "So his lordship hath pledged his word. Let all those who are my friends bear witness that his lordship did pledge his word."

He paused, and once again a look of impish cunning over-spread his face. He seemed to be preparing for a fateful moment which literally would mean life or death for him. An exclamation of angry impatience from Stoutenburg recalled him to himself.

"I am ready," he protested with eager servility, "to do his lordship's pleasure."

"Then speak, man!" Stoutenburg retorted savagely, "ere I wring the words from thee with torture!"

"I was only thinking how to put the matter clearly," Diogenes protested blandly. "The Stadtholder only outlined his plan to me. There was so little time. My friend Klaas will remember that after his Highness's horse bolted across the moor I was able to stop it —"

"Yes – curse your interference!" Stoutenburg muttered between his teeth.

"Amen to that!" the blind man assented. "But for it, I should still have the privilege of beholding your lordship's pleasing countenance. But at the moment I had no thought save to stop a runaway horse. The Stadtholder was mightily excited, scented that a trap had been laid for him. My friend Klaas again will remember that, after his Highness dismounted he stopped to parley with me upon the moor."

Nicolaes nodded.

"Then it was," Diogenes went on, "that he told what he meant to do. I was, of course, to bear my part in the new project, which was to make a feint upon Ede —"

"A feint upon Ede?"

"Ay! A surprise attack, which would keep De Berg, who is in Ede, busy whilst the Stadtholder —"

"Bah!" Stoutenburg broke in contemptuously, "De Berg is too wary to be caught by a feint."

"So he is, my lord, so he is!" Diogenes rejoined with solemn gravity. "But if I were to tell you that the surprise attack is to be made in full force, and that the weight will fall on the south side of the town, what then?"

"I do not see with what object."

"Yet you, my lord, would know the Stadtholder's tactics of old. You fought under his banner – once."

"Before he murdered my father, yes!" Stoutenburg broke in impatiently. He did not relish this allusion to his former fighting days, before black treachery had made him betray the ruler he once served. "But what of that?"

"For then your lordship would remember," the blind man went on placidly, "that the Stadtholder's favorite plan was always to draw the enemy away by a ruse from his own chief point of attack."

"But where would the chief point of attack be in this case?" Stoutenburg queried with a frown.

"At a certain molen your lordship wot of on the Veluwe."

"Impossible!"

"Oh, impossible? Your lordship is pleased to jest. Some days ago, spies came into Utrecht with the information that the Lord of Stoutenburg had his camp at an old molen, which stands disused and isolated on the highest point of the Veluwe, somewhere between Apeldoorn and Barneveld."

"My camp? Bah! The mill was only a halting place —"

"The spies averred, my lord," the blind man broke in blandly, "that vast stores of arms and ammunition are accumulated in that halting-place. And that the attack on Amersfoort was planned within its rickety walls."

Then, as the Lord of Stoutenburg made no comment on this – indeed, he had cast a rapid, significant glance on Nicolaes, who throughout this colloquy had appeared as keen, as interested, as his friend – the blind man went on slowly:

"The Stadtholder's objective is the molen on the Veluwe."

"What? From Ede!" Nicolaes exclaimed.

"No, no! Have I not said that the attack on Ede would be a feint? It will be the Stadtholder himself who, with a comparatively small force, will push on toward Barneveld and the molen, and at once cut off all communication between Ede and Amersfoort."

"I understand," Stoutenburg rejoined, with a grave nod. "But if it is a small force we can easily —"

"You can now," Diogenes assented coolly, "since you are warned."

"Quite right! Eh, friend Nicolaes?" his lordship retorted, and strove to let his harsh voice express a world of withering contempt. "If all this is not a trick you varlet hath served us well. What say you? Shall we let him go to hell his own way, and save the hangman a deal of pother?"

"If it all prove true," Nicolaes put in cautiously. "But what proof have we?"

"None, in truth. Nor would I let this craven vagabond out of Jan's sight until we do make sure that he hath not lied. But there'll be no harm in being prepared. Here, sirrah!" his lordship continued, once more addressing the blind man. "With how strong a force doth the Stadtholder propose to cut us off from Ede?"

But, during this brief colloquy between the two friends, the blind man had begun to nod. His head fell forward on his chest, the heavy lids veiled the stricken eyes, and anon a peaceable snore came through the partially open mouth. Stoutenburg swore, as was his wont, the moment his choler was roused, and Jan shook the prisoner roughly by the shoulder.

"Eh? Eh? What?" the latter queried, blinked his sightless eyes, and turned a pale and startled face vaguely from side to side. "What is it? Where's that confounded —?

"Answer his lordship's question!" Jan commanded briefly.

"Question? What question? Your lordship must forgive me. I am so fatigued, and that tankard of—"

"I asked thee, knave," Stoutenburg broke in impatiently, "with how strong a force the Stadtholder proposed to cut us off from Ede?"

"Call it four thousand, my lord," the blind man babbled, "and let me go to sleep"

"You shall sleep till Judgement Day when I've done with you, sirrah! Will the Stadtholder lead that force in person?"

The blind man winked and blinked, tried to collect his thoughts, which apparently had all wandered off toward the Land of Nod. Then he said:

"The plan was to leave the bulk of that force to menace Amersfoort. But the Stadtholder himself meant to push on as far as the molen, with but a few hundred of his picked men. He thought to seize the stores of arms and ammunition there and then to await the coming of the Lord of Stoutenburg, who, driven out of Amersfoort and cut off from Ede, would make of necessity for his headquarters."

"Ah!"

The exclamation, deep and prolonged, came from three pairs of lips. Stoutenburg, Nicolaes and Jan looked at one another, and there was triumph and satisfaction depicted in their glance. The same thought had occurred simultaneously to these three traitors; the Stadtholder, with a comparatively small force, pushing on to the lonely molen on the Veluwe, not knowing that some of De Berg's troops were holding the Ijssel beyond.

He would be caught like a rat in a trap; and the question was whether it would not be better to allow him to carry out his plan, not to oppose him on his way, to let him reach the molen and then close in behind him, so that he would have but two alternatives before him – to surrender in the molen or to turn his small force in the direction of the Zuider Zee, and therein seek a watery grave.

5

"I must have a little time to think," Stoutenburg muttered to himself, after a while.

The blind man had apparently dropped off to sleep again. His head had once more fallen forward on his chest. Jan was prepared to give him another rude awakening, but his lordship stopped him with a sign.

"Let the muckworm sleep," he said. "I must think out the whole position. If what the knave says is true-

"I am inclined to believe it true," Nicolaes interposed. "The man is too fuddled to have invented so circumstantial a story. And I have it in my mind," he added reflectively, "that when the Stadtholder visited Amersfoort yesterday he said something to my father about devising a plan later on if the city were seriously threatened."

"Then, by Satan! all would be well indeed!" And Stoutenburg drew up his gaunt figure to its full height, looked every inch a conqueror, with heel set upon the neck of his foes. Jan alone looked dubious.

"I wouldn't trust the rogue," he said grimly.

"Would you hang him now?" Stoutenburg retorted.

"No; I would wait to make sure. Let him sleep awhile now. When he wakes out of his booze, he might be able to give us further details."

"In the meanwhile," his lordship rejoined, "keep the men under arms, Jan. I have not yet thought the matter over; but this I know – that I'll start for the molen with a few hundred musketeers and pikemen as soon as I am sure that this rascallion hath not spun a tissue of lies. Do you send out spies at once in every direction, with orders to bring back information immediately. We must hear if an attack hath indeed been made on Ede, and if the Stadtholder is moving out of Utrecht. Have you some men you can trust?"

"Oh, yes, so please your lordship," Jan replied. "I can send Piet Walleren in the direction of Ede, and I myself will push on toward Utrecht. We'd both be back long before dawn."

"And 'tis not you who could be nousled, eh, good Jan?" his lordship was pleased to say.

"If we have been tricked by this tosspot," Jan riposted gruffly, "I'll see him burnt alive, and 'tis mine own hand will set the brand to the stake."

He paused, and drew in his breath with a shudder; for he had turned to look on the blind man whom he was threatening with so dire a fate and whom he had thought asleep, and encountered those sightless orbs fixed upon him as if they could see something through and beyond him, some ghoul or spectre lurking in a distant corner of the room. So uncanny and terrifying did the rascal look, indeed, that instinctively Jan, who believed neither in God nor the devil, remembered his mother's early teachings, and made sundry and vague signs of the Cross upon his breast, with a view to exorcising those evil spirits which must be somewhere lurking about, unseen by all save by the man who had lost his sight.

"What is it now?" Stoutenburg queried with a scowl.

The blind man indeed appeared to be listening – listening so intently, with head now craned forward and eyes fixed into vacancy – that instinctively the three recreants listened too. To what, they could not have told. Through the open casement the sound of life – camp life, of sentries' challenging call, of bivouac fires, and rowdy soldiery – came in as before. A little less roisterous, perhaps, seeing that most of the men, tired after long days of marching and hours of carousing, had settled themselves down to sleep.

Inside the room, the monumental clock up against the wall ticked off each succeeding second with tranquil monotony. It was now close upon midnight. Nothing had happened. Nothing could have happened, to disturb the wonted tenor of the life of an army in temporary occupation of an unresisting city. Nothing, in fact, unless that blind tatter-demalion over there had indeed spoken the truth.

And still he listened. A vague anxiety seemed to have completely banished sleep, even momentarily to have dissipated the potent effect of that excellent Oporto; and on his face there was that strained look peculiar to those who have been robbed of one sense and are at pains to exert the others to their utmost power. It seemed as if his sightless orbs must pierce some hidden veil which kept vital secrets hidden from ordinary human gaze. And these three men – traitors all – whose craven hearts, weighted with crime, were sensitive to every uncanny spell, felt their own senses unaccountably thrilled by that motionless, stony image of a man whose very soul appeared on the alert, and in whom life itself, was as it were, momentarily arrested.

The spell continued for a moment or two. A minute, perhaps, went by; then, with an impatient curse, Stoutenburg jumped to his feet, strode rapidly to the window, and, leaning out far over the sill, he listened.

Indeed, at first it was naught but the habitual confused sounds that reach his ear. But as he, in his turn, strained every sense to hear, something unusual seemed to mingle with the other sounds. A murmuring. Strange voices. A few isolated words that rose above the others, louder than the sentries' call; also a patter of feet, like men running and a clang of arms that at this hour should have been stilled.

The Lord of Stoutenburg could not have told you then why those sounds should have suddenly filled his mind with foreboding – why, indeed, he heard them at all. Beneath the window, ranged against the wall, the men of his picked company were sleeping peacefully. Their bivouac fire fed by those on guard, shed a pleasant glow over the familiar scene. Beyond its ruddy gleam everything looked by contrast impenetrably dark. The river beyond it, nothing; only blackness – a blackness that could be felt. The lights of the city had long since been extinguished, only one tiny glimmer, which came from a small oil-lamp, showed above the Koppel-poort.

But that confused sound, that murmuring, came from the rear of the burgomaster's house, from the direction of the Market Place, where the bulk of his lordship's army was encamped.

"What in thunder does it mean?" Stoutenburg muttered.

Nicolaes came and joined him by the window. He, too, strained his ears to hear, feeling his nerves vaguely stirred by a kind of superstitious dread. But Stoutenburg turned to the blind man, and tried to read an answer in the latter's white, set face.

Jan shook Diogenes fiercely by the shoulder.

"Dost hear, knave?" he said harshly. "What does it all mean?"

"What does what mean, worthy Jan?" the blind man queried blandly.

"Thou are listening for something. What is it? His lordship desires to know."

"Canst thou hear anything, friend Jan?" the other riposted serenely.

"Only the usual sounds. What should I hear?"

"The armies of the Stadtholder on the move."

An exclamation of incredulity broke from Stoutenburg's lips. Nevertheless, he turned imperatively to Jan.

"Go or send at once into the town," he commanded. "Let us hear if anything has happened."

In a moment Jan was out of the room; and soon his gruff voice could be heard from outside, questioning and giving orders. He had gone himself to see what was amiss.

And Stoutenburg, half incredulous, yet labouring under strong excitement, once more approached the window and, leaning far out into the night, set his ears to listen.

His senses, too, were keyed up now, detached as they were from everything else except just what went on outside. The subdued murmurings reached his perceptions independently of every other sound. A hum of voices, and through it that of Jan, questioning and commanding; and others that talked agitatedly, with many interruptions.

After awhile he felt that he could stand the strain no longer. Very obviously something had happened, something was being discussed out on the Market Place, and there was a kind of buzzing in the air, as if around the hive of bees that have been disturbed by a company of robberwasps. And to him – Stoutenburg – for whom that buzzing might mean the first step toward the pinnacle of his desires, the turning point of his destiny, beyond which lay power, dominion, ambition satisfied, and passion satiated, every moment of suspense and silence became positive torture. A primeval, savage instinct would, but for the presence of Nicolaes, have driven him to seizing the helpless prisoner by the throat, and thus to ease the tension on his nerves and still the wild hammering of blood on his temples.

But Nicolaes did, as it happened, exercise in this instance a restraining influence on his friend; quite unknowingly, of course, as his was the weaker nature. But the last half hour had wrought a marked change in Stoutenburg – a subtle one, which he himself could not have defined. Before then, he had been striving for great things – for revenge, for power, for the satisfaction of his passions. But now he felt that he had attained all that, and more. Obviously his stricken enemy had not lied. The Stadtholder was about to fall into a trap which was easy enough to set. The once brilliant Laughing Cavalier had sunk to a state of moral and physical degradation from which he could never now recover. And Gilda! Gilda had but to realize the slough of turpitude into which her former lover had sunk to turn gratefully and with a sigh of infinite relief to the man who had freed her from such a yoke.

In truth, Stoutenburg felt that he no longer needed to climb. He had reached the summit. The summit of ambition, of power, of sentimental satisfaction. He was a conqueror now; master in the land of his birth; the future Stadtholder of the United Province, wedded to the richest heiress in the Netherlands; happy, feared, and obeyed.

That was his position now, and that was the cause of the subtle change in him – a change which forced him to keep his savage instincts in check before his servile friend; forced to try and appear before others as above petty passions; a justiciary and not a terrorist.

6

The minutes sped by, leaden-footed for the impatience of these two men. Nicolaes and Stoutenburg, each trying to appear calm, hardly dared to speak with one another lest their speech betrayed the exacerbation of their nerves.

It was Nicolaes' turn now to pace up and down the room, to halt beside the window and peer out into the darkness in search of Jan's familiar figure. Stoutenburg had once more taken a seat on the highbacked chair, striving to look dignified and detached. His arm was thrown over the table, and with his sharply pointed nails he was drumming a devil's tatoo on the board.

Alone, the blind man appeared perfectly serene. After that brief moment of comparative lucidity, he had relapsed into somnolence. Occasional loud snores testified that he was once more wandering in the Elysian fields of unconsciousness.

Half an hour after midnight Jan returned.

"There is no doubt about it," were the first words he spoke. "An attack on Ede appears to be in progress, and the Stadtholder left his camp at Utrecht a couple of hours ago with a force of four thousand men."

He was out of breath, having run, he said, all the way from the Joris Poort, where he had gleaned the latest information.

"Who brought the news?" his lordship asked.

"No one seems to know, my lord," Jan replied. "But every one in the town has it. The rumour hath spread like wildfire. It started at opposite quarters of the city. The Nieuw Poort had it that a surprise attack had been delivered on Ede earlier in the evening, and the Joris Poort that the Stadtholder and his force are on the move. The captains at the gates had heard the news from runners who had come direct from Utrecht and from Ede."

"Where are those runners now?"

"In both cases the captains sent them back for further information. The fellows were willing enough to go, for a consideration; but the business has become a dangerous one, for the roads to Utrecht and Ede, they averred are already full of the Stadtholder's vedettes."

"Bah!" Stoutenburg ejaculated contemptuously. "A device for extorting money!"

"Probably," Jan riposted dryly. "But the money will be well spent if we get the information. The men are not to be paid until they return. And if they do not return —" Jan shrugged his shoulders. If the spies did not return, it would go to prove that the Stadtholder's vedettes were not asleep.

"I sent Piet Wallerin and one or two others out, too," he added, "with orders to push on both roads as far as possible, and bring back any information they can obtain – the sooner the better.

"They have not yet returned?" Stoutenburg asked.

"Oh, no! They have only been gone half an hour."

"Is the night very dark?"

"Very dark, my lord."

"Piet may never get back."

"In that case we shall know that the Stadtholder's vanguard has sighted him," Jan rejoined coolly. "Nothing else would keep Piet from getting back."

Stoutenburg nodded approval.

"You think, then, that this varlet here spoke the truth?"

"I have no longer any doubt of it, my lord," Jan gave reply. "Though I did not actually speak with the men who seem originally to have brought the news, the captains at the Poorts had no doubt whatever as to its authenticity. But we shall know for certain before dawn. Piet and the others will have returned by then – or not, as the case may be. But we shall know."

"And, of course, we are prepared?"

"To do just what your lordship commands. The men will be under arms within the next two hours, and I can seek the Master of the Camp, and send him at once to your lordship for instructions."

"Mine instructions are simple enough, good Jan; and thou canst convey them to the Master of the Camp thyself. They are, to remain quiescent, under arms but asleep. To surrender the town if it be attacked —"

"To surrender?" Jan protested with a frown.

"We must throw dust in the Stadtholder's eyes," Stoutenburg riposted. "Give the idea that we are feeble and unprepared, and that I have fled out of Amersfoort. The surrender of the city and its occupation will keep the main force busy, whilst Maurice of Nassau, anxious to possess himself of our person, will push on as far as the molen, where I, in the meanwhile, will be waiting for him."

His voice rang with a note of excitement and of triumph.

"With the Stadtholder a prisoner in my hands," he exclaimed, "I can command the surrender of all his forces. And then the whole of the Netherlands will be at my feet!"

Never, in his wildest dreams had he hoped for this. Fate, in very truth, had tired of smiting him, had an overfull cornucopia for him now and was showering down treasures upon him, one by one.

7

It was Nicolaes who first remembered the blind man.

During the last momentous half-hour he had been totally forgotten. Stoutenburg during that time had been in close confabulation with Jan, discussing plans, making arrangements for the morrow's momentous expedition. Neither of them seemed to feel the slightest fatigue. They were men of iron, whom their passions kept alive. But Nicolaes was a man of straw. He had been racked by one emotion after the other all day, and now he was so tired that he could hardly stand. He envied the blind man every time that a lusty snore escaped the latter's lips, and tried to keep himself awake by going to the fire from time to time and throwing a log or two upon it. But he stood in too great an awe of his friend to dare own to fatigue when the future of his native land was under discussion.

It was really in order to divert Stoutenburg's attention from these interminable discussions on what to do and what not to do on the morrow, that presently, during a pause, he pointed to Diogenes.

"What is to happen to this drunken loon?" he asked abruptly.

Stoutenburg grinned maliciously.

"Have no fear, friend Nicolaes," he said. "The fate of our valued informer will be my special care. I have not forgotten him. Jan knows. While you were nodding, he and I arranged it all. You did not hear?"

Nicolaes shook his head.

"No," he said. "What did you decide?"

"You shall see, my good Klaas," Stoutenburg replied with grim satisfaction. "I doubt not but what you'll be pleased. And since we have now finished the discussion of our plans, Jan will at once go and bid the Heer Burgomaster rise from his bed and attend upon our pleasure."

"My father?" Nicolaes exclaimed in surprise. "Why? What hath he —"

"You will see, my good Klaas," the other broke in quietly. "You will see. I think that you will be satisfied."

Jan, at his word, had already gone. Nicolaes, really puzzled, tried to ask questions, but Stoutenburg was obviously determined to keep the secret of his intentions awhile longer to himself.

It was long past one o'clock now, and bitterly cold. Even the huge blazing logs in the monumental hearth failed to keep the large room at a pleasing temperature. Nicolaes, shivering and yawning, crouched beside the blaze, knocked his half-frozen hands one against the other. He would at this moment have bartered most of his ambitions for the immediate prospect of a good bed. But Stoutenburg was as wide awake as ever, and evidently some kind of inward fever kept the cold out of his bones.

After Jan's departure he resumed that restless pacing of his up and down the long room. Up and down, until Nicolaes, exasperated beyond endurance, could have screamed with choler.

Less than a quarter of an hour later, the burgomaster arrived, ushered in by Jan. He had apparently not taken off his clothes since he had been upstairs. It was indeed more that likely that he had spent the time in prayer, for Mynheer Beresteyn was a pious man, and the will of God in fortune or adversity was a very real thing to him. With the same dignified submission which he had displayed throughout, he had immediately followed Jan when curtly ordered to do so. But he came down to face the arrogant tyrant for the third time to-night with as heavy a heart as before, not knowing what fresh indignity, what new cruel measure, would be put upon him. Grace or clemency he knew that he could not expect.

The look of malignant triumph wherewith Stoutenburg greeted him appeared to justify his worst forebodings. The presence, too, of Diogenes, fettered and asleep, filled his anxious heart with additional dread. As he stepped out into the room he took no notice of his son, but only strove to face his arch-enemy with as serene a countenance as he could command.

"Your lordship desired that I should come," he said quietly. "What is your lordship's pleasure?"

But Stoutenburg was all suavity. A kind of feline gentleness was in his tone as he replied:

"Firstly, to beg your forgiveness, mynheer, for having disturbed you again – and at this hour. But will you not sit? Jan," he commanded, "draw a chair nearer to the hearth for the Heer Burgomaster."

"I was not asleep, my lord," Beresteyn rejoined coldly. "And by your leave, will take your commands standing."

"Oh, commands, mynheer!" Stoutenburg rejoined blandly. " 'Tis no commands I would venture to give you. It was my duty – my painful duty – not to keep you in ignorance of certain matters which have just come to my knowledge, and which will have a momentous bearing upon all my future plans. Will you not sit?" he added, with insidious urbanity. "No? Ah, well, just as you wish. But you will forgive me if I —"

He sat down in his favourite chair, with his back to the table and the candle-light and facing the fire, which threw ruddy gleams on his gaunt face and grizzled hair. His deepset eyes were inscrutable in the shadow, but they were fixed upon the burgomaster who stood before him dignified and calm, half-turned away from the pitiful spectacle which the blind man presented in somnolent helplessness.

"Since last I had the pleasure of addressing you, mynheer," Stoutenburg began slowly, after awhile, "it hath come to my knowledge that the Stadtholder, far from abandoning all hope of reconquering Gelderland from our advancing forces, did in truth not only devise a plan whereby he intended to deliver Ede and Amersfoort from our hands, but his far-reaching project also embraced the possibility of seizing my person, and once for all ridding himself of an enemy – a justiciary, shall we say? – who is becoming might inconvenient."

"A project, my lord," the burgomaster riposted earnestly, "which I pray God may fully succeed."

Stoutenburg gave a derisive laugh.

"So it would have done, mynheer," he said with a sardonic grin. "It would have succeeded admirably, and by this hour to-morrow I should no doubt be dangling on a gibbet, for Maurice of Nassau hath sworn that he would treat me as a knave and as a traitor unworthy of the scaffold."

"And the world would have been rid of a murderous miscreant," the burgomaster put in coldly, "had God so willed it."

"Ah, but God – your God, mynheer," Stoutenburg retorted with a sneer, "did not will it, it seems. And forewarned is forearmed, you know."

Instinctively, as the full meaning of Stoutenburg's words reached his perceptions the Burgomaster's eyes had sought those of his son, whilst a ghastly pallor overspread his face even to his lips.

"The Stadtholder's schemes have been revealed to you," he murmured slowly. "By whom?"

Then, as Stoutenburg made no reply, only regarded him with a mocking and quizzical gaze, he added more vehemently:

"Who is the craven informer who hath sold his master to you?"

"What would you do to him if you knew?" Stoutenburg retorted coolly.

"Slay him with mine own hand," the burgomaster replied calmly, "were he my only son!"

" 'Twas not I!" Nicolaes cried involuntarily.

Stoutenburg appeared vastly amused.

"No," he said. "It was not your son Klaas, whose merits, by the way, you have not yet learned to appreciate. Nicolaes hath rendered me and the Archduchess immense services, which I hope soon to repay adequately. But," he added with mocking emphasis, "the most signal service of all, which will deliver the Stadtholder into my hands and re-establish thereby the dominion of Spain over the Netherlands, was rendered to me by the varlet whom, but for me, you would have acclaimed as your son."

And with a wide flourish of the arm, Stoutenburg turned in his chair and pointed to Diogenes, who, sublimely unconscious of what went on around him, was even in the act of emitting a loud and prolonged snore. Instinctively the burgomaster looked at him. his glance, vague and puzzled, wandered over the powerful figure of the blind man, the nodding head, the pinioned shoulders, and from him back to Stoutenburg, who continued to regard him – Beresteyn – with a malicious leer.

"I fear me," the latter murmured after awhile, "That your lordship will think me over-dull; but – I don't quite understand —"

"Yet, 'tis simple enough," Stoutenburg rejoined; rose from his chair, and approached the burgomaster, as he spoke with a sudden fierce tone of triumph. "This miserable cur on whom Gilda once bestowed her love, seeing the gallows dangling before his bleary eyes, hath sold me the secrets which the Stadtholder did entrust him – sold the to me in exchange for his worthless life! I entered into a bargain with him, and I will keep my pledge. In very truth, he hath saved my life by his revelations, and jeopardized that of the Stadtholder – my most bitter enemy. Maurice of Nassau had thought to trap me in the lonely molen on the Veluwe which is my secret camp. Now 'tis I who will close the trap on him there, and hold his life, his honour, these provinces, at my mercy. And all," he concluded with a ringing shout, "thanks to the brilliant adventurer, the chosen of Gilda's heart, her English milor, mynheer! – the gay and dashing Laughing Cavalier!"

He had the satisfaction of seeing that the blow had gone home. The burgomaster literally staggered under it, as if he had actually been struck in the face with a whip. Certain it is that he stepped back and clutched the table for support with one hand, whilst he passed the other once or twice across his brow.

"My God!" he murmured under his breath.

Stoutenburg laughed as a demon might, when gazing on a tortured soul. Then he shrugged his shoulders and went on airily:

"You are surprised, mynheer Burgomaster?" Frankly, I was not. You believed this fortune-hunter's tales of noble parentage and English ancestry. I did not. You doubted his treachery when he went on a message to Marquet, and sold that message to de Berg. I knew it to be a fact. My love for Gilda made me clear-sighted, whilst yours left you blind. Now you see him at last in his true colours – base, servile, without honour and without faith. You are bewildered, incredulous, mayhap? Ask Jan. He was here and heard him. Ask my captains at the gate, my master of the camp. The Stadtholder is heading straight for the trap which he had set up for me, because the cullion who sits there did sell his one-time master to me."

The burgomaster, overcome with horror and with shame, had sunk into a chair and buried his face in his hands. The echo of Stoutenburg's rasping voice seemed to linger in the noble panelled hall, its mocking accents to be still tearing at the stricken father's aching heart, still deriding his overwhelming sorrow. Gilda! His proud, loving, loyal Gilda! If she were to know! A great sob, manfully repressed, broke from his throat and threatened to choke him.

And for the first time in this day of crime and of treachery, Nicolaes felt a twinge of remorse knocking at the gates of his heart. He could not bear to look on his father's grief, and not feel the vague stirrings of an affection which had once been genuine, even though it was dormant now. His father had been perhaps more just toward him than indulgent. Gilda had been the apple of his eyes, and he – Nicolaes – had been brought up in that stern school of self-sacrifice and self-repression which had made heroes of those of his race in their stubborn and glorious fight for liberty.

No doubt it was that rigid bringing-up which had primarily driven an ambitious and discontented youth like Nicolaes into the insidious net spread out for him by the wily Stoutenburg. Smarting under the discipline imposed upon his self-indulgence by the burgomaster, he had lent a willing ear to the treacherous promises of his masterful friend, who held out dazzling visions before him of independence and of aggrandisement. Even at this moment Nicolaes felt no remorse for his treachery to his country and kindred. He was only sentimentally sorry to see his father so utterly broken down by sorrow.

And then there was Gilda. Already, when Stoutenburg had placed that cruel "either – or" before her, Nicolaes had felt an uncomfortable pain in his heart at the sight of her misery. Stoutenburg would have called it weakness, and despised him for it. But Stoutenburg's was an entirely warped and evil nature, which revelled in crime and cruelty as a solace to past humiliation and disappointment, whereas Nicolaes was just a craven time-server, who had not altogether succeeded in freeing himself from past teachings and past sentiments.

And Gilda's pale, tear-stained face seemed to stare at him through the gloom, reproachful and threatening, whilst his father's heartrending sob tore at his vitals and shook him to the soul with a kind of superstitious awe. The commandment of Heaven, not wholly forgotten, not absolutely ignored, seemed to ring the death-knell of all that he had striven for, as if the Great Judge of All had already weighed his deeds in the balance, and decreed that his punishment be swift and sure.

But Stoutenburg, in this the hour of his greatest triumph, had none of these weaknesses. Nor indeed did he care whether the burgomaster was stricken with sorrow or no. What he did do now was to go up to Jan, and from the latter's belt take out a pistol. This he examined carefully, then he put it down upon the table close to where the burgomaster was sitting.

8

A quarter of an hour later the stately house on the quay appeared wrapped in the mantle of sleep. The soldiers, wearied and discontented, had after a good deal of murmuring, finally settled down to rest. They had collected what clothes, blankets, curtains even that they could lay their hands on, and wrapped up in these, they had curled themselves up upon the floor.

We may take it, however, as a certainty that Jan remained wide awake, with one ear on that door which gave on the banqueting hall, and which he, at the command of his master, had carefully closed behind him.

Upstairs, Nicolaes had thrown himself like an insentient and wearied mass upon his own bed in the room wherein he had slept as a child, as an adolescent, as a youth, now as a black-hearted traitor, haunted by memories and the ghoulish shadows, of his crime. He could not endure the darkness, so left a couple of wax candles burning in their sconces. Whether he actually fell asleep or no, he could not afterward have told you. Certain it is that he was not fully awake, but rather on that threshold of dreams which for those that are happy is akin to the very gate of paradise, but unto souls that are laden with crime is like the antechamber of hell. Half consciously Nicolaes could hear Stoutenburg pacing up and down an adjoining room, restless and fretful, like some untamed beast on the prowl.

Then suddenly the sharp report of a pistol rang through the silence of the night. Nicolaes jumped from his bed, with a feeling of sheer physical nausea, which turned him dizzy and faint. Stoutenburg had paused abruptly in his febrile wanderings. To the listener it almost seemed as if he could hear his friend's laboured breathing, the indrawing of a sigh that spoke of torturing suspense.

A few minutes went by, and then a heavy step was heard ascending the stairs, after that, the closing and shutting of a door. Then nothing more.

In that heavy step, Nicolaes had recognized his father's. Even now he could hear the burgomaster moving about in his room close by, which had always been his. Gilda's was further along, down the passage. Everything now seemed so still. Just for awhile, after the burgomaster had gone upstairs, Nicolaes had heard the soldiers moving down below. Rudely awakened from their sleep, they had done a good deal of muttering. Voices could be heard, and then a rattle, like the shaking of a door. But apparently the men had been quickly reassured by Jan.

The silence acted as a further irritant on Nicolaes' nerves. Taking up a candle, he went out of the room in search of Stoutenburg. Outside on the landing he came upon Jan, who was on the same errand bent.

"What has happened?" the young man queried hoarsely.

Jan shook his head. "Which is His Lordship's room?" was all that he said.

Nicolaes led the way, and Jan followed. They found Stoutenburg standing in the middle of the room which he had selected for his own use. He was still fully dressed, had not even taken off his boots. Apparently he was waiting for news, but otherwise he seemed quite calm.

"Well?" he queried curtly, as soon as he caught sight of Jan.

"We cannot get into the room," Jan replied. "After we heard the shot fired, we saw the burgomaster come out of it; but he locked the door and, with the key in his hand he walked steadily up the stairs."

"How did he look?"

"Like a man who had seen a ghost."

"Well?" Stoutenburg queried again, impatiently. "What did you do after that?"

"I tried the door, of course. It is a stout piece of oak, and I had no orders to break it down. It would take a heavy joist, and the men are already grumbling —"

"Yes!" Stoutenburg put in curtly. "But the windows?"

"I thought of them, and myself went round to look. Of course we could climb up to them, but they appeared to be barred and shuttered."

"So much the better!" his lordship retorted with a note of grim spite in his rasping voice. "Let the varlet's carcase rot where it is. Why should we trouble? Go back to bed, Nicolaes," he added after a slight pause. "And you too, Jan. As for me, I feel that I could sleep peacefully at last!"

He threw himself on the bed with a long sigh of satisfaction, and when spoken to again by one of the others, he curtly ordered them to leave him in peace. So Jan did leave him, and went back to his men. But Nicolaes, terrified of solitude, which he felt would for him be peopled with ghouls, elected to find what rest he could in an armchair beside his friend. And a few minutes later the house was once more wrapped in the mantle of sleep.

1

AGAIN it is to de Voocht's highly interesting and reliable "Brieven" that we like to turn for an account of the Lord of Stoutenburg's departure out of Amersfoort. It occurred at dawn of a raw, dull March morning, and was effected with all the furtiveness, the silence, usually pertaining to a surprise attack.

The soldiers bivouacking inside that part of the city knew nothing of the whole affair. But few of them did as much as turn in their sleep when his lordship rode through the Koppel-poort, together with four companies of cavaliers. Jan was an adept at arranging these expeditions, and the Lord of Stoutenburg had made a specialty of marauding excursions ever since he had started on his career of treachery against his own country.

His standard-bearer preceded the companies, carrying the sable standard embroidered in silver, with the skull and cross-bones, which his lordship had permanently adopted as his device. But they went without drums or pipes, and with as little clatter as may be, choosing the unpaved streets whereon the mud lay thick and effectually deadened the sound of horses' hoofs.

A litter taken from the burgomaster's coach-house and borne by two strong Flemish horses, bore the jongejuffrouw Gilda Beresteyn in the train of her future lord. She had offered no resistance, no protest of any kind, when finally ordered by her brother to make herself ready. She had spent the greater part of the night in meditation and in prayer. Her father, hearing her move about in her room, had come to her in the small hours of the morning and had sat with her for some time. Nicolaes, wakeful and restless, had wandered out into the corridor on which gave most of the sleeping rooms, and had heard the subdued murmurings of the burgomaster's voice, and occasionally that of his sister. What they said he could not hear, but he was able subsequently to assure Stoutenburg that the burgomaster's tone was distinctly one of admonition, and Gilda's one of patience and resignation.

Just before dawn, one of the old serving men, who had remained on watch in the house all through the night, brought her some warm milk and bread, which she swallowed eagerly. The burgomaster was with her then. But later on, when the Lord of Stoutenburg desired her presence in the living room, she went to him alone.

That room was the one where, a little more than a week ago, the Stadtholder had held council with the burgomaster and his friends, on the day of her wedding, Her wedding! And she had sat in the little room next to it and played on the virginal so as to attract her beloved to her side. Then had come the hour of parting, and she had with her own hands taken his sword to him and buckled it to his side, and bade him go wither honour and duty beckoned.

My God, what memories!

But she met Stoutenburg's mocking glance with truly remarkable serenity. She felt neither faint nor weak. He communion with God, her interview with her father had given her all the strength she needed, not to let her enemies see what she suffered or if she were afraid. And when Stoutenburg with callous irony reminded her of his decision, she answered quite calmly:

"I am ready to do your wish, my lord."

"And you'll not regret it, Gilda," he vowed with sudden earnestness; and his sunken eyes lighted up with a kind of fierce ardour which sent a cold shudder coursing down her spine. "By Heaven! you'll not regret it! You shall be the greatest lady in Europe, the most admired, the most beloved. Aye! With you beside me, I feel that I shall have the power to create a throne, a kingdom, for us both. Queen of the Netherlands, myn engel! What say you to this goal? And I your king —"

He paused and closely scrutinized her face, marvelled what she knew of that drunken oaf, once her lover, who now lay dead in the room below, slain by the avenging hand of an outraged father and an indignant patriot. But she looked so serene that he came to the conclusion that she knew nothing. The burgomaster had apparently desired to spare her for the moment this additional horror and shame.

Well no doubt it was all for the best. She was ready to come with him, and that, after all, was the principal thing. In any event she knew the alternative.

"Jan remains here," he said, "in command of the troops. He will not leave until I send him word."

Until then, Amersfoort and the lives of all its citizens were in jeopardy. The quick, scared look in her eyes, when he reminded her of this, was sufficient to assure him that she fully grasped the position. Of the Stadtholder's plans, as betrayed by the informer, she knew, of course, nothing. Better so, he thought. The whole thing, when accomplished, when he – Stoutenburg – was made master of Gelderland, the Stadtholder a prisoner in his hands, the United Provinces ready to submit to him, would be a revelation to her – a revelation which would make her, he doubted not, a proud and happy woman, rather than a mere obedient slave.

2

In the meanwhile, he had strictly enjoined Jan to leave the banqueting hall undisturbed.

"Let the locked door and close shutters guard the grim secret within," he said decisively. "Apparently the Heer Burgomaster intends for the nonce to hold his tongue."

In the hurry and excitement of the departure, the soldiers, who in the night had been roused by the pistol shot, forgot that unimportant event. Certain it is that not one of them did more than cursorily wonder what it had been about. Then, as no one gave reply, the matter was soon allowed to fall into oblivion. At one moment, Stoutenburg who was standing in the hall waiting for Gilda, felt tempted to go and have a last look on his dead enemy; but the key was not in the lock and he would not send to the burgomaster for it.

It was better so.

Just then Gilda came down the stairs. She was accompanied by her old waiting woman, Maria, and was wrapped in fur cloak and hood ready for the journey. Apparently she had taken final leave of her father, and had quite resigned herself to parting from him.

"The burgomaster is well, I trust, this morning?" Stoutenburg asked with great urbanity, as soon as he had formally greeted her.

"I thank you, my lord," she replied coolly. "My father is as well as I can desire."

The litter was her own. Oft had she travelled in it between Haarlem and Amersfoort, when the weather was too rough for riding. Those had been happy journeys to and fro, for both homes were dear to her. Both now had become hallowed through the presence in them of her beloved. To Stoutenburg, who watched her keenly while she crossed the hall, it seemed as if once she glanced round in the direction of the banqueting room, and craned her neck as if trying to catch whatever faint sound might be coming from there. She appeared to shiver, and drew her fur cloak closer round her shoulders, her lips moved slightly as if murmuring. Stoutenburg thought that she was bidding a last farewell to the man who she could not bring herself to forget or to despise and an acute feeling of unbridled jealousy shot through him like a poisoned dart – jealousy even of the dead.

3

A mounted scout led the way, to clear the road of encumbrance that might retard progress. After him came the standard-bearer. Twelve Spanish halberdiers followed, the shafts of their halberts swathed in black velvet, behind them one hundred cavaliers, who were armed with muskets, and a hundred more carrying lances. Then came the litter, which was covered in leather with richly stamped leather curtains, at the sides, the shafts, front and back, supported by heavy Flemish horses, which were sumptuously caparisoned and plumed. The Lord of Stoutenburg rode on one side of the litter and Nicolaes on the other, and behind it came two more companies of musketeers and lancers.

The way lay through the Koppel-poort and then straight across the Veluwe, on the road which runs to the north of Amersfoort, thus avoiding any possible encounter with the Stadtholder's vedettes. Stoutenburg's intention was to await Maurice of Nassau's coming at the molen, not to offer him battle in the open.

The road was lonely at this early hour, and a cutting wind blew across from the Zuider Zee, chasing the morning mist before it. Already on the horizon above the undulating tableland, the pale wintry sun tinged that mist with gold. Stoutenburg's keen hawklike eyes searched the distance before him as he rode.

A little after seven o'clock, Barneveld was reached, and a brief halt called outside the city whilst the scouts went in, in search of provisions. The inhabitants, scared by the advent of these strangers, submitted to being fleeced of their goods, not daring to resist. Though closely questioned, they had but little information to impart. They had, in truth, heard that Ede was in the hands of the Spaniards and that Amersfoort had shared the like fate. Runners had brought the news, which was authentic, together with many wild rumours that had terrorized the credulous and paved the way for Stoutenburg's arrival. His sable standard, with its grim device, completed the subjugation of the worthy burghers of Barneveld, who, with no garrison to protect them, thought it wisest to obey the behests of His Magnificence with a show of goodwill, rather than see their little city pillaged or their citizens dragged as captives in the train of the conqueror.

Gilda did not leave her litter during the halt. Maria, who had been riding on a pillion behind one of the equerries, who she roundly trounced and anathematized all the way, came and waited on her mistress. But Stoutenburg and Nicolaes kept with unwonted discretion, or mayhap indifference, out of her way.

The halt, in truth, lasted less than a couple of hours. By nine o'clock the troop was once more on the way, and an hour later on the high upland, out toward the east, the lonely molen loomed, portentous and weird, out of the mist.

4

The spies of the Stadtholder, who had, according to Diogenes' statement, spoken of the molen as Stoutenburg's camp, where he had secreted great stores of arms and ammunition, had in truth been either deceived or deceivers.

The molen was lonely and uninhabited, as it had always been. No sign of life appeared around it, or sign of the recent breaking of a camp. True, here and there upon the scrub in the open, the scorched rough grass or a heap of ashes, indicated that a fire had been lit there at one time; whilst under the overhanging platform, the trampled earth converted into mud, and certain debris of straw and fodder, accused the recent presence of horses and of men.

But only a few. As to whether the stores of arms and ammunition were indeed concealed inside the mill-house itself, it was impossible to say from the mere aspect of the tumble-down building. Whatever secret the molen contained, it had succeeded in guarding inviolate up to this hour.

Standing as it did upon a high point of the arid upland, the molen dominated the Veluwe. Toward the west, whence the Stadtholder would come, a gentle, undulating slope led down to Barneveld and Ede, Amersfoort and Utrecht; but in the rear of the building toward the east, the ground fell away more abruptly, down to a narrow gorge below.

It was in this gorge, secluded from the prying eyes of possible vedettes, that Stoutenburg had put up his camp ere he embarked upon his fateful expedition to Amersfoort, and it was here that he disposed the bulk of his troop: horses, men and baggage, under the command of Nicolaes Beresteyn; whilst he himself, with a bodyguard of fifty picked men, took up his quarters in the molen.

The plan of action was simple enough. The fifty men would remain concealed in and about the building, until the Stadtholder thinking the place deserted, walked straight into the trap that had been laid for him. Then, at the first musket shot, the men from the camp below were to rush up the sloping ground with a great clatter and much shouting and battle cry.

The Stadtholder's troops wholly unprepared for the attack would be thrown into dire confusion, and in the panic that would inevitably ensue, the rout would be complete. Stoutenburg himself would see to it that the Stadtholder did not escape.

"Welcome home, myn engel!" had been his semi-ironical, wholly triumphant greeting to Gilda when her litter came to a halt and he dismounted in order to conduct her into the molen.

She gave him no answer, but allowed her hand to rest in his and walked beside him with a firm step through the narrow door which gave on the interior of the mill-house. She looked about her with inquiring eyes that had not a vestige of terror in them. Almost, it seemed, at one moment as if she smiled.

Did her memory conjure back just then the vision of that other molen, the one at Ryswick, where so much had happened three short months ago, and where this arrogant tyrant had played such a sorry role? Perhaps. Certain it is that she turned to him without any defiance, almost with a gentle air of appeal.

"I am very tired," she said, with a weary little sigh, "and would be grateful for a little privacy, if your lordship would allow my tire-woman to attend on me."

"Your wishes are my laws, myn schat," he replied airily. "I entreat you to look on this somewhat dilapidated building only as a temporary halt, where nothing, alas! can be done for your comfort. I trust you will not suffer from the cold, but absolute privacy you shall have. The loft up those narrow steps is entirely at your disposal, and your woman shall come to you immediately."

Indeed, he called at once through the door, and a moment or two later Maria appeared, reduced to silence for the nonce by a wholesome fear. Stoutenburg, in the meanwhile, still with that same ironical gallantry, had conducted Gilda to the narrow, ladder-like steps which led up to the loft. He stood at the foot, watching her serene and leisurely progress.

"How wise you are, mejuffrouw," he said, with a sigh of satisfaction. "And withal how desirable!"

She turned for a second, then, and looked down on him. But her eyes were quite inscrutable. Never had he desired her so much as now. With the gloomy background of those rickety walls behind her, she looked like an exquisite fairy; her dainty head wrapped in a hood, through which her small, oval face appeared, slightly rose-tinted, like a piece of delicate china.

The huge fur coat concealed the lines of her graceful figure, but one perfect hand rested upon the rail, and the other peeped out like a flower between the folds of her cloak. He all but lost his head when he gazed on her, and met those blue eyes that still held a mystery for him. But, with Stoutenburg, ambition and selfishness always waged successful warfare even against passion, and at this hour his entire destiny was hanging in the balance.

The look wherewith he regarded her was that of a conqueror rather than a lover. The title of the English play had come swiftly through his mind: "The Taming of the Shrew." In truth, Nicolaes had been right. Women have no use for weaklings. It is their master whom they worship.

Just one word of warning did he give her ere she finally passed out of his sight.

"There will be noise of fighting anon, myn engel," he said carelessly. "Nothing that need alarm you. An encounter with vedettes probably. A few musket shots. You will not be afraid?"

"No," she replied simply. "I will not be afraid."

"You will be safe here with me until we can continue our journey east or south. It will depend on what progress de Berg has been able to make."

She gave a slight nod of understanding.

"I shall be ready," she said.

Encouraged by her gentleness, he went on more warmly:

"And at the hour when we leave here together, myn schat, a runner will speed to Amersfoort with order to Jan to evacuate the city. The burgomaster will be in a position to announce to his fellow-citizens that they have nothing to fear from a chivalrous enemy, who will respect person and property, and who will go out of the gates of Amersfoort as empty-handed as he came.

Whereupon he made her a low and respectful bow, stood aside to allow the serving woman to follow her mistress. Gilda had acknowledge his last pompous tirade with a faintly murmured, "I thank you, my lord." Then she went quickly up the steps and finally passed out of his sight on the floor above.

Just for a little while he remained quite still, listening to her footsteps overhead. His lean, sharp-featured face expressed nothing but contentment now. Success – complete, absolute – was his at last! Less than a fortnight ago, he was nothing but a disappointed vagrant, without home, kindred, or prospects; scorned by the woman he loved; despised by a successful rival; an outcast from the land of his birth.

To-day, his rival was dead – an object of contempt, not even of pity, for every honest man; while Gilda, like a ripe and luscious fruit, was ready to fall into his arms. And he had his foot firmly planted on the steps of a throne.

5

And now the midday hour had gone by, and silence, absolute, reigned in and around the molen. Stoutenburg had spend some time talking to the captain in command of his guard, had himself seen to it that the men were well concealed in the rear of the molen. The horses had been sent down to the camp so as to preclude any possibility of an alarm being given before the apportioned time. Two men were stationed on the platform to keep a look-out upon the distance, where anon the Stadtholder and his troop would appear.

Indeed, everything was ordained and arranged with perfect precision in anticipation of the great coup which was destined to deliver Maurice of Nassau into the hands of his enemy. Everything! – provided that blind informer who lay dead in the banqueting hall of the stately house at Amersfoort had not lied from first to last.

But even if he had lied, even if the Stadtholder had not planned this expedition, or, having planned it, had abandoned it or given up the thought of leading it in person – even so, Stoutenburg was prepared to be satisfied. Already his busy brain was full of plans, which he would put into execution if the present one did not yield him the supreme prize. Gilda was his now, whatever happened. Gilda, and her wealth, and the influence of the Burgomaster Beresteyn, henceforth irrevocably tied to the chariot wheel of his son-in-law. A vista of riches, of honours, of power, was stretched out before the longing gaze of this restless and ambitious self-seeker.

For the nonce, he could afford to wait, even though the hours crept by leaden-footed, and the look-out men up on the platform had nothing as yet to report. The soldiers outside, wrapped up in horse-blankets, squatted against the walls of the dilapidated building, trying to get shelter from the cutting north wind. They had their provisions for the day requisitioned at Barneveld; but these they soon consumed for want of something better to do. The cold was bitter, and anon an icy drizzle began to fall.

6

Stoutenburg, inside the mill-house, had started on that restless pacing up and down which was so characteristic of him. He had ordered the best of the provisions to be taken up to the jongejuffrouw and her maid. He himself had eaten and had drunk, and now he had nothing to do but wait. And think. Anon he got tired of both, and when he heard the women moving about overhead, he suddenly paused in his fretful wanderings, pondered for a moment or two, and then went resolutely up the stairs.

Gilda was sitting on a pile of sacking; her hands lay idly in her lap. With a curt word of command, Stoutenburg ordered the waiting woman to go below.

Then he approached Gilda, and half-kneeling, half-reclining by her side, he tried to take her hand. But she evaded him, hid her hands underneath her cloak. This apparently vastly amused his lordship, for he laughed good-humouredly, and said, with an ardent look of passionate admiration:

"That is where you are so desirable, myn engel. Never twice the same. Awhile ago you seemed as yielding as a dove; now once more I see the young vixen peeping at me through those wonderful blue eyes. Well!" he added with a sigh of contentment, "I will not complain. Life by your side, myn geliefde, will never be dull. The zest of taming a beautiful shrew must ever be a manly sport."

Then, as she made no sign either of defiance or comprehension, but sat with eyes strained and neck craned forward, almost as if she were listening, he raised himself and sat down upon the sacking close beside her. She puzzled him now, as she always did; and that puzzlement added zest to his wooing.

"I was waxing so dejected down below," he said, and leaned forward, his lips almost touching the hood that kept her ears concealed. "Little did I guess that so much delight lay ready to my hand. Time is a hard task-master to me just now, and I have not the leisure to make as ardent love to you as I would wish. But I have the time to gratify a fancy, and this I will do. My fancy is to have three kisses from your sweet lips on mine. Three, and no more, and on the lips, myn schat."

In an instant his arms were round her. But equally suddenly she had evaded him. She jumped up and ran, as swift as a hare, to the farther end of the loft, where she remained ensconced behind a transverse beam, her arms round it for support, her face, white and set, only vaguely discernible in the gloom.

The dim afternoon light which came but shyly peeping in through two small windows high up in the walls, failed to reach this angle of the loft where Gilda had found shelter. With this dim background behind her, she appeared like some elusive spectre, an apparition, without form or substance, her face and hands alone visible.

When she escaped him, Stoutenburg had cursed, as was his wont, then struggled to his feet and tried to carry off the situation with an affected laugh. But somehow the girls' face, there in the semi-darkness, gave him an unpleasant, eerie sensation. He did not follow her, but paused in the centre of the loft, laughter dying upon his lips.

"Am I to remind you again, you little termagant," he said, with a great show of bluster, "that Jan is still at Amersfoort, and that I may yet send a runner to him if I have a mind, ordering that by nightfall that accursed city be ablaze?"

He was looking straight at her while he spoke. And she returned his glance, but gave him no reply. Just for the space of a few seconds an extraordinary stillness appeared to have descended upon the molen. Up here, in the loft, nothing stirred, nothing was heard above that silence save the patter of the rain upon the roof overhead against the tiny window panes. For a few seconds, whilst Stoutenburg stood like a beast of prey about to spring, and Gilda, still and silent, like a bird on the alert.

And suddenly, even as he gazed, the man's expression slowly underwent a change. First the arrogance died out of it, the forced irony. Every line became set, then rigid, and more and more ashen in hue, until the whole face appeared like a death-mask, colourless and transparent as wax, the jaw dropping, the lips parted as for a cry that would not come. And the sunken eyes opened wider and wider, and wider still as they gazed, not on Gilda any longer, but into the darkness behind her, whilst the whole aspect of the man was like a living statue of horror and of a nameless fear.

Then suddenly, right through the silence and above the weird patter of the rain, there rang a sound which roused the very echoes that lay dormant among the ancient rafters. So strange a sound was it that when it reached his ear, Stoutenburg lost his balance and swayed on his feet like a drunken man; so strange that Gilda, her nerves giving way for the first time under the terrible strain which she had undergone, buried her face against her arms, whilst a loud sob broke from her throat. Yet the sound in itself was neither a terrifying nor a tragic one. It was just the sound of a prolonged and loud peal of laughter.

"By my halidame!" a merry voice swore lustily. "But meseems that your lordship had no thought of seeing me here!"

Just for a few seconds, superstitious fear held the miscreant gripped by the throat. A few seconds? To him to Gilda, they seemed an eternity. Then a hoarse whisper escaped him.

"Spectre or demon, which are you?"

"Both, you devil!" the mocking voice gave reply. "And I would send you down to hell and shoot you like a dog where you stand, but for the noise which would bring your men about mine ears."

"To hell yourself, you infamous plepshurk!" Stoutenburg cried, strove to shake off with a mighty effort the superstitious dread that made a weakling of him. He fumbled for his sword, succeeded in drawing it from its scabbard, and cursed himself for being without a pistol in his belt.

"Where you came from, I know not," he went on in a husky whisper. "But be you wraith or demon, you —-"

He seemed to speak involuntarily, as if sheer terror was forcing the words through his blood-less lips. Suddenly he uttered a hoarse cry:

"A moi! Somebody there! A moi!"

But the walls of the old molen were thick, and his voice, spent and still half-choked with the horror of that spectral apparition, refused him effective service. It failed to carry far enough. The tiny windows were impracticable; the soldiers were outside at the rear of the building, out of earshot; and down below there was only the old waiting woman.

"That smeerlap!" he cried, half to himself. "Either a wraith or blind. In either case —"

And, sword in hand, he rushed upon his mocking enemy. A blind man! Bah! What had he to fear? The rogue had in truth thrust Guild behind him. He stood there, with one of those short English daggers in his hand, which had of late put the fine Toledo blades to shame. But a blind man, for all that! How he had escaped out of Amersfoort, and by whose connivance Stoutenburg had not time to think. But the man was blind. Every phase of last evening's interview with him – the vacant eyes, the awkward movements – stood out clearly before his lordship's mental vision, and testified to that one fact; the man was blind and helpless.

Crouching like a feline creature upon his haunches, Stoutenburg was ready for a spring. His every movement became lithe and silent as that of a snake. He had marked out to himself just how and where he would strike. He only waited until those eyes – those awful eyes – ceased to look on him. But their glance never wavered. They followed his ever step. They mocked and derided and threatened withal! By Satan and all his hordes! those stricken orbs could see!

At what precise moment that conviction entered Stoutenburg's tortured brain, he could not himself have told you. But suddenly it was there. And in an instant his nerve completely forsook him. An icy sweat broke all over his body. His head swam, his knees gave way under him, the sword dropped out of his nerveless hand. Then, with a quick hoarse cry, he turned to flee. His foot was on the top step of the ladder which led to the room below. A prolonged, mocking laugh behind him seemed to lend him wings. But freedom – aye, and more! – beckoned from below. There was only an old woman there, and his soldiers were outside. Ye gods! He was a fool to fear!

He flew down the few steps, nearly fell headlong in the act, for his nerves were playing him an unpleasant trick, and the afternoon light was growing dim. At first, when he reached the place below, he saw nothing. Nothing save the welcome door, straight before him which led straight to freedom from this paralysing obsession. With one bound he had covered half the intervening space, when suddenly he paused, and an awful curse rose to his lips. There, in the recess of the doorway, two men were squatting on their heels, intent upon a game of hazard. One of these men was long and lean, the other round as a curled-up hedge-hog. They did no more than glance over their shoulder when His Magnificence the Lord of Stoutenburg came staggering down the steps.

"Five and four," the lean vagabond was saying. "How many does that make?"

"Eight, you loon!" the other replied. "My turn now."

They continued their game, regardless of his lordship who stood there rooted to the spot, trembling in every limb, his body covered with sweat, feeling like an animal that sees a trap slowly closing in upon him.

The situation was indeed one to send a man out of his senses. Stoutenburg, for one brief instant, felt that he was going mad. He looked from the door to the steps, and back again to the door, marvelling which way lay his one chance of escape. If he shouted, would he be heard? Could his men get to him before those two ruffians fell to and murdered him? Dared he make a dash for the door? Or — It was unthinkable that he – Stoutenburg – should be standing here, at the mercy of three villains, utterly powerless, when outside, not fifty paces away, the other side of those walls, fifty men at arms were there, set to guard his person.

And suddenly fear fell away from him. The trembling of his limbs ceased, his vision became clear, his mind alert. Even around his quaking lips there came the ghost of a smile.

His senses, keyed up by the imminence of his danger, had seized upon a sound which came from outside, faint as yet, but very obviously drawing nearer. In the semi-darkness and with his head buzzing and his nerves tingling, he could not distinguish either the quality of the sound nor yet the exact direction whence it came. But whatever it was – even if it was not all that he hoped – the sound was bound to set his soldiers on the alert; and if he could only temporize with those ruffians for a minute or two, the very next would see the captain of his guard rushing in to report what was happening: That Stadtholder sighted, the signal given, Nicolaes Beresteyn coming swiftly to the rescue.

Therefore, in the face of his own imminent peril, the Lord of Stoutenburg no longer felt afraid, only tensely vitally expectant. The two caitiffs, on the other hand appeared to have heard nothing. At any rate, they went on with their game, and the flute-like, high-pitched tones of the fat loon alternated with the deep base of his companion:

"Three and two make five!"

"No, four, you varlet!"

"Six!"

"Blank, by Beelzebub! My luck is dead out to-day."

And the sound drew nearer. There was no mistaking it. Men running. The clatter of arms. Horses, too. A pawing, and a champing, and a general hubbub, which those two ruffians could not fail to hear. Nor did any sound come down from the loft. Yet Gilda was there with the miserable plepshurk who, whatever else happened, would inevitably stand before her now as an informer and a cheat. This, at any rate, was a fact. The man had betrayed his master in order to save his miserable life, and the burgomaster had connived at his escape through an access of doltish weakness. But the fact remained. The Stadtholder was approaching. The next few minutes – seconds, perhaps – would see the final triumphant issue of this terrible adventure.

Stoutenburg, like a feline at bay, waited.

Then, all at once, a musket shot rang through the air, then another, and yet another; and all at once the whole air around was alive with sounds. The clang of arms; the lusty battle cries. Men out there had come to grips. In the drenching rain they were at one another's throats.

The two caitiffs quietly put aside their dice and rose to their feet. They stood with their backs to the door, their eyes fixed upon his lordship.

"Stand aside, you dolts!" Stoutenburg cried aloud; for he thought that he read murder in those two pairs of eyes, and he had need of all his nerves to assure himself that all was well, that, though his captain had not come to him for a reason which no doubt was sound, his soldiers were at grips with the Stadtholder's vanguard, and Nicolaes was already half-way up the slope.

But he, Stoutenburg, was unarmed, and could not push past those two assassins who were guarding the door. He bethought himself of his sword, which lay on the floor of the loft. He turned with a sudden impulse to get hold of it at all costs, and was met at the very foot of the steps by the man who had baffled him at every turn.

Diogenes, sword in hand, did not even pause to look on his impotent enemy. With one spring, he was across the floor and out by the door, which one of the ruffians immediately closed behind him.

It had all happened swifter even than thought. Stoutenburg, trapped, helpless, more bewildered in truth than terrified, still believed in a happy issue to his present desperate position. The thought came to him that he might purchase his safety from those potential murderers.

"Ten thousand guilders," he called out wildly, "if you will let me pass!"

But the fat runnion merely turned to the lean one, and the look of understanding which passed between them sent an icy shudder down his lordship's spine. He knew that from these two he could expect no mercy. A hoarse cry of horror escaped his lips as he saw that each held a dagger in one hand.

Then began that awful chase when man becomes a hunted beast – that grim game of hide-and-seek, with the last issue never once in doubt. The Lord of Stoutenburg trapped between these narrow walls, ran round and round like a mouse in a cage; now seeking refuge behind a girder, now leaping over an intervening obstacle, now crouching, panting and bathed in sweat, under cover of the gloom. And no one spoke; no one called. Neither the hunted nor the hunters. It seemed as if a conspiracy of silence existed between them; or else that the nearness of death had put a seal on all their lips.

Out there the clang of battle appeared more remote. Nothing seemed to occur in the immediate approach of the molen. It all came from afar, resounding across the Veluwe, above the patter of the rain and the soughing of the wind, through the rafters of the old mill. Drumming and thumping, the angle of armour, the clang of pike and lance, of metal; the loud report of musket shot, the strident grating of chains and wheels. But all far away, not here. Not outside the molen, but down there in the gorge, where Nicolaes had been encamped. My heavens, what did it mean?

Already the trapped creature was getting exhausted. Once or twice he had come down on his knees. His eyes were growing dim. His breath came and went with a wheezing sound from his breast. It was not just two murderous brigands who were pursuing him, but Nemesis herself, with sword of retribution drawn, in her hand an hour-glass, the sands of which were running low.

All at once the miscreant found himself at the foot of the steps, and, blindly stumbling, he ran up to the loft – instinctively, without set purpose save that of warding off, if only for a minute, the inevitable end.

7

Gilda was standing at the top of the steps with neck craned forward, her hands held tightly to her breast, her whole attitude one of nameless horror. She had been listening to the multifarious sounds which came from outside, and the natural, womanly fear for the safety of her beloved had been her one dominant emotion.

She had heard nothing else for a time, until suddenly she caught one or two stray sounds of that grim and furtive fight for life which was going on down below. She had reached the top of the steps, and tried to peer through the gloom to ascertain whose were those stealthy, swift footfalls so like those of a hunted beast, and whose the heavy, lumbering tread that spoke of stern and unwavering pursuit. At first she could see nothing, and the very silence which lay like a pall upon the grim scene below struck her with a sense of paralysing dread.

Then she caught sight first of one figure, then of another, as they crossed her line of vision. She could distinguish nothing very clearly – just those slowly moving figures – and for a moment or two felt herself unable to move. Then she heard the laboured breathing of a man, a groan as of a soul tortured with fear, and the next instant the Lord of Stoutenburg appeared, stumbling up the narrow steps.

At sight of her he fell like an inert thing with a husky cry at her feet. His arms encircled her knees; his head fell against her gown.

"Gilda, save me!" he whispered hoarsely. "For the love of Heaven! They'll murder me! Save me, for pity's sake! Gilda!"

He sobbed and cried like a child, abject in his terror, loathsome in his craven cowardice. Gilda could not stir. He held her with his arms as in a vise. She would have given worlds for the physical strength to wrench her gown out of his clutch, to flee from the hated sight of him who had planned to do her beloved such an irreparable injury. Oh, she hated him! She hated him worse, perhaps, than she had ever done before, now that he clung like a miserable dastard to her for mercy.

"Leave the poltroon to us, mejuffrouw," a gentle, flute-like tone broke in on the miscreant's ravings.

"Now then, take your punishment like a man!" a gruff voice added sternly.

And two familiar faces emerged out of the gloom, immediately below where Gilda was standing, imprisoned by those cringing arms. The man, in truth, had not even the primeval pluck of a savage. He was beaten, and he knew it. What had happened out there on the Veluwe, how completely he had been tricked by the Englishman he did not know as yet. But he was afraid to die, and shrank neither from humiliation nor contempt in order to save his own worthless life from the wreck of all his ambitions.

At the sound of those two voices, which in truth were like a death-knell in his ears, he jumped to his feet; but he did not loosen his hold on Gilda. Swift as thought he had found refuge behind her, and held her by the arms in front of him like a shield.

Historians have always spoken of the Lord of Stoutenburg as extraordinarily nimble in mind and body. That nimbleness in truth, stood him in good stead now; or whilst Socrates and Pythagoras, clumsy in their movements, lumbering and hampered by their respect for the person of the jongejuffrouw, reached the loft, and then for one instant hesitated how best to proceed in their grim task without offending the ears and eyes of the great lady, Stoutenburg had with one bound slipped from behind her down the steps and was across the floor of the molen and out the door before the two worthies had had time to utter the comprehensive curse which, at this unexpected manoeuvre on the part of their quarry, had risen to their lips.

"We had promised Diogenes not to allow the blackguard to escape!" Pythagoras exclaimed ruefully.

And both started in hot pursuit, whilst Gilda, seeking shelter in a dark angle of the loft, fell, sobbing with excitement and only half-conscious, upon a pile of sacking.

1

PYTHAGORAS and Socrates failed to find the trail of the miscreant, who had vanished under cover of the night. We know that Stoutenburg did succeed, in fact, in reaching de Berg's encampment, half-starved and wearied, but safe. How he did it, no one will ever know. His career of crime had received a mighty check and the marauding expeditions which he undertook subsequently against his own country were of a futile and desultory nature. History ceases to trouble herself about him after that abortive incursion into Gelderland.

How that incursion was frustrated by the gallant Englishman, known to fame as the first Sir Percy Blakeney, but to his intimates as Diogenes, the erstwhile penniless soldier of fortune, we know chiefly through van Aitzema's Saken von Staet. The worthy chronicler enlarges upon the Englishman's adventure - he always calls him "the Englishman" – from the time when a week and more ago, he took leave of Nicolaes Beresteyn outside Barneveld to that when he reached Amersfoort, just in time to avert a terrible catastrophe.

The author of Saken v. Staet tells of the ambuscade on the shores of the Ijssel, "the Englishman's swim for life through the drifting floes." On reaching the opposite bank, it seems that he was so spent and more than half frozen, that he lay half unconscious on the bank for awhile. Presently, however, alive to the danger of possible further ambuscades, he re-started on his way, found a deserted hut close by, and crawled in there for shelter. As soon as darkness had set in he started back for Zutphen, there to warn Marquet not to proceed. The whole of the Stadtholder's plans had obviously been revealed to de Berg by some traitor – whose identity Diogenes then could not fail but guess – and it would have been sheer madness to attempt to cross the Ijssel now at any of the points originally intended.

To reach Zutphen at this juncture meant for the undaunted adventurer two leagues and more to traverse, and with clothes frozen hard to the skin. But he did reach Zutphen in time, and with the assistance of Marquet, then evolved the plan of an advance into Gelderland by effecting the crossing of the Ijssel as far north as Apeldoorn, and then striking across the Veluwe either to Amersfoort or to Ede, threatening de Berg's advance, and possibly effecting a junction with the Stadtholder's main army.

After this understanding with Marquet, Diogenes then proceeded to Arnheim, where the garrison could now only be warned to hold the city at all costs until assistance could be sent.

In the meantime, de Berg's troops were swarming everywhere. The Englishman could only proceed by night, had to hide by day on the Veluwe as best he could. Hence much delay. More than once he was on the point of capture, but succeeded eventually in reaching Arnheim.

Here he saw Coorne, who was in command of the small garrison, assured him of coming relief, and made him swear not to surrender the city, since the Stadtholder would soon be on his way with strong reinforcements. Thence to Nijmegen on the same errand. A more easy journey this, seeing that Isembourg ad not begun his advance from Kleve. After that, De Keysere and Wageningen.

Van Aitzema says that it was between Nijmegen and Wageningen that "the Englishman," lurking in a thicket of scrub, overheard some talk of how the Stadtholder was to be waylaid and captured on his return to camp from Amersfoort. This fact the chronicler must have learned at first hand. By this time the forces of de Berg were spreading over Gelderland. "The Englishman" gathered that the Archduchess's plans were to leave Isembourg's army to deal with Arnheim and Nijmegen for the present, whilst de Berg was to march on Ede, and, if possible, push on as far as Amersfoort. But as to how the coup against the Stadtholder was to be effected, he could not ascertain. At the time he did not know that his Highness intended to visit Amersfoort again. But for him, that little city where Gilda dwelt was just now the hub of the universe, and thank Heaven his errand was now accomplished, all his Highness's orders executed, and he was free to go to his young wife as fast as his own endurance and Spanish vedettes would allow.

This meant another tramp across open country, which by this time was overrun with enemy troops. Fugitives from Ede were everywhere to be seen. "The Spaniards. They are on us!" rang from end to end of the invaded province, and the echo of that dismal cry must by now have been rolling even as far as Utrecht.

It meant also seeking cover against enemy surprise parties, who threw the daring adventurer more than once out of his course, so that we hear of him once as far south as Rhenen, and then as far east as Doorn. It meant hiding amongst the reeds in the half-frozen marshes, swimming the Rhyn at one point, the Eem at another; it meant days without food and nights without rest. It meant all that, and more in pluck and endurance and determination, to which three qualities in "the Englishman" the worthy chronicler, though ever chary of words, pays ungrudging tribute.

He reached Amersfoort, as we know, just in time to see the Stadtholder leave the city in the company of the traitor, Nicolaes Beresteyn, and, struck by that same treacherous hand, fell, helpless for a moment, at the very threshold of the burgomaster's house.

After which began the martyrdom which had ended in such perfect triumph and happiness.

The daring adventurer, left lonely and stricken upon the moorland, did in truth go through an agony of misery and humiliation such as seldom falls to the lot of any man. Indeed, what he did suffer throughout that terrible day, whilst he believed himself to irretrievable blinded, was never known to any one save to the two faithful friends who watched lovingly over him. Socrates, after he had accompanied the Stadtholder, returned to sit and watch with Pythagoras beside the man to whom they both clung with such whole-hearted devotion.

2

It was not until late in the night that a faint glimmer of light, coming from the fire which the two caitiffs had managed to kindle as the night was bitterly cold, reached the young soldier's aching limbs, and seemed to him like a tiny beacon of hope in the blackness of his misery. By the time that the grey dawn broke over the moorland, he had realized that the injury which he had thought irremediable, had only been transient, and that every hour now brought an improvement in his power of vision.

Whereupon, three heads were put together to devise a means for using the Englishman's supposed blindness to the best advantage. One wise head and two loyal ones, not one of them even remotely acquainted with fear, what finer combination could be found for the eventful undoing of a pack of traitors?

Ede was in the hands of the Spaniards, Amersfoort on the point of sharing the like fate. These facts were sufficiently confirmed by the stray fugitives who wandered homeless and distracted across the moorland, and were in turn interrogated by the three conspirators.

With the woman he loved inside the invaded city, and with that recreant Stoutenburg in command of the enemy troops there, Diogenes' first thought was to get into Amersfoort himself at all risks and costs. As for the plan for freeing the town and punishing the miscreants, it was simple enough. To collect a small troop of ruffians from amongst the fugitives on the moorlands and place these under the command of Socrates, was the first move. The second was to send Pythagoras with an urgent message to Marquet to hurry eastward with his army from Apeldoorn, to the relief of Amersfoort, taking on his way the lonely molen on the Veluwe, where an important detachment of enemy troops might be expected to encamp.

The one thing with which Diogenes was, most fortunately amply provided, was money; money which he had by him when first he started out of Amersfoort on the Stadtholder's errand; money which was needful now to enable Socrates to recruit his small army of ne'er-do-wells and to assist Pythagoras on his embassy to Marquet.

Thereafter Diogenes, feigning blindness and worse, made his way into the presence of the Lord of Stoutenburg, who held Gilda at his mercy and the whole city to ransom for her obedience.

To dangle before the miscreant's eyes the prospect of capturing the Stadtholder's person, and thus make himself master of the Netherlands, was the pivot around which the whole plan revolved. The bait could not fail to attract the ambitious cupidity of the traitor, and verisimilitude was given to the story by Socrates' band of ruffians, whose orders were to spread the news of the Stadtholder's advance both on Ede and Amersfoort, and to silence effectually any emissaries of Stoutenburg's who might be sent out to ascertain the truth of these rumours.

We may take it that Socrates and his little troop saw to it that none of these emissaries did return to Amersfoort for the Lord of Stoutenburg marched out of the city at dawn, with his sinister banner flying, with his musketeers, pikemen and lancers, and with Gilda Beresteyn a virtual prisoner in his train.

That the daring adventurer risked an ignominious death by this carefully laid plan cannot be denied; but he was one of those men who had gambled with life and death since he was a child, who was accustomed to stake his all upon the spin of a coin; and, anyhow, if he failed, death would have been thrice welcome, as the only escape out of untold misery and sorrow.

Chance favoured him in this, that at the last he was left face to face with the burgomaster, to whom he immediately confided everything, and who enabled him to escape out of the house by the service staircase, and thence into the streets, where no one knew him and where he remained all night, effectually concealed as a unit in the midst of the crowd. He actually went out of Amersfoort in the train of Stoutenburg; and whilst his lordship's troops made a long halt at Barneveld, "the Englishman" continued his way unmolested across the Veluwe to the lonely molen, which was to witness his success and happiness, or the final annihilation of all that made life possible.

3

All this and more, in the matter of detail, hath the meticulous chronicler of the time put conscientiously on record. We must assume that he was able to verify all his facts at source, chiefly through the garrulous offices of "the Englishman's" two well-known familiars.

What, however, will for ever remain unrecorded, save in the book of heroic deeds, is a woman's perfect loyalty. During those hours and days, full of horror and of dread, Gilda never once wavered in her belief in the man she loved. From the moment when Nicolaes tried to poison her mind against him, and through all the vicissitudes which placed her face to face with what was a mere semblance of her beloved, she had never doubted him, when even the Stadtholder seemed to doubt.

She knew him to be playing a dangerous game – but a game for all that – when first she beheld him, sightless and abject, in the presence of their mutual enemy, and had rested for one brief second against his breast. That his eyes, still dazed by the poisonous fumes, could vaguely discern her face, even though they could not read the expression thereon, she did not know. The fear that he was irremediably blind was the most cruel of all the tortures which she had undergone that night.

When her father came to her in the small hours of the morning to tell her that all was well with the beloved of her heart, but that he would have all the need of all her courage and of all her determination to help him to complete his self-imposed task, she realized for the first time how near to actual death the torturing fear had brought her. But from that time forth, she never lost her presence of mind. With marvellous courage she gripped the whole situation and played her role unswervingly until the end.

Everything depended on whether Marquet reached the molen before the Lord of Stoutenburg, or his captains suspected that anything was wrong. True, Pythagoras had brought back the news that he had met the loyal commander at Apeldoorn, and that the latter, despite the fact that he and his troops intend to take there a well-earned rest, had immediately given the order to march. But, even so, the future of the Netherlands and of her Stadtholder, as well as the fate of the gallant Englishman and his beloved wife, lay in the hands of God.

One hour before dusk Marquet's vedettes first came in contact with the outposts of Beresteyn's encampment in the gorge below the molen. There was a brief struggle, fierce on both sides, until the main body of Marquet's army, four thousand strong, appeared on the eastern heights above the gorge.

Whilst the Lord of Stoutenburg ran round and round the narrow space wherein he was a hunted prisoner, trying to escape that shameful death which threatened him at the hand of two humble justiciaries, his few hundred men were falling like butchered beasts beneath the pike-thrusts and musket shots of Marquet's trained troops.

Nicolaes Beresteyn was the first to fall.

It was better so. Dishonour so complete could be only wiped out by death.

When, a day or two later, after Marquet had driven the Spaniards out of Amersfoort, the burgomaster heard the news of the death of his only son. He murmured an humble and broken-hearted: "Thank God!"

Chapter XVII – The Only Word

1

OUT there, in the lonely molen on the Veluwe, Gilda had remained for a while, half numb with nerve strain, suffering from the reaction after the terrible excitement of the past few hours. Presently her old serving-woman came to her, still raging with choler at the outrage committed against her person by those two abominable rascallions.

With great volubility, she explained to her mistress that they had fallen on her unawares when first she had been sent down-stairs by his lordship – whom may God punish! – The had bound and gagged her, and then told her quite cheerfully that this was an act of friendship on their part, to save her from a worse fate and from the temptation of talking when she should remain silent.

She had been thrust into a dark angle of the mill-house, from whence she could see absolutely nothing, and where she had lain all this while, entirely helpless, hearing that awful din which had been going on outside, expecting to be murdered in cold blood at any moment, and tortured with fear as to what was happening to her mistress. Only a few moments ago, the two ruffians had reappeared, running helter-skelter down the steps and thence out through the door into the open. Fortunately, one of them, conscience-stricken no doubt, had thought, before fleeing, to release her from her bonds.

Maria was stupid, uncomprehending and garrulous; but she was loyal, and had a warm and ample bosom, whereon a tired and aching head could find a little rest.

Gilda, her body still shaken by hysterical sobs, her teeth chattering, her senses reeling with the horror of all that she had gone through, found some measure of comfort in the old woman's ministrations. A mugful of wine, left over from the midday meal, helped her to regain command over her nerves. Holding her young mistress in her arms, Maria, crooning like a mother over her baby, rocked the half-inert young form into some semblance of sleep.

2

And here Diogenes found her a couple of hours later, curled up like a tired child in the arms of the old woman.

He came up on tiptoe, carrying a lanthorn, for now it was quite dark. This he placed on the floor, and then, with infinite caution, he slid into Maria's place and took the beloved form into his own strong arms.

She scarcely moved, just opened her eyes for a second or two, and then nestled closer against his shoulder, with a little sigh, half of weariness, but wholly of content.

She was just dead-tired after all she had gone through, and now she slept just like a baby in his arms; whilst he was as happy as it is possible for any human being to be, for she was safe and well, and nothing could part her from him now. He was satisfied to watch her as she slept, her dear face against his breast, her soft breath coming and going with perfect evenness through her parted lips.

Once he stooped and kissed her, and then she woke, put her arms around his neck, and both forgot for the time being that there was another world save that of Love.

THE END